'Tell me a tale . . . '

'You're a proclaimer too,' she mumbled as the realization came to her: a gentle pressure to perform. 'But I need to sleep,' she protested.

'Of course you do. Start to tell me in your sleep, Jatta. Your troubles will drain away. You'll wake refreshed–'

Tell what first? Tell what before what else? In her mind's eye she saw a circle of chattering monkeys, each holding the handle of the curled tail in front, its own tail held in turn. A circle of tales. But which order did they go in?

'Sleep, sleep . . . '

She slumped stiffly, eager for oblivion, barely resenting the imposition of Juke's will since it was almost in accord with her own. Caressed by his command, she drifted, hardness and ache dispelled. She would talk in her sleep. She knew it. She would dream memories. A proclaimer could make you do that.

Lucky's Harvest

THE FIRST BOOK OF
MANA

IAN WATSON

VGSF

First published in Great Britain 1993
by Victor Gollancz

First VGSF edition published 1994
by Victor Gollancz
A Division of the Cassell group
Villiers House, 41/47 Strand, London WC2N 5JE

A catalogue record for this book is
available from the British Library.

ISBN 0 575 05779 3

Printed and bound in Great Britain
by Cox & Wyman Ltd, Reading, Berks

CONTENTS

PART ONE

PROCLAIMERS

1 · A Cuckoo in the Hall

The banqueting hall was crowded for the Lucky's Day feast and Osmo himself was a little tipsy when two of the town watchmen marched in a fisherman who had berserked . . .

Tapestries of trees largely hid the sparkly pink granite walls of the hall. Along its south-western side six tall windows stood pivoted wide open, admitting some breeze. Narrow hangings dangled bannerlike between embrasures. The bright honey of evening sunlight flooded through upon the much wider tapestries opposite. Upon woven horzma trees, and yellovers, and larkeries. Only segments of pink wall caught the eye, towers of rock glimpsed through illusory forest. Black pot-bellied stoves of cast iron stood at the base of each, like mechanical servants who were currently inert and cold – though the sunlit floorboards of waxed yellover glowed. The slim flues of the stoves rose up the rock.

Those walls supported a high tie-beam roof of tough fireproof purple tammywood. Crystal chandeliers dangled from the braced beams, their lustres prisming the sunlight so that they seemed almost to be lit. Perched upon one of those massive beams, a cuckoo bird gazed down at the assembly out of its large yellow eyes. A scrawny hump clad in a plumage of wafery scales of drab mottled green flecked with rust, it was the size of a largish kettle. Its cupped feline ears twitched and cocked as it eavesdropped on mingled noisy conversations.

Osmo wasn't *keen* on the bird's presence up there. To be sure, he could always tell the cuckoo to go away. He could bespeak it away. Probably he wouldn't even need to shout, since the bird seemed to be listening attentively enough. Yet had it come indoors out of sheer curiosity – or had it been sent here? What *was* there to spy on at his party? Was the cuckoo awaiting some trouble of which he had no inkling?

From where the bird was perched, at least it wouldn't shit on the buffet.

Snooping cuckoo notwithstanding, Osmo surveyed his festive hall with satisfaction. Scores of his own people from the keep

9

and from the lakeside town as well as various itinerant visitors sat around refectory tables nursing pots of dark beer, frosty glasses of vodka, and platters which they periodically replenished.

On the upper shelf of the long serving table reposed several succulent lamb's legs, bedded amidst golden potatoes in the charred, hollowed-out logs in which they'd been baked. Plates of minceballs jostled with pig's trotters, with hams, with mounds of sliced sausage, black and brown and pink, heaps of meat and fish pasties, and tongues. Toasted, speckled bread-cheese sprawled on wooden platters. One bread-mountain remained intact, a ziggurat of flat, crusty barley loaves, buttermilk loaves, dark sourloaf, rye rounds and oat rolls. A cauldron of black blood soup simmered over a clutch of candles. The lower expanse of the table housed slabs of fish, smoked or boiled or baked in paper, as well as pickled in little barrels or set in aspic. Just then one of the cooks carried in a board with split whitefish nailed to it, broiled and browned. Another brought in a roast goose. The town's flautist played melodies evocative of rushing streams and cascades, though most of the partiers paid scant attention to the music.

And then there were Osmo's special guests, at the table on the dais. Inventive Elmer Loxmith had come from the neighbouring keep way across the turquoise lake with his doe-eyed young sister Nikki and his assistant Lyle Melator. From away south-east hailed the dream savant, Gunther Beck, looking very portly. From the southern forests, the lively youngest daughter of the woodlord Tapper Kippan: Tilly. Alvar van Maanen, Osmo's father, was deep in conversation with Gunther. Three years earlier Alvar had yielded up the lordship of Maananfors to his son to concentrate on writing a history of this world, to be called *Chronicles of Kaleva*.

Yes, *writing*, indeed.

Mother Johanna was absent, resting upstairs; her blood pressure remained persistently high, a cause for alarm. Otherwise, all seemed well. Fine, excellent.

That cuckoo shuffled closer to the carved king-post linking the beam with the ridge piece of the roof. The bird hopped around. It shut one eye. It cocked its ear towards the doorway which stood open invitingly as well as for extra ventilation. In the paved courtyard outside, a couple of guards armed with lightrifles meandered. The outer gate of the keep also stood open. Unlikely

10

that any uninvited citizen of Maananfors would presume to claim hospitality! The town itself was festive enough already, and probably tipsy enough; later that night bonfires would blaze on the beach. But the outer gate and the heavy tammywood door of the hall remained open for tradition's sake. Several itinerants, at least, had claimed their opportunity. Some dogs and cats had also sneaked indoors to beg for scraps.

And the cuckoo listened to it all.

'Do you reckon he'll show us the stone man later on—?' This, from the sauna steward, munching a pasty. A phoenix tattooed on his cheek.

'Get him to speak—?' The plump bailiff in charge of town tithes, a trotter in his hand.

'I was told to dust him down *personally* yesterday—' The under-housekeeper, a lively freckled widow only thirty years old.

'How *personal* does you get, Vivi? Does you polish his tackle? Does it ever twitch?'

'Oh, Sep, you're naughty—'

Quitting his seat between Tilly, whom Lyle was entertaining, and the dream savant whom his father was buttonholing, Osmo strolled to stretch his legs and to fetch a freshly chilled glass of spirit. He inhaled the fatty aroma of lamb and the tang of freshly grilled whitefish. Oh, he was conscious of the figure he cut in his embroidered white-silk shirt, his scarlet-striped waistcoat, his breeches with ribbon rosettes at the knee, his vermilion socks and buckled leather shoes. His brass belt-clasp was of a popeyed fish swallowing its own tail. From the belt hung a purse of marks, a ring of keys, and a sheathed knife, as well as a holstered lightpistol of alien manufacture.

Conscious of self – and why not?

Though only of middle height, Osmo had inherited his mother's sturdy build along with his dad's grace of countenance. His chestnut hair was richly wavy. The principal blemish on his skin was a black mole on his upper lip, concealed years since by a full moustache. A little pit in one cheek, as of an invisible nail being constantly pressed into the flesh, seemed merely to be an engaging dimple. Otherwise, he was unscarred by contest and conflict.

'Do you reckon our Osmo has his eye on the Loxmith girl—?'

'Don't be silly. She hasn't enough oomph for him.'

'Maybe that Tilly Kippan, then? An alliance with the woodmaster?'

11

'Our Osmo's a *hero*. He's Kaleva's best bespeaker, right? That's why his dad handed over the reins—'

'Best bespeaker pending the autumn gala—'

'He'll romp it. He ought to go for one of Lucky's daughters.'

'So should I – if I cared to take the risk!'

'A bespeaker like Osmo couldn't possibly become—'

'Become what? Go on, say it.'

'Well, the zed word.'

'I can't hear you.'

'I'm not intending to shout.'

'Zombie, zombie.'

'Shhh!'

Marriageable Osmo. Weddable Osmo, ah yes. Anguished inwardly by his eligibility. Anguished!

Osmo beckoned to his bondsman Sam Peller, an ashen man seemingly his elder by thirty years, though in reality only by thirty months. Whey-faced, with silvery hair and trim white beard, his eyes of ice-blue, Sam seemed perpetually startled as if he had just met with some appalling echo-ghost and been blanched by shock. Sam was usually excellent at security. Alert, and sensitive as a leper tree.

And it was Osmo himself, as a young teenager discovering his strength, who had bespoken Sam thus, earning a thrashing from Alvar – yet gaining almost mystical respect from Sam, who believed himself to have been strengthened and tempered by young Osmo's treatment of him; who was sure that he had been granted a species of timelessness whereby he would never *really* age. For Sam had aged already, in one afternoon, many winters earlier, had he not? And ever since then he had remained the same.

Which wouldn't really prevent Sam Peller from aging more so, once a couple more decades elapsed. Which wouldn't prevent Sam from dying . . . Yet, as Osmo was aware, Sam's superstition was essential to his whole concept of himself.

Some beer had spilled down the front of Sam's full-sleeved shirt, staining the white embroidery, no doubt when he'd clanked pots with an acquaintance, since Sam always held his own drink well.

'Osmo?' (*Ah, that mystic gleam of duty in Sam's eye. He had been blessed.*)

Osmo nodded up in the direction of the cuckoo. 'Any Juttahat activity that I don't know about?'

Sam shook his head and for emphasis tapped the communicator clipped to his belt. 'Scouts haven't sent word of any.'

'If only we had a few more of the things.'

'Scouts?'

'Communicators, Sam. Communicators. Ones made by nimble Juttahat hands for their serpent masters.' But really, this was so much hot air – a sop to Sam's loyal paranoia. The scouts in question were a few scamps whom Sam had 'trained'. Probably they were ensconced in some outlying farmhouse, flirting with the daughters of the house.

Sam frowned. 'For all we know, the Isi may be able to eavesdrop on our calls. Maybe that's why they let us have bits of equipment. The Trojan horse trick.'

'Earth ought to supply us with more gadgets. Not just with dribbles of extra population.'

'Earth's scared of what happens here, if you want my view. Earth doesn't want to spark war in its only colony.'

'Pah, Kaleva's as much a colony as yon cuckoo is a tame pet.'

To be sure, an Earth Resident and her staff were based at the shuttleport. However, the current incumbent, Penelope Conway, didn't in the remotest degree administer Kaleva. She or her officers toured occasionally. No one knew what they reported to utterly distant Earth.

'In my opinion,' said Sam, 'war's essentially a *human* concept. Did lions wage war back on Earth? Did whales?' Sam voiced many opinions. Sam sustained his identity by a shell of such assertions built around the dark hollow in himself which hid his lost youth.

Osmo hoisted an eyebrow. 'How much do you actually know about those creatures?' Lions, whales . . .

Sam's smile was wry. 'What I mean is, the aliens don't play war, or else they could probably put paid to us all. They play games with us from time to time, using their Juttahat slaves. Hell, they even trade us some weaponry. I think we ought to keep an eye on the Brindled Isi.'

'Why? They never caused *us* any trouble.'

'That's why we ought to watch them.' He glanced significantly at the cuckoo.

Shrugging, Osmo returned to his guests.

'Now that I'm really into my *Chronicles*,' Alvar was confiding to Gunther, 'it's rather bemusing to discover the way in which certain events repeat themselves obsessively with variations. To the extent that I can be *sure* of our history . . . !' For the feast, Alvar had donned a striped jacket of black and gold, with a scarlet silk sash around his waist suggestive of some regal award; yet there were ink stains on his fingers which he hadn't been able, or hadn't troubled, to clean.

Gunther nodded. 'The pattern repeats within the pattern, doesn't it just? Beware that telling your stories doesn't lock us in to a cycle of repeating our whole history, to our disadvantage this time round. I'm trying to *escape* from that.' At three hundred years old the dream savant was so youthful in looks especially now that he was plumping out. A cherubic chubbiness softened a once sharp face. He had certainly been putting on weight of late. Remarkably so. Already he had accounted for sizeable helpings of baked lamb, pasties, minceballs, fish and bread, and he was eyeing the serving table ruminatively even as he talked to Alvar. His brown shirt and breeches weren't remotely party gear but at least served to contain his increasing girth.

Gunther's blond hair lapped loose and long upon his shoulders. His grey eyes alone hinted at haunting depths. Gunther's wife had died two centuries earlier, and it was rumoured that he was trying to resurrect her in his dreams; that this was his secret project.

At least he was willing to travel. Tilly Kippan's father, a more recent longlife than Gunther, stayed holed up in his forest redoubt, protective of his extended years, using strange trees as his allies and guards.

Tilly giggled at some joke of Lyle's, and touched his hand. Lyle smirked, perhaps hoping to creep to her bed that night. Affected by this, Osmo toasted Nikki Loxmith with his glass and winked flirtatiously, then felt regret, for her brother Elmer grinned back jovially, and raised his own glass as though Osmo's gesture had obviously encompassed both of them. As indeed it must have done. For Elmer was Osmo's friend, his colleague, as well as his neighbour, merely separated by the width of a lake. At the sight of Nikki in happy harmony with her brother, a squirm of ill-directed lust had possessed Osmo momentarily. Nikki was only a kid, who returned his gaze innocently, fawnlike, seeing Osmo as a kind of elder brother too.

Whatever the circumstances, Osmo vowed to himself, I must never let myself attempt to seduce Nikki. Could he perhaps wed her one day? No, no, and no. Nikki wasn't what he sought . . .

Anguish panged him: a provoking, taunting itch.

14

'What was that Earthbird called?' he interrupted his father hastily. 'The one which could repeat words?'

Alvar recollected. 'Parrot. Or mynahbird.'

'Not cuckoo?' asked Tilly, diverted from Lyle. The presence of a cuckoo *was* provocative.

'No, we call these Kalevan birds cuckoos rather than parrots because—'

'—because we felt *compelled* to call them cuckoos,' stated Gunther. 'And the reason for that is that there were cuckoos in the old stories – but no parrots.'

'*Because*,' Alvar said pedantically, 'a fellow can usually summon a cuckoo by shouting *coo-coo-coo*.'

'If it isn't snooping already. Maybe the cuckoos feel compelled to act as gossips. But sometimes it seems to me, my friend, that they're a cunning species which has a long-term strategy of spying on us – on humans and Isi serpents alike – protected by our taboo about harming them. And where did that particular inhibition come from? From the cuckoos themselves?'

'To my knowledge,' said Alvar, 'no cuckoo has ever spoken to anybody on its own account about whatever might concern a cuckoo. Unless you know otherwise?'

An unkempt chocolate-and-cream spaniel – one of the hopeful intruders – approached Osmo, wagging its tail. It opened its jaws. It uttered awkward words. 'Give . . . food? Give me food?'

Osmo shuddered. 'Sam Peller!' he called out; and his bondsman hurried to the dais.

'Sam: take this *mutant* creature outside.' Osmo searched for a word which the spaniel wouldn't understand. 'Exterminate it.'

'Give food . . . lord?' begged the dog.

'Osmo!' protested Tilly. 'The poor thing isn't doing any harm.'

'I don't trust mutant animals.'

'Is that because you can't "exterminate" the cuckoo?' she enquired pertly.

'Cuckoos aren't mutants,' said Alvar. 'A mutant is a freak among its kind. Cuckoos are all the same as each other. It's their nature to gossip.'

'They must have been so *bored* before we came to this world,' said Tilly.

'Heel,' ordered Sam, stooping to grab the spaniel by the scruff. The dog submitted to restraint.

'Please,' appealed Tilly, 'let me have the dog. Give it to me as a Lucky's Day gift. I'll take it home with me.' Broad-featured, and of generous brow, Tilly's loose tresses of hair were a golden blonde. Her green gown was entirely embroidered with leaf patterns in varying hues so that she seemed to be the very spirit of woodland. A necklace of dark red garnets, cut in broad flat cabochon style, gleamed like capsules of full-bodied wine against the verdure. But no, she was not what Osmo sought.

How could he refuse his guest? Especially not Tapper Kippan's daughter. Kippan who had taken the risk of marrying one of Lucky's daughters, and who had been blessed with long life as a consequence . . .

'Sam: take that out and kennel it on its own until the lady leaves our keep.'

'You're kind,' Lyle murmured in Tilly's ear. Elmer's assistant wore a roan tunic of maroon-dyed sheep's leather dappled with grey, a garment which would hide minor stains or burns caused by engineering work. Gold-rimmed spectacles sat on a somewhat snubby nose, now lending intensity to his hazel-eyed gaze, now emphasizing an air of nonchalant expertise. His hair was a frizzy auburn corona.

'Well, I pity such stray creatures,' Tilly said. 'They're different from their kin, yet they have to live as their kin do . . . until they eventually die, a little bewildered.'

Was Tilly implying that she pitied her own father? Maybe she might feel that way, so as not to blame Tapper Kippan for the fact that she herself would only live as long as any ordinary mortal would.

'If it's to be my dog,' said Tilly, 'it needs . . . reassurance.'

'Dog, or bitch: which is it?' Osmo asked Sam, who investigated.

'Bitch, Lord Osmo.'

Tilly quit her chair and knelt by the spaniel. Fondling its ears, she gazed into its hopeful eyes.

'What is your name?' she asked slowly and clearly. 'Your name?'

The spaniel considered.

'*Out*,' it replied. 'Out. Out.'

'Out,' repeated Tilly thoughtfully. 'Very well, I'll call her that exactly. Osmo, could you possibly bring yourself to proclaim for my dog? To proclaim her a happy life with me in the woods? And maybe a family of puppies?'

'Not puppies, Tilly. One of them might talk.'

'That's a rare mutation.'

'A *freak* one.'

'Unlikely to affect her children.'

'Mightn't her pups seem rather dumb to her? Disappointing? Won't she fail as a mother?'

'Oh, very well, no puppies. That's probably wisest. But please do proclaim.'

Osmo sighed. To proclaim for a mutant bitch, at his banquet . . .

'If that's the wrapping you'd like on the gift, tender Tilly!'

At a signal from Osmo the flautist fell silent (and hastened to avail himself of drink and meat). Most of the feasters paid attention, in particular one good-looking young man wrapped in a grey travelling cloak. Sam tugged the spaniel round to face Osmo, who marshalled himself inwardly. Soberly. Willing away any fuddle.

'What is the origin of this dog?' Osmo asked loudly. His tone was slurred. 'Originally it comes from the wolves of Earth. Alas, its genetic pattern was twisted in transit through mana-space to Kaleva. Mana-space played a joke on its gene line. Ninety-nine of its kind are born true. One is a freak which can talk and is no true dog at all – nor potentially part-way human – but only a wretched oddity.'

Understand the origin of a thing, and you can control that thing. Origin; then destiny.

Usually so! Destiny could sometimes twist as mischievously as had the genes in this spaniel's ancestry. The young man in the audience scrutinized Osmo studiously.

'This dog was called Out because that was what people had always shouted at it. One day it came to a court during a festival where a cuckoo was listening. A kind young lady claimed the dog and took it along with her to the forests further south to live with her. The dog Out would live long and happily and would eat well with her, and she would be the only family it wanted.'

And at this moment, perhaps, Out became barren.

'Out: *this is spoken.*'

Spoken somewhat cursorily – yet adequately.

'Now, Sam,' said Osmo, 'kindly take that thing out to kennel.'

'Wait a moment!'

Unclasping her necklace, Tilly descended a second time from the dais to fasten the chain of gems around the spaniel's neck. The dog shook itself, reorganizing the gift. Some of the carbuncle stones disappeared within the beast's coat.

'Now Out has a collar!'

'What a precious dog.' Osmo smiled at Tilly. She flushed

momentarily and nibbled her lip, as if taken by surprise, now, by what she had just done. Perhaps this seemed a rebuke directed at Osmo, when she should have been thanking him.

'I can't bespeak,' she said lightly, recovering her spirits. 'I *can* at least enhance my dog a little.'

'I fear,' was Osmo's reproachful reply, 'mutation doesn't enhance a creature.'

Scarcely had Sam Peller departed with the spaniel than two blue-clad men of the town watch hustled a bruised prisoner into the hall. The man's bound hands were streaked with blood. The cuckoo flapped its scaly wings and cocked its head attentively.

'We're sorry to butt in, sir,' began one of the watchmen, who sported lavish side-whiskers.

'That's all right, Marko. What happened?'

The prisoner stood moodily, a manic twitch to his stance. A slight individual, though with strong arms. A large black mole high on one cheek stared like a coaly supernumerary eye. The fool had tried to disguise this with a surrounding tattoo of a florid brooch, in which this would be the gem, of jet. The effect was of bloodshot eyelids.

'Hans Werner here stabbed Anna Vainio's cousin, then the girl herself,' explained Marko. 'Midriff and face. They'll both pull through, but the girl might be badly scarred on the cheek. Cousin had a tendon severed in his hand while warding Hans off.'

'Damnation! An outburst of desire and jealousy, I suppose?'

Marko nodded. 'Girls don't look at Hans because he looks back with that black blem. Hans lost control. People are inflamed, so we had to act right away.'

'Quite right, Marko. You, Hans Werner: do you hear me?'

Hans jerked and nodded.

'Why did you stab Anna Vainio and her cousin? Don't give me the anecdotal reason. Give me the true deep reason. *Why?*'

For a few moments it seemed as though there might be no answer, but then Hans cried out, 'I *had* to! The knife came into my hand. My hand slashed at them.'

'Your hand slashed at them.'

'My hand. My right hand.'

'Why were you carrying the knife?'

'I'm a fisherman, Lord Osmo. A knife is natural.' Hans's gaze dropped momentarily towards Osmo's own sheathed dagger.

'We must master our compulsions, Hans Werner. Often we are

too much like fish caught on a hook, dragged by the mouth. Our mouth must regain mastery.' The prisoner was a fisherman on the lake floored with bright blue pebbles, and he had tried to gut his rival and then the girl he desired. If his male member couldn't enter her, his blade could.

'How much more so with our passions and our grievances, Hans Werner! Hear me: their blood is on your hands. Your signature is on her face, carved by your hand. His hand is lamed, and your name is Hans.' The decision was obvious to Osmo. He could smell the vodka in his glass, or was it on his breath? No matter. He contemplated his silver cygnet ring, with a tiny swan of death embossed on it. His thoughts were as crystal clear as the vodka. His own spirit was calm and focused. The hall was entirely hushed.

The fisherman shivered as Osmo spoke. 'So therefore the bones of your knife hand shall be stone. The flesh shall be as rock. For ever. Your hand shall become a fossil of its former self. I fuse your fingers and your thumb.'

Hans listened, with head bowed.

'I petrify your tissue,' Osmo told him. 'I crystallize your blood to veins in marble. Your stone hand shall never fall off, nor shall you hack it off, for the wires of your nerves would agonize then, and blood would spurt from the stump without ever clotting. You will carry your stone hand around till you die. This is beginning now. The hardening starts. For *this is spoken*. And the moment that you assault anybody else unless ordered to by a lawful authority, your left hand will likewise turn to stone.'

Hans Werner groaned as his right hand, still bound to his left, became grey and hard and heavy to above the wrist. His left hand strained to support the weight.

Watchman Marko and his colleague nodded. The punishment would satisfy the people. In the silence a young man unknown to Osmo began to clap slowly. Spurred by this applause, other party-goers banged their beerpots upon the tables in appreciation – while the fisherman was led out to continue his life in Maananfors as best he could.

As if to compensate for the business of the garnets, Tilly was nodding a qualified assent to Osmo's justice; Elmer's sister looked enthralled, though disconcerted.

Yet the cuckoo did not take wing. It stayed. Osmo hesitated, then drained his glass.

'I've another reason for travelling,' Gunther confessed to Alvar. 'My nephew Cully has gone missing.' The dream savant had piled his plate in the meantime with potato pasties and black sausage.

'Cully? Cully? Is this something I ought to know about for the *Chronicles*?'

'I don't expect so. I hope not!'

'When you say "nephew" . . .'

'I don't mean it literally. I took his family under my protection. Mother, couple of sisters. They're direct descendants of mine . . . and of dear dead Anna. My wife, you know.'

'I believe I know all the lineage of Lucky inside out, Gunther.'

The dream savant munched dedicatedly. He was definitely gorging himself. Had Gunther become a glutton? Shouldn't the attraction of food pall somewhat after three hundred years? Really, it wouldn't do for the host's father to mention this . . .

'You're wondering?' asked that man of three centuries. 'About the difference between memory and history? Is Anna memory to me after so long, or is she history?'

'I wouldn't presume—'

'Yet you wonder. I suppose Anna did become an idol to me quite early. She gave me life as well as love. Long, long life. Almost, it seemed to me, obtained at the cost of her own life, as though she were just some *package* of elixir which, once opened, must itself begin slowly to decay.' A potato pasty disappeared into Gunther's mouth.

Alvar scratched his head. 'Are you implying that if one of Lucky's daughters *fails* to wed, then that girl can retain her own youth permanently? *Herself*, as an alternative to bestowing that vigour on a husband?'

'So therefore, but for me, my Anna might still be alive today? I very much doubt it! It's a pointless speculation in my case. Don't you see? For Anna to outlive me, if that were true – and I only say if – we must needs never have become lovers; never have met; never have known each other. It's stupid to torment myself along those lines. I'm tempted to suggest, Alvar, that you're too *young* to understand the feelings I have. Almost everyone is too young.'

'My own wife is ailing,' Alvar reminded Gunther.

'And you're already a retired lord, I know, I know.' Gunther squeezed his glass tentatively as if tempted to crush it, driving splinters into his palm, drawing blood. 'We were speaking of Cully. I could hardly address him as great-great-greatest-grandson or whatever. Too much of a mouthful. Nephew seemed a lot easier.'

'Seemed? Do you fear he's dead?'

'No. I don't believe that. He was – he is – a persistent young man. I'm used to thinking in the past tense, Alvar, because the majority of people I've known are dead. Dreams, by contrast, have no tenses. Or rather they possess a dream-tense all of their own . . . which I wouldn't exactly characterize as an "eternal" one. Not as yet, not as yet.'

'Your nephew,' Alvar reminded him.

'Yes, they lived about twenty keys from my keep. Farming folk. Within my tithe zone, nominally. The father was called Cal. *Was*, yes, *was*. He was killed in a senseless brush with some Juttahats belonging, I think, to the Brazen Isi.'

'Excuse me.' Alvar pulled out an antique black-bound notebook with marbled endpapers. (On the serving table below, the goose had been reduced to a greasy shell and the femur of a lamb jutted nakedly. The declining sun wore an orange veil of cirrus.) Alvar inked a note, and a query. 'How long ago was this?'

'Winter. Five years ago. I took the mother and daughters into my home for a while. The next year, I adopted Cully.'

'Wasn't he needed on their farm?'

'*I* needed someone of my blood who . . . could take charge of things . . . during my absence.'

'Your absence? Absence? Yet here you are, *absent*, searching for your nephew.' Alvar sucked at his pen a few times as if it was a pipe. Obviously Gunther was leaving much unsaid, which he did not intend to confide to a notebook.

'I thought Cully may have decided to meddle with the Isi for revenge, though he'd sworn not to . . . May I?' asked Gunther, and took the notebook and pen.

Alvar's spidery constipated handwriting cramped many thin angular words on each page, most of them abbreviated. The dream savant squinted, foxed by the condensed script, though he remembered well enough how to read. Turning to an empty page, he quickly sketched a youthful face which was frank and open – broad-browed, bold-eyed – though the corners of the mouth

21

drooped somewhat morosely as if doubt had begun to brood. The portrait's lips were full and sensual, so the pout made him appear intriguing, even sultry. Cully wore his hair long in his uncle's style.

'You're an artist—'

On the opposite page Gunther swiftly sketched a free-flowing silhouette. The owner of the book twitched at this prodigal double use of his paper and reached out protectively in case the dream savant might care to demonstrate his pictorial talent further. To be sure, Alvar had amassed plenty of paper, and Tilly – knowing of his pastime – had brought him *reams* as a present from Kip'an'keep. Still, one shouldn't be wasteful.

'Visualization is vital to the dreamer,' Gunther said enigmatically, surrendering the black book. 'If Cully visits here, will you notify me?'

'My pleasure.'

Gunther indulged in a large chunk of blood sausage; and really, this gormandizing did pique Alvar's curiosity.

'You'll lose your figure,' he joked – bumblingly, since the truth of this was already plain to see.

Gunther eyed the would-be historian. 'I suspect it'll be a cold winter. Need to put on some fat.'

A cold winter? Winter was always cold. The lakes always froze so that you could ride horses on them, drive carriages on them.

The dream savant proceeded to hail Elmer, although not, it transpired, to pursue the same enquiry. 'Loxmith, I'd like to commission a piece of *machinery* from you if I might—' Maybe, after three hundred years, a missing nephew wasn't of enormous account . . .

Elmer grinned back at the dream savant. 'I don't know that I ought to have come to this party! Seems I've already agreed to service Osmo's skyboat for him. That'll take me and Lyle a couple of days at least.'

'You *knew* you'd be doing that,' protested Nikki; and Elmer laid a quieting hand on hers. Beneath a mop of black hair which hid much of his forehead, Elmer's face was candid if lean. Those sucked-in Loxmith cheeks and high cheek-bones, which gave his sister a pert elfin countenance, made Elmer seem both cadaverous and ingenuous – older than his thirty years, yet perhaps . . . callow? Yet not unaware of this artless facet of his personality, which went hand in hand with a fine technical virtuosity, an instinct for improvisation. His fingers were long, slender, bony

– skilful manipulators. He was wearing a leather tunic similar to his assistant's though buff in hue and more soiled. Dark mellow liquid eyes gave him the air of some consumptive stag draped in its hide; whereas Nikki was a doe – in a velvet, violet gown, her coiled chignon hair tied with a simple bow of peacock-blue ribbon.

'Ah, there'll be the question of *cost* . . .', prompted Gunther.

'Show us the stone man!' cried a voice from the body of the hall.

Other tongues seconded the cry. 'Make him speak!'

Beerpots clattered on wood.

Osmo stood. 'Yes,' he agreed. 'It's Lucky's Day. Stone Man deserves an airing.'

Descending, he sought out the freckled under-housekeeper.

Vivi arose unsteadily. Bumping some chairs and shoulders, she hurried to join Osmo in front of a tapestry of bottle-green harper trees. Silver threads in the weave mimicked the cords of shiny fibre stretching between trunk and lower branches which a wind would ripple musically. This tapestry hung from a stout brass rod able to swing outward from the wall. Swiftly, tables and chairs were shifted aside. Vivi pulled the arras through a half circle to reveal a deep niche in the pink granite behind. Within stood a pink stone statue of a naked man, arms by his side, fists clenched. He seemed almost an outgrowth from the marble. The stone man's face was heavy-jowled, his lips fat and self-indulgent, his expression brutal yet appalled. Was that a wen on his right cheek or a petrified teardrop?

Lyle gripped Tilly's hand reassuringly; which she allowed.

'A man turned to wood is still alive . . .', she murmured.

'You've seen such in your father's forests?'

'. . . but a man turned to *stone* . . .'

'Do you think Osmo should have spoken that fisherman's hand to wood instead?'

'No . . . Stone was right. Wood wouldn't have been burden enough. He might have screwed in hooks to let him use the hand.' With her free hand Tilly stroked her own soft and unscarred cheek. Tentatively Lyle caressed her other cheek with his fingertips.

'I expect,' she said to him, 'wood can think . . . slowly. Can stone think at all? Maybe only one horrified, petrified thought. The same one always, for an aeon.'

'Oh, Osmo lets the stone man think. For a few minutes, every six months or so—'

*

The sauna steward buttonholed the young stranger who had previously launched the applause. 'You should approve, eh? Great proclaimer. Thorough bastard.'

'Who do you mean?'

'Who do I *mean*?' Little azure phoenix on his cheek rising from a nest of flames, the steward jerked his thumb. 'Tycho Cammon, 'course! Stone Man. *Him*. Who you think I mean? Think I mean Lord van Maanen? That what you think?' Well in his cups, the steward was as ready for a squabble as for conviviality.

'I didn't know the stone man was a proclaimer. I'm sorry.' (But he knew, of course.)

'Where you been all your life? Vagrant, coming here, leeching on our hospitality. Where you from, anyway?'

'The east,' the young man said vaguely. 'I'm travelling around.'

'Woz your name?'

'Juke.'

'Sure it ain't Joke?'

'It's Juke.'

'That your first name or your second?'

'It's how I care to be known. Why a phoenix, if I might ask without causing offence?'

Meanwhile, Osmo stood with arms crossed and one beribboned knee advanced, conscious of his stance, contemplating the man-statue in its narrow alcove . . .

'Why . . . ? In charge of the saunas, course. Hot charcoals. Billows o' steam. A body arises, refreshed, renewed.' The steward hiccuped, his face flushed with alcohol.

Juke nodded at the steward's sagacity. So the tattoo was a brand of office rather than a freely chosen adornment expressing the steward's soul. Deliberately to adopt a stigma of servitude struck Juke as quite absurd, *luxuriously* absurd. He didn't say so, or even let an eyebrow twitch.

No one looking at Juke would have guessed that he was of mutant parentage. Of athletic build – a runner, perhaps. When he tensed, muscle sheathed his neck. Greasy fawn hair jutted back from under a large skull-cap as if perpetually windblown. His blue eyes peered frequently into some distance of which he alone was aware, seeking a target.

That morning, after waking in his grey cloak on the pebbly shore, head on napsack, Juke had bathed in the cool lake and slaked his thirst. Then he had wandered around Maananfors, observing

24

wharfs and jetties and fishing smacks, white sails furled for festival. Charm pennants hung from their mastheads, revealing in a flurry of breeze a hand with an eye in the palm, the silhouette of a cuckoo, a black cat's head. The paddle steamer ferry to Loxmithlinna and beyond was moored to iron bollards polished by the friction of the hawsers. Triangular bunting, snipped from bright old skirts and shirts, decorated its thirty-metre deck. Early-risen crew were playing cards for dried fishbones; loss of money might have kindled ill will, could have caused a knife to gleam.

'—six o' hearts!'

'—ace in the hole!'

'—twenty!'

Women in shawls and headscarves stood on stools in small wooden boats, butt-ended against the low granite quay, fish and vegetables for sale on planks straddling crates. Other more permanent stalls of the morning market plied smoked fish, sausages, fruit, bottles of berry liqueurs. Further along, on rafts, aproned women leaned from recessed galvanized tubs to soak and wring and scrub striped, chevroned rugs. Some rugs were already draped over wooden racks to dry. Everyone was keen to finish business early today.

Juke halted to stare across the achingly blue lake, at tiny islands accommodating half a dozen trees, some with a solitary log-house crouching almost at the waterline; and at the curve of wooded shore wending in and out, similar houses nestling in bays. In the distance the lake finally meandered away behind low leafy shores. Almost all long lakes meandered, sometimes for a hundred keys.

His sister Eyeno would know how to express the soft appeal of this scene. She was the poetess. Read, write, cross out; read, write, cross out.

The savour of grilling fish assaulted him. A fat cheery woman with a face like a merry pig was vending charred rosy chunks of luckyfish on sticks, to dip into waxed paper twists of dill sauce. She had several customers. Juke teetered. Take the edge off his appetite? Ah, why squander pennies when there'd be plenty of free food later on!

Up there above the town.

Not high above; nowhere was particularly high hereabouts.

But certainly set on an upswell of blushing granite, reached by an ascending road cut through the rock: Osmo van Maanen's keep, a sprawling fortified complex of stout walls, roofs, and towers.

Fasting, Juke roamed. He wended his way past white vertical-boarded wooden houses with decorated gutters eaves, past garlanded shops, and shuttered workshops venting no steam or smoke today.

Trestle tables were being set out on some earthen streets. A gang of small boys scampered, rolling barrel hoops along, which they guided with sticks. Awnings bloomed open. A landlord swept dust from his pub. A lad ran past with a wooden gun, pursuing a friend who wore a serpent-mask. Another snake-faced kid was gaining on the junior rifleman, chanting:

'—*isi-isi-isi-isi-isi!*—'

Maidens stepped out in best blue dresses patterned with red and yellow bands embroidered with flowers, tassels of streamers dangling from braided conical bonnets frilled with lace.

Brassy music led Juke to a square shaded by curver trees planted so that their lopsided chartreuse crowns formed archways all around a dusty little park. The navel was a bandstand. Musicians in breeches and candy-striped jackets were tuning up on bombardon, trombone, cornet, and horn. A scattering of elderly spectators eyed the proceedings from irregular rows of wooden slat-seats.

Maananfors was a deal more decorous than where Juke hailed from.

Art, too! Several sculptures stood around the periphery, under the curvers – and also a chain pillory. The neckband and square manacles hung loose from a tall post on heavy long-link chains. No one was a guest in those today.

A girl's head – and her smooth armless shoulders and upper swell of breasts – emerged yearningly from a column of rough-hewn marble, gazing upward. A nude swimmer surfacing from stone rather than water. Or was she *submerging*? Was the stone engulfing the last of her?

A plump, nude woman appeared to be melting as she feebly tugged a towel around her loins. Her chubby face, capped with a smooth foam of hair, had almost lost definition; was almost the twin of her huge breasts. Fat nose, snouty nipple: which was which? Her arms flowed amorphously, hands fusing into paws.

From a rough-cut block of stone a bald man's forceful head emerged, the eyes almost closed, the brow and mouth twisting with the strain . . . of sustaining that last citadel, of his intellect and senses.

'You admire our local decorations?' enquired a gaunt snowy-headed oldster who favoured a cane. He was clad in a black frock-coat buttoned up almost to the throat despite the warmth. A stiff collar showed, though no necktie. His eyes bulged exophthal-micly behind copper-rimmed spectacles.

'My sister might appreciate these,' Juke found himself saying. 'She's a poet.'

'You miss her,' observed the old man.

Juke's hand fluttered. 'That girl's face . . . emerging from the marble . . . somehow it reminds me of her.'

'When Lord Osmo was a kid, sometimes he used to play down here. Watched by his tutor. These marbles might have given him early inspiration, I suppose. A structure for his power . . . You know all about the tyrant he spoke into stone?'

Juke nodded.

'I do like to talk to strangers. A lot of the people here in Maan-anfors *don't* especially.' (Juke couldn't say that he had noticed anything of the sort.) 'But not me, oh no. Fundamentally my fellow townsfolk are a dull awkward sort, except when they lose their tempers and a knife comes out. They're awkward because they're dull. They don't know what to talk about, being unobserv-ant. Now, I pride myself that I never bored anyone with my conversation. I noticed your own feelings for your sister, for example. Spotted those right away, since I pay attention. So she's a poet? I think I could have been a poet if I'd had the time to boil my observations down. That's what poetry's all about.' The talker inclined his head, smiling with a fatuous self-satisfaction which included a hint of intimidation. 'When I was younger, let me tell you, I stood in that pillory a few times stripped to the waist. Quite an experience. Do you wish to know why?'

'I think I can guess . . . sir. Your fellow townfolk didn't want to seem dull.'

The old man frowned, uncertain whether he was being mocked.

'We kept a Juttahat in that pillory once, for a month, but it never said anything. I don't think it could speak. Finally Lord Alvar came to some arrangement, and we released it. It walked away, teased by a pack of boys, though they didn't dart too close to it. I fought Juttahats twice, you know? On the first occasion—'

The tuba *umphed*.

'I think the concert's starting.'

'Oh no, not yet.'

'I think it's rude to leave a performance just as it starts. I'd better hurry along. Good day to you.'

'If we have the good fortune to meet again—'

However, Juke was already walking away, leaving the veteran to subside into a chair and begin to wave his cane to and fro, conducting anticipatorily with a liver-spotted hand.

A handful of festively dressed families emerged from a mana-kirk which was rather more steep saddle roof – shingles of tammywood – than chequerboard stone wall, and considerably more wall than window. The campanile stood a dozen metres to one side, capped with glassed lantern and bulbous cupola, its lych-gate base giving entry to the town's graveyard.

'—for Saint Lucky?' piped a girl, and was clipped gently about the ear.

'—isn't a true saint—'

'—she lives for ever—'

'—by mana-magic—'

'—the serpents' sort—'

These persons must be Christian believers, a rare breed. A mana-priest would control the kirk, but mana-priests were usually tolerant.

Juke wandered into the graveyard, curious whether there might be any memorial statuary which had once been human and alive. But there wasn't. Of course not. Lord Osmo wasn't given to excesses the like of Tycho Cammon's. Lord Osmo was impeccable.

Neat mounds of sun-bleached, pinkish pebbles bore large granite cobbles incised with symbols or names of the dead. One per cobble; as many as half a dozen perched on some graves. Rusty iron holders for candles were spiked in the soil at the head of each. A carved waxed swan of rare ivorywood presided on a plinth, its snaky neck curved back like a handle, a bird only to be found on the other side of mana-space. If ever you saw a swan in a dream surely you would die. Narrowing his eyes, Juke imagined the entire walled area entirely cobbled over, and the swan taking wing at last. He slapped his own cheek stingingly. He had almost let himself imagine death; and that wouldn't do at all.

'Well, Juke-Juke?'

'Well what?' Juke asked the sauna steward.

'What you *think*? 'Course!'

As Osmo splayed a hand dramatically towards the stone man in his niche . . .

Sheer theatre. *Speaking* was what counted. The power of will and intention. Knowledge of origins. Not ostentatious gestures. But then, Osmo was a lord – determined to act in lordly fashion – and Juke *wasn't*. Perhaps Osmo might be vulnerable because of his self-importance . . . A shade more style than substance? When he'd contested against Cammon surely Osmo must have felt apprehensive? A bit uncertain? *No.* He wouldn't have. So therefore Juke must never let himself feel intimidated for an instant.

And Osmo spoke.

'Tycho Cammon: you were once a man of flesh and blood. Oh yes, far too much lust for flesh and too much thirst for blood! You burst pet animals apart as a boy, then later you burst your rivals. You stole women willy-nilly. You were a hero against Juttahats, but then your beard grew blue. Galas became terrible, until a young man stood up to you. Without realizing, you had lost mana-focus through excess. You tried to burst the young man with your words, like a ripe peach, but he thought and he spoke *stone*. And stone was what you became, slowly, from head to foot. That's what the audience all watched that day: the young tyro petrifying you. Now your stone lips are softening for a while, and also the muscles of your cheeks and throat, and your brain can think again for a while, and your eyeballs can see, and your ears grow soft. But none of the rest of you. For this is spoken. Now.'

And it was happening.

Above, the cuckoo shifted agitatedly, then stilled, straining to hear a harsh whisper in the silence.

Eyeballs grew moist and less opaque as if the stone were sweating. Poised at Osmo's side, Vivi shivered. She clutched her gown around herself. The sensual lips of the statue cracked apart. The words were gravelly, dry, though with an echo of mesmeric command to them still.

'Woman,' said the stone man. 'You – touch – me.'

Vivi half raised a hand; Osmo caught it lightly.

'You – dream – me.'

The steward sniggered, and Juke shushed him impatiently.

'I do *not*,' protested the under-housekeeper, half to Osmo, half to the living statue of Tycho Cammon; flushing. Osmo patted the freckled hand he held.

29

'Good try!' he called out to the statue. 'You become aware for a moment. You see a female employee next to me. Evidently she has some slight connection with yourself, in your stone condition. How can you increase that connection? As a potential lifeline – no, a mere thread . . .' He chuckled. 'A gossamer strand will never shift a block of stone. I forbid you ever to speak unless questioned. Do you hear me, Cammon?'

'I – hear.'

'Is not your condition preferable to death?'

'Per-haps.'

'I should have my workers smash you with sledgehammers, but I don't.'

If Osmo was testing, the stone man made no reply.

Releasing Vivi, Osmo slapped her proprietorially on the rump to scoot her back to her seat. Then he clapped his hands together.

'Cammon, I'll let you hear our mana-priest declare Lucky's Day before I put you completely back into stone.'

Could it be, wondered Juke, that Osmo preferred to wait a while? To collect his potency once more? Was Osmo feeling just a shade *lethargic* right now?

A prim-faced man wearing a grey serge suit and stiff white wing-collar arose shakily. Wispy islands of thin black hair descended from a bald polar sea of white skin. His sky-blue eyes were intense.

'Density,' he quavered; then corrected himself. 'Destiny,' he continued in a sing-song tone, 'brought us here to this world – and we are beings dogged by fate in its various guises. Fate which we, which we must fight or cooperate with . . . but never be unaware of. Events foretold strongly enough can come true . . . if not necessarily always as desired or expected. Tellings have power, as we see. Great tellers,' and he glanced at Osmo, 'can directly mould *what is—*'

'Oh, not a sermon,' sighed the bailiff.

'*Have* you dreamed about touching the stone man?' the steward whispered to Vivi, who was attempting to compose herself.

'Of course not!'

'Maybe *not yet*, eh . . . ?'

'—and why is this? Because we came through mana-space – therefore mana drenches our lives on this world. Mana stains our lives, flavours them, scents them. And what is this mana?'

'Ho, now he's asking—'

'. . . a supernatural force, you might say. Not one to worship. But to focus our minds upon – aaah.'

The man was rambling. He too had indulged in chilled vodka. Osmo frowned at him.

The mana-priest squared his shoulders.

'Today is the four hundred and second anniversary of the date when Paula Sariola, whom we call Lucky, discovered the Ukko in Earth's asteroid belt. That's to say, today's the anniversary of when Lucky entered the labyrinths and cochleas – the inner chambers, mm, of the Ukko. Since she wasn't actually the *discoverer* as such . . . in the sense of actually finding it—'

('*Oaf*'), from behind cupped hands. ('*Goof.*')

Vivi dug the bailiff in the ribs.

'Rather to say, Lucky Sariola was the *activator*—'

Just then, a small commotion outside the doorway propagated inward: in the shape of guards gripping lightrifles and an urgent, unkempt young woman with short black hair who was clutching a little child . . .

3 · THE JUDGING OF JATTA

She wore the clothes of the far north: a purple suede tunic to which were sewn many strips of felt, orange, vermilion, and pea-green; over calfskin trousers stuffed into peaked leather boots. The soiled tunic was slashed from neckline to waist as a makeshift sling for the child bursting forth excitedly, and probably cut open to cool her as well. Her boots were splitting. Mud caked her trousers. A broad leather belt girded her waist loosely, sheath-knife dangling. The knapsack flopping from her shoulder looked seriously empty.

'Lucky Sariola was the youngster, the blessed *maiden lass* who told stories to that ancient alien, hmm, entity, winning us our passage to Kaleva—'

'*Blessed?*' exclaimed the newcomer. The word became a spluttering cough, and she spat on the floor – or did she simply stoop over to release her skinny dark-skinned child? The boy scampered barefoot – did not by any means toddle – towards the

31

serving table, nostrils flaring, to grab a fish pasty and stuff his mouth with it. Gobbling, he seized a second.

The woman's spasm subsided. Straightening up, exposing a frilly chemise grey with dirt, 'Oh Fastboy!' she cried. *'Jack!'*

The urchin promptly spun around and incongruously, for one who looked to be only two years old, he bowed towards the dais. Munching, crumbs spilling from his lips.

'I was starving,' he piped. Grubby brown knees poked from under a threadbare cotton vest.

'Thus today we celebrate Lucky and give thanks—' the mana-priest persevered.

'And give gifts?' the boy asked hopefully.

'Wait, Jack!' The woman brushed a hand across her short jet hair in some show of tidying herself. 'Lord Osmo van Maanen?' she enquired, gaze flicking to left, to right, not knowing who was who, settling on large cherubic Gunther.

Osmo identified himself.

'—give thanks for the life of Lucky Paula Sariola, our Queen.'

'What do *you* know about her, baldy?' chirped the boy. The woman's mouth twitched bitterly as she swung round: *'Jack, please!'*

'Who might you be, young lady?' asked Osmo – as Sam Peller's hand plucked the priest back into his seat; he had said quite enough of his piece. 'And who is the precocious sprat?'

'Lord Osmo, my name is Jatta. Jatta Sariola.'

'—*Sariola*—'

'—did *you* hear what I—'

'—I don't believe—'

'—just look at the state of her—'

'—raggle-taggle ain't the word—'

'—you do hear as they're a wild lot in the north—'

'It's *her* daughter!' exclaimed Alvar to Gunther. 'The daughter who *won't!*'

'Won't what?' The dream savant was gazing distractedly at the woman, shaking his head. *She could be dear dead Anna's own sister, but for the butchered hair. She could almost be Anna herself* . . .

'What we were talking about. Haven't you heard any gossip in between your dreams? Won't wed on any account. I thought that's why you were agonizing about your Anna, although you denied it . . . Well well! The Daughter Who Won't is here – and it looks as though she *has* after all.' Out came the notebook again.

32

'Or has she? How didn't I hear? No cuckoo babbled anything—'

Impatiently: 'You aren't basing your *Chronicles* entirely on the sayings of cuckoos!'

'That kid's two years old if he's a day—'

'That kid's a *strange* one, Alvar, I tell you—'

'—May I claim sanctuary with you, Lord Osmo? Here in Maananfors for myself and my child?'

'Sanctuary?'

Prey to a flux of feelings, Osmo scrutinized ragged Jatta Sariola. She – or someone – had hacked her hair as though to deny a glossy beauty. Her pear-shaped face had ripened sunbrowned as a shepherd's. A long scratch arced across one prominent cheek. Her narrow dark eyes without much fold to the lids . . . he could imagine the customary smoothly moulded butter of her features, those eyelids slit so neatly without creases. The face of a Sariola. Of one of Lucky's daughters. Who could give long life to the suitor she accepted.

'Is that boy your own?' he asked. She couldn't of course bestow that bizarre gift again, upon a second partner.

'Jack. Yes, he's mine . . .'

Jack scampered; Jack capered; he kicked a leg high, exposing his bare midriff before the vest slid back down.

'Whereabouts is the father?'

'He . . . I didn't know him long. Only for a few days. My mother expelled me when she discovered.' Head high, Jatta glanced around the assembly of guests as if careless of opinion; or perhaps intent on evoking pity without contempt. She didn't enlarge on her explanation.

The hall buzzed; the cuckoo ducked its scrawny neck.

'—seduced, obviously—'

'—abducted and raped, for my money—'

'—for several days on end—'

'—too fast for a seduction, eh—'

'—some fellow determined to seize long life—'

'—whatever the consequences—'

'—including Lucky's rage!—'

'—must have been a man possessed—'

'Why can't Osmo question her privately?' from Nikki. 'Afterwards?'

'What, when she asked in public?' from her brother.

'Can't he, even so?'

'*I* certainly wish to hear!' Tilly may have saved Out from oblivion, yet mere embarrassment wasn't lethal – *this* vagabond woman's predicament was *very* intriguing.

'Who's she appealing for protection *against*?' Alvar prompted his son. 'Against her mother? We might all be busy celebrating a certain lady – but there's no accounting for Crazy Lucky's cranks.'

Osmo nodded. To enrage the madwoman of the north was impolitic. On the other hand, if Lucky was vexed by what happened here in Osmo's hall then he might never need to approach her about a certain matter . . . *What could it be like to have Lucky Sariola as a mother?* Or as a wife, as Bertel Okkonen-Sariola had her . . . ?

'Lady, I need to know the circumstances.'

'Circumstances . . . ? Aren't they plain? I never meant to . . . take a man. To let a man take me. But one man *magicked* me, there's no other word for it.'

'Who was he?'

'Jarl Pakken: that was his name.'

'I never heard of a Pakken.'

'He's my father,' chipped in little Jack. 'I want to meet him. I think I want to fight him.'

'*Hush.*'

Suspicion blossomed in Osmo. 'How old are you . . . Fastboy?'

Jack flickered his fingers. 'Sixty days.'

'*What?*'

'I don't understand it,' cried Jatta, as, gripping the table, Osmo half rose. 'But I'm glad of it! My mother drove me out. I wandered. I gave birth alone in a forest. If Jack hadn't grown so quickly I'd have had real trouble keeping a baby alive.'

'Now *here's* a story,' Alvar exulted; he scribbled minutely. The whole banqueting hall was agog . . . except perhaps for the under-housekeeper, Vivi. Many people had leapt up to stare at the boy – startled, or fascinated, or superstitiously appalled.

'—two months old!'

'—and speaking!'

'—and *understanding*—'

'—he's a *demon* child—'

In the confusion Vivi was straying from her seat, back towards the alcove . . .

*

34

Osmo's voice tightened with controlled nausea. 'Woman, you – mated – with a mutant! You – wasted yourself – on a freak. And a freak is what you gave birth to. No wonder your mother threw you out.'

'She didn't know how Jack would turn out. She never saw my boy—'

'Cuckoos might have told her a mutant man charmed you, Jatta Sariola. There's a cuckoo right here—' *Sent by whom? By Crazy Lucky, to see that her deceitful daughter reaped suitable justice?* 'It's watching! It's listening! For this!'

'I see the bird. I don't know its intentions, Lord Osmo.'

'*You mated with a mutant—*'

'Jarl didn't seem . . . He was different! Entrancingly, compellingly. Do you understand? He was intoxicating.'

'Do you expect all mutants to have fingers on their feet – or three eyes? Your child's a mutant, lady, son of a mutant. Isn't he?'

'I don't know.' Jatta coughed to clear her throat. 'Maybe Jarl was like you, my lord? A proclaimer can force events to happen. A proclaimer can overwhelm people.'

'If *I* had a son,' Osmo fairly roared, 'he wouldn't start speaking within a few days of his birth! He wouldn't be running around gobbling fish pies!'

'—Our Osmo's right—'

'—one of Lucky's daughters opening her legs to a damn freak—'

'—immortalizing him, I've no doubt—'

'—what I wouldn't have given—'

'—catch me risking it—'

'—well, it weren't *rape*—'

'—gave herself willingly—'

'—at least she's honest—'

'—brazen—'

'—her mum must have hacked her hair off—'

Juke was tempted to shout out that no mutant child he knew of had ever grown so fast. Never ever.

What kind of person could possibly have impregnated this Jatta? Some recent arrival from Earth perhaps? Someone whose seed had altered strangely while the Ukko carried him through mana-space?

A mutant? Juke didn't believe it. No one whom he knew of, certainly! No one whom he could imagine. The true cause mattered less than Osmo's bigoted insistence on *that* as the explanation. Pollution by mutant, ha! Juke kept his counsel, irked to cold fury by that sneer about *three eyes*. His own sister's face haunted him as he stared bitterly at Osmo, seeing his future target starkly and unmistakably verified.

Mustn't betray himself. Flicking his gaze elsewhere, he noticed how Vivi loitered near the stone man.

'How long did you bear this child for, Jatta Sariola?'

'Eight months . . . I conceived him in the mushroom season.'

Somebody brayed harshly. Others tittered.

'I survived the winter, homeless.' A statement – or a plea?

'Unhelped?'

She did not answer.

During snowbound months in the forest in that survival hut which a cuckoo had called her to, Jatta was all alone except for that other life growing inside of her. At noon on calm days when snow mirrored turquoise sky she would shovel up pailfuls of the frozen waterwool to melt. Sometimes snow bled where she walked. Blood-stained footprints followed her. She knew that this was no omen, merely the death by crushing of innumerable tiny algae feeding on the snow itself, chlorophyll cloaked in a pigment shielding them from cold. Still, it was an eerie sight. Her breath smoked in the chilled air. She listened to the silence, the loudest source of sound in the cold-locked forest being her own body.

And her own words . . .

During long hours of darkness, conserving lamp oil, Jatta told herself aloud all the stories which her mother had told her in periods of sanity, the same stories which her mother related to the Ukko entity in Earth's asteroid belt long ago and which patterned out the route through mana-space to Kaleva.

Jatta told herself, not knowing that as winter waned towards the cracking of the lakes and thawing of the trees she had an audience within her, who would speak almost as soon as he was born . . .

'He's a mutant,' repeated Osmo, 'and so was his father. Obviously you must seek your sanctuary with mutants.'

'They do need food,' whispered Alvar. 'Fresh clothes too. And

36

especially a couple of days' rest so I can have a proper opportunity to question her—'

'In the hut outside the walls, then, Dad. Not in this keep of ours.'

'If she has to travel east,' Nikki suggested to her brother, 'we might escort her part of the way.'

'A very small part . . . You're forgetting about our work on the sky-boat, Nik.'

'Maybe Lord Beck could bend his route home?'

The dream savant shuddered. *That damnable resemblance to dead Anna. He would be tormented by this Jatta's company. She would distract him from his dreams. Compelled by that likeness, he might make the error of offering this Jatta Sariola hospitality . . .*

'It's wisest,' Gunther said to Nikki, 'that she's sent away quickly, on her own. Besides, I've business with your brother.'

Thus it seemed that consensus endorsed the judgement which Osmo had, in any case, been intending to pronounce. As to Tilly Kippan, she lived far south – and she already had a dog that talked . . . No, Osmo wouldn't seem severe. Wouldn't seem harsh at all. Merely firm, merely just.

Jatta spoke up. 'I came here, Lord Osmo . . .' She broke off to cough. '. . . because your reputation was that of a fair man. You did oust Tycho Cammon, after all . . .'

The stone man. Who was continuing to witness all of this. Still conscious, still aware. Distracted by Jatta's arrival, Osmo had quite forgotten about Cammon. The flit of his gaze caused Jatta to swing round. As she realized the nature of the statue in the alcove her hand fluttered to her mouth.

Fastboy darted from feast table to niche to peer up at that face of pink stone and flesh – in which the eyeballs shifted, in which the lips massaged one another. Was little Jack about to frame a question? Speedily the under-housekeeper pulled the boy to her and clamped his mouth with her hand as though this interception had been her sole purpose in dawdling next to Cammon's nook.

'Jack!' his mother called. 'You come here now!' Vivi obligingly propelled the boy, and her mother clutched the urchin to her. Sight of the petrified man seemed to have numbed Jatta's spirits; she did not continue with her entreaty.

While Osmo hesitated, the cuckoo, balancing upon one leg, lifted a foot to scrape its claws cat-like on the purple tammywood beam. Next, it manicured its other foot. The bird might have been mocking him.

He's weighing up whether to deal with Jatta or the stone man first, decided Juke. *Too much vodka lowers his potential, bleeds away power ... He already used his talent twice. He needs to measure himself. He can be vulnerable. Why didn't he unpetrify more of Tycho Cammon? Why not make Cammon dance a heavy jig to entertain the gathering? Oh, Osmo's nobility of heart would forbid such mischief. Such vulgarity. But if he softened too much of Cammon, might he be wary of his prisoner breaking free ... ?*

'Fastboy,' proclaimed Osmo, 'I name you *Demon* Jack ... Pakken. Jatta Sariola: hear my judgement. You mated with a mutant man and you bore a mutant child whose future may be ... helter-skelter.'

If it wasn't true that a mutant had bewitched Jatta – of course it wasn't true! – why then, Osmo was falsifying the origins of this present affair in his rush to judgement. His Lucky's Day party was being rudely interrupted – by one of Lucky's own daughters. Was there something about a daughter of Lucky which ... disconcerted him? Scared him? So that he felt impelled to abbreviate her presence in his hall?

'You may remain here till noon on the day after tomorrow, to recover your energy, Jatta Sariola. Take as much food as you need. And new clothing. Then you will leave here and travel east to find where mutants live. *This is spoken.*' Spoken with a passionate energy. Jatta listened, downcast. She touched her sheathed knife fleetingly; her hand flinched away.

'Sam Peller! Show Jatta Sariola and Demon Jack to the storm-hut. See that they're fed.'

'That's the second time,' observed Tilly, 'that the man leads a bitch out to kennel.'

Jack jerked a reproachful finger at Osmo. 'Mummy, *why?*' She tousled his dark hair sadly.

'What happens once can happen twice,' Gunther agreed dourly. The dream savant refrained from watching Jatta depart with guards and Sam and child.

Up above, the manicured cuckoo cackled. Sidestepping away from the king-post, the bird shat upon the beam. Clacking open its scaly green wings, it pitched forward into flight and swooped along the hall, out through the wide doorway away into an evening still undimmed.

'If you ever do finish your *Chronicles*, Alvar—'

'Hush, but I'm still making notes!'

'Perhaps you'll forever be making notes . . .'

Alvar tutted.

'. . . if there's never any obvious conclusion. If events occur and occur, recur and recur.'

'*Shhhh—*'

However, Gunther urgently needed to speak about something, *anything*, other than the young woman who had just been exiled from the hall, and from his view.

'. . . how many people will actually read these *Chronicles* of yours?'

'Tsk! They'll be learned and chanted across Kaleva.'

'And corrupted and embellished, I've no doubt.'

'They'll be *printed* one day, drat it.'

'Down at Kip'an'keep?'

Alvar threw down his pen. 'No, I rather expect the Earth authorities will print them for me – in as many copies as I want. In fact I paid a visit to Penelope Conway a few years ago.'

'Really?'

'She's *keen*. Very keen to have a true record of facts from our point of view to supplement their own data. She gave me several notebooks like this one. Even offered me a *data-pad*, would you believe? And a voicer too. Tiny things, big enough to store ten thousand volumes, so she said. But I don't trust electronics. Mana might warp the memories.'

'Memories,' murmured Gunther yearningly.

Osmo gazed thoughtfully after the bird. For several minutes he steepled his hands upon his chin to compose himself before descending – acknowledging tipsy appreciations and feast-thanks – to buttonhole Vivi.

'Did you ask the stone man anything?'

The under-housekeeper shook her russet, frizzy head.

'*He* didn't say anything either? Couldn't say anything?'

Apparently not.

'Don't let danger fascinate you, my dear. I shouldn't want to dismiss you. You and I . . . well, the flesh sometimes hungers, doesn't it?'

The widow nodded hesitantly. 'Lord Osmo, the stone . . . yearns. I could sense yearning.' Beads of sweat studded her cheeks, dilute liquid gold distilling from her freckles.

'How powerful was his yearning?'

'Like some frozen waterfall before the ice breaks: that was the sight that came into my mind. Shall I come to you later on? After the dancing? During the songs and chants?'

'I ought to talk to my mother. She'll be awake and restless.'

'Mightn't your father—?'

'He'll want to scribble while today's fresh in his mind. Were you offering to share my bed tonight, Vivi, so as to banish the stone man from your mind?'

'A little . . . That's true. But not only that.' Her lips pursed in a muted hint of kiss. She tilted up her chin, though Osmo barely overtopped her; radiating a sensual, if not over-assertive, friendliness towards him.

'Just you carry on enjoying yourself. I'd better tuck Cammon up tight. Oh . . . and in future don't you clean him. Let him dust over, crust over. I mightn't display him again.'

'People will be disappointed. That's sad.'

'Sad, for a human monster? I don't think he's really such a wonderful souvenir.' Osmo's attention strayed to the figure of Sam Peller, returning from outside. White-haired Sam: another trophy? Though a loyal and living one?

Vivi nodded towards the open arras. 'He's a bit . . . awesome.'

'I used to think so too.'

'If I might say it . . . don't doubt yourself, Osmo. What you decided about that woman was wise. It didn't harm her. It might well fulfil her.' Vivi cocked her head, she smiled. A shred of lamb was caught between two of her front teeth that angled apart; and he smelled vodka pleasantly on her breath.

Osmo wended his way to the niche and spoke Tycho Cammon thoroughly back into stone. He himself swung the silver-threaded tapestry of harper trees against the wall once more. A fiddler struck up; the flautist tootled. Streams burbled; the musical trees seemed to twang. Hands stacked dirty platters; arms heaved a few benches up on to table-tops. Prancing and flirting invaded the area by the arras. The summer sun hung low, reluctant to hide itself even for the few scant hours till it rose again.

'You're awake, Mother?'

A single brass tablelamp – one of several large ornate

examples – burned in the wainscotted chamber where Johanna lay on her broad bed in an airy lace nightgown. A window stood open upon a fragrant dark courtyard, admitting faint far chants. The plastered uppers of the walls were painted with floral garlands. Cut-glass bowls of fruits and berries shared table space with the lamps, while one much huger crystal vessel held discarded cores, skins, pith, rind, peel, already rotted or still rotting down into a mouldering goo, releasing a heady aroma of fermentation. Osmo's mother adored the smell of decaying fruit. Spitted on a wrought-iron cuckoo perch outside the window was half of a shrivelled pomegranate. A wooden puzzle lay on the floor; another on the silk counterpane, its notched rhombs and polygons, square dumb-bells, pyramids and prisms of assorted polished woods partially dismantled. The bedside marquetry table held a carafe and bottles of nostrums.

One eye opened in a beetroot face; then its partner.

'My blood pounds too swiftly, Osmo. Annetta already told me about your visitor. A daughter of Lucky's, spurned by her own mother! How could she? She's mad, of course. Intermittently mad. We all know it. Too much living; though that's *not* to say long life's a bad thing ... Too many daughters, perhaps, down the centuries! Growing, wedding, dying. Never a son for variety ... Does she grow careless with daughters? You deserve one of those girls, Osmo. Before too long. I myself don't mind about death ... My blood rushes towards the river where the swan swims.'

'Why not let me try to ease—?'

'*No!* I shan't be proclaimed at. I promised myself long ago when you aged Sam Peller. I'm your mother who bore you, not a puppet.'

Osmo perched by the burly, ruddy-faced woman. Fastidiously he adjusted the ribbon rosettes on his knees.

'When the swan takes me,' she whispered, 'you'll wish for a daughter of Lucky's then, because I'll have gone through a gate into darkness and left it standing open for you too, in time, unless you do something. Stop dithering your days away.'

'I can't believe you're threatening to die just to bring something home to me—'

Johanna chuckled. 'When your father retired, I retired too, you might say. *He* has his hobby. His passion. Now that he no longer needs to be lord he can be a dusty, dandified old pedant. Well, that doesn't involve me, since I won't ever read his screeds. Me,

41

I'm quite commonplace, I'd say. So your talent came from out of the blue. Out of mana. What a wonderful gift.'

'What are you saying, Mother? That I might be some sort of . . . abnormality?'

Johanna hauled herself up, ample bosoms heaving, to recline against pillows which Osmo hastened to plump into place behind her.

'No, no, I'm saying that you have to preserve your gift for *the centuries* for the sake of the van Maanen name. When does one pickle a pepper? When it's starting to shrivel? Or when it's fresh? You might have advantaged yourself with Lucky when she hears of your judgement.'

'Don't imagine it didn't cross my mind.'

Johanna's fingers sought out little wooden rhombs and prisms, twisting them against each other, over, under, without her once looking, as she felt for patterns of events. And for traps, false turnings.

'Though Annetta did feel you were a *mite* fast . . .'

'What right has your maidservant—?' Osmo reconsidered quickly, thinking of his own affinity with Vivi. 'Is somebody else's misery to be entertainment, Mother?'

'Ah now, that does sound truly mature. Ripe for pickling. Even if your real desire was to rush that wayward mother and her demon-child out of sight.'

'Your Annetta does give rather detailed reports . . . But really, to call yourself commonplace! When Dad was lord I swear you orchestrated everything.'

'Now he isn't lord any longer, and now I'm virtually dying.'

'You aren't dying, Mother. Was it totally Dad's idea to retire? You didn't even need to be down in the hall tonight, did you?'

'Oh, the excitement might have killed me. I'd have been intruding on your role as host. One doesn't need a dowager infesting a young lord's banquet.'

'Dad was there.'

Johanna laughed. Her face flushed ruddier; her dugs quaked. 'Oh, I'll burst, I'll burst. The swan will come for me tonight. Osmo, dear, I beg a favour. Of course you can refuse me if you have other engagements . . .'

'Which I don't.'

'You handled Tilly well. Alliance with the Kippans would be

42

of minor value compared with you-know-what. Tilly's a bit of a chit. I imagine she may even have been sent here by the woodlord to look you over.'

'Really? Lyle spent most of his time looking her over. Tilly didn't seem to object.'

'Thus she displayed her beguiling qualities before your very eyes.'

'How perceptive Annetta is.'

'Oh, don't sound sour. A mother needs to consider the future, especially when she's on her death-bed.' Johanna patted the counterpane complacently. Her florid moon face beamed. Wound thrice around her crown, the braided grey rope of her hair which she washed once a year, ceremonially.

'This is *not* your death-bed.'

'Is that a proclamation? Naturally it's my death-bed, silly! Where else shall I die – some day or other? Why, in this very bed! Nor would one want to wait for Elmer's kid sister to mature a little more. That would be quite like marrying Elmer himself. Friendship's *one thing*.' Two pyramids of mustardy yellover wood fitted upside-down, upon a tammywood dumb-bell; a speckled beige prism of horzma wood capped them.

Osmo sighed. 'What favour, Mother? I'm quite tired.'

Concern bloomed; Johanna peered. 'Why are you so tired?'

'I'm not *so* tired. I'm *quite* tired. Long day; and vodka.'

'Several proclamations . . . and the stone man too. Never mind,' and she brushed his hand, 'you look so . . . dapper. Quite like—' Reaching out, discarding the puzzle, she mussed his chestnut hair.

'Don't say it.'

With a fingertip she touched the pit in his cheek as if that were her special private place, the tiny inverse of a nipple, and he twitched.

'—but Alvar's best could never match *your* best. That's what parenthood's all about: betterment. And then the parent can die happily. If he'd forced you to learn to read like him, well! Writing lessens the power of words, doesn't it? I wouldn't let him. I had a *presentiment*.'

'The *favour*—'

'Yes! Will you sleep in my room tonight? On the couch? I feel this may be my last night.'

'You don't mean it.'

'I do too! I feel the swan is coming. Or maybe it isn't the *swan*

43

exactly . . . I'd be so much happier with you here. My blood could slow down. I could sleep.'

'On Lucky's Day,' grumbled her son, 'with guests in our keep, this hero who bested Tycho Cammon – who's supposed to court one of Lucky's daughters – has to sleep in his mama's room . . .'

'To please her. When you were a boy—'

'I was a boy. I admit the awakening of my talent . . . puzzled me.'

'Be a good boy again for one night.'

'To prevent me from seeking out Tilly? I've no interest in her. Lyle has.'

'To save me from the *swan*, Osmo.'

Osmo wrenched one of the rosettes roughly from his knee and tucked it into the top of Johanna's lace gown. 'There's a favour!' Nevertheless, he kicked off his shoes, loosened his waistcoat, discarded   .s belt, and stepped towards the couch where a rug lay folded. In passing, he turned off the fish-oil lamp.

Unbuttoning, he lay down in the fruity reek, his senses dazing. For a while in the darkness pieces of the complicated wooden puzzle continued to click together. Wedges, notches: sliding out, twisting, sliding in.

4 · UKKO IN THE SKY

Distant chanting, faint rattling-bone rat-tat of a drum carried on the current of night . . . Osmo reclined by the open window, hot with spirit, torrid with his own inner fire as much as with the alcohol burning inside him, and cloyed by the bouquet of rotting fruit which seemed to him now to be his mother's breath, exhaled sweetly, sourly, engulfing him.

In the banqueting hall the party should soon be fizzling out; Sam would see to the winding down. Yet now Osmo felt feverish rather than drowsy. His weariness had taken on a hectic hue, robbing him of rest. This could be one of those tiresome nights when he lay brightly and confusedly conscious, forever on the brink of sleep. He lolled inert as a corpse, willing no movement yet sweltering, sweating while images coursed through his head.

. . . of the first time his friend Elmer came to stay, for half a summer, at the keep: a lean mop-headed lad of ten to Osmo's twelve, though just as tall.

The visit was Alvar's idea – or had it really been Johanna's? Osmo was showing signs of, well, *subordination* to Sam Peller. Sam and Osmo were being tutored together companionably in all that a future lord of Maananfors – and a steward of his keep – might need to understand. Mental arithmetic, economics of fisheries and farming, self-defence and tactics, the geography of northern Kaleva ... Sam took Osmo fishing on the turquoise lake. Sam led the young lordling to bag soarfowl in beds of reeds. With crossbows Sam and he stalked scampering leppis in the woods. That son of Alvar's steward was a useful adventurous companion and junior bodyguard ... but not at all a van Maanen.

Elmer quickly filled the subordinate role which Osmo had been slipping into. The mastery returned to Osmo. This Loxmith boy was enthusiastic and guileless – although not in a pathetic fashion. He could be led, persuaded, like a trusterfish tickled out of water. Yet he soon showed how clever he was where machines and tools were concerned. A piece of equipment was a living body to Elmer, and he a masseur who knew it inwardly simply by touch. Its purpose, its proper rhythm, its possibilities. In him, ingenuousness was the twin of ingenuity. Transparent of heart, he saw through mechanical complexities.

Soon after Elmer and escort had crossed the lake to Maananfors in his father's power-launch, *Sea Sledge*, bronze-skinned Juttahats had begun long-distance forays. Apparently senseless ones, aimed simply at stirring the stewpot. A few farmers died, a few farms were looted, but by no means all those lying in their path, by no means. A few girls were captured, abducted away – for what reason? To arouse passions? Anxiety? Anger? To spark a useless war which people couldn't win, and so cull and enfeeble the human population to some extent?

One of the servants of the Brazen Serpents stood in the town pillory – caught by Maananfors scouts during a skirmish. The Juttahat had let itself be caught easily enough.

Since capture the alien had remained totally mute. Many Juttahats simply did not understand human speech, but this specimen could have been a semi-flexible statue. Sudden clashings of metal behind its head had produced not a flicker. Maybe the message this prisoner conveyed, if indeed it aimed to convey one, was: *no communicable reason for hostilities*.

Or else, in itself, it was a bargaining card if Lord Alvar chose

45

to use it as such. This might be a test of Alvar's acuteness.

To appease his people Alvar had the Juttahat pilloried in town in the sculpture park, with orders that it shouldn't be injured and a watchman always on duty to ensure this. Oh, it was pelted with fish guts by relatives of those killed or kidnapped, but nothing damaging, and they desisted once it licked out a maroon tongue and sucked some adhering entrails into its mouth. Otherwise, it was mainly fed with porridge.

Elmer had already repaired a moribund clock in the keep and, according to him, he knew all about his parents' power-boat. Now he begged to examine a smashed gadget taken from the captive. Using tweezers and a bent safety pin – while Alvar and Felix Peller and his son and Osmo looked on amusedly – the boy had probed and pried in that palm-size box of loose cells, beads, wafers, and filaments, jiggling and rearranging.

'It's some sort of communicator,' Elmer decided. 'But it doesn't feel complete. There's a bit missing . . . *here*, about the size of a silver half-mark.'

Osmo's father had chuckled: '*Crafty*, Elmer!' – and handed over a coin. Which, once in place, after a few more tweaks and twiddles, caused the device to buzz loudly, before filaments melted and it quit.

'Or a . . . *beacon*, perhaps?' suggested the boy. 'A signal?'

'Well now, they can already guess their creature's here, if that's all the use this is! A bonfire which promptly quenches itself isn't much use, ha!' However, Alvar let Elmer keep the half-mark. To make the alien box squawk at all was an accomplishment – more than had been achieved with the captive.

The creature was by now on display down in town. Avoiding Sam, Osmo and Elmer sneaked off to the park the next day.

The chained Juttahat wore a tawny one-piece livery of tough scaly artificial fabric of a coppery hue, the formerly lustrous sheen diminished by smear and dirt. Sinuous black hieroglyph on one shoulder.

The servant of the snakes was manlike, though its golden eyes were closer set than most human eyes. A membrane nictitated over its eyeballs, glazing those briefly every half minute or so. Nostrils flaring down from a thin bridge slowly closed and opened. A prim cupid mouth disclosed dainty little teeth, a couple of which had been knocked out. Twin tiny blue gland-slits beaded its jutting chin with salival pearls. A felt-like ruddy mat of fuzz capped its skull, above a tawny face. Its hands and feet were slightly webbed. Bootless, five-toed, the captive stood upon a trampled smear of oddly fragrant gingery excrement moist with urine.

Drizzle misted the air, deterring spectators. A bearded blue-clad watchman sat whistling on a plinth, cudgel beside him, lightpistol at his waist. Perched on the bent chartreuse quiff of a curver tree roosted a cuckoo, its speckled green plumage gleaming with damp – like some rust-diseased, stubby minor limb of the tree.

The previous autumn, Osmo's mother had insisted on a visit with her son to the gala in Speakers' Valley. That was some two hundred and fifty keys to the north-east of Maananfors and eighty keys north of Landfall, where the Earthfolk had their bastion and shuttlefield. Osmo had rather hoped they might travel by way of Landfall, but no, he wasn't to be distracted from events at the gala – where indeed he was thrilled by the bespeaking (this was well before Tycho Cammon soured the proceedings) and even amused by some of the non-mana versifying . . .

Facing the mute Juttahat now, and spurred by Elmer's clever meddling with the signal device, Osmo strove to impress.

He cast his mind back to the bespeakings in the tree-girt valley. Those had sent such a thrill of unexpected excitement through him, a ripple almost of recognition.

He posed.

'I'll make this monster *work*, Elmer! Just as you made its box work. You watch, now!'

He strained, uncertain quite which sinew of the mind to flex, so therefore flexing his boyish muscles. His junior thighs, his chest, his biceps; puffing himself up. Visualizing cords linking himself to this creature that stood shackled before him, imagining strings by which he could pull it – and also strings which led away from its present location, over land, over lake, down earlier days which had passed away into mana. Oh, suddenly to know something revelatory about this enigma!

'You,' he addressed those golden, quick-blurring eyes. Hastily he lowered his voice an octave. '*You*,' he growled, 'Isi-isi-isi snakes sent you here. You will tell me *why*, or else . . .' Osmo cast around. 'Or else I'll turn you into a real statue! Dummy, you will *talk*; for this is spoken.'

The exotic unman regarded the boy and shuddered. It rattled its fetters, it pursed its lips. Toes raked faeces.

47

'*Th'shee sheeloo ¡k'thuu ruvii sa'isi ¡kex'¡keedzuu—*' A sibilant clicking voice . . .

'Elmer, I did it!' Spinning around: 'Watchman! Watchman!'

. . . who had come alert, with cudgel.

'Definitely made some noises,' the bearded guardian agreed.

'Well now,' marvelled Elmer.

'Must tell my mother.'

'Not your dad?'

'Shut up, I'll forget what it said. *Coo-coo!*' he called to the top of the curver tree. The scaly green bird peered down at the boy, head cocked. '*Th'sheee shee—*' Osmo spluttered. 'Did you hear what the Jutty said?' Of course, the bird didn't reply, although it blinked.

'Do cuckoos answer personal questions hereabouts?' Elmer asked.

Osmo was momentarily tempted to kid his friend, but really this was no time for triviality.

'Cuckoo, cuckoo, tell the tale!' Pointing, 'Fly north half a key to keep. Go to perch in inner courtyard. Tell Johanna van Maanen that Osmo bespoke the Juttahat. Tell her what it said . . . if you heard.' A cuckoo's hearing was considered acute.

'*Ukko-ukkoo,*' croaked the bird. Stretching, it flapped a spray of water from its wings. Then it launched itself out of the curver tree, circled the little park lazily to gain height, and headed up away over a vague mizzly red rooftop, northward.

Presumably it was going to do as he had told it.

'Neither an answerer nor an asker be; that's their motto,' quoted Elmer.

'I know, I know.'

'Though you'd *think* if they can understand us directing them they could talk to us properly. It's as if,' said he of the enquiring mind, 'there's a bit missing from their brains the way that silver was missing—'

'Never mind *that*. I made the Jutty speak!'

'I mean, my mum's mutant cat can talk to us—' Was Elmer simply overawed by Osmo's little triumph? He must be.

What Elmer had said registered belatedly. 'You keep a mutant cat?' Osmo spat. 'You ought to put it out of its misery.'

'It does whine about fish a lot of the time. Pleads like a loony.'

'Lame-brained pathetic parody!'

'Be fair, it *converses*, after a fashion. Whereas a cuckoo—'

'The cuckoo has flown. And I bespoke a Jutty.'

48

'You did, you did. Gosh, Osmo—'

'Let's *go*.'

And the two boys dashed back through the drizzle up the hill back to the keep.

In through that great gateway, across the paved courtyard (horses snuffling in their stables), up a spiral stone stairway . . . Along one dim rug-strewn corridor then another, past guest bedchambers, the family sauna, dining room, Lord Alvar's study . . . brushing past a maid, a clerk . . .

Osmo's mother was striding around her chamber in buttoned blue bodice and long purple skirt, embroidered kerchief askew on her head. Her long brown pigtail swung as though with a will of its own. Her big face beamed. Alvar, perched on her bed in breeches and braided jacket, had pulled off one shoe and white sock and was arching his bare foot. Creasing map-lines into the sole, he probed with a neat fingernail at a callus. A dismantled puzzle littered the counterpane.

'Boys!' exclaimed Johanna. '*Osmo!*'

No cuckoo sat on the wrought-iron perch outside the window, which was open.

'Mother—'

'I know! The bird came, it spoke, it flew away. Oh Osmo. It's because of our name, you know, our *name*. Van Maanen spells *mana*.'

'I don't know about that,' said Alvar, who could read. Osmo's father flexed leathery crevices in his foot, a web of cross-wise valleys. Tweezing, he pulled loose a tiny knob of stony skin.

'You oughtn't to do that, dear. You'll harm your flesh.'

'It's like walking on a *pebble*.' Nevertheless, Alvar replaced sock and shoe. 'So, lad, you bespoke a Juttahat. Well, *well*! Impressive.'

'If he'd smothered himself in books – as I warned you . . .'

'I wonder why it only spoke in Juttahat jargon . . .'

'Doesn't know any other.'

'So how did it understand his order?'

'He compelled it, Alvar. Compelled it. A proclaimer can compel a beast.'

'Hmm. Hmm.' Osmo's father stood, not quite as tall as Johanna; nor nearly as burly. 'So, son, we'd better hobble down there and see if we can repeat the performance. The *impressive* performance, yes indeed.'

Johanna's tail of hair swung, hugely catlike. 'It's drizzling outside. We'll need our cloaks.'

After the gentry had departed from the Lucky's Day feast Juke had sat through the drumming and chanting. *Rum-tum, rum-tum*, then *rat-a-tat*, faster and faster. That mana-priest might be a bumbler at speechifying but he was a dab hand on the kettledrum. A shoal of tiny, painted, fish skeletons patterning the vellum drumhead reverberated madly as the wispy-haired, grey-suited fellow took the rhythm up to a couple of hundred beats a minute. Arms linked two by two, guests chanted names and nicknames of a dozen fish breathlessly in a weaving network of voices which finally converged to capture one particular species, all in unison. Sometimes a lone voice boobed, calling out the wrong name. Chanters hooted, and resumed. It was a game; it was a bond; it was a luck-spell. Juke could play no part, but he drummed his fists on his knees and smiled enthusiastically, mouthing.

Lit an hour since by tapers on long rods, candles burned in two of the chandeliers. Lustres twinkled, reduplicating light. Shadows skulked like dark shaggy dogs.

The amity of the occasion eluded Juke. How easily blood could be spilled. A fit of temper, a provocation, a misunderstanding. That fisherman had shown how easy it was to yield to a sudden overwhelming compulsion, to be swept away by the tide of mana. A fellow must control himself before he could control others. So was what Juke now planned – what he now brooded upon and visualized, as the drumbeats raced – a reckless impulse? A piece of folly? Not if he'd thought it through enough times. Not if he avoided being caught.

'Gloweye—'
      'Sweetfin—'
            'Anchorfish—'
                  'Sparky—'

In the panting percussive pause after a triumphant, almost simultaneous shout of *sweetfin-sweetfin*, from across the courtyard came a shrill cry.

'Ukko in the sky! Ukko in the sky!'

A scrambling, agog bustle towards the main door. Drum suddenly mute – the mana-priest part of the rush. But not Juke, no not Juke. Juke darted the other way. For a moment he paused on the threshold of the doorway leading to the kitchens. Then he slipped out of sight.

Vaulted dark passageway. A fierce hiss made his heart thump – a cat skedaddled.

Avoid kitchens themselves; scullions might sleep in there. Broad steps descended leftward.

Knapsack in one hand, sliding fingers of the other hand across a granite wall, probing with his boot-tips, circling downward . . . into utter darkness.

A chilly embrace, hands of cold air, enveloped the hideaway.

Distant bonfires flamed by the lake, scarlet flowers twisting. Low down in the southern heavens the great sickle of silver and pearly brilliance which had once been Kaleva's moon arced outward in space, dimming constellations in a tenth of the sky, quicksilvering water at the horizon, dusting a far forest phosphorescently. By no means blinding the eyes of those who had rushed from the hall to the gleam of a halfpenny moonlet swinging low across the skyvault . . .

'Ain't our Ukko,' commented bailiff Sep amid the crowd of watchers outside the main gate. 'Ours buzzed off ten days ago, didn't it?' He broke wind noisily and hastily shifted his position.

'An Isi one,' said Sam Peller. 'Wonder what they're landing now.'

'Pissmire snakes—'

'*Our* world, bollock it! *We* got here first—'

'Chase 'em away's what I say—'

'You and whose army of Juttahats—?'

'—could cream us all off if they really wanted—'

'Brindleds don't bother us—'

'—Brazens gave old Alvar the sky-boat as reparation—'

'Pah!'

'—needing a spot of repair, so I hear—'

'What d'you expect, after years? Young Loxmith'll spruce it up—'

'Lightguns too, don't forget—'

'Wouldn't need those if there weren't Brazen Isi and Velvet Isi—'

'So why don't snakes get on fighting each other—?'

'In my opinion,' Sam said loudly, 'war's a *human* idea—'

'Isi aren't warlike, snowhead? With their Juttahat troops and guns and *niggling*—?'

'Bless the Ukko, anyway,' pronounced the mana-priest as the bright little oval moon dipped down around the camber of the world. 'Sister of the egg we hatched from here.'

'The *sister* of an *egg*—?'

('Oaf—')

Sighting the Ukko put a convenient stop to the party. His opinion unappreciated, Sam Peller trotted back across the courtyard and shut one door of the hall emphatically. From inside he collected the mana-priest's kettledrum. Drunks returning to town could catch the tail-end of the bonfire celebrations if they cared to . . .

It was exquisitely cool, at first, in the ice-room. After the heat of the hall, Juke revelled in the wintry chill. 'Hoo,' he risked calling sharply just once to hear echoes. *Big enough.* With hands outstretched he began to feel out the span of that subterranean chamber carved into the marble of the hilltop. A mass of straw-wrapped ice blocked his progress in this direction, then in that: bricks of ice sawn from the lake five or six months earlier. Discarded straw was damp underfoot, though the absence of standing meltwater suggested drainage channels somewhere. Or perhaps not. The chamber was frigid.

He bumped into a leaden body, which swung away, then back. A carcass. Of course. On a hook.

And what was this? Shelves, with pots of . . . sniff one . . . roe. None of that at the banquet.

Don't dip your finger in, though . . .

Better still, *stay* still. Don't knock anything over.

So he remained motionless, visualizing how events should unfold for cocky Osmo that night. Despite his cloak, Juke soon began to shiver, and the initial pleasure of being in the ice-room became a pain. But he would need a cool head, wouldn't he?

How would sister Eyeno react to being in this glacial quiet darkness? What kind of poem might she make? One about blindness . . . about the arctic, daylong night . . . about looming unseen objects? About dead bodies standing upright close at hand . . .

And pots of roe. Everything was ordinary. *Don't be spooked.* He needed to be imaginative when he went upstairs again – but with a purpose, not dreamily.

*

The Juttahat prisoner down in the park had only drooled when Osmo bespoke it again. Still, the watchman confirmed that it had definitely made some peculiar hissing and clicking sounds; which was proof enough for Johanna . . .

In the hot retrospect of near-slumber where past events glowed as if inflamed, lying there in that warm daze of fermenting fruit, Osmo brooded whether that shackled servant of serpents might have been *acting*, long ago. Could its masters conceivably have sensed the boy's potential? Known of his trip to Speakers' Valley? Felt inspired to stimulate him? Was *that* perhaps a purpose of the raids? Aside from some inexplicable kidnappings . . . accompanied by mayhem which faded away.

And the smashed beacon-device . . . Had that somehow been intended for Elmer's clever fingers? Oh, the Isi were wily; though this might seem to attach too much importance to the activities of two boys.

One of whom, however, was to be future lord of Maananfors. The other, the inheritor of Loxmithlinna. Isi loved to meddle, didn't they? Often in bizarre ways. One faction trading some alien machine; then a different faction launching a raid.

After what seemed a full hour, Juke crept back up from the ice-room.

The banqueting hall was silent and empty. Candles were dead in the chandeliers. Silvery light from the sky-sickle infused illumination. The main doors were closed, and windows too. The catch of a window yielded. Juke pushed the tall glass slightly ajar. Then he navigated his way between tables and benches, stowed his knapsack, and swivelled that harper-tree tapestry out from the wall.

Tycho Cammon stood as before, and as always, naked, fists clenched by his sides commemorating his final vain resistance to Osmo's will. Muscular thighs . . . and arms too, though his sculptural belly bulged with spare flesh. A heavy oppressive face, selfishly sensual. For the first time, Juke registered a narrow crimped arc of beard skirting the base of Cammon's chin. Above a high protuberant forehead tight curls were dense wavelets lapping a shore of incipient baldness.

Could the stone man register Juke's presence at all? In the faint pearly light Tycho's eyeballs were calcified boiled egg, glittering ever so slightly.

Juke's own gaze drifted down again, over ossified pectorals and bulging polished abdomen to Tycho's tight pubic curls, stubby rock-cock twisted leftward, his stones solidly empouched.

The hideaway brushed back his greasy hair.

Could he really summon Cammon back to life? Fully so? Arm and leg, hand and foot, biceps and belly and bowels . . . This had begun to happen a few scant hours ago. To a certain extent. To a small degree. The stone man should still be resonant with the possibility of arousal. And once partly roused, urgent with yearning? Able to add to Juke's own power any force he still possessed?

Perhaps Cammon only ought to be *questioned*, about that afternoon in Speakers' Valley when he had succumbed. How exactly had Cammon failed? What had he sensed regarding Lord Osmo's weaknesses? How would he recommend a new adversary to pitch himself against that foppish, mutant-hating hero? If Cammon's advice proved accurate, then Osmo's trouncer would promise to come back here and free the stone man . . . And perhaps never keep his promise, for who in the whole world would want Tycho Cammon revived?

This was sheer timidity! By rousing Cammon fully Juke would be matching himself against Osmo van Maanen in advance of the gala. Testing himself; proving himself.

And quite likely – quite conceivably – van Maanen would never get to travel to the gala at all. Van Maanen would be killed or crippled by his liberated victim tonight. Quite so. He could indeed be; though Juke doubted that the stone man possessed too much of his old vigour . . .

Osmo would at the very least be highly disconcerted by what was going to happen. Undermined! Not knowing how Cammon had managed to soften and step from his niche, Osmo must suspect himself of an inexplicable *failure* of his talents . . .

Ah yes. At the very least. While Juke himself would feel quite enhanced.

'I'm doing this for *you*, beloved sister,' murmured Juke. He poised himself and breathed deep, imagining fiercely how events must fall out when, uttered with utmost conviction, the right words prescribe happenings.

'Tycho Cammon,' he announced. 'Hear me, *Tycho Cammon*.' Borrow a little of what van Maanen had said? Yes, why not? 'You were a man of flesh and blood, Tycho.' *Reiterate his identity.* 'You were a hero, Tycho. To your horror a whippersnapper turned you to stone, Tycho, and brought you to his keep to stand naked

54

in his banqueting hall behind a curtain to amuse his guests once in a while. Now older, the whippersnapper wearies. He roused you to speak – and he forgot! He forgot about you. He spoke you back to stone negligently, wearily. You're rousing again, Tycho. You're softening. Soon you'll move – and you'll seek out van Maanen in his bedchamber where he snores drunkenly—'

Alvar decided to negotiate with the Brindled Isi faction of serpents who had their nests to the north-west rather than with the Brazen Isi of the south-east who were launching the attacks. Maybe the Brindled would agree to mediate, or despatch some of their own Juttahats against those of their Brazen cousins. He sent Felix Peller and an escort hastening north-west on horseback on the long circuitous route between a hundred interposing lakes large and small; and Sam went with his father on this presumably safe errand, leaving Osmo and Elmer to deepen their friendship.

When Peller's party returned a month later, it was with the advice: *release the Juttahat.*

Release the alien imbecile from the pillory.

Indeed, the folks of Maananfors had grown sick of this spectre in their park; and ever since that day when Osmo bespoke it the captive seemed halfwitted as well as dumb and alien. Maybe Juttahats wilted if kept too long away from their kin or from the serpents who controlled them.

A few days after the prisoner was chased out of town by mocking if diffident kids, two sky-boats overflew the keep. Half a dozen white flags and banners rippled on each craft. Truce, truce, a surplus of truce. The sky-boats circled slowly for a while, innocuously, while spectators gathered and guards pointed a few lightrifles upward; then the larger vessel dipped down to land on a table of rock not too far from the keep.

Sky-boats! Were there more than three score of these on the whole world? A bronze-skinned Juttahat sat at the controls of the one which had landed. A Brazen Juttahat, no less. A four-seater, the sky-boat was tarnished, its hull somewhat dented, though the white bunting lent it a spurious air of spick-and-span.

This Juttahat could speak comprehensibly in a clipped mechanical way.

The sky-boat was for Lord Alvar. In atonement . . .

*

55

Lyle Melator stepped out of his guest room, candle in hand, dressing gown silky against his flesh, feet bare – slippers might seem fuddy-duddy. He'd forsaken his spectacles too. The corridor was a blurred tunnel, but a steady wedge of oil-light spilled from one half-open doorway.

That would be Alvar's study, the door ajar for air.

Was the old historian still gassing with Gunther? A useful informant on events of the past three centuries, or at least on those that the dream savant cared about . . . Or was Alvar only scribbling notes insomniacly?

Lyle stroked his frizzy hair and thought of Tilly's tresses arrayed upon a pillow while he stooped over her. While she stared up, wide-eyed with expectation, with invitation. Surely he couldn't have misunderstood Tilly's body signals? As he soft-footed along, quiet voices asserted themselves.

'That *girl*, Alvar. Jatta. So like my Anna. As if time has no meaning—'

'Yet you agreed she should be sent away—'

'Oh *yes*. I shan't be fooled. Beguiled. I want . . . I want to tell you about my plan, Alvar—'

Tobacco smoke savoured with rum and nutmeg tickled Lyle's nostrils. Abruptly boots thumped towards the doorway as if the inadvertent eavesdropper had been scented. Lyle spun round and fled, blowing out his candle as he rushed, dodging – in his after-knowledge of what the candleflame had shown him – into a stairway leading to the top floor of the keep . . . He stubbed a toe agonizingly. His mouth opened in a silent mime of a cry. He dug nails into the palm of his free hand while he froze on the third step until the pain diminished to a throb.

He heard the study door shut, and presently patted at the side of his gown to find pocket and matches. Was there a different way round to where Tilly was chambered? Up, along, down? He *thought* there was.

Gunther's *plan*. . . must surely have some connection with the unspecified equipment which he hoped to commission from Elmer and Lyle. What a shame the door had been closed. Instead of seeking an alternative route, should he tiptoe back, crouch, and put his ear to the keyhole for a while?

Business loomed, between Gunther and Elmer. Could be a neat idea to have the *background* clarified in advance. Though Elmer might react askance to Lyle snooping on their host's father in his sanctum . . . And Tilly beckoned. (Or did she?) *I couldn't help overhearing . . .* , Lyle rehearsed. *You see, I was on my way to a certain lady's room. And once I heard whatever-it-is, I was riveted . . .*

Maybe Osmo might have changed his mind about wanting her company? In her under-housekeeper's room below the eaves, Vivi tossed restlessly on a narrow bed. She certainly wanted his company to exorcise the phantom which kept haunting her whenever she dipped towards sleep, and jerked awake again. Tycho Cammon . . . who had taken women, bespoken them, possessed them hatefully. A pearly glow from the sky-sickle invaded her uncurtained window, waxing and waning on the whitewashed wall; clouds must have begun drifting above the horizon.

Osmo would have said goodnight to his mother by now. Perhaps if Vivi were to creep down to his chamber and linger outside for a while she might hear him pacing . . .

'A strand can shift a block of stone if it becomes a string and then a rope!' declared Juke. 'I am that strand, that string, that rope, that cable pulling you. Sly as gossamer, stout as chain. Soften, Cammon, waken. Return from the grip of rock.'

At last the eyeballs moistened. Lips moved tentatively. The breast heaved. Stone fingers uncurled.

5 · THE STONE MAN WALKS

The stone man's left foot jerked forward cracklingly as if his shinbone was splintering, as if stone were finally relinquishing its grip in the explosive manner that ice snapped on a lake in spring.

Juke hyperventilated dizzily, breathing for two people, massaging the living statue's respiration with his own.

'You can move,' he repeated, gasping, flexing his own muscles. 'You are . . . flesh again . . . through my words, Tycho. You can speak.'

'Who . . . are . . . *you*?'

'I . . .' Juke shut his eyes momentarily, refusing to identify himself. 'I'm nobody. In Osmo van Maanen's eyes – I'm no one at all.' Relaxing, he reminded the man who had been stone: 'You'll seek Osmo van Maanen in his bedchamber, for *this is spoken*.'

Tycho Cammon teetered. 'You must be strong,' he observed, voice coarse as hessian.

'Yes . . . But *are you*, Tycho? Are you?'

Cammon lurched from the niche, stepping down thumpingly on to the waxed yellover floor.

'*Shhhh—*'

The statueman rocked; recovered his balance. 'I was stone. Stone's strong—'

Indeed it seemed to Juke that Tycho Cammon, though largely or even wholly flesh again, still partook of the nature of stone, his body fortified against any ordinary blow. A hook to the chin might snap Cammon's beardcurls but break the assailant's hand.

The heavy-jowled man regarded his rescuer intently; then gradually he reached out his right hand to touch. Just as his palm connected with Juke's chest he jerked downward sharply with the heel of his hand. Half the breath was expelled from Juke's lungs. Juke reeled in surprise.

'Strong enough.' Cammon stroked his palms across his chest, down his flanks and thighs. He seemed quite careless of his nakedness as if any clothing might represent a new confinement. He chuckled: a rattling of pebbles. Gorged lips pouted insolently.

'Van Maanen,' Juke reminded him.

'Oh *that* is spoken,' was the derisive, rasping reply. Cammon hawked dryly. 'I'll drink his blood to wet my whistle, brave boy.'

A sky-boat, in atonement for the raids, the assorted murders and kidnappings . . .

Osmo shifted sultrily on his mother's couch, hectic reminiscence possessing him as if he had slipped into a different, tiresome species of slumber seething not with dreams but with memory – while Johanna herself snored softly nearby.

When Alvar demanded the return of those women and children who had been plucked from their homes, the Juttahat pilot finally claimed they had died of a glandfever. An Isi mana-mage had been about to moult its skin; its glands were secreting a powerful lymph to separate the old skin from the new. The people were affected by its emanations . . . Afterwards, their bodies were cremated.

True? Or untrue? Why should human prisoners have been kept close to a mana-mage?

'Why did you kidnap them?' Osmo's father wanted to know.

'Curiosity,' said the pilot in its flat precise voice – either meaning that this was the motive, or else commenting upon Alvar's question. The Juttahat wouldn't elaborate.

A litre of alcohol would fuel the Isi-conceived, Juttahat-built engines at a hundred keys per hour for a distance of fifty keys with four average human body weights on board.

A sky-boat! A great acquisition. Almost as if a trade had at last been finalized, the currency being not marks and pennies but a few deaths. Were the Isi testing the worth of human lives? With a sky-boat Alvar could travel easily, researching into titbits of the past which tickled his fancy. After the pilot showed Alvar the controls, which appeared uncomplicated, a Juttahat colleague landed the smaller machine to whirlwind its colleague away, leaving the larger vessel to be unburdened of its white flags.

Stripped of bunting, the dun-coloured sky-boat seemed tattier. It needed at least a coat of yachtpaint outside and refurbishment within. But still, it was a *sky-boat*. A light alloy pod the size of quite a few cows, set on fat little wheels, with stubby wingbraces supporting tilting rotors, and tail propellers. A canopy slid forward from a capacious cockpit across the squat transparent nose section in the manner of a glassy shield. Aft of the hatchway, bulging air-intake pipes resembled bisected tubas and brassy serpents.

Almost as soon as he could scramble over the craft, Elmer diagnosed that the rotor bearings were worn but a good blacksmith could craft replacements. Was it *bearings*? Osmo had never been clear about machinery. And a fuel line was frayed. The machine might have crashed within a few hundred more keys, but it could be beautifully renovated.

Over the next week, with Alvar's blessing, humming to himself happily young Elmer had pried into the twin engines till he began to see how to tune them. He babbled about compressors, ceramic combustors and fans and mini-turbines, centrifugal filters, mixers, nozzles, ducts. The engines mainly burned oxygen snatched from the air, the fierce suction also reciprocally pulling the machine, so he said. Any birds or leaves pulled in were flash-combusted by bursts of hotlight. Incoming snow became steam became fuel. A person would be ill-advised to lounge near the mouths of those tubas while the engines came to life, a caveat which the Juttahat pilot had neglected to confide, any more than it had mentioned worn bearings. (*Was it* bearings?) Really, young Elmer proved himself invaluable – not that the sky-boat when delivered was in an actively booby-trapped state. But, *well*—!

An upholsterer worked on the seats. The hull became sky-blue. Alvar paid out compensation to the families of victims . . .

Having closed the study door for privacy, Gunther Beck returned to sag into the high-backed leather armchair. On a two-tier dumbwaiter at his elbow, a fluted yellow sodaglass bowl still half-full of gingerbread cookies, and a half-empty bottle of blueberry liqueur. Scooping up a fistful of the gingerbreads, the dream savant chewed one of the soft rich biscuits thoughtfully. As though abruptly re-addicted to that syrupy blend of ginger and orange peel, cinnamon and cloves from the far-south island of Pootara – his appetite renewed – he munched three more in quick succession. Quizzically he held up the fourth between his fingertips. His ancient ashen eyes – set incongruously in that plumping cherubic face – had grown melancholy, and it seemed as if he might not, after all, relate his plan.

He turned the little gingerbread man to and fro.

A flat fat body, buttock-cleft at the base, as though its body were merely a bum bending over. Two diminutive button arms jutting from its waist. A globular head with tiny round topknot.

'The Mandelbrot Man,' said Gunther, 'that's who our gingerbread fellow really is. Suppose you magnify the cleft between his chin and his shoulder many times, presently you discover a bay of spiralling inlets. Suppose you magnify a fraction of that bay, you find fjords indented within fjords. And down there, hidden deep in the hairy curlicues, in the follicles of fjords, a minuscule gingerbread man – who is the selfsame damned insinuating gingerbread man! – lurks, to commence the cycle again . . .'

Gunther nibbled the head off the cookie, then bit its body in half. '*That* is how events flow, my friend. Not onward, but inward, repeating.' He slapped his brown-clad prominent midriff, and belched gently.

Alvar perched on a rocking chair, his leather shoes shucked off, revealing a toe-hole in one of his scarlet socks, awaiting some explanation of this *aperçu* presumably from the olden days. This dream savant could remember three whole centuries . . . a deep well into which Alvar himself could only toss a somewhat leaky bucket on a long rope to haul up the juice of history.

His informant was visibly wavering between disclosure and prevarication. Maybe Alvar should reposition himself more magisterially in the squab-cushioned carver's chair behind his littered desk? Should waken him up too. Half past one, by the ormolu clock over the fireplace; dawn due in another thirty minutes ... This very late hour conspired with the blueberry liqueur to lull him dozingly. Heave himself up from the rocker? No, now was an intimate, confidential moment. He puffed on his droop-bowl tammywood pipe, releasing a discreet billow of congenial fragrance.

What on Earth significance did Gunther really attach to a bowl of gingerbread men? *Mandelbrot* sounded like some exotic sweetbread. Almond bread? Maybe in a past century the dream savant had nibbled almond bread and gingerbread with his beloved Anna, and the exact spicy taste of those cookies recalled the image of her to him teasingly now.

Hadn't Gunther once said something about certain tastes triggering recollection? And about how curiously little sense of taste or smell existed in dreams considering that in dreams the mind seemed pre-conscious, unaware of self, more akin to the ancient brain before self-awareness dawned? Yet the ancient brain was the smell-brain, the taste-brain. Something along those lines ...

Lines... The copied tempera painting, heavily framed in scroll-carved horzma wood between two neatly ordered tall bookcases, hung askew once more. Alvar twitched, froglike, overcoming an impulse to leap up and straighten the painting. Damned silly Amelie! The maid must have tilted the painting again when she brought the gingerbreads. Amelie was sure that a naughty nakki-spirit could sit on a picture which hung straight, whereas the invisible mischievous little demon would slide off a slanted one.

Was Amelie oblivious to the fact that the lake horizon in *The Revenge of Joukahainen* now sloped downhill? And that Jouka-hainen, already leaning forward into the wind in his quilted winter clothes while he squinted (hair windswept back) along the exact line of that horizon and notched a dart in his crossbow, appeared to be overbalancing! Held back from skidding forward over the ice only by his fussy beseeching little mother. Pah!

Gunther patted the varnished spindly dumbwaiter. 'Do you often take meals on your own in here, Alvar?'

Prevarication . . .

'Sometimes, sometimes – to avoid interrupting my flow of thought about the *Chronicles*. Occasionally I do!'

'Ah, your *flow* of thought . . .'

It was Gunther, not Alvar, who rose. Was the smoke offending him? Might he reopen the door, and at the same time close a door on intimate confidences? Instead, the dream savant stepped over to the painted wooden globe of Kaleva standing next to the desk, mounted in a tilted brass sickle. Contemplatively he spun the orb slowly on its axis.

'Day after day after day, Alvar. Year after year after year . . .'

After years of paralysis Tycho trudged across the banqueting hall, recovering a lost art of movement. Freed from stone, his whole body nonetheless seemed grievously bulky, while his surroundings shifted with rubbery caprice, tables and benches altering their positions and their shapes, swelling, diminishing, the walls elongating and heightening. The world had lost its inflexibility.

Oh, its contents had varied during those fleeting quarter hours and half hours of tormented awareness which had interrupted his rigid statuesque trance. People had partied in the hall, drinking, prancing, gawping, grotesque and threatening in their mobility: actors upon a stage. Yet the stage itself had been rigid: floor and roof and windowed walls. Now it flexed and shifted.

The young man with the swept back hair retreated, massaging his breastbone where Tycho had pushed, yet beginning to grin slyly, jubilantly – a parent enticing its offspring to walk. Tycho bumped a table edge and growled, but did not try to hurl the table aside.

How long had it been? How long? After each teasing partial revival of him, such abominable renewed suffocation of his entire being! Such crushing into a stiff residue of suspended existence, exile to a dim static dream of a dark eternal curtain. He was the hanged man, cut down to take a breath, then hanged again. He wasn't a prisoner – but the empty pillory itself. And periodically – after vast petrified vacancy – abrupt bright deafening goading events cruelly swamped his utterly diminished senses.

Diminished, no longer.

He lurched. The hall lurched. Aye, because he moved. Memories of strength returned to him: the strength to squeeze a person till they split apart, a scream at last bursting from them as their spirit took flight. To speak phrases that were steel fingers. Oh the savage joy of rupturing a man; or of invading a woman, cleaving her while she moaned in the captive ecstasy he gripped her with . . . It had been so long, so long.

The young man shifted circumspectly behind a table. 'Tell me how you lost to Lord Osmo. Tell me now. This is spoken.'

Tycho swayed. Surely he'd once possessed other traits too? He must, he must! Yet those had diminished, been crushed, for compulsion had possessed him – the compulsion to *compel*. Thus he had become . . . monolithic, ruled by a single dark passion, inelastic, prey to a lucky whippersnapper who could make him in reality what he had already become in essence . . . This fleeting insight skittered away, shouldered aside by the pressure of a brutal dominance crystallized to marble.

He couldn't tell about what no longer existed. What was absent. What had fled.

'Tell you? Why, he made me what I am! Hard-hearted.' Disconcertingly, rumblingly, Tycho chuckled. 'How ever did I lose . . . ?'

Johanna hadn't wished Alvar to fly herself and Osmo the two hundred and fifty keys to Speakers' Valley. She felt that the journey was too important to abbreviate. They should travel on foot through the forests of larkery, minty, harper, and yellover, around lakes, by ferry across those few which were too big to bypass. This would teach her son nuances. Features of the landscape were forever repeating themselves in shape and scale: variations within a seeming sameness of woodland and water, farm and fen, knoll and vale, keep and township. Was any wood-hemmed lake the same as any other? Was any shore of the same contour? Was any island in any lake? All were simply lake and island, island and lake. Equally they were themselves. No place en route was unique; yet none was the same.

To her the northern continent was a quilt of subtlety; and one moved most boldly across it by perceiving all of its varying, self-similar threads. If terrain became meaningless, then one's own personal terrain might become amorphous, ill-organized.

The long journey would attune her son's senses, the better to appreciate the poetry and mana-speaking at the gala.

The time when the van Maanens travelled to the *crucial* gala, though, nearly two decades later, Alvar had personally piloted the sky-boat to Speakers' Valley. He and Johanna might need to depart hurriedly in the Isi vessel – along with their son, sane or insane, hardy or stricken, alive or dead or . . . perhaps worse than dead. And this later journey, to an impoverished devilish gala, had been one of fearful determination; though the return flight, with a living statue stowed on board, was euphoric . . .

Johanna had known – almost known – that Osmo would beat Cammon, if not perhaps quite so dramatically. Alvar was apprehensive, but he went along; yes, went along at the controls of the sky-boat.

Probably Johanna had been confident of Osmo ever since he aged Sam Peller – she hadn't reproached Osmo for that, even if Alvar thrashed their son – a salutary stroke of discipline aimed at deterring Osmo from indulging himself.

No, thought Osmo hotly, *I would never have indulged myself the way Cammon did. Indulgence was his downfall . . .*

And whom would I be indulging if I aim my hat at one of Crazy Lucky's daughters . . . ?

Sending Jatta Sariola away with a flea in her ear (a flea which would nag her unmercifully till she carried out his instructions) wasn't exactly a token of honest self-denial . . .

His mother's snores were throbbing purrs.

Abruptly, Tycho lumbered towards the young man, the witness of how he had depended upon another person to break free. Not someone whom Tycho had beguiled, but a *fool* on their own account. A fool with a power, but a fool nonetheless. A fool who hoped to use Tycho Cammon as a catspaw, a tool. 'Fool *tool*, fool *tool*,' sneered Tycho, caught up in the mesmerism of the silly rhyme.

To Juke the words were a bizarre disconcerting incantation. *Fuultuul! Fuultuul!* He'd spoken the tyrant alive, but he couldn't control him. Scrambling for the window he'd unfastened, he thrust at the glass, pulled himself up.

Legs, boots disappeared out at full tilt.

Tycho veered away towards a door which would lead further inside Osmo's keep. Because this was spoken? Oh no. Because he wished it with all his tormented, vengeful being.

Gunther brought the well-balanced globe to a halt with a trailing finger which rested, finally, near the island of Pootara, source of Alvar's smoking weed as well as of molasses that made the rum, of nutmeg, of the cinnamon and ginger in the gingerbread men.

Black-skinned farmers and traders, sun-proofed settlers from

Earth, held the large island without any interference from the Isi that Alvar was aware of. The islanders had largely cleared their land of the tangled native vegetation, the rubbery writhings of the sub-tropics. Many other smaller islands in the northern ocean were still unpopulated, mostly unexplored, unvisited; and indeed Alvar's globe – based on Earth-sponsored satellite photography – while accurate, was scant in irrelevant details of nameless places. South of the equator a desert continent accounted for half of the land on the planet. Too hot, too dry, too inhospitable: a yellow swathe on the globe. The sort of place one might expect serpents to prefer, except that the Isi favoured bases in the northern continent, close to people. The further north one sailed from Pootara, the more did islands crowd the ocean – while the low-lying northland was so punctuated with lakes and rivers that the actual final boundary between sea with islands and forested land with lakes was hard to determine on Alvar's globe unless one traced and retraced with a finger. Even further north, beyond the Great Fjord, the forests thinned out into a tundra. *Northland* was what people generally called Lucky Sariola's region, even though the whole little continent was a north land. This whole north land (including her *Northland*) was minutely detailed on Alvar's globe, sufficiently so as to require use of a magnifying glass. This was the real Kaleva, of consequence. Pootara, where Gunther's finger rested, hardly had a history except an economic one. Its sailing ships were of northern manufacture, built of tough tammywood, intended for commerce with the north. On Pootara, mana effects were seemingly unknown. The people were practical, immune to obsessions and wild conceits. They took a pride in the mundane and were definitely leery of the north with its feuds and cuckoos and alien serpents, its bespeakers and freaks, its huge native forests, and its crazy Queen. A Pootaran sailor in one of the ports south of the woodlord's bailiwick, or at Tumio further east, was notoriously a cautious fellow, eager to offload spices and fruits chilled and candied, load fish and timber, and sail home to safety where there were no hereditary lords, only equal worker-citizens. Thus Pootara would only play the most minor part in Alvar's *Chronicles of Kaleva* . . .

Elsewhere on the globe, south of the equatorial continent and drowning the entire far side of the planet, ocean, so much featureless ocean.

'It's my ambition,' said Gunther, 'to hibernate.'

'To *what*?'

'Hibernate. Or estivate. Depends on whether I do so in the winter or the summer.'

'That's what I thought you said . . .' In confusion Alvar spilled matches as he sought to relight his pipe. 'But,' *puff*, 'surely people aren't able to hibernate?'

Gunther tapped that purposeful aquiline nose of his. 'The Isi can. A gland secretes a juice. Between you and me . . . I've managed to lay my hands on some.'

'How?'

Gunther shook his head.

'Please tell.'

'That's why I'm building up my weight. So I'll have kilos and kilos to burn when the time comes. That's why I hoped to have young Cully running my affairs.'

'Are you so desperate,' *puff*, 'to escape from the day-after-day?'

'What? Oh I see . . .' The dream savant chuckled. 'No, Alvar, that isn't why I wish to *hibernate*. I intend to dream more deeply than any human being ever has before – the way an Isi mage dreams during its long sleep, a mana-dream.'

'What's that exactly?'

'I'll know when I dream it. I'm fairly sure that's how the Isi first summoned an Ukko to them.'

'Has one of the Isi,' *puff*, 'ever told you so?'

'And then in my mana-dream I'll be able to resurrect Anna—'

Gunther was mad. He had to be mad. Though not perhaps quite so mad that he wasn't still a little hesitant about this enterprise, desirous of a confidant – who might deter him?

'The Isi also shed their skins,' Alvar said carefully. 'Those gland juices can prove fairly lethal.'

Gunther set the globe spinning again. 'Isi poison? Bah. Mine's a *lucky* body, isn't I? Repairs itself well.'

'Quite a few years ago some women and children whom the Juttahat kidnapped lost their lives because an Isi mage was shedding its skin—' Though had that been quite true? Or a deceit?

'I'm not asking you to discourage me, Alvar. I'm tipping you off as chronicler—'

'*In case!*' Alvar pointed his pipe accusingly. 'In case you die!'

'Do you really think by now I care all that much about dying?'

'So this is your attempt at suicide.'

'Would I be fattening myself up for suicide?'

'Oh you must make it seem plausible to yourself or else you'd be betraying your Anna, wouldn't you?'

'And you're worried you might lose an *informant*.'

'That's unfair,' muttered Alvar. Were the two friends on the verge of a quarrel? How could you be friendly with somebody two centuries older than yourself? Gunther stepped forward so swiftly that Alvar feared the dream savant might strike him, and jerked up his arm. However, Gunther was only intent on raiding the bowl of cookies. Quickly he gobbled one, crumbs spilling from his mouth.

'Down there, deep down there,' he ranted, 'the gingerbread man awaits.'

'In your tummy?' Alvar converted his gesture of self-defence into a thorough scratching of one side of his head, possessed by a pretended itch.

'In my mana-dream, of course. The gingerbread man can restore Anna. The fact is, Alvar ... hypothetically speaking, *if* anything should go wrong I wouldn't want people to imagine I'd been poisoned – say, by the Juttahats. I wouldn't want a feud flaring up. That's the damned nuisance about Cully going missing – you see, he could take over the reins. I just need an impartial witness to my intentions: you.'

Trying to hibernate in order to hunt for a gingerbread man in a dream: Gunther must truly be mad.

'I don't know too much about dreams,' Alvar temporized, 'but as to what our mana-priest was trying to say earlier on – well, it's a question of what propels us, isn't it? He said fate and destiny. I'd say compulsion. Once you feel compelled to do something it's hard to avoid doing it. I mean, it can come from inside you ... or a bespeaker can lay it on you ... or—'

'No one has bespoken me into hibernating.'

'How soon will you be *fat* enough?'

'I don't know, I just don't know. I think I'll need to let my new bulk stabilize.'

'While you're up, would you mind straightening that painting?'

Gunther glanced, then resumed: 'I must ask you to keep this a secret unless—'

A shriek of terror startled them both.

Cursing himself for ineptitude, Juke climbed back through the window just a few minutes later into the deserted hall to recover his knapsack. As he prepared to leave for a second time with slightly more aplomb – less headfirst – he too heard the scream.

A *woman's* cry, damn it all. He accelerated his departure, though once outside he had the wit to push the window shut behind him sharply, hoping that the latch might fall. A dog barked, a hound howled. A wall of trimmed boulders, barely waist-high, capped a five-metre precipice likely to prevent intruders, though not an absconder willing to risk twisting an ankle. Juke dropped his knapsack down to the granite base of the little cliff, softly silvered by reflection from the sky-sickle. He scrambled over, lowered himself, and slid.

A crushing grip held Vivi by the throat, hauling her on tiptoe. An erection, which had to be of stone, it was so rigid and rough, bored into her cambric nightgown. The organ prodded like some mutilated, fossilized wrist bereft of palm and fingers, intent on rupturing her gown in default of raising it. Her candle had fallen but not extinguished itself. A rug was smouldering; shadows danced.

'Be *silent!*' Tycho commanded her as she squirmed and choked and beat at his inflexible body, bruising her hands and not heeding the hurt because of the pressure of asphyxiation. His manic face, his lips were only inches from hers. The scream trapped inside her swelled intolerably, lung-burstingly, edged with jagged iron that would soon claw her chest apart. The world throbbed thunderously.

'*No!*' shouted a voice. And the hand of rock threw her aside, gasping air for a moment, amazed to be sucking rather than exhaling a terrible metallic screech. For just a moment. A black wall obliterated her awareness.

Lyle had set his relit candle down. And flame licked from the rug along the dimly dancing corridor. The naked man had hurled the woman away from him at Lyle's cry; she lay crumpled. For seconds Lyle had no idea who the nude, priapic man was; then he realized, and bellowed, '*Elmer! Osmo! Help!*' Backing away, hands spread emptily, as Tycho Cammon advanced.

A rug was burning lazily. Elmer stood nightshirted, bleary and puzzled in a doorway. Gunther hefted the poker he'd snatched up from Alvar's fireplace. Lyle withdrew, gaze on the burly intruder, snatching then promptly jerking back his hands, a wrestler seeking a hold and refusing to commit himself; challenging, baulking, retreating. With a roar of irritation, Tycho blundered towards Lyle, his cock still prominent.

Gunther swung the fire-iron, cracking against Tycho's suddenly upraised arm.

'Aaaaaach—!' The arm sagged, and Tycho gripped his elbow reflexively. As if to transfer any pain and injury immediately back to the dealer of it, Tycho swung the succouring hand spade-edged at Gunther just as the dream savant was pulling the poker back for a second blow. The blade of the hand caught Gunther under the nose. Blood flowed over the dream savant's crushed lips. He staggered but succeeded in stabbing with the poker. His thrust met dense resistance though not the shock of striking solid stone; Gunther's wrist wasn't sprained.

Where had Elmer gone? But Elmer was reappearing, cocking a crossbow, slotting a quarrel into the shaft.

'Watch out!'

The short square-headed arrow thumped into the nude man's back so that only the feathers protruded. Tycho pitched forward several paces.

Licking blood, Gunther stabbed again – for the head; the blow missing because Tycho jerked. Half a metre of rug had kindled by now, though not flaringly. The flames were polite.

'Cammon!' Arriving loose, unbuttoned, and shoeless, Osmo tugged the lightpistol from the key-jangling belt he was clutching. Discarding the belt, he aimed with both hands.

'Get down, Gunther! Elmer! Drop!'

Gunther collapsed quickly, poker pointing upward at Tycho to ward him off. Blood poured from the dream lord's nose. Elmer dodged behind a door jamb.

A luminous thread stitched the air momentarily, quivering, more afterimage than image. Another pulse. A third. Tycho screamed; his right eye had burst, boiling. Cauterized scar tissue marked his cheek. Gunther struck at the nearest ankle with his poker. Tycho sprawled forward, recovered, windmilling with his one sound arm towards Osmo.

Pulse, pulse. The lightgun quit.

Osmo leapt aside. Ducking, he flattened himself against the wall as a blind man avalanched past to skid, to sprawl, and writhe. Scrambling up, Gunther gimped low, using the poker as a walking stick. Brushing past Osmo, he came alongside the prostrate Cammon. Only then did he check, glancing enquiringly at Osmo.

'Yes,' said Osmo. 'Yes!' Banging the butt of the pistol against the wall in frustration – or as a sign of what to do.

The dream savant brought the fire-iron down powerfully several times till the stone man's skull was splintered open, curls matted with an oozing ruddy porridge. Lyle stooped by Vivi, examining her by rug light. Flame tongued towards the underhousekeeper.

'She broke her neck,' he called.

'*She* broke her neck?' Osmo repeated stupidly. '*She* did?'

6 · A Princess Vanishes

A distant chime. Within a nonplussed moment Osmo's memory resurged.

Mother's couch. *Vivi . . . was dead!* Murdered by Cammon, who was dead as well . . .

Vivi. Vivi. His piss-erection withered to a stub. Above the courtyard, sky was overcast. And so was he. Grey cloud pressed down to smother him with grief and shame. The cloy of rotting fruit sickened his stomach . . . *ching – ching*. What time?

'Ah—' Johanna had noted his stirring. 'That's eleven.' Wallowing abed in her voluminous lace nightgown, she fiddled with a scarlet flower more vivid in hue than her own complexion – no, it was his ribbon rosette. A breakfast tray with giant empty coffee cup: a raft adrift on the waves of the counterpane. Two reassembled puzzles were crates washed overboard.

Osmo groaned, hungover, desolate, grey as the sky.

'Vivi,' he whispered. That hot-spirited, *friendly* widow was lying upstairs abed too, stone dead, bereaved of herself. Bereaving him. And Cammon's corpse was locked in a store room.

'As I told you last night, I'm *so* sorry. Yet maybe it's a sign of sorts—'

'Mother!'

'Well, a stimulus. Not to satisfy yourself with . . . well.'

'*Mother!*' Levering himself upright, lowering his legs, Osmo buttoned and belted and pulled on his shoes, discovering a spatter of dried blood on one toe-cap. Closer inspection revealed several clinging flecks of paler dehydrated tissue. Sprayed from the killer's poker-crushed cranium.

'I know this sounds harsh, but one really couldn't have a Vivi as mistress of Maananfors.'

Spitting on a monogrammed handkerchief, Osmo buffed his soiled shoe thoroughly. 'Yesterday, would you believe, I was being so lordly I even told her I might need to dismiss her! Oh why did I say that? Why?'

'I imagine you know why. Annetta said Vivi was showing signs of undue interest in our stone man.'

'Vivi wasn't going to a tryst with *him* when he surprised her.'

'With you, then?'

Osmo tossed the cloth out of the open window. He didn't wish traces of Tycho Cammon's blood or brain left in his pocket. Somewhere in mana, the tyrant's soul still thought . . .

'I . . . didn't ask her to.' The handkerchief would be found, laundered, restored to a linen drawer. Pulling his lightpistol from its holster, angling round upon the couch, he sighted out of the window up at the sky, squeezed. Nothing happened. 'Damn, but if only I had. Then she'd have been safe in my room.'

'Then *you* wouldn't have been safe. He'd likely have found you. I told you I had a presentiment about something like the swan . . .'

'If I hadn't visited you, who knows?' Glancing at those garlands frescoed on the walls above the wainscot: 'Flowers for a funeral, hmm?'

'*I* didn't cause her death. I did send word a couple of hours ago to Asikkala, to Vivi's family.'

'While I slept.'

'You need sleep if you're going to attend a funeral. Warm weather, fast last rites, mm?'

Osmo thrust himself erect. 'You mean you *already* fixed that for today?'

Gently: 'This evening.'

'Our guests—'

'Can attend. Or not.'

'How is *your* blood this morning?' he asked harshly.

'Flowing fast.'

'So it seems.' Osmo shook his lightgun in bitter frustration. 'I swear I'll burn *him* on the beach in a swan of wood. I'll incinerate him to ashes. Do you think it'll rain later?'

His mother crooked a sausage-like finger, testing a sensitive joint. 'Ah . . .' she said.

'Ah?'

'Tycho Cammon was a lord too. Once,' she reminded him.

'Meaning that I shouldn't burn his bones so that his soul evaporates?'

'That might give people notions of *lèse majesté*. Next thing, any fisherman could be wanting one of Lucky's daughters for himself.'

'Your fisherman can have her. No, he can't – obviously he can't. There aren't enough princesses to go round. Those are fussy girls. Lucky's fussy.'

'When she isn't mad. All the more reason for making your mind up.'

Osmo smoothed creases from his velvet breeches. 'I rather think—'

'Would you like *me* to sew this rosette back on?' his mother interrupted. 'Though maybe people will suppose it was torn off in the fight.'

'Obviously I'll be changing into black. I rather think I'd like Vivi to rest in our own crypt, if you don't mind . . .'

'And in a few months' time when you go down there to sit by my own granite coffin will you be sitting beside me – or her?'

'You aren't dying, Mother. Vivi *has*.' Unconsolable dejection, and a tear, welled briefly in Osmo as he recalled the redhead's uptilted chin, pursed lips which he had neglected to kiss.

He *would* burn Cammon's corpse, dammit. He'd obliterate the murderer's soul along with his bones. *How had Cammon broken loose?* Could it be that Vivi had succumbed to macabre fascination and crept back down to the hall? That Cammon had been able to suck animation from her because Osmo had been careless when he made Cammon back into a statue? No one else hereabouts could have liberated the tyrant.

Afterwards Cammon had hauled a limp Vivi upstairs as a guide? Somehow Vivi had resisted and shrieked – to protect Osmo, to warn him. According to Lyle the phallic nude had only just met Vivi and was about to rape her. Lyle's mind could have been preoccupied with sex at the time. Why else had he been corridor-creeping?

Cammon's arousal would probably remain a disquieting enigma . . . unless Sam could throw any light on what had happened . . .

Johanna was right. Vivi shouldn't rot to bones in the van Maanen crypt. That wasn't right. The town cemetery would acquire a new inhabitant, and a new granite cobble, a soulstone; unless her family preferred to sail her body home the fifteen keys to Asikkala.

The armoury smelled of grease, solder, fishy lubricant. Circular windows with iron bars – their porthole glass wide open – were graticules sighting on the walled bailey where the sky-boat stood. An oil lamp with reflector mirror acted as bright spotlight for Sam Peller's makework. Shirt-sleeves rolled up, the steward was desultorily stripping a projectile rifle while Elmer perched on the end of the workbench, boots swinging to and fro. Racks with more gaps than guns held a dozen rifles of human and alien manufacture. A standful of blades were wrapped in oilskin adjacent to a rack of long knives. Brackets supported crossbows; shelves carried boxes of cartridges, quarrels, and power cells. Stock, barrel, magazine, bolt . . . The silver-haired bondsman cursed softly.

'How, dammit, how?'

Elmer peered. 'You just need to—'

'Not *this*. The attack on Osmo! If the young woman hadn't been in the way . . . and that's a cruel blow to Osmo . . . because, well you know—'

'What do I know?'

The iron-bound tammywood door was ajar. 'Because those two—'

'Ah, I *see* . . .' Elmer brushed back his black mop of hair.

Suspicion haunted Sam. 'He never told you?'

'Why should he especially? I'm Osmo's friend but I'm not part of his household. Things like that sometimes escape me.' Elmer's long fingers quested vaguely, wishing to manipulate some tool. He sucked in the caves of his cheeks.

'That's Osmo's business, I'd say, Sam. You're upset.'

'Sam?' Accompanied by Gunther, the lord of Maananfors stepped through the doorway, only one knee sporting a rosette. The dream lord, face scarcely bruised by now, tugged at a tooth. At last he tore it loose to toss on the bench, a misshapen cracked bullet of ivory.

'Grow again in a year or so,' he muttered dolefully. 'Long in the tooth's the word for it . . .' He looked around while Sam tried to interpose. 'Quite a modest arsenal, really.'

'What's here isn't all of it, sir,' Sam assured the dream lord. 'Though why one should suppose an inventory is in order—' Sam's expression reproved Osmo. 'Unless the attack was part of a plot, and in my opinion that's far-fetched.'

'Morning, Loxmith,' said Gunther. 'Could we have a word later?'

Elmer nodded, whereupon Osmo held out his lightpistol. 'Charge gave out. It wasn't delivering a full beam anyway.'

'I noticed.' Glad of a device to worry at, Elmer snapped the Isi weapon open. His hand groped for tiny tools in a frayed leather satchel clipped to the side of his belt.

'An Ukko came across the sky last night,' Sam mentioned. 'Everyone rushed out to see. I *think* everybody rushed out. There *were* several strangers, though that's hardly odd. Afterwards I locked up and looked round. Everything was still shut up tight this morning, 'cept the ways into the main house of course . . .'

'I'm going to burn Cammon's corpse to ashes tonight on the beach. Do you hear, Sam, do you hear? After the ceremony for Vivi. Do you hear?'

'Well . . . yes.'

'Elmer? Elmer?' Lyle popped his head round the door.

A belly chuckle issued from Gunther. 'We must feel quite defensive, all skulking in the armoury. May I propose a visit to the sauna, Loxmith? Followed by some nourishment?' He slapped his tight-stretched brown girth. 'I'm curiously famished. Considering the splendid feast,' he hastened to add.

With a spanner slimmer than a pencil Elmer beckoned his assistant. 'Take a look at this now—'

Lyle flashed a quick smile of apology at the dream savant. 'Could we shift to my room?' he suggested to Elmer. 'Can't concentrate in a crowd.'

In mulberry dressing gown and cool leather slippers, Alvar perched himself on his wife's couch, fidgeting.

'I was hoping to question witnesses, my dear,' he complained mildly, 'before memories become confused.'

'Oh, I think everyone involved will *remember*.'

'Except poor Vivi. And maybe she's the key.'

Annetta, of the keen hearing and big observant brown eyes – now bloodshot – snuffled; while the housekeeper, Mrs Holmberg, rested a hand on a trembling white sleeve. Dumpy, gingham-frocked Mrs Holmberg had plainly shed a tear too, though she

74

was a firm and frumpish woman who had never quite approved of Vivi. Really, her chequered frock resembled a tablecloth with buttons.

'Now,' said Johanna sadly to the housekeeper, 'there's the question of whom to recommend my son to appoint to poor Vivi's position in due course . . .'

'I hadn't given it a thought, madam.' The housekeeper's owlish countenance remained unruffled.

'Suppose you were considering . . . Amelie . . . even though she's your niece?'

Alvar groaned. '*Amelie?*'

'Since you mention it, madam, Amelie's very dutiful and particular.'

'*But my love,*' protested Alvar, 'how many times—?'

Johanna gestured hush. 'Perhaps a little too particular, in a compulsive dippy way.' She beamed at Alvar. 'I'm referring to the paintings.'

The housekeeper flushed. 'I've spoken to Amelie about those. I'm sure she can break the silly habit.'

'She'll break an imp's leg first,' muttered Alvar, glancing at the single small, framed reproduction hanging on his wife's wall, then swiftly, guiltily, averting his gaze, for it was a painting of the river of death. A naked man climbed grimly into a rowing boat beached by that black stream to join a hunched sorrowing nude woman. A young girl disrobed morosely, revealing her budding breasts. Other reluctant passengers waited, wearing the clothes of life as yet. In the distance the swan cruised.

'Well, possibly there *are* nakki-spirits, madam. Not here, of course. In the countryside . . . What's more, a painting tells a story, doesn't it? Stories can cause things to happen. So a painting can have a power, can't it, if it isn't, well, tipped a bit askew from the lines of the house? That's why my niece gives pictures a nudge. In her opinion!'

'Hmm, Mrs Holmberg.' Johanna picked up a wooden puzzle. 'An eccentricity can become a mania if it's given the nod. I really think Annetta would be a far more suitable choice . . . don't you?'

Mrs Holmberg took a pace away from the chubby-cheeked, pigtailed maid, who stared down diplomatically at the rug, hands crossed over a starched pinny.

'Annetta knows what's going on.'

'Oh, I'm sure she does, madam.'

'Well, then.'

75

'As I said, I hadn't given it a thought.'

'Now you have.'

The housekeeper shuffled. 'Seems a terrible thing to step into a dead girl's shoes; I think Amelie might have scruples on that score . . . But I'll need to decide if Miss Annetta can cope with the extra duties.'

'Of course. Annie: run along to Mrs Holmberg's parlour with her, hmm?'

When the two had departed, Alvar sprang from the couch. 'Bravo, my love. And thank you.'

'Hmm,' was the reply. 'Osmo won't repeat his indiscretion with Annetta, not while I'm alive. Which mightn't be long; and much you care.'

'My love, I *do*. I just become . . . preoccupied. Some real history happened here last night.' Her husband frowned, nagged by some absent item.

'You too limp along, Alvar, and interrogate for your silly *Chronicles*.'

'That's it! Interrogate. *Jatta Sariola*: I almost forgot about her.'

Eyes closing in exasperation, bosom heaving: 'How can someone *almost* forget? Either they do or they don't.' Alvar was already leaving, slippers slapping on the bare waxed wood by the door.

'I were drinking with her just last night,' confided Sep the Bailiff, as if this gave him unique insight into Vivi's death. 'Mana, my bleeding *head*.' He chewed a leftover pasty, swigged ale, and surveyed his kitchen audience of cook, scullions, stableman, laundress, baker. 'Cammon's last victim, eh! It's like a death had to happen. The Watch nabbed that fisherman, but the swan was still swimming. Right?'

No one presumed to disagree.

'I were joking with her, not knowing as the swan had its beady eye set on her—'

Perspiration beaded Sep's tubby features even though both windows stood open upon the inner bailey, where another stableman was exercising a mare in a wide circuit around the sky-boat. Steam and grease! Brass ceiling fans stirred the air, their blades propelled by the pull of chain-slung weights descending grooves in the plastered wall. High time for a scullion to ratchet one of those lumps of lead back up, in fact. The waft from the fans stirred suspended bundles of insect-repellant herbs. Copper pans

76

and pewter measures hung in regiments. A spitted half-lamb roasted before a glowing hearth, juices dripping into a blackened tray. From an oven wafted warm yeast. A cauldron of potatoes simmered vigorously. The stack of minty logs could well be higher. Hangover-sweat dripped from the bailiff's face on to a scoured, scrubbed tabletop.

'Far as I can recall, I were kidding her 'bout that damn statueman, her having to dust him down—'

Leather slippers slapped on flagstones. 'Ahem—'

Alvar van Maanen had slung a purple cloak around his floor-length silken dressing gown. With his delicate features he seemed like a long-skirted elderly lady – clutching a notebook.

'Lord Alvar!'

'Not lord any longer, Septimus. Sir is quite sufficient. Did anyone here take breakfast to the lodge outside the gate?'

'Sir, sir, I did, sir,' piped a skinny blond lad in soiled dungarees. 'I took clabbered milk and barley porridge and cheese rolls, and some cheese and sausage sandwiches for lunch too.'

'At what time was this?'

'Nine o'clock, sir?' the boy suggested hopefully.

Some blobs of excited water leapt out of the cauldron and danced on a hot hob, sizzling.

'And were the mother and her talkative infant there?'

'No, sir, nobody was there, sir.'

'You didn't tell anyone?'

'Cook didn't ask me. We was busy, sir.' The lad gestured at the scullery, where cleaned platters and polished pans piled up high.

'Well, that same food's still all there, boy, under a net!'

'I did that, in case of flies. Thought as they'd gone for a walk, sir, whoever they are.'

A log cracked in a hearth, spilling a red cascade. Overheating, Alvar shucked off his cloak on to the table.

'It seems they went for a very long walk!'

'You don't pass up a breakfast,' mumbled the scullion, as Venny the cook waddled over, smearing her hands on her apron. She clipped the boy across the lug.

'Go and get the food back. That's your next few meals.' Close up, she smelled like a goat, fattily acidic.

'I don't care about the *food*,' cried Alvar. He wrinkled his nose. 'That woman was important. Where's she gone to?'

'Away, I s'pose,' said Venny. 'Weren't she s'posed to go away?

77

That's what I heard. Lord Osmo ordered her 'way, didn't he? Overnight, then off, with some grub in her belly and her mutie brat's?'

Alvar backed away from Venny and her lactic bacteria. 'Damn it, but the compulsion must have been too strong.'

Venny noticed the fan-weight. 'Crank that, sprat.' The dungareed boy hastened to haul on the chain, ratcheting the lead weight back up to the ceiling where it pulled a thick wire that powered the blades around.

'Septimus, I needed to talk to Jatta Sariola – for several hours. Who's that on a horse out there?'

Circling on a grit track. Spilling brown dung as it trotted. A flock of squawking little scaly blue scavengers descended from nearby eaves to peck. Sep peered. 'Hannes, on Dewdrop.'

A vibrant-winged suckerfly with branching feathery antennae, almost a tiny bird, buzzed in from the bailey, trailing a threadlike tube. The fly veered up towards the aromatic herbs and butted into them then began to spiral down erratically till it crashed upon a flagstone where a scullion squashed it with his sandal. Most insect intruders would simply have quitted the kitchen.

'Send Hannes after her right now. On the eastern road, yes, *east*, that's the way. Stop the woman and put her up in some farm. Maybe you ought to go along with Hannes.'

'Me?' Now Sep perspired at the prospect of a brain-bouncing ride. 'But—'

'Ach, you're right, it's funerals this evening. Was Hannes in the hall last night? Will he recognize – oh he can't mistake that Fastboy. Have him take a communicator.'

'I'd, I'd have to ask Mister Peller, sir—'

'Hmm, no, I'm not lord. Hmm, that's true. This is really irritating. Still, the pictures won't all be crooked.'

Steam billowed as Lyle tossed another hissing snake of water across the top of the sunken brazier. Sweat slicked his rosy flesh. A glance at the thermometer satisfied him, so he clambered to the upper slatted bench of mellow yellover where naked Elmer and Gunther sat together very still, pinkly, the dream savant virtually twice Elmer's rawboned mass. On Gunther's bulging thigh, a silver tattoo of a swan pierced by a long arrow, contorting in its death throe into the shape of a heart. The dream savant wore gold rings through both nipples, a slim chain linking them, locket hanging midway. The outward pressure of fat tautened this chain so that Gunther's nipples pulled towards one another. On Elmer's elbows brassy hinges were tattooed and on his forearms little blue flat-nose pliers like crayfish, talismans to hone his skills. On Lyle's left shoulder, the sapphire tattoo of an eye.

'So you'd hibernate,' mused Elmer, aping a degree of surprise (while Lyle winked covertly at him). The engineer shifted his pelvis on the yellow slats. 'A machine to monitor your metabolism, eh? And rouse you after three months? I suppose by electro stimulation of the heart and brain and muscles . . .'

'Can you do it?'

Elmer brushed back his mop, still damp from a preliminary dunking in cold water so that the heat shouldn't burn his scalp. Despite the slick of sweat, hairs on his legs were crisping.

'I'd prefer to ask for some advice from the Earthfolk at Landfall before I design this. Thing is, Gunther, I'm perfectly aware of what makes machines tick, or fail to tick. But living bodies . . .' His hand warded off the dream savant's incipient protest. 'I'd be discreet. You have my word I wouldn't mention dreams. They wouldn't know it's intended for you. I'd say this is . . . well, research into longlife . . . from a new angle. I wonder whether your nipple rings will need to come off . . .'

'They stay.'

'On account of the locket?'

With a tubby knuckle Gunther knocked at the little golden box. 'This holds a tiny piece of my Anna's skull. While I wear it I'll always be close to her. If my keep burns down completely along with her bones—'

'Fierce fire, I'd say!'

'—there'll still be this fragment of her left.'

'I'd like to sound out the Earthpeople—'

'What would they want in return?'

'—and maybe conduct an experiment first, say with a dog or a sheep, if you could spare some of the Isi hormone.'

'Tommi!' suggested Lyle. 'He's smaller – should take less hormone, I guess. He talks – just like his grandsire. He can report. Cats love sleeping almost as much as eating.'

'How would Tommi put on enough weight? Assuming weight's needed . . .'

'You know Tommi's as much of a glutton as any dog is. Always whining for more and different and better. He'd fatten up. Anyway, we'd have him bespoken.'

79

'Nikki might be distressed.'

'What would the Earthfolk want in return?'

Lyle eyed the dream savant's rolls of pink plumpness which wasn't quite obesity. Not yet. Gunther Beck was a great podgy long-haired baby. *If Gunther did resurrect his Anna in deep dreams, would she meet the man he had once been? Or this semi-monstrosity who seemed to be reverting, after three centuries, to a bloated second infancy? Or a slack-skinned starveling figure who had consumed his accumulated fat during hibernation and was burning up his muscle and flesh?*

'In return,' suggested Lyle, 'we could give them a blueprint for our modifications to the sky-boat engine. Just to show willing. Not to seem over-anxious. Or else you could offer to take a look at their orbital shuttle.'

'Earth does have its own engineers—'

'Not an *instinctive* engineer, though.'

'That shuttle engine's based on Isi design—'

'Bet you can improve its performance. Well, Gunther, we'll think of something.' Lyle stepped back down to the yellow water bucket and tipped half a ladle over hot charcoal, explosively. The air clouded stiflingly.

'It'll all take a while,' Elmer cautioned.

Beck raised one rump-cheek as if to fart. 'I'll mortgage myself if need be.'

'Mortgage?' Some ancient idea ... *Could it be*, wondered Elmer, *that the dream lord was relatively poverty-stricken? That he didn't bother himself overmuch with tithes and rents and harvests?*

Too busy dreaming his extended life away ... Too busy brooding about a lady dead more than two centuries since ...

Gunther powered his fat-creased haunches forward, stooping so as not to crack his head on the hot wooden ceiling. 'I need a dip—'

They all did.

The heatproof tammy door gave on to a short deep pool of black-veined snowy marble surrounded by glacial tiles. The pool-room was already occupied. Osmo and Sam Peller were shedding shirts and breeches – and old Alvar his mulberry dressing gown – to hang on vacant pegs, eyed by a tall gruff sunpickled stranger. Switches of curver twigs in leaf dangled from hooks. Soft white towels towered on a bench. In the anteroom the steward with the phoenix on his cheek was neatly assembling glasses, jug of beer, carafe of currant juice, pot of mustard, tureen of steaming link sausages.

'It's water from a deep spring,' Osmo was mentioning to his guest. In his late fifties, the man's curly shock of hair was of a faded ginger hue.

Into the pool, feet first, plunged fleshy Gunther, then gaunt Elmer and Lyle; bobbing, gasping.

The stranger, shedding black breeches and starched white shirt, revealed torso and legs tattooed with a tumble of mushrooms large and small: brown morels mimicking convoluted brains, horns of plenty, milky caps, yellow chanterelles, funnel chanterelles, champignons – and Osmo sniffed, as if a carnal forest musk were assailing his nostrils. Spores from Earth had taken so well in the soil and humus of Kaleva, and on some native trees and amidst their roots, though mana had varied some varieties, making mutants. In Tapper Kippan's forests especially, freak specimens grew, so one heard . . .

'You're a mushroom cultist, Rintala?' asked Osmo sharply, scanning the man's skin for dubious toadstools. 'I didn't know!'

'Just a gatherer,' replied the man levelly.

Alvar's only tattoo was a maroon monogram of a small v within capital M, set inside a shield, on one scrawny shoulder. Bony – yet delicately fleshed, even though the flesh was aging. A ladylike shoulder. His son sported speaker's lips on his biceps. This farmer Rintala had certainly gone to extremes with such a multi-coloured fungoid cornucopia . . .

No sooner ducked in cold than out again, the trio hauling themselves from the pool – Gunther uttering a sharp little cry and hastily scrutinizing the heel of his hand from which a thread of blood welled briefly.

'You cut yourself?' Lyle stooped to run a finger along the waterline. 'Ah . . . it's the marble. Black veins are beginning to stand out. White must be softer. This pool's a hundred years old at least . . .'

Bony Elmer seized a switch and flicked at Lyle playfully before briskly scourging his own limbs and his back. After licking his wound, hefty Gunther belaboured his body with twig and leaf. Whistling, Elmer whipped Lyle across the buttocks a few times. Lyle retaliated. The dream savant joined in the horseplay. Two switches were quite stripped of leaves, several sticking feathery to skin, others floating in the pool.

The raw-boned engineer laughed. 'How hard do women do this to each other?' he wondered, and sniffed at the fragrant curver sprigs.

Osmo's gaze flicked to the farmer's groin, where his tufty pubic hair was as richly red as Vivi's. 'May I present Victor Rintala, Vivi's father—?'

'So I've lost my speckled red hen,' Rintala said sadly amid the steam, to which they had all resorted.

'Mine too,' confided the lord of Maananfors. 'Mine too.'

'Yours, sir?'

'Yes, I actually *thought* of . . . wedding her.'

'Of marrying my red hen?'

The white lie might console the father in his stoical grief. 'And because of that affection I felt for her, and because this tragedy happened here, I wish to remit your tithes for . . . ten years, Victor.'

Alvar winced, but needn't have felt qualms.

The farmer shook his bleached gingery head. 'No, sir.' Impossible to distinguish between sweat and a teardrop. 'A dowry goes the other way, don't it? Lord Osmo, if you ever want a right arm, I'm yours.' He shrugged bleakly. 'My mischievous hen didn't bring much joy to her previous hubby, though, did she now? Or the swan wouldn't have carried him off.'

The logic of this evaded Osmo.

'Maybe that was fated so that *you* could know my hen,' Rintala pursued. 'A great bespeaker like yourself. Now her destiny's snipped, because a bespeaker should seek . . . more than a mushroom hunter's hen.'

Was the farmer reproaching Osmo? Hence his refusal of Osmo's offer of compensation – at the same time as he promised loyal service.

'Maybe my hen flew too high, Lord Osmo! Maybe. And speaking of high, when I saw that Ukko cross the sky on Lucky's feastnight I shivered inside of me. My hen's death was a glint from that rushing wee moon up there.'

'I'm going to burn Cammon's body, Victor, I swear,' vowed Osmo. 'Burn his bones and his soul.'

'Aaah—' The farmer massaged his mushroom tattoos appreciatively.

Alvar fidgeted. 'Son, couldn't we possibly send someone after Jatta Sariola and her Fastboy?' Several varicose veins corded

82

the former lord's shanks. Otherwise, from the knees upwards, he was almost dainty, his aging flesh hardly blemished.

'Why, Dad, do you imagine *she* revived Cammon, out of pique? She couldn't possibly. I spoke her away towards the mutants, so now she's gone. Try to halt her? We might make her sick. I spoke strongly.'

Gunther Beck shifted his creased rump on the hot buttery yellover slats. The thought of Jatta had discomposed him. He rose stoutly, with the caution of someone who was heavier than accustomed. 'I could devour a few sausages—'

A *few*. How could he?

7 · BLAZING BONES

Jatta's thin, dusky child had been scampering ahead along the forest track for half an hour now. He disappeared out of sight. He reappeared, spurring Jatta to tramp faster than was comfortable. Still, this pace matched her craving to distance herself from Maananfors. Propelled by an almost tangible, repelling hand she marched onward, stumbling occasionally over rocks or roots.

Harper trees in the overcast woodland hummed; and a cloud of sizzleflies might follow her sweat for twenty or thirty paces before streaming back to their previous haunt to dance aerially above azure tubes of chimney flowers. From behind the broad bole of a tree dangling an emerald umbrella of fleecy fronds, a leppi darted. Like some tawny fur glove frantic to avoid its own self the animal scurried to and fro. Jatta's hand fell to her knife as a snake-tailed musti sleeked through the fuzzy herbage on short swift legs.

'Jack! Fastboy! Stay where you are!'

The khaki carnivore darted at where the leppi would likely be – and almost was – a moment later. Prancing on its fingers the glove veered behind its attacker. Musti's tail whipped into a noose, snaring leppi. Lithely twisting itself, the musti bit at its prey, snapping its spine. Slender, it reared to glare at Jatta . . .

. . . whose fast boy was scampering back along the track, not very much taller than the upright, quivering predator. Since their night at Maananfors he was wearing soft little boots and castoff dungarees.

'Jack, *stay!*'

Jatta loosed her knife, and spied a stick, which she plucked up. Her gaze flicked from musti to Jack, and back.

'Mummy, what is it?'

'It's dangerous.'

As beady-eyed as the musti itself, her boy peered at the inert bundle coiled like some counterbalance in the poised killer's tail. 'It killed a lep, a quick little lep.' Fellow feeling possessed Jack. 'I'll catch it and spank it.'

'No!'

Stick and knife stopped her from snatching Jack. He jinked into the herbage, ahead of her, arms windmilling. Hissing, the musti launched itself – it was clinging to him, squirming. No, Jack was gripping it by the scruff. Its thin bald tail looped his arm. Teeth like little nails glared, jaw and neck strained. A claw-foot raked. He pivoted, half triumphant, half terrified. The slim creature was heavier than he'd bargained. He tottered.

Jatta jerked her knife into the beast's arching side. The musti screamed, contorting. She thrust again, careful but urgent. Its belly wept blood. Spine arched. Its tail sprang clear of Jack's arm – ah, to whip up momentum.

'Throw it!'

Stumbling, Jack tossed his burden. Stick abandoned, Jatta pulled her boy away as the musti writhed, snarling, on a bed of purple moss.

Mother and son decamped, only pausing a hundred metres further along the track.

'Eat it, Mummy? Make a fire?'

'We can't eat mustis.' She panted. Sweat coursed. 'They're sour, they'd make us sick. Stay still a while, Jack! Let's see your scratches.'

Claws had caught her boy under the wrist, raising angry ruby ridges. Laying down her blood-slicked knife, Jatta sucked his flesh and spat, licked catlike, then wiped her blade clean on herbage. 'Oh Jack. You'll wear me out.'

Echo-like: 'I'm tired, Mummy. Carry me? I'm hungry.'

Sweltering and drained, the sunbrowned, pear-faced young woman eyed the cloudroof, trying to guess where the sun might be hidden above that dismal ashen canopy. A drenching wasn't *immediately* imminent, she suspected. But must surely come.

How far had she come since early morning – thirty keys or more? And now: late afternoon? Would the impetus of her flight ever slacken? Was she clear of van Maanen's territory or not? Her feet ached dully in their hand-me-down leather boots, and she was certainly overdressed – fresh chemise and gaberdine shirt under the soiled slashed felt-bright tunic which she hadn't felt inclined to abandon; not to mention a heavy buff corduroy skirt smelling of fish in place of her dirty trousers. When she coughed her left lung ached. Under cropped jet hair her scalp prickled.

Briefly the odour of Jarl Pakken haunted her, a ghost aroma compounded of cinnamon, roast kasta nuts, mushroom gills . . . She even looked around for her seducer of eleven months since, in case miraculously he might step out of the forest to lend a hand with his prodigal child.

Jack was sturdier by the hour, though prone to abrupt exhaustion and equally sudden hunger pangs – and why not indeed? Delving in her knapsack, Jatta pressed a fish pasty into eager hands, and herself bit into a chunk of sausage. The boy wolfed so quickly that Jatta surrendered the snub-end of her snack. How much remained from last night's bounty? She rummaged, found cinnamon buns – Jarl's fragrance, *of course*, part of his charm. Jack gobbled, gulped sweet berry juice from her canteen. As she devoured a bun, her son leaned against her, clutching, rocking, snoozing.

Eleven months earlier had she changed Jarl into a longlife? Presumably! Maybe. That was what usually happened to the lover when one of Lucky's harvest of a hundred girls and more first shed her chastity girdle and lost her virginity with a man. He had magicked her girdle open. He must have known what else to do, exactly right – though how had he ever learned? So, yes: a longlife now. Unless the man was very ill-destined and became . . . zombie. Maybe Jarl Pakken deserved such a fate! (Oh no he didn't. He'd made her *glad* to toss her gift away instead of simply withholding it.)

On the third occasion when she saw Jarl, he was stooping naked in that hidden little lake, washing himself from head to knee. And then with such natural grace, with such godlike grace he had stood beautifully erect and had vented his seed into the waters as if that too was a part of purification – not offending her at all, no, not repelling her but rather reassuring her, for surely he would

85

be drained; tempting her to approach him in his dark, golden nakedness, summoning her . . .

Wearily, Lucky's hundredth-and-some daughter hoisted her boy. She tucked his limp legs into the sling of her fancy soiled slit tunic, and marched on. A cough tried to rack her but, staggering, she stilled the spasm. A harper thrummed as though the vibrations of her bark had stirred its strings. Sizzleflies haloed her briefly, outlining the absent hair she herself had hacked off. Then the insects gusted away. The dreary skycap thickened, squeezing heat upon the forest.

A hundred candles brightened the kirk. Frescoed upon the plastered walls and tammy vault was a vast green vine. It branched and rebranched into sprigs, into twigs, all bearing at their final tips a white cinquefoil flower. Thousands of flowers, with a fair scattering of names inked in minuscule letters around the petals. Anchor, hook, horseshoe, comb: a hundred emblems represented many more monikers. So many tiny black beetles, this communal genealogy of Maananfors. The dead were finally all of one family. A heritage mostly unreadable, either from lack of the knack or forgetfulness of who this fishhook had been, who that spindle.

A pile of huge white soulflowers lay on Vivi's yellover coffin. The grey-suited mana-priest rested his hand on the coffin for support as he prated well to a packed congregation. His wisps of hair were lank and his blue eyes bloodshot, but he prated well.

He spoke to Osmo and Alvar clad in their black frock-coats, and to snowy-haired Sam and Mrs Holmberg and Septimus and many other staff from the keep, and to Tilly Kippan who'd tethered her carbuncle-collared dog outside to Osmo's irritation, and to gorbellied Lord Beck in a borrowed, dark-purple cloak; to Victor Rintala and his stout melancholy wife and her sister and a mature red-headed daughter who was a dull burlesque of Vivi, and to her strapping husband who'd sailed the mourning party from Asikkala in his boat; and to many bleary townsfolk abridging their work on the excuse of this tragic postscript to Lucky's Day, prelude to the final end of Tycho Cammon's long-suspended career of cruelty. Word had spread of the swan-shaped mass of incendiary mintywood which keepsmen had piled high on the shore near one of the last night's circles of ash.

'For as long as her bones endure,' the mana-priest assured his audience, 'her spirit survives beyond the black river, reliving her days in memory, dreaming the life that she lived—'

Gunther listened sanguinely, nodding to himself, chubby hands cradling his growing girth. Alvar squinted up at that painted vine peevishly. So many unorganized names and emblems of names lost to remembrance over the centuries – not that the possessors of many of those had likely ever participated in any notable event! Yet even ordinary folk experienced in miniature, quite as intensely, the echoes of larger happenings. From the circumstances in one lakeside town, the acute chronicler might perhaps deduce greater patterns . . . From the midget gingerbread man, to borrow Gunther's peculiar allegory, one might proceed to his giant twin . . . Ach, Alvar must never let himself be seduced by a paltry cameo perspective! That would be to declare his whole undertaking a failure. Mock as Johanna might, who else was chronicling Kaleva satisfactorily? Earthfolk were trying to. Longlifes knew a lot, though often only about their own concerns. Lucky Sariola was too wayward to trust. Who else but himself could carry it off? Strands of the painted vine snaked across walls, across the saddle ceiling . . . Looped. Twined. *Snaked.*

A horrid thought struck Alvar. Could the *Chronicles* conceivably be incomplete without insights from the alien serpents? Might the Isi have such a thing as archives maintained by their Juttahat tools? Narratives – which he needed to know about to complete the picture, a picture that seemed forever to expand, exposing more and more blanks? Ach, no trust could be placed in meddling enigmatic alien snakes, even of the Brindled kind. The embryo *Chronicles* were a human record.

'And when her bones at last decay, her spirit vanishes from that black shore and dissolves into mana unknowably. So we who aren't longlifes live not thirty-three years, as Vivi Rintala did – nor forty or fourscore – but a thousand, two thousand, and more, on that ebony shore while our skeletons rest intact—'

Sweat dribbled down the fat-swollen dream lord's back as he sensed the gaze of numerous townfolk prying into his neck and spine, wondering how it felt to be longlife, not resenting or envying but appraising blearily, itchily.

'So we too endure for centuries on end—'

A fine consolation for all those who hadn't wedded, and never would woo, a daughter of Lucky Sariola's. Who were short-lived not only on account of being commoners but because only half a handful of princesses – two or three fingers' worth – were available every half-decade or so; and those were often headstrong girls, as capricious as Lucky herself. As witness Jatta Sariola. The dream savant burrowed within his cloak to claw at the lump of the locket box under his shirt. The link-chain tugged at his nipples, exciting them to stiffen.

A skeleton resting *intact*. . . how completely intact? The scrap of Anna's skull nestling amid velvet in the locket couldn't possibly diminish her memory-life on the black shore. Gunther's local mana-priest had been sure of this. Why, a person could lose a hand or a leg in life . . .

A dream had instructed Gunther what to hang by his heart to ward off any further peccadilloes, any more . . . Mariettas. How had the locket allowed him to feel so disturbed by Jatta Sariola? Why, the codes in his dead wife's chip of occipital bone and in her living *sister's* skull would almost be the same. Her *sister*, distanced by over two centuries, and almost – almost – her twin as if the hand of time had ticked round to the selfsame number once again. A nearly identical gingerbread girl, lurking deeper down the gulf of years. But not the same Anna! Not Anna Sariola the unique! Remembered still by himself – and by her father perhaps? By Bertel Okkonen, oldest of all longlifes? Anna's image stored somewhere in an attic of Okkonen's mind?

'—for the bones are the armature of the soul—'

The audience stirred. When Tycho Cammon's bones burned would a wail arise from the dancing flames? Would sensitive people glimpse a breach opening briefly into mana to suck a decomposing soul away?

The prim-faced toper of a priest mopped his brow with the same hand which had been resting on Vivi's yellover box then restored his moist fingers to the coffin; and beckoned.

The priest and Victor Rintala, with Rintala's son-in-law and Sam Peller, hoisted the box. Disturbed, the soulflowers reeked fragrance as the pall-bearers shouldered the box outdoors into the hot, pallid, early evening, tailed by the congregation.

'Why, the soul's *eternal*,' declared an earnest, lace-capped woman who was dallying with two spruced little boys near the railing where Tilly had secured Out. '*Eternal spirit*.' Her testimony was more stubborn than strident. Her sons shuffled, intrigued by the spaniel with the gemmed collar, which began yapping, 'Tilly! Tilly!'

Tilly Kippan had claimed that the beast was pining. Out was scared of being kennelled alone. Equally, she did wish to pay her respects before witnessing the bonfire. So she had begged Osmo very sweetly to let her bring the dog along. Really, a mutant dog suddenly seemed a trivial thing – as trifling as her somewhat thoughtless request, perhaps. No point in his slapping her face figuratively . . .

'Bones don't matter!' the black-frocked woman assured her sons. 'Your soul is always.'

'Bones good,' barked Out. 'Want bones.' The boys giggled while the leaf-dappled daughter of the woodlord hushed her dog.

Despite himself, Osmo uttered a solitary snort of laughter, for Vivi would have appreciated this absurdity. 'Do you hear that, Mrs Lundahl?' (. . . who turned away embarrassed.) 'Out of the mouths of dogs! Or even *into* them! Bones!'

Yet, as the parade proceeded under the lych-gate into the pink-pebbled graveyard, angry gloom shrouded the lord of Maananfors. Up in the cupola of the campanile a bell clonged sombrely.

Cloud blanketed forest, and exhaustion had finally supplanted Jatta's immediate urgency to be away, well away from van Maanen country. She must have covered forty, maybe fifty keys that day, on dirt road and forest track, skirting farmsteads and settlements when possible, circuiting lakes by the shoreline wherever trees did not crowd too close to the water, wading some streams and shallows. The lie of long, thin lakes to the northward of the great turquoise pond between Maananfors and Loxmithlinna had mainly been in her favour, channelling her eastward. Perhaps as the cuckoo flew she was thirty keys from Lord Osmo's keep. Enough for compulsion to abate from a raging toothache of the soul to a mild easterly ache, almost mellow, familiar, and comforting. She'd seen a few woodmen, riders, and farmers en route but avoided those by hastening aside into woods or undergrowth. A demented, crop-headed vagabond with child, armed with a knife, a livid scratch across her cheek, was best left alone if she wasn't soliciting help.

Now she could use some shelter, what with the drab sponge of the clouds almost full to bursting. And food too; more food for hungry Fastboy and herself.

A small lake lay leaden, skirted by fleecy-fronded horzmas – potential umbrellas – and glossy, spade-leafed larkeries from which the rain would cascade. Blue-chevroned soarfowl upended themselves, waggling among reeds. The gloom muted their usual iridescence. The birds hauled up strings of weed. Where fish snatched insects, ripples pocked water as though the first few fat raindrops were pattering. Lustrous fat harnies cruised, stabbing their long necks down to snatch minnows. Succulent greasy harnies with poisonous livers; tasty but mainly indigestible soarfowl ... Uncatchable, anyway. Were there any trusterfish in this lough? Could she weave a mesh of reeds? If only she could spy a waterside woodsman's hut. Setting her son down on a sandy strand, she knelt to lap, careful not to stir grit. 'You too, Jack. Drink.'

'Can't I have juice?'

'None left.'

'I'm *hot.*' So he scampered past her, stamping knee-deep, soaking soft boots and dungarees. Soarfowl leapt aloft noisily and glided away.

'If you'll come out I'll try and net a fish. Take a drink first.'

Her little boy froze, poised like that hungry musti, while moments passed.

'Come *out.*'

'Fish!' he cried, and threw himself headlong, spray fountaining.

'*Jack!*'

Knees powering, he struggled up, clutching a pink-streaked truster half as long as his arm. Back he hip-hopped to the beach to toss his catch down at Jatta's feet. The wriggling fish scraped a dish for itself in the sand. 'See! I don't need you to catch me a fish!'

Stunning the truster with the nearest stone, wearily: 'Oh Jack, you need me all right.'

His eyes widened.

'*Ho, Fastboy! Ho, Jatta Sariola!*' Emerging from a grove of larkeries, pushing sleek spade-leaves aside, came a tall, well-muscled young man with pale yellow-brown hair spilling back, a skull-cap perched atop like a criss-crossed spiced bun. A grey cloak swept wide open to ventilate grimed brown leather breeches and corduroy shirt. Such blue eyes. Such suety hair. Long knife strapped to a thigh. Bulging oilskin knapsack.

The man approached diffidently. 'Name's Juke – I was in Lord Osmo's hall. I'm travelling back east.'

Jatta stooped to hack off the truster's head with her own blade, blooding the steel conspicuously. Straightening up, she challenged the man: 'You followed me! *How?*' Jack hovered on tiptoe intently, sniffing, his little fists clutched.

90

Juke spread empty hands. 'When a person's compelled, they leave a faint trace.'

'*Do they?*'

'For me they do. I'm a child of mutants.'

'A child? Don't tell me you're only six years old or there-abouts—'

'—or you'll think van Maanen was right?' Juke shook his head. 'Your Fastboy's unique in my experience. Since we're travelling the same way, might I share your burden?' He smiled lavishly. 'Or your blessing? Nice truster, lad! Still, I've plenty of food. Stuffed my sack at the feast.'

'Juice?' Eager Jack.

'Some.' As soon as Juke produced a canteen, the boy rushed – Jatta clutching for him in vain – and guzzled; before distancing himself once again, eyeing the tall man, nose twitching.

'There's an outcrop of rock back that way, Jatta – excuse my familiarity—'

'Oh you'll be *familiar* with this fallen woman's story, won't you just be?' If Jatta intended bitterness, though, she spoiled the effect by yawning.

Gently Juke shook his head. 'I can't say as anyone in that heartless hall heard enough to understand your plight. Van Maanen was so hasty to judge you.'

'I have no more gift to give away! Do you understand *that?*'

'Your child's our chaperon, princess. As I was about to say, there's a bit of a cave back there. Decent-sized overhang, anyway.'

Crooning and rocking, Jack clapped his hands over his ears. Seconds later thunder rolled over the lake, a booming, reverberating rumble.

'And we'd better race for it!'

'Come, Jack!' Jatta snatched up the decapitated fish. The fast boy darted. No sooner amongst the sleek leaves of the larkeries than Juke jerked Jatta to a halt. Oh but she waved that fish-blooded knife in his face.

'No, *look!*'

Swooping low under the ocean of cloud flew a long mauve craft, the hue of a livid bruise. Deltoid wings jutted above fluted side-pipes. Propellers a blur. Strange vanes. Antennae bristling from the nose . . . no, could those be *lightguns*? The sky-boat slowed. Downward jets of air blustered dents in the lough. Waves rolled outward, colliding and mingling in a choppy swell that rocked the panicking harny birds – stroking for the shore, necks outstretched into bowsprits. The round-windowed craft hovered over the squall it tossed upon the water. The low, thick, stratus clouds acted as a soundboard. Juke pressed Jatta low among leaves, and her boy – fortunately – chose to cower. Ports framed tiny vague dark heads. Lookouts were staring.

The three fugitives crouched.

As if the boom of those engines had split the sky, rain cascaded. Sheets of water marched across the lake, wobbling the craft, and it was laundry day for the forest. Mother and child and mutant began to soak. The sky-boat became vague – it could have half-dissolved. A fanning searchlight leapt from its snout, biliously staining the deluge as the vessel rose, to drift away.

Huddled wet under that outcrop, curtained from the forest by rainsheet, Jack contemplated the headless fish. Jatta coughed phlegm and spat at the cascade, a gobbet of herself immediately lost in a million others from the sky-sponge.

'A sky-boat,' marvelled Juke. Had he never seen one before?

Defiantly: 'Mama says Grandma has one!' *So, Mister Juke, don't be nasty to me.*

Gazing at nowhere in particular, Juke pulled off his skull-cap and wrung it between strong hands. 'Is that so?'

'Maybe that *was* my grandma's sky-boat.'

'Different colour, sharper wings.' Lucky's hundredth-and-some daughter hawked again. 'That one was Isi.'

'I want to fly it.'

'In it, you mean.'

'No, *fly it.*'

'Your grandma's? You can't. Can't ever go to her. She doesn't know you. She stopped knowing me.'

'Why,' asked Juke, burrowing into his waterproof sack, 'didn't you go to one of your married sisters?'

'But I did go to two sisters. After a few days they turned me away because of Jack talking so soon. Their beloved longlife husbands thought Jack might endanger them by becoming famous. Attracting attention. Everybody turned me away before too long. I want nothing Sariola, nothing. Maybe I'll be happy with mutants—'

Juke cocked a damp fawn eyebrow. Producing a great wedge of toasted cheese-bread, he broke it into three equal portions.

'—if they're all like you!' The boy snatched and devoured.

92

'Not outwardly they aren't.' Juke chewed. 'See, I'm by way of being a freak mutie – I look normal. And my sister's lovely. Well, you mightn't get to meet her.'

'Won't we come to live with you?'

'We can cook that fish tomorrow morning or we could eat it raw now . . .' Next the sack yielded a greasy leg of goose. 'Bites for each! Share.' Juke bit off a mouthful, handed the leg to Jatta, rubbed his lips and wiped his knuckles across wet breeches. 'Do you think those Jutties in the warboat were looking for you, princess?'

'How could they know' – *munch* – 'and why should they care?'

'Because of that cuckoo in Osmo's hall.'

'I didn't see one!'

Jatta's son – and Jarl's – was soon sucking bare femur. Curling up, he nodded into torpor with a bone dummy in his mouth.

'Perched up high, the bird was. You already said yourself why they'd care. On account of Jack, your demon fast boy. Why don't you tell me about this Jarl Pakken?'

'So you remember his name! You followed me to find out the story.'

'I'm travelling east myself.' Cheese appeared, of eggs and buttermilk, the van Maanen monogram imprinted on the fat soft white tile. Juke leaned intently towards the pear-faced young woman, the angry scratch across the swell of her sun-browned buttersmooth cheek now only visible as a faint inscription.

'*Sing me a story . . .,*' he cooed.

Tiny green glittery beetles, phosphorescently aglow in the gloom, hoisted cheese-bread crumbs in microscopic pincers and dug themselves backwards into the shallow mattress of humus under the rock.

'*Tell me a tale—*'

The towering swan of mintywood flared, wooden wings enclosing the oil-drenched sack wrapping Tycho Cammon's corpse, and the crowd shrank back from the furnace.

'Let stone bones burn!' bellowed Osmo. He raised his arms dramatically. The tails of his frock-coat gave him the look of some great inky bird confronting sullen lake and dense lowering sky. At the request of the Lord of Maananfors, as conveyed by bailiff Septimus, the paddle steamer, still draped in bunting, had only departed tardily on its journey to Loxmithlinna at what proved to be a dreary dark hour. Puffing outward, paddles churning, its passengers staring back from the rail at the conflagration on the pebble shore, the ferry was a boat of death cleaving a flat, leaden waste. Not a mere rowing boat as on Johanna's wall but a substantial steamer which Cammon's soul would dearly regret missing.

Scarlet flames ruddied Sam Peller's hair and sallow face, his whole head florid in the firelight. Osmo's bondsman seemed to be blushing at the lapse which had brought death to Vivi. *Osmo's* lapse – which was now being redeemed. A mistake, nevertheless. A fatal error. Tilly's spaniel sniffed a billow of smoke. 'Meat – burning,' it yapped.

'*Soul eternal . . .*'

'. . . *burn in hell!*' quavered Mrs Lundahl, engrossed in the spectacle. Hot smuts settled on her lace cap till her sweltering boys pulled her further away.

'I thought you believed in *bliss*,' snapped the mana-priest, impassioned by this destruction of a soul before his eyes; or at least in his mind's eye.

'Cammon was evil,' declared the black-frocked mother. 'He was a devil. Everybody knows that.'

'You mean he was a *nakki* in human form?'

'Oooo,' chorused the crowd as the swan radiated whiter heat – scorching, searing – and still kept its shape. The furnace blaze greedily sucked in air. Incandescence blistered. A pungent tang of mint teased nostrils: a false note of illusory coolness.

'A devil! Have you never read your *Bible*?'

'*Read . . .*? No wonder your head's full of nonsense, woman.' Alvar harrumphed.

'In the book of *Chronicles*,' began Mrs Lundahl. However, the mana-priest was already shouldering away through the crowd.

'Chronicles?' the historian exclaimed alertly. Mrs Lundahl swung round. 'Lord Alvar!' Her sons gawped.

'Lord no more, Mrs Lundahl.'

'You once chained a *demon* in the sculpture park!'

'No, Mrs Lundahl, that was a Juttahat.'

'And Satan's a snake.'

The great bonfire roared, drowning her ramblings. Shaking his head sadly, Alvar absented himself too. Did the woman not realize she was in another world where the stories which mattered were different? Gunther ought to have been here to see Tycho Cammon's soul-pyre. It was the dream savant, after all, who had finally put paid to the stone man with Alvar's poker. Obviously longlife bred little respect for history in the making . . . Or was Gunther badgering Elmer and Lyle while they worked on the sky-boat? Negotiating for his hibernation monitor. Nikki Loxmith hadn't cared to witness the tyrant's bones being burnt, to which Vivi's funeral had been prelude. Her brother had decided to forgo both occasions.

'Fire burn bones to ash!' bawled Osmo, proclaiming, dripping with sweat. Mintywood burned searingly and persistently. Still, the temperature needed to incinerate a skeleton was formidable. Again, he swept his arms aloft, how much more like a priest than the mystic sot in the grey suit. And why not indeed? reflected Alvar. That was only right and proper. Hobbling back from the increased heat, the former lord recalled Johanna's insistence that Seppo Hakulinen would be a perfectly adequate priest for Maananfors. Oh, the bogus balm of mint on the fierce scorching fire-breeze.

'Flames crack and crumble, as lightning splits a rock!'

From offshore the gloom-dusked ferry passengers would be watching on the beach a radiant sun-bright swan illuminating the nearby wool mill and tannery.

8 · GIRL WITH A CHOCOLATE EGG

'Sing me a story, tell me a tale . . .'

Juke's lulling conjuration brought memories welling back of Jatta's mother and of the tale of how young Lucky had entered the secret inner chambers of the Ukko in Earth's asteroid belt centuries ago to be greeted by that same request; and the legends which Lucky had told to the Ukko; which Jatta in turn retold to herself in that dark wintry hut, and to Jack gestating in her womb . . . Her head spun with stories. Rain sluiced down, spattering stray droplets under the eaves of the rock. Her son snoozed against her like some cat abed whom she didn't wish to wake. How stiffly she reclined while their new companion crowded her in the gloom, watching intently.

'Tell me a tale . . .'

'You're a proclaimer too,' she mumbled as the realization came to her: a gentle pressure to perform. 'But I need to sleep,' she protested.

'Of course you do. Start to tell me in your sleep, Jatta. Your troubles will drain away. You'll wake refreshed—'

Tell what first? Tell what before what else? In her mind's eye she saw a circle of chattering monkeys, each holding the handle of the curled tail in front, its own tail held in turn. A circle of tales. But which order did they go in?

'Sleep, sleep . . .'

She slumped stiffly, eager for oblivion, barely resenting the imposition of Juke's will since it was almost in accord with her own. Caressed by his command, she drifted, hardness and ache dispelled. She would talk in her sleep. She knew it. She would dream memories. A proclaimer could make you do that.

That jigsaw of monkeys was an import from sultry Pootara where the mana-free rationalists remembered about apes from some country on Earth. To them all northerners were the apes of mana. Jatta's mother had given her the jigsaw on her ninth birthday. It wasn't an easy plaything, this flat variation on the puzzle boxes and puzzle spheres. So many possible permutations of tail and hand, hand and tail. But which was the *right* one? Which was the order which would arrange all those different monkeys into the shape of a horned snake starting to swallow its own tail? Perhaps none! If you juggled and concentrated long enough, said her mother, that was the hidden design you would discover. A serpent. Lucky could easily have been lying. Pootarans produced puzzles as exercises of the intellect, as witty logic tools. As exorcisms of mystery, not revelations. And so as to use up all their offcuts of northern timber frugally. A ring of apes becoming a serpent, ha! Probably Jatta had been searching for the impossible.

Though finally the impossible had found *her* – in the form of her fast boy.

Winter at Sariolinna, in Pohjola Palace. Two months of darkness; and her mother pregnant again – with the foetus who would become daughter Ester. Jatta was nine and a bit. Flighty Flicka had just wedded, back in the late autumn. Which left Kay and Helena, Jatta's elders, Jatta herself then Eva and little Minnow. Five daughters, and one more in the making. Always one more. Always. Lucky and Bertel made daughters compulsively.

Sisterhood was spoiled by being of Lucky's lineage; for sooner or later a daughter realized that there would always be half a dozen daughters growing up in the palace, as there had been for centuries. Affection from mad Mum or sad Dad could only be a whim, a quirk, a flower doomed to wither. Your elder or younger sisters were actually *you yourself* at different stages. So you became jealous for yourself, resentful, and you expressed your alienated feelings in foibles and fancies. You were at once romantic and fractious towards suitors who sought your gift. Usually you were glad to marry and move away, so as to be yourself, well away from the monkey-chain of sisters; though you might make a fuss when it came to accepting a particular suitor. You might create difficulties which served to amuse Lucky, your volatile keeper and custodian of the word which would unlock your chastity. Or else serve to infuriate her. To fall in love with a suitor could be folly when your betrothed might, just might, become zombie, an everliving corpse. But daughters were readily foolish.

Thoughts of suitors were far from Jatta's mind at the age of nine in the winter-locked palace as she puzzled with chilly fingers over jigsaw pieces on a tray in her lap. Burning peat warmed but did not wholly heat her lamp-lit bedchamber, high up a tower, as she huddled in the curved windowseat in thick blue trousers and a blue cloth dress banded with red brocade. Comprising almost a semi-circle of turret, the room was a stone breast with bulging oriel window as glass teat. A brown woollen rug on the yellover floorboards. A soft narrow bed, thick duvet embroidered with watchful eyes large and small, headboard carved with a complicated frieze of keys.

The green satin curtains were wide open. A slight chill fondled the girl. Tiring of intractable monkeys, she peered through the bow of panes at rimed forest and ice-capped menacing mountains. Though the sun had set seemingly for ever for midwinter, the far edge of the sky-sickle, unshadowed by the world, shone brightly silver. Snow sparkled on the wide frozen fjord and on the blanketed rooftops of Sariolinna.

And then her mother – her *young* mother, in a velvet gown of peacock blue – came in as unexpectedly as ever.

'Jatta? My Jatta? Let's yatter, let's natter, let's chatter!' Spilling from the girl's lap, little wooden monkeys clattered to the floorboard between windowseat and rug.

'It *is* Jatta, isn't it?' As if Mummy had forgotten who her own daughter was! Well, Jatta didn't see her mother every single day,

97

that's true. Tutors, servants, guards, maids, and Nanny Vanni
– *Nannivanni*, as till quite recently she'd thought the stout
woman was called – comprised her social universe. And Eva,
pretty much; though hardly toddling Minnow. And twelve-year-
old Helena, to a large extent; though hardly Kay, at *fifteen*, and
quite the woman. Jatta sometimes missed seeing her mummy
and daddy for weeks on end, and at other times for days. Or
perhaps she did not *miss* them, since this condition was usual.

When she was just a bit younger, Jatta had reasoned that her
parents always continued to look exactly the same, and youthful
– compared with other mummies and daddies in the palace who
had daughters as old as Flicka – because they only lived on
certain days, once a month or once a week. Whereas everyone
else lived all the time. Some nights before going to sleep Jatta
had whispered to Nakkinook, her pigtailed doll who shared the
bed, 'I'll miss tomorrow out!' But she never did.

Mummy could be loving, bouncing or cuddling Jatta in the
same way that Jatta cuddled or bounced Nakkinook; and she
could be scary. Sometimes both at once.

'Oh it's *me*,' agreed Jatta, wriggling.

'Is your girdle troubling you, daughter dear?'

'No!' The girdle was practically part of her, as her mummy's
big ruby ring seemed part of Mummy's finger. A padded hip band
and two delving prongs, blessed by a proclaimer so that it would
be flexible and never chafe or soil yet would prevent . . . something . . . which could steal her gift. This was the third such
girdle Jatta had worn, handed down to her from Helena who
needed a larger one, as Helena's would have been handed down
from Kay, and as Jatta in turn had handed her last girdle down
to Eva . . . a chain of diminishing monkeys' tails. Yes indeed,
Jatta had a little tail, and a wedge in front. It was Mummy who
fixed the girdle in place, after muffling her daughter's ears so
she wouldn't hear the secret word she whispered. Sariola women
never visited a steam-room, so Jatta rather assumed that all
female people wore girdles just as they wore rings or necklaces
or bangles.

With a sudden swoop Mummy settled beside Jatta on the windowseat. Mummy's peaked bootees crunched tiny monkeys. Her
arm tightened around her daughter. Jatta might have over-
balanced if Mummy hadn't clutched so firmly. The regally
gowned woman stroked her daughter's shiny cascade of coal-
black hair, already streaming beyond the girl's shoulders.

Mummy's own jumbled, straying raven hair was pinned up by several curved silver combs. The effect was part coronet – and part as if Mummy's cranium was clamped in a metal corset. Mummy's skin was so baby-fresh – firm butter flushing to rose on the chubby swell of cheeks faintly laced with the softest of down – and she smelled faintly of spiced buns with an unsettling piquant shrimpy hint. Jatta had seen that the smoky narrow eyes in that full oval face were wild.

'Tell me a story, Mummy!' begged the girl. Or else, what mischief might Mummy make?

This appeal was in vain.

'No,' came the reply, '*you* sing me a story and tell me a tale, little leppi! I want you to chatter about how your mummy came to Kaleva and we'll see how much of it you understand, for I'm sure I don't understand much any more; and maybe that's because I'm not quite wholly here at all but left my echo in the Ukko. Or maybe only my echo came to Kaleva to give birth to all Bertel's daughters, echoing one another down the years. So the real Lucky's still enjoying herself for ever and ever in manaspace, hidden away. Surely not in *my* Ukko any more, oh no, or someone would have noticed by now, wouldn't they, little leppi? So where else? Do Ukkos connect deep inside themselves down where the echoes are?' Jatta's mother laughed hectically at her daughter's perplexity and ruffled her hair.

A yearning for kindness, aflutter with panic, took hold of the girl.

'Mummy—' she pleaded.

'Call me Paula, not Mummy. A mummy is a dead body preserved by cunning.'

Jatta didn't understand.

'Paula . . . ?'

Only Daddy called Mummy that. Was this a trapdoor rigged for Jatta to fall through, or was her mother suddenly favouring her above Kay and Helena and Eva and Minnow? Frantic as a cat overwhelmed by petting, Jatta arched her neck to stare out at the silent snowy darkness of the day and the scintillant sky-bow always hanging low beyond the far horizon. Her mother, Daddy too, had come from the deep cold darkness of unimaginable space, somewhere beyond the world, empty but for drifting rocks, some the size of mountains, a kind of endless sea as deep as it was wide, a sea without shores in which you could float for ever and ever, but without any water in it, or even any air, a sea of nothingness except for those ever so seldom encountered boulders and wandering rock-bergs and icebergs which the family ship had been hunting – for the treasures in them, not treasures of rubies and emeralds but of iron ore, nickel, tungsten . . .

Her ancient, young mother held her effortlessly. Was she Jatta's succourer or her tormentor? How easily tenderness could turn into torment, warmth into waywardness.

Jatta squinted at the constellations. Archer. Cow. Harp. Cuckoo. So many stars, muted by the mirror-arc of the sky-bow. How crisp and clear the air was. Stars – and a bright planet too, a tiny silver lamp. Gassy Otso with its dozen moon-cubs?

'Paula . . .' Jatta tested out the name on her tongue. '. . . you lived in a ship in the dark nothing, a ship of steel that hunted rich rocks for the great whale-ships to melt—'

'The factory ships, yes.' Her mother's free hand plunged into the purse at her hip. 'Look!' Out came an egg, which she popped into Jatta's palm. This hen's egg was heavy. Jatta rotated it till she found the little chocolate plug, yet her fingernail scraped in case there was shell beneath and she might crack the egg only for sticky yolk and gluey albumen to drench her fingers and her dress.

'You don't trust me much,' her mother's voice lilted slyly in her ear.

'I do, Mum – Paula.' Jatta crushed the egg so that chocolate nougat oozed through ruptures. Tummy fluttering, she set the mignon egg on the windowledge, and breathed deep. 'You lived near one of those stars up there,' she resumed.

'None of those! None. Hasn't your tutor told you a thing? Who is she?' (Didn't her mother even know? Had she known so many tutors – and daughters?) 'No one knows where in the star-sea Kaleva is.'

'But,' and Jatta smacked the upholstery in protest, 'Kaleva's *here*. I only meant a star *like* those, because they all look the same.'

'Behind those stars are further drifts of stars, and behind those are a hundred more veils of stars, and then a thousand more. Nobody knows where Earth is or where Kaleva is – in *relation* to each other. I was once going to be a navigator, my little mignon . . .'

Mignon was a cracked egg with sweet dark nougat bursting out.

'I loved the dark,' her mother whispered; and maybe she was

lying. 'The dark was my home. The cold, and the empty. Even though it could kill me, and kill anyone.'

'Surely your ship was bright and warm inside?'

'The *Katarina* was an eggshell. We all knew that. We all lived with terror, in case the egg ever cracked. So we had to love that terror, love the dark. That's why I adore it here in Sariolinna at this time of year when the sun hides away. This reminds me of who I was.' Her mother's haunted face magnetized Jatta, for Paula Sariola was seeing . . . *space.* And deep time. 'You'll wed a handsome suitor, little Jatta, and you'll gift him with long life like mine. He'll not age, but you will.' A shiver chilled Jatta's spine. Her mother was taunting her with what was incomprehensible. 'He may take a mistress. He may throw you out. It has happened! I wreaked *havoc* on a husband who did that seventy years ago. I don't think it'll happen again.'

What was a mistress? 'You're the mistress of Pohjola Palace . . . Paula.'

Oh yes, of the parlours, kitchens, storerooms, workshops; the whole roofed-over village of servants' and guards' quarters. The great cellars. Halls and galleries and onion-domed towers. Courts and colonnades beneath cupolas aflicker with lamplight in winter, in summer lanced with day-long sunbeams. Corridors that were indoor streets. Apartments, closets, attics, refectories, nursery, buttery, pharmacy, armoury, treasury – mistress of all, and of Sariolinna town too, and of the forests and the mountains and the fjords and the lakes and the cold deserts and bogs of the tundra.

So what could this menace of a mistress be? Some powerful, fickle, moody woman more important than a wife? Full of mad passions and dark glooms. An invading queen . . . invited into his house by a husband? But why?

Paula was Bertel's *wife*! They'd been married so long. And Paula had given birth to dozens of other daughters who grew old and died . . . The girl's head spun, and she stretched to press her palm against the cold windowpane. Brushed by her thin wrist, the egg of shell and nougat nearly rolled off the slight slope of the windowledge.

'Tell me the story, Jatta! You *are* Jatta, aren't you? Chatter, Jatta.'

The girl had to ask: 'Did you ever call any other daughter Jatta?'

'No . . .' Mummy hesitated. 'Surely not, not even one who died

101

as a baby. I wouldn't have forgotten that. Bertel would have reminded me. Maybe I'll forget in another two hundred years' time . . . How long will it be, how long? That's what Bertel bleats at me – he'd better not try to leave me on my own. Who would father Lucky's daughters then?' The Queen stared out bleakly at the snow-fleeced roofs of the town and the frozen fjord. 'This world's my harvest for as long as mana insists. Or till I find the echo of myself; and I shall. Now tell me the story,' she hissed.

Tell, so that Mummy would know who she was; who she had been.

'Your kin were searching for rich rocks—'

'Yes, rich. A fortune. The search cost a fortune too. As much as Earth could afford.'

'Families lived far from the sun—'

'Out in the darkness, in eggshells. The stars stayed as far away as ever. Way out of reach, moated by an infinity of nothing. For an eggshell to cross even the smallest abyss would take a thousand years, and the great-great-grandchicks inside would have gone mad and bad. As mad and bad as me, little Chatter?' Her mother squeezed her abruptly so that Jatta squeaked.

'Is your girdle tight?' Paula stroked the lustrous coaly hair of her hundredthsome daughter, and tilted up her chin. She kissed the tears which had started from the girl's eyes. Mummy's body was so oppressive against Jatta, yet the pressure filled the girl with a giddy lightness as if she was drifting in a void – in the vacancy of her own existence.

'I can talk to you because you're still so young,' breathed Paula. 'Because you don't know life yet, mignon.'

'I do know what happened to you in the Ukko—'

'Do you indeed *know*? Do *I* know?'

'Listen!'

'Ah, you're becoming assertive, little Natter. Impetuous. I think I like that. Today I do.'

'Your ship found the Ukko which looked like a big egg-shaped rock but was only a rock on the outside,' gabbled Jatta. 'It was a whole key long and a half a key high and wide and far too regular for a rock and it had a hole in it—'

'Was the hole plugged with chocolate?'

'No, it was a big door like the iris and pupil in my eye. But inside, your Ukko was more like an ear, a complicated ear—'

'With chambers and caves and cavities and curvy, curly tunnels.'

'Inside there was air, sweet air—'

'Not the pong of old *Katarina*, a pong we knew and loved like a leppi its burrow—'

'There was proper weight too—'

'Gravity, girl. Oh the muscle-suits we had to wear in *Katarina*! How could such a rock have three quarters of a gee inside it, or air, unless it was a dormant alien base, we asked ourselves?' The tip of her mother's forefinger circumnavigated the auricle of Jatta's lug, tickling her shiversomely. When finger met thumb at the lobe Lady Sariola tugged at the lug-flap, prompting her daughter.

'Your Ukko was like an ear inside—'

Her mother's yeasty yet faintly tart, salty aroma: she smelled of baking bread and things from sea pools. And of course the Ukko had altered her body. It had made her once-blonde hair dark as night, the reverse of a bleaching by fright, as if she were the negative of the person she had been before.

'It was like an ear with great cavities and chambers and twisty channels and tubes and labyrims.'

'Labyrinths, Chatter. Cochleae. Huge inner spirals akin to curious snail-shells. Spirals spurring off spirals. At first we had no notion how much inner space my Ukko contained.' Thumb and index finger tweaked.

'That's because a lot of your Ukko was closed off. Then you went exploring – without your suit.'

'We moved into the rock like nomads to breathe the fresh air and feel our true weight.'

'You went off to play inside the stone ear. You were fifteen.' How old fifteen seemed: Kay's age.

'Oh we all played about a bit – cautiously, of course. You could easily die in the darkness. We capered because we'd made the greatest discovery of all time, a hundred times greater than Tut's tomb even if this one seemed quite empty at first. We assumed it was a creation rather than a creature. A forsaken alien base? A drifting alien monument or sculpture? In a way we were right on both scores. But wrong, so wrong. We didn't realize the half of it.'

Lulled by the memory of herself, Lucky sighed, and her hold on her daughter's ear slackened and fell away. Her boots scuffled the fallen wooden monkeys. She inhaled noisily.

'There's so much air here, isn't there? Air everywhere. I still love the wintry dark.'

She didn't sound as if she did but rather as if the darkness was a demon which she'd decided to adore so that it wouldn't consume her.

'Then deep inside, your Ukko spoke to you—'

'Deep inside it. Or what I thought was deep inside it, little Natter. And deep inside me as well. My kin had already been to that part and found a cul-de-sac. Nothing odd had happened to them. But now sounds started to *squirm* in my mind, hissing, clicking noises making me sick and dizzy. I reeled and fell down, dropping my torch, smashing my lovely light. Thin soft fingers crept around inside me, in my belly and my head. I convulsed. A hundred voices all chanted at once in my brain, my own and my mother's and father's and uncle's and aunt's a dozen times over in a maddening pandemonium of senseless babble, spewing out words, words, words. I was a sponge being squeezed. Pictures flashed so fast I only saw a blinding, nauseating blur. I thought I must die. I wriggled and writhed and I clutched myself up tight, bent around as if I was unborn. But then the booming madness faded and the sickness drained away. The smooth rock tube around me was luminous, pearly, with an archway leading onward, inward, downward. So I rose. I would have raced away, but no, I knew I must walk on down another spiral.'

'And your Ukko spoke in your head, and you could understand it. It said, *sing me a story, tell me a tale*—'

'Mustn't forget about the skeletons.'

'Bones and bones of what looked like human people but weren't because the ribs were all different. Juttahats! And half a dozen serpents. The Isi!'

The wick of the oil lamp on Jatta's table began to gutter, pulsing up spurts of blue flame, making ghosts dance in the room, but the girl plunged on. 'You started to tell the walls the stories from the *Book of the Land of Heroes* that your mother told to you, and her mother on Earth told to her—'

'It cost so much to go back to Earth, it was so far.'

'First, you told how in the beginning Vainamoinen spread trees across the bare land, including the curver tree for the cuckoo to perch on; and how the dwarf who became a giant helped him fell the tammy that grew too high so it was shading everything – after which every other kind of plant sprouted. Then Vai prayed for rain so there'd be a good harvest—'

'Prayed to what, little Natter?'
'To the Ukko in the sky, 'course—'

Jatta stirred, mumbling. Her small son was pressed damply against her. She'd been reciting in her sleep. Someone else, who was not her fast boy, was snoring very close to her. *Unnnngkr, unnnngkr.*

Juke the proclaimer.

She'd been dreaming of her bygone turret bedroom in Pohjola Palace – and of her mad mother whom she'd learned to hate.

The rain had ceased, though drips still plopped from the lip of the rock. The cloud-lid was breaking apart above the darkened spade-leafed larkeries and stout fronded horzmas. Vague grey castles were uncoupling. Their battlements smouldered orange and cherry in the first glow of the wee-hour dawn. Warm air was on the move, less stifling and humid than when she'd fallen asleep, but her chemise clung clammily to her. She suppressed a cough, hoping not to wake Jack at this exceptionally early hour. Half-two? Three? Could she lie still enough? The prickle to get on the move again might goad her. Would she doze again?

Unnnngkr, unnnngkr.

She timed her breathing to Juke's snores as if those might massage her back into a dormant stupor which could serve as sleep. Her nipples itched annoyingly. For the first week after Jack's birth she had suckled her fast-growing baby, disconcerted and drained by him. By then Jack was focusing on her face, recognizing her as herself, not as a mere extension, a source of comfort to be wailed at. Within another week he was lisping his first words, and before a further week passed he was almost coherent. He was struggling upright on bow legs already grown skinny, his prior plumpness consumed and transformed; carolling *Mamamamama* or sometimes *Jattajattajatta* like a projectile gun.

'What are you?' she had once exclaimed in wonder. 'Have you been reborn?'

To which her baby replied, uncomprehendingly, 'I'm *Jack*, Mama. *Jack.*'

The name she had cooed to him during the first evening of suckling and snoozing after he slid out of her. Her own name, with a hard ending.

Jack scared but enchanted her. How had this prodigy come to be hers? Why, Jack was Jarl Pakken's prodigy too, of course!

105

The sheer rush of their courtship – if you could call an almost peremptory seduction by such a name – seemed reflected in their baby's haste to grow, now that he was out of Jatta's belly. After the long dreamlike wintry gestation Jack sprouted apace. How much more life-saving this was – even if exhausting for Jatta – than if Jack had remained a helpless, wordless burden. Ah, Jack was springtime itself. Inspired with a sense of miracle, Jatta's thoughts had skittered away from dark doubts . . . which Osmo van Maanen had brusquely rekindled.

My marvellous mutant . . .? she mused. *Does your origin really matter as much as it mattered to Lord Osmo? You are you!* Somehow she was sure in her flesh that Jack wasn't *mutant* at all. Not merely because he showed no visible sign of deformity. Why, neither did Juke. No, because Jack was a miracle.

Flesh tickled, flesh ached . . .

She had quickly stopped suckling Jack, who needed – and called out for – solider food than milk. At first she chewed this for him, and kissed it into his mouth, there in that hut of sanctuary which the cuckoo had called her to and which was so well provisioned and fuelled far beyond any other such refuge. Jack's neat little milk teeth grew through, and he could munch for himself and grasp hold of his victuals. She'd had to squeeze some milk from her breasts with her fingers, but the little milk-berries which grew within her bubs, rooted inwardly from the nipples, soon dried. Only an occasional creamy bead and a tickle and ache, as tonight, reminded her.

When Jack was a month old she left the hut, loaded with her child and with the last provisions which would soon give out. For a week or more she tramped through forests in what she supposed was the general direction of her sister Helena's keep. Presently, charitable woodmen and farmers pointed the way; and some not so charitably.

What did being a *sister* count for, in a succession of so many? Very little, when Jatta had brought a nakki child with her! Helena set her and her talking infant on a week-long hike to sister Kay's. Kay sheltered the refugees for just a few days till her husband baulked at the bumptious bairn and issued marching orders. Kay advised her younger sister to appeal to van Maanen. On the route there, a ruffian assaulted her. But Jatta had her knife, and Jack bit the man.

Was Kay's advice a sop to conscience, or a malicious prank? Was Kay aware of Lord Osmo's prejudices? Maybe her sister thought that confronting van Maanen might force Jatta to face the reality behind her miracle boy . . .

Unnnngkr, unnnnnngkr.

Drip, drop.

9 · BATHERS IN A LONELY LAKE

The boy scrambled away from his mother, waking her. He careered towards Juke. Their new companion squatted on wet herbage, shirtsleeves rolled up. He was laying out rosy slices of trusterfish on three large larkery leaves. Trees glistened, well washed. Unseen insects chirred, and on a nearby bough an iridescent robberbird croaked to itself impatiently, betraying its camouflage of shifting greens and blues. The would-be snatch-thief eyed the breakfast on those impromptu plates. *Crukk, crukk.* Woolly, white cumulus floated in a calm, sapphire sky.

Jack snatched raw fish to cram into his mouth as his mother staggered from under the overhang, uncramping herself.

'One leaf-full only, lad. One each,' said the chef.

To Jatta: 'Wood's too wet to make a fire. Come and eat your share before robberboy gobbles his.' Juke's overnight stubble was fuzzy rather than bristly. Jatta imagined a wispy, curly beard which would not grow quickly.

'Robber?' the little boy asked as he munched. 'Me caught the fish.'

'*I* caught the fish,' Juke corrected.

Ambery eyes – *Jarl's* eyes – were huge in protest.

'You didn't, you liar!'

Juke's hand lazed out to cuff the boy. Of a sudden Jack was two metres away, poised on tiptoe.

'*Stay*, boy! I was simply correcting your words. I say *stay*.'

Jack shuddered. His mother glanced keenly at the proclaimer. Would she soon be accompanying him like an obedient bondslave, with her son a capering trained monkey?

Juke smiled reasonably.

'You'll have to help us, lad, if we're to have an easy journey. You mustn't dart around so, and snatch, and run off.'

'I *need* to move,' cried Jack. 'Or I won't grow. I'll burst.'

'Is that so?'

'Yes!'

'If you say so,' Juke agreed mildly. 'Have you thought that you might grow so fast, like an overnight mushroom, that your whole life's over in a year or two?'

'*No*,' protested Jatta, 'that can't be. Don't say so.'

The boy stared at Juke, quivering.

'*I* was too big,' he said, making his mouth gape wide demonstratively with the first word. 'Fish could fall out. *Me*'s smaller.' He pursed his lips.

Juke chuckled. 'You mean you think about your words? Well, well.'

'He's a miracle,' declared his mother.

'He's certainly *something*, and that's a fact,' Juke agreed. 'When I've heard your whole story I might have an idea what that something is.'

That insinuating sense of insistence . . .

'Didn't I talk half the night, and you fell asleep?'

Crukk, crukk.

Juke jerked his thumb.

'There's our real robber, boy. Bird'll be in my knapsack next.'

Jatta's child erupted into action. He spied a stone, he seized it, he shied it.

CRUKK! The robberbird took flight then crashed to the leaf-mould. It spun around, one wing beating, and the other crumpled. The boy scurried to where the bird rotated like a broken wind-up toy. He balanced above it uncertainly.

'Poor birdy,' he wailed. 'Naughty birdy!'

'Jack—'

Juke's hand brushed Jatta. 'Don't prompt him, let's see what he does.'

Indecision twisted the boy around, to left, to right. He spun several times while the robberbird gyrated, glinting blue, green. Then Jack pounced. Hoisting the injured bird, he swung it around and threw it along a narrow glade of full apricot bell-flowers between the tall, flopping, fleecy umbrellas of the horzmas. The bird travelled further than any such throw could possibly have sent it. It was flying again. Finally it collided with a stout trunk and tumbled, inert.

Fascinated, Jack ran after it.

'He forced it to fly,' said Juke softly. 'Even with a broken wing. He's like a tight coil. If he can keep calmer he'll be able to do strange things, I'd say. Or maybe he'll always be half out of control.'

Jatta stared after her son.

'And how long will *always* be?' Juke asked.

'Don't say that!'

'Don't say, don't say,' he mocked softly. Contempt for a once-privileged daughter mingled with a stern pity. 'You're spilling the fish I sliced for you.'

This was true. Raw fish had slid off the glossy leaf in her hand.

Jatta recovered the morsels. She cleaned each on a cushion of moss and popped it into her mouth before devouring the remainder from off her improvised plate. See: she was not proud like some of Lucky's offspring. The soft, succulent, oily mouthfuls hardly needed chewing. They almost melted.

'I need to know about your lover,' said Juke, 'if I'm to understand your miracle fast boy.'

'Have I asked you to understand him?'

'I need to know about Lucky's court as well.'

'Because you're an outcast.'

'Outcast, eh? Why, so are you now.'

Jatta tried to visualize a community of mutants. Of freaks.

'Lord Osmo's mana-priest is a buffoon,' said Juke. 'He ought to have been praying for the harmony that lets our livestock and our crops flourish here on an alien world.'

Jatta's feet and calves itched. Walking further away from Maananfors would soothe the itching. She shuffled around. 'Jack, come back – we should be going!'

'I gather it's van Maanen's bed-ridden mummy who calls the tune about mana-priests in his neighbourhood. She wouldn't want her precious son overshadowed. No, he must eclipse all others.' His insistence on talking, talking, when they ought to be on their way.

She paced, she fidgeted. 'Jack!'

Her boy skittered back, a scaly feather in his fist.

'Now who,' Juke asked in seemingly fine humour, 'do I have a bread-box for in my sack?'

'For me!'

Juke ruffled the boy's ebon locks. He was a groom gentling a skittish foal. The foal twitched but stayed with the man as they both ambled back towards the overnight den.

Why was Jatta holding an empty leaf? Why else but to wipe her bum. Tearing off a couple more leaves, she hastened behind a thicket to empty her bladder and bowels as quickly as possible. When she returned, Jack was biting his way through a crusty shell of rye packed with fatty pork and tiny baked sprats. Juke had shouldered his own knapsack and Jatta's. But Jatta was wrong to imagine that they were setting off for distant parts just yet.

'I think,' said Juke, 'we should all have a bathe in the lake before we even think of going anywhere.'

She stared at him in bewilderment.

'A thorough wash begins the day.' Winking: 'We mutants aren't necessarily dirty, you know, fine lady.'

'But . . .'

'We'll be wasting time?'

'Yes!'

Juke stroked his chin. He glanced idly in the direction of the sun.

'You'll enjoy a leisurely dip.'

He had her knapsack, so she couldn't just seize hold of Jack and hurry off with him.

'The boy's our chaperon. No hanky-panky intended.'

Jatta squirmed.

'You're itchy. Sweaty. We need a wash.'

'You're tormenting me.'

'Probably saving you from a flush of prickly heat.'

'But we just ate.'

'It was quite a light meal.' Laughing, Juke strode off in the direction of the lake. Jatta had no choice but to follow.

'Jack'll get a cramp,' she protested. The boy was dashing ahead through the grove. 'Jack, wait!'

'No, he won't,' said Juke. 'Strip off and wade in, lad!' he called.

'Well, I'll stay on the shore. I washed at Maananfors.'

'Today's today, Jatta. You'll soak yourself too, and float about a bit, and not pace the beach like a madwoman.'

Mist lazed serenely on the lough. A few harnies were cruising distantly, their enamelled plumage muted to pastel. Vapour drifted: lace veils tinted faintly blue. Jack's boots and dungarees and tan vest lay discarded. Her skinny, dusky boy already bobbed in the shallows, chortling to himself. A cough racked Jatta. She spat out sputum on the sand. 'I'll chill myself—'

Juke's hand steadied her. 'No, you're feeling much better. You're strong. You're healthy. That cleared your lungs nicely.' He dumped the knapsacks, shed his cloak, unbuttoned his shirt.

'What if the sky-boat comes back?'

'They already looked here, didn't they?'

His robust chest was smoothly devoid of hair, a firm creamy breastplate. Around both nipples red lips were tattooed. Speaker's lips. The lips seemed huge and sensual. He glanced down at those, and smiled.

'I speak from the heart, Jatta.'

There was nothing provocative to her about his flesh and muscle as there had been with Jarl. Really, the double tattoo was too much. One would have been quite adequate. Two made it seem as though . . . he was a mutant, with actual lips in his chest. If any mutant was deformed in such a fashion!

'Undress,' he insisted.

Did he wish to see the body of one of Lucky's daughters stripped bare, so that he might imagine himself as a successful suitor one fine day? She doubted that he had any intention of ravishing her in the water or there on the silvery sand.

But still, jitters had seized her. She was trembling – with frustration, at not being able to continue the journey immediately.

'Personally,' he said, 'I wouldn't try for one of Lucky's daughters. Not with mutant seed in me. I'd be chary of becoming . . . you know what.'

She knew. She did not wish to know.

'But you need a wash. *This is spoken.*'

Perhaps this was the closest he would come to such a consummation: bathing with a Sariola, and remembering her unclad physique.

Yes, she must bathe. She had no choice. And in the lake, she could hide from his gaze. Moving away from him, she kicked off her boots. Hastily she jettisoned tunic, skirt, shirt, chemise, and panties – no chastity girdle now, not any more, a bone missing from her body. She slapped into the water, wading till she could sink to her neck. Discarding his breeches, he followed: oh handsome in a homespun way. He sank down near to her. He rubbed water under his armpits. Jatta's itchy breasts bobbed, but his were the blushing nipples hereabouts. She imagined her abandoned clothes rising up of their own accord and stalking off impatiently, continuing the journey without her. Jack was trying to learn to swim, flailing his slender brown arms and legs.

'So tell me,' said Juke, 'what tales Lucky told to her Ukko to

111

win us our world – just as you told them to your mother when you were a little girl.'

'No, not now. Please. Later, while we're hiking.'

'*Now*. And calm yourself. Let the water cool your racing heart. There'll be no rushing off yet a while.'

'You must already know those tales, Juke. Everyone does.'

'Then they'll be easy to tell, won't they? You'll hardly need to strain yourself.'

She realized that he was pitting himself against the impress of Osmo van Maanen in her, against the print of his brusque proclamation – by delaying her, frustrating her. He was testing the stretch of van Maanen's power to see how well he could counter it, and maybe even snap it. Did he care that he was being unkind? That she was suffering anxiety? Did he even consider the effect he was having on her? Oh yes: he considered it carefully, studying it. Almost innocently, as though he was helping her, easing her. How much better it might have been if he'd behaved lecherously! His damned chaste concentration on her. He was like an obsessed adolescent who was saving himself up abstemiously for some imaginary future bride.

Well now, hadn't virginity been *Jatta's* very own saintly foible? In rejection of Lucky's game of daughters and to spite her mother, Jatta when adolescent stubbornly swore that she would never give herself to any man. Lucky's daughters must wear girdles. They must remain chaste until they wed. She would remain chaste for ever!

Until she met Jarl ... upon whom she tossed her gift away gladly.

'We really ought to find some better refuge than a cave tonight,' she said. 'Somewhere drier. A barn. And food – we'll run out of food. That'll all take time.' This was itchingly obvious.

Juke eyed her closely. Were those beads of water on her face, or nervous sweat?

'I do have some money,' he told her. 'I don't suppose you have any marks left, rich girl?'

She shook her head.

'Well, I do.'

'*Some*? You don't want to squander your *some* on Jack and me.'

He snorted a laugh. 'Tell me a tale, Jatta Sariola, here in the cool, calm water. And don't you fret. Your boy's enjoying himself. We'll leave in half an hour or so ...'

112

He was daring Osmo van Maanen – from a distance. He was matching himself, remotely. But was that all? A mutant in normal guise, claiming hospitality at a Lucky's Night feast; asking questions of Lord Osmo's staff when they were in the cups. Watching, probing. Juke hadn't followed her simply so as to learn her own story but also to use her as a probe into the state of Lord Osmo. Did Juke imagine that some change might have come over van Maanen since she left the keep, and that this might be detectable through Jatta on whom the lord had imposed his will?

Had Juke done something sinister while he was in Maananfors? Had he arranged some unpleasant surprise for Lord Osmo?

Her nipples itched, and she clutched at her submerged breasts. 'Before you left Maananfors did you—?'

Juke slicked back his matted hair. 'Don't ask me things, Jatta – *you're* wasting travel time. Just tell me, and you'll feel so blithe about it, so buoyant . . .'

How his voice lulled her now. Her curiosity slid away, dissolving in the waters of the lough.

'After Vai sowed all those trees and plants,' little Jatta piped to Paula Sariola in the tower bedchamber while the lamplight leapt and sank, 'he sang such lovely proud songs that another minstrel who was called Youkahainen got jealous and challenged Vai to a singing contest. After a bit of a contest Vai got fed up with Youkahainen. Vai really chanted his best, and the ground under Youkahainen turned into quicksand. Youkahainen began sinking. The sand was as greedy as if it was alive, quick to gulp down Youkahainen's knees and thighs and chest. The sinking man promised Vai all sorts of magic treasures if Vai would spare him, but Vai only scoffed—'

Phut, phut, from the guttering wick.

'—until Youkahainen promised Vai his own sister . . .'

'Like a desperate pimp, a panicked pander,' snapped Lucky. 'I'm no procuress, no bawd! Not Saint Lucky, oh no. I'm the Queen of Pohjola Palace.'

Little Jatta was scared. What did all those words mean? 'Yes, you are, Mum. I mean, Paula.'

Mummy's head jerked to scan the frozen fjord with a gaze of ice; and then she patted her daughter's midriff. 'I'm the lady of the lock.'

Hastily, Jatta resumed the story. 'Yes, Youkahainen promised

113

Vai his sister. So *then* Vai released Youkahainen. Youkahainen went home, disgusted with himself, but his parents were delighted at the bargain because it was a real honour to wed someone as powerful as Vai. You see, Vai had already seen Youkahainen's sister and he really liked her; which is why he said yes to the bribe. The sister didn't want this. She hated it. She thought Vai was horrible—'

Mummy gripped Jatta by the wrist. '*My* daughters can all refuse husbands if they don't fancy them.'

'Can they?' gasped the girl. The base of the ruby ring was pressing upon a bone, rocking to and fro upon it. 'Youkahainen's sister threw herself into a lake and drowned herself.'

The pressure relaxed. Mummy simply held her daughter's hand limply, little palm in large palm.

'And how did my Ukko like my tales? Deep down there in its huge phosphorescent cochlea, amongst the bones of humanoids and serpents! I feared if I didn't tell a good tale then I'd be bones too . . .'

Tiring of her daughter's recital – or satisfied by it – Lucky Sariola herself continued telling Jatta about the inside of the Ukko, and of how she had glimpsed echoes of the dead Juttahats and Isi: maroon-tongued unmen carrying snakes coiled around their chests, rearing, hissing silently. The spectres of the aliens terrified her. But those wraiths fled from her into a space she knew she couldn't enter.

'A space . . . ?' Her daughter was confused. Space was the dark vacant endless sea, empty even of air, though with lonely jagged mountains and boulders and rocks adrift in it now and then.

'Don't you understand? Don't you listen to my mana-priest? That's the black shore, where the spirits stay as long as the bones survive.'

'Yes! Yes!'

'The Ukko's previous passengers still existed inside it as spirits on their own black shore.'

They had died, and the Ukko had drifted, inactive. How and why had they died? No one knew even now, centuries afterwards.

'Maybe it had heard all their stories?' suggested the girl.

Mummy's hand squeezed. 'Think! The Ukko likes to hear stories over and over again. That's how it directs itself. It finds a place in the galaxy where the stories can belong, and come to life. Then it heads back to the origin of the stories. To the world where they were born. It travels to and fro. And people emigrate in it, like fleas in a dog's coat. Talkative fleas – telling it over and over again the stories that please it and propel it. Always the same stories. It insists on that. Different stories might lead elsewhere.'

'Maybe it heard the snakes' stories too many times? Maybe it wanted new ones.'

Mummy patted Jatta approvingly on the knee. 'That's good. That's bright. But is it right, my Chatter? The snakes are still using their other Ukkos. Ukkos bring them here with their black and bronze and amber servants to meddle with us. I'll meddle with them, oh I shall!'

That fifteen-year-old, who would become known as Lucky on account of her find, had told the Ukko stories from a land of forests she had never seen herself except in holograms aboard the *Katarina*, and of trees and lakes and rivers and fjords and islands and of ice and day-long wintry dark and night-time summer sun.

Shall Ukko take you to a world like that? it had asked. *To a world sufficiently like that?*

Maybe in the same galaxy, maybe not. Maybe in the same universe, maybe not.

'*Yes,*' Lucky had answered. She dearly wished to see those landscapes which had only ever been bright images to her out here in the steel eggshell, in the great dark which she nonetheless loved since not to love it could be lethal.

'*All of us. All of us who want to go.*'

Ukko would take as many as wished, as often as they wished. They only had to tell Ukko the same stories, again and again.

But first it must . . . adjust her. Alter her a little.

Would she like to live for a long time and still be young? Would she like to grant long life and youth to the partner she fell in love with? Why yes. Who wouldn't?

Would she like to conceive many daughters who would do likewise to their own first loves? Well, this seemed wonderful.

So the Ukko made Paula sick again. She sank to the stony floor of a tunnel and lay feeble with nausea while thin feelers seemed to quest inside of herself as though she was a home for worms.

Eventually she returned past the skeletons to the cavern where most of the crew of *Katarina* had camped. She was bursting to tell her story.

Who was this girl?

115

Paula Sariola had been blonde-haired before. Now her hair was jet black. Paula had been missing for a day and a night and a morning. Her father and mother and the others had been searching and could find her nowhere. Her mother was frantic with worry. Everyone else was uneasy. How could Paula have disappeared? Disappeared where to? Now Paula came back eagerly as if she had only been away for an hour or two. She came back. Or did she?

Who was this black-haired girl who looked so like Paula of the chubby cheeks, pear-shaped face of peachskin, narrow dusky eyes?

Her mother, centuries dead now, had started forward – then halted, staring in bewilderment. Was this Paula's twin? Paula had no twin. No sister. No brother.

'Listen, everyone!' Paula sang out. Words bubbled from her about her Ukko, a fountain of talk, a rushing stream.

Still, she didn't realize that her hair had become jet black.

'We wore our hair very short in the *Katarina*, you see, Jatta. And I had no mirror with me.' Mummy fondled Jatta. 'I went in, but was I the same one who came out? No, it kept me in there, and sent my echo back, my dark echo. I've been suspecting this for years. Bertel doesn't agree – though he pretends to humour me – but I *know*, you see. It's as plain as looking in a mirror.'

'That you're not really you . . . ?' How dangerous this was, if Mummy was pretending not to be herself. She might do anything at all.

'If you're not you,' the girl mumbled, anxious to appease, 'then maybe I'm not really me either.'

And this was almost true. For who was Jatta among a hundred and more sisters?

The Queen laughed in a crazed expression of sorrow. 'Whenever one of my daughters dies I think a part of me returns to the black shore to keep up the link with my lost self, wandering there, still alive. You're my messengers. Where do you go to? Where is the real Paula hidden? I think I know, I'm sure I know.'

'Where?' Jatta asked miserably.

Her mother's tone became crafty. 'You won't find out from this Paula, to tell your husband and give him power over me. How soon are you getting married, Chatter?'

'I'm *nine*—' The girl darted a glance, of appeal, towards her doll on the bed. 'Nakkinook,' she whispered.

Her mother swung round. 'You're going to marry a doll? Why, so did I, I suppose. A man who became a doll.'

116

Daddy wasn't a doll.

'He'd better not try to leave me. I need him in bed. The way you need your doll. Don't turn against me, Yatter, the way they all do. I'm not to blame for half of what I do, because it isn't me who does it. No, it's my dark echo. Young Paula's still inside. Somewhere. Not here. I'll find her. She loves you, Jatta.' The compulsion of her mother's presence! She was so powerful, mistress of town and tundra, forest and fjord. Jatta feared for Nakkinook.

What could she say? 'I love you, Mummy, I won't leave you, I won't ever get married to anyone.'

'That's what you think, my little leppi. All my daughters are free to choose. They *have* to choose; and I, to approve.'

'I shan't choose,' insisted the girl, not understanding that when eventually she would refuse to accept any suitor, her motive would be quite the opposite: not the product of pretended love for this ancient young woman whom she saw only every so often, but of rejection of Lucky's régime and rules.

Arising urgently, the Queen hurried to the bed which was embroidered with eyes and carved with wooden locks. Her hand hovered over the blushing bisque boy-doll dressed in a red-striped jacket, a mustardy waistcoat and pea-green breeches. The once natty outfit was scuffed and faded. Nakkinook's moulded curly hair was blond. His wrists and hands were of bisque. He had lost both thumbs. The rest of his body under his clothes was firm stuffed leather. Mummy prodded, and Jatta's heart skipped. Nakkinook's pivoting blue glass eyes flicked sideways flirtatiously.

'Who's this in your bed?'

'Did any of my older sisters ever refuse?' Jatta was desperate to distract Mummy from Nakkinook. To save him from being shaken, spanked, broken.

'If you don't give life to a man do you suppose you'll live for ever yourself? Is that it, Natter?'

'Would I, would I?'

'Two and a half centuries ago one of my earliest daughters, Rita, had that idea. I was curious too, in case my Ukko had misled me. Though it didn't cheat me about anything else, except for hiding the real me away. I can't remember what Rita looked like, but she must have been rather like you. You all are. Soon Rita began to look old. Quite quickly, I fancy. She'd put off choosing. After a while she was eager to wed, I remember. Your doll thinks I'm upsetting you.'

117

'Oh he doesn't, honestly.' Jatta swung her head. 'Look, there's a cuckoo—'

Gown swirling, the mistress of Pohjola hastened to the window. 'No there isn't, I'm wrong. It was just a shadow.'

'I wonder if the fools are remembering to hang food out just in case? A snow cuckoo might tell me where the real me is. I must go and check!'

'It wasn't a cuckoo – it's too cold.'

'I love the cold, little Chatter.' Lady Lucky glanced, strickenly, at the peat glowing in the hearth. 'It's so warm in here.'

Please go, Mummy. Go and impale dead chicks on the cuckoo perches.

Jatta's itchy tension had dwindled. She felt quieted.

Long ribbons of azure mists lazed, lending a charming modesty to the morning lake and to whatever transpired in it. Cumulus clouds up above were benevolent behemoths grazing on air. Trees around the shoreline glowed, refreshed. The silence was emphasized by an occasional *crake* from a distant harny. Even her boy lolled hushed in the shallows, staring up transfixed.

'Beautiful,' she sighed. Her hand arced. 'All this . . .'

'A poetess would think so,' agreed Juke.

'The mist . . . Some things look best when half-seen.'

Jatta fretted immediately that this remark might strike him as provocative and flirtatious, a hook for an unwanted compliment on her own charms which were cloaked by water. Juke shut one eye. He did not look at her at all but stared around the shore at the ranks of trees, emerald, lustrous.

'Half-seen,' he repeated, and seemed to tremble. He was paying no attention to her. Just then, the irksome pestering urgency returned to Jatta. She struggled from the water, angry at the heaviness of flesh no longer buoyed up. Slapping ashore, she used the gaberdine shirt as a perfunctory towel. She bundled it damp upon her knapsack and quickly dressed in the cast-offs from Osmo's keep and in her own mutilated northern tunic. Juke had hardly looked at her while she dried and dressed. Now he strode naked from the water to gather up his own cloak as a towel.

'Come, Jack,' he called, and the boy came scampering out of the shallows, kicking spray then sand.

'You enjoyed your dip in the water, didn't you?'

Busy with drying and dressing Jack, Jatta failed to realize that Juke was addressing her rather than the boy.

'You enjoyed your dip, Jatta.'

'It eased me . . .'

More than that.

A different lake, a different man . . .

Jarl.

Who had abandoned her.

But perhaps he'd had no choice?

Jarl had brought her bliss and rapture. Panic stirred as Jatta realized that the unfolding of her story, now unavoidable, would lead to her needing to clarify ecstasy for Juke, perhaps in exquisite detail.

'Where's Nakkinook now?' her boy piped. He'd been listening to everything with his preternatural sharpness. Soaking her sentences up like a sponge, digesting them.

'Somewhere in the palace, I suppose, with a younger sister of mine. And spruced up again. I lost interest in Nakkinook.'

'Why's that, Jatta Mummy?'

What could Jatta say? That she had soon disdained the doll because he was a boy? With those flicking ogling eyes of his, and his brown leathery body under the natty costume. Boys became youths became suitors. That was why the boy-doll had been given her in the first place, so that the little girl would confide in him, reveal herself to the little gentleman in secret.

'Why?' pestered Jack. 'Why lose in-ter-est in Nakkinook? Why why?'

'Don't you know that a nakki is a naughty spirit?'

Jack considered. 'Am I naughty? Am I your Nakkinook now?'

At last his shuffling boots were tied. 'No, you're my Jarl child,' she muttered. What if her miracle did continue maturing at such a pace?

'I think I want to *beat him* some day.' Jack began punching at his own chest, then wrapped his arms around himself in a clinch which could as easily have been a passionate hug. 'What did Vai do next after the singing contest? What did he do?'

Jack very likely already knew from the womb, but was no more averse than Lucky's Ukko to being told all over again.

A frown creased Juke's forehead as he crammed his skull-cap back into place upon hair as matted as felt. 'The singing contest,' he murmured. 'The quicksand. His pitiful sister . . .'

Jatta glanced sharply at the man. 'You're going to speak against Lord Osmo at the gala this autumn, aren't you?'

'If he's there,' said Juke evasively.

10 · TROUBLED DREAMS IN THE AITCH-HOUSE

Sometimes it was hard to know what an animal wanted, even when the animal in question could speak.

Thus, with Nikki Loxmith's pussycat Tommi.

'Me want,' the pet whined plaintively. Tail erect and spine arched, the mog rubbed its black and white person against Nikki's shank as if intent on tripping her. Then it promptly wandered off to nuzzle a chair, quite turning its back on her.

'Me waaaant,' Tommi complained to the chairleg. Perhaps the cat had missed Nikki during her trip to Maananfors but couldn't quite adjust to her return. The white tip of its sturdy black tail twitched petulantly. Hairs ridging its spine suggested that Tommi was hosting a few worms.

The guest chamber provided for Gunther Beck was on the third floor of the south wing of Loxmithlinna keep, overlooking the water-yard. The six-storey granite residence formed a massive letter H. Its south and west wings actually jutted into the turquoise lake. Water flooded the space between the wings, forming a protected harbour rimmed with a quayside pathway. At the lakeside end of the aitch reared a pair of onion-domed towers. Between the domes, stout chains stretched tautly. Suspended beneath, a covered wooden bridge with a dozen windows effectively formed the top of a giant gateway. The bridge housed winch-gear for a portcullis a hundred metres wide. This massive grating rode on vertical rails riveted to the granite on either side. Ceremonially, once a year, the barrier was lowered. An hour later it was raised again.

Built two and a half centuries earlier, architecturally the huge aitch-house was a monument to paranoia. Dread had played a large role in its design. Shortly prior to its erection the Isi and their Juttahats had first appeared on Kaleva. At the advent of these aliens anxiety had gripped that portion of the human populace which lived to the west of the turquoise lake. Irrational fear infected people like some bout of influenza. Alarm was in the air, amplified by mana, out of proportion to its cause. Those ancestors of the Loxmiths and their retainers hadn't themselves *seen* any aliens as yet. They only knew of the Isi and their

120

Juttahats from travellers and from cuckoo tales. Nevertheless, keep and village (as it then was) must be united under one indomitable, defensible set of roofs. At considerable sacrifice, the hulking fortified aitch arose.

The mood of anxiety had long since drained away. Subsequently the town expanded out around the keep, spreading along that shore which had for a while seemed so nakedly vulnerable.

Numerous ordinary families lived and plied trades in the east and west and north wings of the aitch-house, since otherwise much of the edifice would have stood empty. Those wings housed lacemakers, tailors, saddlers, shoemakers, bakers, even a brewery. The presiding Loxmiths and their household and staff only occupied the six-storey south wing; that was quite spacious enough. The result: a bustling conviviality. Paranoia had resolved into sociability. This reflected itself in the attitude of Elmer, who could easily be prevailed on to assist an Osmo or a turnspit whose spit wouldn't turn smoothly. No doubt the air of industry in the aitch-house had favoured the flowering of Elmer's mana-blessed talent for machinery. Nowadays his mother Lokka presided as châtelaine of the whole keep and lady of the region. Her husband Henzel had contracted a paralysis, and could only move his lips and his fingers – with which he guided an ingenious mechanical wheelchair made by his son.

Gunther Beck's belly rumbled. To be sure, his gut was expanding; but could there be room left in it for a rumble?

'A hundred and ninety years since I was last in this keep!' he announced as he seized a pear from a fruitbowl by that massive tammywood bed in which he would sleep. Juice ran down his doubling chin.

Nikki stared at him in some awe.

Gunther sucked the pear slurpingly. 'Yes, a hundred and ninety, if I'm not mistaken. The sense of panic still hung about. My dreams *mocked* me. They taunted me. They jeered at me, as if gibbering nakkis were in charge of them. As if this was their own private castle which you'd obligingly built for them.'

Stimulated by the sound and sight of someone eating, Tommi ran to Elmer, gaping up at that candid, lean face.

'Want *fish*!' the mog appealed, green eyes wide in its furry black mask.

Elmer pursed his lips.

'Sooooon,' he cooed – a sigh of wind to soothe the cat's wishes.

The cat continued staring intently, waiting for *soon* to happen.

'The panic?' Elmer shrugged it away, somewhat embarrassed. 'That's all over long since. Our dreams are sweet.'

'Sweet as a pear,' confirmed his sister.

'Anyway, I wasn't aware that our people used to suffer much by way of nakki-nightmares here in the house. Not once the house was completed.'

'One of my talents, or curses,' said the dream-lord, 'is to be able to sense the spirits imbuing a place, and to dream those. I can control it nowadays. I can suppress it.'

'Let's hope you won't need to.' Elmer rubbed his chin thoughtfully. 'I'm not sure I believe in nakkis. I've never sensed any nakki hiding in a recalcitrant piece of machinery.' He chuckled. 'Any *knack's* in me myself.'

The purple tammy headboard of the bed was carved with stylized waves in an oval lake. Not tempestuous billows but gentle, though exaggerated, undulations. This motif repeated itself in the bedspread which was all the hues of blue, and in a tapestry which partly cloaked one wall.

Gunther tossed the pear core into a hearth grey with ashes. He licked his fingers, dried them on a kerchief, then caressed the carvings. 'At least this bed won't burst into flames while I'm in it . . .'

Innocent-eyed, Nikki Loxmith enquired, 'Do you sometimes set beds on fire with your dreams?'

Gunther chuckled, though his expression was melancholy. 'That would be something, wouldn't it? No, in this bed I'm more likely to feel seasick.' All those waves were, of course, intended to soothe a sleeper, gently rocking him.

'Oh,' asked Nikki, 'doesn't this room suit you? We could put you in the armoured suite, but that's—'

'—panelled in cast iron,' said Elmer dismissively. 'From the panicky times.' He spoke as though he couldn't credit what such frights had been about.

'No, this is a perfect room,' Gunther assured Elmer's sister. 'With its incombustible tammy bed.'

Nikki's laughter tinkled as she realized her misinterpretation of his remark. He had simply been alluding to the flameproof qualities of the purple wood.

'Spacious. Airy. Fine view of your harbour-yard, and your *Sea Sledge* – in which I felt no stomach qualms at all on the trip here, I assure you.'

122

It had taken Elmer and Lyle the previous two days to service the van Maanens' sky-boat. That morning the party had crossed a somewhat choppy lake in no great haste while Gunther snacked on cold sausage, the ballast prolonging his breakfast. The plan was that after a few days spent at Loxmithlinna Elmer would pilot the ten-metre powerboat onward along the chain of lakes and linking rivers to Landfall which lay some two hundred and fifty keys east-south-east. Lyle Melator would be going along, and Elmer's sister had practically insisted on visiting the Earthfolk's base. How could Elmer disappoint Nikki?

There at Landfall, Elmer and Lyle would take counsel – discreetly – about how to build a certain piece of equipment which the dream seer required. Gunther Beck himself would have disembarked after the first hundred keys of the journey. He would head home on foot in a more southerly direction. At keeps and villages and farms he would pursue further enquiries about his missing nephew Cully.

Nikki did not yet know the exact nature of the piece of equipment. Her curiosity was piqued at the air of secrecy, but it would be childish to ask outright. The apparatus which Lord Beck had commissioned was something which apparently wouldn't be used until the following year. Long before then Elmer would surely have confided in his favourite, his only, sister.

However, Nikki did not have nearly as long to wait to discover what Lord Beck and her brother and Lyle were hatching.

Since the bed had become a focus of interest, Tommi leapt on to the wavy blue coverlet and sprawled. The cat stretched luxuriously. Its front paws flexed, catching on threads in the weave.

Lyle tickled the cat's soft white belly. 'Do you like to sleep a lot, Tommi?'

'Yesssss,' agreed the cat. 'Sleep.'

Elmer's assistant adjusted the gold-rimmed spectacles upon his snubby nose. 'And what do you dream?'

Tommi yawned, showing sharp, brown-stained teeth. His mouth closed like a trap. 'Dreams,' said the pet.

A frown clouded Gunther's chubby cherubic face. 'Language *possesses* a talking animal like some nakki-imp,' he said. 'It's in them, but it isn't *of* them exactly. I wonder whether your cat would talk if cuckoos didn't talk?'

'How do you mean?' asked Nikki. She pulled the peacock-blue ribbon from her chignon, about to play with Tommi. Let him

123

snatch at the ribbon. Let him claw, let him bite. Let him be saved from the embarrassment of talking. Half the time she was convinced that her cat was a genius – for a cat, that's to say – and the rest of the time Tommi seemed an imbecile.

Lyle stayed her hand politely. 'Tell me a dream,' he coaxed the cat.

'I mean,' Gunther went on, 'how does it know what *dream* means? You can't point at a dream as you can point at a fishhead. Yet the animal seems to know from within.'

'Thanks to mana.' Nikki wound the ribbon round her hand so that she looked bandaged, vulnerable to bruising.

'It's as if one in a thousand animals accidentally echoes the talking of the cuckoos, but in a more communicative way, really – since a cuckoo never answers a direct question. Strictly speaking I don't *believe* in nakkis,' Gunther told Elmer. 'Not in the sense of imps with a will of their own. Still, there are always forces loose in this world. Surges of mania can affect anybody.'

In the same fashion that the dream lord was forever bewitched by his dead wife? After two centuries, dead Anna Sariola continued to obsess Gunther unshakeably. Being aware that one was prey to a craze did not generally help to abate the passion.

Elmer looked non-plussed. Machines and mania might both begin with the same sound but there the resemblance ceased.

The cat stared at Lyle and lisped, 'I hunt you.'

Taken aback, Lyle ran fingers through his frizzy halo of hair. 'Do you indeed?'

'I never catch you,' the cat added regretfully.

Laughing, Elmer snatched Tommi up by the shoulders so that the bulk of the cat's body dangled helplessly. Elmer nuzzled his cadaverous cheek against Tommi's. '*You*. You'll sleep for a lovely long time and you'll tell us all about catching people!'

'What's this all about?' asked Nikki. 'Put Tommi down. He doesn't like that.'

Elmer dumped the cat back on the bed. Elastically Tommi sprung off. Growling, he scuttled to claw the tapestry.

Gunther shifted from foot to foot, as if weighing the matter. He smiled appeasingly.

'Miss Loxmith, the truth is I'm planning to hibernate in the way the serpents do. I wish to dream the deepest possible dreams, though I don't want *everybody* on Kaleva to know what I'm up to in case my keep gets raided while I'm snoozing. Your brother has promised to construct a monitoring cradle for me.'

'I'll make a smaller model first to test the design. That's where Tommi comes in,' Elmer said guilelessly. Fingers itching in anticipation of the project, he toyed with the scuffed satchel of tools clipped to his belt. The cat continued shredding the bottom of the arras.

'Should Tommi be hearing this, do you think?' Nikki asked indignantly.

Lyle shrugged. 'He won't understand. He doesn't understand the future. Just *soooon*.' Nonchalantly he imitated Elmer, and both men grinned.

'No wonder Tommi wants to hunt you, Lyle,' cried Nikki, hurt. 'You're intending to put my cat into some *sleep machine*!'

'No, no, Nik,' her brother assured her, 'the machine won't make Tommi sleep. It'll safeguard him and wake him.'

Her elfin face registered bewilderment. Her eyes were wide with mystified alarm. 'So how does Tommi manage to hibernate?'

Gunther cleared his throat.

'I think a word of, mmm, apology's in order here, since Tommi's definitely *your* cat rather than the family cat or the keep cat, or its own cat for that matter.'

How boyish the tall dream lord seemed just then, with his long blond hair and his fresh countenance, so chubby and rosy. Despite his gorbellied girth, he could have been a huge anxious lad at his first dance.

If one disregarded his pensive eyes . . .

To Gunther's mind the point at issue wasn't whether the hibernation elixir would prove safe for a cat to use; and thus presumably for a human being too. Gunther was convinced the elixir wouldn't kill him. Blessed by his beloved Anna, his own body was supremely resilient.

He had obtained the Isi juice from a shaman of his domain, who was dying. The prize did not *appear* to have been planted mischievously in Gunther's way for him to find. It had come – indirectly – from a serpent pariah. As he proceeded to explain . . .

Several years previously a sorcerer named Taiku Setala had received a flask of the gland-juice from a mutie monster of a serpent. This prodigy had been expelled from the Brindled Isi nest; or maybe the snake had become a voluntary hermit. Taiku was never able to decide which of these two explanations was the correct one, or whether the truth was a mixture of both.

This Isi monster had its abode far to the north-west, deep in wild forest way beyond Maananfors and the Brindled Isi nest. It inhabited what Taiku described as a *death maze*, or *mana-trap*. Whether this maze was of the monster's own conjuring so as to safeguard its privacy, or whether it was constructed by the Brindled serpents to confine this prodigy, was also ambiguous. The giant serpent was known as Viper.

Occasionally cuckoos would cackle about Viper, but very few people had wished to search it out. Of those who wished, how many could find it? Of those who found it, how many had returned?

Taiku Setala had gone in search of Viper, hoping to gain wisdom. He had negotiated the death maze, had found the giant snake and had returned to his village in Lord Beck's domain. In addition to his previous weather-weirds and leechcrafts and conjurings, Taiku now began to dream the dreams of other people in his community.

At this point Gunther interrupted his story.

'I'm given to understand,' he said, 'that when people dreamed in the old days back on Earth generally they lost all self-awareness. So how could you tell someone else's dream from your own? Whereas we usually retain a sense of ourselves while we're dreaming, don't we? We mayn't be able to control the dream in the least, but at least we're aware that we're the dreamer. Dreams don't disappear easily from memory. I gather they did disappear back on Earth.'

His listeners nodded. Yes, one was generally aware of being in a dream, even though the dream events might be bizarre. To forget one's own dreams must be a sort of partial death, an eclipse of a whole swathe of one's life.

But Taiku found it very difficult to remember *other* people's dreams. He had to struggle to recall them when he awoke. None of the dreams were his own. Disconcertingly, each such dream aged Taiku disproportionately. At first, the shaman failed to realize this. Within a year he could hardly deny the evidence of his own wrinkling flesh and shrinking frame. This must be why Viper had given Taiku the flask of gland-juice. If Taiku were to *hibernate* – to hide himself away in a cave or be buried in the ground or laid in a coffin – obviously he wouldn't age any further. He would dream all the dreams of his community, perhaps for centuries. Though not his own dreams, inspired by his own existence. Thus Taiku would lose his own self. Where would his own self be?

126

Lord Beck was well known to villagers in his domain as the dream seer. Taiku Setala appealed to him. While staying in Lord Beck's keep Taiku began to dream Gunther's dreams, but never his own. He dreamed the dreams of nephew Cully and of others in Gunther's keep. Never his own. He was bereft of his own dreams, but endowed with hundreds of others.

The shaman's condition fascinated Gunther, yet the dream lord was unable to help the rapidly ageing villager. Should Taiku drink the elixir of hibernation? No! Taiku resolved to die of premature old age. Therefore he gifted the elixir to Lord Beck.

This was the story which Gunther told Nikki and her brother and Lyle, though the dream lord was reticent on some aspects; just as shaman Setala had been reticent about many details of his visit to Viper's lair.

Of course the juice would make Gunther hibernate successfully – and Elmer's apparatus would rouse him again successfully after three months. The Earthfolk would believe that Elmer merely intended to build an experimental apparatus for a mog, to investigate longlife. That enclave of Earthfolk at Landfall wasn't generally regarded with a great deal more fellow-feeling than the rationalist Pootarans. They were perpetual strangers, with the motives of strangers. After the test on the cat, Elmer would scale his equipment up to accommodate an increasingly obese giant of a man. By now Tommi had assumed importance in Elmer's scheme and Lyle's and Gunther's, as a false scent.

'Your Tommi won't be playing the role of poison tester, you see,' Gunther assured Nikki. 'I beg you to give your consent so that I can find my long-lost wife again deep in my dreams. That's what this is all about, you know. *Do* you know?'

Nikki nodded. Yes, she knew the story of his adoration of a woman centuries dead. Not well. Did anyone but Lord Beck know it intimately? Still, she knew – and felt thrilled to be involved in such a quest.

Gunther plucked a Pootaran banana from the fruitbowl and peeled it. 'You're very gracious to a guest, Miss Loxmith.'

Nikki stood, lost in thought.

How must this man of three hundred years really view her? As a mere snip of a girl? Wet behind the ears? Barely weaned? No experience of life worth mentioning? No right whatever to impede someone so possessed by a dream of resurrecting a lost love somewhere in the realm of mana . . .

Lord Beck didn't act arrogantly. After so long, perhaps there was only irony and sorrow left. And a residue of hope, if one could snatch at any hope at all.

The dream lord could hardly behave disparagingly to Elmer's sister if he wanted a favour from the engineer – presumably to be paid for. True enough! Yet there was about Beck, she felt sure, a nobility of heart which alone could account for such enduring loyalty to a woman dead so very long ago. Questions bubbled in Nikki. At the same time, she was determined to be dignified and generous. How could she quibble in the face of an obsession which was really so tragic, so romantic? Notwithstanding the grossness he was inflicting on his body, for a very noble purpose, as she now realized.

While the dream savant munched the banana, Tommi sidled up to rub against his boot.

'Me! Me!' mewed the cat. The mog reared high up his leg. It inserted a claw into Gunther's brown breeches. Inclining sideways in lieu of trying to bend his belly, Gunther held the remaining thumb's length of yellow fruit down to Tommi's nose. Affronted, the animal dropped, eyes blinking as if stung.

'Nasssty sssmell,' the cat hissed. It glared at Gunther.

'Tommi'll be all right,' Lyle coaxed Nikki.

For a moment she thought that Lyle was referring to Tommi's encounter with a banana. Of course Lyle was encouraging her to accept putting her pet to sleep for a few months.

She nodded curtly as if to say, *I'm not a child any more.*

Maturity had arrived; and she felt proud of herself. Questions still bubbled – about Beck's dead wife and his dream abilities, about Viper and the shaman. However, Nikki subdued these questions. She wouldn't wish Lord Beck to imagine a tattling chit-chat going to Landfall with Elmer and Lyle, or else the dream lord might ask her brother not to take her.

'*Fish*,' nagged Tommi.

'Soooon,' cooed Lyle. 'In fact, very soon! Time to fatten you up, Tommi. Feasts for you. Feast after feast. Fish and cream and best mince five times a day till you can hardly stagger.'

'*I'll* take care of that,' Nikki told Lyle in her most sophisticated tone.

Lyle was definitely an attractive man. One day, might she and he wed – almost by inadvertence? Without his ever having seemed to manipulate his way into such a position of trust, or into her affections? Lyle never *openly* manipulated her brother, nor had he made a play for Nikki. In Osmo's keep, Nikki had watched Lyle flirting tipsily with Tilly Kippan, establishing himself as a fellow who was hot-blooded, though well versed in polite behaviour. Had he been on his way to Tilly's bedroom along that corridor when the stone man intervened? Perhaps. Quite probably. Circumstances had saved Lyle from either a conquest or a rebuff.

How calculating a man *was* Lyle? Sufficiently so, to avoid stirring suspicions that he might be a bit of a schemer? Only very recently had Nikki begun to realize how Elmer – bluff, candid, straightforward Elmer – benefited by the company of someone who wasn't quite so ingenuous. When her brother inherited the lordship, Lyle would be a valuable right-hand man.

Lyle Melator came from a family of boatwrights and had been her brother's technical assistant for the past six years. He helped Elmer in the extensive workshop which the two of them had fitted out on the ground floor. Down there, there was *electricity*, from a steam-machine fuelled by fierce-burning mintywood. A place of marvels to Nikki when younger – and still so, really – the workshop housed Isi contrivances and Earth gadgets which her brother had been able to lay his hands on. A few of Elmer's dilettante inventions remained half-finished but many others were in use in the aitch-house. Automata, music machines, engines which pumped water.

It might be best for all concerned if Nikki were the lady of that trusted helper at Elmer's side. Thus spake her new sense of maturity. Lyle wasn't in the least unpleasant. Who on Kaleva was *Elmer* going to wed? Probably no one. Nikki's own children would carry on the Loxmith line. Her brother might always have seemed supremely competent to her, yet his competence wasn't really with people at all – otherwise he would have asked her first about Tommi's role in this experiment rather than simply assuming she would take this all on trust. Well, she wouldn't protest shrilly and childishly.

At a candlelit dinner of baked lamb and savoury pancakes that night, a brass automaton linked by a cable to Henzel Loxmith's wheelchair fed the paralysed lord of the aitch-house with mouthfuls whenever his finger commanded. Activated by powerful clockwork in its pelvis, four arms of the skeletal automaton telescoped in and out, slicing meat and potatoes, loading a fork, pivoting this to Henzel's lips, dabbing those lips with a napkin, raising a bottle of dark mustaberry cordial fitted with a suction tube.

If Elmer was gaunt, his father, in a blue satin dressing gown, was positively withered. Henzel's face was of wrinkled yellow parchment and his dark eyes were sunken, yet still alert, constantly shifting to and fro. Since Lord Henzel could no longer move his head, an additional arm of the brass servant tilted a mirror this way and that to enhance his field of view. Whenever he spoke, which was in a rusty whisper, the other diners duly fell silent.

'What's dream drama?' echoed Gunther in response to one croaked enquiry. 'Why, I mesmerize myself with a mana-mirror before I lay me down to sleep. I choose the actors for my pageant, and the topic, and let the spectacle unfold of its own impetus. I serve as an actor myself – a performer subject to the play of circumstances. Often I surprise myself, which is welcome after these hundreds of years, believe me.' He halved a golden pancake stuffed with minced chicken and devoured one side of it.

Henzel's voice rustled.

Munching, Gunther stared out of the mullioned window at the lake of gloomy darkest purple. The departed sun still cast some ruddy ember-light upon banks of cloud, faintly pearled by the hidden sky-sickle. The dream lord wiped a hand across his lips.

'Yes, that's right: a mana-mirror, bespelled by the shaman who taught me two hundred years ago. I can also peer into someone else's dream by using my mirror in a particular way—'

'Do you have that mirror here?' Elmer's mother interrupted. Her tone was shrill and challenging. 'I wouldn't wish anyone to snoop on my dreams.'

Lady Loxmith wore a pink silk robe iridescently sequined with the wing-cases of hundreds of glitterbugs. Once upon a time as she walked about the aitch-house she used to sing. She would laugh aloud. She had enjoyed the bustle of the building. Due to her husband's paralysis and the onus of responsibility for Loxmithlinna and environs she had become fraught recently. As if to emphasize that her insistence upon privacy was not a bee in the bonnet, or to abash Gunther, she brushed a cascade of greying hair back from a long, equine face which was painted and powdered disconcertingly white, and masklike; and gazed at the dream lord. This was her facade of equanimity, of calm composure, which her voice occasionally denied.

*

130

Elmer had inherited his mother's substantial if lanky frame and features, whilst fawnlike Nikki took after Lord Henzel. Whenever Elmer visited Maananfors, he was at least marginally aware of the similarity – amid dissimilarity – between his own parents' situation with respect to their son and that of his friend Osmo's. As regards ruling the roost, Elmer's father and Osmo's were both out of the running. Yet Lord Henzel in his wheelchair still played the role of figurehead. Alvar, though spry, had resigned in favour of Osmo to pursue his hobby as a chronicler. Johanna van Maanen, who had always orchestrated affairs at Maananfors, claimed to be an imminent candidate for the swan; though so far as Elmer could tell she still revelled in manipulation behind the scenes. Lokka, who had put on such startlingly pallid anaemic make-up to present a cool and composed face in public, used to be much more relaxed. Nowadays she acted the role of serene châtelaine, but it was a role requiring make-up – which she applied exaggeratedly. By now Elmer was sure that he himself wouldn't become lord until his father actually died. In itself this didn't worry him, leaving more time as it did for his engineering. Yet perhaps Lokka had arrived at some assessment of him – by contrast with, say, magisterial Osmo – which she had refrained from confiding?

His mother's presumed view of him did not bother Elmer unduly. People's motives and sentiments were so confusing compared with the sleekly oiled meshing of gear-wheels in a machine.

'I left the mirror at my keep,' Gunther told Lokka. 'I wouldn't wish to spy on people's dreams uninvited. Or on their memories. Or on what they see while they're awake.'

'Your mirror can do all those things?' Lokka asked.

'A mana-glass can do many things if a great shaman so disposes. But I'm not a mana-mage, you know.'

Gunther downed many glasses of wine. Occasionally he fingered a lump beneath his shirt. Prompted by husky whispers from the paralysed lord of Loxmithlinna, he talked ramblingly about categories of dreams. About kaleidoscopic mushroom-dreams, over which Mister Fungus presided. About meditation-dreams, locked in focus upon the image of another person. About dream-projection, to influence someone else. Dream-journeying, too. He sounded dismissive, as if all these arcane skills were trivial ones which he had long ago explored and rejected as ways of resurrecting the lost wife on whom he was fixated.

'Dream-journeying? Ach,' exclaimed Lord Beck, his voice slurring. 'On Earth they could travel in dreams to real places to talk to living people. But here some strange mana-domain attracts the journeyer. Yet never far enough! So no, Lord Henzel, I can't find Cully by dream-journeying ... As to Anna: never far enough. Not yet. I need to dream my way right into the belly of mana.'

And lo, his own belly groaned; and he burped.

The automaton had long since quit feeding Lord Henzel with morsels. The motionless cripple sat in silence now. Yet his eyes shifted and the mirror tilted in response. Outside, the night was as dusky as it ever would be. The sun was below the horizon. Clouds had thickened, muting the radiance from the sky-sickle.

'I'm not from the Northland, you realize, even though my name's Lokka.' In the candlelight the face of Elmer's mother was as white as snow.

'Beg pardon?' The logic of her remark had escaped Gunther.

'There's a village called Lokka up in Lucky's domain. I'm not from there at all. I'm not one of those women who gives longlife to a man.' Lokka glanced at her husband, her features a blank veneer but sorrow in her tone. 'Would that I had been! If Henzel's condition should prove inheritable ...' Her gaze veered towards Elmer. 'The local mana-priest says it isn't. He's sensitive to people's bodies.'

Chilled vodka and purple siniberry liqueur stood upon the table now. Gunther replenished his glass from a frosted carafe of the former.

Perhaps Lady Loxmith wished to hear about Queen Lucky's daughters from a man who had known one such daughter intimately? With her own son in mind as a possible suitor? Though without tipping guileless Elmer the wink? Let Elmer win a Sariola daughter, then Lokka could be content to surrender the reins of Loxmithlinna to her son, safe in the knowledge that he would be viewed with some awe rather than merely with amiable regard as at present. That was her tentative drift. Did she drop such hints to Elmer?

He mustn't have his head filled with such fancies or he might neglect the dream lord's commission. Elmer might fail to produce the hibernation cradle.

In apparent denial of his dead wife's supreme importance to

132

him, Gunther scoffed: 'The line of Lucky goes on and on, doesn't it? An endless set of life-giving daughters – with the occasional trickster in the pack, remember!' He gulped spirit, and choked momentarily. 'Queen Lucky is *iterating* daughters. She's repeating them down through time just as the damned gingerbread man recurs. As events echo events – if you live long enough to see the resemblances! Almost identical daughters – or so some people might imagine.' Already a sense of betrayal desolated him. 'Anna was unique to me!' he blared. '*Unique*, I tell you! No one echoes my Anna.' He had begun to rant. 'Not Jatta Sariola, oh no not her, damned semblance that she seemed! I can't find Anna's true echo anywhere. Not till I sleep deep—'

Of a sudden, Lord Beck was seriously drunk.

And he ought to sleep deeply, thought Nikki. She almost wished she had excused herself when the vodka and sweet siniberry arrived. Quickly she rejected this qualm as craven and immature. She must strive to understand. Her mother's frame of mind was unguessable. The white mask showed neither disapproval nor sufferance. Elmer was toying with a fluted glass of siniberry, faintly embarrassed. Lyle was eyeing the dream lord shrewdly with an air of attentive sympathy.

Why was Lord Beck so intent on emphasizing his eternal devotion to his dead Anna? Could he really have been so shaken by the sudden advent of Jatta Sariola at that banquet? In rags, with a wayward and abnormal brat? Maybe he had been deeply shocked, mocked by a seeming apparition.

The dream lord's inebriation reminded Nikki of an incident a year earlier when her own brother himself had got drunk late at night at a party in the aitch-house. Nikki had never seen Elmer out of control before – or since. Yet on that night, Elmer had definitely gone 'over the hill', as the saying went.

Way over the hill into a different valley entirely. Elmer had propositioned the young wife of a shopkeeper from the town with such intensity and persistence that it seemed Elmer imagined himself suddenly as a proclaimer who could bespeak the young lady between the sheets simply by talking at her seductively and grossly. Her brother had behaved quite crazily. Madly so – possessed by a nakki of desire. That naughty nakki had overwhelmed Elmer as surely as he tried to overwhelm the woman whom he had fixed upon almost randomly.

On that occasion, to Nikki's relief, Lyle had led the young

woman away on his arm practically from under Elmer's nose –
while Elmer bellowed what he no doubt thought were hilarious
insults at his smiling assistant. When Nikki begged her brother
to retire to bed and not shame her in public, he had been almost
offensive to her, as if Nikki was some meddling stranger. Thank-
fully Elmer had then staggered away obediently to sleep the
nakki off.

The next day, Elmer was the same mild sweet brother as before
– apparently oblivious to what had occurred, or to what had
failed (thanks to Lyle) to occur.

Whether Lyle had enjoyed the favours of the young woman
instead, or had merely rescued her, remained a mystery to Nikki.
She simply knew that her brother *could* become intoxicated
beyond the bounds of sane behaviour – if a nakki held the reins
of his will. Elmer really wasn't cut out for such passions! Mischievous nakkis ought to look elsewhere.

Until now Nikki had avoided thinking too deeply about
Elmer's behaviour at that party. Surely it had been an aberra-
tion. Faced by Gunther Beck's fervid drunkenness, though, and
equipped with her own fresh new sense of maturity, she was
thankful to note Elmer's embarrassment at such expressions
of infatuation as Gunther's. An object lesson to her brother.
She was glad that Lord Beck had become as inebriated as he
had.

When a swaying Gunther, assisted by Lyle Melator, collapsed
on to the stout tammywood bed, the dream lord harboured every
expectation of sinking swiftly into a black void bereft of any
dreams at all. When he drank heavily such was almost always
the outcome.

Briefly, as he lay flat on his back, still fully dressed, apprehension gripped Gunther, a lingering hint of the dread which had
once permeated the aitch-house, seemingly given a new twist of
energy by his presence. Probably the spectacle of the paralysed
Henzel Loxmith being fed by the brass automaton accounted for
his disquiet. Gunther himself was intending to become even more
inert inside a mechanical cradle designed by Henzel's son.

He realized that Lyle had already departed. Wasn't going to
haul Gunther's breeches off, and tuck him in. Neither was
Gunther himself. His head spun. He almost heard his own first
snore.

*

To Gunther's surprise he was aware of blackness. This total darkness wasn't a temporary obliteration of himself, an absence of awareness, but a presence in its own right. Maybe for the first time he had become conscious of nothingness? Aware of void?

Already that blackness, which at first had seemed to include him absolutely, was shrinking, receding from around him.

As it distanced itself he recognized the outline of . . . the *gingerbread man*, jet black, set against a purple and mauve background. Gingerbread man, almondbread man . . . a tubby little nakki monster . . .

Fiery, golden, electric discharges prickled around the figure. It seemed to dance, hanging there in a space filled ever more with scalloped cascades and curlicues of happenings, efflorescences of circumstance.

The discharges were jagged strings of energy. Like zigzag flashes of lightning repeating and repeating, they led to tiny silhouettes of people whom they jerked about as puppets on strings.

A silhouette of Elmer Loxmith cavorted in thwarted passion beside the outline of . . . Anna? Of Jatta? Of a Sariola, certainly! A silhouette of Elmer's mother slumped slackly. Surely there was a puppet of Cully too, of Gunther's nephew . . .

If only Gunther could once again become part of the gingerbread man. If only he himself could dangle those cut-out figures at his fingertips! When all had seemed black, dark and null he had actually been within that mischievous presence. If only he could pull Cully to him, and retrieve his nephew. If only he could pull upon another string, a Sariola string, and attract Anna back to him at last, and so reclaim his love . . .

Another silhouette dangled on a scintillating string – another bewitching version of Anna.

It was Marietta.

Marietta, whom he had taken to his keep, and into his bed. Marietta had borne a haunting resemblance to Gunther's Anna when middle-aged. After the Marietta episode Gunther had taken to wearing his breast-box with Anna's skull-bone in it. In all the many previous years Gunther had never been emotionally unfaithful, spiritually unfaithful.

All those figures at the gingerbread man's electric fingertips! If only Gunther himself could be the gingerbread man at the heart of events!

He would do so, he would – when he hibernated! By then he would be as roly-poly as the gingerbread man itself.

Anna would cease to be a silhouette and would become solid again, alive. She who was dead would attain flesh again, in some guise. As the dreaming Gunther's bulk diminished during hibernation, so he would transfer part of his obesity to her, somewhere, in some manner – enough mass to fashion a new body for her from out of his own flesh; flesh donated to her ghost.

Of a sudden Gunther was on fire.

His body blazed.

His skin was being flayed from his flesh. It was peeling from him agonizingly. The elixir of hibernation was causing him to shed his skin as a serpent sheds its skin. A human being was not supposed to slough its skin.

Aflame with tormented nerves, Gunther shrieked. Sheets of skin flapped away to cloak Anna's silhouette. Red raw, he arose, roaring, a maddened bull.

Glittering with energy, which was an image of his own pain, the black form of the gingerbread man pulsated mockingly.

Troubled dreams beset all the tenants of the aitch-house. Nakki nightmares made sleepers sweat and mutter. Asleep in his arrassed chamber filled with little automata and gadgets, Elmer saw lying upon a floor strewn with chartreuse curver fronds a glossy human-like machine, cream in colour. Its pelvis vibrated. Sleek, raised legs pistoned to and fro as if to gather Elmer into their crook-kneed embrace. Between those legs a valve throbbed open, trickling lubricating oil. Although the lower half of this mannequin lay supine, confronting him, from the waist upwards the machine-creature was prostrate, the bumps of its spine on display. The animated dummy had twisted at the belly through a hundred and eighty degrees. Any face, any bosom, was buried out of sight in all those twigs cut from a curver tree.

Elmer was a machine too. A limp dribbling siphon lolled from his loins. Sinking upon his knees, he slowly shuffled forward. The smooth, parted legs kicked towards him, drew back, kicked out again to enfold him. This body-machine was at once abominable and enticing. He crept closer, appalled. If only he could twist the upper half of the machine around so that the whole automaton faced him – revealing what facial features?

He must know.

Surely he could revolve the machine if he inserted the tap at

his groin into the valve between the legs. A key into a keyhole!
Yet his tap was so soft and slack.

Awake suddenly, Gunther found himself standing naked beside
the topsy-turvy tammywood bed. Sheet and coverlet were tangled
and twisted. He had torn off the shirt and breeches in which he
had collapsed earlier on.

The bed wasn't on fire. He still retained his skin, a great stuffed
bag of slowly expanding skin. Reflecting from the lake, the light
of the sky-sickle silvered him coolly. Anna's locket dangled
between his chained nipples as ever.

Plumping his blubber down upon the mattress, Gunther rested
his head in his hands – a head hammering with hangover. This
dream which had surprised him by emerging like a raider from
darkness . . . what did it promise?

Surely something strange and dire would happen in the aitch-
house to torment the Loxmiths. Though not yet, not yet. Not
before he had hibernated.

In the morning, all was genial and benign. Perhaps over-polite.
Nikki's cat alone shunned Gunther.

11 · WHAT ROUGH BEAST

The Kitajoki was a broad belt of river-muscle thrusting north-
eastward through woods mainly of tammy and minty. Magenta
pillars of tammies, with scale-leafed foliage of bottle green –
and broad-crowned pea-green minties. The tammy tree was the
fireguard of the minty, as the saying had it.

Just before Juke and Jatta and Jack reached the river they
had passed a burnt-out clearing where fast minty saplings were
already hoisting bright wands through the ashes of their predecessors. Lightning must have kindled an inferno – contained by
scorched tammies on which healervine had already taken root.

'Stay, Jack, you'll get all grimy!' Juke hoisted the boy.

Within a few minutes the forest had opened upon the river-
bank. Their path veered northward of necessity, though a bend
was in view. The swift sinews of the current rushed between

bouldery banks. Minties and tammies jostled one side of the track. The day was breezily bright. High mares' tails drooped their hairs in farewell to morning showers. The sky was suddenly large, and their route seemed to expand vastly.

'It's about another thirty keys to Forssa where the rapids are,' said Juke. 'Then the river forks. A couple of rivers drain from Forssajarvi Lake. We might catch a ride on a boat. Do you still feel urgent?'

Jatta shook her head. No, not oppressively so.

'He only said you need to find where we mutants live.' Again, he was chipping away at her sense of coercion, unravelling van Maanen's command. 'Being with me is a kind of discovery, isn't it?'

During the past few days the refugee and her custodian had fallen into a superficially easy relationship. Jack could almost be their own son. Generally, Juke relieved his mother of the burden of carrying the boy when he wasn't scooting ahead and back, and to and fro. Her cough had cleared up. Her step was light. His questions and promptings were soft, if insistent. Often, now, there was a hesitancy to those questions which maybe marked the extent to which he was now treating her as a substitute sister.

Jatta hadn't learned the name of Juke's sister. A poetess, apparently – he hadn't quoted any of her verses.

'There's one mutie fellow I know,' he'd told her, 'who can only hear words, nothing else. His world's silent except when people speak. His brother can only hear the noises of nature, and never any words at all.' Was his sister perhaps deaf or dumb in some peculiar way?

Yes, in Jatta he seemed to see a demi-sister, who opened her heart to him. Perhaps *because* she opened her heart, albeit at his own sometimes diffident urging, he saw her as resembling his sister; and he hesitated now and then, for fear of violating something within his own self, or for fear of opening an inner door which had stayed locked until now. He reserved himself. He had also withheld any offer of sanctuary under his own roof. So maybe Jatta would never now meet this sister, who surely had some oddity about her.

Under his softening pressure Jatta had told him about her adolescence in Pohjola Palace. She had described that giant onion-domed multi-mansion of cupola'd courts and corridors and branching cellars and chamber after chamber, many of them rich with tapestries, paintings, gilded furniture, sculptures, dowry after dowry. She spoke of hands jutting out of walls and people made of wood, of doorways with eyes, and of peering into mana-mirrors to see through the eyeballs of roaming spitz dogs. She told of the snow sculptures sung up by conjuror-shamans from the tundra during the winterfest, and wild dances; of raspberry tarts for the Runebergfest, whomever *that* was supposed to commemorate – no doubt Lucky and Bertel still knew. Some ancient warrior, probably. Red jam sometimes flowed from wounds. She recounted Lucky's tantrums, and the festival for the giving away of sister Helena; and her own chaste resolution not to be given away to any man, but to stay as a sweet-smiling thorn in her mother's side.

The pressure to tell did not need to be rough. Once begun, her story grew muscles. Like the Kitajoki, it surged along towards distant rapids, towards that cascade – unrevealed as yet – of her glad ravishment by golden Jarl.

In recounting her tale thus far a shy entente had bloomed between Jatta and Juke such as she hadn't known previously. Not with Kay or Helena, to be sure. Nor with Jarl, about whom she'd experienced nothing less than an irresistible intimacy which quite transcended the particulars of himself or herself. The implicit currency of this entente, its climactic payment, could be none other – she realized – than the fullest description of her incredibly brief liaison with that magnetic man, Jarl, which brought her a baby, and blight, and abandonment.

Was Juke merely subtler in his manipulation of her than van Maanen had been, guiding her with queries which were actually imperatives? No, he had become an emotional ally rather than a controller. At times his face was boyish, and she saw right through his veneer of adroit guide and bespeaker – to a lurking apprehension about his intended challenge to Lord Osmo. By now he freely admitted his ambition. She saw within the man an adolescent heroism built upon noble, embittered promises to himself. Always a sense that he was somehow championing his sister prowled within Jatta whenever he alluded to the poetess, often abruptly as though scratching an itch. He had pledged himself to challenge van Maanen so as to dignify the mutie sister. And to obliterate some alternative outcome which he refused to see, just as he refrained from uttering his sister's name. (And Jatta refrained from asking.) Hence the farness of Juke's gaze at times. He wanted to see grand perspectives, not discrepancies.

Was he perhaps by now her friend? Yes, and no. Yes, in as much as she had come to reflect that sister. No, since his true ideal friend – his protected ideal – was that young woman whose name Jatta was determined never to ask, as long as he avoided volunteering it.

Jatta had never known a brother. When Juke had shaved that morning in a wayside pool for the first time since they'd met, using his knife and sharp words, she had watched fascinated as fuzz fell away. No, his wouldn't be a very manly beard. Definitely he looked more impressive clean-jawed.

Occasionally, a pang of jealousy pierced Jatta on account of that sister who meant so much to Juke that he must hide his feelings even from himself. Only once or twice did Jatta wonder whether the nameless sister might just be a phantom in Juke's mind.

Crashing through the undergrowth from the left came a bulky rufous body the size of a bull. A browful of horns ripped through pea-green minty foliage.

The hervy halted on the path.

Strings of saliva dangled from its wide mouth. Mucus oozed from its floppy, pulsing nostrils. Its high, tufty ears twitched towards the travellers. Its burly muzzle swung. Hooded long-lashed bloodshot eyes glared blearily. The shaggy beast flinched and snorted gluey strands. Cleft hooves grated the pathway. Horns, decked with torn minty sprigs, were menacingly pronged and hooked.

'It just wants a drink,' Juke murmured.

The little boy strained in his tightening arms.

'Me want a ride!'

'*Hush, Jack—*'

'A ride?' The hervy's tufty back was long and broad, three saddles' worth of back. 'I wonder. I'll try. It has to drink first or it'll be unruly.'

'Try to compel *that*?' Jatta was appalled at this braggadocio. Oh, try anything risky to impress a reflection of his sister, especially if the exploit might gore him and inflict a punishing wound! He might seem the soul of sobriety, obsessed with self-set duties, but he had a reckless streak. But of course Juke mustn't be a cringer, or how would he ever face up to van Maanen? The beast offered a fine impromptu test of mettle.

'You're wearing your madcap this morning,' she remarked.

140

In momentary puzzlement Juke adjusted the criss-cross cloth topping his head.

'Can you stay perfectly still and quiet?' whispered Juke to the boy.

'Don't set Jack loose—'

'*Hush! Hwisht!*' Juke had already sat Jack down. The boy obeyed, standing rigid, staring at the animal fifty metres ahead. The hervy lumbered over the great stone eggs along the riverside and lowered its muzzle to bite mouthfuls from the swift water. It slurped litres down its burly throat. Liquid cascaded from its wide slobber-lips.

Sated, the beast returned. Juke began to pace forward, knapsack still on his back. He pitched his voice with soothing insistence.

'Hervy, hervy! You're strong and gentle. You'll carry three on your back, all the way along this path. For this is spoken. Your thirst is quenched, hervy, you're satisfied. You want to travel, exercising your strength by carrying us; this is spoken—'

Jack stole after the bespeaker. He dodged his mother's apprehensive hand once, then twice, as she followed him. Regaining the path, the hervy snorted. Blood-eyes glared at Juke. It lowered its leafy hooks and prongs.

'Hervy, you're bowing down to us—'

The beast wasn't. It merely rocked its rack of horns from left to right. Hooves raked. Its rancid grease odour reeked towards the hikers. Wavering, Juke glanced back.

'What—'

Why were the boy and his mother so close?

'Go back. It doesn't know what I am. It's too wild.'

Jack slipped past Juke, reaching out a small brown palm.

'Get back, lad, this isn't a truster! Hervy, *stay!*'

Of a sudden the boy dropped to all fours. He arched his back. Snuffling and dribbling, keeping his head high, he was an absurd diminutive beast. He scuttled forward on booted tiptoes and angled fingers. Juke seemed frozen – and if Jatta rushed past him she would surely provoke the beast to attack.

Aaaannnggg: the hervy's call was a twanging nasal bell note. Its teeth were bared, its nostrils flared. Leaves throbbed loose from tines. Jack sprawled before the creature. Chin scraping grit, the boy stared up at one of the animal's ruby eyes.

And the hervy crooked its knees.

Heavily it subsided on the pathway. It laid its thick neck out on the dirt, horns erect like a stiff parched bush. Its flanks heaved. It snuffled, spraying beads of mucus. Leaping up, the boy scurried round to scramble on to the beast's shoulders, where he clutched at its rank shag.

Juke swallowed.

'Hervy, hervy, you'll carry him and us; for it's spoken, and it's shown to you. You'll bear us on your brave back. Now that you've been shown.'

He beckoned Jatta. 'Jack augmented me, that's what! He showed Hervy by posture. That *isn't* speaking at all. It's wordless. I don't understand it – when he spoke so young.'

'He didn't have any doubt at all,' said Jatta.

Juke flushed as if she had reproached him for cowardice. 'I think my being with you is bringing this out in the boy . . . Yes, I think that's it.'

The rough beast wallowed in dirt, blaring *aaaannnggg*. Its ruby eyes were wide with a submissive panic which might still erupt into random flight. Drool pooled.

Cautious of the beast's horns, the two adults mounted. Jatta behind Juke, Juke gripping Jack. The hervy responded by staggering to its feet, moaning nasally, flicking spittle. Its matted rouge coat reeked of tart sweat. Jack tugged on a tine to turn the beast's head.

'Watch your eyes, Jack!' yelped Jatta.

Their mount turned and trotted along the track. Soon it began to lope.

At first the boy giggled at the tossing, rolling motion. Then he began to gulp and huff.

'What's wrong with him? Should we get down?'

'No, no, the beast's set on its course.' Juke braced the lad through his spasm. 'Calm, calm. Feel calm. You strained yourself bringing the beast to its knees.'

'I'm hungry!' cried the boy.

'Jatta, reach in my knapsack. Give him the truster we baked.'

As she clutched and unbuckled: 'What's he *becoming*, Juke?'

'I don't know. His movements affect other creatures. Words aren't involved.' Dirt sped by under the hervy's hooves.

'So he *is* a weird mutant after all!' She thrust the paper-wrapped fish up over Juke's shoulder. 'Not a mana miracle but a mutie!'

Bitterly, as he loosened the paper: 'What's the difference? Most muties happen to look freakish, so people reject them.'

The smoked fish, a two-pounder, was in Jack's hands; he wolfed, teeth snacking along the browned fishflesh like some manic harmonica player.

'You don't look freakish.' As their shaggy reeking mount lolloped, she lugged the straps of Juke's sack to yank confessions out of him.

'No, but I don't pretend! I don't turn my back on my folks. I want honour for us. Van Maanen's no different from me apart from normal birth and privilege, and of course he won't have a mutie brat if he weds. Maybe that's why he puts off deciding – in case his wife does give birth to a freak, and pulls the soft rug from under him!' He was searching frantically for Osmo's flaws. 'Maybe the rug's already out from under him! Maybe he cracked his handsome head when he fell!'

Jack's teeth raced along the exposed spine-comb of the truster. The bounding hervy snorted and chomped the air, whiskers of glutinous drool elongating from its muzzle till those snapped and flew on to its hairy flanks. The wind of its motion whistled through its high sharp horns. The riders jounced and bounced. Spitting out little bones, the boy rotated the fish to gobble along the other side of the fish.

'What do you mean? What rug?'

Juke ignored her question. She yanked fiercely. The man's splayed knees clamped on the beast.

'Hey, you'll pull me off, Sis!'

He stared round in sudden fury at the jet-haired, crop-headed woman who rode behind him.

'Damn you.'

His tone softened instantly, caressingly. 'You lay with someone—'

'Just *someone*?' Jatta responded with vehemence. Jarl's image still magicked her.

'—and you had a very weird child. What if you made your Jarl weird instead? You reminded Osmo how it's possible for a Sariola girl to turn her husband into—'

Drowning him: 'Don't say it!' A colonnade of tall tammies rushed by.

'His mummy wants that for him, but he's scared of it. So he kicked you out helter-skelter. My sister thinks there's some sense to that zombie curse of yours. Living death once in a while instead of longlife.'

'We don't talk about this . . . My mother taunted me with it.

No wonder I wanted to love no man! Until love *took* me utterly.'

'Don't talk,' he taunted, 'in case it comes true.'

Jack had bitten and sucked all remaining flesh from the spine of the truster. He held the skeleton of the fish aloft like some banner on the pole of his arm.

'Weeee!' he cried, as the hervy careered along the riverside path.

'The intermittent curse deters all but the brave and the best and the utterly besotted from wooing one of you princesses, Jatta. The gift isn't wasted on inferiors. Of course rank and riches count! No one from mutie country would fare any better than a flea in a bonfire. Longlife ought to go to a brilliant—'

'Poetess, perhaps?'

'My sister's a *woman*! She can't wed—'

'Yes, yes, of course. She's a woman. She would be.' Well now, here was the thorn in Juke's flesh. His ideal woman was also his sister. Hastily Jatta sidestepped the issue. Recalling his squeal of protest, she couldn't help adding, 'When you were little you larked around a lot with her. I never larked around with any brother. I don't know what a brother is.'

'Weeeeee!'

And Jack let go of the skeleton. A too-heavy, too-slender kite, nevertheless it scooted off into the river as though there it might replenish its tissues, putting on muscle of water. The hervy began slowing its pace from a headlong gallop, back to a lurching canter.

'When I started to bespeak,' muttered Juke, 'I couldn't say the same things to her, because they would happen. Oh she always had the pretty words.' He shivered. 'When I was ten I became able to *speak*.' The very word dizzied her, in the way that he uttered it. 'Stronger words welled up in me. The same old words – but bold, illuminated, dazzling. I saw them as shapes in my mind, though when I sketched those shapes in charcoal to show my sister she said that wasn't how words are written. She knows how, you see. She has books, and the fellow I told you of who can only hear speech had shown her how to read because he had the knack and he liked the way she said words.'

Now Jack was flying the stained wrapping paper as a flag. It rippled noisily, annoyingly.

'Do you read, Jatta? Do well-bred Sariola girls get taught the trick?'

'Why should we? Didn't I have my jigsaws and Nakkinook?'

'My sister says we don't (WHRRRRR) so that some of us can *speak*—'

'What's that?'

'We don't read so that some of us can (RRRRRRR) fully and powerfully. And the rest of us can listen and heed.'

A fount of wisdom, this sister whose bodily flaw remained as much of a secret as her name. Jatta was sure the sister had a flaw. So did Lucky's harvest of daughters. Very occasionally a marriage resulted in the happy husband becoming one of the living dead, those creatures with moribund bodies that exhibited all the signs of death and decomposition except that the inhabitant remained on the move. And increasingly detached from human concerns. Terrifying.

Don't think of it.

Suitors for longlife didn't. Suitors obsessed with winning one of Lucky's daughters. They would laugh at the risk, dismissing it.

Don't think of zombies.

The thought had lodged in her head, stubbornly persistent. Her mother had taunted her. She had vowed herself to chastity. Until . . .

Other people did become zombies once in a while. Those would be descendants of Sariola marriages, several generations later.

Only a Sariola daughter gave true longlife. Healthy longlife. What might happen to some unlucky great-great-grandchild out of dozens in a future century was too far off to bother about.

But if a husband himself became zombie . . .

It rarely happened.

Brave suitors dismissed the risk. Daughters likewise. Unless Lucky taunted them. What was spoken might come true.

A farm appeared ahead, in a great clearing amidst tammies. A stout farmhouse and barns of purple logs. Their roofs were shingled with bark. Vegetable gardens and a herb garden. Gold-spangled hens with vivid vermilion combs pecked about. A youth armed with a stick was driving a long spotty pig back into the forest to forage. Two bare-chested men and a long-skirted woman in bright blue blouse and headscarf looked up from hoeing.

They gaped.

The men brandished eye-tattooed palms at the loping hervy and riders to ward them off. But the woman beckoned eagerly. Her face lit with wonder as she called out some indistinct greeting. At that moment Jack released the paper which had wrapped the truster. It fluttered towards cabbages. Dropping her hoe, hitching her skirt, the radiant woman hurried to retrieve this soiled blank souvenir.

Already they had ridden past.

'Me tired,' the boy complained. Almost at once he was drowsing against Juke. Their mount lowered its head, nodding, though still pursuing the pathway doggedly.

'I was confused and sick, too, when I went through my own change,' Juke told Jatta. 'When words became powers. When I started telling how things should happen, and consequently they would. Though not always as I told them. Tales could sprout legs and run off in their own chosen direction wilfully. Wayward variations on what I hoped for happened. I had to learn to focus with all my heart. She helped. She had *in*-sight.' Juke stressed the last word oddly as if it had a special private meaning for him.

'I don't have any insight, and my boy's changing.'

'But differently. He's a real oddity.'

'How do I guide him?' Could Jatta hope that this man's sister, the poetess, might offer assistance from her fount of wisdom?

'Locked up in your memories of Jarl is the key to your boy's nature, Jatta.' Juke was wanting to know about her most intimate moment.

'Jack'll soon wake up,' she said, to delay. 'He'll probably be hungry again.'

Hunger.

One day last autumn she had become so hungry for one marvellous man, Jarl, that he might have been a savoury feast, and herself starving. The wooing had been brief enough. Jarl had told her stories . . .

'. . . telling stories in the woods,' she found herself saying. 'Sharing a bowl of roe and a flask of mustaberry wine.'

'Tell me, Jatta. Tell me now.' While the hervy bore them onward. The rippling muscles of the Kitajoki were a silvered dull blue like the sheen on the tongue of an ox; an enormous endless thrusting tongue.

She was staying at Lokka on the Lokkajoki river. Until early summer the river was in spate, draining snows from mountainsides. By this season it only meandered through a broad course of boulders. Sariolinna was a hundred keys to the south, a bunion on the foot of the Great Fjord, that long leg of the western ocean marking the frontier of Northland. A hairy leg, abristle with lesser fjords. Lokka also marked a frontier of sorts between forests of evergreens – kusies and veras, katies and sylvesters – and the starker moors and boglands where trees became wind-twisted dwarfs foretokening naked, undulating tundra.

Jatta had left the sprawling village of log houses on that sun-bright morning along with a gaggle of old women in long skirts, red shawls, and headscarfs. Pungent sprays of herbs were slung round their necks to deter gnats and gadflies. Each carried a basket made of woven wood strips. Jatta herself wore her favourite tunic of purple suède sewn with contrasting strips of brightly-dyed felt. A couple of Lucky's men, tubby Marti and lanky Olli, accompanied the virgin princess, one armed with a lightpistol. Those two lagged behind, locked in a complicated Pootaran peg-game which they passed to and fro. Soon they were passing a flask of berry liqueur, just for a nip, mind. Escorting this daughter of Lady Lucky's was a sinecure. Jatta was no mischievous minx. She was the one who scorned men.

The bow-legged biddies began yoiking a mushroom chant as they ambled along.

'*Milky cap, Plenty-horn,*

'*Chanterelle, Chanterelle!*' They swung their trugs in unison.

Jatta liked to travel the Northland, secure in the girdle hidden under her gown. She now rejoiced in this hip-cage as a symbol of defiance on her own part rather than a psychotic imposition by her forever young mother. Quite often Lucky gave Jatta leave to roam. Perhaps Lucky reasoned that pent up in the palace her daughter might become cranky and cobwebby. Wanderings could instil a desire to journey further afield – south of the Great Fjord, which Jatta could be sure she would only ever cross as consort of a successful suitor. Perhaps liberty (though supervised by a couple of guards), and mixing with all sorts of people might infect Jatta with an itch to shed her chastity girdle. Besides, the girl was receiving a fine apprenticeship in practical landcraft which should stand her in good stead as châtelaine of some keep south of the Fjord.

'*Brain-morel,*

'*Champignon!*

'*Milky-cap,*

'*Plenty-horn!*' yoiked the bundled-up beldames. Jatta joined in their chorus as they trod a track wending through

147

groves of hoary sylvester trees, viridian-needled veras, and win-terbare larixes whose scales had flushed from jade to henna-orange prior to shedding.

Yes, Jatta had travelled far and wide from Sariolinna in all seasons, guided by villagers and nomads under the supervision of such as Olli and Marti. Over moors with quake-bogs where swollen spongeweed hid oubliettes of foetid stagnant meltwater. Across heaths where the heat quivered and solitary warped trees grew at any angle, even slumping along the ground. She had learned to pack her boots with dried beaten marsh-sedge, folded round her fist to make a smooth glove for her foot.

In deep winter she had helped bore holes through half a metre of ice in locked lakes, her breath smoking. Gullible fish hurried for the new supply of oxygen only to be hooked or speared out. On sunless mirror-days when the edge of the sky-sickle silvered the frozen land, she had ridden in boat-shaped sledges through herds of arctic goats and skittish tundra tarandras, altered from Earth livestock by the Ukko during transit through mana-space, so it was said. She had stayed in tepees of poles and bright blankets, steepled on snow which glowed softly gold. On aurora-nights she had watched the shimmering gassy green and scarlet dancers in the sky leap and swirl their diaphanous electric skirts. Oh, she had explored Lucky's domain. Lucky seemed determined to expel Jatta from the nest. To see her wedded, and on her way.

Jatta wasn't feeling any signs of premature senility; so maybe what her mother had said about daughter Rita had been rubbish. Lies.

‘Morel,

‘Chanterelle!

‘Morel,

‘Chanterelle!’

The yoiking of the grannies drowned any zizzing of midges in the otherwise silent woods. Their posies of tart herbs repelled hovering amber gadflies. Way behind, Marti and Olli in their camouflage-dappled leathers thrust the peg-board, and the flask of sweet spirit, to and fro. Occasionally they slapped at an insect. Herbal prophylactics were pinned to their lapels but the smell of the liqueur was a sweet lure.

This bow-legged, stumping hike continued for several kilo-metres through the trees till Ganny Ritva announced to Jatta, ‘Now we split up. But we'll yoik so we know where we are, and to make Mister Mushroom swell into sight.’

Forests such as this were deceptive. Once you were away from a path, direction soon became meaningless and distances deluded you. Jatta hurried away from the track amidst veras and sylvesters all like one another, quite happy to lose her escort. The trees were widely enough spaced for ground cover to flourish – glaucous cushions, tufts, and rosettes. She glanced back presently. Trunks hid any sign of grannies on the prowl. No, there was one: a fleeting flash of red shawl.

'*Chanterelle!*' – a distant call.

'*Champignon!*' – a faint reply. Jatta didn't bother to yoik a response. She swung her trug jauntily as she wandered quickly on. Here, a cluster of golden cep mushrooms, nakki houses; she harvested them.

'One day a maid,' cooed a baritone voice overhead.

Jatta's trug slipped, spilling the mushrooms.

'—met a serpent, a truly *resplendent* serpent—'

For a moment she couldn't see the source of these words at all and wondered with a lurch of excitement and mild panic whether one of the trees itself might be talking – she'd heard tales of bizarre trees down south in the territory of that forest lord Tapper Kippan whom an earlier daughter of Lucky's had blessed with longlife. Trees with mouths. Trees with tongues and teeth.

'—while she was walking in the woods,' lilted the voice.

The cuckoo shifted its stance and she saw it: a bulge of mottled green among the scaly green fingers of a vera tree. Big yellow eyes blinked. Cupped ears twitched. It was watching her, hearing her heartbeat.

('*Chanterelle!*') A far tree-muffled call, could be half a key away.

'Coo-coo?' she queried, thinking of dead day-old chicks impaled on the spikes of a perch. Surely the bird was here in these wilderness woods for some purpose, and that purpose none other than her. Had her mother sent a cuckoo to find her? Yet what a strange message.

'The teller of the tale is near,' resumed the voice, and momentarily she thought that the bird was referring to itself. 'Follow the cuckoo to find him.'

The bird launched itself from concealment and clung to the upright branch of a larix painted a lurid copper hue by autumn. Now the cuckoo stood out as a green blaze, a routemark.

'Hear about the girdled maid who loved the serpent.'

149

The girdled maid: how could it know that about her? Was this some joke of Lucky's?

'Curious enough to follow the bird?' called the cuckoo, flapping to a tree further off. 'Bold enough? No harm comes. He only wants to tell stories. Stories burst from within him, never heard before.'

'He? Who is he?'

Useless to ask. The cuckoo was saying what *he* had commanded. Jatta was already following the bird with empty basket, her other hand on her knife butt.

'People may look for the lady. But a cuckoo tells them she went that way, not this.'

Tantalized and wary, the virgin princess pursued.

Jatta realized she hadn't coughed all day, except perfunctorily when she first woke. Her child still snoozed, rocked by the hervy ride. The Kitajoki pulsed with an onrush of liquid force. Up ahead foresters were winching a trimmed tammy trunk towards the river with chains. Horns high and nostrils flaring, flicking flecks of mucus, the gingery shag-beast cantered towards them. The woodmen scurried to retrieve stacked axes. They dashed to picket the path.

'Me hungry,' Jack sang out, awake.

12 · A FINE RACK OF HORNS

'Whoa, Hervy!' shouted Juke.

Axe-blades flashed.

The woodmen had pitched a sun-bleached pink tent in the clearing cut beside the river. Half a dozen tammy trunks lay tumbled from their broad purple stumps. A hillock of lopped branches awaiting trimming might have been the nest of some giant eccentric bird. Those hand-winches and chains had been hauled to the site by cart. Sweat slicked the woodmen's bare torsos. Did the five idiots imagine they were stopping a runaway hervy from *abducting* its riders? They swung steel, they bellowed.

Juke hauled on the beast's coat.

'Whoa, damn it!'

Jack pulled on a tine.

'Me hungry!'

The beast slowed to a snorting, maddened hobble, eyeing the woodmen balefully.

'Let us past, fellows! I can't hold this brute long.'

The foresters gawped. Blades sliced slowly to and fro like horizontal pendulums.

'How you get Hervy to carry you, eh?' asked the shortest and broadest of the men, a squinty eye wandering unpredictably. 'A fellow could use yon horns. Fine set.' A ribbon tied back his chestnut hair, and on his right bicep was an axe-head tattoo.

'Bit of a proclaimer, hmm?' guessed his neighbour, whose chest was laced with healed scars. Souvenir of an ill-felled tree? Or of a knife fight? 'You don't wear fine duds as some speakers do. Have to be *quite* a speaker to gentle a hervy.' Indeed the foresters' attitude was perhaps only superficially belligerent. The hervy-riders had invaded their space on this wild beast, and the wood-men could hardly have let such a thing simply pass by without challenging.

Scarchest nodded. 'Quite a bit. Not making much display of it, except by bounding breakneck along the banks of the Kita on a bloody mad shag-back with the biggest bracket o' horns I ever saw.'

Two tall blond men – twins – nodded to one another. 'Doesn't look *gentle* so much as chained up inside.' Their axes drifted lazily from side to side.

'Your wife and kid?' one twin asked Juke.

'We want food, sirs,' piped Jack. 'Me tummy's empty. I'm a growing lad.'

Juke squeezed the boy's shoulders to silence him. But it was too late.

'*In mana's name!*' exclaimed Squinteye. 'He ain't normal.'

The last of the foresters was a shaven-headed piggy fellow, plump and pink. On his wobbly pectorals a cross was tattooed, embellished with smaller crosses.

In wonder he declared, 'It's the Holy Family, lads. And the Child.'

'Oh shut up, Seppo.'

'I knew it would come true, if other stories do! They're fleeing from Herod.'

'That's all right, Seppo, of course it's a holy family with a spelk

151

of a – what, a saviour, that's it – already spouting all grown-up like.'

'Rations, rations,' the believer exclaimed. Dropping his axe, he scurried off towards the tent.

The hervy uttered a choked *Aaannnggg, aaaannnngggg.* Its horns swung. It frothed.

'Stay, hervy, stay!'

The beast pawed in an attempt to drag itself forward.

'Can't *hold* it, can't *hold* it,' warbled Juke. He heaved on fistfuls of shag.

'We stay till the food comes, Hervy!' Jack wrapped skinny arms around himself as if to crush the breath from his chest. The hervy gasped, and quit pawing.

The plump man was hurrying back, bearing a great wedge of emmental cheese in one hand and links of black blood-sausage in the other.

'When you reach Forssa—' advised Scarchest.

'We intend to, after you step aside,' Jatta said to him.

'—they could use yon horns ... What a lady's tone, and from far north too, I'd say.'

'She's *the* Lady.' The plump man pressed the cheese and sausages up to Jatta.

'Hey,' objected one of the twins. 'That's our food,' protested his brother. He lifted his axe. 'Slice the sausage for you, lady?'

'I can pay something,' Juke said quickly.

'No,' cried the plump man. 'Not money. No. Preach to me, Child! Proclaim the word. The others are all false proclaimers. Preach, preach!' He moved right in front of the hervy to stare through its sharp horns at Jack.

Jack had begun rocking to and fro, clutching his belly. '*Want food!*'

'Give him some sausage, Lady, so he can preach.'

'Don't disappoint our Seppo, will you?' said Scarchest, his tone grown menacing. 'Kid should sing a bit for his dinner. That's only fair.'

Jatta cut off a lump of black sausage – so as to flourish her knife? She thrust the piece forward. 'Here, Jack.' Her son's hand snaked back to snatch. He gobbled. Another big share followed, to disappear just as quickly. Jack was such a clamorous fledgling.

'Any preaching will do,' Scarchest declared with a spurious equanimity. 'But not nothing. We want to remember this occasion, don't we? Tale to tell to our grandkids.' He snorted a laugh. 'A holy family passes by, complete with tatty proclaimer, and we feed them. In't that just it, Seppo?' Respect seemed to be diminishing, except on Seppo's part. Juke could hardly bespeak these pickets out of the way while he was concentrating on the beast.

'Please preach, Child,' begged the plump man.

Jack burped. He stared at his expectant audience. He glanced at the rushing river.

'Yes, my fast boy,' coaxed his mother. 'Tell him a tale. That's what he means, that's what he wants.' Those sharp, long axes! The possibility of sudden violence. . . . What could her child say to this dotty devotee?

Jack began to recite: 'After Youkahainen's sister drowned herself, Vai got very upset. He wandered around. He went to the water-maids for a cuddle. They said to go fishing. And he caught a lovely big leaperfish. He was just about to stick his knife in the fish when it cried, "I'm *her*! You're so cruel!" That leaper was really Youka . . . hainen's drowned sister. But she jumped back in the water again for ever and ever.'

Piggyman's brow began to furrow, though Scarchest seemed content.

'Next, the echo of Vai's mother told him to go north to find a fine wife. So Vai—' Jack gulped a breath. 'So Vai jumped on his magic horse and flew off northward, but Youkahainen was waiting in ambush with poisoned arrows 'cause Vai had made his sister drown. And he shot once, and missed. And he shot twice, and missed. But the third time he did shoot down the horse—'

'Threes, things come in threes!' The scarred forester applauded by thumping a hand against his leather-clad thigh.

'We didn't,' chorused the twins with a double chuckle.

'What about the trinity? The Father, the Child, and the Holy Echo?' Piggyman was becoming disgruntled. None of his colleagues seemed to care. The squat, pigtailed woodman called out, 'Carry on talking, kid. That's only one bite's worth of boiled blood so far.'

Jack clamped the shoulders of the hervy tight between his little knees. 'So the steed crashed in the sea but a fierce bird from the northland rescued Vai and flew him there. In the northland Vai met a lovely maid whose mother was Queen Louhi—'

Jatta glowed with pride. How well her boy was speaking this simple version of those womb-words which he'd heard during the winter in the sanctuary hut. Between her legs the beast's ribbed flanks expanded and deflated like a bellows.

'So Vai asked Queen Louhi if he could wed her daughter—'

'This isn't the Word! This isn't right!' cried Seppo.

Jack abruptly speeded up. He began to gabble so that no one should interrupt him.

'Louhi-wanted-a-magic-mill-to-make-all-sorts-of-things. Vai-could-have-her-daughter-if-he-could-make-the-mill. But-Vai-couldn't-so-he-promised-his-brother-Ilmarinen-would-do-it. So-Louhi-gave-Vai-a-new-steed-to-go-back-to-his-brother-on. But-Vai-mustn't-look-aside-on-the-way. Well-he-did-and-saw-a-rainbow-maid-weaving-with-a-shuttle. Vai-wanted-her-but-she-didn't-want-to-be-a-wife. So-Louhi-set-Vai-three-hard-tasks. To-tie-a-knot-in-an-egg. To-split-a-hair-with-a-blunt-knife. To-make-her-shuttle-fly-like-a-bird.'

The boy gulped air. A wind had sprung up along the river, creaming it with curly waves. Resentment curdled Seppo's features; a bitter pique at the way this preaching was proceeding.

Each sentence was one single word now.

'Vai-succeeded-twice-but-then-he-hurt-himself. He-couldn't-stop-bleeding-so-he-had-to-search-a-long-time-how-to-cure-himself. When-at-last-he-got-home-Ilmarinen-didn't-want-to-go-north-till-Vai-bamboozled-and-bespoke-his-brother-into-it. Then-Ilmarinen-made-the-mill-for-Queen-Louhi. The-magic-mill-made-wonderful-things-and-Louhi-hid-it-inside-a-mountain. She-said-Ilmarinen-could-wed-her-daughter-but-her-daughter-swore-she-never-would-wed-so-Ilmarinen-went-back-home-unhappy.'

Gasp.

The daughter who would never wed . . . A pang pierced Jatta's soul.

The boy's voice sang zanily, mesmerizing his listeners, stalling Piggyman from open outrage. Words tumbled over words.

'Vai-set-out-north-in-a-magic-boat-along-with-young-hot-head-Lemminkainen-who-then-kidnapped-Louhi's-daughter. She-said-she'd-marry-Lemminkainen-if-he-gave-up-fighting-and-wild-ways. He-agreed-but-he-wouldn't-let-a-wife-mix-with-village-girls. When-she-did-this-Lemminkainen-left-her. Back-he-went-to-the-north-where-he-enchanted-everyone-except-one-singer-who-he-trounced-and-sent-to-the-river-of-death. He-demanded-Louhi's-next-daughter-instead.'

Gulp.

'Jack, *stop*,' begged his mother. 'Please stop him, Juke.' She shook the proclaimer. She pounded him on the shoulder.

The tale was fairly thumping along now.

'Louhi-SAID-he-HAD-to-CATCH-a-TERRIBLE-wild-HERVY. He-DID. He-HAD-to-BRIDLE-the-FIRESTEED. He-DID. He'd-HAVE-to-SHOOT-the-SWAN-of-DEATH. But-WHEN-he-WENT-to-SURMA-river-WHERE-the-SWAN-swam-OH!-the-SINGER-waiting-CHOPPED-him-UP-and-THREW-him-IN.'

Mucus flew from the hervy's flappy nostrils. Piggyman's outrage was mounting – he twisted his axe shaft around in his hands. Sweat sheened him. He flushed pinker than ever as the boy rushed on.

'IN-the-SOUTH-his-MOTHER'S-hairbrush-BLED. She-RUSHED-to-QUEEN-Louhi's-THREATENED-to-BREAK-the-MILL-so-MUM-learned-LEMMINKAINEN'S-fate. MUM-begged-ILMARINEN-to-MAKE-a-RAKE-went-FISHING-in-SURMAJOKI-caught-CLOTHES-and-LIMBS-of-LEMMINKAINEN-brought-BACK-to-LIFE—'

'No!' howled Piggyman. By now his companions were all exhibiting distress . . . and panic. Wind whipped the river, spuming it. Gusts tore scarlet leaves from minties on the far shore, whirling them over the Kitajoki like tongues of flame or dashes of blood.

'He's the Antichild, the opposite of all—'

'*Demon child!*' Scarchest retreated, wild eyed.

Demon Jack Pakken: the name that Lord Osmo had bestowed on Jatta's boy.

The moment that Scarchest brayed out those words Jack halted his hectic chant. The boy threw himself back against Juke. Then he plunged forward. He might have impaled his face on one of the hervy's sharp tines if Juke hadn't caught him. The beast burst into motion, its hooves scoring pits in the path.

Jatta very nearly pitched backward over its rump. Her fingers clutched at the shag, seizing hold just in time. She almost lost her grasp on the greasy hairs. She clamped her knees fiercely. She arched her spine forward, tightening her grip as the animal careered. The foresters were fifty metres back, a hundred. They were calling out incomprehensibly.

'What did the fat man mean?' her boy asked once he had polished off a large fistful of emmental. 'Calling us a holy family?'

'The only holes were in that cheese,' said Juke, 'and you just ate it.' He barked a couple of short laughs to signal *witticism*.

'Oh don't confuse him—'

'I'm sure I don't know, lad. He'd be what's called a Christian. They expect a miraculous child. Or maybe the child already came and went long ago.'

The hervy slowed. Arching its raggy tail, their mount squirted a stream of stinking loose stools, some of which splattered on its hock. The beast proceeded onward at a less brisk pace. It was wearying. Minties and tammies continued to hedge the rushing river, which swung in great curves from left to right. A floating tammy trunk had lodged itself against a spit of boulders and would need to be poled loose before it could pursue its course towards Forssa.

'But I'm Mummy's miracle child,' said the boy.

'You are, you are,' agreed Jatta.

'What's a demon?'

'You aren't,' said Juke. 'You're something else.' His tone was troubled. Glancing back, he asked Jatta, 'Was your hair as short as that when you met your Jarl? Was that part of being a virgin?' He was beginning that gentle pressure again.

A shake of the head. *No*, not now, please. Not with Jack awake, and so weird. She clamped her jaws on a butt-end of sausage, though the reek of discharged excrement from the rear of the hervy almost made her gag.

Abruptly the trees ended. Simmental cattle – burly-shouldered and white-headed – and teeming sheep grazed a plain of scrubby pasture. Some distant farmsteads of plank barns and steep-pitched beige timber buildings punctuated the vista. The Kita-joki broadened into a long lough, losing impetus.

Jatta sat up high to survey the pastureland, nostalgic of a sudden for tundra. 'An open view. Such herds.' Scenting the hervy, a Simmental bellowed. Their mount groaned *aaannnggg*, shaking its horns. A young herdsman, blond curls peeping from under a pillbox skull-cap, shaded his eyes to stare at the wild beast – with riders on its back. He swung a curved horn to his lips. His quavering mournful hoots found answer a couple of keys away, and then a couple further.

'What lovely beasts compared with this one.'

Juke gazed at cattle near and far. 'Meat and milk,' he said, 'and leather and buttons and fertilizer, and oil and glue and tallow and gall dye.'

'I know, I know. I didn't loll about on perfumed cushions.'

'I know you didn't, Jatta.'

'I was admiring their beauty – as your sister might.'

Was he going to offer her a home, after all? But as what? A family servant for a mutant household?

'In the town we're coming to you'll keep quiet, Jack,' Juke told the boy severely. 'Do you hear?'

Jack's head nodded up and down.

Back in the forest they had passed a couple more loggers' camps without incident. Trunks from those camps bobbed along the reed-fringed lough to end up in a log-jam. Beyond the log-jam the lough narrowed suddenly into river once again; and the plain ended, dropping away into a valley as yet unseen.

Log-drivers emerged on to that shifting raft as the trio rode closer. Those men held poles acrobatically for balance while they stared at the oncomers. A neck of water separated the log-jam from the track, but a boom of chained timbers offered a slippery causeway. When the log-drivers hallooed, Juke plucked out his long horn-handled knife to wave. The blade flashed sunlight.

To their right, the Kitajoki dashed itself noisily down bouldery spray-smoky rapids towards the lake, now revealed to view. Along the north shore spread the roofs of Forssa, tiled yellow or orange or rose: a great trayful of crusty buns. A keep of grey stone thrust an L-shaped pier into the lake, a crooked arm to shelter and supervise boats. Along the southern shallows of the Forssajarvi a raft of roped logs proceeded serenely, kitted out with a squat red sail and a tent. Two tiny figures poled it.

On the far side of the river, water also poured down a slipway fendered with staked logs. This was how timber bypassed the rapids, chuting down to a holding basin in the lake. Over there the log-drivers were stripping off their shirts and breeches. One after another they vaulted into the waterchute. This man on his belly, that man on his back, they rushed down towards the lake. The fender of logs must be worn smooth by decades of friction.

Where the downrush of river spumed into Forssajarvi Lake, a rickety jetty thrust out on piles. Some men were casting a net into the churning foam. Several large silver fish gleamed in long baskets. It seemed insane that any creature would try to mount those rapids. But this they did, compulsively, jumping from lee of boulder to lee of boulder, often swept back exhausted. Compulsions prevailed.

Children were running alongside the beast, playing tag with its smelly coat when it stumbled into the market square of Forssa. Surrounding the square were shops vending woollen sweaters, oil, tallow candles, leather breeches, herbs and medicines. Two lines of low carts faced one another on the worn flagstones, stalls for eggs and fish and beef and mutton. Tethered in the shafts, placid big-boned Ardennais mares of bay and dapple grey and red roan snuffled in their nosebags. Squabbling little scaly-winged scavengers pecked at accumulating dung, and at one another, ignoring the scuffle of bare feet and sandals and finer shoes. Housewives in frocks and shawls bickered with farmwives perched long-skirted on the sides of the carts. A fiddler was sawing away, his cap set down for pennies. A tinker, hung all over with spoons and knives and copper pans, juggled some of his wares, his farcical armour clinking and clanking. A hulking, egg-streaked youth was chained to a pillory. A high stone plinth sported a horse's skull and a sharp-horned bull's, both daubed with stars of red paint.

'Whoa, Hervy!'

And everyone in the square turned to stare. More spectators arrived by this street and that alley. Men crowded around the frothing beast as Jatta slipped from its back, to lift Jack down. (*Now don't say a thing.*) The heaving hervy swung its horns, eyes maddened, nostrils slapping open and shut.

'Here's a gift for Forssa,' shouted Juke. 'We'd appreciate a boat ride towards Speakers' Valley.'

'*Quite the proclaimer—*'

'*That's plain as the nose on your mush—*'

'*Bit soon for the gala, though—*'

'*Get the mana-priest here!*'

A lad was sent scampering. A leather-aproned shopkeeper came trotting with a heavy hammer, and a cutler with a long knife. Passing by the tinker, the cutler darted his blade mischievously and merrily at the man. The itinerant jumped back jangling, grinning nervously.

The shopkeeper hauled a box alongside the beast and climbed up. Jatta tried to cover her boy's eyes with her hands, but his head ducked clear. Juke sat back invitingly upon their exhausted mount.

'A gift for Forssa!'

And if he hadn't made a gift of the beast . . . ?

Swinging the hammer two-handed with all his force, the shop-keeper struck the hervy on the back of the neck below the horns. The beast slumped beneath Juke; and he stepped clear nonchal-antly. Already the cutler was plunging his long blade into the hervy's heart.

Those log-drivers had arrived clad only in wet breech-clouts. They must have swum across the spume to that fishing jetty. By the time the beast's horn-racked head had been sawn off by them their bare arms and legs and chests were piebald with the gin-gery gore of the slaughtered hervy, and flagstones were slick. Two of the bloodstained men hoisted the dripping glassy-eyed head on to the plinth alongside horse and bull skulls. The quick azure scavvybirds would flock to peck the bones bare, though this might take hundreds of busy birds several days.

The crowd chanted softly:

'Skull-soul,
'Death's eye,
'Bones alive,
'See us thrive . . .'

The charcoal-suited mana-priest ordered the headless corpse cut open. Axed, sawn, sliced! A bronze amulet of a pierced serpent hung down his fine linen shirtfront to ward off the attentions of Isi, and the bright brass buckles of his leather shoes remained quite unstained throughout. Soon the beast's large maroon heart and purple liver were spitted upon its own horns. Draught-horses snorted uneasily in their bags of oats. Their shoes scraped the flagstones. Carts shifted forward and back, but the press of the crowd restrained them.

The priest wore silver-framed spectacles, and a silver ring on one manicured hand. A trim moustache and oiled curls completed the impression of fastidiousness. He was slight in build but all the townsfolk deferred to him. Spotless, he assessed the organs impaled on the tines. He composed himself. He raised his arms, exposing chunky silver cufflinks. Then he called up at a sky where a few woolly cumulus clouds floated far below the ghosts of mares' tails:

'Coo, coo, cuckoos come, to spread word of Forssa's prosperity, prayed for in harmony with mana, the energy which imbues all Kaleva, letting this be our world, daunting the Snakes. We honour this king of native beasts which came here in the reins of mana, guided by man, with a human family riding on its back. This is a story to tell, so that our custodianship of field and forest will continue reinforced.'

Jatta nodded. It was well put. She hugged Jack to her closely in case he burbled out some interruption. Her clothes and his stunk of hervy yet this seemed appropriate. Juke inclined his head politely if broodingly. He certainly wanted a boat ride.

'We saw the Isi war-boat pass over last evening. Yet here's a sure sign that the Snakes shan't injure our well-being—'

The same sky-boat which had appeared over the lake where she and Juke met? With its crew of Juttahats seeming in search of . . . *what*? 'Coo, coo, come when you can!' called the priest. He cocked his head then shrugged deprecatingly. A cuckoo would come when it came.

But the crowd gasped. Two green birds were fluttering over the rooftops.

They flapped in a circle above the square, eyeing the pack of people before plummeting down. Alighting on the horns of the hervy, one cuckoo tore at its liver, the other at its heart. Their hooked beaks clipped out gobbets to toss up, catch, and gulp. After the first sating of appetite each threw some pieces for the other to take. Perched on the tines they fed one another.

The spruce priest waited till the birds paused and looked at him with their yellow orbs.

'Cuckoos, cuckoos, tell the tale,' he began. Two on the same perch together!

However, one bird already had a tale to tell. In a clipped, automatic tone it cried, 'Osmo van Maanen banished Jatta Sari-ola and her freak bastard to live with the mutants—'

Jack jerked against Jatta, growling softly. Juke planted a steadying hand on the boy's shoulder. 'Easy, lad, easy. They needn't know it's us.'

'Jatta's bastard is only two months old—'

The other cuckoo interrupted. 'Tycho Cammon the Tyrant revived.' A maroon sliver of hervy heart slipped from inside its beak. The bird flicked the offal away with a swipe of its claw. 'Revived, and murdered van Maanen's mistress Vivi Rintala. Van Maanen burned Cammon's bones to ash—'

The bird which had eaten liver eyed its perch-neighbour. '—and Demon Jack Pakken already looks two years old, or three, and scurries and prattles. Van Maanen gave him that name—'

160

'—then he bespoke Jatta,' said the heart cuckoo.

'Van Maanen had a bonfire built on the beach for after the burial of Vivi,' the liver cuckoo said.

What was this? A *dialogue* of cuckoos? They were telling one another's story now – just as they had fed each other bloody tidbits. In astonishment the mana-priest gazed at the birds.

'Cuckoos, you're talking to each other!' he exclaimed.

'Ukko-ukkoo,' croaked the heart bird. 'Ukkoo-ukko,' its companion.

'No, of course you aren't!' The priest's excitement mounted. 'You're each saying what the other knows – without the words being spoken yet. Your minds are passing the words to and fro. What one thinks, the other can think. How far apart can you be for this to happen? Were you two birds at Maananfors at all?'

His spectacles glittered. Rightly he could expect no answer, but still he hesitated for a hopeful few moments before plunging on.

'Cuckoos, cuckoos, tell this tale of how mana-priest Jussi Haavio of Forssa discovered that cuckoos can think at one another, and know the messages in each other's minds at once.'

He considered what he had said, then meticulously added: 'Maybe only when they're close together, but maybe not. Maybe when they're far apart. We see them fly off fast to their destinations, but how far do they actually need to go?' The priest clapped his hands together. 'Cuckoos, I pray you, fly to the mana-bishop at Tumio. No: *send word* to mana-bishop Papin Jumala. Tell him the words of Jussi Haavio. Beg him to send me the message . . . the message that Jussi Haavio has become his curate, to the honour of Forssa and of Lord Fors. Beg him to send word immediately.'

The seaport of Tumio was four hundred keys south-east. So if that message came back rapidly . . .

People in the crowd were regarding Jatta and her boy with mixed feelings now. *Mischievous* cuckoos.

'But first,' and Haavio's voice soared, 'tell us a tale in full of van Maanen and Jatta Sariola and her bastard, and the stone man.' He peered at Jatta anticipatively. The priest didn't seem ill-intentioned, only excited. Her tanned pear-shaped face, her dark narrow eyes – and that ripped northern tunic, oh yes . . .

Jatta winced. Had Tycho Cammon revived of his own accord? *The rug on which Osmo might crack his head . . .*

Had Juke done *that*? To undermine, or destroy, Osmo van

161

Maanen? Resulting in the death of some woman who must surely be classed as innocent, although her murder as surely wounded van Maanen himself ... After his brusque treatment of her, Jatta held no brief for the bespeaker lord; but to attack a future opponent in such a furtive style was diminishing of Juke. In seeking to weaken van Maanen, Juke exposed weakness in himself. Lack of confidence. A streak of cowardice. How would he treat herself and Jack in a moment of crisis – which might be close at hand? Juke's face was bitter as he stared at the two cuckoos perched on the horns of his gift to Forssa.

'Why's her bastard boy a demon?' cried a farmwife from a cart.

'What kind of nakki, eh?'

'What did she *do*?'

'Who sired the demon bastard?'

They weren't too interested in how cuckoos communicated news. This was something juicier. By now many onlookers were putting two and two together where this northern lass and her little boy and male companion were concerned. Hadn't they ridden in like devils on the back of a wild hervy buck?

The two scaly green birds shuffled on their sharp perches.

'Tell us the tale,' Haavio bade them. '*Then* send my message to Tumio.'

First one cuckoo began to recite, then the second took over the story. Alternately, as if swopping voices or memories, they betrayed Jatta and her fast boy to the priest and to the crowd. But not Juke.

13 · DINNER WITH A MANA-PRIEST

At last the two cuckoos fell silent and turned again to rending heart and liver. Their audience jabbered.

'A *Sariola*—'

'Tossed herself away on a mutie—'

'On him—'

'Doesn't look much like a mutie—'

'Who says it's him?'

'Oh really!'

A finger poked Jatta investigatively. Jack shrunk close to his mother, dwarfed by the pressure of big bodies, almost suffocated. Juke's hand was on his knife. Nothing that either bird had chirped had connected Juke in any way with the freeing of Tycho Cammon, an omission which haunted Jatta yet for which she was very grateful. News that this man had freed the fossilized tyrant for his own selfish purposes could have spawned deadly consequences. Though had he done so, had he indeed? She wasn't totally sure.

'Kid looks normal enough—'

'For two months old? Who you kidding—?'

'Can't damn well see the little tyke—!'

'Proclaimer fellow brought us yon hervy—'

The gutted body sprawled cumbersomely in a pool of congealed gingery blood, attracting the attention of a cloud of flies and scavvybirds. A hand pushed experimentally at Jatta. Juke growled a warning.

'He can't bespeak us all at once—'

'If what, mate? If what exakly—?'

Jussi Haavio removed his spectacles and polished the lenses lovingly on his pocket kerchief as if to perfect his vision of events.

'Our guests,' he said, 'our *guests* have brought us a fine hervy to honour Forssa. Isn't that so? And two lively tales have followed them. Those two messenger birds have shown how cuckoos can communicate without talking aloud. All thanks to our *guests*—'

Jatta began to relax.

The birds had devoured as much of the maroon and purple offal as they cared to. They flapped aloft, rising above the roofs. One to head off north, but the other south. Haavio eyed their departure eagerly.

'Our *guests*,' he resumed, 'are in need of hospitality and a ride down the river tomorrow. How far, by the way?' he asked Juke.

'Somewhere near Speakers' Valley will be fine.'

Of course Juke would want to go by way of the venue for his duel with van Maanen this autumn. To reassure himself; to imagine a future triumph while nobody powerful was actually confronting him.

Jatta found herself hauled off to a public sauna by townswomen grown friendly to the point of officiousness. Jack and Juke were to visit the men's counterpart before rendezvousing at the mana-priest's mansion for an evening meal.

Being separated from her son hardly appealed to Jatta. She

foresaw a frantic tantrum on the boy's part, and her confidence in Juke as a custodian had suffered a sharp knock. If his fixation on Lord Osmo could cause the death of one unoffending woman, how reliable was Juke should he spy an advantage which could harm Jack or herself? What if Juke had deliberately aimed the stone man not at Osmo but at his woman friend, his consolation, thus to devastate him but leave him alive till the autumn with a thorn in his heart? That would have been despicable. And yet Jatta could still not swear that her companion had actually caused the stone man to break free. The cuckoos hadn't mentioned any reason why the calamity had happened.

Jatta's thoughts swirled while a gaggle of eager women sped her along a cobbled street. They passed a sweet-smelling bakery, a dusty flour mill, a granite warehouse for grains. Protests at leaving her boy had been quite overruled. Actually, her boy appeared eager to be off with the men. To show off? To gabble. *Did he love her?* Jatta couldn't help feeling love for him, protective devotion such as she recalled once feeling for Nakkinook, though far stronger. Why should she shun this feeling? One of natural mother love? Not totally . . . No, it was bound up still with feelings of ardour for Jarl. It might well be a splinter from the passion she had experienced in regard to Jarl, a sentiment which remained undiminished by his abandonment of her. Oh her maddening, tiring, demanding, adorable miracle boy! Was he going to rush away from her soon for ever? She feared, she feared. She had lost Jarl. Let her not lose Jack too. Yet what kind of prodigal might he soon become?

The women's sauna was a low-slung, plank building backing on to the Forssajarvi. Grey keep and sails of the boats in its harbour loomed beyond. The women hastened Jatta into the ablutions room to strip her, and themselves. Her fishwife's corduroy skirt, ponging of hervy, her sweaty chemise and gaberdine shirt: all, all was rushed off to be laundered. Laughing, women poured wooden buckets of water over their naked selves and Jatta. They soaped, they worked up a lather. Flesh slapped. Breasts bounced. Thighs quivered. They rinsed off, and led her into the hot-room, stunned, for Queen Lucky's daughter had never been in such a situation before.

Never in a sauna room. Never naked with other women.

Fresh steam exploded in sizzling billows from the charcoal brazier. Women stared along and down and upward unabashedly at Jatta's body, at her curly coaly short muff of pubic hairs covering the part which could give longlife once to a man. Might she be visibly different down there? In one respect she was. Years of wearing a succession of chastity girdles, padded and blessed though those had been, had left slight permanent indentations. A faint impression remained in the flesh. Juke hadn't remarked on this when they bathed in the lake. Perhaps he hadn't even noticed. These women had more time to observe. But perhaps Juke was entirely virgin in his knowledge of women's bodies? Could that be? Could it be so at all?

There was a babble of introductions, a jostle to be closest to Jatta on the tiers of yellover benches.

Syleilla was a substantial rosy middle-aged blonde. Squeezing beside Jatta, she brushed the delicate curved imprint of the girdle with her hand as though accidentally, puzzled by it.

'Oh that hervy was so bruising,' said Jatta, though the mark in no way resembled a bruise. 'I'm aching.' She regretted her words, which made her seem a milksop.

'Steam'll set you right, dear.' Syleilla patted her.

Steam was opening the pores in her breasts. The areolas, abandoned target for her baby's appetite, were still significantly browner. Wormhead nipples prickled as some last trace of creamy exudate emerged.

Jatta tried to steer the conversation away from the women's obvious object of interest, a Sariola daughter stripped bare. 'So a war-boat went over last evening?'

'Yes, and our keep loosed off its lightrifles as a warning,' said her other immediate neighbour.

Sleek freckled Sudella's left breast was tattooed with a little yellow narciss bloom. 'Just to show we had some rifles, mind you. They weren't fired *at* the Jutties – that would be crazy. No, they fired at some minties on the ridge to set them alight. That looked wilder. Tree-torches blazing up!'

'Is that proclaimer with you a longlife now?' demanded Syleilla. 'Did your mother hate him because he's a mutie?'

'He doesn't look it—'

Sudella stroked the flower on her breast. 'Oh you must have been consumed by *love*!'

Crowded in this steamy space where she could hardly breathe, Jatta strove for a light tone. 'Is your Lord Fors . . . vigorous?' she asked with a smile. 'Firing on Juttahats!' (May she not encounter any more lords!)

'He's a longlife, you know. Fors of Forssa. A hundred and forty

165

years old. And he stays in that keep of his like an oster in its shell. Fors collects clocks. Hundreds and hundreds of clocks, so he can keep an eye on the time. Ding-dong, cling-clong: the noise in there when all those strike! We can almost hear it from here. Guests don't even see Fors on Lucky's Day.'

Thanks be to mana, Fors was a recluse, obsessed with his own longevity. Obviously no Sariola wife was left alive. There'd be no moody hag-sister roosting in Forssa keep.

'Well, I mention Lucky's Day. Old Lucky's your very own mother!'

'How *do* you make a man into a longlife?' pestered Syleilla. 'I've always yearned to know.'

'Honestly, I've no idea. How do you make a baby? How do you breathe? Do you tell yourself: in-out, in-out?'

The ample blonde elbowed Jatta in the ribs. 'In-out in-out's how a fellow becomes a longlife, though. Must be a special kind of in-out in-out, eh?'

Was it?

When Jarl had ravished her he had manipulated her into a somewhat unexpected position. Was his preference unusual? She hadn't known and hadn't cared. But she hadn't generalized from this to imagine a trick to the love-making till Syleilla put her cheeky question. Jatta had no intention of answering her. If there was a trick, how would Jarl have known of it? Yet he had known how to free her from her girdle! She hadn't questioned any of this. She hadn't been remotely interested, because he was godlike to her at the time. Of course all these women misunderstood the nature of her relationship with *Juke*.

'Penny for them?' said Sudella.

Syleilla guffawed. 'Oh, a mark, at least a mark!'

'What . . . ?'

'For your bosom thoughts, of course.'

The assembly of naked, perspiring women was agog. But Jatta wasn't going to tell *them*. She couldn't bear to. They couldn't bespeak her to. Yet the pressure of so much flesh seemed to pile upon her. A score and more pink thighs and buttocks and arms both chubby and lean, all beaded with hot dew. Here a hand-slap of a birthmark, there a delicate floral tattoo. Firm breasts, sagging breasts, little tits, large. Blonde hair, brown hair plastered to heads, bushing and wisping from groins and armpits. Faces, faces: smooth ones, furrowed ones, ageing ones, younger ones, florid, flushed, silky. Eyes, eyes, gawking keenly in the swelter-

166

ing vapour. She wouldn't couldn't shouldn't. The tale pushed to be told, as if en masse they were proclaiming that she confess to them. Words might have welled up if she hadn't found herself struggling to breathe. The humidity was stifling. All those other mouths and noses, stealing what air remained in the torrid mist and exhaling warm dead gas. Her head swam. The vague room spun. Stars floated, sparkling. Her muscles had slackened to jelly.

Hot bodies were enfolding her. Lugging her here and there like a carcass.

'*Fainted*,' she half-heard.

'*Passed out*—' All those disappointed women.

She was glad to float senselessly, rocked on a sea of hot clutching flesh, dreaming foggily of Jarl.

The mana-priest's wife had baked lamb and potatoes in a charred hollow log, with red cabbage salad and carrot casserole to accompany. Leena Haavio was birdlike in features and build, with bright inquisitive eyes. Plumed in black lace, on first glance she seemed like a spry widow till one registered her flawless delicate complexion. Serpentine bangles wound around her slim wrists. She was only in her late twenties, a good two decades younger than the mana-priest. Mrs Haavio perched on her dining chair. She fluttered to serve Juke and Jatta, cleaned and spruced, and her adored Jussi. Lacking any table manners, Jack gobbled ravenously through in her kitchen. A silver candlestick stood unlit on the polished speckled beige table. The carved fireplace surround was a mass of tammywood birds. Outside the wide-open window: the lakeshore, a gilded evening mist lazing over the water.

'So why didn't you people already have a hervy skull?' Juke was asking. He glanced at Jatta to check that he was manipulating his cutlery correctly. All his niggling *doubts*. Mutant whelp in a mana-priest's mansion.

'One had to *come*, not be shot in the forest. I'm indebted to you. Ah, those cuckoos!'

Cuckoos turned out to be a major obsession of Haavio's. One of his life's ambitions was to tame one, talk to it, and hear it talk back intelligently, not just relate stories the bird had gathered like a beakful of twigs.

'They understand us. Why don't they answer questions about themselves?'

'Maybe they don't want to become tame like sheep and horses,' suggested Jatta. She pronged a golden potato.

'What I heard today riveted me. Those two birds shared a mind in common. Maybe they also share a mind in common when they're far apart. If so, they don't actually need to fly great distances. Cuckoos all look the same, so how can we tell one from another? If they have a common mind, that must be a huge mind. That must be how they learned our language, not merely as noises but as meanings. Maybe they're the mind of mana itself. Its voice on Kaleva.'

Juke carved a wedge of lamb and transferred it, wobbling, to his blue faience plate. He gulped from his pot of ale.

'How does a cuckoo learn its tricks? Well, how does a bespeaker learn? Words begin to glow – to have energy. The energy directs itself. It shows you how. Another proclaimer can give you advice if you're lucky. Your dreams help a lot. You dream yourself bespeaking. But in the main *it simply happens*. Why not the same with cuckoos too? The pressure of circumstances ... A proclaimer's a conscious concentration of this pressure.'

'I could catch a cuckoo,' piped Jack from the kitchen doorway, a drumstick in a greasy paw.

'I swear he's taller than when we met,' said Juke softly across the table.

'You could keep it in a cage, sir, till it tells you what you want!'

'That's blasphemous, boy,' snapped the mana-priest. 'We mustn't harm a cuckoo.'

'Why not? Why not?'

'He doesn't understand—'

'It's the worst luck,' said Leena Haavio. Hastily she kissed one of her brass bracelets. 'Brings the nakkis on you.'

Jack gnawed the chicken bone clean and dropped it on the checkered rug. Haavio winced, and adjusted his cufflinks.

'Couldn't you have taught him how to behave himself?'

'I'm sorry, we were in woods so much – he's growing up wild.'

Leena fluttered her hands dismissively. A bone on the floor didn't matter too much. Though bad luck did.

'Maybe you ought to go to Landfall,' Jatta suggested to the priest. 'The Earth people might be investigating cuckoos. They could be fascinated to hear what you're saying, Pappi Haavio.'

'Oh no,' his wife exclaimed, 'it's Tumio we'd go to. I'd love to see the sea. If Jussi can become a bishop's curate, and he will now—'

Haavio's fragile young wife might be his own beloved talking bird, his human cuckoo in the house, but she had ambitions too. While Haavio continued doing justice to the succulent lamb on his plate, Jatta slipped from the table to gather up the gnawed drumstick then usher her boy back into the kitchen. Like a puppy banished from a dining room? Well, not quite.

If the cuckoos hadn't arrived in the market square to tell of her banishment – by her own mother and by van Maanen – that crowd wouldn't have begun to seethe troublesomely. There would simply have been glee at the delivery of the hervy. If the birds hadn't told their tales in the way they had told them, then, notwithstanding the hervy, Haavio mightn't have become fascinated enough to host the travellers. This priest with his passion to understand cuckoos. Had a ripple of sympathy for Jatta passed through mana even as it brought bad luck to her, betraying her?

Jussi Haavio wasn't any more interested in understanding Jatta's troubles than Lord Osmo had been. What preoccupied the Pappi over dinner was the 'voices of mana', as he'd begun with increasing conviction to call the messenger birds. That, and his chances of promotion to Tumio. And mana, always mana.

He addressed his guests dreamily as if they were a miniature congregation.

'Mana's the otherworld, the otherspace. It's the realm the Ukko travels through to bring us here to Kaleva. It's the region where wish becomes will, where tale becomes event. Mana is the force of fate. But it's a fate which fortunate ones amongst us can foresay, and bespeak into happening.' He eyed Juke and added the caveat: *'To a certain degree.* Mostly the currents of fate sweep us along, don't they, spilling from the old stories which Saint Lucky told to the Ukko? Reflections of reflections; aspects of aspects!'

Jatta stared at her plate, unwilling to acknowledge her mother as any sort of saint. Haavio hardly heeded her indifference.

'Mana is the spirit force which moulds this world for us and moulds our lives on this world, yes indeed. The compliant inscrutable god-creatures that inhabit mana are the Ukkos – Saint Lucky's, and the demon serpents'. Cuckoos are the voices of mana.'

Haavio was intoxicating himself with words, trying to preach a prophecy into existence. He glanced through the open window from time to time, expectantly. A verandah overlooked the lake.

169

From the railing jutted his very own wrought-iron cuckoo perch – a spiked crown set on a disc at the end of a hinged arm. Little chunks of raw lamb were impaled on the tines of the perch. The meat was drying in the breeze, attracting waterflies.

No cuckoo had settled there with a message from the bishop far away.

Not yet.

No doubt the old bishop might need to think a bit before sending his reply.

'Leena, will you take what's left of the lamb leg out and stick it on our perch instead of those scraps? Quite delicious, wasn't it?'

Jatta agreed.

'A cuckoo should think so too. We only offer them raw meat and offal. Well, the hervy's offal certainly attracted them. But maybe one should cook for a cuckoo too. Then it'll speak more sophisticatedly about itself.'

Obediently Mrs Haavio bore the hollowed log and meaty femur away.

'Isn't it a fact,' said Juke, 'that there aren't any cuckoos in Pootara, and there's no mana-magic there either?'

'How could there be the magic without the voice?'

Juke probed between his molars with a fingernail. Jatta frowned at him, shaking her head slightly. Why should she care if the killer of Osmo's housekeeper betrayed a lack of table manners?

'I mean, correct me if I'm wrong, but mana doesn't flood the whole world.'

Dainty lace-clad Leena emerged upon the verandah. Jack was tagging along, sniffing at what she carried.

'That's why I wish to be at a port, where there are Pootaran sailors to question! Not just any port, but Tumio with its bishop's palace and the mana-temple.'

Leena balanced the hollowed log on the railing. Then she pulled at the black iron arm to swing the spiked crown within reach.

'Besides, some old longlifes chose to live in Tumio for the entertainments. One of those might know when the first cuckoo told the first tale. Was it as soon as the first people landed on Kaleva? Was it later?'

When Leena had discarded the raw meat she lifted the half-eaten leg into position, careful not to stain her sleeves.

In memory Jatta saw those dead chicks spitted on her mother's cuckoo perches. If anyone knew when the first cuckoo had spoken it was likely to be Lucky. Sly, crazy Lucky. Or Bertel.

Jatta had no wish to emphasize her parentage. 'Your own Lord Fors—'

'—is only concerned with his clocks. Anyway, he isn't *ancient*.'

'*Shun, skavvies, shun!*' Leena chanted at the new cuckoo food. '*Eschew, robberbird, don't chew!*' She pushed the perch out again from the verandah. After Leena had carried the empty log-dish away, Jack on tiptoe clung to the rail, struggling to peer along the iron arm at the offering.

'—and some longlifes went to live in Pootara, would you believe?'

This surprised Jatta. But thus Haavio had learned during his novice years in Tumio. Did they know he had been trained there? Hadn't he already said? In his opinion mana must hold sway on the garden island far in the south. But it lacked a voice: the cuckoos.

A few of the earliest longlifes had killed themselves when the endless years began to appal them. A few others had been killed by enemies. Yet some had definitely fled to the balmy lush shores of Pootara, where reason ruled the roost and where random violence was unlikely to cut their long lifelines short.

To live for ever more among black men who looked like the Juttahats of the Velvet Isi? Among the fruit growers and puzzle makers? Those rationalists who regarded the whole northland with wariness? Ah, the longlifes in question had long since outlived their own generation. Perhaps they were happy enough – or alienated enough – to dwell without illusion among people who were blatantly strangers.

'Mana still sustains their lives,' said the priest. Which puzzled Jatta. Surely longlife, once granted, was intrinsic?

Once a bee was in someone's bonnet, it set up a buzzing which could seem to fill the whole world. In the priest's case: a cuckoo in one's cap. On Leena's return she brought black mustaberry pie and Pootaran coffee.

'BOY!' roared Haavio.

Jack was dangling from the arm of the cuckoo perch. Legs waggling, he was inching clutching little hands along the perch as he strove to reach the crown and the lamb bone, as if this had been placed out of his reach as a test of initiative.

'Oh Jack!' Jatta hurried to the open window. Juke eased her

171

aside. He slung a long leg over the windowsill, knocking a brass bowl of herbal pot-pourri to the floor, to Leena's dismay, and ducked his shoulders through.

Too late.

The wrought iron snapped.

Perch and lamb and boy fell to the lakeside pebbles a couple of metres below.

Frigidly, Haavio had decreed a recitation from the *Book of the Land of Heroes*. The momentum of tale-telling might still attract one of those absent cuckoos to his home in spite of the broken perch. Where *was* that bird with its message from the bishop? Jack's mischief couldn't have happened at a worse time.

Juke had recovered the spiked crown, and the lamb's leg from the lad's lips, and the lad himself, whom he now held on his knee. Leena had hurried to fetch a blacksmith. Coffee grew cold; mustaberry pie was quite neglected. The evening sun shone blithely through the window, illuminating a leather-bound volume which Haavio had lifted solemnly from a small tammy chest and opened upon the dinner table.

The priest launched into his recitation:

'Vainamoinen, old and steadfast,

'Had not found the words he wanted—'

Nor had the mana-priest. No message had yet come from the distant seaport to prove that cuckoos could communicate mind to mind across hundreds of keys! Haavio had chosen a suitable text.

'—In the eternal realms of Mana,

'And for ever more he pondered,

'In his head reflected ever,

'Where the words he might discover,

'And obtain the charms he needed—'

Charms, in this case, to help Vai finish making a magic boat in which to revisit Louhi's far northern realm – just as Haavio hoped to move to Tumio further south. Jack was spellbound. The priest's occasional glances showed plainly that *he* wasn't at all enchanted at the presence of this demon child. Yet having the boy here in the dining room for the recitation seemed to keep him quiet. At the correct intervals, which he'd memorized as a novice, Haavio turned the pages of unreadable print. Finally a shawl-clad Leena ushered the blacksmith along the verandah. Oilskin toolbag in hand, he was a stocky red-faced fellow. A replacement iron rod, tucked tight in his armpit, made it appear as if he'd been pierced by a metal shaft.

'Ah, Paul!' Haavio hurried to the window. 'Can you fix that perch quickly?'

Jack squirmed impatiently. His left hand finger-walked in the direction of the mustaberry pie. Haavio craned through the window while the blacksmith examined the damage.

'Me want pie.'

'*Hush, Fastboy,*' begged Jatta. Juke clamped the boy tight. Leena's face puckered with sour censure. Her pot-pourri still lay scattered like chaff.

In frustration Jack began to chant:

'Vai-TORMENTED-the-DEMON-from-WITHIN-with-FIRE. He-WON-the-MASTERWORDS-and-ALSO-his-FREEDOM. Vai-COMPLETED-the-BOAT.' Jack raced helter-skelter, abridging the story to its bare bones. 'Ilmarinen's-SISTER-discovered-WARNED-her-BROTHER-that-VAI-would-STEAL-his-BRIDE. So-VAI-gave-CHASE-by-SLEDGE-and-CAUGHT-his-FRIEND.'

Jack was like a crazed cuckoo himself. A freak breeze whipped through the window, riffling over leaf after leaf of the book.

'Fastboy, don't—'

'They-AGREED-the-MAID-would-FREELY-choose. In-POHJOLA-the-DAUGHTER-favoured-ILMARINEN-who'd-MADE-the-MAGICMILL-work. VAI-went-BACK-home-HEAVYHEARTED—'

Page after page after page whipped over. Swinging round, appalled, the mana-priest banged his oiled curls on the windowframe. Out on the verandah his wife uttered a series of sharp squeals. Her hands fluttered to her lips as if squeaking mice were issuing from her mouth and must be caught. Her brass bangles were hungry little snakes gobbling the mice.

'—Ilmarinen-HAD-to-PASS-three-TESTS. To-PLOUGH-a-FIELD-of-SERPENTS-to-MUZZLE-a-BEAR-to-CATCH-a-GIANT-fish-SWIMMING-in-DEATH's-river-WITHOUT-any-NET—'

Juke finally clamped his hand over the boy's mouth. Jussi Haavio swayed as if on the verge of apoplexy. The leaves of his precious book, pages of his memory, had quit flipping over. Clutching at his amulet, Haavio hastened to the leather-bound tome. He shut his eyes briefly. He circled a finger thrice before plunging a manicured nail on to a page. Brow knit, he examined the open volume for specks in the paper, for creases, for past marks of fingernails. Then he mouthed coldly:

'O thou wicked, wretched eagle,

'What a faithless bird I find you . . .'

Haavio shouted out to the verandah where Paul was shuffling to and fro, the spiky crown loose in one hand. 'That means the cuckoo, doesn't it? Hurry up, man, hurry up!'

Juke relaxed his gag on the boy.

'Sir,' piped Jack, 'I tried to hurry the cuckoo for you. Can I have some berry pie now?'

But Haavio glowered at Juke and Jatta.

'Off with you all to the public hostel! Right away, do you hear? You'll have transport downriver tomorrow because I promised that in exchange for the hervy head. Kindly get out of my house this minute. *Get out.*'

Outside, Leena began to cry softly. Emitting little birdlike cheeps, she dabbed at her eyes with black lace cuffs.

14 · RAVISHED

The hostel was on dusty Satama Street, down by the harbour which nestled near the keep. A grey-bunned, wrinkle-rutted granny admitted Juke and Jatta and Jack. A black patch masked the old woman's left eye. Her hostel proved to be vacant of other travellers.

'Towards gala time it'll be four to a room and a couple more on the floor,' declared Granny. 'Folks traipsing to Speakers' Valley for the fair and for the fancy words. Fair and fancy, fair and fancy, that's it. Take your pick.'

Of guest rooms in this resthouse, she meant. More than a dozen doors opened off a dingy corridor lit poorly by a pair of skylights. The sun had finally been setting when Juke thumped on the front door.

'Except mine, that's the end one.'

Stomping along, she shoved one door open then the next, to reveal neat spartan rooms each furnished with two-tier double-berth bunks, pot-bellied stoves, table and stools. Juke kept stealing sidelong glances at the woman's black patch.

'Oh, this? Lost my peeper gutting fish, I did, when I was just a girl. Wicked nakki of a hook flew out and snagged me in the glimmer. Slipped on guts with the pain of it, I did. Hook tugged me jelly out so now I know how a fish feels.' She cackled as if this was a great joke.

'I see,' said Juke.

'Oh but you see double, young man! And twice thirty pennies is what you'll pay to Granny assuming you can afford it. Child's free. And weary – shouldn't be up so late.' Jack slumped foetally, half inside Jatta's tunic, his head lolling.

Reluctantly Juke hauled out his purse.

'That's my pension, young fellow,' explained Granny. 'Pay up and I'll give you a key to the privy.' She scrutinized him. 'Maybe you'd like to see me eye socket too for another ten pennies?'

Juke flinched.

'I could light a candle. I've a lovely little opal in the socket. It's to pay the swan of death.'

'*No!*' In distress.

Granny chortled mischievously. 'Didn't think as you would somehow. Big strong squeamish chap. Me patch bothers you, hmm? So you behave yourself, cause Granny's watching with her blind eye. No hanky-panky on me blankets, if you take me meaning.'

As soon as Juke had counted out the money, the biddy plucked a key from a frock pocket, showed her guests where the privy was, then retired, chuckling to herself.

Jack was already tucked on the top bunk by the wall, sound asleep. Jatta had lit a candle stub so as not to bump her boy while manoeuvring him to bed. She would climb up, to pen him in. But she sat for now, blocking the lower bunk.

'Your sister,' she said to Juke. 'It's her eye, isn't it?'

'Never mind about that. We've other things to talk about.'

'Such as a housekeeper's murder? Osmo's housekeeper?'

Juke pulled a stool close to Jatta and squatted.

'Look, I did set the stone man free. To needle van Maanen a bit. The stone man was a bit more than I could cope with. He was Tycho Cammon, after all! So I shinned out of a window. Does that satisfy you?'

'I shan't tell your sister, Juke, I promise.' No wonder he'd been chary of promising her sanctuary in his community. 'Cuckoos don't seem to know.' *Was he touching his knife? Was she in danger?* 'What a lot of empty rooms there are in this hostel.'

'And we're sharing this one. Lie down, Princess Sariola.'

'I'm no princess any more.' Oh no, she was quite dishonoured.

'It's time, Jatta.'

Time? She knew what for. Jussi Haavio hadn't been much concerned with questioning her. Cuckoos had preoccupied him: the messengers, not their message. This moment had been building for ages now. This was the sharp tip of the arrow of Juke's interest.

'Jatta: lie and doze, and tell me how it was with you and Jarl. This is spoken. You'll talk about the climax. You must, or you'll never know what Jack is.'

Oppressed by him, she retreated within the lower bunk. Discarding his cloak and belt before quenching the candle, he swung himself in beside her. She already smelled ghostly whiffs of cinnamon, mushroom gills, roast kasta nuts. Memories.

The cuckoo had flitted ahead from henna-scaled larix to hoary sylvester tree to green-needled vera, for a key, two keys, three. She became lost in a pleasant labyrinth of trunks rising and dipping with the undulations of the land. Soft tufts and rusty rosettes and pea-green cushions carpeted the woodland floor. Not the faintest yoik to be heard. She didn't pick Mister Mushroom though she passed him many times in numerous shapes.

Of a sudden, a voice other than the cuckoo's warbled through the woodland. Such a throbbingly musical voice, such a richly human voice.

A dell cupped a modest turquoise lake. On the bank a sturdy young fellow with curly red head sang to himself out of sheer joy in a resonant baritone. He slapped his rolled-up brown breeches while he sang. On his head, a cap of the four winds, tassels of red and orange ribbons hanging from each corner. His full-sleeved embroidered shirt seemed lily-white by contrast with the golden tan of his face. His shanks and feet were bare, and of a lovely honey hue as if his whole body must be gilded.

> 'Did the saint slay the dragon?' he sang.
> 'Did the saint save the girl?
> 'Did the girl cheer the saint?
> 'Oh no, roll over!
>
> 'While the dragon lay a-dying
> 'Did the girl kiss her hero?

> 'Did the hero kiss the girl?
>   'Oh no, roll over!'

A tiny tent stood pitched nearby, its green and brown stripes almost hiding it from view. It couldn't accommodate more than one. The singing man must be quite alone. Wearing that cap, surely he was a young magician from the tundra. Off on a journey of insight. Seeking his own special tree in all the woodlands of the world – the secret tree which hadn't yet been named – in the branches of which he would fast himself to delirium till he spied the star that was his soul, till he plucked the bead of amber resin which reflected the star, and swallowed it.

Yet his face wasn't decorated with a picture of the skull beneath his skin. Nor were his hands and shanks painted with the bones underneath his flesh. And his debonair jubilant song! Maybe he'd come down weeks since from his tree of transformation to put on brawn again and become sleek. He'd swallowed his nugget of amber long since, and that hue suffused the whole of him.

The cuckoo had sped away.

> 'No, the girl loved her dragon
> 'So she spat at the saint
> 'So the saint slew the girl,
>   'Oh yes, roll over!'

Jatta descended into the dell, fascinated, her hand on the silver hilt of her knife.

'Hullo!'

The young man didn't rise. He simply slapped a cushion of moss beside him. 'Do you want to hear this story?' he invited as though Jatta's arrival was the most natural, destined thing in the world.

'Who are you?' she asked.

'Why, Jarl. Jarl Pakken.' As though she should know. As if she should have met him long since in a dream. Indeed Jatta felt that she had walked from wakefulness into a dream, crossing some boundary where no yoiking biddies or Martis and Ollis could possibly intrude. She settled some distance from the man, palm still on her knife.

'But who's Jarl Pakken?'

'I am born of dew at dawn, I'm the sweet berry that bursts from the flower.'

177

'A *nakki*?'

Surely spirits didn't show themselves like this – if spirits existed at all! Nakkis were farmwives' explanations for why milk soured, maidservants' excuses for a broken plate. Or for a stroke of luck, of course! Could all the nakkis of Kaleva have come together blissfully in this radiant young man, to present a smiling face to her, maybe to bless her?

'Nakki, no . . .' He laughed, and slapped his thighs. 'Am I woven of water, am I sewn from smoke? A man is what you see.'

A man with tufty red hair which she would love to knot her fingers in. A dimple on either side of his chin, where her little fingers could rest. A graceful nose, cupid lips, such clean teeth. This redhead wasn't speckled with freckles, not a single one that she could see. His tanned copper complexion was perfect. His eyes were green flecked with gold, and quite close set. She could smell roast kasta nuts and cinnamon and the earthy gills of mushrooms. Perhaps his skin was spun from scent.

'Do you want to hear a story never told before?'

'Never ever?' What could it be?

So Jarl Pakken told how a dragon serpent abducted a terrified maiden. But when brave Georgi turned up to rescue the maiden he found her writhing ecstatically in the dragon's embrace, besotted with her captor. Whereupon, in a fit of jealous pique, Georgi ran his sword through the woman instead of through the dragon.

In another version the dragon ate Georgi to protect the woman from her would-be rescuer's spite.

Next, Jarl told Jatta the true story of the copperman who came out of the sea to help Vai destroy an evil tree. That fellow's hat wasn't made of copper at all, nor were his boots made of copper nor his mittens nor his belt nor his axe. The man himself was made of copper. His flesh was copper, and his bones. He wore no clothes at all. When he first waded on to the shingle shore he was small and condensed – as heavy as a boulder. Then Copperman began to swell, because his copper body was wonderfully flexible . . .

Jatta listened, intoxicated, her hand soon straying from her knife to stroke the moss of this dream-dell.

Presently Jarl rose, so flexibly, and padded down to the water. He fished a glass jar out of the shallows, then another one. Orange fish roe and ginger fish roe, cool from the lake. And a pot of sour cream.

He placed the jars and the pot near to Jatta. From his tent he brought some rusks, a bowl of chopped onions, and a bottle of black mustaberry wine, its cork already pulled.

The fish eggs tasted *exquisite* on the rusks, smeared with cream, sprinkled with onion. The wine was so sweetly vibrant with just the right tangy aftermath to cleanse the palate.

'A man is what you see,' he repeated. 'Perhaps you've never seen a man before, to think me a nakki?'

Humour twinkled – a glimpse of the hilarity of a god. The saline tang of roe, the smoothness of cream, ferment of mustaberry, and the fragrance from him: oh she was banqueting, on so little and so much. She could have reached out already to brush against his lustrous skin.

No, she mustn't. Of course not. Absurd notion.

Yet dreams were absurd, were they not?

'I think you're a dream,' she said.

Immediately she regretted her words. Though what she had said was true. No other man's presence had ever affected her in remotely this manner. Certainly not on first meeting! So this was indeed like a dream where one accepts as impeccable and obvious – as unarguable – what would otherwise be challenged and resisted. Inconspicuously she touched the padded firmness of the girdle through her tunic and breeches. Still there, reassuringly there! That hadn't vanished.

'A dream?' he asked. 'In the mind of mana, perhaps? Now there's a fine fancy for a lovely lady to entertain.' His words jostled her gently, as if those were a hand he held out to tame a wild, coy foal. To coax, and conquer. Then to command.

Though not yet. Not yet. First she must become thoroughly captivated, spellbound.

Jatta found her curiosity as to *who* he was lessening – for the simple reason that *he was*. This Jarl was, unarguably – as the sun was or the sky-sickle. Nevertheless she stood up, and he nodded his approval of her decision, his understanding of this young woman whom most other people misunderstood.

'I'll be here again tomorrow morning,' he told Jatta. He spoke as if in the meantime he might simply disappear from off the face of the world.

His emphasis, *be here, be here, be here*, echoed in her mind, so that she thought those two words back at him as if it might be in *her* power to summon *him* to appear. Be here. Be here.

'I'll be here by this lake.'

He would, she would. Him and her. Their hands might well

have been clasped in a promise, their fingers interlinked, except that Jarl was still seated on the moss and she, determined to depart, wasn't touching him at all.

Roast kasta nuts and mushroom gills and cinnamon. Be here, be here.

Cinnamon.

Mushroom gills.

Nuts.

The cuckoo guided her back through the undulating woodland till she heard a granny yoik, till she spied a flash of red shawl. Hastily Jatta plucked a dozen of the nearest mushrooms and sniffed at their gills.

And on the next morning, which was foggy, Jatta slipped out of Lokka early, evading Marti and Olli without any bother. She'd brought them a large flask of spirits the evening before.

Along the same track – to follow a cuckoo through the hazy, vaporous forest – and to strain her ears for the sound of Jarl's song.

Yes, there it was:

> *'Did the snake love the girl?*
> *'Did he wind round her waist?*
> *'Bruise her breathless breasts?*
> > *'Oh yes, roll over!'*

This time her red-headed friend was lying on his back, carolling at the coiling curling fog. Mist-shrouded, she tiptoed. Beside Jarl, another bottle of wine, dry pink valleyberry this time by the look of it. A broiled truster fish lay on an impromptu platter of bark garnished with chopped mushrooms. Fish-eggs and cream yesterday, flesh and fungi today.

> 'Did the snake lick her loins
> 'With his fork of a tongue?
> 'Did his head slide inside?
> > 'Oh yes, roll over!
>
> 'Was his body as smooth
> 'And as slippery as silk?
> 'Did he flex and twist?
> > 'Oh yes, roll over!
>
> 'Was he firm as could be?
> 'Did his tail grip her knee?

'Did she moisten his neck?
    'Oh yes, roll over!'

'Jarl,' she said, 'my name's *Jatta.*' She knelt on the damp moss where he was lolling blithely, and plucked up a mouthful of crisp brown fish-skin and tender flesh. The broiled truster was still warm. She couldn't see where he had built his fire – oh, an hour before and more? It took that long. The result was deliciously sweet. Licking her fingers clean, she raised the cool bottle to her lips, the glass still slick with lake water. Or with fog.

He propped himself on an elbow, and sang jauntily:

> 'Did the snake shed his skin
> 'Owing to her juices within
> 'Thus shutting her wombdoor,
>   '*Jatta?*'

His audacity, at once languorous and carefree, was beyond any mere impudence.

'Don't be naughty,' she told Jarl. 'Did my mother send you here as a suitor? To spin stories and serenade me so brazenly?'

'No woman sent me here; nor any man either, Jatta. I'm quite free to act as I choose.'

And to do as you choose with me? Ah, no. Not with me.

She touched her knife absent-mindedly. Cinnamon and kasta nuts. And mushroom gills. He could have grown out of the ground: a huge golden king of mushrooms had become a man, a coppery-foliaged tree had sprouted legs and mellowed from solid wood to flesh to roam the forest.

'And as you choose too, of course,' he added, 'Jatta.'

You choose, you choose. Be here, be here. Choose me, choose me. Mushroom gills and cinnamon.

'Is there any more to your song?' she asked nonchalantly.

In answer his baritone burst forth:

> 'Did the maid touch her knife?
> 'Did she bare her breast?
> 'Did she prick her skin?
>   'Or else roll over?
>
> 'Did her red blood flow
> 'All down to her toe?

'Did her dark hair cascade?
'Was Jatta afraid?'

The song disoriented her ever more.

Those motes of gold in his green eyes, so close set for peering deep within her. Those blushing twin bows of his lips – was she herself flushing hectically? Such dainty nibbly teeth. His tongue, almost cherry in hue – an organ choked with blood, firmly flexible – thrust words like sprouting seed into her open ears, into her mind.

How coolly clammy the fogged air was. Reptilian. Yet his heat: she warmed herself before the oven of his presence. His hair was wiry flames. Gold melted in his eyes.

'Did her heart beat fast?
'Was a lover forecast?
'In the space of a dream,
'Oh yes, roll over!'

She wrenched herself away again that morning.

Jarl wasn't holding her or even making any attempt to reach for her, except inwardly. Inside her a ghostly body, the spirit-sleeve around her aching bones, reached for him. His jaunty, sensual song was weaving such a cage of strings. One string floated here. Another, there, another elsewhere. Soon these might tie her down upon the moss. Into her mind came an image of an oval-faced, dark-haired girl corseted by a mesh of such frail-seeming strings which tugged this way and that in response to words. Strings of words commanded the movements of her limbs, and of her feelings, of her nerves, and the juices of her glands. If only she could pluck the string corset in such and such a way it would fall apart, freeing her. Those strings moved her hands and her limbs otherwise. The girl writhed, smiling, welcoming. Only her eyes were somewhat appalled.

'Will she come the next day?
'Come grey, or sun's ray?
'So what will her dragon say?
'But: roll over!'

Would she come again? Yes.

The fog was lifting, its veils fraying into a faint lemon haze. Of course Jatta was safe, quite safe. She could allow herself to feel bizarre desire welling. So she walked away from its source through the henna and viridian woods, following an obligingly fleeing cuckoo.

The third morning was sunbright once more.

No song of summoning sounded through the trees! Had Jarl Pakken packed up his tent and gone? If so, she was glad, for she would not now need to make an impossible choice, impossible because at root it was useless. She grieved in case Jarl wasn't there. Had he been a creature of her imagination, her imagination was now the emptier. From behind the chalky bark of a sylvester tree she peered at the lake.

Jarl stooped, kneedeep and naked, throwing handfuls of water over his shoulder, rinsing himself clean. He straightened up and stared at the far shore. A golden man. So beautiful. So foreign to her, so disconcerting.

Flee, Jatta, flee!

Now why would she wish to run away?

Come, Jatta, be here.

With the surety of a sunrise, his penis arose of its own impetus, a pointer swelling stiffly – quivering, shuddering. Oh so was she too, at this sight. His right hand gloved that cock of his. His fist slid to and fro, till soon, so soon, seed spurted. Jatta relaxed, breathed out.

Jarl's solitary massage of himself had been so *natural*, so purificatory. Yes, pure. And reassuring. It expressed joyous vitality. But a man wasn't a ram who could tup a herd of ewes fifty times in a morning – as she'd gathered from the jokes of grannies. Had Jarl wanted her to see his performance? And to be . . . reassured? He was so unlike any other man she could imagine. Godlike in his indifference to the ordinary.

He turned, his manhood limp, to beckon to her.

And to sing out:

> 'Did Jatta shed her clothes?
> 'Did she romp in the lough?
> 'Did the gold splash her skin?
> 'Oh yes, roll over!'

No picnic was set out upon the shore this morning. *He* was the feast, was he not?

Laughing, she stripped to her girdle, to which he paid no attention. His organ lolled diminutively, a harmless thumb without a bone, slack and stumpy. Ginger pubic hair was a tangled wet

183

ribbon. His seed pouch was tight as two shrivelled russet apples. No, she wasn't giving it more than a glance. The polished contoured copper of his chest . . .

Under her bare, flooded feet, her toes moulded sand. Jarl held out his hand. Together, they waded until their waists were hidden. They ducked neck-deep and bobbed up close together. Puréed kasta nut and mushroom gills . . .

He was lifting her almost effortlessly, he was carrying her ashore. It was as if great soft wings bore her, with delicacy and power. His lustrous satin skin, so warm.

His cupid lips were kissing her, a nectar-eater feasting on flowers, as he laid her down upon a bed of moss. His mouth roved to her nipples. His fingers stroked her thighs. She moaned. Her palms patted his shoulders as if his flesh might burn her. That golden crucible was melting her. Between her legs she was moist, but she was safe in spite of her weakness, in spite of her yielding. He would never breach her defence, and never breach her. All wasn't stripped away, no not all.

His odour intoxicated as much as his touch. She glimpsed that naked girl writhing in the web of strings which were words and caresses, turning this way, that way, unable, unwilling to resist.

No, that wasn't a net. It was some strange revealing garment clinging tight to the girl's whole body, manipulating her just as Jarl manipulated Jatta herself, his limbs coiling around her, soft and so strong.

> 'Did the girl turn her back?
> 'Whatever did she lack
> 'But a thumb in the crack?
> > 'Oh yes, roll over!'

She lay on her breasts as he raised her hips, kissing her, whispering in a fast slurred voice which seemed dazed by desire. What was he but desire itself? The tumult in her mind deafened her to his hot jumbled words. Unbelievably, she felt her girdle sliding free from her, slipping away, exposing her assailable nakedness.

His hips covered hers.

'How?' she gasped.

She gasped again as the shaft of his loins slid deep within her tenderness to inflame her.

Soon the whole land was loving her. A glory of joy flooded Jatta. She clawed the moss as a cat might, revelling in its own muscles. Her nerves glowed; she moaned. The centre of her was the crucible now, cupping hot gold, melting that gold to flow through her belly, through her fiery veins, and as delirious vapour into her brain.

Unseen behind her, upon her, Jarl pressed and caressed. His nakki rod drove the engine of her body steadily towards a bright exquisite spasm, to be clutched by her buttocks.

This was only the first aspect of her panting ascent to some ecstatic astonishing summit. Was this ordinary? Was this usual between a man and a maid? How could it be? No, she was *possessed*. Surely mana was co-operating with his desires. This ravisher was indispensable to her.

'Jatta, Jatta, wake up.'

She was squeezed in a bunk, fully dressed. A hand shook her.

'Jarl?' she mumbled. 'Jarl?'

The candle was glowing again. Juke had roused her.

'I know who Jarl must have been, my fine lady,' he whispered. 'With his golden skin, and those twin dimples in his chin – what else were those but scent glands? And his stories of seductive serpents. He was a Juttahat.'

Juke might as well have thrown icy water in her face.

'No! That's impossible.'

'Is it?' he sneered.

'Juttahat don't look like Jarl did. Their eyes have haws like a cat's.'

'Cut out. Or never allowed to grow in your lover.'

'Their chin glands drip—'

'Suppressed in him somehow.'

'Their eyes are golden. Their hands and toes are webbed. They're *aliens*!'

Juke's hand clamped her shoulder.

'*Listen*: your Jarl Pakken must have been bred by the Isi, or dreamed up by them, or however they go about farming their Juttahat slaves—'

'No, no . . .'

'—with the aim of seducing a daughter of Lucky's, what else? Ah yes, something else indeed! To make her pregnant with a half-breed of Juttie and human.' He jerked his thumb aloft. 'Him up there. Jack. If only van Maanen had known the half of it. Not any old mutant as a lover, nothing as trivial. A freaking Juttie. That could have been you and your boy on the bonfire instead of Cammon, Jatta.'

'That's insane! Jutties are slaves. Jarl was free. He could act as he chose.' Jatta felt she was suffocating, squashed inside this bunk as if it was a coffin, and Juke's body the lid, eclipsing the feeble candlelight and about to close on her.

'In that case he was a very special specimen of Juttahat. I think Juttie brats normally grow up very fast, more like animals than men.'

Jatta grasped at any straw. 'How can an alien breed with a woman? Can a hervy breed with a cow?'

'The serpents made him that way. No woman sent me, nor any man, remember?' His voice mocked. 'Conniving Isi sent him, that's who. They knew a way of magicking your precious girdle open.'

Juke's diagnosis of her fast boy's origin was so cruel. So barbarous. His words had slapped her face; they punched her in the womb.

'You're just saying this because you killed van Maanen's mistress so sneakily! And I know about it – so you're trying to drive me mad!' She struck back at him from the confines of the bunk awkwardly with her fist, and lashingly with her tongue: 'You're in love with your mutie sister, you virgin! You tell lies to yourself – and to me!'

He seized her wrist and pressed her backward. He was snorting like that frantic hervy.

'So rape me,' she yelled in his darkened face, 'and get in some practice. Rape the girl who last opened her legs to a Juttie! Maybe Jarl put something in there besides his seed! Something to burn you up and shrivel you. Then your sister'll be safe.'

Uuuuunnngh, was the bestial noise Juke made. A wordless moan.

'Why don't you strangle me as well? Before, or after! Jarl, *Jarl*, you possessed me!' she cried. 'You still possess me!'

It was Jack who was trying to strangle someone. Jack had shinned down from the upper bunk. With his little hands Jack was clutching her persecutor by the neck.

'Stay!' snarled Juke. 'Little devil, get off me!'

The mutant proclaimer was shuddering violently, his grip on Jatta slackening. Jack's pull was affecting him, as if the boy had the strength of a man, as though the man's own strength was being turned against him.

'This is spoken, this is spoken,' Juke roared. 'I'll turn you to jelly, I'll annihilate you.'

Jatta wrenched her hand free. Should she stab Juke in the eye with a finger?

Jarl, Jarl! Her desire, rekindled by the telling in slumber, went out to him wherever.

The room brightened; the door was wide open.

Granny stood with a candelabrum in one hand – four flames dancing side by side. In her other hand was a stout stick. She thrashed this against the pot-bellied stove, a wooden clapper clanging against a bell. She was wearing a shapeless nightgown and slippers. But no eye-patch.

'Disgrace, disgrace!' she bawled. 'I'll fine you, so I will. Haven't you any decency? I definitely said no hanky-panky. Thirty pennies for Granny. Otherwise you're out on the street right now.'

The furrowed old woman brandished her stick. Deep inside her left eye socket, mounted in some spidery silver clamp, her opal flashed green and blue in the backwash of candlelight. The jelly of her peeper might have shrunk down to the dimensions of that stone, its humours drying out and hardening.

Juke stared at the gem in horror.

Though Jack still clung piggyback, Juke stumbled away from the bunk. Muttering pleas to her to leave them be, he counted out three tenpenny pieces into Granny's hand. He avoided meeting her one-eyed, one-opal gaze.

Granny wasn't sure whether to feel mollified or justified in further indignation.

'Yes, well,' she said. 'I'll call the watch if there's any more bother.'

Jack craned past Juke's head. 'Why do you have that shiny stone in your head? Is it a bit of your brain?'

'*Nakki-spawn!*' the ancient concierge yelped. Dropping her stick, she clapped a liver-spotted hand over the little treasure cave in her head as if the boy might dart little fingers in to thieve.

Her candelabrum swaying perilously, she beat a retreat.

Jack slid down from Juke's back. Jatta lay gnawing on a knuckle. Chastened and shamefaced, she and Juke regarded each other.

'You angryangryangry?' warbled the boy.

'No, we aren't,' Jatta said, with tears in her eyes. 'We just hurt each other a lot because that's what people sometimes do when they open their mouths.'

'Words bite,' agreed Juke. He was shaking.

Jack rushed from door to window and back and around and around the table, a pygmy whirlwind. 'Me hungryungryungry!'

In the morning, one of the log-drivers who had hoisted the hervy's head arrived at the hostel. He'd been sent by Pappi Jussi Haavio to fulfil the promise of transportation downriver.

The log-driver did not conduct the three travellers further along Satama Street to the harbour, though. He led them in the opposite direction.

Jatta and Juke and the boy were to sail down the lower reaches of the Kitajoki not in the cabin of some boat or even on the deck, but by working their way on a raft of logs. A raft with a bright-red steering sail to warn oncoming vessels, and long poles to keep clear of the bank. No cuckoo could have brought any news from the bishop in Tumio overnight.

PART TWO

POET
AND
PASSIONS

15 · AN EYE FOR AN EYE

Eyeno sat outside the ramshackle dwelling at midnight on her favourite stone. She was rereading her latest poem in the wash of silvery light from the sky-sickle which had once, aeons before, been Kaleva's moon.

The sloping sweep of the sickle dominated the clear southern sky. It arched low from horizon to horizon and beyond, quenching stars with its brilliance. Some people regarded that curve of light as a great ice-bridge in the sky under which the black river of death must pass. Others saw it as a bubbling mercurial viaduct down which mana spilled sparklingly from out of the cosmos. As if mana could be visible.

If she squinted her right eye she would espy the illusion of a giant world in almost full eclipse. The upper limb of such a world, at least. Seemingly a huge planet hung adjacent to Kaleva. Light spilled around its vast dark camber. Her own Kaleva could only be a little moon accompanying that colossal phantom globe. Eyeno would strain to discern faint partial shapes of oceans and continents on that wraith-world which no one else saw.

Her inward eye saw it, the eye hidden inside her head.

What did her *other* eye see? Her imitation eye, which occupied her left eye-socket? That false eye of Juttahat manufacture? Why, it saw nothing at all of which she was aware.

Sickle-light laid bare a rugged, tangled landscape of jutting cloven rocks and trees. Trees thrust from amongst great boulders. Trees sprouted up from cracks. Bygone winter storms or weight of snow had tumbled many such trees from their precarious nooks. Some were locked together in death. Others flourished at a slant. Thousands more stood to attention downslope for as far as any eye could see.

Sickle-light shone on the raggy thatch and shingles of nearby cotts and barns. Mocky-houses, with mocky-people in them. This settlement, Outo, comprised a hundred such homes.

The sickle-light also gleamed on the pages in Eyeno's hands. The words thus illuminated were large enough and bold enough to read by night, the letters rotundly formed like necklaces of moons.

Eyeno thought she understood eclipses and moons well enough, even though she had never seen the disc of a moon or an eclipse gnawing it. The notion of an actual moon fascinated her: a neighbour world, a twin in the sky such as the original home of humankind had possessed.

Her latest poem was about a moon. She had called the poem *Otherwhys*; and now she read it over to herself once again by sickle-light, wondering whether it was suitable to recite at the gala.

She had all the words in her memory, but actually reading those aloud in this silvery light – this offspring of ancient moon-light – might reveal faults. Her poem should be perfect. If brother Juke was going to proclaim at Speakers' Valley this year, why so was she in her own silkier way: the way not of power-words which could impose one's will, but of poetry which might enchant the soul.

> '*Why does Sun?*' she read aloud slowly.
> '*Why, Moon?*
> '*Ah, those are two different whys.*
>
> '*One why is of gaseous fire*
> '*—Trembling meniscus*
> '*On gravity's deep pool.*
> '*The other why, of that harem-captive*
> '*Marble odalisque*
> '*—Body of passive stone*
> '*So cold while Sun's gaze*
> '*Is turned away, yet*
> '*Agonizedly incandescent*
> '*If caressed.*
>
> '*Worlds are only moons of a Sun;*
> '*Yet the lover, the empress,*
> '*Visits her World daily*
> '*Not fortnightly*
> '*In rotation.*
>
> '*Sun's touch warms World,*
> '*Does not scald.*
> '*Hence that jealousy*
> '*Of Moon towards World,*

'Envy that steals the breath
'Away, crusting acne
'On Moon's skin.

'Moon would throw stones at World,
'Flail World with the hair
'Of comets . . .'

Would connoisseurs of words understand? Only immigrants
from Earth had ever seen a real moon. (You couldn't count an
Ukko up in orbit; it looked no larger than a lamp rushing by in
the distance.) That glowing band of rocks and stones and dust
was all that most people knew about a moon. Its debris. How did
Kaleva's one-time moon become debris? Long ago, it spiralled
too close and was torn apart. She at least knew that. But then,
she had been able to read a book.

'Why else,' Eyeno read on, 'does Moon conspire
'To seed nightmares?
'For Moon is vexed
'If Sun is peering elsewhere
'—Staring avidly out
'At those others
'Whom Sun truly adores:
'Sun's flame-sisters
'Stars lost so far away
'Except to a gaze
'Always centuries
'Out of date.

'Why, is the sigh
'Of the sea-tide seduced
'By bitter Moon . . .'

And on Kaleva there were no such tides as on Earth. Once,
there *would* have been tides. Seas would have surged. The largest
lakes might have lapped and slurped. But then Kaleva's moon
shattered and spread out in a ring around the world's waist,
further out from that waist than twice the world's width. In her
room under the raggy reed-thatched eaves, Eyeno treasured half
a dozen volumes which were tatty with thumbing, their pages
breaking loose. She owned three giant compendiums of verse.
She owned a dictionary. And the *Book of the Land of Heroes* –
which she used for fortune telling. There was also an ancient
volume about stars and moons and worlds.

'One day,' she resumed, 'Moon will plunge
'Into warm World,
'Shattering herself
'In a rapturous and
'Forced embrace.

'What shall issue
'From this genocidal union?
'Eventually, some aeons afterwards?
'Perhaps a new race
'Of tortoise-roaches,
'Of armoured ants
'—Or of sapient spiders
'That dream
'And ask why.

'Yet one why will be missing
'From their understanding
'—Being sunk in the bowl
'Of a new ocean
'Around which the breasts
'Of lunar mountains rear.'

And that was it.

Her fat book about worlds contained pictures of tortoises and ants and spiders and roaches. Instead of *spiders* should she refer to hammockis, spinners of nets which could coat a field with dewy floss of a spring morning . . . ? Ach, her poem was about a different world than this one. It was about an Earth and a moon of *almost* and *never*, an invisible world within the embrace of the sky-sickle.

Perhaps a new race . . .

. . . of mutant things. Muties. Mocky-folk.

Who all slumbered just now, this midnight, except for herself.

The Lord of Saari tolerated mocky-folk in this wilderness, and of course taxed them as the measure of his tolerance. Lord Johann Helenius took tithes from their economy of goats. The mocky-folk paid him with animals and cheeses and kid gloves. Since earliest adolescence, Juke and Eyeno had helped drive the tribute and other saleable beasts and produce all the long way from Outo and neighbouring Halvek to Niemi or Threelakes or Saari itself. Juke and his sister were presentable mocky-folk.

Juke was completely so. Eyeno had become so to all appearances now that she wore a plausible false eye.

Where was her brother, this midnight? Sleeping in his cloak on some lake shore? In a bed in a hostelry? If only her inward eye would show him to her. Yet what the eye inside of her skull almost always saw, albeit hazily, was vistas of lacy trees, lush meadows, bubbling streams, creamy waxen flowers, gauzily-clad young maidens laughing and skipping and dancing.

Could it be that inside her head she was spying upon blissful pastures of death where echo-souls sported for as long as their bones endured in the soil? What her inward eye perceived was a beauty so poignant that she must needs prevent most of it from spilling into verse, or else her lines would be too sweet by far, cloying and winsome. Fortunately for her poems, the terrain around Outo was severe and rugged – goat-land. And her mocky-folk kin were grotesque.

Except for her brother, of course. Except for Juke who craved power through words, and honour. Whom she loved; whom she feared for.

Eyeno gazed at the sky-sickle a while longer, then went yawning into the ramshackle cott to climb creaky stairs as quietly as she could.

That night once more she dreamt the memory-dreams of how she had gained her false eye.

It was as if, while she slept, that imitation eyeball of Juttahat manufacture was peering within her, obsessively rummaging through the same set of recollections associated with its own origin. Eyeno did sometimes wonder whether this *bauble* of the serpents possessed some ulterior (or more properly, interior) purpose aside from its role as a skilfully matched and comfy filler for her empty socket. Serpents were such unpredictable creatures; though they did grant favours. Maybe Eyeno's mild worry on this score was what prompted her dreams to search for some hidden motive which might well not exist at all.

Her memory-dreams usually followed the sequence of actual events faithfully for a while, then spun permutations. Well, dreams usually sprouted legs and ran off wilfully in their own chosen direction. She dreamed the dreams perhaps once a week. As the dreamer she remained aware – though in an uncritical fashion – of discrepancies between what had actually happened, and the dream variations.

What a quest hers had been, for the imitation eye. A true quest. *Her* quest; her own. No wonder she dreamed of it, the unmind of slumber fertilely embellishing what her waking mind had experienced, the imagination of sleep concocting event-poems.

Eyeno had been born to Arto and Ester Nurmi almost as wonderfully well-formed as her brother Juke, who had been born a year earlier. The baby girl's left eye was missing, that was all.

Glove-maker Arto possessed six slim functional fingers on each hand. His legs were short and bowed. His ears were as long and pointy as a goat's, with hearing which was preternaturally acute. Each creak and groan of the cott, every sigh of wind through a crack, was a familiar spirit to Arto. That was why he could never endure the thought of any improvement or genuine repair. His home was growing older along with him. When he finally succumbed, so might the house likewise, to a storm. Until then it would hold out.

In this regard Arto resembled the other mocky-folk who lived in Outo. For a swathe of reasons they all neglected their dwellings.

'Look poor; pay less tax.'

'This cott's no more warped than me.'

'You want to look like some Prince of Outo lording it in your palace?'

'We knows our place; an' our place knows us.'

'Keeps the Jutties away.'

'Saarifolk would get riled if they didn't feel *vastly* grander than us.'

When Eyeno first saw smart, tiled houses at Niemi she could hardly believe her eye and thought fancifully that those might be dwellings where the maidens of her inward vision lived.

Her plump hirsute mother Ester had the eyes of a goat, with rectangular pupils. Ester's sense of smell was as keen as Arto's hearing. Eyeno's mother wouldn't sweep or scrub a familiar odour out of the cott. On that score she saw eye to eye – rectangular pupil to rounded pupil – with Arto. The cott was her den.

Shortly after Eyeno's birth the crookbacked wisewoman from Halvek examined the baby girl. She diagnosed that the missing eye was inside of the baby's head, within her brain. The lurking eye ought to be reminded of its absence from the usual place. It shouldn't be left in the dark but be encouraged. Or else it might harden. It might turn to stone and give the girl megrims.

Hence the choice of name for the baby. Eyeno. Naturally such a name caused the growing girl to be preoccupied by that hollow in her cranium in a way which otherwise mightn't have occurred to quite the same degree. Surrounded in Outo by many varied distortions of the human form, in what way was her deformity unique? Ester seemed almost comforted by her daughter's absent orb. *Two* perfect offspring could have amounted to impudence. Eyeno's flaw, emphasized by her name, redeemed the Nurmi family.

So Juke and Eyeno grew up, and played hide and seek among the mazes of boulders, and they herded goats. Ester made cheeses of subtle delicacy which were powerfully pungent to her. Arto nimbly sowed soft gloves of four fingers and a thumb apiece for ladies of the court at Saari a hundred keys distant and more. Eyeno began to glimpse dancing damsels with her inward eye. Juke began to proclaim – at recalcitrant goats to begin with. His powerful words quickened beauty-words in his sister, words inspired by phantom meadows and by the sky-sickle.

One day, squash-headed, bulgy-eyed Arni (who could only hear voices and no other noises) told Eyeno he suspected she was a poetess. The mocky-man brought from his cott a brass box containing a stained leather-bound *Book of the Land of Heroes* and began to teach her to read the runes, to figure out the letters. Arni had learned to write to help his brother Kuro who could hear the bleats of goats and the whistle of the wind but no human speech at all. Kuro was thin-headed, sunken-eyed, web-fingered. Arni would chalk any important communication on a slate for Kuro. Kuro would lay a webbed palm on the slate and, thanks be to mana, absorb the import. Kuro never framed a syllable with his lips yet he would guide Arni's hand to inscribe a reply.

Together Arni and Kuro guided Eyeno to read and write.

Presently Pieman, whose skin resembled crusty pastry all over, returned from a goat-droving trip to Saari with a bundle of yellowed old paper, and pencils too. In Saari he'd been laughed at for such purchases. Just the sort of thing a mutie would need! Maybe he was going to make a paper bag to cover himself?

Pieman was thick-skinned, but the mockery he'd endured led soon enough to Juke, now fourteen – and his thirteen-year-old sister – becoming the front-people for the communities of Outo and Halvek in their relations with the wider realm of Saari. Fellow mocky-men would accompany Juke and Eyeno and the

197

goats and the gloves and the cheeses for most of a journey. Then the mocky-men would bivouack out of sight. The two Nurmi siblings would proceed onward into towns. No normal folk stared askance at Juke or made jinx signs. No kids threw fish heads. And Juke could direct a herd of goats ably with his words.

As for Eyeno, she was growing long-limbed without gawkiness. Juke's hair was fawn and greasy, but hers was silky and yellow. Her single eye was a less vivid blue than his two eyes – which caused less of a shock that there was only one on view. Her skin was creamy, with a few milk-chocolate moles on her cheeks and neck – those seemed adornments rather than blemishes. Her features were dainty though determined, almost provocative in their poise. The lack of a left eye, the limp-lidded hollow of the socket, was unsettling rather than nauseating. It served her as a protection. A stranger's gaze would slide off her rather than him ogling her.

Goat-drovings infected Juke with a taste for wandering and a growing vexation at the lack of respect for mocky-men. He certainly counted himself as a mocky-man. Arto and Ester had raised their two children devotedly. Often their son or daughter found a lucky almond hidden in their rice pudding. No, he would not desert the community.

Eyeno began to yearn for a false eye at the same time as she composed her first real poems, a cycle of bittersweet lyrics on the theme of eyes themselves. As was often the way with words, these poems impelled her to consider completing her visage by filling that hollow orbit with a suitable and attractive *globe*. (From a crypt below the mana-kirk in Threelakes she had liberated an ancient dust-covered volume on worlds and suns and moons, globes all of them – just as eyes were globes.)

This ambition in no way marked a desire to alienate herself from her mocky kin, and mother and father, or a wish to pass as a pure person (though this had its uses to the community) but rather a commitment to the idea that her own peculiar poetic perception – her illuminatory perception – deserved some proudly worn token, worn where nature had already set a frame, allowing Eyeno herself to choose the trinket.

Meanwhile, the one-eyed girl also told fortunes, not only in Outo and Halvek, but when droving took her further, in Niemi and Threelakes and Saari. An enquirer must, with their fingertip, choose five random words from that *Book of the Land of Heroes* which Arni had given her. Eyeno would invite a short poem to compose itself. Fortunes were poems by another name. Poems were fortunes, though in an allusive way quite unlike the proclaiming which Juke was striving to master.

In the first memory-dream Eyeno, at the age of sixteen, was visiting a glassmaker in Niemi. Niemi was southernmost of the three principal towns in the straggling domain of Saari. It was certainly poorer than either Threelakes or Saari itself, though Eyeno hadn't thought so initially. Compared with the village of Outo, Niemi appeared sumptuous.

White-painted wooden houses with tiled roofs – the paintwork not peeling too scabbily. Gravelled streets. A few fountains which might yet spout again. Shops and a market, a public hall and a mana-kirk. The town occupied an upthrust of land which lined the northern flank of Lake Lasinen with modest cliffs. A promontory housed a tumbledown keep. Zig-zagging flights of steps, a snaking roadway, and a rusty funicular railway (which always seemed out of action) linked the town proper with a long sandy lakeside strip of boatsheds, fishermen's shanties, and sauna huts. The serene lake, often as smooth as a mirror, was landlocked, though there was desultory talk of a ten-key-long canal to link it to the artery of the Murame river, thus with Threelakes and Saari.

This glassmaker was a sweaty balding tub of a man. His surviving slicked hairs seemed likely to float away soon enough from his scalp. He was also a genial fellow, otherwise his products might have fractured. He was happy to turn his hand to Eyeno's commission. He too had a daughter who was quite a beauty. The glassmaker could sympathize with what he presumed was Eyeno's motive for wanting a false eye.

'My little hen'll find herself a fine nest,' he boasted, there in his workshop amongst barrels of sand and potash and soda, furnace and moulds and marvering slab.

'No less than the Dame of Niemi's own son has kissed my hen at a dance, quite ruffling her feathers,' he bragged. 'He's a handsome lad, that Minkie Kennan. Has quite a way with him. The Kennans have fallen on hard times, 'tis true, what with Minkie's dad making himself so many enemies as he had to run away for years – then Ragnar Kennan got himself killed anyway. Their keep's a bit of a ramshackle. But I say as a keep's a keep, and it's breeding that counts, don't you think?'

Eyeno emphatically didn't think so, except in the negative

sense that mocky-men counted for very little indeed. However, she understood discretion.

'The Dame's a tough bird, so we'll all see better times when young Minkie gets in his stride. We'll have our canal at last.'

Did Eyeno know what a paperweight was?

She did not.

The glassmaker, Mr Ruokokoski, hastened to fetch a hemisphere of glass from a cupboard. The bulging little dome filled Eyeno's palm, weighing heavy. Deep inside, hundreds of tiny bright flowers gleamed. It was the loveliest creation she had ever seen – a lyric in glass, enduring, immortal, the souls of all those flowers perfectly preserved. The fat, sweaty man deserved a poem for showing her this. But what flowers were those?

'Ach no, those are slices from rods of coloured glass,' explained Mr Ruokokoski. 'You gather molten glass from pots of different colours. You roll, you marver, you do that all over again, right? You mould your layered glass into a star shape, you pull the star out into a rod, let it cool, and cut. You arrange your pattern in a pan the size of the paperweight, pour clear glass, knock the pan off, reheat and shape; gather another clear layer then reshape with a wooden paddle, right?'

Right; and if he told her half a dozen times more the process might become perfectly clear.

> *The marver man,* she thought,
> *Paddles in a lake of molten glass,*
> *And fishes out rainbow flowers.*

Such 'paperweights', he said, had once been used by people who could read, to stop breezes blowing their pieces of paper around. Using just such a technique of paperweight-making he could embed a black pupil within a blue iris within an eye-socket-size paperweight.

'Couldn't I have a flower inside, instead?' Eyeno asked him. 'A single, lovely flower? A daisy?'

'You'd look odd.'

But I am odd, she thought.

As to the price, how about a fortune for his daughter?

'No, not in money!' Mr Ruokokoski laughed. 'A fortune in words.'

She *was* the fortune-telling goatherd, wasn't she? He wanted the fortune told to *him* privately, not to his pretty little hen.

*

Eyeno and Juke were staying in a decrepit hostel which out-ranked their own home in Outo by several rungs. What a surprise it would be for her brother to see her with an eternal glass daisy in her right eye, a corolla of white petals for an iris around a golden pupil. Next noon, she hurried back to the glassmaker's, clutching her box containing the *Book of the Land of Heroes*.

The paperweight eye was ready. It perched upon a china eggcup, tilted so that the daisy eye looked at her when she first entered the hot workshop.

'The actual glass flower's quite small,' explained Mr Ruokoko-ski proudly. 'Magnification swells it.'

With thumb and forefinger she prised her sunken eyelids apart. He inserted the paperweight for her. How solid and how enormous the glass eye felt. Released, her lids clasped it.

He held up a mirror.

Beautiful, yes. A poem of a pupil, and iris. The majority of the eyeball was clear glass so that a flower seemed to float in that small cave in her head. Did it matter that the effect might be disconcerting? People wore tattoos, did they not? A poem ought to disconcert a little, otherwise it was banal.

Time to settle accounts. Mr Ruokokoski summoned his daughter from the house behind the workshop.

Ellen Ruokokoski proved to be a whimsical wisp of a teenager of undoubted fragile beauty. Large-eyed, her flaxen hair in pig-tails, Ellen looked as though she habitually starved herself in case she put on lard like her father. A necklace of lovely glass beads complemented a loose, low-cut cream frock. She glanced once, twice, then a haunted third time at Eyeno's daisy eye.

Eyeno placed the leather volume on the iron marvering slab where glass was rolled. At Eyeno's bidding Ruokokoski's daughter opened the book at random, and dipped her finger on to a different page, five times. Silently Eyeno read the words that the girl's fingernail touched. As each word entered Eyeno's imagina-tion that word leapt to join its companions in a dance within her mind, a dance which summoned other words to join it willy-nilly.

In spite of Ellen's protests her father dismissed her.

'What's my little hen's fortune?' he asked when Ellen had gone.

The verse spun in Eyeno's mind. She already heard it clearly in her head. Sometimes a fortune-poem took her quite by sur-prise. She didn't know what it would be till she uttered it. On this occasion she knew; and what she overheard disconcerted it.

If only the verse had organized itself differently! Alas, it hadn't. Such was the way with fortune-verses. There was mana in words taken from that book.

'Sometimes,' she warned, 'words use a person – rather than a person using words. This verse has put itself together of its own accord. Do you understand that?'

'I'm all ears.'

So she recited, stressing those words taken from the book:

> '*Simpering* daughter, dancing, *kissing*,
> 'Father finding daughter missing,
> 'Comes the *rascal* from the *tower*,
> '*Thinking* only to deflower.'

Mr Ruokokoski was very much taken aback.

'You're jealous of my little hen's prospects, that's the nub of it!' The fat man fulminated. 'Deflower, deflower indeed? Decent girl like Ellen. I've a mind to deflower *you*!'

Not sexually. No, simply by demanding the return of the glass eye. The glassmaker held out his hand. He glared. He accused her of false pretences. Of abusing his kindness. Mischief-making mutie, that's what. He would summon the watch.

Her lower lid drooped and tears leaked. When she squeezed out the eye, Ruokokoski placed his creation on the marvering slab. With a heavy hammer he hit the bauble, shattering it into pieces, liberating the daisy which was suddenly so much smaller. Bye-bye, eye.

And this event was true . . .

In her dream she fled from his workshop without surrendering the paperweight. Guided by her false eye she chased a trail of daisies through the town. Larger, creamy blooms appeared ahead of her, then disappeared once she reached them. More flowers materialized ahead. Those promised that she must soon arrive at a meadow where maidens could dance without fear of assault or mischief.

Instead she came to a halt on the clifftop overlooking the calm mirror of Lake Lasinen. The dream-cliffs were so tall, far higher than Niemi's real bluffs. This cliff she stood atop was a plunging precipice. The lake was so far below. Nor did any beach exist with cabins and shanties and boat sheds. Rock dived directly into water. Underwater, there spread a meadow dotted with a million milky blooms.

Eyeno pitched herself forward, cartwheeling down. Poems took

202

wing as she fell, a stream of white birds with black words written on them, deserting her.

In her second dream she was at Threelakes. The cloverleaf lobes of the triple lake reflected a sky of blue porcelain. A fine purple tammywood bridge straddled the narrow neck of the southern lobe. This bridge joined the older stone town with the newer wooden town, which housed a fair number of settlers who had been born on Earth. Some of those settlers could still speak tongues other than Kalevan. Occasional flurries of exotic words at first intrigued then disappointed Eyeno – there seemed to be no mana in such babble.

Some mocky-folk of Halvek had been panning gold from a river in the wilderness, so they entrusted Juke and Eyeno with the task of turning the accumulated grains and morsels into coin on their next droving trip. The brother and sister were less likely to be cheated, less likely to stir up resentment that outcasts had access to a little wealth. In spite of the derelict appearance of settlements such as Halvek and Outo, mocky-folk weren't out and out paupers. This fact wasn't to be advertised.

Thus Juke and Eyeno exchanged a fat leather pouch of grits and bits for a passably plump purse of silver marks at Missieur Pierre's establishment in the Street of Crafts.

He was a jeweller by trade, a dehydrated spidery fellow with long bony fingers and a long thin nose on which magnifying spectacles rested. His whole physiology seemed to plead straitened circumstances, despite the evidence of trays of glinting rings and brooches.

His premises were of stone, with stout shutters for the windows. By day a wary if quiet Spitz hound lay chained to a kennel in an adjacent yard.

How he haggled over the gold. Business was dire, even if he did travel by appointment to the court at Saari with his trays of gems. Frivolous ladies craved jewels to wear, but sensible ones favoured paste. Sometimes frivolous customers likewise preferred paste since then a jewel could be more ostentatious.

Paste? What was paste? Why, paste jewels were false ones made of glass backed with quicksilver and coloured with metallic oxides. A lot of lead oxide in the glass increased the lustre, so said Missieur Pierre.

Did Missieur Pierre produce this paste himself? No, he bought it all to cut and polish from a *verrier* in Niemi. A glassmaker.

'Would that be from Mr Ruokokoski?' asked Eyeno. It was a full year since she had watched the peeved glassmaker shatter her paperweight.

So she knew Ruokokoski? Shame about his daughter – not that Missieur Pierre was one to gossip. A visitor (by appointment) to court should be discreet. Still, Ruokokoski wasn't exactly high-born, and now his little *poulet* never would be noble. In Missieur Pierre's original lingo *chicken* also, aha, meant *love-letter* – not that this charming young one-eyed lady currently visiting his premises would likely know what a love-letter *was*.

On his sister's behalf Juke flushed at this slur. Temper smouldered in her brother. Anger threatened to flare until the jeweller clarified his meaning: that people generally didn't send *amatory epistles* to each other since they could neither write 'em nor read 'em. Back on Earth – at least when he'd quit that festering, overcrowded world – thinking machines half the size of your palm did most of the reading to people who cared to be read to. If this brother and his sister cared a hoot about the old homeworld.

But Eyeno could indeed read.

And what was this about Ruokokoski's little hen?

The little hen had hatched an egg, if they took Missieur Pierre's meaning. The cock who took advantage of the hen was reportedly none other than the Dame of Niemi's son, Minkie Kennan, just sixteen years old and handsome as hell but certainly not intending to be a husband too soon. Nor would his strong-minded mother want her family's honour scratched by alliance with a glassmaker's daughter . . .

Later, Eyeno returned on her own to Missieur Pierre's to negotiate for a bright eye made out of paste. A savoury smell wafted downstairs from his apartment.

'It wasn't by any chance *you*,' he asked, 'who cursed Ruokokoski? He mentioned a one-eyed mutie girl.'

'Cursed? I did no such thing!' protested Eyeno.

'I thought all muties were fearful freaks. You, on the other hand . . .' The dry, spidery jeweller inclined his head gallantly.

'I thought Mr Ruokokoski was affable – at least until he lost his temper after he heard his Ellen's fortune.'

'Her pregnancy soured him.'

'And *he* couldn't be to blame for stupid negligence. So he blames me instead. I see.'

'Whereas you were actually warning him?'

'I was saying the words that came into my head.'

Eyeno had predicted Ruokokoski's misfortune quite comprehensibly if only the glassmaker could have accepted what he was hearing from her. Possibly – no guarantees, only likelihoods – she could perform a similar service for the jewellery trade. She wasn't greedy; an eye made of paste would be fine. To carry a real gem in her eye socket could be a risky proceeding, not that any genuine gemstone would be likely to fill up that space.

But if a fine jewel were mounted frontally on a sphere of thin copper hoops? suggested Missieur Pierre. He scented a possible tour de force of craftsmanship.

No, no, she wanted a false jewel for a false eye; and one as big as an eyeball.

In exchange for a simple little piece of prophecy?

However, Missieur Pierre was definitely impressed by the words she had uttered to Ruokokoski. The jeweller would like his fortune told, as comforter or as caution.

Missieur Pierre brooded. 'Business is bad. I have to feed the dog and me. And a woman. Do you see how lean I am? So do I really need my fortune told? Better to have some of the marks back that I lavished on your gold dust.'

Eyeno sniffed the aroma of cookery appreciatively, so that he would be aware she knew otherwise about his finances.

'We had to pay all our community's tithes to the Saari bailiff's office, Mister Pierre,' she said. 'Our marks are almost all gone.' This wasn't quite true. There were also marks from goats and cheeses and gloves: some to be spent on necessities for the mocky-folk, some to be taken back and buried safely. 'I can only afford one mark, and a fortune. A paste gem's just glass, you said.'

'I still had to buy the glass from Ruokokoski in the first place. There's the skill of shaping it. Wear and tear on tools.'

Surely it was a liver casserole which was wooing her nose?

'A fortune might prove invaluable, Mr Pierre.'

'You can't guarantee it.' She could see he was hooked. 'Two marks, and a fortune,' he proposed.

'When you're getting a fortune, two marks on top is *irrelevant*.'

'One mark fifty pence, mam'sell.'

And so, early on the morning of their departure from Threelakes, Eyeno presented herself at the jeweller's. Missieur Pierre presented her with a large imitation gem three quarters nestled in a protective satin sheath. Bright rays beaming through an unshuttered front window made a glossy pool of the glass-topped counter. Rings and brooches twinkled like sunken treasure.

The exposed facets of the eye-gem sparkled blue and white and green, the predominant colour being a weak blue. Missieur Pierre held up a silver-framed mirror. Eyeno prised her lids apart and pressed the false eye into place.

One eyeball, perfectly curved. The other, faceted, without any pretence of a pupil or iris.

The effect was subtle and strange as if her left eye had crystallized. In spite of the satin a sense of intrusive bulk discomfited her. Bizarrely she thought of some faceless man pressing his swollen organ some day into the cleft between her legs, invading a different portal of her body intrusively. Bulkily. But beautifully? Small chance of that. She was sure she would never lie with any of the mocky-males of Halvek or Outo, fine fellows though those might be. As for men from other communities . . . how would they treat a daughter of the mocky-folk? No, she was wedded to *word*. To her vision of maidens in a meadow. Might one of those dancing maids be a lover to her, perhaps? Unintrusively? Delicately? The idea thrilled her. The vision of someone very like herself, a twin, embracing her gently and caressing her, beckoned to her as those maidens habitually beckoned. Someone without a rude invasive lump of meat jutting from their loins. Someone unlike a randy billy goat.

She closed her eyes – she *tried* to shut both – yet she sensed that her lids hadn't come together all the way across the hard gem. Her eye-lashes hadn't shaken hands.

Her inward eye seemed to respond to the complex prism lodged in her orbit. That visionary meadow fractured into a dozen repetitions of itself, spinning around. Gauzy-clad maidens rushed towards her and away. Towards – so she reached out. Away – so that she gasped in distress.

A thin hand clutched her. Her eyes jerked open.

'Thought you were going to faint,' said Missieur Pierre. 'It shouldn't feel painful.'

'What shouldn't . . . ?'

The gemstone had been affecting her like the fungus drug the mocky-men occasionally used to escape into a confusing kaleidoscopic beauty. She had only once ever tried the drug. The experience had made her inner eye *sore* for headachy days on end.

'The satin pads it. It's glued tight to the satin—'

'I just felt dizzy, Mister Pierre.' Yes, dizzy for the damsels . . . for their cordial soft embraces, for their wild and tender kisses.

She had laid her *Book of the Land of Heroes* on the counter. The jeweller had chosen his five words, which now cavorted in her head, summoning other words together willy-nilly.

Eyeno spoke:

> '*Flash* of emerald and sapphire,
> '*Eager* fingers would acquire,
> 'Fingers *black* and bodies velvet,
> 'Pompous *serpents* send their *pets*.'

'Do you mean,' exclaimed the jeweller, 'that Juttahats will want to buy gems for the Velvet Isi? That the snakes want sparklers?'

'I don't mean anything, Missieur Pierre. It's the verse itself that means something.'

'Why, that's wonderful news . . . except that Juttahats can't come into town . . . There'd be riots. Surely they wouldn't attack us in force here in Threelakes just to rob my shop! Should I take my wares to them? All the way north of Saari?'

'I don't know, Mister Pierre.'

'Trade with the Isi? What an idea. I might become rich!'

Eyeno left the jeweller to his excited new dream. She herself felt dizzy as she retraced her steps along the Street of Crafts, clutching her book box to her. Passers-by glanced at the sparkle in her eye.

'What happened to you?' gasped Juke.

She hadn't forewarned him.

Standing guard over several knapsacks packed with purchases in the panelled lobby of the hostel, her brother seemed as hard and angular as the faces of the false gemstone at which he gawped, befuddled.

'I bought an eye from Missieur Pierre,' she said lightly. 'I paid a mark and a half, and a fortune. Do you like it?'

'That's . . . a gemstone? So big?'

'It's just an imitation one.'

'I thought it was a growth from inside you! I thought your secret eye had forced its way out – *cut* its way out – and that's what your secret eye really looks like. A blue crystal . . . Oh Eyeno, have you been yearning for this for all these years?' His voice caught. 'I'd have pulled out my own eye if it could have taken root in you.'

She hurried to embrace him. She laughed, even as a sob shook her. How chivalrous he was.

'Then *you* would only have had one eye, dear Juke.'

Her brother held her awkwardly. His fingers strayed towards her cheek, tracing a route towards her hard false peeper. His fingertips drew back.

'Touch it if you want to, Juke.'

'No, I might put some dirt on it . . .'

His fingers were sweaty. He pulled away.

They had several knapsacks to shoulder.

One of the mocky-men with whom they rendezvoused in the forest was Pieman. Eyeno's dream had loaded the boughs of kasta trees with jewels instead of nuts. The crusty-skinned fellow stared askance at her new eye as the waiting trio heard how she had come by it.

'That's meant to be an *aquamarine*,' declared Pieman. 'I've been to Saari where fine ladies like their baubles. I know! Miners can dig up huge crystals just like it. They don't cost too much at all. So why imitate one in glass? I'm thinking that's a real one he's given you—'

'Unlikely!'

Juke glanced at his sister suspiciously, and she flushed. Surely he didn't imagine for a moment that she had *pleased* that scrawny jeweller in such a way that he would give her a genuine gem!

'You don't know what you're blethering about,' Knotty told Pieman. Knotty's skin looked as though it was made out of brown rope and string in which a thousand tangles had been tied, and he wore a tunic of hessian to match.

'I do too! I've talked to miners.'

'It's paste,' insisted Eyeno. 'It's just glass with metals added to colour it.'

'Maybe it was a shot at making glass look like *emerald*. But the wrong metals got mixed in, or not enough of 'em. Emerald's a cousin of aquamarine. I'm thinking your jeweller's passed off a botch. Nobody would want a fake aquamarine.'

Juke caught Pieman by the collar. 'Don't say that! It's what my sister wanted.'

'Easy, easy,' intervened Lammas. He only wore shorts and

sandals since his body was coated in tufty grey wool a finger's span thick. Wool sprouted from his scalp. 'Aren't you the know-all, Pie-face? Let's not spoil the girl's pleasure.'

Her dream diverged. In the dream she plucked out the glass aquamarine. Clutching the paste gem in her hand, Eyeno sprinted back into town, arriving there almost immediately. But the Street of Crafts had changed. In place of Missieur Pierre's there stood a *money shop* – a shop where you could buy coins with coins, which in her dream seemed to be a perfectly just and equable arrangement. A mark for a mark; a penny for a penny. Consequently coins circulated quickly and the town prospered. This money shop was crowded with richly dressed people all brandishing coins. She swiftly found herself in the forefront, clad in a gown which was dingy and raggy. She was facing a brawny apron-clad shopkeeper. Behind his counter buckets and buckets of coins overflowed on to the floor. The man's moon-shaped face was the bronze of a penny, on which his features were merely engraved. His was a crescent mouth. Coin-eyes were miniatures of his whole face. Within those eyes, a tinier crescent mouth and tinier eyes. Would those tinier eyes also contain his whole face in minuscule?

'Mister Penny!' the eager shoppers clamoured. 'Mister Penny!'

Eyeno thrust her glass jewel at Mister Penny. She was consumed with a desire to wear a bronze penny in her eye. She wanted a metal monocle of visible value squeezed between her lids. The other customers burst out laughing. They guffawed, they brayed. Mister Penny's crescent mouth cracked open in a grin. He quaked with merriment.

'Gold for glass!' he hooted.

No, she didn't need a golden one with Lucky's head on it. A bronze penny would be fine. An ordinary penny minted in Saari, stamped with an anchor on the front for security and an eye on the rear for prudence. An eye, to fit in her eye, why of course!

She had thought of this before. When she was younger she had several times privately pushed a penny into her empty socket. But unless she kept her head tilted right back the flat coin would never stay there. It would quickly fall out. You couldn't walk round staring straight up at the top of the sky. In her dream she forgot all about such silly contretemps. She flourished her paste gem which had cost a mark and a half and a fortune.

'Please, Mister Penny!'

The keeper of the money shop chortled. 'Bronze for a botch, bronze for a bungle!'

'I coin words too,' she cried in appeal. 'I'm a poetess.' She realized that her feet were bare. She was a pauper, in rags, with a cheap chunk of cut glass in her hand.

The bronze-faced man leered at her. 'Which word will you pay me,' he asked slyly, 'which you can never ever use again? Will you pay me *I* – he struck his chest – 'or *eye*' – and he pointed to one of the coins in his face – 'or *love*, or *true*, or *twice*?'

Horror invaded her heart. She couldn't possibly hand over to him any word that would be lost to her for ever. Fighting her way through the crowd, who plucked at her rags and stamped on her toes, she fled.

In reality, the false aquamarine had begun to tarnish after only a few months. Its initial brilliance faded, so maybe Pieman had been right after all.

Eyeno remembered the fortune with which she had paid Missieur Pierre: Fingers *black* and bodies velvet, Pompous *serpents*... Next year when they drove goats and took those gloves and cheeses as far as Saari, she would travel onward, east by north, into the territory of the Velvet Isi and their black Juttahats to ask the serpents for a false eye. She had tried to obtain one too easily, too frivolously. A daisy paperweight eye, an aquamarine eye ... gewgaws! She would get herself an eye made by aliens. *That* would be a worthy one.

16 · JUTTAHATS

Eyeno's was a crazy scheme, though it appealed to the wanderer in Juke. For her safety's sake he felt obliged to dissuade her. Alien serpents and their servants were unpredictable.

Eyeno only became more quietly determined, more obsessed with this brainwave of hers. Juke could not bring himself to impose his will on his sister. That would be tantamount to a violation of her.

Juke even consulted the crookbacked wisewoman of Halvek who had first detected Eyeno's inward eye. By now that woman was elderly and almost bent into a hoop. Surely she would snap in half soon. Her opinion was that infatuation would lead to frenzy if frustrated. Obsession demanded satisfaction if at all possible. If quite impossible, then you must commit yourself to something perilous and earth-shaking as a distraction. Obsessions were the fevers of mana. Such a fever must burn itself out like a minty tree on fire. Why was she herself so crookbacked except from denying herself motherhood long ago, sensing that fruit of her womb would be born without any limbs at all?

This consultation persuaded Juke that his sister needed a true adventure to reconcile the poetess to her future life among the mocky-men.

The year after Eyeno's purchase from Missieur Pierre of that eye of paste (which was now dulling) she and her brother set out north-east from splendid Saari with its paved streets, its spraying fountains and canals, its palace of Johann Helenius fronting the wide Murame river.

Tithes had been paid in kind, gloves sold at a profit, and goods acquired. Juke persuaded the mocky-man escort to trek back to Outo and Halvek without the two Nurmis.

Brother and sister themselves walked for several days through field and forest. By now little villages were stoutly stockaded. Each was a minor stronghold. The crammed buildings formed one single fortified interconnected home. Black Jutties roamed these reaches where the velvet serpents set them loose.

But there was trade, as well, with the servants of the snakes: a *game* of trade, almost. Isi gadgets and souvenirs were prized for their resale value to Lord Helenius, even if in themselves those gadgets might be perfectly enigmatic. The Lord of Saari believed that a to-and-fro of trivia across his border helped to define that border and distract the Isi from random mischief.

As to what caught a Juttahat's amber nictitating eye, that might be a belt-buckle of unusual design or a Pootaran puzzle. It might be an embroidered shirt which no Juttahat would ever wear, or a lucky charm. Here to the north-east of Saari people habitually dressed interestingly, hanging themselves with amulets and earrings. They always wore knives, with a second knife tucked down their boot. No one tattooed him- or herself in case a Juttie coveted the decoration. A century earlier, Jutties had demanded tattoos from village folk – and had taken them, using some humming slicer which painlessly flayed off the fancy patch

211

of flesh, replacing it with an adhesive pseudoflesh on which strange symbols later emerged, without any obvious consequence.

In the men's sauna in one rustic stronghold, Juke was advised to be wary of those tattoos of speakers' lips which newly framed both his nipples. He'd had the tattooing done in Saari just days before to fortify his confidence as a proclaimer. He might need to exert his will over a hostile Juttie. He had imagined himself tearing open his shirt to lay his chest bare as he *spoke*. Not now he wouldn't.

Where would his hosts advise him and his sister to head for?

The naked sweating men nudged and winked and nodded. Hermi's bone-cabin, way out in the forest, was where. Hermi fancied himself as a broker and mediator with the servants of the Velvet Isi.

'Fancies? But he is—'

'Hermi's halfway round the corner—'

'Hermi's holy—'

'Wholly crackers—'

'A honeypot for Juttahats—'

'Good thing too. Hermi's our mascot. Hermi's our good fortune, fellows—'

Steam swirled. Many earrings dangled, dripping. Several nipple rings too. A couple of men wore slim silver rings through their noses.

A few days earlier, it transpired, these villagers had given the same directions to a skinny man who was kitted out in a posh striped suit. This traveller wouldn't reveal his business with Jutties, nor would his bodyguard who carried a crossbow. Both men rode ponies with bulging saddlebags. Busy days for Hermi in his cabin. In his house of beast bones.

That cabin was deep amongst curver trees and hoary sylvesters. Chartreuse quiffs brushed the roof as if dedicated to sweeping it clean, or fanning it. The morning was muggy, bug-hot. Sizzleflies buzzed.

Eyeno felt sick, despite being forewarned. The walls of the cabin consisted of row upon row of bones roped and twined tightly together: femur, scapula, humerus, tibia. Many were too large to be human bones. Those must be cattle bones or horse bones. Others would be pig and sheep and goat and dog. Were there

212

actually any human bones here at all? That would be a terrible thing. The hooped door was all of ribs. The irregular shingles of the roof were a jigsaw of jaw bones large and small. There mustn't, there couldn't, be human bones here. Shutting her eye, Eyeno feared she might see skeletons dancing in her secret meadow. Yet the maidens cavorted faintly as usual.

No sign of any *living* ponies hereabouts. Nor of those other two travellers. No sign of Juttahats slinking among the trees . . .

Inside the cabin of bones they found a naked man seated cross-legged.

How could this person be called naked when he wore so much? Rows of metal balls hung from hooks planted in his bare chest. Heavily they tugged on his flesh. Chains wrapped his arms. Around his neck, a metal collar was linked to great leaden epaulettes resting on his shoulders. Circling his waist, a skirt of burdens hung from a metal band. Ballast dangled from his nipples and stretched earlobes. Brass rings encased his penis and scrotum. At least his buttocks and legs were bare.

'Are you Hermi?' asked Juke, non-plussed.

The man laughed.

'Are you blind?'

Hermi's face was long and lean, dog-like, toothy. His deep-set eyes were dark. Dirty grey hair coiled around his crown, held in place by long pins which seemed to transfix his skull. He must be about sixty years old.

Blind? Blind? There was so much to see! A pot-belly stove, its black chimney rising through the battened jaw-bones of the roof. Open cupboards crammed with pots, pans, jars, chronometers, dolls, pieces of puzzles, statuettes, coils of rope, balls of twine, hoops of wire, tools, scrolls, combs, brushes. Spiral-patterned rugs covered much of the earthen floor. Eyeno stooped, and stroked. Surely the rugs were woven of human tresses. Blonde and grey and black.

'Yes, people's hair,' the naked, weight-clad man agreed. 'We don't need our hair in the grave. Is hair a bone? Does the soul live in hair? I hardly think so. That's your first question answered, young lady with a glass gem for an eyeball.' Hermi's voice was husky and merry. Breeze filtering through the battens brought a peculiar odour.

'Warm dry bone's what you're smelling, my dear. The souls of animals. One learns to smell a soul.'

She stepped closer. He himself seemed to possess no odour at

213

all. Actually, his body was very clean, and his metal weights were polished.

'These stop me from floating away,' the man remarked. 'The more I wear, though, the lighter I seem to become. I think by now my only weight is theirs. I'm simply a soul equipped with an illusion of a body. I puzzle the Juttahats who visit here, don't I?'

'Do they often visit you, Mister Hermi?' asked Juke. 'Can you help us negotiate with them?'

'For a real eye, for your sister?'

Hermi proved more than willing to talk. Honesty was his stock in trade, said he. A single glance would show him something revelatory about a person, so he claimed. (But he was wrong about Eyeno wanting a *real* eye. She already had that other real one hidden away inside her skull.)

Armed with such insights, Hermi prided himself on answering questions before they were asked. Yet his inspired frankness could seem like a subterfuge to people who were guileful. So he felt perfectly safe being visited by servants of the serpents. The more he told Juttahats about himself, the more mysterious and fascinating he became to them: a kind of human mana-mage, a magnet. Their Isi masters had been playing a game with human-kind ever since the aliens arrived on Kaleva, and Hermi had become part of that game.

'You see, my dears,' he said, 'for the most part people play games of power and sex and prestige and riches. But there's also a game of the *mysterium*, which involves insight and perception. That's what the Isi try to play. It's the one I play by myself, here in this cabin. I'm sure the Isi could send their slaves to massacre us all if they wished. They probably have devastating weapons at their disposal. This isn't the game they're playing with us – and with each other. They only niggle us the way you might stir a nest of formicks with a stick to watch what happens. They have a deeper goal.'

'What's that?' asked Juke.

Hermi rocked from side to side. His weights shifted like bulky pendulum bobs.

'Mastery of the mysterium. Of mana and Ukkos and Cosmos. The serpents guess something about this world that we don't guess. They watch our mana-manipulators pranking and pro-claiming, imposing their will on other people in such petty power-mongering manly ways. What goes on here is like convolutions in a dreaming mind – a mind which must awaken one day. The Juttahats don't manipulate mana, you know. I can tell! Serpents have bred a peculiar compliance into their slaves for thousands of generations. Very intrigued by this bone-house of mine, the Juttahats are! They circle all around it. They stare at the bones as if some day they might recognize a particular one.'

Hermi swayed about on his rug of human hair.

'Ah, the draft is trying to blow me away! Hold me down, hold me down.'

Despite his load of weights and chains the naked man was rising.

No! Of course he wasn't floating. He was simply standing up. His feet and the muscles of his calves and thighs were powering him erect.

Hermi chuckled – upright now, his bare body cloaked in weights to the groin.

'I'm so light I believe I could fly.' Grandly he raised his chain-clad arms. What a trickster he was.

In the doorway there stood a black Juttahat. Its twin lurked behind it. These Unmen wore seamless sable livery with a velvety nap to it. Swirly silver hieroglyphs were appliquéd upon their left shoulders. Their skin was ebon and glossy as if oiled. From clips on their garment hung a number of little pouches, and each wore a sheath with a dagger. Close-set ambery eyes glazed and unglazed as the Juttahats gazed in. Their nostrils valved open and shut, giving a false impression that they had been running and now were panting; whereas they were perfectly poised.

'Who being these, Hermi-*maaginen*?' The voice rattled and hissed as if the throat had been injured.

'Ah, this is my gift to the Velvet Isi-*maaginen* today: two mutant travellers who seek me because I'm here—'

Juke's hand slid towards his knife. 'We aren't gifts . . .'

'Calming yourself,' snapped the naked man. His weights clinked against one another.

'There are certain protocols to observe. Travellers who seek your masters, gentle Juttahats,' Hermi resumed. 'I have devised my own etiquette,' he explained to brother and sister. 'All life is balance and burden and buoyancy. How can you repay *me*, who wants nothing beyond beast bones and metal balls, if you are not gifts I can pass on?'

Hermi seemed quite capable of carrying on two conversations simultaneously, for he said to the Juttahats, 'This girl seeks a new eye.'

With her good eye Eyeno skimmed those cupboards over-flowing with dolls and tools and puzzles and whatever else. Hermi claimed to own nothing?

Seemingly at random, the trickster moved. He seized the hand of a little pink girl doll dressed in a grubby lace smock. The doll's tresses had been half torn out, leaving tiny holes exposed in a pierced tin scalp. He thrust the doll at Eyeno.

'Here: my gift to you. Take it.'

The doll was missing its left eye. Its other eye was blue. He had known exactly where to reach.

'Mind that you bring it back to me.'

Bring it back?

'She will be bringing it back,' said one of the Unmen.

Swivelling, Hermi plucked another little doll free. This was a bisque boy doll with moulded blond curls, clad in tattered dunga-rees. He tossed the doll to Juke, who was obliged to catch it with both hands.

'He will be bringing it back,' said the black, spruce Unman.

Safe-conducts: that's what these dolls were – by some eccentric protocol which the Juttahats and Hermi both understood.

A ring had fallen from the boy doll's garment upon the matting of hair. A blue and green opal mounted on gold. For a moment it seemed to Eyeno that maybe this belonged in her own doll's eye.

'Look—'

Hermi scuffed the opal ring dismissively into the tangled hair with a toe.

'Some seek wealth and some seek vision,' he said airily. 'The game of vision interests the Isi rather more.'

'Your most recent visitor – on pony-back, with a hired guard – was called Missieur Pierre, wasn't he?'

Hoisting a chain-wrapped arm, Hermi scratched his brow. 'Do I know *your* name, girl?'

'You can probably guess it,' she said wryly. 'Your last visitor was a jeweller, wasn't he?' She pointed her doll's tiny head at the hairy floor. 'Will *he* come back for that ring he left behind?'

'It seems you have visions already.' Hermi flicked fingers along the metal balls hooked to his chest, banging them together to make music.

216

'I can tell your fortune from the *Book of the Land of Heroes*, Mister Hermi.'

'And send me off to sell ice to the tundra-folk, perhaps? Far from my well-ventilated house of bones and hair? As you sent a jeweller to sell gems to Jutties! It is I who send you, dear girl with a vision. Tell the fortunes of serpents, if you can.'

One of the Juttahats had produced a small spy-glass half the size of its own thumb. It stepped towards Eyeno.

She awaited it, clasping her doll.

The Unman's lips parted, displaying neat little teeth and an almost purple tongue. Was it smiling? Sticky beads welled from the gland-slits on its jutting chin. She smelled cinnamon. Holding the spy-glass in two fingers, the alien examined both of her eyes, the natural one second. She saw a tiny, shimmering circle within the instrument where minuscule hieroglyphs danced.

'We being Tulki-nine and Tulki-twenty,' the Unman said. A tut and a click, a tut and a click.

It took two full days' march through woodland to reach the nest of the Velvet Isi. After the first ten keys, a narrow black roadway snaked through the trees. The surface was of some stiff rubbery substance. Juke had tested his blade along the edge. With difficulty he shaved a thin strip loose, whereupon Tulki-nine asked incongruously, 'Are you hungry?' This Tulki's shoulder hieroglyph was more convoluted than its companion's. Otherwise there was little to tell the two Unmen apart. Juke quickly threw the scrap away.

As they proceeded, one or other of the Unmen would periodically crouch and press an almost human ear to the road, harkening – to what? To vibrations from the distant tread of other Juttahats? When Juke and Eyeno knelt to listen they could hear nothing but the hum of sizzleflies in the woods and a soft sigh of breeze.

Eventually Eyeno asked the Tulkis what they were listening for. It seemed that she would receive no answer. When she had almost forgotten the question, Tulki-twenty said, 'Hearing the voice in our ear, against the road.'

A voice like a poem composing itself?

'What voice?' she asked.

'Of the Lord that is speaking in our heads,' replied Tulki-twenty. 'The voice being the Lord of ourselves.'

'Do you mean that the Isi speak to you in your head while you're far away from them?' asked Juke.

'No, only when close by. Here, being our other self that is speaking to ourself.'

'So you have two different selves in you?' he asked.

Again, it seemed as though there would be no reply, but then the Unman said, 'We are having our unit-self, and our Isi-self which was raising us from savagery. We being the hands and the feet and the voices of our Isi-self.'

Juke thought about this a while longer. Neither he nor his sister had been anywhere near to Juttahats before. Really, the aliens did not seem any more outrageous than mocky-men. Less so than some of his and Eyeno's kin! Of course everyone was leery of Juttahats . . . Even Hermi felt obliged to boast how unperturbed he was by the visits of aliens to his bone cabin.

A Juttahat wasn't exactly its own person. It was a tool of serpents. A trained voice. A trained body. Eyeno had obviously been thinking along similar lines.

'It must be like having a proclaimer within yourself all the time,' she suggested.

Juke frowned. 'Do you enjoy being *instruments*?' he asked Tulki-twenty somewhat roughly.

This prompted a long, peculiar discourse from the Unman as it marched.

'Man,' said Tulki-twenty, 'there being a story about the Juttahat who was lacking a second self. When this Juttahat was being told by its kin to be doing anything it would be continuing the same task for ever, unable to stop. Nothing inside was telling it to stop. If it was beginning digging it was continuing digging. If it was starting to walk it was continuing to walk. Lacking its Isi-self it was being a mere mechanism. One day its kin were tiring of telling it to be starting and stopping all the time. They were wanting rid of it, so they were saying to it, *be eating yourself.*

'And it began eating itself, until only its mouth was remaining. Its mouth was sinking upon the ground. Its lips, swollen with nourishment, were becoming part of the ground.

'Then it was beginning to consume the ground itself. Sand and soil were flowing into it. Those lips were growing ever larger. The mouth was devouring trees and boulders. The mouth was drinking streams. The whole world was flowing into those lips. Its kin were crying, *Stopping*, but the mouth having no ears to be hearing them. The mouth was sucking them in too when they were venturing close.

'Then along was coming an Isi mage, asking, *What is happening here? Why is there being a vast hungry valley with no bottom to it? Why is it eating the world?*

'When the surviving kin had been explaining, the Isi mage was throwing herself into that mouth. It was swallowing her away out of sight.

'What was happening then? First the eyeballs of the Juttahat who had been eating itself were flying out. Next, its nostrils. Then most of the rest of its body, and finally its ears – till it was standing there whole again, except that its mouth was still missing.

'The flesh beneath its nostrils was splitting. Like a flower opening up, lips were parting. As they were parting, so the great valley of the mouth was shrinking till it was closing up, pulling the world tight again.

'So *where* being the Isi mage?' Tulki-twenty paused.

'Swallowed up,' hazarded Juke. 'Buried deep.'

'Where being the Isi mage?' repeated the Unman, its third eyelid flickering.

'Inside the Juttahat,' said Eyeno. 'And somewhere else too.'

The Tulki's chin-glands leaked fragrantly.

'The Juttahat was speaking to its surviving kin of its own accord for the first time, and was saying, *You shall be doing this*, and *You shall be doing that*. And the kin were obeying it.'

'That's a strange story,' said Eyeno. 'Almost a poem.' A poem in a strange timeless tense.

It could become a poem. *The person who was swallowing himself* . . . The story only made confused sense otherwise. Maybe to the Juttahats the tale was beautiful and true. Maybe it had persuasive force. Force, almost, of law. Of authority.

The Juttahats seemingly had an Isi-mind inside them, a part of them which thought what the Isi would wish them to think, and advised their main mind accordingly. In a sense the Juttahats had swallowed the Isi. In another sense the Isi had swallowed *them*.

'Did the Isi first tell you that story?' Eyeno asked Tulki-twenty.

'No!' The reply was sharp. 'That being our story.'

The eyes glazed over.

'The great Isi narrations being quite different and magnificent.' Tulki-twenty seemed to be reciting a received truth –

219

received from the other part of its mind. 'Being narrations that are shifting an Ukko through mana-space.'

'Can you tell me one of those?'

A sudden longing kindled itself in Eyeno: to transform one of these supposedly magnificent narrations of the serpents into her own poetry. To speak *that* out some year to the amazement of an audience – at the famed gala at Speakers' Valley perhaps, if she was ever so lucky as to visit it. One year or another. Sometime. Already this desire seemed like a grand resolution arrived at by night but betrayed and derided by the coming of daylight.

'Only our masters can be singing those long songs,' said Tulki-twenty, 'and in the Isi tongue.'

'Teach me some of it!'

'Being forbidden,' the Juttahat said mechanically.

The road swung sinuously from side to side. That black ribbon constantly revealed itself a couple of hundred metres ahead, and concealed itself to their rear. Towards the end of the first afternoon mist began to seep from the roadway. A miasma spread outward and upward through the trees. Soon this masked all but the closest trunks and hid the location of the sun. A party of half a dozen Juttahats loomed, but they trotted by without a word. Without even glancing at Juke and Eyeno they vanished into the mist. By now the territory they were passing through seemed like a dream indeed.

The travellers spent that night in a bulbous dome of black metal set in a rubbery-paved clearing near the roadway. The Tulkis' touch had opened an oval door which was scratched and scorched as if forced entry had been attempted but had failed. Inside, curved walls were luminous, and the bone-coloured floor supple, almost spongy. Cabinets yielded warm cakes of food and chilled flasks of sweetened water. A toilet cubicle concealed a thrumming hole in the floor flanked by two flexible shoes to stand in, and thus squat. Moist wiping fabric jutted from a slot. Another cubicle would shower hot water then dry with a blast of air – though none of the four were to shed their clothes. Beds were rolls of soft springy material which would cling around a body, cocoon-like. A pit of raked sand would be the resting place for a serpent. A circular blue line on the blanched floor suggested a hatch giving access to space below.

How different this was from a mocky-house or any other human dwelling. Eyeno felt that she had left her world behind.

Though when she shut her eyes the maidens capered in the meadows.

Next day, the road and its surroundings remained just as miasma-shrouded. Vapour drifted from that dark surface to hide its whereabouts and its direction.

Presently the travellers came to a fork where twins of the road curved away to left and right into invisibility.

Tulki-twenty crouched and listened. The Unman chose the leftward route.

The road divided again.

Then again. Always it was cloaked in drifts of thick mist. The nearest trees were faint ghosts.

'If the wrong feet are walking these roads,' said Tulki-nine, 'they will easily becoming lost. This being mana-mist.'

Juke stamped his foot on the rubbery road from which all those concealing vapours seemed to issue. 'I thought it was a trick of the serpents.'

'It is that too. How many roads do you think there are?'

If these roads were a vast spiralling maze laid out through dozens of keys of forest, there might be . . .

'Dozens?'

A Juttahat did not smirk. Its eyes glazed. One of its chin-glands dribbled, releasing a fleeting acrid scent.

'Only one. There is only one road for it is all of the same substance.'

Juke cleared his throat of fog and spat at the road.

They came to a lake athwart their path. Mist hid its width. Harnies honked invisibly. The road led out across the water, afloat now, extending like a long tongue. For the next many minutes they were completely out of sight of trees or land, lost in a realm of liquid. Water lapped the black roadway but did not submerge it. The rubbery surface vibrated faintly and the lake seemed to thud like a pulse of blood in the ear. The travellers' boots were drumsticks marching across a drumskin. Might the river of death be akin to this? Might you trudge on and on for ever across a waste of water, remembering your passionate past in mirror detail, unable to return to the shore of the past, unable to reach any further shore? Eyeno found herself watching out for the swan, but only a harnie hove in sight, its lustre diminished by the fog.

Then the road was crossing a gravel beach. Vague trees beckoned again.

So did a figure – part way up the trunk of a minty. A black-liveried figure hung from under the pea-green foliage. It dangled upside-down, by one leg. It was a dead Juttahat. A rope from its ankle stretched up into the leaves. Rusty blood stained the black face and had drained through its tight mat of hair. Blood had streaked its arms right to the fingertips. The Juttahat's throat had been cut. A placard was pinned to its belly. On the placard, a drawing of a swan flapping its wings. What pinned the placard was a crossbow quarrel.

The Tulkis pulled out knives. They stepped off the road.

Juke pushed his sister clear of the bare road, too. He thrust her into shrubbery.

'Crouch down! Some people must know their way through this maze.'

'Isn't it better that we're seen?' She resisted him. 'Juke: proclaim peace as loudly as you can. Or we might lose our guides in an ambush. I wouldn't ever reach the Isi. I wouldn't get my new eye.'

The Tulkis were treading softly and slowly. Alertly their heads turned this way and that. The mist-veiled forest was silent.

Till Juke bellowed out, '*Pax!* This is spoken. Peace: I proclaim it!'

The Tulkis swung round as one, accusingly. But since all continued to be calm the Unmen turned their attention back to their hanged alien kin, dangling down within their reach.

Eyeno shut her eyes. She saw a misted meadow where a solitary maiden danced, waving gaudy red fireflowers. Of a sudden the blooms became flames. Her hair and gauzy garments blazed. The mist flushed rosy as if it were a fog of dilute blood.

That pea-green tree from which the corpse hung . . .

A minty.

One of the Unmen was contemplating climbing it.

'Tulkis!' she cried. 'Don't touch the body. Don't touch the tree. It's a trap.'

The black Juttahats stared upward for a while. One of them delved in a pouch to spill out thin cord, tens of metres of silvery cord. Warily the Juttahat made a loop to slip around one wrist of the corpse. As the cord paid out, both Unmen retreated back to where brother and sister stood. When Tulki-twenty reached for Eyeno's hand she accepted the cord. *She* had declared there was danger. *She* should prove it.

She pulled the thin cord taut.

The corpse swayed.

With both hands she hauled, leaning backwards.

The minty tree exploded in a ball of fire as if lightning had struck it.

Heat gusted. A vertical furnace roared. Eyeno had sprawled upon a bush. Juke was ducking over her. Tangled together, they rolled as they used to when wrestling as kids – kids among four-footed kids and goats – crushing shrubbery. They scrambled up, to shade their faces from the oven-heat.

When the rope suspending the corpse burned through, the body fell. Its livery hadn't caught on fire. The Unmen pulled the dead weight of their kin towards them with the silver cord. Mist glowed rosy in the fierce firelight.

'Peace!' called a voice.

A skeletal man sat on a pannier-hung pony. He wore a rumpled black suit with slim grey stripes. The stocky animal looked tired but it was fretting at the blaze, scraping the road with a hoof and snickering. The man slapped his mount across the neck with the reins.

'Peace!' appealed the scrawny rider.

'Missieur Pierre—'

And then he knew her.

'Why, it's you! It's my conniving mutie fortune-teller. False eye, false fortune!' The jeweller noticed the two Unmen crouched over their scorched kin. He flinched, and his pony shied. Juke darted and snatched the reins.

'You're in league with the Jutties,' Missieur Pierre accused. 'You sent me to them just to be robbed,' he croaked at Eyeno, grief in his voice.

'I did not send you anywhere! You sent yourself.'

'You, and that madman with weights hanging all over him. Hermi, that's him. All of you in league.'

Juke wrestled the boy doll from his knapsack to brandish at Missieur Pierre.

'He didn't give you one of these, did he?'

The jeweller goggled at this grown young man thrusting a bisque doll in tattered dungarees at him. Tulki-nine straightened up and stared at the jeweller. The tree continued to blaze, its plume of grey smoke losing itself in the mist. That fiery beacon couldn't be visible from more than a hundred metres away.

Missieur Pierre called out to the Unman: 'I warn you, I've been rescued once already. You Jutties killed my guard – but two brave lads saved me. They're watching over me even now. If you do me harm, they'll attack in a trice. That applies to you too,' he snapped at Juke and Eyeno. 'Don't you shove that demon doll at me, *cochon*.'

Tulki-nine trotted over.

'Who was killing our kin and hanging it up?' the Juttahat demanded.

'The lads must have done it, mustn't they?'

So they must. That highly combustible minty tree had been rigged with an explosive charge which would detonate when the bait was shifted. Those 'lads' had set a booby-trap for Juttahats. The same lads had apparently interrupted some Juttahats in the process of plundering Missieur Pierre, though the jeweller was far from lucid about what exactly had occurred somewhere further along the misted road.

'Telling their names,' insisted Tulki-nine.

The jeweller protested that he didn't know their names. The lads could be listening at this very moment, hidden behind some nearby tree in the dense mist, waiting to fire their crossbows . . .

Lads . . . Heroes of humankind who engaged in minor mayhem and murder – of aliens who were no weirder to look at than mocky-men. Self-appointed rogues, out for a giggle and glory. Roustabouts who might pick on mocky-men next. Crowing roosters. Quite competent ones, though, who could cope with mana-mist and a maze of misleading roads . . .

Juttahats also could rampage, of course. Juttahats of the very same breed who were guiding him and his sister had waylaid Missieur Pierre on his daft greedy journey to sell jewellery to serpents. Missieur Pierre sat quaking on his pony, though in a peevishly defiant fashion. What did Juke owe this man who had given his sister a dull false eye, a paste gem which proved a dud? On the other hand Juke might be obliged to sell the mocky-men's gold to Missieur Pierre again at Threelakes . . .

Let the jeweller feel thoroughly intimidated! The gratitude of Juttahats could help ensure a fine false eye for Eyeno. So Juke bespoke the jeweller, to identify those two bravos who had come to his aid.

After brief resistance a pair of names popped out of the jeweller like pips springing free from a squeezed orange, so fast that the listeners almost missed them:

'Minkie-and-Snowy—.'

Minkie. And Snowy.

The name Minkie was familiar. Of course it might be a different Minkie . . .

'He's the Dame of Niemi's son,' confirmed Missieur Pierre.

The same Minkie Kennan who had got the glassmaker's daughter in the family way apparently liked to hunt Juttahats as well as nubile girls. What a collector of trophies this Minkie must fancy himself as. How far from home he'd ranged to harass the servants of the snakes.

Juke proclaimed Missieur Pierre on his way across the hidden lake. Then he asked Tulki-nine, 'Will the Juttahats seek revenge?'

'Are you meaning,' asked the alien, 'will we be rewarding you for the names as well as for saving us from the explosion?'

Juke flushed, and enquired no further.

The Juttahats listened to the road again. Afterwards, they carried the corpse back along that rubbery causeway into the dense mist curtaining the waters. A few minutes later they returned empty-handed.

'Its bones will be sinking into the mud,' said Tulki-twenty. 'The mud will be burying its bones. Its echo may be guarding the bridge, here in the mana-mist.'

From now on the Juttahats walked between Juke and Eyeno, who clutched their dolls in full view. Presently another squad of Juttahats trotted out of the mist, armed with crossbows of Isi design and long knives. They conferred with the guides in clicks and sibilants. Tulki-nine received a crossbow. The bow was fastened to the stock with a steel bridle which a tommy-bar would tighten. It was of a kind which fired bullets from a barrel. Bullets, one at a time. Explosive ones, though. Tulki-nine fired off a trial shot. Hitting a yellover tree, the bullet detonated with the force of a grenade, spraying a shrapnel cloud of wood chips from the gashed trunk. Nevertheless, Tulki-nine could only fire single shots.

'Don't you have guns that fire faster?' asked Juke.

'The balance being wrong,' replied Tulki-nine.

Balance? What balance? The symmetry of the contest, of course . . . Minkie and Snowy were using crossbows. The Juttahats armed themselves accordingly. The aliens' bows might fire explosive bullets, but the conclusion to the hunt was far from foregone.

225

A game was under way. If it proved lethal to some of the Jutta-hats, their masters must be content to accept losses.

They hurried onward through mana-mist along the twisting rubbery highway, protected by dolls and a single-shot crossbow.

17 · A NEST OF SNAKES

Instead of mutating, Eyeno's dream of the past fractured. It lost its sequence.

Already Minkie Kennan was saluting her on the road between Saari and Threelakes. The dirt road, at that point, passed through a tree-choked gorge. A timber bridge spanned a spuming little tributary of the Murame. The heir to tumbledown Niemi Keep lolled nonchalantly against the rail of the bridge. He was clad in a long tawny leather coat of many sagging pockets and enormous collars. Propped by him was a cocked crossbow. Its winding handle would have done justice to a mangle.

'Where have *you* been all my life?' he exclaimed with warmth and wonder. He scooped a floppy corduroy cap from his chestnut curls.

'Oh bless me.'

It was as if his whole existence was instantly devoted to Eyeno, opening to her as a flower to the sun. He acknowledged Juke's presence with a disarmingly friendly nod.

'Delighted to see you too, sir.' Minkie might have been waiting specially for this brother and sister to come along.

His eyes were nutbrown, his mouth and brow generous, while a slightly snubby nose suggested an affectionate humour. Stubble lent him a raffish, roguish air. This sturdy, sparkling fellow wasn't tall, yet his long coat suggested that he *might* be.

Ah, a watchful crony lurked in the woods: a mop of blond hair so white it could have been bleached, a rotund red face keeping squinty eyes on the scene.

How Minkie admired Eyeno's neat, sweet countenance, so poignantly resolute. Those few beauty-moles on her creamy cheeks. The yellow silk of her hair . . . No man had glanced at her before in such a bewitched style. Glanced, and glanced again, whilst contriving also to defer to Juke.

Was this what she must come to expect now that the cleverly fashioned Isi eye completed her appearance? An appearance of normality . . . ? No: rather, a visage of perfect loveliness – or so it seemed from the bashful smitten gleam in Minkie's nutbrown eyes. Eyes that looked at her adoringly, with a captivating diffidence, almost a virginal modesty.

'My name's Minkie,' he confided, offering her – and Juke too – a simple, innocent, heartfelt gift, of himself, to be their trusted friend, defender, provider. He was a thorough charmer.

'Snowy!' he called. 'Come out. It's safe.'

That bleached young crony ambled into view. A crossbow with hefty cranequin handle hung from his paw. Snowy's broad face was completely blotched with bright acne. It was a weepy rosy ocean crowded with inflamed red islands. His affliction was really extreme. His face seemed flayed raw; yet he was grinning cheerfully at the reassurance. How comely Minkie was compared with his comrade. How loyal of Minkie to consort with someone so disadvantaged in looks.

Doubly disadvantaged; Snowy also stuttered.

'Hu-hu-hu-hullo there—'

Eyeno must bear in mind that this same Minkie Kennan was an unscrupulous seducer. And that the *other* hobby of this pair was the murder of oddities.

Naturally the four of them would travel together as far as Niemi.

On the way, Snowy let slip to Eyeno that Minkie was something of a hero, returning from his latest exploits about which modesty wouldn't let him brag. A Dame's son, too; an heir to a keep, though in no way a snob. Why, Snowy himself was just a farmer's boy . . .

Raised amongst mocky-men with wool and pie-crusts on their skin, Eyeno wasn't averse to mentioning a case of acne to Minkie while he strolled along with her, later, dewy-eyed and beguiled. Snowy was diverting Juke's attention with his stutters.

'Shouldn't he dye his hair dark, don't you think?'

'So that his phiz wouldn't look so awful? He wouldn't be Snowy then. Ah you who have such a fine face . . .' Minkie gazed into her eyes, quite failing to realize that one of those was false, such was the skill of the Juttahat artisans.

Somehow Snowy heard her comment, and caught up. 'Ca-ca-ca-can't use dye. D-d-d-dye hu-hu-hu-hurts.'

Minkie's look reproached Eyeno, begging that she make amends – to Minkie . . .

It seemed that Juke couldn't help liking Minkie, or indulging Snowy – who was, after all, almost a kind of mocky-man – even when Snowy more and more acted as a decoy bird (broken-tongued rather than a broken-winged) to help Minkie monopolize Juke's sister.

Snowy's pace constantly lagged, so the journey became a stroll which might last a week or more. Whenever a cart passed by, or when riders overtook the walkers, Snowy would step shyly aside into the trees and linger there, regaling Juke in staccato whispers with tall tales about Juttahats. Snowy compulsively *had* to complete these anecdotes before he could move another pace. His speech impediment stalled him from finishing stories for up to half an hour. Juke began to guess at the words for which Snowy was clutching. Wrong guesses only reinforced the stutterer's stubborn determination.

While this was happening, Minkie was raptly attentive to Eyeno. He didn't enquire much into her background. He was the soul of meek courtesy. But the disclosure that she was a poet entranced him. Poetry was the language of love. Would she teach him – purely as an exercise – how to compose a love poem, aimed, say, from him to her? Phrases which could express the silkiness of her hair, the magical subtlety of a certain tiny mole upon her neck?

Minkie murmured of his shyness, of his search for self-expression, of how easily wounded he could be (just like Snowy!), and of how long this mere adolescent that he was had searched for a soul-mate, and maybe he had found her. What price his bravado against aliens? That was purely a distraction from the quest for love – for a hen he could hold to his heart.

One soft sultry evening they bivouacked in a glade. Minkie persuaded Eyeno to stretch her legs. Soon *he* would try to stretch them, too, as she lay supine. While Snowy stuttered urgently at Juke, Minkie lured Eyeno half-bemused to a bower far enough away. This young man wasn't a proclaimer, yet he radiated such a sensuous and endearing promise of joy. To help him rejoice would be a delight. And very appropriate. Didn't he deserve it? Wasn't this his due? Her very own brother was looking the other way intentionally.

When Eyeno relaxed on moss she closed her eyes and saw the maidens giggling in the meadow. Minkie was striding amongst them, naked, strutting, beckoning. A beast in rut.

Those were *her* maidens! Hers, not his. How dare he?

The gauzily gowned nymphs were frisking like foals. Bestial Minkie captured a maiden, skittish yet compliant. He hoisted her. He frisked her garment clear up around her waist. He planted her upon the jutting pommel of his loins so that she rode him, her bare legs wrapped around the saddle of his waist. Threads of virginal blood trickling thinly down Minkie's thighs as he bucked and snorted. And Eyeno shrieked – as the maiden surely ought to have shrieked, once at least. How she shrieked at this rape of her private paradise.

Juke burst into the bower.

Snowy blundered after him, stuttering, crossbow in hand.

Minkie was protesting perfect innocence while fumbling with his belt in haste to buckle it. He hadn't let his breeches down far. Eyeno's gown wasn't even mussed. Well, not much. Only rumpled up to the knee, or a jot higher. What could have distressed the young lady so?

'A cramp in her calf made her cry out. Honestly! I was massaging it to relieve her discomfort, wasn't I?'

Didn't Eyeno know how much he respected and adored her? And what good-fellowship he felt towards her brother? Eyeno had filled his soul with poetry, not with furtive passion.

'Why else did she wander with me to this pretty nook?'

'Liar. Mesmerizer.'

Juke's accusations glanced off Minkie like stones skipping over water before sinking with barely a ripple.

Debaucher of a glassmaker's daughter. *Assassin* of Unmen.

Skip, skip, and scarcely a mark made on Minkie. He blinked beguilingly at Eyeno.

'Your brother's spoiling something precious and dear,' he protested. He swallowed, choking with sentiment. 'I hoped ... to share my life with you, Eyeno.'

'The life of a marauding womanizer!'

'Hey,' Snowy interrupted Juke, 'he's the heir to a keep.'

'Your influence would gentle me, Eyeno,' pleaded Minkie. 'In these past few days I've discovered beauty.'

But Eyeno had seen Minkie's true self rampant in the meadow of her mind. She scrambled up, affronted.

'I'm *not* wicked,' insisted Minkie. 'I feel compelled to – vent my high spirits, that's all. Oh, I admit I do some things which seem mischievous. A little selfish, maybe. It's only because I can't find the lassie to fulfil me. When I do, I'll be a lamb, suckling milk.'

'Not from me,' said Eyeno.

'I'm laying my heart bare before you. And before your good brother.'

'You won't lay *me* bare before you. Oh no. Never.'

Frustration twisted Minkie physically.

'I doubt if you know what such pressure's like. Or how I control myself – as a well brought-up lad ought to – except in my dreams, which I can't avoid. To live in dreams might be fine; but where's dreamland? Where's the wench of my dreams? I believe you're her, Eyeno. Please help me.'

How sincerely he persuaded himself. If Eyeno hadn't seen the beast strutting in the meadow she might have been persuaded. Even now. For a while – till he had used her, then betrayed her. She had known pressure too: the compulsion to seek a false eye that would suit her. Every poem was a small compulsion.

'I can't help but love you, Eyeno! My father couldn't help but make enemies. Enemies killed him in the end. If love should make enemies for me, it's a curse. Don't lay this curse on me, dear friends.'

Minkie's strawberry-faced crony was toying with his crossbow. Juke breathed deeply.

'Lay your bow down, Snowy. *This is spoken.*'

Reluctantly, Snowy lowered the weapon. He bunched his fists, and thumped his thighs in mortification.

'I'll help you control your desires, Minkie Kennan,' promised Juke.

'You're a proclaimer . . . Never said you were.'

'You'll forget about my sister, do you hear?'

Panic flitted across Minkie's engaging face. He struggled.

'Don't put a lid on my life or I'll burst. How can I forget her while she's still here?'

'Our ways are about to part, Minkie Kennan.'

Minkie flapped his leather coat petulantly as if to waft away Juke's words. He gawked at Eyeno, craving her.

'You'll be mine some day, poetess. You'll be my living, loving poem that sets me free from the pressures I suffer. You'll be a poem as potent as a charm – which is what you are: a *charm.*'

'Shut up, Minkie,' said Juke. 'After we walk away from here, any future glimpse of this particular hen will shrink your cock to a button. *This is spoken.*'

*

The dream rocked. Like liquid spilling from a bowl, images cascaded of Minkie flaunting himself flagrantly in her private meadow of maidens, amidst her secret sisters. Why did they sport with him, throwing off their flimsy garments? Was it to sate the insatiable fellow so that he wouldn't find Eyeno herself? Did they sacrifice themselves for her, since otherwise Minkie would have raged madly?

Some days earlier, though later in the memory-dream, Eyeno was telling the mana-mage of the Velvet Isi about the meadow in her mind . . .

The Tulkis had eventually brought Eyeno and Juke through the perpetual mist to the source of the road. Vapour cleared to reveal a barren expanse, black and glassy as obsidian, fringed by forest. This dark glossy tract seemed full of rivers and pools of liquid sunlight and mana-mirages. Within the surface moved sluggish shapes which might have been magnified images of serpents. Or reflections of the billows above. For the sky was now restored to view, densely packed with roller clouds.

Twin domes flanked the gape of a tunnel which delved underground. Slits in those domes were probably for weapons. The two Juttahats were leading Juke and Eyeno towards that mouth when part of the glassy surface began to swell upward. The area was pregnant with something about to emerge – something bulky, something black. Glossy darkness bulged into a hill. The mound encysted an inky slug of huge proportion. That bloated cyst was splitting open, parting like jelly . . .

'Hurrying,' said a Tulki. 'A shuttle launching itself.'

Indeed. A dark craft had risen from the strange ground. An Ukko must have come into orbit, bringing more serpents, more gadgets from a snakeworld. The shuttle would soon leap upward to rendezvous with the living moonlet.

'Hurrying.'

They passed between the domes into the downward tunnel. Behind, the false ground vibrated. Light glared, thunder rolled.

Soft apricot light diffused from ceiling panels. Tunnels coiled away in all directions, serpentinely. There were levels below levels of this nest. Liveried Juttahats trotted to and fro. They laboured in workshop chambers over strange purring engines and mechanisms, amid vats, pumps, pipes. The noise of their talking was a crackling susurrus, of claw-clicking crustaceans

231

in a hissing surf – and often they were totally silent. Junior Jutties in black elastic scampered along corridors clutching utensils. The tiniest Juttie-brats could run and chatter. These offspring paused to stare at the two intruding humans but only briefly, as if their Isi-mind had told their ordinary mind to disregard the novelty. Mature Juttahats barely flicked a glance, enough to note Juke and Eyeno's ushers. Occasional twangs and chimes sounded through the nest as if it were some enormous timepiece. The air was warm and dry and redolent of unripe fruit.

In a bright chamber floored with golden sand a serpent basked sinuously. Its purple skin was aswirl with indigo ideoglyphs. The scales of its upper body wore a faint downy nap, of former barbs now soft and degenerate. The serpent's personal Juttahat sat cross-legged, eyes shut. However, the Isi's glossy eyes watched the human couple pass by.

In a gloomy, guarded hibernaculum another Isi slept, coil balanced upon coil like some thigh-sized hawser.

Brother and sister glimpsed barely a fraction of the convoluted underground keep before the two Tulkis brought them to a mana-mage in a yellow-lit cavern.

This purple and indigo Isi reposed on a deep shelf of rock. Its horned head was erect. Lustrous eyes stared into an indefinable distance, two plums of black glass. Its personal Juttahat stood near it. Two other Juttahats sat at a low shiny desk of buttons and lights, talking to themselves rather than to one another. The desk faced in the direction of a white marble pedestal, on which there sat a great glassy egg twice the size of a human head. Within the egg were vague tubes and cells. Elfin blue lights flickered inside the egg like luminous flies.

Also on the pedestal stood a glass flask holding a long-stemmed flower, waxen and creamy. The spoonlike petals were slowly flexing in one direction, then another, as though the bloom were trying to fit its shape to the play of lights within the glass ovoid. To her great surprise, Eyeno recognized the strange flower. She had seen such blooms as those growing in the meadows of her mind. Occasionally a maiden had plucked one and waved it.

Holding out their dolls, the visitors approached. A thin pronged carmine tongue flicked through an opening under the Isi's rostral scale, emerging to taste the air even while its mouth remained shut. The serpent's entire body expanded and contracted with each breath it took. A scent of green fruit wafted strongly from the mana-mage.

Tulki-twenty took up position close by the mana-mage next to the Isi's own body-servant. The Tulki's musculature slackened. Its mauve cupid lips fluttered rapidly but no sound emerged.

Eyeno felt *pressure* emanating from the serpent. A pastel aura glowed about the sharp little horns which jutted from its flat scaly brow. Now she smelled vanilla and an oily attar. A disconcerting cascade of sensation coursed through her. Her nipples stiffened. Yet the hot tingling faded almost at once. Beside her, Juke was shivering. His hand clamped tight around the bisque doll. His breathing was noisy, exaggerated.

The body-servant questioned Eyeno while the Isi watched lazily. So she is being a poetess? Searching for a new eye? Isi and servant already knew what Tulki-twenty knew.

Her brother must be leaving the mage's cavern, and waiting elsewhere. 'Intending no harm,' promised the mouthpiece. 'Being obliged to you. Grateful. The study of obsession and desire being dear to us. Making us aware that human people are requiring privacy even from their bloodkin. Obliging your sibling to withdraw. That probably being his true desire.'

Juke protested feebly.

'Go, Juke, go,' urged Eyeno. 'This is my quest. And my request.'

Juke looked relieved to be leaving the vicinity of the serpent.

Now the flower could be mentioned. And the meadows. Eyeno felt no qualms at telling an alien snake her secrets.

'A poetess with an inward eye is seeing a meadow where maidens are dancing and where flowers such as *that one* are growing?' The mouthpiece sounded amused and pleased.

'Beholding the flower,' it advised.

Clutching her grubby damaged doll, Eyeno turned to the pedestal. Azure lights twinkled in the recesses of the ovoid, hovering and flitting. The waxen flower flexed. Hair-thin tendrils were sprouting from the base of the cut stem. Those filaments twisted and turned slowly in the sustaining fluid.

The Isi reared up, watching Eyeno steadily as she turned back towards it.

'Being a bloom growing in Ukko caverns, often among bones and echoes,' said its voice, from beside it. 'A flower striving to copy the curvings within an Ukko. We are calling it the ear-flower. Ukkos being the ears of the cosmos, in which fragments

233

of the *logos* are reverberating. A multifold word moulding all events.'

Words moulding events. Yes. She understood – at that moment. Though later her understanding would blur.

An Ukko, moulding events . . .

The glass egg was a model of an Ukko, or an attempt at a model. Those shifting lights were mapping spaces inside the model. The flower's petals responded to the play of lights – to be recorded by the Juttahats at their shiny, winking desks.

Black pupils narrowed to vertical slits within sickly yellow orbs. 'Why should a woman be seeing ear-flowers in her mind's eye?' enquired the mouthpiece. 'Why?'

'Maybe because I was due to see one of those flowers here,' suggested Eyeno. 'I can tell fortunes. Maybe I saw those flowers as part of my own fortune. Me being here – and gaining a fine eye from you.'

'All Ukkos are surely connecting,' the Juttahat puppet mused. 'Yet we are losing the way. Within an Ukko, desire is becoming reality. Routes are becoming illusion, bending back upon themselves . . .'

Sparks winked within the model, appearing here, then there. The flower swayed, its waxen petals twisting.

Tulki-twenty spoke. 'This woman being the new Lucky perhaps? This poetess being due to find what we are seeking, wherever it is hiding itself from us—'

Eyes dilated, pools of ink. The Isi hissed fiercely. Tulki-twenty staggered away from the stone shelf, drooling in distress.

Surely something untoward had happened. Tulki-twenty had been so close to the Isi mage, so much within the ambit of the mage's mind, that it had uttered the serpent's secret thoughts? About herself being . . . a new *Lucky*?

'Poetess! Be reciting a poem in exchange for an eye. Without delay.' The mouthpiece spoke urgently. '*Reciting it now.* Or failing in your quest for a new eye.'

A poem? What poem? Why? To divert her from thinking of what Tulki-twenty had said. To distract her. Panicked, Eyeno stared around for inspiration. That flower upon a stem without any leaves . . .

'*At once. A poem. Or be taking your leave.*'

She recited:

> '*Dried leaf*

'with stalk as rudder
'scuttles like a mouse's
'brown body in the breeze;

'flees
'the cat of the wind
'which will soon shred it
'leaving only the tail to drag

'into a worm hole.
'If people's ears
'crisped to crêpe by frost
'fell off and blew about in flurries
'would winter be the silent season, then?

'Will spring shriek anew
'while fresh ears grow from nubs?
'Will summer play the mad harmonica
'but autumn bring us anaesthetic deafness?

'That's when the worm
'which hides within the brain
'plugs up our hearing canals with golden wax,
'with roots of dead nouns, with the flaked claws

'of verbs that wounded.'

'Verbs wounding with claws,' said the mouthpiece. 'A worm hiding in the head. If words are dying, they are still leaving roots behind. Ears being routes to the brain. Eyes likewise. Your poem lacking any obvious reference to limbs, being polite. We are accepting your poem. Giving us your doll. Taking out your false eye.'

Had she succeeded?

Eyeno handed the one-eyed girl doll to the mouthpiece. She removed the dull paste aquamarine from her eye-socket. The Juttahat accepted the gemstone too. It laid gem and doll on the recessed dais where the coiled serpent reposed, head rampant. The Isi's sleek long velvety head swayed forward. Dipping, it flicked its tongue across Missieur Pierre's gem which must be flavoured the taste of Eyeno herself. Rearing its chin, the Isi opened its mouth for the first time, exposing a wet pink cave lined with hindward pointing teeth, short and sharp.

That dislocated gape was capacious enough to accommodate a

235

human head. Long curved fangs slid out from plump violet sheaths at the forefront of its upper jaw. Surely she wasn't supposed to lie her head in its mouth as an act of submission!

The Isi's voice stepped smartly around Eyeno. It fetched the ear-flower in its flask. Careful not to bruise the bloom, it thrust the lip of the flask under one of its master's fangs.

An oily golden bead of fluid swelled at the tip of the serpent's fang. The liquid bead dropped into the water of the flask. Quickly the Juttahat milked the other fang then it stepped back as the Isi mage shut its pink yawn. A pastel glow played around the serpent's little horns.

Was that what nourished the Ukko bloom – serpent venom?

The waxen petals were closing up, folding around one another. Soon the flower had become a tight bud.

'Standing perfectly still.'

The voice slid the waxen bud into Eyeno's eye-socket. She clenched her fists, nails biting into her palms. She felt petals tremble open and flutter within her orbit like a trapped moth. She trembled too.

When the Juttahat carefully withdrew the flower, the petals were packed in a globular configuration. The Isi's voice hissed and clicked at one of the desk-servants – which rose, to carry the flower and the flask away.

Tulki-twenty said: 'Taking you to your brother, to be waiting for your new eye.' Its spasm had abated. Indeed it semed unaware of any spasm.

Without thinking, Eyeno moved to retrieve her doll from the stony dais. Immediately the Isi's voice blocked her.

'Keeping your manikin.'

'But I was meant to take it back to Mister Hermi—' She didn't want the dirty one-eyed doll to stay with the mage. In some way that doll represented her. A shrill squeal stilled her objections. A small hatch had swung open at the side of the mage's lair.

A curly-tailed pink piglet scampered out – the source of the squeal. Lissomly, the Isi mage swung and seized the baby animal's head and shoulders in its jaws.

'No!' protested Eyeno.

Haunches wriggling, hind legs kicking, the piglet was already writhing down the serpent's gape. Its squeaks were high but muffled. Dislocated jaws marched across its body, puncturing and propelling.

'Are you not eating animals?' asked the voice. An Isi could speak with its mouth full.

'Are you only eating alone in secret?'

'We don't eat animals alive . . .'

She still heard stifled squeaks. The disappearing piglet continued to squirm and kick its hind legs. How long till the wretched animal suffocated? Would it survive long enough to drown in stomach juices? Would its dead throes make the Isi's belly heave?

'Swallowing,' said the voice placidly, 'being an irreversible event.'

Had she in some sense been swallowed too?

Tulki-twenty guided Eyeno away without her doll.

She waited with Juke in a bright, spacious chamber half floored with soil and half with red tiles. A little stream separated the two sections. In the soil grew gaudy variegated shrubs unfamiliar to Eyeno and Juke. Large patterned leaves suggested fanciful maps crayoned by children. On the tiles were table and chairs of polished grainy kastawood, a cushion-strewn sofa and a large brass bed surrounded with golden satin curtains. A screen concealed a sanitary cubicle. This peculiar guest room conveyed reassurance and unease in equal proportions.

Tulkis brought baked trusterfish garnished with nuts and mushrooms, carrot casserole, and a flagon of pink valleyberry cordial.

Eyeno was famished. The act of eating horrified her, but brother and sister ate.

And waited.

Waited.

How long must they stay here? The Tulkis had gone away without saying.

Eyeno whispered to Juke about the ear-flower and the piglet; but she made no mention of her secret meadows.

On the way to this garden-room to await his sister, Juke had glimpsed a chamber flooded with blue light. Within, the skeleton of a serpent lay curled in a tunnel of ribs upon a glassy platform. Liveried Juttahats sat motionless on high stools grouped around the skeleton.

Fascinated, Juke had paused. 'Don't you bury bones in the earth?' he had asked Tulki-nine. Without answer his usher had gripped him by the arm and propelled him onward.

What had Juke seen? A funeral rite? Whatever was happening had looked so static and enduring – like a tableau, as if Juttahats might sit there motionless day after day.

Had their master died? Were they obliged to watch over it for as long as its bones endured? How had the flesh and organs been stripped from those bones? This enigma preoccupied Juke. It was wiser to contemplate a dead serpent than the living ones which infested the nest.

He toyed with his bisque doll – its moulded blond curls resembled his own fawn hair. So far he had failed to notice that his sister no longer had her doll with her.

Why *were* those Juttahats grouped around the bones of an Isi in silent reflection? Were they trying to summon its ghost into their Isi-mind?

Eyeno realized how anxious her brother was. Thus the riddle of the skeleton – if it was really a riddle – riveted him. Juke wasn't really brave, but he tried to behave as if he was, buoyed up by his ability to bespeak other people into obeying him.

Time passed.

Eyeno thought about the fine false eye the Juttahats were busy making for her at this very moment. It *would* be fine, wouldn't it? Unlike the paperweight and the phoney aquamarine. It had to be fine; it was the climax of her quest.

What had Tulki-twenty said about a new Lucky? About Eyeno finding something which the Isi sought? A riddle! She wouldn't even *try* to puzzle it out. Perhaps it was a piece of Isi mischief similar to eating the piglet alive before her very eyes.

After perhaps two hours Tulki-nine returned, accompanied by a silent Juttahat. In its black palm this Juttahat carried an eyeball nested in blue silk.

A perfect human eye. Its blue iris matched Eyeno's own. Short adhesive eye-strings were attached to the orb at top and bottom. An adhesive stub jutted from the rear, a stump of imitation optic nerve. To her wonder she discovered that the pupil even responded to light and dark. By some gyroscopic wizardry an inner core would swivel.

Firm and lightweight, the eye slid easily into her socket and secured itself. Of course she could see nothing through it. The world remained as flat as ever. She would still be obliged to veer her head from side to side more than two-eyed people did.

The light in the garden-room began to dim. Too late to leave the nest, to resume the rubbery road back through the mana-mist.

Brother and sister napped in that garden-room overnight, Juke on the sofa, tossing and turning, Eyeno in the curtained bed.

The dream of memory twisted mischievously. Eyeno awoke to find herself stretched out in the brass bed alongside the skeleton of a serpent. No such occurrence had taken place on that night spent in the garden-room. But now a skeleton lay beside her, such as Juke had described.

Emitting a raucous squawk, a scaly green cuckoo alighted on the brass curtain rail. The bird cried out a fortune poem.

> 'Ukko's child is for the finding,
> 'Lucky seeking, serpents looking.
> 'Lasses playing ardent games:
> 'So its meadows are in flames . . .'

Elongated glassy organs began to form within the skeleton alongside her. The stretched tube of a lung, a protracted stomach and liver . . .

As these changes occurred, the blanket which covered Eyeno became vague and vanished away. Her gown likewise. Stiffness numbed Eyeno's denuded body. Flesh and purple scales now cloaked the serpent's head, though the rest of its body remained ghostly. Glossy eyes reappeared within their sockets, glaring at her.

The cuckoo peered down and cackled. As if that cry were a signal, the partly-resurrected serpent reared. It came crashing down upon Eyeno. The bones might have been mere compacted powder. Ribs and vertebrae collapsed into dust. She smelled such an odour of antiquity. Released from their fragile cage, its vague organs slithered lightly upon her bare skin. The head had fallen off to lie next to her own head. That head alone had achieved solidity. As the mouth gaped wide, Eyeno stared down the gullet, bewildered to see a tunnel curving away into the distance. The floor of that tunnel was littered with skeletons – of serpents, and of bipeds with odd bone structures which must be Juttahats.

She was drifting along that tunnel – so the serpent had indeed swallowed her. The wonderful eye it had given her throbbed with a pulse of life. Of a sudden she was seeing true *depth*, as she imagined depth to be. The tunnel stretched *away* instead of merely being inscribed upon the surface of perception.

That passage opened out into a cavern carpeted with emerald moss. Mist swirled densely, hiding any walls or roof from sight. Tendrils thrust from the moss, to become succulent green herbage. Twists of mist pirouetted, congealing into gauzily clad maidens who capered away from her, luring her across a sward. Trees were appearing. A spring fed a stream.

She saw a Juttahat skeleton stagger erect from the bank of the stream, shedding soil. Mana-mist wove around its bones, bandaging those swiftly in ghostly flesh. A second Juttahat was already being resurrected. The maidens had vanished.

Eyeno shrieked. Her scream was hot and bright. It set a tree on fire.

Morning light flooded through the cracked panes of Eyeno's bedroom window under the shaggy eaves.

In Outo, where else?

After the memory-dreams, she sometimes needed to remind herself of where she really was.

Before she and Juke had journeyed north-east of Saari to the home of the Velvet Isi she had never dreamt memories which might kink and twist capriciously. These dreams had begun during the year after she had gained her beautiful imitation eye. At first they were infrequent. Now they came as often as once a week. Dreams of her quest, all of them – and why not? And often of the maidens in that meadow.

If only she could meet someone who truly understood about dreams.

She *loved* the Isi eye passionately, inseparably.

A commotion erupted outside. Cries of 'Come, come!' were calling the mocky-folk from their cotts.

Had Juke turned up? Oh, let him have returned!

When she pressed her cheek to the cracked windowpane, she saw her neighbours hastening towards the dead harper tree. One branch was perch to a scrawny green bird.

When had a cuckoo last paid a visit to Outo?

Dismay clutched at Eyeno. She dreaded that the bird was about to tell something awful about her brother. She dressed in a rush. Barefoot, she hurried down the rickety stairs. The wobbly front door stood open.

Her mother and father had already joined the gathering. Maybe Arto and Ester likewise feared bad news.

'Come, come!' cried the cuckoo.

Upwards of thirty souls had assembled near the harper tree. Crusty-faced Pieman was there, amid half a dozen kids. In a state of high excitement, lanky Kuro was elbowing bulgy-eyed Arni in the ribs – could Kuro hear a cuckoo uttering words of language? Head, with his baby-sized body, sat on top of his hulking brother, Shoulders. Head clung with tiny strong fingers to his supporter's topknot of red hair. This sprouted from a flattened cranium sunk in a saddle between peaks of shoulders. Head often sat high in that same dead harper tree, seeking enlightenment, hoisted up there by his dim-witted twin. During Head's reveries Shoulders would amble amongst boulders, pitting his muscles against one or other of the great stones that littered the land.

'Come one, come all!' croaked the scaly green bird. The dead harper had lost most of its strings. Some still clung between trunk and bare branches, dry white ribbons which could only muster the feeblest rustle.

'Sing us a story, tell us a tale,' piped Head in squeaky tones.

'Tell us a tale,' demanded Arto gruffly. His pointy ears twitched. 'Hurry up about it.' Stout hairy Ester clutched her husband's arm anxiously as Eyeno joined her parents.

'Don't let the story be about Juke,' Eyeno begged quietly.

'Hush, girl. Won't be 'bout our boy, Mother, nor you fret. Nowt much happens to mocky-men that a cuckoo would ever care for.'

'Zing uz a ztory!' bellowed Shoulders, to amplify his tiny twin's demand.

'A story, a story!' squealed mocky-kids – one with speckled red feathers sprouting all over his skin, another with lustrous fishy scales.

The cuckoo fluttered its green, rust-speckled plumage. Its big yellow eyes winked. It cocked its cupped ears.

'The Dame of Niemi's lad has stolen himself a fine bride,' the bird began; and Eyeno breathed out in relief.

The cuckoo eyed Head and Shoulders. 'Minkie Kennan went to serve at Johann Helenius's court in Saari just a year ago—'

'Whooze ziz Minkie?' Shoulders interrupted loudly.

'The Dame of Niemi's lad, of course,' Head told him. He pulled on the topknot as if to lift the lid of his brother's brain-pan.

'Whooze ziz Dame of Niemi, Head?'

'Shhhh,' implored Eyeno. 'It'll fly away.'

Minkie Kennan. That pest. That the scallywag had actually wedded a bride pleased Eyeno very well. Since that meeting in the woods some years before she had dreamed several disconcerting things about that scamp and lecher and, oh yes, terror of Juttahats. If the heir to Niemi had truly fallen in love, a bride might distract him from mischief. What was this about him *stealing*, though?

'Tell us the tale,' she called out.

The cuckoo swivelled to focus upon her.

'Loverboy kissed the girls at court and made them sigh,' it craked. 'They couldn't resist our Minkie. He rolled them all in the hay, you might say. Within a twelvemonth he had those court girls thoroughly under his thumb – both the thumb on his hand and the thumb somewhere else. They'd help him do whatever he wished. Well now, *courting* was his main intention—'

Shoulders had raised both his paws to inspect his splayed fingers. He guffawed.

'Ze *thumb* on t'other hand! Zat's it!'

'Hush, you great lunk!'

The messenger bird continued to gaze at Eyeno.

'The courting of rich little Miss Snooty-Nose, Kyli Helenius, who else? A marriage with the Lord of Saari's lass could fluff up the Kennan family's fortunes from a flat pillow to a plump bolster. Whatever her girlfriends said in our Minkie's favour, Kyli Helenius still looked down that neat little nose of hers at our insolent scallywag, immune to his allure—'

'Thumb on one hand, thumb on t'other.' Puzzled, Shoulders fitted his left hand against his hip, then upon his waist. 'Unlezz 'iz hand woz zumwhere elze!'

'It was, it was,' teased Pieman, 'it was down in the bird's nest.'

'What nest's zat?'

'The hairy one, Dunderhead.' Tiny Head belaboured his twin. 'The one with all the hay in it. Where the egg hatches out.'

'—So what does our Minkie do?' asked the bird. It blinked rapidly. 'Why, he kidnaps Kyli Helenius and ravishes her, that's what. Well, now that her honour's undone—'

'—and so is her bird's nest!'

'—she decides she'll make the best of a bad job, and the best of a bad boy too. No more rousting about for Minkie. So now our rapscallion is a wedded husband. He repairs the Kennan keep with a bit of grudging dowry from his Dad-in-Law.'

'—caught in the birdcage!' Pieman applauded.

'What's that to us?' Eyeno's father grumbled. 'Why should the likes of us care about such goings-on of the high and mighty?'

His wife nudged him in the ribs. 'Oh Arto,' said Ester, 'don't you see that this new châtelaine will want nice kid gloves – if only to handle her naughty husband with.'

Arto waggled six fingers derisively. 'An iron gauntlet sounds a better bet.'

'You don't understand, Arto, 'cause we're *ugly*. Away from her posh court, in a half collapsing keep, that spoilt lass'll be bound to yearn for gowns and kidskin gloves. Especially gloves, to keep her fair hands soft. She brought a spot of money with her, didn't she? Don't you agree with me, daughter?'

Eyeno winced. She would never peddle gloves at the door of a keep where *that person* ruled the roost. Not likely. Never, ever.

'Sung is the story, told is the tale.' The cuckoo flapped its wings by way of finale. It fluttered impatiently.

'Wants feeding, it does,' observed Pieman.

Eyeno darted back into her home, to return with a drippy lump of goat liver, wrapped in a discarded draft of a poem. She tossed this up at the dead tree. A soiled page of verse unfurled half-way and fluttered free. With a hop and a skip the bird nimbly caught the offering of offal in its beak. Balancing one-legged, it held the liver in its claws while it tore and swallowed. Nothing ever made a cuckoo sick.

Bulgy-eyed Arni had picked up the paper. '*Shattering herself*,' he read aloud, '*in a rapturous*, no, make that *rupturous* . . . *enforced*, no, cross that out, *and forced embrace*. Hmm, hmm.'

His web-fingered brother seized the slate which hung on a thong from Arni's belt. Crumpling the page into his pocket, Arni snatched a stub of chalk out. Kuro guided Arni's hand to print: *I HEARD EVERY WORD OF THE BIRD.*

'Wonderful!' exclaimed Arni, while Kuro stared from his sunken eyes at his brother's lips. Arni clapped his brother on the shoulder, in response to which his acromegalic brother cuffed him amiably.

'Cuckoo,' called Eyeno.

The bird cocked its head, a last morsel of offal hanging from its mouth.

'Cuckoo, why did you come here?' Far from dismissing Minkie Kennan finally from her mind, the unexpected news had suddenly revived her apprehensions about him.

The bird glared. 'Ukko, Ukkoo,' it said, and took wing.

243

Speakers' Valley was a fertile bowl some three keys wide. From around a central hillock, terraces rose gently to a rim crowned with harper trees. Upwards of a thousand sheep were grazing those slopes, keeping the vigorous herbage trim. Stocky, hardy, prolific sheep. Susceptible to footrot, though, in lush conditions. A few lame ewes grazed on their knees. A couple of shepherds worked on one tumbled captive. The first man restrained the ewe while his partner trimmed her hooves with a knife prior to daubing with tar from a pot. Two perky Spitz dogs crouched intently, bushy tails coiled over their backs. A trio of riders ambled on ponyback, crossbows slung over their shoulders. This wealth of livestock could attract thieves or the attentions of a verrin. The larger relative of the musti could easily slaughter ten or twenty sheep in succession. Sensing something uncongenial about the flesh and blood of its first victim, the verrin would promptly desert the corpse to attack a second prospect – then another, then another, all killed in vain. Verrins mightn't care to give themselves belly ache, but nor did they ever seem to learn the principle that people's livestock were indigestible to them.

The riders paid only scant attention to a man and a woman with a boy. Sightseers were common enough. Anyone passing through Yulistalax might hike out from the lakeside town to admire this valley, to listen to the mingled melody of so many harper trees, to imbibe the mana which must imbue the site after so many galas. Come gala time, most households in Yulistalax teamed up to offer accommodation.

Come the autumn gala, too, the foliage of the harper trees around the valley would have flushed to gold and bronze and apricot. As yet, they were jade-green. In the mild breeze their massed strings thrummed softly. Shadows ambled across the bowl below, dappling gleaming slopes with greyer glaucous smudges. Some of that multitude of sheep seemed to have been transported, magnified, into the sky as woolly clouds. Prior to the gala, of course, these flocks would be herded away to pens to make room for masses of people, grandstands, marquees, stalls, booths, and sideshows.

In his mind's eye Juke was already anticipating that autumn spectacle.

'I want to stand down there on Speakers' Stage,' he told Jatta, nodding to the knoll at the heart of the vale.

'And proclaim to the sheep, perhaps?'

Lightly said, and sympathetically. Her riposte wasn't a mocking one.

Since their fracas at Granny's hostel Juke hadn't once mentioned his sister, nor the subject of Juttahats either. Nor had Jatta. During the long raft journey their mutual wounds had healed in common, as it were, the raw tissue uniting the two of them in a complicity to avoid further injury to the feelings. Juke was practising an affable courtesy. She was determined to be supportive, and not falsely so in the way of a charade. Some banter was even beneficial, so long as they avoided certain topics. Areas forbidden to contemplate – not because Juke had proclaimed that so, but out of common consent. Areas best left cloaked in fog.

Oddly, young Jack never piped up about what he had overheard on that night in the hostel. Maybe he'd been too confused, or shocked and frightened. Maybe he hadn't understood. His mother and her companion may have sounded like two drunks raving nonsense at each other. Or perhaps his mind was pregnant with new thoughts which needed to gestate, rather than be blurted out prematurely.

'I'll make the trees sing for you, princess,' Juke offered grandly. 'I'll tune the valley for Osmo's downfall.'

A downfall which she did rather desire. If only she herself could be here to see the gala. What finer sight could there be anywhere south of the Great Fjord? If Juke were to be hailed as a proclaimer, and she was under his patronage, but not under his thumb . . . well!

Another four hundred keys remained till they reached mutant homesteads in the southernmost wilderness nook of the domain of Saari. As regards tithes at least, the mutant settlements were part of that vast landholding. No longer did Jatta feel any overriding obsession to arrive there. Sheer distance from Maananfors, and travelling with a mutant, had drawn that sting. What replaced it was mere pressure of necessity to find a safe berth for herself and her miracle boy. Already Jack was a knuckle taller than when they had rafted away from Forssa.

'Can you really make the trees sing?' she asked.

245

'Well now, the presence of a large audience would help me somewhat. All minds have a glimmer of mana in them. A thousand glimmers is a mirror to magnify the speaker's will.' He laughed sharply. 'An audience of sheep mightn't quite serve the purpose. Though maybe Jack can help? He stirred up quite a wind for those foresters.' Juke tousled the trotting boy's hair; Jack dodged.

They began their descent through a flock which lumbered and hobbled bleating out of the way.

In another couple of months proclaimers would be challenging each other on this tabletop of a knoll – watched from the terraces where only woolly bodies grazed at present; and where two tiny shepherds pared hooves; where a few riders kept watch for roving verins or rustlers.

'Sing, harpers!' Juke called out to the wooded brows of the valley. 'Play your strings!' Acoustics were excellent. A shepherd looked up and waved.

'Feel the wind of my words! Stretch tight and sing! This is spoken, spoken.' He yodelled. Echoes of his voice returned. He began to dance like some tundra shamans she had seen. He cavorted, he skipped, he faced the four winds in turn.

Jack goggled a while then suddenly he crouched. He hunched over on his knuckles. Like some puppy hound the boy howled a reedy parody of Juke's noises at the encircling hilltop.

Juke paid him no heed. 'Harpers, sing!' he warbled, shuffling around.

Something stung Jatta's hand. In astonishment she stared at a melting snowflake. Another snowflake fell. Impossible, on such a warm summer's day. Those fleecy clouds couldn't contain snow.

'*Harpsing, harpsing, harpsing-ho,*' bellowed Juke, all his attention on the wooded ridge. Little Jack wailed his juvenile imitation.

Hundreds of sheep were turning to face in an identical direction. They didn't face the knoll but lined up clockwise along the broad terraces. All around the valley sheep were aligning themselves like fat white fish in a current.

Single-mindedly, thousands of animals began to walk and hobble in unison, clockwise.

Still Juke didn't notice, so intent was he on the distant circuit of harper trees. The proclaimer was blocking out all else. Jack had raised a hand from the turf and was circling it in the air as he hooted. Flurries of snow flew by. Almost all of the sheep were on the move now, surging. Pony riders and shepherds were alarmed. Horn calls rang out: *hoo-hoo, hoo-hoo.*

A slow stampede was under way all around the valley. Bleats blended into one quivering plangent babel. The collective cry of blundering sheep was a voice that filled the whole vale, reverberating from slope to slope: *MAAAIRRR-MAAAIRRR-MAAAIRRR—*

It was more than the noise of the herds. The harper trees had taken up the same outcry, amplifying it. At last Juke snapped out of his private trance. His face went slack – he was scared.

The din resounded: some great alarm call which might be heard keys and keys away. Flocks were in full flood around the gradients of their pasture. Some sheep tripped, some were trampled. The white mass poured pell-mell, bodies leaping, colliding. *MAAAIRRR*, sang the trees.

Jack crouched tensely, one fist on the ground, the other stirring the air. The boy was bleating in tune, sounding subhuman.

'Stop it, Jack, stop it,' cried Jatta. He grinned back at his mother crazily. And at Juke. Juke certainly hadn't unleashed this maelstrom of madness upon the animals. Consternation was written on the man's face – perhaps a trace of greed too, a desire for such power. But alarm won out.

Should Jatta seize her boy and shake him? Maybe all the sheep would stumble at once, breaking their legs. Up on the ridge to the west other riders were emerging from the baaing trees. Crossbow in hand, rifle in hand, they struggled to control their rearing ponies.

The riders only scanned the swirl of sheep briefly. Their attention was on the sky to the south.

The clamour was masking the noise of a sky-boat floating slowly from that direction. A long sky-boat with sharp delta wings, vanes, fluted pipes, whiskery antennae. It was descending above the harper trees: a mauve sky-boat with a row of portholes.

'That's the boat we saw at the lake,' cried Jatta. 'It's the Isi boat!'

She and her boy and Juke were exposed in plain view on that mound at the heart of the valley. The stampede had separated into several rivers; one bleating stream rushed around the base of the knoll. Snow flurried again from nowhere.

'Shite it,' swore Juke, 'we must hide among the sheep.'

'Among *those*?'

More likely to be bowled over. To have a few ribs broken. Or an arm.

An Isi sky-boat . . .

Cuckoos were spreading word of her demon child. Maybe Jarl was searching for her. Jarl hadn't been a Juttahat – she rejected Juke's guess. Maybe that mauve sky-boat wasn't an Isi one at all. Perhaps the sky-boat was an Earth one, come from Landfall to find her and her child. A cuckoo had told the Earthfolk about her miracle son and they were fascinated. They would offer her sanctuary. Why hadn't she thought of this possibility?

'That might be an Earth boat.'

'Don't kid yourself! They're Jutties, and you know what they want.'

'Don't talk about that,' she said urgently. Wounds would be torn open again.

'Let's hide, damn it.'

'Jack'll be crushed—'

Jack jumped up. 'Hiding's fun. *Maaaairrr!* Riding's more fun.'

Her crazy fast boy would ride a sheep now. Gallop off on its back. With herself straddling two sheep? And Juke two more? Or clinging under their bellies, thumpety-bumpety, being dragged around the racetrack?

The descending vessel's air jets ruffled the stampede. To clear a space for landing, hot light lanced from rods mounted under the war-boat's nose, scything to and fro. The result could hardly have been what the crew expected. Instead of sheep falling over dead or disabled, while the rest scattered, a score of animals burst into flames as though their wool was soaked in oil. Saturated by mana-mania, more like. The blazing sheep plunged onward, shrieking, passing the torch to others in the mob. Flame leapt from ewe to ewe. Greasy smoke streamed back in smutty plumes, a cloud of confusion for the pilot. The sky-boat thumped down clumsily, crushing a couple of sheep beneath its long sprung skids. It lurched, settling at an angle. Pony riders were descending into gaps in the stampede, readying their crossbows and a rifle or two. The burning sheep did not fall. They fled with a furnace on their backs. Tongues of flame clung to the animals, goading them to gallop faster, bleating wildly. Yet none of the tormented sheep had collapsed.

'Poor lammies,' cried Jack. 'All sore, all cooking. All wanting to be cool!' He gyrated both fists in the air. Showers of snow swept across the frantic herd as it passed by below. What could better fight hot fire but cold?

Juke heaved the boy by the arm.

'Down the other side!'

Down where the knoll could hide the three of them from the sky-boat – for a while at least. The sky-boat's propellers had halted. A hatch sprang open. Out darted Unmen dressed in lustrous tawny livery, the scaly fabric suggestive of hammered copper. Several carried lightrifles.

Juke and Jatta and Jack hurried down from the knoll.

But a *second* sky-boat was coming in from the north. The vessel was aiming to land on a vacant swathe of terrace several hundred metres away. Half a dozen sheep had fallen, forming a jumbled barricade. Not quite as long as the mauve war-boat, with more rounded wings, this other vessel was winter-white. Painted around the pupils of its portholes, the vermilion outline of eyes peered like bloodflowers from a bank of snow.

A spasm twisted Juke's face. 'We're boxed in. Nowhere to hide.'

'To hide, to hide,' chanted Jack.

Jatta exclaimed, 'But that's my mother's sky-boat!'

By now the vessel had settled. Sheep raced past it, one on fire. Streamers of snowflakes chased after the ewe like clouds of hungry white flies.

'Your mother's? Your mother kicked you out. She had you dumped in the forest. This is an Isi trick. That sky-boat's only painted to look like Queen Lucky's.'

Jatta saw its hatch sink down to make a ramp. At the top of that ramp appeared a tubby figure in camouflage-dappled leathers, waving a lightpistol.

'He's human, he isn't a Juttie.'

'Wait for a second one to show.'

'That's Marti – my guard at Lokka.'

As the podgy man plodded down the ramp, a lanky guardsman followed.

'And Olli.'

Other northern guardsmen dressed in camouflage leathers spilled out in the wake of those first two. Marti collided with several charging sheep and disappeared. Olli beckoned frantically across the milling herd in the direction of the knoll. *Come here, come here.* Around the bottom of the hillock a loose carousel of ewes circled, several blazing and streaming thick smoke.

Juke gripped Jatta by the arm. 'We shan't set on fire. We shan't

249

burn. Do you hear, this is spoken! Listen to me, Tycho Cammon did this to a challenger here one year. I heard it from a spectator who was here when it happened. Cammon made his rival into the burning man. Burning, burning. Running round burning and screaming for ages while Cammon laughed. The valley remembers. Mana remembers. It's mana-fire that's afflicting the sheep. I won't let it touch us.'

Juke hoisted Jack.

'Hide us, seek us!' yelled the boy.

Gaps opened in the carousel of sheep. Within seconds Juke and Jatta were in their midst.

'Poor lammies!'

Abruptly a full-scale blizzard blew. Stinging, swirling snow engulfed the three of them. A burning sheep lumbered past, eyes wild, teeth bared. Flames sizzled as they flicked at fat frozen flakes. A crowd of ewes crashed into Juke and Jatta, spinning them around, carrying them along. *MAAAIRRR, MAAAIRRR* was the voice of the snowstorm.

A corridor of sunshine. A shaft of sky above. Green herbage underfoot. *Walls of blizzard.*

Exhausted sheep blundered from winter to summer to winter. Jatta glimpsed a marquee draped in multicoloured bunting, decorated for the gala. Of course the big tent wasn't really there. It would have been here last autumn, yes. It would be here in the autumn to come. Not now, not now. It seemed as if the year had stumbled and tripped forward, missing out months. Falling into winter, recoiling into autumn. Juke had been dreaming so possessively about the future, hadn't he? Now seasons were jumbled with Jack's help.

A Juttahat trotted into view, lightrifle held at the slope. The Unman's head was capped with snow but the front of its livery gleamed. Sunlight glanced off the wall of blizzard to reflect from the alien fabric. A snaky hieroglyph on the Juttahat's shoulder was a zigzag of spilled ink. The Unman cried out in a clicking and hissing voice. It headed towards the trio, although it didn't lower its weapon to menace them. It must be under orders not to, if the aim was to capture them. If the aim was to capture *Jack*. A blunder of sheep blocked its path. The Unman swung the weapon frustratedly.

Two more of its kind stepped into the bright clear corridor. A pony appeared. Its rider reined in. Snow flecked the man's shirt and breeches. One-handed, he aimed a cocked crossbow.

The quarrel lodged in an Unman's neck, throwing the alien aside. A burning ewe barrelled into one of the other Juttahats. The sheepguard tumbled from his pony to scrabble towards the fallen lightrifle. What a prize that weapon was. Neither of the reinforcements had carried one, but the Juttahat who was still upright whipped a knife from a sheath behind his leg.

Juke and Jatta didn't wait to see the outcome. They hurried into winter. Jack chortled as he snatched snow from the air.

Shivering, they reached a broad hub of summer where two sun-dappled corridors crossed. Jatta sneezed convulsively. Snow melted into her clothes, into her cropped hair. Not far away two Juttahats were guarding a third who supported on cradled arms – a serpent of burnished gold.

An Isi in the flesh. One of the masters of the Unmen slaves whom they directed with their minds. It had directed its carrier to bring it out from the safety of the sky-boat. So as to test the nature of this fragmented tempest personally? To guide its troops? Was it as lost as Jatta and Juke?

The Isi seemed to be some monstrous extrusion from the snake-bearer's livery, or a great brass tuba which the Juttahat was about to blow a blast upon. Hands locked together, the Unman sustained the coiled weight of its lord's fat, scaly tail. The main mass of body looped twice around its servant's shoulders, their girth that of the Juttahat's upper thigh. Ochre brown and rusty ferric glyphs patterned the Isi's glittering body. Its horned head wavered beside the porter's own head. The serpent's large jet eyes stared. Its thin tongue flickered in and out. The serpent was artful intelligence – it was peril, and authority. And something else besides. Puffs of light – pink, blue, and rose – popped from the sharp little horns jutting from above those night-black eyes. Energy ascendant? Drifting up, bursting like bubbles ... The serpent's head swayed. It seemed discomfited. Confused. Its Juttahat called out, 'Waiting! No harm to you!' The voice made the reassurance sound sinister.

Juke and Jatta didn't linger. They ran away along a summery corridor. One of Lucky's guards and a Juttahat fell through, cloaked in snow. The fighters rolled over and over. Human hand on alien wrist, human wrist in alien hand, each tried to stab, each struggled to hold the other's knife away. A glow in the snow: a ewe staggered into summer, heaving and maddened, flames gushing from its fleece. The wool still appeared no more than singed.

251

Juke thrust Jatta into the snowstorm. They stumbled uphill through that swirling yet stationary blizzard.

Here was a glade of sun, with honey-bright lanes leading away up the terraces, down, along. The snow could have been so many high tumultuous white hedges. Defeated by the absurdity of their surroundings, thirty or forty sheep huddled together trembling. Mavericks continued to lurch into sight, and out of sight, one or two ablaze.

This little herd had its shepherdess.

A young woman.

Her naked body was crisscrossed with tight strings. Her figure was graceful, though her skin looked curiously glassy. That face, with large dusky eyes, might have been lovely had the woman's mouth not hung open slackly. Her dark hair was greasy and unkempt. Jatta recoiled at this apparition who seemed to have stepped from her own imagination. No, not from her imagination at all, but from her *memory* – of a girl corsetted by a network of lines which moulded her and moved her and manipulated her this way and that, steering her emotions too. *What memory? From where?*

From when Jarl was setting about seducing her. Yes, that was when. When Jarl was busy intoxicating Jatta.

The seductive, weary shepherdess looked somewhat older than the girl whom Jatta had glimpsed in her fleeting and delirious vision. As if she were sapped by being ... employed, in those strings which commanded her. She wasn't really naked at all. All those strings, and that glassy cast to her flesh ...

Puppet-like, the woman lurched forward. She stretched out her arms.

'Come to your nurse, Jack,' she called.

She knew Jack's name.

'I shall be your nurse, little boy.'

The words jerked from her awkwardly. She was echoing phrases, reciting words that someone or something had taught her that she must say. She wasn't delivering her words at all well, as though she could no longer hear them properly in her mind – or perhaps did not wish to repeat them except to be rid of them from out of her. That young woman, who resembled Jatta as if reflected in a distorting glass – Jatta with her jet hair and pear-shaped face – strained towards Jatta and Juke and Jack with such craving to be with them – with a yearning which was

quelled by *strings*. The wish surged within her. To join them.
Rather than they should come to her.

'Whoever you are, go away!' the woman shrieked. 'But take
me with you!'

Those were her own frantic words. No one had told her to say
them. *Baaaa*, said a sheep.

'That *net* she's wearing,' said Juke. 'I'll swear it's – a snake
skin. A sloughed-off skin. She's wearing Isi skin.'

'For the love of Lucky!' cried the young woman. She staggered.
She attempted to dart forward but was unable to. Her arms
reached.

'Something's been done to the skin to make it into a garment.
It's been stretched—'

Expanded. Treated. Made into a body-glove. Into a network
webbing the woman's limbs, much of the tissue transparent.

Of course: Jatta saw that now. When, in that flash of vision
on that second day of Jarl's strange songful wooing, the same
girl had writhed so heedful to lust, she hadn't been wearing
strings at all but a second skin over her own. A skin that moved
her. Moulded her. A skin moulted by a serpent.

'We must help her,' said Jatta. Yet she was utterly unconvinced of this.

Juke's hand restrained her; it only took a touch to do so.

'For the love of Saint Lucky!' How frustratedly the skin-clad
woman craved. How her hands implored.

'Lucky's my grandma,' piped Jack. 'My grandma who looks so
like my mummy, says Mummy!'

'She thinks *you're* Lucky Sariola?' Juke was flummoxed.
'Because that's Lucky's sky-boat? She wants your boy, she wants
your Demon Jack. Mana help me, I'm heeding Jack as if he talks
sense.'

'*For the love of Lucky!*'

'She's *praying*,' snapped Jatta.

The woman was some poor peasant. Kidnapped from some
lonely farm. Jutties kidnapped people from time to time. Hadn't
Juke mentioned some veteran telling him tales of bygone abduc-
tions, in a park in Maananfors? This woman had been snatched
by Juttahats of the Brazen Isi. She'd been made to wear the
cast-off skin of one of the sorcerous serpents as a web of control.
She must act as a nursemaid for Jack when they seized or lured
the boy. Control was wearing thin in the swirl of mana which
had brought the snow from another season. Jatta imagined an

253

icon of Lucky hanging in a hovel. Seeing Jatta emerging out of the inexplicable snow, the young woman must have seen the family resemblance, despite hacked hair and sunburn. Did she imagine that the mistress of the Northland was miraculously before her eyes, complete with blizzard?

The Sariola sky-boat was indeed close by. Illusion was reality.

'Where's my mother's sky-boat? If only we can find it—'

Jatta stared along one narrow sunny vista then the next. Those swarming snow-hedges masked so much. *MAAAIRRR*, blared the valley. A sheep raced by, on fire, smoke streaming. In what direction was the white sky-boat, and where was the mauve war-boat? A muffled shot rang out. A blurred voice cried in pain. People were shouting confusedly. The meaning was lost.

'No, we must get right away,' said Juke, 'up the slopes, and out of here.'

To seek sanctuary with muties in a wilderness? When her mother's sky-boat had come at last with Olli and Marti and others from Pohjola Palace?

'Confusion's our friend, Jatta. Your mother's guards mightn't win.'

They mightn't. Why had her mother sent the boat in search of her? To collect Jack, of course. Cuckoos had told Lucky about the miracle child. Was Jatta to be brought home too? Or abandoned once again!

Juke seemed as paralysed as Jatta felt. To move down any sunny avenue seemed senseless when right now they were concealed – except from that pleading soul-sister. Veiled by snow, dazzled by sun, beckoned to by a distraught woman in a snake skin, amidst outcry, invisible skirmish, and sheep in flames, what course of action made any sense?

A man stepped from the snow-shield, close by the peasant girl. He wore a cap of the four winds. Orange and red tassels flapped. Snow sat on the cap. Fat flakes embroidered his white shirt and stippled his brown breeches. Snow masked his face: white cosmetics slapped on zanily.

Yet Jatta knew him at once.

'Jarl!' she sang out. 'My Jarl!'

Heart thudding, she launched herself towards her lover.

To embrace him? Or to pummel him for deserting her? What jaunty song would be on Jarl's lips today?

'It's *Daddy*!' Jack became a wild thing in Juke's hold. The boy tore himself free. He tumbled to the turf. Springing up, he sprinted after Jatta, bunching his little fists.

The mask of snow fell from Jarl Pakken's face – and Jatta staggered to a halt. That well-remembered face was grey instead of golden. Her lover's skin was papery. His eyes were a sickly yellow hue. His cupid lips had lost their blush to become a bruised blue. Dimples in his chin were ulcers, oozing rheum. The whiff of sour milk and dung wafted from him. Jatta stared, aghast and dizzy.

The young woman in the snake skin flinched. Her nipples, her navel, her squeezed black pubic hair: all was glassily visible, all was exposed, and all was confined. All was visible, all was restricted. Her nostrils flared. Her face twisted in a crazy grin as she turned towards Jatta's former lover.

'My darling Jarling,' she cried, 'you can't have me now. You're *dead*. Your prick's dead. Your tongue's dead.'

'Silence, Anni. Be quiet.' Jarl's formerly resonant voice was now rustling dried leaves stirred about in a bucket.

Zombie.

Zombie.

Zombie.

The little word pitter-pattered within Jatta's skull. Some tiny evil insect which had flown in through her ear.

Zombie. Zombie.

A scream was rising to drown out that vile insistent insect-word. That scream had to ascend from deep down within her. The howl had a long way to climb before it could evict that dreadful word. For a moment Jatta must have seemed almost serene.

Jarl's gaze slid from mother to boy.

'Sonny, let pretty Anni hold you—'

That crackle of dead leaves.

Jack threw himself at Jarl, fists flailing in anger and frustration.

'Daddy's dead already! Jack can't kill you!' The boy's fists left slimy imprints in that shirt.

This walking cadaver was what Jatta had made Jarl into. It was this corpse-to-be who had ravished her so deliriously. And had begotten her boy in her. A half-breed boy. Hybrid. Half Juttie. This well-bred, slyly hatched *Juttahat* had stolen her precious gift. Its odour nauseated her. In a spasm of comprehension Jatta understood that Jarl had *practised* on this girl in the

255

snake skin. Exercising himself in the skills of seducing a human woman. Training himself in lovemaking. Singing to her, mounting her. Again and again and again till he was perfect. That little word zombie had stopped Jatta from grasping immediately what Anni had snarled at Jarl. Now she understood.

Now the scream erupted from her.

And the walls of whirling snow suddenly subsided.

The blizzard swiftly settled into flat white tracks, a maze of melting paths.

Giddy sheep were still stumbling around like mobile bundles of snow. Smouldering sheep bleated inanely. Skirmish suddenly was no longer blind. People crouched and scurried. Guards, brazen Jutties, dismounted riders. The crumple of a pony corpse here, a Juttie corpse there, a shot ewe. The Juttahat who bore the serpent stood a full fifty metres from any other Jutties and a long way from their sky-boat.

Out of the white sky-boat there bustled a plump woman of youthful looks splendidly dressed in a purple velvet gown and scarlet suede boots. A twinkling jewelled tiara perched on her spilling black hair. Lucky Paula Sariola, queenly as could be. Jatta's scream died.

Her mother was risking a lightbeam from the Juttahats. Maybe she was sure that no alien would aim at her. Maybe she was right. Jatta knew well enough what her mother's plumpness implied. Another pregnancy in that long sequence of a hundred and more daughters.

Lucky had rushed from the sky-boat because she had caught sight of . . . Jack and Jatta?

Jack's tantrum had weakened the boy. The wild energy had fled out of him when the snow collapsed. He slumped against the thing which had been Jarl.

'You'll be raised by your real kin,' said the zombie.

'I'll nurse you nice,' promised Anni. She snatched Jatta's boy up, clutching him to her bosom.

She was carrying him off, showing Jatta her snakeskin-netted rump. Jarl staggered in her wake. Other Jutties were paying attention. Jutties were converging on Anni.

Jatta started forward but Juke had hold of her.

'Let go!'

'They'll take you too – they'll use you.'

'Save my boy, Juke – let me *go*.'

He wouldn't, he wouldn't. He wouldn't risk his neck.

'*Damn you!*' She struggled with Juke. What a coward he was.

'Don't be a fool,' he scolded, 'the kid's half alien.'

'I don't care. He trusted you, *mutie*.' Jutties were shepherding the nursemaid with her burden and the zombie who'd been Jatta's lover.

'Mother,' she shrieked, 'save my boy!'

The queenly woman was also shrieking orders, to her men.

'*Catch the snake and its Juttie! Bring me the mana-mage and its mouthpiece!*'

Jatta could hardly believe her ears. Lucky had altered her priorities on the instant. That's why she'd rushed from the sky-boat: to stop her men from wasting time rescuing the miracle boy now that a greater prize was at hand. That's why she was risking her centuries-old, ever-youthful skin.

For a mana-mage. Northern guards raced towards the lone serpent-carrier as its burden reared, glaring. Juttahat were hustling the nursemaid towards their war-boat, wading through sheep. A sheepguard loosed his crossbow. The man pitched over his pony's mane as his mount crumpled, blood spurting from a throat sliced by light.

'Save my boy!' screamed Jatta.

One of Lucky's men swung a net over the serpent-carrier.

'Jarl,' bawled Jatta, 'we're catching your mage!'

Anything to divert the Jutties from rushing Anni on board the mauve boat. But quite in vain. Why wasn't their serpent-master more important to them than a demon child? Because there was only one Jack in all the world? Jack's abduction mattered more. Maybe the mage wasn't sending clear thoughts to the servants it controlled. Still muddled by the mana-storm. Four Pohjola guards were lugging the loaded net along as fast as they could. A net which might have held her fast boy in it! What did her mother think that Jack was? A junior wild beast?

Juke was thrusting her towards the white sky-boat. Her boots scuffed turf. He lifted her off the ground. He hobbled along with her crushed to his chest while she kicked and fought. Lucky beckoned imperiously.

'Come with me, daughter,' she yelled. Jatta's mother retreated up the ramp ahead of her guards. 'Hurry yourselves!'

'We'll go with your mother,' Juke blabbered in her ear. 'This is spoken, it's spoken.'

Kyli Kennan, neé Helenius, looked out over placid Lake Lasinen through an embrasure. She practised smiling as if the lake might mirror and magnify her smile, filling her heart with felicity.

The windowframe was rotten and empty of glass, though the inner shutters had been repaired. Winter, when it came, wouldn't howl into the tower room and load the bare floorboards with snow. A soarfowl lay in one corner, reduced to plumes and bones and rubbery feet, a rusty flèchette lodged in its rump. That corpse must have been there for months or years.

This abandoned chamber was certainly the worst one in the ramshackle keep. If Kyli could contrive to smile here, why, she could smile anywhere.

As she stared at the inactive funicular railway linking dusty clifftop Niemi with the shanties along the shore, she subdued her grief for Saari with its fine canals and fountains. She reined in her nostalgia for the riverside palace of her father overlooking the busy broad Murame. Only a few fishing boats plied this lake; it was locked in by land rather as she was now locked in to a humbler life away from her sisters and the glittering girls at court.

From now on this keep would be *her* court!

Presided over by staunch Dame Inga Kennan, attended by strawberry-faced Snowy and other retainers, with Minkie's kid brothers Kosti and Karl as squires. She would find herself soulmates in the town. Oh yes, she would still be able to play. Not splendidly, but satisfactorily.

'Kiki-liki! Kiki-liki, where are you?'

Her heart beat faster at the sound of her husband's voice.

Her ravisher's voice.

'I'm here, Minkie,' she called. 'Top of the tower.'

The door groaned open, and there he stood. Minkie beamed blissfully at his bride. His nutbrown eyes were moist with sentiment and adoration. How handsome he was with his chestnut curls in cultivated disarray. Generous, humorous, valorous. And how hardworking now at fulfilling her every fancy – or a fair fraction of those – with regard to refurbishing the keep, using her dowry as his purse.

He had also quite frankly raped her, after his attempts at seduction failed – seduction which, she suspected, had also embraced quite a few of her intimate circle as a way of gaining accomplices by guile and blackmail . . .

Minkie crossed the room to enfold her in his arms. He rubbed his snubby nose affectionately against her own neat little upturned nose.

'What a lovely hoity-toity button,' he murmured. 'I adore it. I worship every bit of you.'

He held her away by her shoulders so as to inspect her for the thousandth time. He appraised her slim oval face framed by a cascade of yellow ringlets. His hands slid slowly down her sides, clad in a pink satin gown. Quivering fingers barely brushing her small high breasts before delicately caressing the gentle swell of her hips. He seemed almost in ecstasy, as if any further increase in intimacy might make him swoon. Her gown was a sacred vestment; she was a goddess – yet one with whom he was on friendly, droll terms.

How unlike the occasion of her kidnapping when he had forced her skirt up to her waist in the woods, and had buried himself in her with such a prolonged clamour of release, such an agony of rapture, that you might have thought *he* was being violated by her.

He had been possessed – bewitched and demented. His life and sanity were at stake. She was the cure. He had smothered her, not with a hand upon her face (his own outcry adequately drowned her protests) but with such an outpouring of exalted devotion as stupefied and fuddled and overwhelmed her. Minkie projected such passion that her very feelings were rearranged within her. That was his knack, of which he seemed at such a time to be purely the tool rather than the master. It was a talent beyond mere lechery. It could bewitch the object of his desire, and himself too.

Kyli Helenius had been his greatest challenge – with a difference that this time he was seeking a noble wife not just a night of fun. Yet she had baulked. She had resisted his appeals. Somehow, corsetted by snobbery, she had found the strength. Finally he had needed to abduct snooty Kyli and impose his desire at the closest proximity, himself inside of her.

Shaming her. Infuriating Lord Helenius, into whose good graces Minkie had been inveigling his way for months while acting as a sedulous squire.

How many fine girls and ladies at the Saari court interceded on Minkie's behalf, and Kyli's, for fear of revelations about their own misconduct? A good few, perhaps.

In the end: frosty reconciliation. Swift marriage. A moderately liberal dowry which was wealth to the Kennans of Niemi Keep.

These days Kyli basked in Minkie's admiration. His jocular adoration nourished her like nectar. Being with him day after day was mesmerizing. *Forgiving* him did not exactly enter into it.

'What are you *doing* in here, dearest heart?' he asked.

'This room needs a completely new glazed windowframe, don't you think?'

'I suppose so,' he replied innocently. Her presence had blinded him to such an obvious deficiency. 'I'll get Snowy to see to it, darling hen. He'll measure up and rush into town to the carpenter's and the glazier's, clutching some of your daddy's money. It's yours to dispose of.'

'Speaking of the glazier, Minkie, that new mirror in my dressing room has a warp in it. It makes me look squinty. Almost ugly, from some angles! You must take it back. Demand a replacement.'

'It was fine when Snowy bought it—'

'It isn't now. I think there's some nakki sitting on it, making the glass flow funnily.'

'Ruokokoski,' muttered Minkie.

'What did you say?'

'Nothing, my bliss.'

'Surely you did, Minkie. I hate secrets if I don't know them.'

'You're my secret, Kiki-liki.' Leaning forward, Minkie stuck out his tongue to touch her white neck. 'I want to lick you all over tonight till you purr as loudly as a waterfall.'

She laughed, delighted. Why ever had she been mourning the palace of her girlhood when her own body was a palace? Still, something must be done about that looking glass.

'You *must* complain about my mirror having a nakki on it. Why should it? Why?'

'A mystery . . . Snowy will *belabour* the glassmaker.'

'Why don't you yourself, my bold daredevil? Or are you observing your vow very faithfully?'

Minkie looked genuinely puzzled. 'My vow . . .'

'Not to go off fighting now that you have a wife. Not to go

hunting Jutties. Not to stir up enemies gratuitously as your dead dad did. Remember?'

'Ah yes. That vow. Of course I remember, darling hen! The promise is etched on my shoulder blade.'

'Where you can't see it.'

The court tattooist at Saari had indeed pricked the symbol of a small padlock upon Minkie's back, and a discreet little key upon Kyli's palm during their wedding while the mana-priest was cooing enchantments. This tattooing, at the insistence of Lord Helenius.

'I wouldn't want to upset my dad-in-law by causing trouble on his borders . . .'

'Your vow applies to needling the Brazen and Brindled Isi quite as much as the Velvets.'

'Of course, of course. In any case, the Brindleds live so far away.'

'The principal point of your vow is to keep you alive, husband.'

'So as to worship you always from close by, dear Kyli. What more could I want? I'm fulfilled. Incidentally, my dad didn't make enemies of everyone. Mum says he once performed some service for Lucky Sariola herself. Lucky was grateful. At least I think she was, though Dad had to scarper before he could collect his reward.'

'What service was that?'

'Mum said she would tell me when I'm wise and wouldn't hare off.' Minkie gazed dotingly at his bride of five weeks. 'That must be now, all thanks to you, precious hen! The time must have come for the family secret!' Delighted, he was on the point of departing.

'Wait, Minkie.'

'Wait? But of course.' He dropped, exaggeratedly, upon his knees. His breeches grooved dust on the floorboards. Gently he stroked her gowned hips, and moaned in pent obedience.

'Why won't you confront this glassmaker yourself? Instead of stuttery Snowy doing it?'

'My vow – of docile ways! Anyway, I'm noble. I'd be embarrassed.'

'You, blush? I think, naughty Minkie, I spy the tip of some past indiscretion which accounts for the nakki on my mirror.'

'You see right through me, Kiki-liki – for you enclose me inside of you.' His caresses grew firmer, moulding her. 'Only you will do that, ever more, in the secret wet warmth within you, in the hot sleek harbour.'

261

She swayed, weakened, and mumbled, 'The secret . . . tell me.'

'She was only the glassmaker's daughter,' Minkie confessed, 'and it isn't much of a secret, I'm afraid.'

'You don't want me to mix too much in town in case I trip over indiscretions right and left . . . I shall just turn up my nose at those peccadilloes. So there!'

A serious aspect clouded Minkie's face.

'Do you really feel that you need some girlfriends, just as at Saari, dearest? Whilst I'm with you, which I will be always! I beg you, let your girlfriends be ugly ones, at least. What am I saying? In your shadow, all other female flesh is stale bread. Alas, some people suffer from a restless itch and a wander-bug in their pants. Not that I do so any longer!' Minkie clasped her left hand and planted a kiss on the palm. 'Here's the key to my heart from now on,' he promised.

He rose, dust on his knees. Kyli was more than content to be led from the draughty, neglected chamber. Though, as she passed the dead bird, for a moment it looked to her as if a pierced heart lay there upon the floor.

'Mother, mother,' clamoured Minkie, later. 'Will you tell me my father's secret now that I'm a steady married man who'll roam no more?'

Inga Kennan regarded her son with a fond smile.

The Dame of Niemi's chamber was hung with tatty tapestries of wild, windswept men waving swords. Warriors on horseback blew long horns amidst mayhem and massacre and the settling of scores. She was embroidering a pillowslip with flowers of silk. Her wide window, where she sat, looked out upon the serene lake and the far tree-clad shore. Her bed was a great carved boat, stout masts at the four corners, sagging sail aloft. The speckles in the beige horzma wood camouflaged perforations which were the work of miner-beetles. Within the heroically proportioned bedstead and headboard and corner-posts would be a network of needle-thin galleries and shafts. Most of the rugs on the floor were threadbare.

Minkie's mother sighed. 'Some day I'd love bright new wall-hangings instead of these dowdy feuds.'

'You shall have them just as soon as we fix the front hall. No, sooner than that! Draw your designs. I'll send Snowy to Saari to commission the work toot-sweet.'

'No, we shouldn't squander too much on decorations.'

'On beauty!' protested Minkie. 'I brought beauty here, so her whole setting must be beautiful, not grim. Would you set a diamond in rotten wood or rusty iron?'

Inga shook her head. 'No, I think I'll keep the old hangings for a while. Let them remind me of what put paid to Ragnar.'

Mother and son talked for a while. Dame Inga, in thick black woollen skirt hung with trinkets like stars in a dark sky, and bodice of black lace studded with spangles, was the source of Minkie's good looks. Greying chestnut hair spilled upon her shoulders. Her mouth was full and sensual. Her skin of sculptured butter wore the faintest lattice of wrinkles. Her hazel eyes were bold and challenging. Her nose – unlike Minkie's mischievous sniffer – was straight and firm.

Minkie's nose was his father's. A painting of Ragnar Kennan hung over a once-bloody though now washed-out tapestry. It depicted a blustery scrunched-up defiant man with a scowl in the offing – maybe due to glimpses of the painting in progress. Behind him thunderclouds bunched on a horizon riven with lightning. In startling contrast Ragnar's right hand rested lightly not on a weapon but on a child-sized alabastrine statue of a nymph.

Presently, Inga said, 'I'd have told you the secret when you were younger, Minkie, except that it might have made you thoroughly reckless . . . Even so, I felt tempted. Hunting girls is one thing. Angry fathers and brothers can sharpen their knives. But you always had winning ways, unlike poor Ragnar with his genius for provoking people. Harassing Juttahats as a hobby was something else.'

'I shan't be doing that again, Mummy, though I think maybe the Unmen appreciated it.'

'*Appreciated* it? What do you mean?'

'It kept them on their toes. They probe at us, so it's only fair—'

'No more.' Inga cut him off.

'No more,' he agreed.

'The Isi lay long plans, Minkie. They don't necessarily retaliate at once. Cuckoos will have told them who you are. You and Snowy didn't exactly keep your, um, heroic exploits secret—'

'I suppose those *were* rather heroic, now that you mention it, even if that's all over now.'

'You gained us back some respect that your father threw away. As to your seductions—'

'—which are all over now, Mummy.'

'—I suppose most people forgive a young champion. But if you ever get into *terrible* trouble—'

'How could I, now? How could I?'

'If the serpents take it into their skulls to punish you and decide to pursue the matter . . . well, your father once found a place to hide right outside of this world of ours. The pity is that he came back out of his hiding place.' Distress afflicted Inga. 'He came back. Because. He. Missed. Me. I would miss you if Jutties ever killed you to even up scores. I love Kosti and Karl dearly.' Her voice caught. 'But I couldn't bear it if you died. You seem on the verge of being *safe* at last.'

'You didn't tell me the secret in case I became brash . . .'

'For another reason,' she said. 'What I'm going to tell you shouldn't be squandered as part of a juvenile escapade, in the way that men are prone to squander what's precious. This is women's wisdom I'm disclosing, even though it was your father who stumbled across the source.'

'How do you mean, women's wisdom?'

'It's to do with creation, not destruction.'

Intrigued, Minkie knit his hands together as if to protest his own new sense of restraint and self-discipline.

Laying aside her embroidery, Inga told him the true tale of how her husband found a place to hide himself where no cuckoo would babble his whereabouts. But she prefixed this with another tale.

'When God first made Man and Woman, Minkie, they lived in a paradise beside the Loom of Creation, which was a bottomless lake. Every day Eve gave birth to a new daughter. She didn't want her offspring to go out into the wild world. So she hid each new one in the lake. God would come walking by each evening. He would ask Eve how soon she would have some children. Eve always said, "Not yet, God, not yet." So God would rebuke Adam for his lack of ardour and potency, much to Adam's embarrassment.'

Minkie grinned. 'I'm not surprised.'

'Every night when God had gone, Adam would impregnate Eve again as passionately as he could. Then Eve would sing him to sleep. In the morning, before Adam was awake, Eve would give birth and hide yet another daughter in the Lake of the Loom.

'One morning thunder woke Adam early, and he saw what Eve was doing. That evening, he told God.

'God was annoyed. He declared that a skin like ice would grow

264

over the Lake of the Loom so that nothing should be able to enter the water. Nor anything leave it, either. Adam and Eve would need to move away to find water to drink and fish to eat. From now on Eve would give birth to many sons and daughters. But the beloved daughters she had already borne would remain hidden away in their underwater paradise deep in the bottomless lake.

'Well, Minkie,' continued Inga, 'when your father was fleeing on horseback through the wilderness beyond where the muties live, and when he was running out of provisions and hope, he happened to come upon that same Loom Lake. It was among a hundred other lakes. Mana-mists drifted confusingly thereabouts. The Loom Lake, which was shaped like a rhomb, lay below cliffs which were steeper than here at Niemi. These cliffs ran along two sides of the lake, and at their highest actually overhung the waters.

'Your father camped on the highest part of those cliffs so that he would have a good sight of any pursuers.'

'And they of him?'

Minkie was aware of his father's impetuous and self-defeating decisions, even though much had faded from his mind. It was twelve years ago, while Inga was beginning to swell with his two sprats of brothers, that a knife had finally caught up with Minkie's dad. At the time Minkie had been a lad of eleven. Prior to Ragnar's ill-fated return to a decaying Niemi Keep – circuitously, and encountering no less than mad Lady Lucky en route – Minkie's father had been missing for the best part of five years, a stranger to his son.

'There were big boulders up there!' retorted his mother indignantly. 'That night in his fraught state your father dreamed that all those hidden daughters of Eve were beckoning him to their sanctuary underwater. He must have stood up in his sleep and walked. In his sleep he leapt off the clifftop – to find himself hurtling down through midair towards the surface of the lake.

'What a blow he struck the water. He clove down deep, so deep – and the water dragged him deeper still.

'Those maidens' hands were heaving upon his ankles, hauling him further into the depths of the bottomless lake. Ragnar feared he would surely drown. Yet then there was sweet air, and brightness. He'd entered the paradise of the daughters of Eve.'

'Are you really telling me the truth?'

'Yes, yes, I am. If Ragnar was telling *me* the truth; and I'm sure he was. Where else could he have been hiding for so long? Among the muties? In his despair, he found the Loom Lake. It's real. Though it isn't easy to stumble across unless you know where to look.'

'The boulders on the clifftops.'

'Mana-mists hide it. But paradise truly did invite him in.'

And that was where Ragnar the runaway had holed up for a number of years.

'At first, Minkie, Ragnar thought he was dead. But no. He was simply outside of this world, in a corner of paradise left behind after this world was made –'

'With all those daughters of Eve residing in it, eh?'

'Don't think that way, son. Ragnar found adventures in paradise. Paradise was like a dream where he could do whatever he wished, except that latterly the dream began to have its own ideas. It turned against him. He left, and swam back up to the world.'

'What happened to the horse?' asked Minkie.

'What horse?'

'The horse Dad was riding.'

'Naturally that wasn't still there!'

'A lake shaped like a rhomb,' repeated her son, 'with cliffs along two sides and great boulders perched at the highest point, well to the south-east of the muties.'

Minkie scratched the back of his neck, then his right arm as fiercely as if formicks had taken up residence, tickling and stinging him.

'A truly bottomless lake?'

'How else could paradise have fitted in beneath the waters?'

An array of copper pans, china bowls and tureens caught a percussion of drips from a downpour assaulting the arch-braced roof of the dining hall. Two dozen receptacles stood about on tables and floor as rain seeped through cracks between the rafters aloft. Rain oozed through windowframes to pool on sills. A candelabrum relieved the gloom of the cloudburst as Minkie and Kyli and Snowy and Kosti and Karl and beldame Goody dined on fish pie at the one undripped-on table. The rain drummed monotonously, almost masking the *plink, plop, ping* of drips.

'It's a rare deluge that sneaks through the ceiling,' wrinkled Goody assured a glum Kyli. This, despite the alacrity with which

266

the two boys had rushed all those utensils to predetermined positions. 'To this extent, anyhow,' she said. The hall could accommodate a hundred guests. That evening it seemed desolate, rather than grand.

To cheer Minkie's bride, the old housekeeper told a tale of a water-nakki who fell in love with a handsome young fiddler who had built a hut by her lake . . .

'She didn't wish to drag the young fellow forcibly into her embrace in case she drowned him,' said Goody, toothlessly. 'After thinking a while, the nakki invaded the lad's hut in the form of raindrops which soaked his bed while he lay in it. Alas, this merely annoyed and embarrassed the young man and even gave him a cold. He nailed tin over his roof of reeds.'

Rain plopped into the pans. A waterfall was sluicing off the roof, past the windows. The housekeeper raised her voice.

'Next, the nakki made herself into a woman of shimmery warm water held together by a skin of woven water. She knocked on the door. The lad was entranced by her silky beauty.' Goody winked at Minkie. 'He embraced her; he led her to his bed. Alas, she had neglected to think what the consequence might be when he penetrated her. Another soaking wet bed, and no other sign of her!' She cackled.

'What a silly story,' objected twelve-year-old Kosti. His brother Karl flushed and disagreed.

Kosti, curly-haired and charming to the eye, could all too easily leap to impatient conclusions. Karl, whose brown hair hung like lank string and whose thin, pinched countenance was spotty, already tended to brood about notions, tormenting the pith from them as pus from pimples.

'*Next* time,' continued Goody, 'the nakki wove a cunning flap between her legs . . .'

Inga's fingers drummed on the table in time to the raindrops but she didn't tell Goody to hush.

'The enchanting visitor didn't burst in the young fiddler's bed when he took his pleasure. But when he drew back to admire her, lo and behold, to his amazement he saw a host of little fishes darting about inside her body. Magnified by the curves of her belly and breasts and limbs, his sperms were so many sprats and minnows and elvers! What's more, they were gulping her water and growing. Soon she would no longer be a woman, with an aquarium inside her body, but one huge communal wriggling fish. That nakki lady had to hurry back to the lake to liberate all that life inside her by dissolving.' Goody gleamed at Kyli, who giggled.

'*Next* night, the nakki came to the fiddler as a jelly-woman. When our fiddler drew away after lying upon her, what did he see but the negative imprint of himself? Not her face, but his own. Suddenly, flip-flop, the jelly thrust outward into relief. In place of her sex, he saw a stiff jelly imitation of his own organ swell. She squealed, and so did he.'

Kosti wriggled about impatiently, but Karl was all ears.

'Well now, the night *after* that—'

'It's a ring o' monkeys story,' exclaimed Kyli.

'Each holding the tail of the one in front,' piped Karl.

'Let's see,' Minkie's bride improvised, 'the next night the nakki went to him as a snow-woman, and she chilled him frigid. So the night after that she visited him in the form of scorching sauna-steam. Scalded, he ran out of the hut and down the shore and plunged into the lake, hurling himself into the cool arms of water—'

Goody clucked. She forked fish pie into her toothless gob. Munching, she chortled, 'Oh that's far too soon.'

Snowy, his bright pink face weeping acne-rheum, guffawed.

'Sh-sh-she mu-mu-might ku-ku-come to him fu-fu-first as slippery fu-fu-fish-oil—'

Rain blurred the windows utterly. Drips plinked and plunked into tureen and pan. Minkie scratched himself. Did *Goody* know about those underwater daughters of Eve? he wondered. He shouldn't think too much about those; not now that he had Kyli.

'When can we hold a dance in this hall?' Kyli asked. She closed her eyes, imagining young ladies and gallants spinning around. 'Something festive?'

'I know a special jig,' whispered Minkie. 'Though it's just for two bare-skinned partners.'

His bride swayed in her seat. Just then an errant raindrop struck her upon the tip of her nose.

'*Oh*,' she squeaked in dismay, 'now it's leaking here too. How can we possibly have a ball, even if,' she added haughtily, 'there aren't any glassmakers' daughters invited to it?'

'I know what,' Minkie offered grandly. 'I'll take my goddess to the gala in Speakers' Valley.'

'Do you mean it? Will you?'

'Can I come too?' cried Karl.

'And me?' from Kosti.

Minkie ignored his brothers' plea. 'While we're away, Snowy will repair the roof completely. Won't you, Snowy?'

'I'd mu-mu-much ru-ru-ru-rather—'

'There's a good fellow. Of course you'd rather fix the roof.'

Speakers' Valley was in quite the opposite direction to the mutie villages and those hundred lakes far beyond.

'That's a splendid idea, Minkie,' said Inga. 'Kyli'll be in her element at a gala. You'll be right beside her, won't you?'

'Besottedly,' Minkie agreed, with full sincerity.

'Speaking of galas,' said Goody, 'there was once a cuckoo used to keep a special watch on Tycho Cammon all the time, quite as if it was fascinated by all of his awful deeds—'

'One special cuckoo?' asked Karl. 'How can you tell them apart?'

'I was coming to that, young man. This cuckoo had a crippled foot. One day Cammon decided to try and use the bird as a voice to proclaim a horrid woe at a lord who had shut himself up in his keep—'

'But what can I *wear* at the gala?' Kyli exclaimed.

20 · A BLOT IN THE MIRROR

Jatta's sister Eva was her immediate junior. Then there was Minnow, followed by Ester, followed by Sal, followed in turn by Kaisa and finally by Martha and toddling Mary. This was the sheaf of Lucky's Harvest presently in residence in Pohjola Palace – excluding that newest daughter-to-be currently gestating within Lucky's ever-fertile womb.

Eva, at eighteen, was the ranking maiden now. Slight spare Minnow, at sixteen, was also of marriageable age. Eva Sariola didn't wish to gush naively but she *was* consumed with curiosity at all that had happened to her prodigal elder sister. Till now, Eva had rather looked down on Minnow as a chit who ought to hang out with Ester rather than with her own mature person. Really, Minnow looked not much more than Ester's age of thirteen! But Minnow could ask leading questions while Eva played the role of tactful, supportive confidante who tried – without *too* much success – to mellow Minnow's curiosity. Eva couldn't bring herself to send Minnow away with a flea in her ear. It was *so* important for the girl to associate with a marriageable elder sister. Distraught at the loss of her son, Jatta was vulnerable to sympathy.

The three daughters sat over Pootaran coffee and cream and cinnamon buns, in the nook of a small refectory within sight of the counting-house court. In the chambers around that glass-domed plaza (with its terracotta pots of fragrant shrubbery) clerks were busy muttering calculations, humming mnemonics like sizzleflies. They inscribed numbers and symbols in ledgers. They counted bronze pennies, silver marks, and golden ors. At this mid-morning hour the refectory itself was deserted but for the three Sariolas in their flamboyant tunics and an aproned waitress arranging lunches at her counter. A ceiling fan stirred the warm pastry-scented air with blades of lightweight wood, its clockwork clicking. Oil lamps with shades of tinted mica cast a soft light.

Two stiff hands protruded from one white-plastered wall. The palms were upright. Higher up the wall, a mouth gaped and a nose jutted. A clerk who had stolen from Lucky's treasury decades ago was submerged in the wall. A potent proclaimer had fastened him there on the orders of the infuriated mistress of the Northland. Customers would count out the cost of their meals into his hand for the waitress to collect. She would scrape leftovers into his mouth; those would disappear. Did he feel the tickle of money? Did he taste or smell the scraps?

'I've always been a mite scared I might make my man into a – well, into a *zombie*,' prattled Minnow. 'Me particularly, being – well . . .' Being so elfin and petite, so dainty. Maybe she lacked enough mana to immortalize a spouse properly.

The three sisters were alike in their pear-shaped faces, prominent cheeks, and dark narrow-set eyes without a crease to the lids. Minnow was a miniature, her black hair worn in a frizzled bush to magnify herself and suggest an aura. Eva had fleshed out more lushly than Jatta. She favoured a glossy coiffure piled high with the aid of spangled combs, and decorated by golden ribbons. On one cheek, a tattoo of a tiny violet starflower. On her neck, and on a wrist, other such blossoms. Where else on her body might little blooms or buds be found? Jatta's hair was as short and spiky as a worn-down broomhead. Once massacred, it proved almost impossible to readopt a style. Jatta was forever snipping at unruly new growth.

'If it happened to you,' said Minnow, 'it can't happen to another sister so soon, can it?'

'How should I know?' Jatta asked bitterly.

'She'll hardly wish to unburden her heart about that,' Eva said. 'Not *quite* yet, anyway. Your poor hair, my sweet . . . Mother didn't shear you, did she?'

Jatta shook her ravaged head. 'More practical this way during the winter. Less desirable's safer when you're a tramp.'

'Did men assault you?' pursued Minnow. 'How does it feel not to wear a girdle?'

Inevitably, Jatta thought about Juke, who had seemed quite unqualified to assail a woman in that fashion . . .

Jatta's 'rescue' remained a sharply-etched confusion in her mind. The shattered images were vivid but lacked connections.

Guards in camouflage leathers had hauled the netted golden serpent and its Juttahat to a compartment at the rear of the yellover-panelled sky-boat. Somebody was cursing the ten seconds it normally took for a lightrifle to recharge itself.

'A slug rifle would have been better—'

'Not with mana about. Bullets can soften in mid-air—'

'The crossbow's me best man—'

Apparently four of Lucky's guards, including Marti and Olli, lay dead in Speakers' Valley. Thus Marti and Olli had redeemed their negligence at Lokka.

Lucky had welcomed Jatta effusively. What a gift her little girl had caused to fall into her hands: an Isi mana-mage. Lucky wanted to play with her present at once. Actually this must wait till the sky-boat returned to Pohjola Palace. Hence her impatience. You'd hardly have thought that Lucky had ever spurned this daughter of hers; or that a previous trip in this same vessel had marooned Jatta in wild forest.

The sky-boat duly fled up and away, pushing passengers back into padded leather seats. Juke's fingers punished his knees. Was he terrified at his first ever flight? Was he intimidated by the plump Queen in her fine gown and sapphire tiara? Juke had lost his skull-cap. He stared through a porthole towards the east, where his sister was waiting.

'Mother,' said Jatta despairingly, 'when you've played enough with the mage, will you trade it back for my boy?'

'You've been very wayward, Jatta. Did you refuse to wed all along because you suspected you'd create a zombie?' This taunt came as a cold blow to Jatta's belly. Lucky had spied the living corpse accosting her daughter. She had fathomed the significance. Jatta's seducer was claiming its offspring back. Did Lucky make up her mind to abandon the bizarre boy as soon as she saw what had become of Jarl? Intoxicated by cuckoo tales about Jack, Lucky must have flown south with the initial intention of retrieving the boy.

Juke spoke up gruffly in Jatta's defence. 'A real man mightn't have become a zombie. Your daughter's seducer was a special breed of Juttie, out to deceive and deflower her.'

'Whatever were the Juttahats playing at?' cried Lucky. 'Trying to steal longlife for the serpents, I'll be bound. With my daughter's help! That's treason to Kaleva. The mage must know the reason. It's much more important we bagged the mage. Why did it expose itself to capture? To distract us? Or was it intrigued then dazed by the mana-snowstorm and the burning sheep? Caused by *that demon child of yours*, Jatta! Don't say I received the worst of the bargain!'

The boat throbbed its way through a cloud into a gulf of bright air, over forest and a narrow twisting lake.

'Jatta, Jatta, do you remember your monkey puzzle?'

What in mana's name made her mother mention that? Was this a suggestion as to how Jatta might spend her time in future in the palace now that her own mischievous little monkey was in the hands of Isi and Juttahats?

Her lost boy . . .

Her lost Jarl . . .

Jatta began to weep.

Queenly Lucky quit her seat. She embraced her daughter. Tears trickled from her eyes too.

'I forgive you, my chatter, my natter. With a mage to question I might find my own real self again, and that's all thanks to you.'

Lucky hugged her hundredth-and-some daughter joyously. Jatta could only grieve, mystified by whatever her mother had in mind. The yeasty tart scent of Lucky made Jatta feel sick.

Abruptly, her mother rounded on Juke. She quizzed this fellow who had escorted her daughter and miracle brat all the way from Maananfors.

Juke told Jatta's mother a very abbreviated version of events, in which he starred as a modest, chivalrous protector. A mutie hero.

272

Why, decided Lucky, Juke deserved to be flown home, not carried far out of his way to Sariolinna!

The Isi sky-boat probably wouldn't give chase. If there had only been one serpent on board, the Juttahats mightn't have the initiative to pursue Lucky's sky-boat and the kidnapped mage. They would return to their starting point, carrying their prize. Sensibly enough! In all Kaleva there were many serpents but only one demon child.

The pilot must change course right away for the far south of the domain of Saari. Where was the harm in a detour?

Juke protested that he would just as soon be set down a hundred keys short of his home. Lucky quite overruled this suggestion. She would take him all the way back to – where was it, Outo? – to reward his kindness to a Sariola in distress.

'You don't want to land among misshapen muties,' Juke insisted. He was verging on a certain tone of voice.

'Don't ever try to proclaim at *me*!' Lucky raged. 'You can't, no one can. I'm the mother of Kaleva. You're being honoured.' She raised the ruby ring on her finger as if to blood him with it, or perhaps expecting it to kissed.

If the visit to Outo was spied by a cuckoo and tattled about, this might bring a raiding party of the Brazen Isi down upon the mutants' village. Juke might be viewed as an accomplice in the abduction of the mage. Lucky was laying a false trail, of sorts?

'I'm sorry,' Jatta whispered to Juke, wet-cheeked.

'Nobody cares a hoot about muties,' Juke muttered. 'Everyone leaves us alone.'

'By the way,' said Lucky to her daughter, 'I'm expecting another child. Aren't you happy for me?'

Jatta had shrunk up in her seat.

So Queen Lucky had descended in her sky-boat upon the cotts of the mocky-men. She escorted Juke on her arm, displaying herself at the head of the ramp for at least half a minute. An impromptu audience of freaks gaped. Freaks with pie-crust skin or lamb's wool, with sunken heads, bowed legs, capricorn ears, goats' eyes. A long-limbed, silky-haired young woman of perfect features came running from a thatched hovel. Through a porthole Jatta watched Juke embrace his sister fervently. The poetess. His fixation.

*

273

'What was the word that loosed your girdle?' asked Minnow urgently.

'I didn't hear it,' mumbled Jatta. 'There was such a roaring in my ears.'

'A *roaring* and a *rushing*,' echoed the girl. 'As if you were carried away by a torrent. So that's how it was. So that's how it is. How wonderful.'

'He was indispensable . . . But he was an alien semblance.'

'Men *are* aliens,' suggested the girl. 'Every woman gives herself to an alien, don't you think?'

Jatta moaned. 'What do I do, what do I do?'

'You used to roam about a lot, up country,' said Eva.

'Do you think I ought to go back to Lokka, where it happened? What good would that serve except sorrow? Would I find an alien zombie waiting there? I can actually say that word aloud! Would I find my fast boy there? He's far far south. Mother *must* trade for him before they manipulate him into someone who isn't mine at all. Something that isn't mine.'

'Before your Jack grows up as fast as a mushroom and becomes the image of your Jarl.' Eva laid a hand on her suffering sister's hand. 'My poor darling sweet.'

As so often, Minnow began muttering to herself in an undertone. 'That's really important, I mean, that's really important,' Minnow assured Minnow without anyone else being any the wiser. As if by this means Minnow might double her presence.

'I survived all winter,' said Jatta. 'I gave birth alone. Only to be robbed by my mother, my boy given away for a snake when she could have saved him instead. She says she wants her real self back—'

'Nobody knows what Mummy wants or means,' said Minnow. 'But I want the handsomest, bravest suitor ever.'

Eva slapped Minnow on the wrist. Her fingers lingered so that the smack did not seem quite a smack. Briefly the sisters were all connected like a trio of monkeys.

'*I'll* be wedded first,' said Eva, 'in my own good time. I might even scout for a man on my own account. *Daddy* might just well be taking me to the gala at Speakers' Valley this year . . .'

'You can't do that, Evie! Sariola daughters don't go south of the Great Fjord till we're wedded. Not unless—' Minnow glanced pityingly at Jatta. 'I don't believe you. Mother wouldn't allow it.'

Eva winked. 'Wait and see, little sprite.'

Exhaustion began to overwhelm Jatta, a tiredness quite distinct from the bygone fatigue of journeying with her fast boy. Was it merely depression? Minnow and Eva were conspiring about something or other. Temporary allies. Eva was hushing her diminutive, doll-like sister. All Lucky's daughters were precious jewels. Jewels with flaws resulting from being precious, and being at the same time only pieces in a string of similar gems spanning centuries. Jatta had thought she was otherwise, a free spirit, her own unique self. Then she had lain with an alien impostor. What had she lost, after all, but a freakish hybrid, a boy who sprouted up like a mushroom?

Or like a miracle.

Her own dear miracle – even if Jarl had become ZOMBIE.

Her marvellous boy, her prodigy, her mana kid.

Lost, now. Missed. Oh yes, *missed*.

Did she ache for Jack?

'*Yes*,' she said fiercely.

'Yes, to what?' enquired Eva. 'Another cinnamon bun?'

Jatta stood up wearily.

'Let's go,' said Minnow. She was anxious not to lose the company of such a repository of intimate secrets.

'It's quite true about me going to the gala,' Eva said serenely. 'Well, *probably* so. Bertel hasn't exactly promised yet. I've asked and asked, and he isn't refusing.'

Jatta at last realized what her sister was saying.

'Speakers' gala? There'll be people from all over, and cuckoos telling tales. Eva, promise me you'll listen hard for any word of my boy Jack. For any clue.'

Eva hugged Jatta and patted her. 'Maybe that's why Mother might let Daddy go there this year. With me as his excuse.' Eva contrived to sound modest.

'Gosh, the gala,' breathed Minnow. 'To seek a husband there, as if it's your very own marriage market. The world *is* changing. Maybe Mother's afraid that otherwise you might *do a Jatta.*'

'Don't be crass, sprite.'

'Pennies for the hand, noble young ladies?' the waitress called out, her way of reminding them to pay. She calculated quickly. 'Thirty-nine of them.'

'My treat,' insisted Eva. She burrowed in the purse that hung from her waist. Naturally, their mother never paid for anything in the palace, or in town; she already owned everything.

Daughters must pay – until a successful suitor paid for them. Daughters collected an allowance from the counting house.

'Quite right,' muttered Minnow to herself. 'Too true.'

Eva placed a silver half-mark on the palm of the paralysed, engulfed embezzler. The waitress grinned.

'He can't give change . . .'

Eva waved airily and the waitress curtseyed.

Sister linked with sister, little Minnow bringing up the rear.

'You know,' Eva drawled, 'I really do admire your mettle, Jatta. Myself I'd be crazy with agitation and, well, shame isn't the proper word at all . . . I apologize for even saying it—'

They strolled along an arcade housing the palace furrier's. A score of women were steaming and beating, cutting and combing and sewing the hairy skins of tundra tarandras and arctic goats.

'May you marry a simple-hearted man who'll cause you no . . . pain,' said Jatta.

Eva inclined her head. 'I think I fancy a dignified fellow of whom I can be proud. Dignity is so important. Oh dear, but what am I *saying*?'

'Beware of men's masks,' Jatta warned her. Juke had worn a species of mask to conceal his feelings for his sister – even from himself. Jarl had sported the most deceitful mask of all, the guise of a human being. 'Dignity can be a facade, Eva.'

A five-year-old Sariola girl romped through an archway, tugging at the hand of her lanky stooping governess who was draped in a spartan grey frock. From the woman's scrawny neck hung a silver pomander of herbs. On her nose perched scrutinizing spectacles. The little girl was dressed in blue with red brocade. In her free hand she clutched a battered bisque boy-doll. The doll sported a brand-new red-striped jacket, verdant breeches, and sunny waistcoat. Nakkinook, no less, his outfit refurbished. A bearded guard ambled, as escort.

'Naturally, of course,' Minnow told herself.

The girl – Martha Sariola – plucked her hand from the governess's. She held up the flirtatious doll to stare blue-eyed at the elder sisters. Martha whispered in Nakkinook's chipped ear. Mrs Simberg stooped to hiss in the girl's little pink lug and was about to lead her away. But all of a sudden the governess rushed towards Jatta. She clamped the errant daughter by the shoulders in bony hands, her eyes bulbous to bursting point behind those spectacles.

'I lost a child once,' she said harshly, squeezing Jatta quite painfully. 'Simberg left me the year after we wed, and I miscarried. Now you know.' She pivoted, seized little Martha, and stalked off, sniffing at her pomander. Had Mrs Simberg been offering consolation, or the contrary?

'Well yes, *presumably so*,' Minnow told Minnow, her own finest confidante.

Along from the fur factory, a spiral stone stairway ascended to a picture gallery. Jatta let Eva coax her up into the long skylit pinacothek. Dozens of portraits of their mother lined the walls. The mistress of Pohjola Palace appeared composed and lucid in this oil, unhinged in the next. She seemed shrewd, wise, hectic. In none had she aged by one whit. The repetition of that selfsame face time and again was soporific and oppressive, mesmeric and megalomaniacal.

The furthest frame held a milky mana-mirror aswirl with mist. A fat old lady custodian sat dozing opposite, a duster of goose feathers resting across her lap. The woman was supposed to keep an eye on that final amorphous blank space. Supposedly some year the blank glass might clarify to reveal a spontaneous new image of Lucky. A mature Lucky. An elderly, venerable Saint Lucky. A Lucky who was barren at last. So claimed the shaman who had enchanted the glass. Supposedly. Thus the story went, but no one other than Lucky or Bertel would have known the long-dead shaman personally. Of more interest was the fact that the mirror would sometimes show visitors their futures.

'You must have special mana in you,' Eva said to Jatta, 'otherwise, how could you have conceived such a child, even if a Juttie *was* the father? Can a Juttie really breed with a human woman? Maybe he caused you to breed with *yourself*.'

'With myself?'

'Our mother gives birth to herself over and over again, doesn't she?' Eva gestured along the gallery as if all those portraits were images of Lucky's offspring rather than of herself. She nodded at dainty Minnow. 'With variations,' she added. 'But always girls, who give longlife. Or sometimes, longdeath. Your boy sounds like longlife compressed, longlife turned into fastlife.'

'*Jack mustn't burn out like some quick candle*,' Jatta said, distraught. 'Not all those hundreds of keys away from me. Did Mother come for him because she feared he was some rival to her? Did she abandon Jack for the mana-mage because the Isi won't ever let my boy go free to bother her?'

'Hush, hush.' Eva stroked Jatta's shorn, spiky hair cautiously

277

as though it might scratch her fingers. 'You must have had special mana in you. I bet the Juttie never expected you to have a child at all. It just wanted your gift. If you'd mated with a normal man I'll wager you wouldn't have borne a fast boy. Mother has special mana in her and she gives birth to herself with Bertel's assistance.'

'I'm not her. I'm *me*.'

'In your case a boy popped out. Look in the mirror. Maybe it'll show you your Jack grown up.'

'Grown up *already*?' Jatta cried.

'No no no, dearest. If you're worried, look in the mirror with me. Try to imagine . . . well, you were at Speakers' Valley.' A hint of jealousy coloured her tone. 'Try to see me there this autumn, as a test.'

'And who she's *with*,' added Minnow, earning a frown.

'I'm sure you're very special, Jatta,' said Eva.

'It's flatter-Jatta-time,' Minnow remarked quietly, and Eva pinched her.

Lucky claimed to have lost herself inside her Ukko long ago, emerging from its inner spaces with her hair as black as jet. Maybe Jack was Jatta's own secret mana-self, liberated. No wonder Lucky often seemed so deranged. For the first time perhaps, one of Lucky's daughters could imagine how Paula Sariola felt. Jatta's own inner self had been torn away from her.

'The mirror,' Eva prompted. 'Just a test. Try to see me.'

The swirling whiteness within the frame was so like the blizzard which had engulfed Speakers' Valley before Jack was snatched away. At any moment an aisle of sunlight might open, clearly displaying an aspect of galas past or future.

What came into sight was the foggiest image of Eva's face.

Eva's lips were clenched tight, so it seemed. She seemed to be doing her best not to squeal.

The image was double, though. Within Eva's visage lurked an even vaguer scene. Did a naked woman lie on her belly, rump upward, her head hidden by her mass of hair? Were her wrists tied to the head of a brass bedstead? Did a nude man stand beside the bed, a thong in his hand? So hazy, so blurred.

'Ach, tut!'

Aroused, the custodian woman thrust her way between the sisters. 'Shame on you, young ladies, sneaking up while Granny's snoozing without slipping her a copper.' She swept the white plumes of her duster across the face of the mirror. Promptly the reflection and the faint strange scene within it vanished back into fog.

'Damn,' swore Eva.

'Well, that's one way of looking at it,' Minnow commented to herself quietly.

Below the palace was a vault lit by massive candles perched on wax-cloaked sconces. Here the captured Juttahat stood backed against a rough-hewn granite wall. A stone ball shackled to one ankle by a length of chain would limit its mobility. In its arms and around its shoulders the Unman bore the looping brassy burden of its Isi master. The serpent's jaws rested broodingly upon the Juttahat's fuzzy rufous cranium, the snake's eyes half-dilated. Through the sand which carpeted the flagstones to a thumb's depth a shaman from the tundra shuffled to and fro. Decked with pelts and harnie wings and tinkling tin discs, the shaman wore upon his head and shoulders the massive decapitated head of a hervy. He banged a rattle on a broad drum slung around his neck.

He bellowed. He darted his load of jagged horns towards the double prisoner as if about to disembowel one or the other. The Juttahat flinched, bouncing the Isi it carried. Then it froze. Its eyes blurred. Like resin, glutinous beads welled on the gland-slits of its chin.

The shaman stepped back. He grunted, he panted, he drummed. Superficially it might have seemed that a manic entertainment had been arranged for the involuntary guests ...

Lucky and her husband and the priest stood watching the display. A pair of leather-clad guards held lightpistols at the ready. Lucky's mana-priest – square-faced and ruddy-cheeked – clasped his hands upon a corpulent belly. He wore the customary grey serge suit and stiff white wing collar. Lucky was in her purple velvet gown, tiara, and scarlet boots. She tapped a foot impatiently to the rhythm of the drum. Her consort of four centuries had assumed a crisp white uniform decorated with much golden braid at the cuffs and ostentatious epaulettes upon the shoulders.

Bertel had charge of a pouch of indigo baize. Hardly a wrinkle creased his frank fresh features. His blue eyes were rueful. His sandy hair sprouted profusely, forever in vigorous riot, though his beard was a wispy goatee.

The flamboyant epaulettes of his princely uniform accentuated the breadth of Bertel's shoulders, making him seem temporarily

279

top-heavy – though whenever he walked, with a bounding and elastic gait, the impression was rather of someone determined to launch himself free of the chains of gravity, someone forever gathering himself up to float free, of life itself perhaps. A little pot of a tummy – product of ale – swelled his waist-band, suggesting a mimic pregnancy.

The Isi's tongue flicked out, tasting candle smoke and the rancid odour emanating from that huge shaggy taurine head which confronted it, bowed and menacing.

'The hervy lost its head,' called out the priest. 'Now we wear its head. With its head we control you. This is spoken.'

Puffs of pastel light drifted up from the serpent's horns, to pop like bubbles.

'Quite useless tormenting my servant,' recited the Juttahat, about itself. The Isi-mage was speaking through its lips. The snake's long scaly head rose, swaying. Its mouth opened, displaying sharp hindward-pointing teeth within a pink mouth, fangs at the fore. Its eyes dilated to inky pools. 'Damaging pain can be drugging an Isi into a chosen oblivion.'

'Is that so?' enquired Lucky. 'You can choose to go into a coma if we hurt you? We wouldn't dream of tormenting either of you, Honoured Mage.' She gestured grandly around the vault. 'See, we have a fine den for you, with fresh sand on the floor – you do like sand to writhe in, don't you? – and a special alcove for you to roost in.' A deep recess was carved into one wall. For the Juttahat, there was a sanitary cubicle. 'A home from home, I think. Maybe a little primitive. But then, we are a bit primitive, aren't we?'

The shaman shook his rack of horns, thumped his drum, chanted a hex-rhyme.

'A bit close to the well-springs of mana, maybe.'

'And correspondingly far,' said the Juttahat, 'from a true knowledge of the mysterium.'

'Ha!' said the portly, suited man. 'The *mysterium*. Oh yes.'

'If some of your priests will be submitting to our guidance—'

'So you're a negotiator now?' Lucky asked the serpent. 'Let's speak about the everything machine.'

'Being where?'

'Certainly not here. Did you think I would house an everything machine in my own palace, not knowing what it might produce?'

'Being our machine.' The brassy serpent's pupils narrowed again, to slits in yellow orbs.

'How is the machine activated?'

The alien mage held itself rampant, defiant – and supercilious. 'Perhaps by desire, Queen Lucky.'

'Whose desire? How?'

'What are you seeking from the everything machine?' A scent of vanilla and oily attar wafted from the mage, almost lost in the reek of smoke and hervy. The shaman rattled his drum.

Lucky hesitated. 'Oh, a locator for lost treasure,' she said off-handedly. She polished the ruby ring upon her velvet sleeve. 'Bertel, dear—'

Her husband lifted a mana-mirror from its baize pouch. Within a hoop of silver was a lens a hand-span across, so clouded it was quite opaque.

'Paavo, if you please,' said the mistress of Pohjola.

Accepting the tool of inner vision, mana-priest Paavo Serlachius held that up between himself and the mage.

'A mirror having *two* sides?' the serpent queried.

'Ha!' from Serlachius. 'When is a mirror not a mirror? When it's an eye of the mysterium.'

He chanted softly:

'Mana-cloud,
      'Part for me;
'Mana-cloud,
      'Let me see
'Secrets of a soul;
      'Such is spoken.'

'Eye of mystery,
      'Disc of destiny,
'Charm thou this snake,
      'To freely relate—'

An acrid odour drifted from the mage. Bubbles of rose and violet light popped from its horns. The Isi's eyes dilated fully. A nimbus sparkled around its head. Its Juttahat's eyes nictitated rapidly. The Unman's nostrils panted open and shut. Dainty teeth clenched tight in its prim mouth.

A black blot appeared within the lens. Swiftly this blemish put out tendrils. The cloud within the glass became inky as if the cracks were propagating throughout its substance, fissures which forbade and banished light.

With a sharp cry, Serlachius snatched the mana-mirror away from his eyes.

281

'Such being broken,' the Juttahat mouthpiece said in a slurred and laborious tone.

Swelling, those smudges in the lens cohered until they all became one larger oval of darkness. Blackness occupied half the area of the mana-mirror. One of the mage's dilated eyes might well have been captured, magnified within.

The shaman rattled and jangled and drummed. The leather-clad guards pointed their lightpistols at the Isi, coiling up from its bearer, its mouth gaping like a fat brazen horn. Lucky stamped her foot exasperatedly.

Serlachius squinted cautiously.

'No, it isn't broken at all,' the tubby priest assured Lucky. Brows knit in concentration, he warbled:

> 'Dark grow light;
> 'Bring us sight;
>   'This is spoken.

'Ah,' he said, 'the stain will surely shrink and disappear in time. I feel it in my waters.'

'How *long* a time?' Lucky asked petulantly.

'Maybe a week, two weeks ... a month at the most. Yes, I'd definitely say a month at the most. Glass is a kind of liquid, you see, my lady. It's a solid liquid. That's how I feel this in my waters.'

'Being fortunate,' said the glaze-eyed Juttahat, 'that your mirror is possessing two sides, or the *macula* might be staying sunken deep in its pool. Now I am about to be sleeping. My servant is requiring food daily. Myself being content with a sleek live piglet or shaved lamb once a fortnight.'

Lucky tugged Bertel to the far side of the vault. He bent, lowering a gilded epaulette so that she could whisper in his ear.

'A month; then the mage might hex our mirror again, hmm? I suspect Serlachius isn't a match for it. Our shaman's all very well at neutralizing bad mana—'

'But probing opens a channel, inviting a backlash?'

'So it seems, Bertie. We could really use a drug that can bemuse a mage – fed to it in a piglet or lamb. A well-shaved lamb, of course.'

'Our mage doesn't want wool caught in its teeth.'

She rubbed her belly, where the latest daughter was gestating.

'So I'll take Eva to the gala,' he murmured.

'Right, let her dazzle all eyes. Some Earthfolk will be there. Observers always are. They might know a drug.'

'Fungus pharmacopoeia?' (*Let him not seem too eager to escape from his splendid wife's clutches for a while.*)

Lucky pursed her lips.

'Be stupid to poison the mage,' Bertel hinted. 'Suppose it could cope, could neutralize—'

'Bertie . . .' A tinge of paranoia in her voice, now. 'We don't wish to blab too much to Landfall, too eagerly.'

'Of course not.'

'The mage may have let us capture it, to lead the Isi to my—'

'To your—' He nodded.

'We merely want a . . . treasure detector.'

'From the everything machine. And then—'

She frowned. 'Events can begin to move towards a conclusion for you? You'll come back here, Bertie! Don't take risks.'

'What, with Eva accompanying me?'

'Don't think I'm blind. I need you for daughters.'

'Your own jaunt to Speakers' Valley—'

'Wasn't *much* of a risk.'

'You went for Jatta's fast boy in case *he* could find your—'

'The mage is a more likely route to taming the everything machine.'

'Maybe Earth science could . . .'

'Not with regard to the machine, no no. If it's activated by desire.'

'If that's true.'

'We need Kaleva's best proclaimer.'

'Eva at the gala. Longlife, the reward.'

Murmur, murmur.

'Earth shan't get hold of the machine. Don't take risks, Bertie. We shan't be hasty. I'll curb my impatience. I've waited hundreds of years to find myself. Not to lose *you*, Bertie, oh no. Don't even think so, or I shall be very angry . . .'

Tamely, Bertel nodded.

The mage's head reclined upon its servant's. Chain clinking, the liveried Juttahat edged its master past the shaman to the recess in the wall, to unload those glistening coils dappled with ochre brown and rusty ferric glyphs.

'Serpents can slither swiftly,' Lucky shouted to her guards. 'Don't be fooled—

'On the *other* hand,' she murmured to her consort, 'I might just

283

give the everything machine to Landfall once it has served me. I'll have no further use for it, will I? I'll be reunited.'

Bertel stroked his braided cuff. 'Haven't been to a gala for . . . well, must be going on sixty years. I'm wondering whether this regalia is quite—'

'It's *dignified*, Bertie.' Impulsively she hugged him. 'You're my very own Crown Prince of Kaleva, don't forget it.' Dusky eyes narrowed further in her ripe oval face. 'Don't forget any of my wishes!'

'Even if they're in conflict, my love?'

'*Especially* not then.' She grinned zanily. 'How else do we keep the Isi and the Earthfolk guessing? Caprice is my sceptre, Bertie. Sometimes I know it, sometimes I quite forget it. It doesn't forget me.'

Bertel sighed, a draught from the chasm of the centuries.

'Neither do I,' he said, haunted. 'To love a person for hundreds of years – it's the dream of poets, I suppose. It's . . . devastating, this slavery of the heart.'

'Poor Bertie. So richly fulfilled.' Lucky stroked her belly. 'A father, time and again. Though never of a son.'

'That doesn't matter to me—'

'Deep down, though,' she teased, 'it may make you feel just a little effete in a world of heroes?' She flicked a gilded epaulette with a forefinger. 'This really is a very nice costume.'

She could be at once pitiless and tender. How his love for her ached, an enchantment.

21 · LIFE AT LANDFALL

'Every few weeks,' Penelope Conway confessed to the newcomer, Wex, 'I feel a wave of sick consciousness sweep over me like a nausea.' The black woman sat up straighter behind her cluttered tammywood desk. Penelope was fifty years old this year, and her tight coaly hair showed a few white threads. For summer she favoured a plain olive sari, elegant but in no way ostentatious. The looseness of the garment flattered her figure which had become portly of late. Matronly.

'But I can cope perfectly well,' she insisted. 'I just remind myself of harmony.'

'Seems this whole planet needs a therapist,' said Wex.

'And you're it?'

Wex wore a wig, she was sure. His curly, lustrous, black hair had an unnatural, artificial panache to it. Penelope imagined tiny metal sockets studding a depilated scalp underneath that wig. Or perhaps criss-cross sutures where his skull had been opened up. In his forties and of wiry build, he wore loose purple silks beneath a green gaberdine cloak with many sealed pockets in it. High tooled tan boots. His face was prim, the dark-brown eyes close-set.

'Not exactly,' he said.

The Earth Resident leaned forward. With a hint of paranoia in her voice, and perhaps a note of pleading too, she asked the meta-man, 'Have you come to replace me?'

Wex laughed. 'Where do you wish to retire to? Warm, sensible Pootara? Amidst the farmers and sailors and carvers of crosswood puzzles?'

'Crosswood?'

'By analogy with *crossword*, though without any words involved. Back in the days of . . .' Wex shut his eyes momentarily as he consulted his data-mind.

{*Newspapers.*}

'. . . newspapers; papers with news in them, selling by the millions every day.'

'So many trees . . .' A sigh of regret escaped from Penelope.

'Plenty of trees on Kaleva.' He glanced significantly at the files of assorted text which piled her desk, and at similar labelled stacks heaped on tammy shelves towering from floor to ceiling. 'Quite a citadel of literacy, your sanctum.'

She shifted a ledger, exposing a recessed screen with voice and keyboard input.

'Everything's in bubble-memory too, Wex. Backed up, and backed up. We're scrupulous.'

'You worry that bubbles might burst . . .'

'It happens.' Penelope gazed at him. 'Especially in transit through mana-space. The Ukko is choosy about what apparatus arrives in working order.'

'I came through unimpaired. Aware of mana effects, but hopefully immune.'

'Hopefully. Unlike me. So you have censor circuits in your mind?'

'Kaleva's most popular export: puzzles,' he said sarcastically.

Instead of rising to the bait she retorted, 'And its prime import: people. Hitherto! But Earth's cutting back on immigrants, isn't it? Just enough to maintain the link. Enough to provide sufficient passengers for the Ukko ferry. Hardly a torrent to fill this virgin land. I admit the value of the escape valve is primarily psychological.'

Wex reached for the ledger she had shifted.

'We need access to more worlds. We need to know what makes an Ukko tick so we can *build* ones of our own. Breed 'em, build 'em, not be reliant. How many Ukkos do you suppose the Isi operate? Earth's scared of Kaleva, Pen Conway. A world where magic operates. Proclaimings. Enchantments. Cuckoos. Kaleva mightn't be in our own universe at all.' Wex read the title lettered on the ledger. '*A Catalogue of Obsessions*. Hmm . . . Would you rather retire to Earth, Pen? Back to our own enlightened crowded world?'

'Pen? Pen?' she echoed.

By way of explanation Wex picked up a stylus from her desk and waggled it at the mass of documents.

'I'll call you Wethead,' she said mischievously. 'Wethead Wex, our secret weapon . . . with a protoplasmic computer in his brain. According to a cuckoo story, the Isi sneaked in an everything machine a few years ago. A device for manufacturing whatever you wish. Isn't that magical?'

Wex shut his eyes briefly. {*Presumably nanotechnology*—} 'Nanotechnology device. Using programmable molecule-size assemblers. *We* don't have nanotech. If only we did.'

'It's just a rumour. Supposedly Lucky Sariola captured the everything machine. Or the Isi let her capture it, so it probably doesn't work reliably.'

'Maybe not after coming through mana-space in the womb of an Ukko.'

'The *womb* of an Ukko – odd you should say that . . .'

Penelope Conway's sanctum looked out from the topmost tier of the Earthkeep towards distant Harmony Field. No herbage greened that field. It was a great flat circle of pink granite and black obsidian arranged in a yin-yang pattern. In the centre, a shuttlecraft ferry pointing skyward. Boomerang-shaped Lake

Plentiful lapped one shore of this huge amulet, mirroring heavenly blue. Forest fringed the rest of the field, green beard sprawling lavishly away from its rounded chin. Two widely-spaced eyes, one pink and one black – one of granite, one of obsidian – stared upward from a twisted grin. That was how Harmony Field seemed to Penelope after fifteen years' service on Kaleva.

Closer to her headquarters a squat old building of rose-red brick supported a satellite dish. The surveillance satellite up in orbit – codenamed Carter on account of its cartographic function – had mapped almost the whole globe long since but it had never succeeded in peering through mana-mists at the forested haunts of the three Isi factions and *their* shuttle depots. Currently Carter was idle. Gun-towers stood around, but had never been used.

A domed building was an observatory. But the stars had been charted without yielding a clue to their position relative to Earth or to known quasars or nebulae. At night the glow of the sky-sickle provided its own nearby milky way.

These and other science buildings might have formed the kernel of a University of Kaleva located here at Landfall, except for the mana-massaged moods of the people. Their involvement in a life of lords, passions, mana-priesthood, nakki notions, was almost mesmeric. Likewise, their acting out of metamorphosed variations on old folkways. Wasn't such behaviour well suited to a virgin world and to an economy just a few rungs above subsistence? Lucky's Ukko continued to require old wives' tales and fantasies as the price for travel from Earth orbit to Kaleva-space and back again. That obsessive, vital cruise . . .

The frustrations of Kaleva, the exasperations! A Penelope must try to remain aloof and retain a clear consciousness – and ensure the same harmony of consciousness in this enclave of several hundred Earth personnel. She must attempt to decipher the long-term schemes of the aliens. She must brood about the gossip of the native cuckoo birds. She must meditate about mana while trying to remain free from the lusts and jealousies, the conspiracies and cravings, the neuroses and the violence, all the charismatic sexism enshrined in Lucky Sariola's breeding of an endless succession of daughters who could immortalize a hero. All those qualities which Earth, for the sake of sheer sharing survival and decency, had done its very best to educate away.

Kaleva often seemed mellow, lovely, and fresh. But passions forever simmered. Monsters emerged, of the stripe of a Tycho Cammon who could have been somebody from out of Earth's dark bloody old history, a Bluebeard. Penelope frequently felt corrupted. Yet as a woman she trusted that she was less corruptible than a man might have been in her position. Thus Earth's consistent choice of a female resident. Less potential for aggression or for random rampant bullying desire.

Now here came Wex: a covert new player in the centuries-old game of Kaleva. Game, indeed. A game played by mana, with people as its pieces. A game initiated by the star-faring Ukko entity, whose kin had ferried aliens and their humanoid servants to Kaleva to trade and intrigue, and presumably to *study* people – as Penelope and her staff likewise studied the situation.

Something was certainly learning lessons from what transpired on Kaleva. One generally learned lessons for a purpose, not out of sheer playfulness. Kaleva had been relatively quiet of late. Now there were *signs*. Cuckoos cackled about a battle in Speakers' Valley. Lucky had taken an Isi mana-mage prisoner. A miracle boy had appeared. Tycho Cammon had revived and murdered the proclaimer Osmo van Maanen's mistress before being killed and burned to ash. Dreams were more nonsensical than usual, with blazing sheep stampeding through them. Surely something was coming to a boil.

Who was learning those lessons? The Isi, with their mana-mages? The telepathic cuckoos? The visiting Ukkos?

And what was *Earth* learning, at the end of its long umbilicus? To fortify people's brains with supplementary neural networks woven of programmed protoplasm? So that a second, better informed opinion could reside within a person's skull?

Jesuitical cleric, assassin, thief, or diplomat: which was Wex?

Already she was telling herself stories about him. She must focus on the man himself. This meta-man. A man with an extra, artificial mind. A man equipped with an encyclopedia in his brain – and with an internal moral overseer too, she supposed? Given his double mind, in what style would Wex dream? And what was he? Her inspector from Earth? Her successor, her supplanter? Ach, she was thinking like a lord! *Be lucid in spirit, my daughter*, she told herself.

One wall of her office was crowded with scores of little pictures – paintings, pen-and-ink drawings, photographs taken by roving agents of her predecessor – showing scores of keeps across the continent. Strongholds. Including the red brick ziggurat she sat in.

Be lucid, my daughter. Be clear.

Was it an error on the part of Earth to send a resident whose skin was a dark shade of chocolate? Kalevans frequently treated her as a Pootaran. Earth had hoped she might resolve the enigma of why the quota of black immigrants remained immune to the dizzy foibles and atavistic neo-feudalism of the north. Why, on the contrary, they had developed a rational and almost utopian community. That was how people *ought* to live, in harmony, moderation, and respectful equality.

'Harmony,' said Wex, 'is the art of mutual respect.'

He might have been reading Penelope's mind, or prompted to this observation by his implanted organic circuits.

'The word *polites*,' said Wex, 'meant a citizen, a social being, respectful of all others – and thus of oneself. Of course for a while politics came to signify artifice and cunning and the exercise of power, which I suppose is more relevant here. You must often be in two minds, Pen Conway.' He grinned briefly, vulpine. 'Rather like me.'

Leaning forward, he asked suddenly: 'Do you have *any* Isi or Juttahat skeletons left to trade to the snakes?'

Penelope hoped that she reacted suavely.

'You'd know about that, of course,' she acknowledged.

Of those skeletons which had been in the Ukko long ago, the final two lay in sealed caskets locked in a vault beneath the ziggurat. The bones of one serpent and of one serpent-servant were hidden below the Earthkeep. Below the *administration building*, to be less quasi-feudal in one's terms.

A century and a half earlier the Velvet Isi first made approaches regarding those skeletons found aboard Lucky's Ukko. The aliens had learned of those from the tale of young Paula Sariola's entry into the innards of the entity, as chanted by mana-priests at feasts marking the anniversary of the event.

When Lucky had made contact with the Ukko, it had transported her and her family of asteroid miners – and their ship the *Katarina*, sucked against its rocky side – through mana-space. It had emerged into orbit around the planet whose northern continent corresponded approximately to the landscape of the folk tales she had told to the Ukko. Lakes, forests, fjords, tundra . . .

The prospectors had photographed Kaleva from orbit. But the *Katarina* wasn't built to land on any world.

So the Ukko returned those first starfarers and their ship to the solar system, into orbit around Earth, causing amazement. And provoking much debate – which really could only have one outcome, unless Earth wanted to forgo such a gift.

To replace the *Katarina*: several spacious shuttlecraft. These would carry a stream of settlers up to the starfaring entity. After transit through mana-space, the shuttles would take the settlers down to the surface of the new Earth. Principally the emigrants would be Northern Europeans and West Africans so as to utilize most appropriately the Finland-like northern continent and the sub-tropics. And for the sake of global yin-yang. And because the Ukko entity heeded Lucky's wishes as to who and what it would convey. Lucky was already queen of the new world.

Those much-examined bones of serpents and humanoids were kept on board the Ukko, sealed in one of its chambers. They belonged aboard this creature which had become their catacomb. Lucky was adamant about this. She had seen ghosts in inner chambers – echoes of the aliens when they were alive. The Ukko itself was totally reticent about bones, aliens, and much else. It would ferry colonists who retold it Lucky's stories. It wouldn't explain itself.

In transit through mana-space certain animals exported from Earth were altered. Certain people too, though mutations might not show up till the next generation. En route the old heroic tales of desires and jealousies and magical exploits, of rage and obsession and superstition, massaged the emigrants' dreams.

When Kaleva had been settled to a significant degree, groups of Isi and their Juttahats had dropped down upon the new world to start their cryptic meddling. Eventually the Velvet Isi requested the return of their dead. Alien skeletons, taken from the Ukko, were shuttled down secretly to Landfall. Thus commenced the protracted, procrastinatory trade in alien remains in exchange for items of Isi technology.

Cuckoos seemingly remained oblivious to this barter. Or did the Isi not *want* the birds to tittle-tattle about this furtive topic? Always the suspicion lurked that the serpents understood more about those enigmatic garrulous birds than did any human being. How often did cuckoos gossip about the private lives of the Isi? Rarely! True, they told anecdotes about a monstrous Isi pariah which had taken the folkloric name of Viper. But otherwise . . . ach! Penelope always felt deeply perplexed about the cuckoos of Kaleva. Foul luck to kill one or catch one to cage: everyone knew it. Two of her predecessors had provoked riots in Landfall itself. All cuckoos knew of a captive cuckoo ar. I could taunt people into tantrums. Hadn't some poet written, *A captive cuckoo in a cage puts all Kaleva in a rage*?

Perhaps the birds were primarily interested in human beings because human beings had arrived here first and far outnumbered the serpents and their slaves. Cuckoos had imprinted upon people. Yet what had cuckoos chattered about before the advent of humanity? In what sort of avian speech, before human words first fell upon their feline ears?

'Why do you suppose the snakes want those old bones?' Wex asked.

Penelope chanced her hand; she'd had dreams.

'To communicate with the dead. With the ghosts, the echoes.'

'Ha!' Was he mocking her? Diagnosing her as infected by local superstitions?

'I've slept down there in the vault beside the caskets . . .' Of which only two now remained. When the last one was traded, what then? Penelope was loath to lose this remaining edge over the Isi.

'And, Pen Conway?'

She shrugged. 'I dreamed that skeletons put on flesh again. Then they talked nonsense. Obscene drivel.'

Penelope was celibate. Avoiding passion was essential to the composure her mission required.

'The Isi must want to know how their kin died in our solar system aeons ago.'

Wex wagged the stylus. 'Not necessarily *aeons* ago, Pen. That's an assumption based on the fact that we only found bones, and not a scrap of tissue. There ought to have been *some* tissue, no matter how shrivelled. It's as if those bones were picked bare, totally cleansed of anything perishable.'

'Cleansed by what, Wex?'

'By Lucky's Ukko. By our Ukko. So that we would find it for ourselves some time.'

'We might never have found it.'

'Maybe it put itself in our way. Then we could be introduced into the Ukko game. Other Ukkos haven't brought serpents to our solar system, have they? They transported some Isi to Kaleva once we were reasonably established here. Ukkos love stories, don't they? Soak 'em up like food and drink. Like fuel. You need an antagonist in a story, don't you?'

'Though of course,' said Penelope diplomatically, 'the best stories are about co-operation—'

'The *safest* stories, Pen. The fashionable ones.'

She nodded. His other mind must have prompted those words – permitted them. Story-telling on an Earth of enlightened consciousness might mainly be about harmony and co-operation, partnership, sharing, custodianship of the ravaged ecosystem, the overcoming of obstacles. About correctness of heart, loving awareness, the rapport of brown and black and white, male and female, people and animalkind – amidst the strict budgeting of living space, foodstuffs, water, mobility, energy, human fertility. Would such stories stir an Ukko and move it between the stars?

Negotiating with Juttahats of the Velvet Isi had been the hardest part of Penelope's career as resident: the need, for security's sake, to treat those mouthpieces of the serpents as *things*, not persons. As a kind of living clockwork machinery.

'When you meet your first Juttahat,' she began.

Again, that quick feral grin on his prissy face.

'There's a theory,' said Wex, 'that human beings weren't properly conscious until just a few thousand years ago. Our brains are divided in two, right? Right – and left! Originally people heard hallucinatory voices originating in the right hemisphere telling us what to do; and we obeyed those God-instructions like automata. That's how the Juttahat are, except that their voices come telepathically from the Isi.'

'*Wethead*,' she said softly.

He nodded. They understood one another. This man Wex was an attempt at a Juttahat, but with something other than a serpent sharing his brain. With programmed protoplasmic circuits.

'It must have been comparatively easy and natural for the serpents to tame the Juttahats, back in their past,' Wex mused. 'To use 'em as hands and legs and voices. Then improve them, enhance them, breed 'em up.'

Penelope's deepest fear . . . must be faced.

'The Isi want to make us into new Juttahats,' she whispered. 'So that we'll serve them. So the whole human race will serve them. They still don't know enough about how to mould us. How to speak to our minds.'

'Like little gods in our brains.'

292

'They probe and pry.' Fury gripped her. 'Whatever was Earth thinking of sending you here, Wex, with wetwear in your head? What are you but an example of how to graft a god into a human mind!'

Momentarily he looked annoyed. Promptly his irritation was erased as if it had never existed.

'On the contrary, Pen Conway, I'm a sovereign person – guarded against any mental meddling by the Isi.'

Her heart fluttered.

Om, she said silently to herself in a calming ritual. *Om, Om.*

And aloud: 'You're . . . a prototype – aren't you? – of how we might all safeguard ourselves against snakes if the need arises – by implanting our own controllers inside our heads . . .'

Earth's population could be guaranteed a compelling purity of mind for ever more . . . No more struggles to do the right thing, no more soul-searching to achieve impeccable conduct, no more conflicts between self and society and the ecosystem . . . This was what Wethead Wex presaged.

Om. Om.

Was this how Earth would ensure the survival of the harmonious human species in future? Not by the enlightened conscience but by artificial circuitry censoring consciousness itself?

'Can you think corrupt thoughts?' she probed. 'Can you harbour evil desires? Is bad consciousness suppressed automatically?'

Once again, that quick feral grin.

'*I'm* here on a mission, Pen Conway – to safeguard the human heart, the integrity of humanity. We need more worlds to settle people on, so that an exodus has an impact. We need control – of more Ukkos; of mana phenomena.'

If the Isi could find a route to Earth, then Earth would clamp its people tight for their own protection, with programmed protoplasm presiding inside their skulls.

How easily was wetwear inserted? Maybe not by sawing the skull open at all, but merely by an injection into the bloodstream – whereupon the protoplasm might multiply, thrusting tendrils throughout the brain . . .

'Maybe,' she said hopefully, 'Lucky's Ukko killed its earlier crew when it sensed Earth was inhabited so as to stop the Isi from becoming our gods?'

Wex rubbed his slim nose. Eyes slightly glazed, he said, 'You

293

mustn't trade every last skeleton no matter what they offer. Keep the last snake as insurance.'

'Are you saying the Isi can't communicate with their dead until they have them all back? Every last one of them?'

'No, but I don't believe they've communicated yet. They're waiting. They're searching for something—' He broke off. 'Why was it odd I should refer to the *womb* of an Ukko? You've forgotten what you said, Pen. I never forget what I say. I can't. It's all stored.'

She strained to recall her exact words. Her original train of thought had *almost* fled.

Ah . . .

'When I came here fifteen years ago, Wex, my fellow passengers in the Ukko all thought of the space creature as a great convoluted ear, listening to them. I felt I was in a many-chambered womb. Can an Ukko give birth to another of its kind?'

'Go on, Pen.'

'Huge stone ears flying between the stars, and never bored with listening . . . What are they, Wex? And how do they come about?'

'How do new ones come about?' he prompted.

'Yes indeed. Could an Ukko gestate a baby Ukko inside itself? Would the Ukko divide in two? Would it maybe implant its essence in some asteroid in such a way that the rock was transformed?'

Wex's eyes gleamed. 'Might Lucky in some way have *fertilized* the Ukko – is that what you're saying? Might the encounter with a new species help an Ukko to breed? I should respect the instincts of people who've been living in this mana-drenched, dream-besotten place. Speak on.'

Penelope spread her hands.

'Where would this baby be? Back in Earth's asteroid belt? Coagulating together somewhere in the sky-sickle? Hidden somewhere on Kaleva itself? Maybe on this very *continent*? A residue of Lucky's Ukko, always here. The source of mana, the focus of mana . . . Pootara isn't affected, but *we* certainly are.'

Swinging round, Wex pointed a slim forefinger towards the distant shuttle. He squinted along the finger.

'Will this baby Ukko *leap* into orbit from the ground? Will it persuade a volcano to hurl it into the sky?'

'An Ukko flies through mana-space,' Penelope protested. 'Why can't it travel directly into space from the surface of a world?'

'You've had dreams,' suggested Wex.

She nodded reluctantly.

'You never had a baby of your own, Pen Conway.'

'Before I came here – you probably know this too – I was sterilized. To avoid belated obsessions about motherhood. It was sensible. Kaleva isn't the place to begin brooding compulsively about something. To be vulnerable. I surrendered my womb but they gave me a world.'

'Now you dream about worlds becoming pregnant and giving birth. And Kaleva is the nursery . . .'

Just then a buzzer sounded. Shifting aside a file labelled *The Summoning of Cuckoos*, Penelope uncovered her intercom. A bespectacled Chinese woman's face regarded her, owl-like, from the little screen.

'Yes, Yü?'

'You have visitors. Elmer Loxmith, the instinctive engineer, heir to Loxmithlinna, and his assistant Lyle Melator.' Yü looked mischievous. 'Young Lord Loxmith wishes to discuss how a talking cat might most conveniently hibernate.'

Wex's eyelids fluttered. Some internal dialogue went on between his wetwear and his natural brain.

'Is this a code?' he asked. 'A riddle?'

Penelope permitted herself a brief smirk. 'Welcome to Kaleva, Wethead,' she said. 'A nursery full of children getting up to mischief.'

Nikki Loxmith took in the sights of Landfall town, that first staging post for fresh arrivals from Earth.

The great ziggurat of red brick and little glinting rows of windows on the far edge of town, to which Elmer and Lyle had headed, suggested to her a tit of the home planet, a swelling rosy bosom which might offer succour or at last a compass point to the disoriented. The fact that the Earthkeep was on the outskirts of the sprawling burg also hinted at a certain loosening of apron strings, a progressive dilution – already – of Earth's influence from that nipple point outward.

Nevertheless, Earth officials supervised Landfall. Olive uniforms were in evidence, worn by men and women some of whose features were exotic to Nikki's eyes. Brown faces, and black, and yellow. Those of persons who, so Elmer had told her, would return to Earth after ten or twenty years' service. She heard a few strange languages on the lips of townsfolk. She felt exotic in her embroidered finery, ribboned bonnet, and long pocketed apron. Some young men eyed her but also noted the knife at her belt.

Three sides of the market square were lined with shops, one crammed with defunct 'tronic junk from Earth. Her brother would enjoy browsing here. She bought a chunk of rosy smoked fish and chewed. Gluttonous goats and truculent geese roamed amidst vendors' carts, scavenging spilled grain and cabbage leaves. A cuckoo preened on one of several tall wrought-iron perches, a green flame on a flambeau. A knot of gaping kids stood below as the bird alternately prated about some murder, and ducked its beak beneath its wing as if to disinter new shreds of information. A family were pushing a barrow of possessions in the direction of the wharfs, where *Sea Sledge* was also tied. Friends accompanied them, chanting resolutely if tipsily about travel.

A sumptuous mana-kirk of white marble dominated the north side of the square. Licking her fingers, Nikki wandered up the wide steps.

Inside, several dark-suited priests were instructing separate little knots of congregation to fluency in Kalevan. Another priest tossed molten tin into a broad low font of water for the benefit of a family whose time had come to leave Landfall. After scrutinizing the resulting metallic sketch-map he compared this with a framed map upon the adjacent wall. Symbols represented place-names. A trefoil signified Threelakes. An open mouth, Yulistalax. Stooping, eyes shut, the priest inhaled a whiff of vapour from a bowl of liquid tin simmering upon a brazier. He jerked the handle of the ladle at the silhouette of a head with protuberant brow, up towards the north-east of the map.

'You'd be best advised to settle in Niemi up the Murame river,' he told the father of the family. He began to sing softly.

'Travellers, travellers, homeseeking safely . . .'

A stout man with skin of shiny ebony sat in the puzzle shop, wearing a blue pleated gown with huge sleeves, and a beaded red fez on his head. Shelves and counter were crowded with wooden boxes and spheres and pyramids made of many inter-locking parts. Doors stood open upon triangular rooms crowded with merchandise, from which flights of steps could be glimpsed leading up and down into other rooms of irregular shape. A couple of black sailors in striped blue jerseys, wide creamy trousers, and peaked caps sat in such one room with a high skylight, sipping coffee and smoking pipes. A staircase ran up to a crooked gallery from which dim corridors led off at oddly acute angles.

The proprietor beamed at Nikki, who was staring about in some confusion. He lifted up an ovoid made of half a dozen different woods, which completely filled his large hands. Even the surface of the puzzle must have comprised almost a hundred segments, and still more pieces would lurk within.

The black man pressed with his thumb in a certain way, so that a tiny section popped free, opening a route to dismantle the construction. His fingernails were long and manicured.

'We call this puzzle the Ukko. It's new.' How very white his teeth were.

The building was a puzzle in itself.

'I expected a Pootaran shop to be . . .'

'Neater? All straight lines and right angles? Perfect symmetry?' His accent was rich and vibrant.

'Something of the sort.'

'We don't subscribe to illusions, miss. You need a sense of balance to find your way about in here.' His eyelids were heavily hooded, lending a drowsy cast to his countenance, but he winked roguishly.

'Meaning that nakkis can't take up residence?'

He chortled. 'Something of the sort.' He set the heavy ovoid down. 'This'll be your first visit to Landfall, from out of the wilds?'

'Wilds, indeed! I'm from Loxmithlinna. My brother's an engineer.'

His name was Bosco. Apparently he was a representative of Pootara in Landfall, equivalent in some way to Penelope Conway whom Nikki's brother and Lyle were presently visiting in the Earthkeep. Bosco saw to the speedy transport of any immigrants of his own race to Tumio and onward by sailing ship to the garden island far south.

A tall black woman had drifted down a steep narrow stairway which Nikki hadn't noticed hitherto. Though the woman was singularly thin, a voluminous pink blouse loosely knotted around her chest mimed an ample bosom. A purple skirt hung in a lavish mass of drapes and folds. Her head supported a massive mauve turban.

The two sailors had also gravitated into the shop area, and were toying with puzzles.

'African houses aren't in the least like this,' Bosco told Nikki, gesturing around the crooked complicated building. 'You won't find mud huts in Pootara, though. We aren't copycats acting out old habits at the behest of Momma Ukko. Hoodoos and voodoos, no ma'am. No mambo priestesses. No orisha echoes of the dead. It's you folks who run around banging on your magic drums.'

'She won't follow you, Bosco,' said the woman.

Follow? Follow Bosco? Nikki frowned. Was he trying to convert her to something?

'Wouldn't that be something if we did? The old worldview of us Africans is really quite befitting.'

'You've been here in the north too long.' The woman laid a slim hand on Bosco's arm. 'It's time to go back to the isles.'

'I do want to understand,' said Nikki.

'No, let me have my say, Miriam. According to *our* old world-view, miss, there's a whole world of forces, though only if we could call a halt to everything would the driving power be revealed. The power that is word and blood and seed and water. A fellow can strengthen or weaken another fellow, or make him or her do things, or mould the world itself by tapping that power. That's what we used to believe. But there has to be mutual respect and well-being – that's really more important than exercising any powers. Humanity before mana.'

Nikki nodded encouragingly. Maybe what he was saying in that attractive accent would make sense some other time in recollection.

One of the sailors thrust a puzzle into Bosco's hand. Without even looking at it, Bosco began to take it apart, prising with his long nails. The exercise was calming.

'Puzzles are cool,' he said. 'They take the mischief out of fingers. And out of minds and hearts. Now if it had been African spacefarers who found Lucky's Ukko instead . . . dear me. Basically, we're here as labourers. To grow bananas, ha! To feed all this madness in the north. I mean, basically that's why we're here. We aren't going to dance and drum and conjure any *loa* spirits. We aren't falling into that trap, miss, not that Momma Ukko quite invited us to. Joyful reason is our guide. You say your engineer brother's visiting Penelope Conway – though not why, and I'm not asking. That woman actually had her womb cut out to stay correct, so how can one tell her anything? It's far better to do puzzles to occupy one's mind. Once upon a time there was a revolution, and people made reason into a goddess.'

'It surely is time to be heading back south,' the woman called Miriam said.

And maybe it was time for Nikki to be heading back to the hostelry where she and Elmer and Lyle were staying overnight and probably for a few more nights.

'Don't pay him no heed, sister,' Miriam said. 'Buy a puzzle. Calm your mind.'

Oh, was she just a shopkeeper, after all?

22 · HIS FACE IN THE FIREWORKS

Autumn had come to Yulistalax, staining the orchestra of harper trees along the ridge north-east of the town to a braid of apricot, gold, and bronze. On the gentle slopes below, fronds of horzmas were tarnished copper, while larkeries tilted a million rusted spade-blades from their boughs.

The town had also put on finery. Each lane vied with rainbows of bunting to welcome guests as pollenflies to flowers. Yulistalax was a maze of such lanes. Blocks of half a dozen timber homes were united at festival time by candy-striped canvas porches and awnings and outdoor corridors to form single connected hostelries, all in amiable rivalry. Here was the Sign of the Goose; there, of the Sky-Sickle. Here were the Hervy's Head, the Lady Lucky, the Sky-Boat, the Goat, the Bellflower, and daringly the Serpent's Head.

No one visiting Yulistalax could miss the direction of Lord Maxi Burgdorf's – and Lady Mitzi Burgdorf's – keep. A tall slim tower of pink granite soared above it. Originally, this tower had borne a tammywood dome in the style of a toadstool cap. A mushroom-doting ancestor of Maxi Burgdorf had designed it but the cap had succumbed to gales a century and a half since.

So Gunther Beck recalled, while he rambled through crowded festive lanes. The populace of this lakeside town had swollen sixfold or sevenfold thanks to the gala. Half of Kaleva seemed to have come (though indeed it hadn't). Harbour and shoreline were dense with sloops and yawls, cutters, luggers, barges. Down at the waterfront: a fish-fair. Verandah-fronted houses had become cafés where beer and spirits flowed. Lord Burgdorf's watchmen patrolled politely with cudgels. A drunk raved from a pillory. Street stalls sold fried doughnuts, pancakes with berry jam, pasties, link sausages, gingerbread men. A brass band marched around town in single file. Kids scampered, teenagers flirted; old folks hobbled, a sparkle of youth in their eyes.

Elsewhere in Yulistalax, Bertel Okkonen-Sariola was pointing out that same tower to an inquisitive Eva, and telling her about eccentric Burgdorf, the would-be Mushroom Lord; for Bertel also remembered the long-gone tammy dome. In his braid and epaulettes he felt like some glorified bandsman . . .

Silver-haired Sam Peller was hauling Osmo van Maanen's port-manteau, of tapestry strapped with leather, into the costly Lady Lucky where Osmo regularly stayed for gala. Their sky-boat was at the field below the Burgdorfs' keep.

'If you want my opinion,' Sam was saying to Osmo with a puff and a pant, 'you ought to twist that ring of yours around so that the swan's definitely under your finger—'

Elmer Loxmith had already found a chamber for himself and Lyle to share in that same hostelry, with a nearby room for Nikki.

'I do hope Tommi *will* have sweet dreams,' said Nikki.

'A cat's sweet dreams,' said Lyle, 'consist of killing things—'

Minkie Kennan, in his trusty long leather coat of many pockets, was squiring Kyli into a room in the not quite so costly Serpent's Head. The mischievous – audacious – name definitely appealed to him. Its clientele were likely to prove amusing.

'Here we are, my love: a fine feather bed for my hen!'

Juke and Eyeno, with slimmer purses, had found rooms at the Sign of the Goat, a name redolent of home. Eyeno had suggested they simply rent a twin-room tent in the extempore encampment along the foreshore. To sleep out under the stars with the sky-sickle silvering the far side of Lake Yulista! But Juke had demurred. The surrounding company might prove boisterous. He was going to be proclaiming at the gala. He hoped for a modicum of rest. As should Eyeno too, since she would be reciting. Bitter nostalgia for the night he had spent on Maananfors strand before releasing the stone man had tweaked at Juke, urging him to spend the night on the beach. Yet the awakening of Cammon had gone askew. Eyeno deserved a decent bed. So did he, so did he, if he was to outmatch van Maanen. *He must not feel intimidated. . . .*

Wex was prowling Yulistalax in the company of bespectacled Yü. Penelope's Chinese assistant was wearing her olive uniform so that gala-goers would be sure someone from Earth was present. She drew constant glances from passers-by, who also then noted her lightpistol.

Their accommodation was Pen Conway's sky-boat . . . Ah no, not *hers*, any more than the Earth Resident was a feudal châtelaine! Rather: Wex and Yü were billeting themselves in an armed operational white dovecraft from Harmony Field. Their dovecraft was parked on the meadow below Lord Burgdorf's keep in company with half a dozen other aerial vessels originally of Isi vintage. One was a Sariola flier (so Yü had said). Another was the more modest van Maanen sky-boat. A third, the Burgdorf family's own; but grass grew high around that tarnished hull.

Were there protocols as regards a formal visit to the Lord of Yulistalax and Speakers' Valley?

{*Unnecessary.*}

'Not during gala,' Yü assured Wex.

{*Confirmed.*} But Wex had preferred to ask Yü, and not appear omniscient.

Lord Maxi and Lady Mitzi would hold court anywhere or nowhere. During the three days their town was all one great house, as witnessed by the temporary uniting of neighbouring homes to form communal hotels linked by canvas. The Burgdorfs' ceremonial duties up in the valley – judgements, arbitrations, awards – pre-empted the time or the desire for any receptions in their keep.

Dressed in mufti, a couple of North Americans from the Earth-keep took turns to look after the dovecraft and to venture out to study this year's celebrations.

Apart from one stormy intermezzo caused by the execrable Tycho Cammon, the weather had in mortal memory always been fine during the days of the gala, as if mana smiled on the event. That afternoon a flurry of rain teased Yulistalax, more by way of settling dust and tidying up unfinished meteorological business.

Stray clouds wept teardrops, but already a shimmering spectrum arched over Harpers' Ridge.

That shower chased Elmer and Nikki into a crowded café under an awning. To Elmer's surprise he spied Gunther Beck working his way through a plateful of whipped cream buns, washed down with buttermilk. A gross cherub, the dream lord was at once wistful and vehement in his dedication to the task at hand.

'I thought you were staying home at Castlebeck?' Ever practical, the engineer spied spare stools and quickly secured them.

Generally careless of dress, Gunther had made an exception for gala. He wore a cambric shirt embroidered with loops of silver. He munched.

'I got restless . . . Besides, since you'd most likely be here to cheer Osmo on . . .'

Elmer laughed.

'Don't worry, I had a long talk with Conway's technicians. The cat'll be in the casket in another month or so. You could have used a communicator to check up. You *do* have one, don't you?'

'Might as well tell a passing cuckoo our business. Anyone can listen in on communicator chatter.'

'Anyone who has one, and that isn't many. You could have phrased things vaguely enough.'

'Pooh,' said Gunther. 'Would you care for a bun, Miss Nikki? They're delicious.'

What, deprive him of a target he'd set his eye on? Or perhaps save him from bursting? Stretched tight, the lavish embroidery did not wholly disguise the chain between his nipple rings. The bone-locket could have been a peculiar cyst.

'Oh I've eaten, Lord Beck,' she said diplomatically. 'But Tommi's gobbling insatiably. I bought a stimulant from a wise-woman. And we had him bespoken too. He'll be ready for fine deep dreams. Months of dreams. About fish, I suppose. Or about chasing Lyle and catching him. Do you think prolonged dreaming might reshape Tommi's mind in some way?'

'*Hush, child.*'

The dream lord glanced towards the nearby balcony rail where a refugee from the shower lingered. A willowy young woman, she was wearing a simple blue gown. Her eyes were a milder blue. She shut one, then the other. Again, and again. The better to focus on what she was overhearing? Could she be winking – slowly – at Gunther? Was there grit in her eyes?

'I'm staying at the Bellflower, Loxmith. Maybe you could have dinner with me in my room tonight to tell me about progress – in the design.'

'Ah but I already promised Osmo . . . He's at Lady Lucky's as well as us. *Tomorrow* night, Lord Beck. Where's the Bellflower, by the way?'

The dream lord told him, adding, 'I thought I saw Cully going into the place. It seems I was mistaken.'

This café they were in overlooked what served as a main thoroughfare through the meanders of Yulistalax. Here, if anywhere, one ought to see most visitors pass by sooner or later. Where more conveniently could Gunther station himself, in sight of the strolling crowds?

'It occurred to me that my nephew might visit the gala, since he doesn't seem to be anywhere else . . .'

Impertinent young woman. Not that she seemed *saucy*, as such . . .

The mingling scent of Pootaran tobaccos – one cloud nutty, the other spicy – drifted from two old codgers puffing on pipes. A tiled roof opposite gleamed as if newly enamelled when sunlight beamed upon it, putting paid to the final spray of rain. The woman in blue, with such silky yellow hair, was edging closer.

'Pardon me.' With a preliminary smile at Nikki. 'I couldn't help hearing you mention *dreams*. I'm by way of being a poetess.' Her smile shifted to include Gunther, warmly and appealingly.

He responded with a growl. 'Is it in the nature of poets to snoop on people?'

He picked up a bun and chomped it in half. He could do without some young woman of a few scant years vintage figuring on him now that his quest for dead Anna was edging at long last towards a culmination. Let there be no second Marietta, no gala indiscretion; not that this chit reminded him remotely of Marietta. This poetess *was* figuring on him. Something slightly *nakki* about one of her eyes . . . ?

No, those were lovely eyes, bewitching eyes.

'Do other people's words belong to you by rights?' he asked roughly.

'I spoke out of turn,' apologized Nikki. 'Sorry, Lord Beck!'

The young woman . . . chilled.

'Damned lords and their ways,' she murmured to herself. Yet she made no move to leave.

Gunther rubbed cream from his lips and licked his hand. Some of the cream remained stuck on his long blond hair.

303

A Marietta? Not remotely. Anyway, she was beholding some-one gross and boorish. Yet she lingered. Something about her posture suggested that she had been in more intimidating presences.

'Do you know much about dreams?' she persisted.

'Silly, he's the *lord* of dreams—' Nikki clapped a hand to her mouth.

Gunther was about to express regret for his brusqueness – though why should he offer this stranger his counsel, as if he had set up a booth in a fair? – when Elmer waved.

Elmer beckoned from the verandah. He called out, 'Osmo! Osmo! We're over here.'

This ought to have been a timely intervention . . .

As soon as Osmo entered the café – cutting a dandy figure in his rain-spotted peach silk shirt and breeches with rosettes upon the knee – he spied the tall slender woman in blue.

To his astonishment he broke out in a sweat. Heat enfolded him, intensifying the mellow autumn warmth torridly.

He knew that his cheeks flushed hectically. It was as though he were being proclaimed at by someone trying to set him on fire – except that he was the object not of incendiarism but of ardour, of an almost unquenchable passion, urgent and com-pelling.

Osmo trembled, virtually ignoring Elmer as he struggled to master his feelings. Why, this was terrible – to be so affected by a stranger on the eve of gala. Not since Tycho Cammon had attempted in vain to transform Osmo into a living torch had he experienced anything quite as disconcerting. He saw Vivi before him, standing naked and inviting in his bedchamber. Vivi was a freckled redhead, though. The exquisite woman hovering beside Gunther (*Gunther*, here in Yulistalax? Oh, that was irrelevant!) – she was taller, and her hair was flaxen. A stranger? Already she was no stranger to him. She *must* not be a stranger.

'Who *are* you?' he asked.

Insensate craving coursed through his blood. Could someone proclaim wordlessly, to such effect? With such oblivious non-chalance?

'—that's van Maanen,' he heard vaguely, from far away.

'—prime proclaimer, and posh with it.'

'—and why not, when he trounced that bastard Cammon?'

The woman was regarding him with a tense scorn, if anything.

Her gaze flicked down – not coyly, but derisively, taking in the popeyed fish of his belt buckle, the full purse hanging from that belt, the ribbons on his knees, the polished buckles on his shoes.

'She says she's a poetess,' remarked Gunther.

This young woman in no way resembled the vivacious widow, yet she triggered acute longing and desire – far more than he had ever felt for Vivi Rintala. Desire, amplified shockingly. Sentiment of such intensity. It was as if some tangible bond connected the dead woman and this purported poetess. (He glimpsed Vivi beckoning, lips pouting in a mimic kiss . . .) As if this young lady poetess was replacing Vivi utterly in some manic economy of the emotions, deliberately thrusting Vivi aside, expelling her memory from his heart. Oh, but those fascinating little milk chocolate moles on her cheeks and her creamy neck enticed his lips, his tongue, to taste her!

'I want,' he began.

Crass and peremptory. Did he not have time to get to know her? But he wanted instant knowledge.

'I'm Osmo van Maanen,' he said. She winced.

No, she couldn't possibly have winced! She *must* be experiencing some of this same maelstrom of longing which affected him. *What is your origin?* he almost demanded. Know the origin of a thing; and command it. That approach would be too rough by far.

'I'd love to know your name,' he said.

'It's Eyeno Nurmi . . . my lord.' Her lips pushed out the last word leisurely, taunting herself with it. Or teasing, maybe.

Her lord. Yes yes. If only.

Teasing herself. And him, abominably so.

She shut her right eye quizzically and seemed almost not to be seeing him at all.

'Can you say one of your poems now, Eyeno Nurmi?'

'Recite right now, merely because you're a lord?'

His desire raged.

'Osmo,' said Elmer, but Osmo paid no attention to his friend.

'Make a new poem. A one of meeting, a one of greeting.'

'Just like that? On the spur of the moment?'

'I have to proclaim on the spur. I'm a proclaimer, you know.'

'Oh I know that.'

Would he perhaps proclaim her into his arms? The current ran fiercely enough from her to him. Or from him to her. No, don't do that in a café in public . . . She must *give* herself as poor dead

Vivi had done in order to occupy that blessed place in his heart.

'Words sometimes need to rub together for hours, Lord Osmo. Unless it's just a fortune poem, of course.'

To rub together. For hours. Yet he caught the drift of her meaning. He thought of his red-faced mother, surrounded by Pootaran puzzle-spheres and paradox-boxes.

'Till they slot into the only possible shape that's perfect.'

Reluctantly, she nodded. 'In a sense, my lord.'

'You must call me Osmo.'

'*Must?*'

Was she seeing him at all, his wavy chestnut hair which her hand could ruffle, his moustache which would surely tickle? Or was she somehow ignoring the flesh in front of her, the body, and only harking to the words?

'Yours is a rare name, Eyeno.'

'I doubt anyone else in Kaleva has it.'

She was rare. Had anyone else possessed her? And was she here on her own for the gala? How could he best confess his sense of erotic affinity!

'Might we have dinner tonight at Lady Lucky's, Eyeno?'

'But Osmo!' Elmer exclaimed reproachfully.

A mild hubbub had sprung up among the patrons of the café.

'—it's Sariola himself, I tell you!'

'Who else would look like that—?'

'Ain't he magnificent—?'

'Don't he look daft—!'

'Be quiet, don't say so—!'

'—with Queen Lucky on his arm!'

'That ain't Paula Sariola, it's a daughter of theirs—'

'A Sariola daughter, longlife giver, *here*—'

'What a gala this'll be—'

'Reckon she's the prize for best proclaimer?'

'Best proclaimer's over *there* right now—'

Distracted, Osmo swung round.

Mounting the steps to the verandah came a youthful-seeming, goatee-bearded man in a white uniform ablaze with ornamental braid and epaulettes. The newcomer seemed at once sheepish and truculent. A lightpistol hung from a gilded belt around his waist. On his arm was a buoyant young Sariola woman in an orange gown coruscating with glitterbug sequins. Combs and ribbons ornamented her hair. She was fleshier than that miscreant Jatta had been. Flashier too. In fact she was making a fine

306

show of chic. The little starflower tattoo on her cheek ... oh, and one on her neck too. A gorgeous girl, on the verge of voluptuous. Two guards in dappled green and brown stayed below.

A spontaneous round of applause greeted the advent of Lucky's consort in his finery (and the daughter too, ah yes the daughter). Bertel responded with a few self-conscious nods. Osmo swung round.

The poetess had gone.

She had slipped away like a shy foal while Osmo's back was turned for a few careless moments.

A blue gown and long yellow hair were departing the café by a different flight of steps. Eyeno Nurmi was escaping. Osmo almost started after her. He almost thrust his way between the tables of clientele who were goggling at Bertel Sariola and his daughter. He nearly called out an appeal, even to passers-by, to halt the woman in blue. But Prince Sariola was at hand. Wistful. With a little pot belly.

Gunther lumbered upright. In an undertone he muttered to Osmo, 'I've rarely seen anyone *come on* so heavily to a lass they just met ...'

Poetess. Poetess. Naturally he'd be able to find Eyeno in Speakers' Valley next day, or the day after. She was here to recite her work in public. She couldn't escape him. Not a chance.

'Van Maanen? It *is* van Maanen, isn't it?'

Flustered, Osmo nodded.

'May I present my daughter Eva?'

'I'm delighted, I'm honoured ...'

Eva Sariola presented not a hand to be kissed but her chubby cheek with that charming violet flower upon it. Osmo's lips dutifully brushed those illusory petals on her skin. He thought not of her but of the poetess who had departed. He imagined a pink flower opening up within that other girl's most private flesh. Opening for him.

'May I wish you all success in the gala?' Sariola said heartily. 'After you've triumphed I've a proposal I'd like to discuss ...'

Eva gleamed at Osmo appraisingly.

'Yes of course,' agreed Osmo. If only he had rushed from the café a couple of minutes earlier. He hardly noticed glances of envy from people in the vicinity, but he was aware belatedly of Eva's fragrance – attar of starflower, what else? Wicked Jatta Sariola had only been a raggy caricature of this woman.

Eva herself appeared to be interpreting his relative unconcern

307

at meeting her as dignified behaviour, laudably polished conduct.

Osmo struggled to compose himself. 'Might I present my colleague and friend, Elmer Loxmith, instinctive engineer? And his sister Nikki.'

How polite not to attempt to monopolize a Sariola daughter. Elmer bumped into Eva when he pecked her on the cheek. He fumbled and blushed and seemed dizzy at her attar. So it fell to Nikki to steer the conversation with this fine girl from the far north.

'Is this your first time south of the Great Fjord, Eva?'

Osmo said longwindedly to Lucky's consort: 'I was obliged, sir, to speak in judgement over another of your daughters recently . . .'

Bertel shrugged. 'I know about that. Her own mother did banish her, after all. Paula could only applaud your decision. Our little hen's back with us now—'

'Bertie, don't you *recognize* me?' broke in Gunther. 'Or are you refusing to recognize me?'

'My God, the old dreamer himself! I must say you've put on a bit of weight . . . Gunther, dear fellow!' Bertel stuck out his hand as gladly as if he was drowning and the dream lord might haul him ashore.

They clasped one another. Gunther grinned. 'You're looking very smart.'

'Actually, I feel rather stupid. Needs must, when one's in Lucky's thrall. There's nothing I'd like more than to sink several stiff drinks with a fellow longlife who understands what it's like. Dear God, all these years and years—'

'My naughty sister's child was taken by *Juttahats*,' Eva was telling Nikki. 'I promised Jatta I'd ask if anyone knew anything.'

'The fast boy? Elmer and I saw him at Osmo's party . . .' Indeed this was an ideal ice-breaker of a topic.

Nikki quite took Eva's fancy. And her brother too – even if he *was* a trifle gauche. In itself this could be an endearing trait. Elmer would hardly turn out to be a brute! His blue breeches and jacket showed rub marks and a few oil stains. On the other hand Osmo van Maanen was a man with some mystery to him. A man of passion and punctilio. A bit puffed up with himself? Yet there was little sense of braggadocio. Osmo wasn't *displaying* undignifiedly for her benefit like some rooster intent on impressing a hen. Eva felt very conscious of Osmo's presence while she chatted with Nikki, and thus with Elmer.

'My dear,' said her father, 'Lord Beck and I really must get together tonight for old times' sake. Seeing as you and the Loxmiths and Lord van Maanen seem to be getting on so well—'

'How about us all having dinner tonight at Lady Lucky's?' Nikki made so bold as to invite.

Elmer nodded agreeably. Almost immediately he deferred to Osmo, though a hint of pique creased his brow. It was only a scant few minutes since Osmo had been on the verge of disregarding their own prior dinner engagement quite cavalierly. Still, circumstances had changed. The girl had bolted.

The Sariolas were staying at the Hervy's Head. The guards would escort precious Eva to Lady Lucky's that evening.

'The Burgdorfs are hosting a sheep roast and fireworks on the beach,' Gunther mentioned to Bertel.

'A sheep roast!' exclaimed both Eva and Nikki in unison. 'Fireworks!' They giggled at their mutual ventriloquism.

Bertel wouldn't countenance his daughter attending an al fresco event at night when she might rub shoulders with anybody, and anybody with her.

Early evening saw Lucky's crown prince and the dream lord navigating through the throng on a gritty foreshore beside sauna chalets.

A breeze from off the lake ventilated trenches of radiant, blistering mintywood charcoal. Lamb carcasses sizzled on spits. Sweating cooks sliced and slapped flesh on to split sourdough rolls. Several beached boats were vending smoked and salted and pickled fruits of the sea all the way from Tumio. Sausage booths traded, and beer stalls. The sky was a darkening turquoise hatched with some high rose-flushed cirrus. Fiddlers played. Jugglers tossed knives. An upcountry shaman thumped his drum, conjuring pastel visions of fish swimming through the air. Everywhere, laughter and babble, impromptu dancing, chanting and swaggering.

'Why *are* you eating so much, if you don't mind my asking?' Bertel enquired of Gunther who was now chewing his way through a black blood-sausage.

Gunther belched. 'Ballast for the liquor we'll put away later, eh Bertie?'

This was no answer. The dream lord must have been gluttonizing for months.

'What really brings you to this year's gala, Bertie, if you don't mind my asking? With a daughter, too? Whom you're happy to introduce to Elmer and Osmo.'

Bertel looked vague. 'The past's our real province, old fellow.' *Let's not talk about the present. About current schemes and ruses.*

'The past repeats itself, Bertie.'

'Daughters repeat themselves, apparently ad infinitum.' Bertel chuckled bleakly. 'Like cuckoos repeating what they hear, repeating what they see . . .'

'Like gingerbread men.'

'What?'

The dream lord gripped his companion by the elbow. He pressed grease marks on to an immaculate sleeve.

'Loxmith's engrossed in his mechanical wizardry,' he said urgently. 'He isn't a fellow to be lured by love. No, he won't be distracted by passion. Not our instinctive engineer.'

'Meaning that . . . *he mustn't be*? Are you warning me off him, by any chance?'

Bertel's amusement kindled Gunther's comprehension. 'I *see*. Eva is bait for *Osmo*! Well, you ought to have seen him just before—'

Before you turned up at the café.

Lucky's husband mustn't be deterred from any designs on Osmo. Hastily Gunther wrenched his sentence askew. '—before he judged your Jatta, why, he was fairly intoxicated by the idea of wedding a Sariola. Then of course the truth came out . . . Anyhow, the past's our province, as you say, Bertie.'

Eyeno had not yet told her brother about Lord van Maanen's seigneurial solicitation of her, so as not to upset Juke. Maybe she wouldn't tell Juke at all. Her brother would be enraged. Fury might unbalance him. At the sheep roast she kept her eye open for *that man*, whom her brother would be challenging during the gala – quite justifiably, even if Lord Osmo was the darling champion who had defeated Tycho Cammon. The dandy lord was nowhere to be seen.

'You're on the lookout,' Juke said to her.

'Am I?'

'Almost as if you'd made some acquaintance this afternoon whom you expected to see here.'

'There's so much to see. Why should I have met a *him* rather than a *her*?'

'Women have a special way of watching out for men.'

'What claptrap, Juke.'

'When people hear you recite they'll admire you.'

'When I recite my claptrap?'

'I don't mean that – you know I don't! You're wonderful. They'll admire the hell out of you. You did meet somebody special, didn't you?' Oh his instincts were keen.

'I met a rude glutton whom someone called the lord of dreams. I didn't meet him for very long.'

'Lord of dreams? That's Lord Beck. Eyeno, he's a crony of van Maanen's. You didn't tell him about yourself, did you?' *And about me . . . About me being at the Lucky's Day festival in Maananfors when Tycho Cammon broke free . . .*

'I didn't get much opportunity.'

'Was he very rude to you?'

'A bit offhand.'

'A longlife lord. What can one expect? My innocent sister, what *did* you expect?'

'I'm not innocent . . . I have dreams.' This sounded totally misleading. 'Dreams about how I got my eye, as if the eye's scrutinizing me.'

'You never told me that.' He was wounded.

'I wanted to ask somebody who understands dreams . . .'

'And *somebody* pointed Beck out to you . . . Why didn't you ask a shaman about those dreams of yours?'

Through a rift in the noisy crowd, she spied the tall cherubic fat man for a moment. He was ambling along with Lucky's white-uniformed prince whose arrival at the café had allowed her to escape. The gap closed before Juke could notice either of the nobles.

'Well, *you* hobnobbed with Jatta Sariola, didn't you?' she said to her brother.

She might almost have slapped Juke. 'What do you mean by that? What are you implying?'

'I can speak to a lord, can't I? That's all. It's nothing.' She hugged his arm. 'Juke, Juke, there'll be fireworks later, won't there?'

'I might just proclaim some pyrotechnics too. Damned lords . . .' He became tight and taut.

*

311

Juke was remembering sheep on fire. He was remembering how it had felt when little Demon Jack amplified his proclaiming. At the time he'd been disconcerted. Scared. As well as hungry for such power. Panic had won out. If he could recapture the taste of the mana-flow which had kindled those sheep. The rich aroma of roasting lamb was already pervading the air. Panic mustn't win out ever again . . .

'Ain't that the proclaimer as set fire to our flock from Speakers' Stage just afore the Jutties came, and the northerners too?'

'Can't say for sure, Carl. I was a long way off—'

'Swear he is. Thirty ewes dyin' from shock even if not from flames. Thirty! An' here he is strutting it at our sheep roast—'

'Different woman with him, though—'

'Bloody cheek, showing his mug. Deserves a blooding—'

'Mightn't be him at all. Why don't you lend me your knife for a while, just for safe-keeping—'

Now who's *that*? Sam Peller asked himself as he leaned against a sausage booth. Though he held a bottle of brew he only moistened his lips now and then. He was engaged in his habitual wary scrutiny of whatever vicinity he found himself in.

Athletic fellow, fawn hair swept back, staring off into the middle of mana, mindless of the girl with him . . .

That very same young man had been present in the banqueting hall of Maananfors Keep during the Lucky's Day feast prior to the fatal event which still shamed Sam.

From a feast to a gala: no great coincidence? In the absence of any other matters which could feed Sam's vein of paranoia, Osmo's white-haired bondsman decided to follow that itinerant stranger around. Vigilance! Sam owed that to Osmo, who had made him look old in his youth so that he should never actually age . . .

'If you want my opinion,' he said to himself, 'that fellow's fishy.'

Lyle Melator threaded his way through the press of people, hoping to find an unescorted girl or couple of girls.

'Excuse me.' A man in a green gaberdine cloak accosted him. 'But weren't you at Landfall recently?' The enquirer had a very *precise* face and a fine head of dark hair.

'Along with Loxmith the engineer?' The man lowered his voice. 'Well, we both know why you ostensibly visited Landfall. Oh, do excuse me, I'm *Wex*. From Earth.' Fleetingly, Wex shut his eyes. The lids flickered as if he had fallen asleep momentarily and was dreaming.

'I'm a kind of investigator, to be frank. I could always use sources of information – about anything, really, that's odd.'

'Is that so?' asked Lyle neutrally.

'And repay a favour, of course, in whatever way's most appropriate now or later . . . Penelope Conway – our Resident – seemed to take the notion of,' and Wex whispered, a '*hibernating cat* in her stride, but,' he tapped his head, 'I'm not so sure. Word to the wise: there might be changes at Landfall. A more vigorous attitude.'

'What does that mean?' Lyle asked sarcastically. 'A resident roosting in each keep? Backed up by militiamen with brown and yellow faces? We got the distinct impression at Landfall that very few pioneers are arriving from Earth nowadays.'

'You have an analytic nose, Mister Melator,' said Wex evasively.

'Why don't you and I investigate some girls, eh Wex?'

Wex winced fastidiously.

'What's the matter? Do you find my suggestion coarse? Maybe you prefer boys?'

Eyelids fluttered briefly. 'I can be very adaptable. Maybe your hibernating cat's of no special significance? Merely a charming eccentricity?'

'I wish you wouldn't wink at me like that, Wex. It's as if your taste runs more in the direction of, well, *me*. In less tolerant company you might well end up with a knife in the ribs.'

Wex's posture stiffened on the instant. His hands became . . . hard instruments. 'I shouldn't wink,' he said to himself. 'Just some smoke in my eye, Mister Melator.'

Lyle laughed. 'Why, Mister Wex, they let you out without a nursemaid.' Whistling, Lyle walked off.

Wethead Wex communed with himself.

Gunther and Bertel had returned to the Bellflower shortly after a fracas broke out between visitors from Forssa and local foresters who had been swilling down fermented minty sap. 'Lord Burgdorf's *peace*!' was the cry as cudgels descended.

Bertel brought two bottles of vodka up to the dream lord's bedroom. There was only one chair, a comb-back specimen made of at least five kinds of wood. A rowing boat, mounted on chocks, served as a bed – it was stuffed to the brim with a mattress. Strongest bed in the Bellflower, they'd promised upon eyeing Gunther. 'We'll put you in the Poop Room, sir.' Strongest, and silliest he had seen in a while. He had guffawed at the discovery. What dreams might such a crib conjure?

This was a lad's room, its regular occupant now crammed into some attic for the duration of gala so that the house and its neighbours could become a hotel. Model sky-boats, fancifully constructed, hung from the ceiling on cords. The window, open for breeze, peeked between rooftops in the direction of the lake. The sky-sickle pearled far waters amid purple twilight. Before sinking down, Gunther had lit an oil lamp which hung from a pole at the stern of his bedstead.

Bertel occupied the seat, and Gunther the bed.

Soon enough the two men were in their cups.

'Of course I fell wildly in love with Paula,' Bertel was saying. 'It's all so long ago it seems like a dream. The magic in her, the fact that she'd opened the way to another world, her wild tenderness and her captivating desire . . . So vivid a girl, so enchanting and enchanted, choosing me as her prince and promising me immortality, undying love. I couldn't help but adore her, since she adored me. I was once a botanist, you know?'

'Some of us still remember,' Gunther agreed gruffly.

'Till she became my only flower, and I her devoted pollenfly bemused by her soft sweet warm petals.' Bertel struck his chest with a braided wrist in salute or in affliction. 'It's all still alive in here. God, the beautiful anguish. Lucky's still alive and surely I know her better than my own self – though her passions are such strange dark storms. Maybe that's good because she changes like the face of a lake: a blinding mosaic of lovely light, or hauntingly serene, then wild and stormy . . .' He swigged.

'There's no monotony. She's with me, *here*,' where his heartache was, 'yet she's also searching, scheming to find some girlhood self she's sure she lost, sure was stolen by the Ukko. What was stolen? Why, just her previous life which would have otherwise ended long ago. How can a gift be a theft? But I always must agree with her. I'm so weary of all these *stimulating* years.'

As if inflamed with sudden fever, Bertel rose and tore off his splendid jacket. He tossed it towards the prow of Gunther's boat-bed and slumped back into his seat to hoist the bottle higher.

'I can't bear to kill myself, Gunther. My love won't allow me to . . . Both what's here in my heart, and the sheer force of her existence, her needs.' Lucky's consort was on the verge of tears.

Gunther swigged too. 'Damn it, Bertie, I know very well what it's like to continue loving for centuries – in my case without the loved one even being alive . . . Recently I thought I might *distract* myself. She was called Marietta, and she bore an uncanny resemblance . . . What a delusion. Now I wear our Anna's skull on my heart.'

'Anna? Anna?' Bertel hiccuped. His almost empty bottle wavered. He seemed sincerely puzzled as to who the love of the dream lord's life might have been.

'You haven't *forgotten* giving your daughter Anna to me two and a half centuries ago?'

A firework exploded above Lake Yulista showering green and golden stars.

'Oh,' exclaimed Eva. Glowing stars slid down the sky. Lovely sparks seemed to strike from the sky-sickle which was certainly more elevated here in Yulistalax than in Sariolinna. Pootaran islanders must be seeing that great sickle fully halfway up the night sky – reaping the constellations of the Cuckoo and the Cow, the Archer and the Harp. Over the scorching desert continent still further south the sickle would bisect the zenith . . . though it might be less visible when seen edge-on? Not that anyone lived in that hot wasteland to crane their necks and see . . .

Eva's thoughts roved, ignited by the display over the lake. Stars were falling into the lake, to quench themselves.

Just as disobedient Jatta had been quenched . . .

And the candles likewise, by Nikki, in anticipation of the fireworks.

As well as a dinner table, littered with cracked crustacean shells and broken toast, the spacious horzma-panelled chamber here in Lady Lucky's housed Osmo's bed, which was a four-poster. Brocade curtains were discreetly closed around the bed. At its foot, on the floor, lay a blanket-shrouded pallet. Osmo's bondsman would sleep there later like a grizzled, alert hound. Windows were wide open into the cool autumnal night. Elmer's room, with Nikki's adjoining, was further along the upper corridor. Eva's two guards were taking their ease down in the common room which wouldn't be at all crowded. Most of the guests were at the roast on the foreshore.

Here was Eva sitting in Osmo van Maanen's bedroom –

315

although it was Elmer who had paid court of sorts to Eva while they were all cracking the crustaceans open and sucking flesh from inside them. Somewhat bashful court. Fuelled by frequent sips of spirit and encouraging smiles from his friendly sister. Nikki could obviously visualize a closer bond between herself and this Sariola daughter. As indeed could Eva herself. How pleasant it might be, thought Eva, to have a different sort of sister than any of Lucky's endless copycat lineage. Yes, a sister-in-law such as Nikki.

Osmo was mysteriously preoccupied. Well, quite soon he was due to defend his status as a proclaimer, wasn't he? How would it be to wed a proclaimer? Might he prove overbearing by nature?

Osmo. And Elmer. And no chaperon present at all, unless Nikki counted as such. But wait, reflected Eva. Her father wasn't reckless! Osmo and Elmer were *both* her chaperons – as regards one another.

Osmo was hardly betraying much of the jealousy appropriate to a contender for her hand in such a situation . . . Still, plainly enough it was Osmo whom her father favoured. Nikki might be disappointed in her hopes.

Another firework exploded. Yellow smoke ballooned, a-prickle with twinkles as of phosphorbugs in a fog.

'That's a dud,' said Elmer.

The bilious cloud hung where it was.

It took on human features. Those of a man.

With wavy hair, with a moustache. With a graceful counten-ance, and a dimpled cheek. The face hung suspended ghostly and jaundiced high over the lake.

'That's *you*, Osmo,' Nikki cried out. 'How ever did you arrange—'

'Bravo,' declared Elmer. 'Perhaps a *touch* ostentatious?'

'I didn't arrange it—'

The face writhed. Those phantom features leered with an ugly despotic malevolence, lustful and brutal.

'It's me – made into Tycho Cammon, damn it! I burned his bones. His soul's gone for ever . . .' Osmo shook. 'This doesn't have anything to do with Cammon. It's a challenge, a public insult, that's what.'

Still the warped yellow face hung on high.

Osmo actually growled, deep in his throat, and Eva shivered. 'More of an insult than a decent challenge, I'd say. And more impressive in appearance than in substance,' he said to Eva. 'It's

316

only smoke and sparks, after all.' In the darkness it was difficult to see how shaken Osmo might be, but his tone suddenly sounded tranquil. Eerily so. He was breathing deeply.

Quitting the table, he rested his hands on the windowsill for a few moments.

'What?' asked Eva.

'Hush,' said Nikki.

Then Osmo raised his fingers to his cheeks to stroke the contours.

He called out into the sky over the roofs of Yulistalax:

'Smoke, so light, restore my face. Hold no trace of this disgrace. Smoke so fine, erase those lines. Restore my smile . . .'

Concentrating, he proclaimed into the night.

'For this is spoken. Mana be my helpmaid, be my mistress too.'

The smoke gradually regained its earlier configuration. Osmo's spectral visage looked down once more upon the town. Nevertheless, the impression which lingered, like a foul taste in the mouth, was that the wraith of Tycho Cammon had merely altered back into the guise of Osmo without positively repudiating the association. Spectators numbering thousands must surely realize that a contest – a premature one – had just concluded in Lord van Maanen's favour?

Perhaps Osmo ought to demonstrate this more dramatically? Could an accusing voice boom down like thunder, unrolling from the din of the next aerial explosion? Could Osmo somehow detect his slanderer and depict him on high, derisively? Before he could decide, a rocket exploded amidst the face of smoke. A fusillade of crimson stars tore through the face. Each star in turn detonated, spraying streamers of green. Maybe Maxi Burgdorf had ordered the pyro fired to conclude this impertinent, if daring, charade – which cuckoos would surely tattle about as far away as Tumio.

Osmo's hold on the smoke was quite disrupted, as was the smoke itself. *Presumably* he was further away from the firework than the initiator. His hold, correspondingly more tenuous. To that extent he was more than a match for his unseen rival . . .

His hidden opponent had managed to sculpt the cloud of smoke in the first place. Then warp his creation. Osmo had merely restored the original.

'I must apologize,' Osmo said to Eva, 'for this unfortunate interlude.'

Personally, she was thrilled.

Harper trees murmured melodiously. The valley itself was a-hum with voices, to which five, no *six*, scaly green cuckoos cocked an ear. Three birds perched on feeding poles spiked with offal and hung with merry ribbons. One sat high on the grandstand of purple tammywood – as yet half full – which fronted the knoll. Up on the mound a choir of old women were yoiking. Another bird roosted on the largest of the striped marquees. In front of this a shaman wearing a bird-suit was shuffling about in his rooster-shoes, banging his drum.

A hundred gaudy stalls sold bread-boxes stuffed with baked fish and pork, pancakes, tangled snake's nest cookies, stiff yoghurt, pickled fishes, ale and hot grog and coffee and juices. Booths housed fortune-tellers, tale-spinners, mana-conjurors, mana-puppeteers. One tent boasted of housing a mutie pig-girl. Another, a genuine zombie. A third, a captive Juttahat.

The sky was of blue silk. There'd been a touch of frost at dawn; now a sun of molten butter basted the thousands of all ages gathered for gala.

Osmo thrust his way through the crowd to reach the poets' terrace.

Currently a bearded young man was chanting his verses. Enthroned in a well-padded fauteuil Lord Burgdorf's laureate was chairing a jury of three masked garland-wearers on a dais. Lady Mitzi looked on, wreathed in smiles. An audience of as many as five hundred stood around attentively or squatted upon the herbage. The laureate Lutainen was robed in green brocade sinuously threaded with silver. A four-peaked black velvet cap sat upon his greying head. Bespectacled, he had rutted ruminative features and a chin so sharp and long that his face seemed to be continued downward by a flesh-hued beard. Sunlight twinkled from his glasses as he nodded, appreciative to the words. Dumpy Lady Mitzi, in her lustrous green taffeta gown, inclined her head and beamed. She sighed such jolly sighs of connoisseurship as the young fellow recited.

Osmo quickly spotted the slim woman in blue. Her hair was such golden silk. Her cheap gown was of finest quality when it clad that willowy shape, inexpressibly enticing to him. Oh but her clothing was trivial – a teasing frail impediment to the craving which seethed once again in his blood, far intensified beyond the previous evening when she had fled from him. Osmo's cock hardened and throbbed for this hen.

'Little man, be still now; this is spoken,' he told his body.

How could she simply *stand* there among other hopeful wordsmiths – a little nervously yet otherwise composed – when she was such an object of desire? She ought to flush ecstatically to be within such a body; to be that body herself. Her skin should be thrilling with sensation, her nipples throbbing, her sex radiant with rapture.

His lust was lunacy. It was mania.

It *must* spring from some strange, intimate link between herself and his desires, which dead Vivi had salved . . .

How could such hunger be overwhelming him, when it was he who must overwhelm other proclaimers? That young woman seemed like such a befuddling nakki wile – as well as a gleaming goal, a perfect prize.

The bearded youth had finished his performance. Her name – that exotic name Eyeno – was called out. She was being beckoned to the fore by a juror in an orange cat mask.

Osmo listened intently.

Eyeno's voice was clear and precise.

Standing before the jury she recited to Lutainen and to Lady Mitzi about leaves and cats and seasons. About ears falling off to sprout anew. About nouns that died and verbs that wounded. The verse was at once delicate and sharp, playful and pensive, minor yet maybe widening out some way beyond itself.

Odd stuff. Not heroic at all. Sultry, it was not. Ardent, never. Charming, perhaps, in an offbeam way. What worm hid in *her* brain?

Ach, whatever was he thinking! Of course her verse was appealing. The poem simply sneaked up on you like a sip of fermented minty sap. As to *physicality*, why she evoked the body and ears and pursuit and squeals.

Osmo's verbs would wound her ecstatically. The raging appetite to possess her was blended of an adoration and a brutality both of which equally disconcerted him. If such sensations were to continue intensifying with each encounter, how could he possibly control himself?

Be calm. For mana's sake, control yourself.

319

(Yet why should he, when such a proclaimer as himself was surely a demi-god?)

(But a gentleman too!)

Eyeno Nurmi's audience reacted variously. Some clapped; some shook their heads. Jurors and the laureate conferred. She was handed a slim bronze bracelet to slip on to her wrist. She would recite again that evening.

Osmo forged through the onlookers.

Eyeno had returned to the side of an athletic young man with his fawn hair swept back as if his own personal breeze forever blew against him.

Smiling, she displayed her newly-bestowed bracelet. Who was this young man – who recoiled as Osmo approached? Who braced himself as if expecting an assault? Maybe Osmo looked to be on the verge of assaulting Eyeno.

'That was beguiling, Eyeno Nurmi,' said Osmo.

'Oh it's you, my lord . . .'

Shock blanched the young man's face. 'You've *met* this one? *Met* him? You know him in person?'

Eyeno nodded distractedly.

'In *person*! When was that? Yesterday? Tell me!'

'Dear brother . . .'

Relief gusted through Osmo. This fellow was only her brother. His inner fires were fanned anew.

'Eyeno, I'm enchanted, and I tell you the truth. You enchant me.'

Shouldn't this loitering brother of hers be flattered? And Eyeno Nurmi too? She might have tried to flee again; in which case Osmo would have been obliged to catch her. She *might* – had her brother not also been present like an anchor to her boat.

'If that's so,' she said sharply, 'you're enchanting yourself . . . Dear mana, why is this happening?'

Her brother's face was rigid in disbelief.

'It's because we're linked, you and I,' Osmo told her. 'Mana knows this. I know it in my blood, in my pulsing blood. Eyeno, it's spoken . . .'

Eyeno's brother bared his teeth. Like an animal.

'Juke . . .' Eyeno appealed.

Those little moles on her cheek and neck, so delightful, so bewitching. That long caress of hair, those light blue eyes . . .

'Yes, spoken by the very woods and lakes. By Kaleva herself—'

320

'Damn you, you searched her out!' snarled Juke. 'You found out. You knew. Did a cuckoo tell you?'

Found out what? Knew what?

'He didn't search me out,' protested Eyeno. 'Yesterday I went into a café. I approached—'

'*You* approached him! To beg for me? To spare my life?' The young man laughed hectically. 'Have you already given yourself to him – or only promised to do so providing he spares me?'

A tear welled in one of Eyeno's eyes, though not in both. 'No, no, no—'

'I'll annihilate you, van Maanen,' vowed Juke, to Osmo's astonishment.

'Because I'm addressing your sister?'

'Addressing, undressing!'

'*Hush, shhh*—' from nearby appreciators of verse. Some tubby fellow splendid in multicoloured leathers was commencing his performance before the laureate and the jury.

'What are you?' hissed Osmo. 'One of those brothers who loves a sister beyond all decent bounds? Is that the origin of this?'

Juke lurched. He shook his head, not so much in denial but as if his head had been slapped and pummelled and he must clear it – and Eyeno gaped at her brother, wide-eyed.

'Lord Osmo!' It was Sam, more ashen-faced than ever, his hand resting on his holstered lightpistol.

Sam was staring at Eyeno's brother with such an intensity that, could eyes alone proclaim, the young man might have withered on the spot.

'This is *him*, Lord Osmo. This is the joker who put your face up in the firework show and *mutated* it! Aye, into Cammon's. He was in our keep last Lucky's Day to see that face brought alive—'

As if a knife of ice had raked his soul, Osmo understood.

'Vivi . . .' he whispered. 'That's the link . . .' He gazed wildly at this Juke. 'You set Cammon free to kill my red hen! It was you!' he screamed.

Wex had been shadowing Bertel Sariola. The prince of the Northland was promenading with his daughter, a couple of guards in attendance. Sariola pointed and commented, wearing a smile which was at once charming and sickly. A studied smile, well learned over the past several centuries. Food vendors and gala-goers gawked at him and his elegant young hen who could give

321

longlife to the first man who bedded her. Such stares could be construed as homage.

Eva wore her raven hair brushed back from her ample Sariola forehead and piled like a turban. Pearl-studded combs pinned this coiffure. Larger pearls were sewn on her bodice. The long sleeves and neck of her creamy dress were lavishly trimmed with lace.

Bertel still smiled as he exchanged a word with one of his guards, a plump fellow who hustled through the crowd towards Wex . . .

{*Alert! He spotted you.*}

The guard jammed the snout of a lightpistol discreetly into the Earthman's belly.

{*Do not defend.*}

'The prince wants to speak to you, mister.' The guard grinned as if Wex was an old acquaintance, and stood very close so as to hide his weapon. The man's breath smelled fruity {*Diabetes?*} and a tiny pink tattoo of a phallic mushroom amid tongues of flames decorated his neck. {*Prophylactic against excess urine production due to the disease.*}

Moments later Wex was face to face with Lucky's consort. The gun had migrated round to his backbone without onlookers being much the wiser. The guard's free hand roved over Wex's gaberdine cloak of many pockets as if admiringly, feeling lumps and bumps. He and Wex might have been old acquaintances.

'He's carrying a lot of things, sir.'

'You've been dogging us like a tail,' said Sariola. He still wore that insipid public smile. 'So now's your chance to wag the dog.'

{*We will tell the whole truth.*}

'At ease, Ben,' Sariola told the guard. The prince nodded him away, and Ben retired a few paces, keeping the gun almost hidden between his hands. When Sariola nodded the weapon away too, Ben eyed Wex's cloak of secrets dubiously. He shuffled. He rubbed one boot against the other vigorously.

{*Ulcers on his feet.*}

'At ease,' repeated Bertel. Reluctantly Ben holstered the gun and after some consideration pulled a potato cake from his pocket.

'Well, wag the dog, won't you?' the prince said to Wex.

{*He is inviting assassination. He wishes someone would kill him. However, he has almost lost hope of this ever happening.*}

322

'I'm from Landfall, your Highness,' Wex introduced himself. 'Newly from Earth. Name of Wex.'

Eva surveyed Wex with a radiant fascination. His lustrous curly hair, the loose purple silks under his cloak.

{This exhibition of a marriageable virgin daughter at a gala is undoubtedly provocative. No record exists of a similar visit. Does Bertel Sariola hope that males may attack him to abduct her and murder him in the process? Low probability explanation. The daughter seems self-assured. Of course she exhibits false consciousness of her status as a sexual commodity.}

'Mister Wex,' said Eva, 'have you Earthfolk heard anything of a boy called Jack who has powers? A mana-kid who's growing up as fast as an overnight mushroom? The Brazen Jutties kidnapped Jack from here.'

{Reference: cuckoo reports.}

'You mean Demon Jack Pakken,' said Wex. 'Jack's your nephew, Princess Eva.' Bertel looked mildly disappointed that apparently he wasn't in danger of homicide.

{Sariolas do not constitute a strongly bonded and cordial kinship dynasty; otherwise this continent would be more unified.}

'All *we* know is stories,' admitted Wex.

'You're here as a spy, aren't you?' asked Bertel. 'What's your full name, anyway?'

'It's Roger Wex.'

{Wethead: we like Wethead.}

'*Rogue* Wex,' Bertel said with his customary smile.

'I'm also called Wethead.'

Eva laughed. She stared at his locks which were glossy but by no means sleeked with brilliantine. 'Why's that?'

{Tell them the truth.}

'The wet's *inside*,' said Wex. 'I have auxiliary organic circuits in my brain. The Juttahats hear Isi voices within their minds. I too have another mind within my mind, vaster than my own.'

Eva shuddered. Diabetic Ben choked on his last mouthful of potato cake.

Yet Bertel appeared delighted. 'Can you eavesdrop on a snake's thoughts?'

'That might be possible with practice,' Wex allowed cautiously.

The prince rubbed his hands together enthusiastically. Then he frowned. 'Can you read *my* mind, Wethead?'

{We can <u>deduce</u>. Deny it absolutely.}

'Not people's minds, no never, and I don't know about an Isi's mind yet, to be honest, but I'm hopeful.'

Bertel nodded to himself.

'Hush it!'

'Hwisht!'

The fellow in harlequin leather had faltered. His ode evaporated, words dispersing. Lutainen raised his long face, and his hand. A serge-clad bodyguard wearing a crimson-cockaded cap had appeared beside Lady Burgdorf who was beaming happily no more. The guard cocked a crossbow. A couple of grey-suited mana-priests were consulting urgently, expostulating about the strong currents they sensed. A cuckoo swooped overhead and circled to perch on the laureate's chair just as Lutainen vacated his throne indignantly – whereupon the bird shat on the padding. This definitely marked a pause to the poetical proceedings.

Already curiosity was bringing more witnesses. Curiosity, and the imminence of violence, an acrid exciting tang in one's nostrils, a thrumming of the heart which communicated itself. The shaman in his bird-suit had arrived, squawking and drumming.

Another cockade, and the glint of a rifle . . . a watchman with a cudgel, another with his sword still scabbarded for use as a bludgeon – or blade, if called for.

Around the terraces away from this flurry, the ebullience of gala was undiminished. The valley was wide. The overwhelming majority of visitors were unaware of this local contretemps. Down on the mound old women, dolled in their best, still yoiked.

Here where the poets were, however . . .

. . . Osmo and Juke stared at one another in mutual loathing. In Osmo's case this passion interlocked jaggedly with the infatuation he felt for the man's sister. Desire and hatred consumed him. Hatred and desire gnawed. Fury and erotic fascination gripped his whole being. These, he must discharge so that they served him – not he them. Otherwise he might be lost, in a way that he scarcely comprehended. He might become a tool of tumult – just as Cammon had become the servant of his own colossal egotism.

This sneaking challenger, Juke Nurmi, had taunted Osmo with that very fate publicly over Lake Yulista on the previous evening.

'You killed my red hen Vivi!' he fairly screamed at Juke. Words flew, battering Eyeno's brother.

Juke gathered himself to jeer.

'Lord Burgdorf's peace!' a voice bellowed.

A guard brought a rifle to bear. Another shifted his crossbow.

'*My* peace, if you please, Lord van Maanen,' announced Lord Burgdorf, as he waddled from behind the rifleman. 'The peace of this gala, ahem. Except,' and he gestured, 'down there on Speakers' Stage, of course. Except down there.' Maxi Burgdorf's tone was at once scolding and appeasing.

Maxi Burgdorf was distinctly bow-legged. To ameliorate this defect, he wore a shank-length tunic of burgundy velvet. Not exactly a dwarf, he was nevertheless markedly short of stature. So he also wore a tall conical fur hat, though he eschewed high-heeled shoes which in no way would suit his rolling gait. All male descendants of the erstwhile mushroom lord suffered from a similar buckling of the body, yet they were all defiantly blessed with names which might encourage loftiness. Maxi's father had been Titus. His grandfather had been Hugo. His uncle, Hercules. Maxi's sons were Goliath and Otso. No one giggled about this; the Burgdorfs were well-loved.

This scandal shouldn't be happening, was Lord Maxi's opinion. Whatever it was that was happening! Not involving such a bespeaker as old Alvar's son. Tycho Cammon had been another matter. Quite out of control until this young hero tamed him and flew him home with him, turned to stone. Maxi had been terrified of Cammon, and the gala and Yulistalax had suffered accordingly. What could he have done? Suspend the annual jamboree? If Cammon would have let him . . . ! Everything had gone so well till now apart from that bestial face in the night sky, which reminded Maxi of past horrors. A competitor becoming a slow-burning human torch. Another unsuccessful proclaimer compressed alive into a bloody block of meat and splintered bone. Cammon's amusements.

Lady Mitzi, half a head taller than her husband, was clasping her hands in consternation.

'We meet in rowdy circumstances, van Maanen,' said Maxi.

'Disorderly,' his wife agreed. 'I was so enjoying the recitations.'

Osmo struggled to control the frenzy in his heart.

'I must . . . challenge this person now. I must. He murdered my mistress.'

'I did not,' said Juke. 'The stone man did. But I'm ready – ready any time.'

325

'He sent the stone man to kill me, Lord Burgdorf, because he's *scared* to face me in person.'

'How so,' sneered Juke, 'if I *mastered* Tycho Cammon?'

Maxi, master of ceremonies, looked from one to the other sharply.

'Don't start yet! This is very out of step. Other proclaimers ought to compete before last year's victor. You, young man, must wait your turn. Today isn't the day. What, the climax at the very start?'

Osmo said tightly, 'And the prize is . . . *his sister.*'

'Oh no,' cried Eyeno. 'You shan't!'

'Never fear, I can easily take him,' Juke assured her, to her greater disgust.

Eyeno cried at Osmo, 'What do you think was going through my mind in that café and while I was reciting just now and during most of the rest of my life till now? Unfulfilled lust? Is that it? Aimed at anyone and everyone I meet? I'm not a *man*, my lecherous lord!'

Osmo laughed grimly. How could he let her rebuff him publicly? A rebuff would diminish his whole potency. It could geld the efficacy of his bespeaking. He was swept up in a rampant delirium of inevitability, of flagrant necessity such as had never seized him before. Power was in him, not to be denied. The terrace, the gawking audience, the shaman drumming in rhythms with Osmo's thudding pulse, the cuckoo on the laureate's abandoned throne: all was luminous, heroic, mythic. It was as if Osmo had entered a fable, a fabulous nexus of events which now guided his words and actions, not to be baulked except at the cost of catastrophe. He was only flimsily in control. To twist the helm askew could lead to capsizal. To steer this course he was set on was to engage in the superhuman.

'You captivated me, Eyeno,' he called out.

'I did not! I'm not a proclaimer! Has any woman ever been a proclaimer? Has any woman ever been able to impose their will on people in that way? Or wanted to?'

Osmo pursued the logic of what he was saying. 'So you must be *my* captive instead.'

'Women have their ways,' someone called.

'How about Queen Lucky?' someone else interjected.

'Can all men be like you?' Eyeno retorted. 'Goats in rut? Cocks a-crow? Oh, dandily dressed – so is the screeching rooster! Is this what any man is under the skin?'

'No, no,' yelped Maxi Burgdorf.

'Only those who are rapists at heart,' Juke scoffed at Osmo. 'Men who are *scared* of women. Who *despise* them. Men with *flawed spirits. Inadequate* men who should have their brains *washed out.* Who don't respect women's hearts – who see only breasts! Men who suckle on *pathetic* secret fantasies – of *impossible power* over other people who would spit on them if they knew, who would vomit in their faces, or just guffaw in *scorn.*' The words were wounding and unmanning, as Juke intended. Power words.

'All men can't be like you, my lord,' cried Eyeno. 'My brother isn't!'

'Wanker,' jeered Juke, fairly beside himself. 'Jerk-off.'

'I say!' squeaked Lord Maxi.

'Unless,' murmured Eyeno, 'Jatta . . .'

'No!' Juke howled. He goggled at his sister. *You*, was in his look. *You*. Nakedly in his look, veils of pretence torn away.

That look on her brother's face, so revealing, sickened Eyeno. Nausea rose in her.

How could she not have realized? How could she have been so blind, so half-sighted, for so long? Her brother, her paladin, was in love with her. Love wasn't a suitable word for such a feeling as he nursed – as he hid away secretly like a hungry maggot in a fruit.

Sister-lust.

What was this bestial wrangle between van Maanen and Juke, but a contest to ravish her?

'No wonder,' she said so softly and bitterly to her brother, 'you know what to accuse him of.'

Juke was bound to deny this as hotly as he could.

'Filth pours out of him and messes me! I'll sweep him away—'

His gaze begged her to overlook the insight she had glimpsed. To disregard it. To erase it from her awareness. To erase the reproach, the contempt.

He begged her: 'What other mirror did I have to look into?' He strangled his own sentence.

What other mirror among mutants? What other object of ardour? Don't mention mocky-men; no one else knew that yet. Eyeno's world was collapsing as surely as their hovel in Outo ought by rights to have collapsed long since. Her poems were mere glitterbugs trampled under a hervy's hooves. They were the gossamer webs of hammockis which a billygoat blundered through obliviously.

'I was right,' shouted Osmo. 'I was right about you straight away. A brother who loves his sister beyond decent bounds. It's true.'

Osmo swaggered, a defiant coxcomb. Sweat trickled down his face. How much had the *scared* and *flawed* and *washed out* weakened him? Why, nothing had really been spoken yet. Nothing as yet!

'It seems we have little alternative,' said wee Lord Maxi.

'None,' agreed his wife with regret.

'Speakers' Stage it is, then.' He grimaced sympathetically at Eyeno. 'And you too, lass. Being the subject of dispute.'

'I'm not . . . Really, I'm not.'

'Being the booty.' Lord Maxi ducked his high-capped head. 'And being the beauty.' He winked.

'You sound like a Juttahat,' Eyeno said tonelessly. '-ing this, -ing that.'

'And when,' asked Lord Maxi icily, 'have you been hobnobbing with Juttahats?' He pulled a silver flask from within his tunic, uncapped, and swallowed several times; then he thrust his flask at Osmo as though this had been his main intention all along.

Distractedly Osmo raised the flask to his lips and gulped.

'Don't,' Sam Peller said to him urgently. 'Don't drink liquor.'

'Milk's best for a fop,' taunted Juke.

'Don't heroes drink fire, Sam?' Osmo's voice resonated bombastically as if he was the mouthpiece of mythic warriors. He swigged again. His bondsman reached to intercept the flask but was thrust aside.

'Drain it dry and crumple it,' urged Juke. He aped Osmo's tone.

Osmo blinked and eyed the flask. Uttering a roar, he hurled the silver heirloom away, to Lord Maxi's astonishment.

Kyli Kennan felt perfectly elated as Minkie squired her courteously and cockily through the crowds in search of none other than Bertel Sariola. Minkie's father, Ragnar, had been personally acquainted with the prince of the north, and now – unprecedentedly – Lucky's consort was here in person at this very gala. It would be an easy enough matter for Minkie to introduce himself, and his young wife. Kyli dearly wished that a cuckoo might spout of this meeting to her father back in Saari. Then he'd be obliged to feel proud of her, consorting with a prince.

Such a relief to be well away from that *rattly* keep with its threadbare carpets and smell of mould. Not to need to see the oozing pink face of Snowy every day and strain to understand his stutters. Still, Niemi Keep was being spruced up at a decent pace – with her money. By the time they returned, her husband's crony would have the hall roof patched. Dame Inga would make sure that Snowy rolled his sleeves up. Inga was a tower of strength, and indeed for this gala Kyli was wearing a low-cut gown of lace over muslin which Inga had sewn specially for her daughter-in-law.

Kyli's first reaction to the gift had been delight, which doubt then qualified. The gown was really rather revealing of her form when silhouetted in sunlight. Since her breasts weren't *big* the scant bodice all but exhibited her cherry nipples.

When Minkie first saw her arrayed in that gown, captivated wasn't the word for it. Minkie's gaze could be guaranteed not to stray too far from her. Of course he had turned over a new leaf, as big as the leaf of a larkery tree – did Inga still think of her son as a rambunctious rapscallion?

Men, and women too, glanced (and glanced a second or third time) at Kyli and Minkie as they navigated the terraces together. Kyli had prevailed on her husband to leave that long coat of his – his adventurer's coat – behind in the Serpent's Head. A name rich with associations. Not that even Minkie boasted of having ever hacked off the head of an Isi! So far, fortunately, he hadn't bumped into any old associates from bygone Juttie hunts.

Natty in a new striped waistcoat of scarlet and green, lavender breeches, scarlet kneesocks, and black leather shoes, Minkie acknowledged the glances of fellows (though not of girls) with a fine aplomb. Those might all have been acquaintances of his or admirers of past escapades, irrespective of whether they were actually appreciating his bride in her lace and muslin creation.

He *wouldn't* be hot-headed. His 'trousseau' for the trip (Kyli's phrase, and funded from her dowry), was the harbinger of delightful future balls in a fully renovated keep.

Kyli was aware that Minkie had concealed a knife inside his waistcoat, but that was purely precautionary.

'Here we are, Kiki-liki, here we are. And there, if I'm not mistaken, is Prince Sariola. Come *along*.'

How could the prince of the north be mistaken for anyone else in that showy uniform of his? A bushel of sandy hair, blond goatee beard, broad shoulders prolonged by golden epaulettes

. . . Such a stately man, and so youthful-looking too apart from a somewhat tubby tummy. Bertel Sariola was talking to a fastidious-seeming fellow who wore a cloak reminiscent of Minkie's own capacious long coat. Beside him stood a very striking, well-fleshed young woman with a turban of comb-pinned black hair. Her bosom was all bobbled with pearls. She was the daughter, Eva, about whom word had been buzzing. Two guards loitered. No riff-raff need approach.

During an obvious pause in whatever discussion might have been occurring Minkie bustled right up to the group. He cleared his throat deferentially, as well as to draw attention.

'Sire, may I present my darling wife Kyli, daughter of Lord Johann Helenius of Saari? May I, her lucky husband – heir to Niemi Keep – remind you of your past acquaintance with my father Ragnar?'

'What?' said Bertel distractedly. 'Lucky husband? *I'm* Lucky's husband . . .'

Eva giggled, and Minkie really appraised her.

Oh what a wonderful succulent hen. What a choice chick. He'd need to be a capon not to respond smittenly to this magnificent young lady. But he mustn't, mustn't.

'You're funny,' she said.

And you can give longlife to the man who beds you, can't you just?

Bertel extended a hand. With a quick bow, the prince raised Kyli's hand to his lips perfunctorily. Had he not also closed his eyes during this sketchy courtesy he would surely have glimpsed her nipples. The consort of Paula Sariola seemed immune to such a temptation. So he should be!

'The Lord of Saari's daughter . . .'

Kyli simpered. Let him not have heard cuckoo tattle about her disgrace – which was now being redeemed.

'This is my daughter Eva . . .'

Eva actually kissed Kyli upon the cheek as if they had been bosom friends for ages. All those pearls. How gracious, yet jaunty too, with starflower tattoos. What a chum she might be in other circumstances.

Minkie draped an arm around his wife. He drew her close to him and nuzzled her momentarily, chuckling, as if he too might partake of that brief brush from Eva's lips.

'You must have *so* many suitors,' Minkie said nonchalantly to Eva. In so saying he paid her a raffish compliment, and distanced himself from the mere possibility that he himself could even contemplate being one, had circumstances been otherwise.

Bertel humphed. 'Ragnar Kennan ... Yes, I remember very well. Quite the confidence trickster, if you'll permit the expression. Stringing people along. Then he decamps all of a sudden. Got himself killed, I hear.'

Unruffled, Minkie projected all his charm. His voice was pleadingly sincere.

'My father did have an attitude problem, sire, that's true. But he was of some assistance to you, wasn't he? I'd hate to think that I'd been labouring under a delusion. If he let you down maybe I can atone for this. Was it some information that he had? Maybe I could lay my hands on the same information.'

His gaze had tracked again to Eva.

'Are you by any chance on a grand tour? Could we invite you to stop by our wretched keep for a night? For several nights? It might take several nights to uncover your desire. Sire,' he added, only glancing back at Bertel then.

Eva regarded Minkie with amused appreciation.

Oh what a splendid hen, with the secret of life between her legs. And she couldn't fail to feel a soft spot for our Minkie ... Could she?

'My lady and I would be overjoyed to host you and your daughter.'

My lady. Not my wife. Not now. Not just at the moment.

He mustn't do this.

'Oh we'd be very honoured,' Kyli concurred enthusiastically. Naturally she concurred. 'Ours is still rather a wretched keep, that's true enough ...'

'And your guards are welcome as well,' added Minkie. 'Goes without saying.' He glanced at the silent man in the cloak, uncertain as to the fellow's status, and whether he needed to be included too.

The stranger's eyes and lips twitched a few times. He appeared to be talking to himself without actually talking at all. That was *his* problem. The man didn't introduce himself.

Just then, other guards hove through the crowd in company of a tiny bow-legged man wearing a high hat.

'Lord Burgdorf!' Bertel called out, perhaps to rid himself of unwanted invitations. Eva's gaze lingered on Minkie, tantalizingly, or so Minkie trusted.

A willowy young blonde woman was preceding the lord of the

331

gala. Her eyes were downcast, not in any modest manner but in misery. An image of melancholy. Of loveliness too, assuredly. Beauty, abashed.

Minkie knew that he knew her, yet somehow failed to know her. Then memory flooded back . . . of failure.

That dolly chick on the road to Threelakes . . . and subsequently in that wooded dell!

Eyeno: that was her name.

Minkie felt his manhood fade.

His cock tried to shrink inside of him to hide. His perception of female charms simply ebbed away. He could not comprehend why that person – why someone with such limbs and hair and such a face – should seem in any way seductive to a man. Utterly preoccupied, Eyeno had not so much as noticed him, yet her melancholy had infected Minkie to his marrow.

Or rather . . . her wretched brother's hex had stricken him. Yes, that was it: Juke's curse that Minkie's cock would dwindle to a button.

More had dwindled than that. Minkie's very understanding of how he could have desired Eyeno had fled away, emptying him of something precious, which now he could hardly remember.

What is beauty? Minkie asked himself in bewilderment. He stared up at the choir of gilded harper trees against a turquoise sky. That was still beautiful. One couldn't desire a tree. Yet if the scene was lovely, and if he didn't desire it, then desire wasn't a component of beauty at all, and a person whom he desired might not therefore be beautiful; so how could he desire such a one? His head ached.

Panicked, he gaped again at sumptuous Eva in her pearls and combs. Her gown delineated such softly swelling contours. Yet the jinx of apathy appeared to have spread. Eva was overblown, too lush, too much for him, too glamorous. Her regard seemed condescending now. She was still amused but purely in a playful way.

'Burgdorf, dear chap! What's up?'

'Oh, you'd hardly believe it!'

Minkie risked another glance at Eyeno. She appeared as stunned and disconnected as he felt. Simply couldn't bear to raise her eyes. She was sunk in demi-oblivion. A bronze bangle on her wrist was like a fetter.

Cold chilled his groin, and he swore *not* to glance again.

That awful fellow, her brother, might be nearby. He might

332

blather slanders about Minkie, disillusioning Prince Bertel and—

—and Eva Sariola, too.

Just so long as he paid no attention to that other person! Her face had been so blank, inducing a blank in him, a void where his essence had been.

If her brother brayed about Minkie, this might upset Kyli too. His bride beside him.

His bride.

Could the jink have dulled his adoration of her too? Unmanning his vision of her bloom?

'Precious Kyli—' Minkie's wife tilted up her nose so pertly, still dreaming of hosting the Sariolas. 'We mustn't prevail further on Prince Sariola's good nature, Kyli, not just right now.'

Bertel was in a huddle with the master of the gala.

'Later,' Minkie told Kyli. He mouthed the same message towards Eva, who opened her eyes wider, teasingly. Surely she wasn't too lush? Surely she was magnificent? Thank mana, Minkie was recovering himself a little.

Were all Lucky's daughters such imperious virginal flirts? The nameless stranger in cloak and silks was frowning prissily as if he had some profound criticism to make – damn his superior silent insolence.

Hastily Minkie shepherded his wife away. Her body protested. Her muscles were reluctant to move at first. Arm around her waist, he marched her. Presently he brushed Kyli's long ringlets back to expose her bare left shoulder and became fascinated by the bump on her shoulder girdle just below and to one side of her windpipe.

The collar bone bent her skin upward in a little rounded mound. To the right of her throat was its twin. Those two bumps were like tiny hard nippleless breasts, unnamed hitherto by any imaginative, poetical lover. Of a sudden those bumps were erotically fascinating to Minkie. He wanted to stroke them, kiss them, lick them, suck them. He was safe, restored; and with his bride. Carefully he stroked Kyli's hair back into place so as to hide this anatomical and sensual discovery which must have stared countless men in the eye, upon countless girls, without men ever really perceiving it. Those bumps should have a special name all of their own. The nubs. The darling bone-buds.

'How can Eva Sariola's hair be so black when her father's is so blond?' enquired Kyli.

'Well, Lucky Sariola's hair is jet black in all the icons. Lucky's dominant.'

'Women don't usually have much mana, do they, Minkie?' What was she hinting at?

'*Eva* Sariola must have mana, to make a man immortal. I suppose that doesn't help her personally . . .' She hastened on guilelessly. 'Do you think they'll really accept our invitation?'

'I did try to be charming enough, my hen.' His finger touched one of the endearing bone-buds.

'What are you doing? Do I have a spot? Has a fly bitten me? Oh, my skin's so exposed.'

He rolled his finger over the hard nub, the nub of desire hardening within him.

The long tammy benches of the grandstand were a-jostle with persons of quality and their kin, with visiting mana-manipulators and a scattering of mana-priests. Watchful cuckoos perched on three separate pennant poles. The railed judgement box was hung with banners emblazoned with icons of golden ears, attached, winglike, to azure eyes. It accommodated both the Burgdorfs, their pint-size adolescent sons, Sariola and his elegant daughter, and a herald clasping a tasselled bugle. Brass gleamed in the sunshine as that yellow-liveried fellow with the strapping chest – Maxi's bellows – raised his instrument to tootle, then to cry out:

'Peace, in Lord Burgdorf's name—'

Riflemen and crossbowmen kept an eye on the crowd, which was still eddying and humming with speculation. A few scuffles broke out as the bottom ranks, closest to the knoll, were propelled still nearer where they mightn't be able to see fully what transpired on top.

But presently – '*Peace!*' – several thousand attendees subsided. Bodies squatted and sprawled on the tiered slopes rising gently from around the green mound of Speakers' Stage . . .

. . . where Eyeno stood, to one side, attended by one of Burgdorf's cudgel-men in case she felt tempted to dart away.

If only the pressure of all those inquisitive gazes could stun her mercifully to death. She was humiliated and devalued utterly. She had come as a poetess – as well as to applaud her brother – and maybe, maybe (though she rather doubted it) on the final afternoon of gala she might have been standing up here in her own right to recite into those fine acoustics at the entire valley. Now she was a prize, the stakes in a contest – to all intents – between someone whom she had known all her life (and maybe never known at all!) and a lascivious arrogant popinjay with the power to impose his will on her.

All because he was a proclaimer. And a man.

Might he even be another Tycho Cammon who liked to be watched by selected spectators while he ravished?

She must hope with all her heart that Juke won. Yet that heart of hers was broken. Oh, to close her eyes and see instead the meadow of the merry maidens. She stared back at the prying audience to defy one spectator then another. Some people looked away when they realized that it was themself, yes *yourself* in person, that she was fixing upon. Others smirked as if she were standing naked. So she gazed up at the far harper trees, bronzed and rubicund, hairy with strings.

If only she could proclaim her way off this mound! If only a woman might bespeak. If only.

At last the audience hushed to hear the herald explain the reversal of normal proceedings. His voice even raised an echo from the uppermost slopes, yet almost all gala-goers had deserted those to gawp at Eyeno in her distress. A rustle of talk sped like wind on water.

Osmo van Maanen mounted the knoll from one side, Juke from the other. Van Maanen lurched. Was he tipsy? Or driven by inward pressures which he was struggling to steer?

Van Maanen, of course, was the popular hero. Could he do any wrong?

'—accepts the challenge of Juke Nurmi,' cried the herald, prompted by little Lord Maxi. 'Being a matter of honour – mercy is waived. Even so, we counsel moderation. Let Speakers' Valley never again witness scenes such as van Maanen himself put a stop to, ahem.'

The two men stood thirty paces apart. They considered one another. They breathed deeply. The surface of the knoll was springy. Several flat stones were embedded as markers. Eyeno's hair crackled. Her custodian muttered. Mana was in the air.

'You banished that Sariola daughter because you loathe anything to do with muties,' Juke called out brusquely. 'Muties terrify you. Don't you realize, my pompous fool, that all proclaimers are muties? *You're a mutie yourself with a mutie mind!*'

This unexpected accusation shocked van Maanen. He shook

his head in appalled denial. For several seconds he looked as if he might actually vomit. He clenched his teeth.

Keep those teeth clenched . . .

'All you need, freak,' and Juke rushed onward, 'is a *mutie body* to go with your puny talent! Let a mass more *fuzz* sprout on your face. Let wool grow so long that it blinds you. Let your voice become a sheep's that only bleats. This is spoken.'

Juke was thinking of Lammas, the werewool, back home in Outo. He was visualizing that mocky-man intently (and exaggeratedly, since Lammas could talk perfectly well). He was projecting his vision upon van Maanen – here where sheep had been possessed by mana (as he'd told his sister), here where the harper trees had bleated in tune to those animal cries. The valley would remember.

'This is your voice from now on, mutie-mind!' Juke bawled at the ridge: '*MAAAIRRR, MAAAIRRR —*'

The trees heard. Their strings quivered. *MAAAIRRR*, they echoed faintly. Then more insistently.

Still Osmo van Maanen uttered no more than a strangled gasp. If Juke could paralyse his opponent's throat by this wily and inspired assault so that his enemy couldn't proclaim . . . then he could reduce the self-important popinjay to the condition of a sheep, facing slaughter. Van Maanen looked much less debonair: hairier, as if he hadn't shaved that morning. His moustache, stragglier. His wavy locks were riotous.

Despite her mortification, Eyeno couldn't but pray for her brother's ruse to succeed.

MAAAIRRR, MAAAIRRR, bleated the harper trees.

Juke didn't let up for one moment as he wove his web of wounding words.

'You gave a certain Sam Peller white hair when you two were younger, poor dupe that he is! You're Tycho the Second, Ozzy! Except that you haven't the courage. Ozzy will turn white too, white and woolly as a lamb, his throat full of fleece – outside, and inside too. This is spoken; and you can say *nothing*.'

Osmo shuddered. Sensations convulsed him, of an invasive choking palsy, and of fury and disgust, and yes, urgent unappeasable appetite too, a hunger for that delicious woman dressed in blue who was the female embodiment of this proclaimer from nowhere who was strangling him.

He remembered now why he had made Sam into an old man: the real reason.

That sudden ageing of his boyhood companion, bespoken so potently when Osmo was twelve and a half and Sam was a mature fourteen, hadn't simply been an act of boyish braggadocio with unforeseen consequences. It hadn't only been an impetuous discharge of Osmo's fledgling powers as a proclaimer. Nor had Osmo merely aimed to put Sam in his proper place – as underling – now that he had acquired Elmer as an impressionable friend, and appreciated the pleasures of authority after being under Sam Peller's sway for so long.

Young Elmer had returned to Loxmithlinna at the end of his summer holiday. Sam, who'd been somewhat neglected, had cajoled Osmo into yet another leppi hunt in the woods. Hot with racing after the scampering little animals – less intent that day on stealth and shooting than on working up a lather – Sam had proposed a dip in a pool to cool off.

'There's no one else about,' the older boy had said; his sense of security was already keen. 'We can put our bows down, Ozzy.' Yes, Sam had called him that when they were alone; but the nickname had begun to irritate Osmo. As, too, had the business of running after Sam.

Once they were both in the water Sam asked, 'I wonder if a proclaimer can make himself breathe like a fish if his mouth's full of water?'

Unaccountably Sam had seized Osmo and ducked him under, naked limbs wrapped around naked body, clutching him tightly.

He held him under while Osmo flailed.

Till Osmo felt that he was on the point of bursting.

Sam's arms and legs were wrapped around him. Was Sam trying to drown him? Trying literally to *liquidate* him? Then pretend that Lord Alvar's heir had met with an accident? If only Osmo could cry out. Water flooded into his mouth. Water was a burning brick in his chest. Frenzy possessed him. His eyes must be bulging like a sufferer from goitre. Like a fish . . .

Suddenly he was hauled up into air, retching and gasping, coughing pebbles of water.

'I'll squeeze it all out of you,' promised Sam, panting wildly. 'Massage you, Ozzy, till you feel fine.'

Frenzy climaxed in Osmo as Sam held him so supportively. He had vomited more water – and then these choking words: 'Be

337

old, Sam, old for ever.' It was frightful to be old. Old age was a punishment, a pain. No one old would thrust him underwater. 'Grow old *now*,' he spewed out. 'It's spoken, I've spoken it. As I live, I tell you!'

A shock had seemed to stab Sam. A spasm coursed through his whole frame. Osmo struggled from his companion's grip and from the pool, to stagger to his clothes.

'Unawares,' yelped Sam. 'I took you unawares.' As if by half-drowning Osmo he had been demonstrating that an heir to a keep must be more wary.

Had that been Sam's only intention? No. Osmo knew now that there had been possessive jealousy at work, on account of Elmer and Osmo's emancipation from Sam's influence. There had been a sensual physicality to Sam's seizure of the younger boy, unacknowledged by Sam perhaps, deflected into this dangerous horse-play in the water. To squeeze Osmo, to massage him while he was incapacitated . . . How else might Sam have held Osmo so intimately?

On the way back home to the keep Sam and Osmo had walked side by side through the woodland in silence. The time for words seemed past, long gone. Only gradually did Osmo realize that Sam was changing. At first he thought this might be some trick of the light and shade, of the chiaroscuro of sunshine through leaves. He did not wish to stare pointedly at Sam. Presently he began to steal glances.

Sam's step remained spry. It would continue to remain so. Nevertheless his features were losing their youthful hue, becoming pale and subtly wrinkled. The colour was bleaching out of his auburn hair.

How soon did Sam himself grasp what was happening to him? Surely some while later than Osmo, and not by direct observation but through some inner process of realization which was almost dreamlike. At no specific stage did Sam cry out in horror or clutch himself to try to retain his hold upon the person he had been. At no point did he halt in denial, to cling to a tree, refusing to take another step in this journey through the autumn-tinted horzmas, yellovers, and kastas, and through the years. As if in a trance – a trance of time – Sam had tramped onward while his hair silvered and his flesh aged, until he who had begun the trek homeward as a strapping lad of almost fifteen years, big for his age, completed the walk as a man seemingly of six decades, and of the same stature.

Osmo observed this transformation with a contrite elation, a thrilled remorse at what he had caused.

It was finally with awe, not bitterness, that Sam had turned to Osmo, to whisper in wonder, 'For ever . . .'

Finally Sam wept, and laughed.

'For ever . . .'

That was what Osmo had said. For ever. Osmo had only meant *lifelong*. Sam was suffering from a great delusion – perhaps an utterly necessary one unless he were to go mad.

Thus Sam had passed through his crisis.

'For ever, as I live!'

For ever older, always that age, undyingly, barring accident or violence. Forever bound to Osmo, whom he had loved in one fashion, and now loved *otherwise*.

Sam retained his stamina – and his alertness too. His watchfulness was much intensified, to an almost over-scrupulous degree. Neither accident nor violence should intrude, if Sam could possibly avoid these on his own behalf and Osmo's. Osmo had made him live for ever – at the cost of being old.

On their return to the keep, Alvar had thrashed his son. Johanna hired a shaman as mentor to the boy for a couple of years.

However, Sam Peller couldn't avert danger from his lifegiver while this Juke Nurmi was bleating out his curses . . .

'You can say *nothing*!'

His opponent's potent words . . .

Here on this very spot Cammon had almost enslaved Osmo to his will, except that Cammon had become rash and careless.

Osmo was suffocating, taken aback by the speed of the assault. An all-at-once attack, abetted even by the harper trees. Fury and carnal hunger were bottled inside him, ablaze. He was choked. His skin writhed.

You can say nothing.

Well, then, so he would!

'*Nothing*,' he roared – and a hairy ball of phlegm erupted from his throat, 'is what you'll be in a few more moments!'

He mustn't try to harden his opponent, to petrify him, as he had petrified Cammon. His enemy would be expecting that same party trick. Another statue to stand in a niche in the banqueting hall, to be softened once a year for the entertainment of his midsummer guests. Osmo could stiffen a man to stone but he could also soften a statue too – which was what his present enemy had done at Maananfors that night.

'The very ground you stand on is nothing. You *softened* the tyrant in my hall. You melted his marble, you moistened his rock. Rock and soil, soften! Suck this murderer down into you. Be quicksand and quagmire, swallowing stickily. You have no ground to stand on now, Juke Nurmi, it's *mutating*' – yes, turn the absurd, hateful accusation back upon him – 'into quag and slime, mire and sucking muck.'

Juke's boots were indeed sinking into the surface of the mound. His ankles were covered. Now, his shanks. The victim tried to wrench his feet free to reach firmer ground. But that wasn't the way. Already he was engulfed to his knees.

'Speakers' Stage is greedy for you, Juke Nurmi! Absolutely gluttonous. It has wanted you to come along for ages to eat you up.'

Juke was beginning to panic.

'You're a mutie, and you're softening too! You're changing, I tell you. You're flowing.'

'No, no, laddie, it's the soil that's flowing – up around your knees.'

As it was.

Now that the hillock had a hold on Juke, Osmo could hold himself together too. His hirsutism was fading away, vaporizing in the breeze. The harper trees had stilled their bleating. Juke was much shorter now, much diminished, just a laddie. The sucking earth submerged his enemy's waist.

'Eat dirt!' shouted Osmo.

Juke babbled rather than bespoke with any purpose. He threw words which burst ineffectually. With lazy gestures and quick phrases Osmo batted those forays away. Within himself he was ablaze with domineering fever. Raw surges of a dizzy intensity coursed through him, bizarrely oblique to common feelings: sideways to rage, crosswise to delight.

The bubbling soil oozed up Juke's chest.

'You know what you need to give me if you're to break free,' Osmo called out teasingly to his opponent. 'You know what you wish me to take from you, don't you? Given freely, taken gladly.'

Juke craned his chin upward as muck lapped it. Fleetingly his gaze sought his sister, and instantly veered away. Veered away out of shame. And in terror at her expression.

'Take my sister,' the sinking fellow cried. 'Yes, take Eyeno!'

This was all he had time to say. Dirt poured into his mouth, silencing him. His features distorted forward, eyes goggling. He struggled to expel the filth, and hoist his nostrils as dirt closed them too.

For a moment longer Osmo hesitated.

Then he shouted:

'Ground, spew your meal out. Vomit it, I say.'

He glowed with such a sense of vehement accomplishment – and abandonment. He was master of the current of mana, and it, in turn, of him. This was one of those perfect moments which dovetailed with legend, adding another layer, strengthening the power of the old tales. Consequently of words as well, in which tales were told, and bespeakings were voiced. Hadn't old Vai the hero dealt with an upstart antagonist in just such a fashion? Of course Vai had, of course. Gripped by passions, Osmo had been blind to the mirror-like nature of this event until the moment of convergence. Now he stood on the cusp of fortune as surely as he stood on this hillock. Whatever he asked for, whatever he demanded must occur. Fellow proclaimers and mana-priests and the multitude must even now be realizing this. That was a hushed multitude. What a gala this was proving to be.

Obediently the earth regurgitated Juke Nurmi. Juke was disgorging dirt as he sprawled filthily, coughing and retching, clawing at his mouth. Abject, the loser crawled towards the edge of the knoll.

Still the spectators waited hushed, for Osmo to swagger towards Eyeno.

The turf seemed to undulate beneath him as he strutted, craving the beguiling girl. The knoll was a vessel bobbing on a mana-sea in tempest. He was its captain, drunken with his own command of affairs, his unsinkable prowess.

'My adorable young lady, he betrayed you—'

Utter helplessness overtook Eyeno. Her situation had moved way beyond humiliation towards the virtual annulment of herself as person and poetess, the deconstruction of herself into reward and mistress.

Submit gladly, a voice seemed to tell her, transforming van Maanen's words within her mind. *Accept, embrace, gain dignity again. Learn to adore this handsome lord. Learn joy and rapture in his arms.*

Her brother was dirt. What *brother*, indeed? Lord Osmo had

341

shown her Juke's true quality. The emotions in her were like worms moving through her substance as if through soil, sifting it within themselves, rendering her flesh – and her spirit – manipulable, fertile, soft . . . and hot. And forgetful. Salvation beckoned, redemption from her misery. So this was enchantment?

Her inner eye panged her, because it perceived none of this. It saw meadows and maidens. Her Isi eye was a hard awkward lump lodged in her head, abominably intrusive and blind. Lord Osmo would intrude upon her with a delirious invasion.

She wasn't going to be redeemed as a pawned trinket is redeemed! If he as much as laid his hand on her – soon, so soon – she would be raped in public before a host of onlookers.

Her fingers flew to her face. She prised the artificial eye from its socket. She brandished this at Osmo to ward him off – and he jerked to a halt in his journey to claim her. He caught his breath in shock.

A gasp flowed across the terraces. Even those furthest away saw the gesture and thought that they understood . . . that she had torn the living eye from her head. This was what everyone thought they saw. Even if there was no blood.

Osmo gawped at the eye in her hand and at the hollow in her face.

'You fool,' she shrieked at him, 'I'm a mutie myself, of course! A mocky-woman! That's who you want to mate with. This eye's false – as false as your fantasies. The real eye's inside my skull. It's a lump of demon-jelly lurking in my thoughts. See how false *this* is!'

Raising the Isi eye, she hurled it down as hard as she could upon one of the embedded marker stones.

The eye shattered.

Osmo staggered, stupefied. She was a mutie? Her brother too . . . And he hadn't suspected till now. Sam hadn't warned him – Sam hadn't found out. Nor had he. Know the origin of a person, indeed! He hadn't suspected. Hadn't dreamed – his treacherous enemy and his enemy's sister had both looked normal enough. He had lusted madly for a mutie *witch*. Eyeno laughed at him so bitterly. Bedlam seethed in Osmo. Echoes of her words gibbered. The valley was a vast whirlpool spinning around, and he at the centre about to be sucked under, drowned in chaos.

Instead, he must send *her* into that whirlpool.

To banish the horror. His desire had become a hateful mockery. Unspeakably so? No, speakably . . .

'Mocky-woman,' he shouted, using her very own word. He was almost within reach of her. 'Get away from me! Lose yourself! Go to the end of the world and throw yourself into the deepest lake you can find! This is spoken, spoken, oh yes.'

Such a pressure arose in Eyeno, so swiftly. She ran from the mound as if a strong wind propelled her. And no one would hinder her.

'Mutie, mutie,' some voices called, but she didn't care about anyone in that vile valley to which she had come with her pathetic hopes. She didn't care about anything else except to escape from it.

Heart pounding, she ran up the slopes. She dodged between blurred, half-seen figures who shrank away.

Could she simply drown herself in Lake Yulista by stealing a rowing boat and weighting herself in a net with stones? No, that wasn't allowed to her. Her punishment, her penalty for attracting the lechery of a lord, must be a prolonged one. She must go to somewhere sufficiently far enough away and lonely enough that he would never even hear about her suicide.

If she must flee a long way from him – and how she yearned to with all her being – equally her suicide beckoned so that she would rush towards it willingly. It beckoned from afar. Her suicide would be her friend, walking beside her on the way, a cold watery companion who would at last let Eyeno sleep in its embrace, a chilly comforter. And on the shores of the waters of death she would perhaps at last meet the maidens of her vision, even if those meadows might be grey. To the dead perhaps greys were bright enough. Her own gown seemed lurid now.

Her gown, her gown . . . Return to the Goat to change, to collect her knapsack? To meet Juke, so soiled in his person and in her estimation, sneaking into the hostelry? No, no.

She wanted nothing any more. Nothingness was her goal. She would beg her way to her destination. Her bleak ally, death, could find a way to feed her.

She trotted uphill between stalls and booths which were mostly deserted on account of the spectacle which had just been enacted down below. The harper trees on the ridge wailed plaintively: *away, away.*

*

343

Sam Peller had hastened up the mound to lend support to Osmo. Many of the spectators were already beginning to applaud, to clap and cheer and whistle. Lord van Maanen had entertained his public capitally. In the grandstand, Maxi Burgdorf's herald blew the bugle. Osmo turned dizzily to face the midget patron of the gala – eye to eye, though at a hundred metres remove.

As he turned, his boot crunched an intricate fragment of false eye which lay upon the stone, reducing it to splinters.

24 · Do the Dead Forget Dying?

On the evening of the day after Osmo had disposed of the abusive, incestuous mutie and his seductress sister who had posed as a poetess (such at least was the wisdom of the world) Bertel held a party in the Hervy's Head to celebrate van Maanen's victory and to repay Osmo's hospitality to Eva. Oh, the Loxmiths' hospitality too, to be sure.

Gala still had one more full day to run. Poets picked by Lord Burgdorf's laureate would declaim from the knoll. Proclaimers would make the harper trees sing and conjure tableaux in the air. They would pit their power words against one another till the loser submitted, checked and enchanted. Osmo's supremacy was hardly in doubt. He had rather pre-empted the outcome, hadn't he?

Not long after Osmo's victory over the mutant, the disgusting zombie which had been on show in a tent had escaped and attacked passers-by.

Its assaults were relatively feeble, but people feared being tainted contagiously. Hence an outbreak of hysteria, a mana-mania which resulted in injuries and a child's sad death. This incident tarnished the glitter of gala for a while, and Osmo himself had very nearly been caught up in the panic.

Rumour spread that the defeated mutie had slipped into that tent shortly before the living corpse went on the rampage. At first the shocked proprietor claimed not to have admitted any such person. When questioned by Maxi Burgdorf, the showman seemed deeply confused and might have been bespoken. Nothing proven, and the mutie couldn't be found anywhere. Surely Osmo's former antagonist would have been too enfeebled to pull a wily stunt?

Nonetheless, Sam Peller had conceived a phobia about Osmo's diet in case his lord might be poisoned. Sam insisted on nibbling a morsel of his food and sipping a drip of his drink. Thus silver-haired Sam was sitting in on the private party that evening in a candlelit dining room in the Hervy's Head. Gunther Beck was also present, though not Lyle Melator – he had a pressing appointment with a young lady.

A fire of minty logs glowed in the hearth. This had overheated the room by a few degrees. Now a window stood open. The autumn night had become cool outside, and the hoteliers were fussy about the comfort of Lucky's consort, eager that he might renew his patronage on some future occasion.

One charmingly amateurish mural on the plasterwork depicted a chunkily naked female harpist against a background of spuming rapids. The harp seemed like an upright net with the woman's hands two large white fish caught in it. Another mural showed a contorted skeleton biting a thin tall sapling and shaking leaves loose from the spindly branches. The leaves, as they fell, became fat flakes of snow.

The feast on the linen-draped table was a goose with roast potatoes and carrot casserole; with a rich mustaberry wine to wash it down. Bowls of black blood-soup had already been drained.

Sam tasted a morsel of the bird.

'What exactly might our food be poisoned with, by this mutie who has slunk invisibly into the kitchen?' Bertel asked exasperatedly. Really, what a breach of etiquette at a dinner in a fellow's honour. Did one feel *reassured* by such a procedure? Did one feel that one's guests were properly expressing their gratitude for a fine goose? But Osmo's composure seemed shaken by events. Or drained by his efforts on the knoll. Just at present he wasn't capable of handling his bondsman's sudden phobia.

'What's our poison?'

'Skull-cup fungus maybe,' suggested Sam. 'Or Isi venom.' He concentrated on the juices in his mouth, like some connoisseur savouring a fine vintage at a tasting prior to spitting out into a cuspidor.

'You'll know immediately?' Bertel's expression was sarcastic, though even as he spoke a certain fascination with the import of Sam's behaviour crept into his tone.

'I mean, wouldn't the venom take a certain while to act?'

'I'll know,' Sam assured him.

It was ludicrously unlikely that Bertel – and all of them – might die of poison due an excellent dinner cooked at the Hervy's Head. Skull-cup fungus was rare; Juke Nurmi would hardly have found a clump to hand among the harper trees. How would he have come by serpent venom? Yet that normal-looking mutant had seemingly attacked Osmo sneakily three times now, if one counted the episode of the zombie and included the business of the face in the fireworks – as well as the freeing of Tycho Cammon. Sam Peller's self-sacrificial paranoia wasn't wholly without a basis. It was merely rather inappropriate at this moment. Bertel did not wish to react ham-handedly if the proclaimer were ever to come to Pohjola Palace to target his powers upon a certain machine. Eva, still in her pearls, giggled at Sam's solemn performance which she wasn't treating seriously at all.

'Is one's appetite enhanced?' she asked all those around the table. She forked some greasy flesh into her mouth regardless. 'Oh yes! Yum, yum.'

Osmo smiled gratefully. Perhaps he *was* embarrassed. Bertel's daughter returned a grin of amused complicity. Her eyes sparkled. Van Maanen's temporary fixation upon that chit of a poetess – a snub to Eva, in a sense – hadn't totally been Osmo's fault. Rather, it showed his readiness for a grand passion such as might sweep a young lady off her feet. He had most certainly disposed of the hoyden, quite put paid to her. Eva continued to regard Osmo speculatively in between tucking into goose and potatoes.

As did Nikki Loxmith, still forkless.

'How *could* you, Osmo?' she asked, to her brother's dismay. Obviously she was pursuing some previous difference of opinion.

'How could you blame that girl?'

'Hush . . .' A soft appeal from Elmer.

With linen napkin as glove, Gunther had torn a hot leg from the bird and was about to sink his teeth in. He paused.

'It was an outstanding performance,' the dream lord assured Osmo, and Eva too; especially Eva. 'Masterful. Osmo was caught up in the heroic.'

'Was that heroic?' queried Nikki. 'Telling the girl to go and drown herself – after she'd disillusioned him?'

'Hmm,' mused Eva. 'Perhaps it *was* a bit harsh. Still, it was electrifying. Don't you think so, Nikki?'

Eva was genuinely concerned about the opinion of Elmer's sister, Gunther noted. The good opinion. He brandished the goose's leg.

'Oh not harsh,' he said.

'In my opinion,' Sam Peller declared at last, 'it's safe to eat.'

Gunther raised his voice. 'Didn't you see how crazily she tore out her false eye? Sister to that villain who set Cammon free! Murdered Vivi. Incestuous sister too, by the sounds of it all.' He bit, and fatty juices dripped. 'No, no, Osmo acted appropriately.' The dream lord practically thundered his opinion. He seized a roast potato in his fingers. Frowning, he quickly dropped this on his plate and speared it with his fork instead.

'You aren't often so emphatic, Lord Beck,' said Nikki.

'Well young lady, in this case I have to insist.' In case Osmo seemed diminished in Eva's eyes, to Elmer's advantage. Thus distracting Elmer from his machinery, and perhaps delaying Gunther's hibernation.

'I'm sorry,' said Nikki, 'but I disagree. Was it noble or romantic to treat any woman in that way? Indeed, should we even be talking about *treating* women one way or the other?'

'You're being treated tonight, by a prince, may I remind you?' Gunther's bluster sounded unconvinced. He clutched contritely at the little box under his shirt.

Reviewing events since his arrival in Yulistalax, Osmo admitted to himself that he had veered out of control in that café on the first afternoon. He had remained deranged until he had banished the poetess from his sight and from his soul and from his senses. Mania had seized hold of him – until he had purged his infatuation in a veritable frenzy up on Speakers' Stage.

'You still aren't eating,' said Eva.

'It was as if . . .' Osmo sighed. 'I felt as if I was a child, with all of a child's urgency for instant pleasure. A chocolate egg *now*, at this moment. Except that my appetite was a man's.'

'Gingerbread man,' Gunther said to him.

'What?'

'You were a hero. Of a sudden you were the hub round which legend was spinning. You were acting out a tale willy-nilly steered by mana.'

'It's true . . .'

'Heroes have such fierce elementary appetites. Such childish ones! You were the junior gingerbread man deep down inside the

347

greater fellow. The junior one's just as complex. Then what had converged diverged again.'

'I don't understand.'

'A hero can't understand. He has to act.'

Softly, Bertel applauded this *bon mot*.

Osmo continued: 'It's as if I was within the world of a child, Gunther, an invisible child existing somewhere all around us, within whom we act out our fortunes. It's a child which harbours' – his gaze drifted from Eva to Nikki – 'sexuality and murderous violence.'

Osmo's craving for the mutie's sister had vanished. That brief frustrated torrent of passion had been linked, he was sure, with Vivi's death, which Eyeno's brother had brought about. Of this he was positive. The poetess had been compensation for his loss – in some uncanny, emotional economy of which he had at first been oblivious, yet must have sensed through his mana faculty. A mother might direct her lamenting child's attention to a glitterbug in lieu of the mignon egg of which it was deprived. She might offer her squalling brat a peach or plum as substitute. What had happened to him was similar, only much more – intensely more – peremptory. The substitute mistress designate was his enemy's own sister.

He might have gladly embraced this successor to the under-housekeeper – fought for, and won, and bespoken to please him! – if she had not torn out her eye. If she had not revealed what her brother had the gall to taunt Osmo with – the mutie curse. That was Juke Nurmi's own guilty secret and the likely source of his grievances. Namely, that he was mutant-spawn.

Yet although Eyeno Nurmi was expelled from Osmo's feelings, an unfocused, desirous mood remained.

Eva waggled a finger at him. 'Your food's getting cold. Cold poison's simply awful compared with hot.'

Yes, she was sumptuous. Vivacious. And witty.

He remembered the zombie blundering malevolently. Might have been a spouse of one of the Sariola daughters who'd been unlucky. Could have been so quite easily. A couple of centuries old, moribund, rotting, still alive in a lunatic fashion.

Osmo at last cut some goose and ate. He reached for the purple mustaberry wine.

'If there's some powerful childish thing that's playing with us,' Bertel said carefully, 'one might be able to find it and control it.'

'Only deep in our dreams,' said Gunther.

'There might be other means to find it too.'

'Such as?'

'Using a . . . machine, perhaps?'

'Oh, but those are *Earth* thoughts,' protested the dream lord, anxious at the way Elmer's interest was kindled.

Gunther had no further need to divert the engineer. Fluttering fussily, a cuckoo alighted on the windowsill. Its large yellow eyes peered into the candlelit room. It cocked its ears. It rustled out its scaly dull green plumes.

'Ukko-ukkoo,' croaked the bird. 'Hear the tale of the death of Johanna van Maanen yesterday morning while a cuckoo sat at her window.'

Osmo's wine spilled right across the tablecloth. Anguished, he arose, jolting the whole table. 'What?' he choked out. 'My mother? My mother?'

Could there be any other Johanna van Maanen?

'How?' he cried. 'Did Cammon—? No, he's all cinders now. What *happened*? Sing me the story, tell me the tale!'

The bird blinked. 'Johanna who fed food to cuckoos,' it chirped – and shut its beak tight as a trap.

Osmo gripped the table. 'In the name of mana tell me the tale!'

'Wait, Osmo . . .' It was Nikki who had the wit swiftly to carve a chunk of goose breast, slap it on her plate and speed this to the window to dump before the bird. The cuckoo tore and gobbled while she retreated to her seat.

'Late morning at Maananfors,' the bird said in the jittery style of a creature plucking words from hither and yon to compose its report. 'Abed, Johanna sat bolt upright suddenly. Face bright with blood. Fit to burst. She cried, "My son, my son! On Speakers' Stage so soon? Such a storm coming my way. Such fierce feelings. Do not die, Son! Never die!" A seizure. She slumped. Her brain had burst.'

A terrible remorse seized Osmo. On the knoll the morning before such a storm had swept through him. Such a rage of passions. Such a deadly whirlpool. It had outstripped anything that he felt when he aged Sam impulsively all those years ago. It wasn't comparable to his sensations when he faced Tycho Cammon, contesting for his own life. Then, by comparison, he had almost been calculating calmly.

Amazing, really, that he hadn't killed the mutie, suffocating him in the soil . . . Ah, but he was a fair-minded lord, not a

349

savage tyrant. So instead he had sentenced the mutie's sister to a delayed death.

His energy had rebounded through mana upon the one who had first given him life, provoking apoplexy in her. In a backlash of power he had killed his own mother.

This, he knew.

He sat down helplessly. Tears welled. He sobbed, and hid his face.

'*I* killed her,' he moaned. 'I killed my mum. What do you think of me now, Prince Bertel? What price my precious mana-talent?'

Gentle fingers were unpeeling his hands from his damp face. Nikki's fingers. She was compassion itself.

'How can you be so sure you caused your mother's seizure? With her blood pressure, this could have happened at any time . . .'

'Of course it could,' agreed Gunther. 'She was *ill*.'

'How ill was she? How do you know? She realized I was on stage. That's when she died! My own rage swept through her . . .'

'So says the bird.'

'Cuckoos don't tell lies.'

'They might tell what they've heard, and it could be wrong.'

'This cuckoo was a *witness*. Who back home would have sent such a cruel message if it wasn't true?'

'Nobody,' Sam Peller said grimly. 'This is the final blow from that mutie. He caused this – him and his sister – by provoking you intolerably, and that's the heart of it. Don't you see?'

Tears still blurred Osmo's vision. 'I caused it myself, Sam. I'm the one.'

Carefully, Bertel said, 'It was a mana-phenomenon, that's for sure. If something childlike is playing with us on this world, feeding on our sorrows and our joys, and maybe also bringing the Isi here to stir the pot—' He glanced at the harking cuckoo; he had said too much. 'Mana's the maker of your misery, not yourself.'

Elmer was directing helpless candid sympathy from those dark mellow liquid eyes of his.

Nikki laid a hand lightly on Osmo's shoulder. 'There should be a better way to live,' she murmured. 'Lust and revenge, greedy desires and obsessions. They're like diseases, fevers. On Earth they've learned how to cure these sicknesses, so I've heard.'

Her brother ran his long bony fingers through his black mop of hair. 'We can do without dread and bad dreams at Loxmithlinna, that's for sure.'

'Osmo,' said Gunther, 'your mother's words were, "Son, don't die. Don't *ever* die." That's what was uppermost in her mind. Her last wish, as it were. Bear it in mind, and you'll respect her memory. Don't – ever – die.'

'I've half a mind to forswear any more proclaiming . . .'

'And half a mind not to,' Eva said knowingly.

Oh, he was a fascinating fellow, tormented by his feelings. She had never seen a man weep – for love. Love of a lost mother. Who would ever weep over Queen Lucky? These tears, from a mana-master who could consign a mutie girl to a watery grave far away . . . Elmer was gentler than Osmo, but could Elmer ever weep impassionedly? Could he ever be thrillingly fierce?

As if tuning in to her thoughts, Osmo gazed blurredly at Eva. He craved a bosom to rest his brow against for comfort. Desire, directionless since the mutie girl's expulsion, stirred in him even despite the news about his mother. Perhaps even liberated by it?

What had his mum meant by that last cry of 'Never die'? What else could she have meant but 'Seek a Sariola daughter'? Why, there was Eva!

He needn't reproach himself for this impulse, seemingly so at odds with grief. Not if his desire was his mother's desire too. Nikki was touching him in a nurselike fashion, a sisterly style, so he supposed. Her fingers alerted him to flesh and muscle and skin. *She* had reproached him, as if some mature adult now inhabited that fawnlike, adolescent body. Bertel's daughter was . . . appreciating him. Nikki would gentle him; she would steal away his potency – of mana, and of man – until he was another Elmer . . . He shook loose.

At this hideous, heart-stopping time how could he bear to think of a woman other than his mother? Why, his overwrought soul sought relief. Such was man's nature, to seek relief.

With those big yellow eyes, the cuckoo watched the consequences of its news inscrutably.

Through tears which still seeped, Osmo saw Eva's ample butter-sculpted brow and fruitful chubby cheeks and dusky eyes blur into Vivi's freckled countenance. Those ghostly freckles swelled till all of the face was flushed redly. Till the features were those of his mother, dead too. Like a huge high collar, almost a cowl, a bird hovered behind. Its wings were spread back to back, tips downward. That wasn't the swan of death. It was a cuckoo, the cuckoo which had come to watch her die. All colour leached from his mother's face. The flesh became grey and mouldy, the eyes rotten eggs, lips livid, curling back from blackened teeth.

Zombie, zombie . . .

Might you do that to me, Eva Sariola? Might you?

'Sam, we must fly back . . . right away.'

'What, by night? You're tired. You're shocked.'

'You can handle the sky-boat.'

'At night? I don't know. It's foolish to. I'm not up to it.'

'I shall fly.'

Sam argued. 'It'll be different at night. There'll be no landmarks. I couldn't forgive myself. If you want my opinion—'

'The sky-sickle shines, Sam, and the stars.'

'Please wait till the morning,' begged Nikki. She still lingered by Osmo.

Gunther's great cherubic face was perspiring. 'No – until the morning after,' he urged. 'Unless a cuckoo comes from your father. Gala's still on. People expect—'

'—me to concentrate on tricks? What if my grief spills, and bereaves somebody innocent?'

Sam was staring incredulously at the dream lord. 'A cuckoo call from Alvar?'

'I know he's obsessed with his *Chronicles*. Even so, he might have noticed that his wife has died!'

It was Elmer who realized why Sam was amazed – and now trying to pretend not to be. 'But Gunther,' he piped up, 'there's a powerful communicator in Osmo's sky-boat. It works fine. I checked it out. What they need to do is call home.'

'Call home, of course.' Osmo spoke distractedly. 'Of course that's what we'll do. Then fly home. I'm stupefied. Why didn't you remind me, Sam?'

Sam scowled. 'In my opinion you're in no fit state. I wish I hadn't—'

Bertel banged a hand on the table. 'He oughtn't to leave.' The dinner party was a ruin. So were his immediate hopes regarding Osmo and Eva and the everything machine. Lucky might fret and fume. 'You oughtn't to!'

Osmo laughed weirdly. 'Before dinner's over? I'm sorry but I couldn't eat another scrap. That'll leave more for Lord Beck and the cuckoo, won't it?'

Bertel nodded insistently to his daughter, and then in Osmo's direction. Gunther was betraying considerable signs of agitation until Eva rose and set Osmo's capsized glass to rights. She refilled it for him.

'You must drink,' she said. 'Drink deep to steady yourself.' Eva winked slyly at Nikki, making her an accomplice as she held the wineglass up for Osmo. 'We should all drink.'

'Oh yes indeed.' Gunther hoisted his glass. 'I propose a toast, a salute, a libation in memory of Johanna van Maanen, a wonderful woman.' The dream lord gulped.

So did Osmo. It was as if he had been bespoken by Eva. Bertel's daughter topped up Osmo's glass again while he held it. Then she guided his hand in hers, raising the glass to sip from it herself. Her smoky eyes gazed into his from so close. Her breath mingled with his breath, her lips stained purple so unlike a zombie's lips yet of similar hue. Releasing his hand, she withdrew to her seat. Osmo drained the rest of that second glassful of wine. He rocked, disoriented. Gunther looked relieved. Bertel smirked at his daughter.

'Now you won't fly by night,' said Elmer. 'I wouldn't let you.'

'Tomorrow,' murmured Osmo. He stared at the scrawny green cuckoo perched on the windowsill.

Her face bright with blood. Fit to burst. Such fierce feelings. Her brain burst.

Never die, son.

'In my opinion,' said Sam, 'you ought to try to eat something.'

'That's very wise,' said Bertel.

The prince brooded.

Eva had intoxicated Osmo, hadn't she? Osmo would think about her. But not yet. Of course not yet. Osmo had to come to terms. Time must pass. The proclaimer would wish to visit Sariolinna. In all likelihood the engineer would nurse the same ambition. After the frigid winter? In the spring when the sap rose? Seed had been sown; it would sprout in its own good time, lustily, demandingly. After all these years, Lucky knew that there were tides not in the Great Fjord nor the sea but in the great pool of human beings itself. Events flowed swiftly, then ebbed slackly, then they quickened again. In the meantime, Wex might unlock the secrets in the mana-mage's mind. Lucky would have to admit that this had been a successful jaunt to the gala. Really, Eva was an excellent daughter.

Gunther swigged. 'I know how it is to lose someone worth all

353

the world,' he announced across the table. 'The hollow has to be filled somehow.'

At last, Osmo took a desultory bite of cooled goose as if this was what the dream lord was advising.

The cuckoo ruffled its plumes huffily. It hopped around. And then it flapped away into the spangled night to spread its tale of Johanna van Maanen's decease by apoplexy . . .

Eyeno's trek eastward was assisted by the absence of her left eye. Only a few farmwives warded her off when she called to beg, and screamed about nakkis. Most countryfolk were only too willing to give her bread and milk, sometimes meat and fish, even to let her doss in a barn. The disconcerting floppiness of those eyelids averted the interest of menfolk from this vagabond who was increasingly frowzy and tangle-haired. This, and her air of despair, at once vacant yet purposeful, desolate but urgent.

She did not speak about herself. In fact she hardly spoke at all, often only mutely holding out an empty palm. Ousted by Osmo's bespeaking, she had virtually banished words from her existence. She concentrated upon the nullity and silence which awaited her. Poetry had perished.

The aura of purpose imposed upon her communicated itself to the countryfolk, prompting them to help her on her way – with food, with an old smock to replace her blue gala gown which was too flimsy for chilly nights, then with a soiled cloak too. Her benefactors smelled tragedy, which must be fostered, helped along to its finale. Her hollow eye-socket augmented the impression that her gaze was set inflexibly upon some far-off and fatal horizon which she must reach without fail. She hardly needed to see her way in full detail. She was summoned – propelled, like a wrecked skiff down rapids. This was poignant mana-magic to many who saw her. They fed it.

Juke had gazed too, into the distance . . .

She had once had a brother. A brave brother. A brother who loved her. Who loved her, loved her . . .

She had no brother at all. She had never had a brother. No such word existed. Nor did any such word as love.

Her ears were plugged with wax. Verbs were wounded incurably. Nouns had died by the dozen. Why does the Sun? Why did her feet march onward? *Why*, is the sigh. Seduced by bitterness. Why was missing from her understanding. When she closed her right eye she saw only a black eclipse. Let words

354

likewise become extinct and cease tormenting her. Let her make her way like some speechless animal whose thoughts have no words at all to kindle memories. An animal, migrating.

Somewhere she lost the bangle which someone gave her to wear on her wrist, for some reason she now forgot.

A week passed.

Two weeks.

Three.

Winds were lashing the last leaves from most trees. Veras remained defiantly green, though theirs was a cruel green, of needles. Hoary sylvesters were harbingers of a winter world bleached by snow. Mists stole many mornings now. A certain wilderness of jumbled rocks seemed familiar. Familiarity wouldn't fool her into homesickness. A cluster of cotts called Outo and another called Halvek might be a day's hike to the north, or two days'. *Don't go near any mocky-men, mutie girl. Forge on, forge on.* Through mist, through curtains of rain blowing down valley slopes.

No more hermit homesteads now. She was carrying an ever-lightening parcel of cheese and rusks and roast oats, and somehow some chocolate and a smelly smoked fish too, which it was high time to eat.

After several days more, she was carrying no food at all. She was scavenging berries and fungus like a bird.

As to drink . . . why, there were lakes everywhere.

Lakes little and large. Lakes beyond lakes. It seemed that the land had all but lost its connectedness and she was hiking hungrily through an archipelago from island to island, islands which somehow remained joined. This must indeed be the end of the world, or almost the end; and almost her own end too.

Mists drifted, paling the sun.

The skeleton of a horse lay picked clean and whitened. The remains of its reins were still tangled on the crooked broken limb of a collapsed dead tree. Caught, the horse had starved to death. She would never starve; cold water would fill her belly first, and her lungs.

She was climbing. Rock tilted upward through thinning haze, till she stood upon a bluff in the sunlight.

Cliffs circuited two sides of a great cauldron of woolly mist. A rift let her glimpse leaden water into which the scarps plunged. The highest part of the escarpment overhung the shrouded lake as if giant teeth had bitten the rock away below. Some boulders

355

rested just back from that beetling brow as though inviting somebody of superhuman brawn to try to roll one over the edge.

She made her way towards those boulders, knowing that she
had arrived at the end – of everywhere, and of herself.

Boulders dwarfed her. For a long while she rested against the
most precipitously poised. She stared vacantly down at creatures
of mist, vast, fleecy, and amorphous, grazing the field of the lake,
exposing gaps, and closing gaps.

All words were dead in her now; even her name.

She ran forward into emptiness.

The abrupt smash of the water against her feet, legs, chest was
stunning. Already she was deep underwater, reaching the nadir
of her plunge.

A current seized hold of her. Liquid hands laced around her
ankles, her knees, her waist, pulling downward impetuously.
The first bubbles gushed from her nostrils. She was rushing
underwater, feet first, her sodden smock rucking up. A lulling,
dazed bewilderment made her forget to breathe. Light had died
away above. She plummeted, the sleek obscurity squeezing her.

She was passing through . . . an opening?

Water became bright sweet air . . . of a smooth cave in which
she bobbed, buoyed up and gasping. The rounded chamber glowed
gently. A passage curved away, softly luminescent.

Words awoke, sickeningly.

*You have come to sing me a story, tell me a tale, to say a poem
to me. Come in, come in. Tell a tale of an eye that was a glass
flower, and an eye that was a false gem, and the falsest eye of all,
an Isi eye that spied from your head and showed the serpents
what you saw within you and without you. Come on, come on. Let
your other eye lead you into me.*

She stood up giddily, knees still awash.

She must be dead. Without having noticed her death. The dead
mightn't notice that they had died. They might merely be puzzled
by their altered circumstances . . .

Her smock and cloak clung burdensomely, waterlogged, sop-
ping. Despite this, her weight seemed less. It was as if she had
lost some element from herself. Life itself, perhaps?

A ghost's garments shouldn't drip so soggily on the shore of
death. Her ears popped, her nose ached.

She waded on to dry stone. The soles of her feet left wet prints.
The air was warm. Even so, she shivered.

Close your eye.

Eyeno had found her voice. She asked aloud, 'Where are you?'
All around you, was the answer. *More so, once you come inside.*
'What are you?'
Curiosity.

Was that a comment, or a reply? Behind the voice other voices
seemed to gibber privately and quietly like disobedient echoes.
Atrocity-generosity-monstrosity-osity-osity-osity . . . These sounds
weren't insistent at all. They faded fast into a meaningless murmur, a mere hum which was comforting if anything, a hum of life
and energy.

'Who are you?'
*The moon that fell to earth. The seed of a new moon fell. Now
I grow in my womb of mana. Nourished by passions I quicken. I
drink; am drunk. Jealousy, envy, vexed, adored, a rupturous
embrace.*

It was plucking words from a poem inside her.

'The embrace will rupture,' she found herself saying, as if part
of a prophecy had popped into her head. Those words were all
too true. Osmo van Maanen's embrace would have shattered her.
As for Juke – whose name she remembered – she couldn't bear
to contemplate the incest which had hidden in his heart, muzzled
shamefully, so that in the end he had spurned her shockingly as
an alternative to a throat plugged with dirt, and to her contempt.
Don't contemplate it. Let me. Close your eye; come on in.

This moon-seed had said something about the Isi spying
through her artificial eye . . .
Discovering your dreams of me; hoping they would discover me.

'So I was hoodwinked by the snakes . . .' Bitterness seemed
inappropriate, so she promptly closed her right eye.

Her inward vision was no longer eclipsed. She saw gauzily into
the vastness of the moon-seed. She saw spiralling tunnels and
cavities and misty chambers. Those seemed of no certain size at
all as if they might be as small as a nut one moment, and the
next as huge as a valley. One route in particular shone for her:
towards a cavern within.

Blind in any ordinary sense to her surroundings she followed
beckoning light.

Until she entered that cavern, luminous and densely misted.

Mists cleared from her inward eye.

Meadows of lush herbage, fronded trees, a stream. Clouds
above, and something like a sun, or a yellow eye. Creamy waxen

357

flowers. The edges of the world curved gently upward, crowded with forests and lakes – becoming ever more miniature and at once intricate and similar so that there was no horizon and no end; so that no eye could arrive at a conclusion, but only at ever tinier continuance. If she opened her outward eye none of that vista could possibly be there.

In the meadow beyond the stream half a dozen young women in loose diaphanous lacy frocks were larking about. All the lasses but one had dark hair. The other was blonde. All larking, just as Eyeno had always seen them. If she opened her outward eye . . . She could hardly walk around for ever with her eyelids shut.

'Do I open my eye?' She ached at the prospect of losing this vision.

No answer came. One of the lasses, then two more, waved to her.

So Eyeno looked.

Her outward eye and her inward eye saw exactly the same sight.

She sped towards the stream. The brisk water wasn't deep. She splashed through it. She mounted the bank and headed up the meadow to the knot of lasses.

'I'm Maria—'

'I'm Anna—'

'I'm Inga—'

'I'm Gretel—'

'I'm Gerda—'

'I'm Paula.'

Paula was the blonde. The lasses were surely close cousins, or even sisters. Chubby-cheeked peachy-skinned Paula wore pigtails. Her face was full and oval, her eyes close-set and smoky, with hardly a fold to the lids. She smelled of spicy buns.

'We're echoes,' Paula said pertly. 'But not *dead* echoes. Echoes in the mind of the moon-seed. You'll play with us, won't you?' she asked Eyeno. Paula gestured around her grandly. 'There's everywhere to play, and everything to play at. We live in a lovely village just over the hill.' She reached to touch Eyeno's sleeve, and wrinkled her nose humorously. 'You're soaking.'

'I happened to jump in a lake.'

'Oh no, you forded the stream down there. We saw you. What a splash. What's your name? Why do you only have one eye?'

'Eyeno's my name.' As though that was the answer to both of the questions. 'Eyeno Nurmi, from Outo in Saari.'

'Saari? How curious! That's almost my other name. Sari-ola. Paula Sariola.'

'*We* don't have other names,' chorused Gerda and Gretel and Inga and Maria and Anna. 'Not that we know of.'

'Maybe we can find you a new eye,' suggested Paula. 'We can find almost anything we want.'

Eyeno shook her head.

'That's thoughtful of you. But no – I see you all more clearly than I ever saw anything before.'

She held out her hands to Paula.

How sweetly the echo-maidens welcomed Eyeno in that meadow of her heart's desire under the bright yellow eye of something quite like a sun.

PART THREE

PALACE

25 · THE ROPES OF LOVE

A long gallery occupied the fifth floor of the south wing of the aitch-house. The inner wall was hung with sun-dulled tapestries of woodland. Frayed faded carpets of variegated greens suggested a glade stretching into the distance, complete with woven flowers: starflowers and heartbells. A couple of centuries had bleached the violet and pink petals to pale faint pastel.

Originally this gallery had been used as an exercise corridor by many inhabitants of the house during the time of the Dread. A score of mullioned windows overlooked the lakeside district of Loxmithlinna town and the lake itself. When snow lay on the ice-locked lake, the green walkway – brighter then – would have been busy with people strolling to and fro, jostling together for comfort, staring out from a safe height over that lake in case the servants of the snakes came a-calling . . . which never happened. The gallery soothed Nikki with its calm reminder of past anxieties which had faded away.

Today the noontime sun of high summer was shafting into the artificial glade. Pools of brilliance, blocks of shade. Shadows of mullions were dark fallen logs embedded in moss. The hot still air smelled of fusty bygone herbs scattered to deter suckerflies.

In another few weeks Lucky's Day would be coming round again. Preparations were afoot for a feast here in the aitch-house. How could Elmer fail to celebrate his own mother-in-law's festival right here with a Sariola bride at his side? Even if the terrible killing of Eva's father cast a dark shadow . . .

No, more than a shadow: a fearful apprehension. Queen Lucky had been dealt a blow which could have rocked the sanity of a well-balanced person. How was this affecting a woman who wasn't balanced at all to begin with? Cuckoos tattled about her crazy laughter at a world turned upside down. Would she try to replace Prince Bertel with some other man so that she could carry on breeding daughters? Would those new daughters, sired by some other fellow, have the same power to immortalize their husbands?

Just as Elmer was now immortalized.

Presumably immortalized!

Doubtlessly.

Yet the other night, when restless with the heat and roaming, Nikki had heard a faint cry of pain issue from the armoured suite which Elmer had refurbished for himself and his bride. An armoured suite was appropriate – to a man's way of thinking – to house his treasure in. Masses of soft silky fabrics now covered the cast-iron panelling. All was luxury within. Nikki had heard a cry, and not one of joy.

At lunch yesterday, Eva had wiggled uncomfortably in her seat until Lyle took it into his head to fetch a soft cushion for her. Elmer had flushed abashedly.

Maybe Nikki had simply heard Eva giving vent to a pang of grief on account of her father's death. So much that was unsettling had happened . . .

Even if Osmo returned home to Maananfors from wherever he had disappeared to, Nikki wondered whether she or her brother would *ever* again visit Osmo's keep.

At either end of the gallery carved yellover panels had once concealed twin hidey-holes: cubicles with little high skylights and peepholes with lenses to spy into the glade. Within these, trapdoors gave access to tight spiral stairways winding downward. Elmer and Lyle had gutted one of those cubicles and all of the stairwell beneath to install a pulley-operated elevator. Now Lord Henzel could have access in his wheelchair to all six floors.

A brass dwarf stood sentinel by the yellover lift-door – one of Elmer's automata. It was three years since her brother had brought this toy up to the gallery to put it through its paces. Powered by an Isi power-cell and guided by an adapted communicator, the brass dwarf could clank along quite merrily, rubbing caster-feet over the carpets. Here it remained. He had improved the model since then – made one fit for a Queen.

When Nikki reached the far end of the gallery, she heard a sob from behind the panel where one hidey-hole remained. She twisted a volute in the moulding and pushed the disguised door open.

Eva sat on the single item of furniture in the cubicle, a soft deep-buttoned pouffe. Elmer's bride, in gay scarlet-striped skirt and full blouse – jewelled combs in her hair – was dabbing at her eyes with a lace kerchief.

Entering the hidey-hole Nikki swiftly shut the false panel behind her. Eva snuffled.

'"My goose," he tells me lovingly, "I'll finger your nipples and I'll whip your buttocks and I'll tickle your loins. That's how a daughter of Lucky has to be loved if her man's to achieve his goal. That's the way. That's the right ceremony! A bride is bridled with a silken gag. The ropes on her wrists bind her – to the one who loves her."

'But actually to the bed! Do you believe me, Nikki?

'I lie with my belly over a couple of plump pillows, my hands tied to the bedstead, and my bum in the air. At first he smacked me with a curver switch to work up a sweat. Now he has graduated to a little leather whip. It doesn't feel so little when it tickles me.'

Nikki was aghast. 'My brother's whipping you?'

'Are you my real true friend, Nikki?'

'Oh Eva, this is *vile*.' Nikki knelt to hug her sister-in-law. 'How could Elmer bring himself to—? The other night I heard – it's humiliating.'

Sobs racked Eva. 'It's the s-s-ceremony,' she stammered. 'My mother told him that, damn her.'

'It's pain-rape, that's what I call it.'

Eva choked out a giddy laugh. 'If it was *rape* it might be over by now, but it isn't!'

'However do you mean?'

'He's your brother.' Eva rocked from side to side on the pouffe.

Nikki clutched her tighter. 'I'm not going to take his side about this. I've seen how Osmo treated that other sister of yours – Jatta – and then that poor one-eyed poet girl too—'

'Elmer *can't*, he *can't*, that's the bottom of it. He whips me harder to goad himself, and he's so apologetic and manly about it.'

'Apologetic! Manly!'

Eva's teeth chattered. '*I'm sorry if I'm hurting you, my goose, my duckling.* He wasn't hurting me at first. Not on the wedding night, and nights after. It seemed more like a game. It's the s-s-ceremony, you see. He told me so. My damned mother gave him the word to unlock my girdle—'

'Your *what*?'

'All of us Sariola daughters wear special girdles to preserve our gift.'

'Sweet mana!' Was there no air in this hidey-hole?

'She gave Elmer the word and told him the ceremony. Of the ropes of love. Whipping my buttocks, tickling my loins. Using a sauna switch. What a sport! A giggle, really, to start with!'

'I wouldn't giggle—'

'He couldn't . . . couldn't harden, Nikki. Couldn't take my gift. So he whips me more. Now he's using a thong, and apologizing for it—'

Nikki was stifling. 'Elmer's gone over the hill – into another valley!' A horrible valley with slippery sides.

'If only Elmer hadn't pleased my mother! If only I hadn't accepted him – did I really have a choice? Though it's true what you say about Osmo. Jatta must have understood all this.'

Nikki kissed Eva on a dim starflower tattoo. Gently she rubbed her cheek against Eva's tear-dampened cheek. 'I'll talk to Elmer. I'll try to talk to him—'

'Please don't.'

'He's humiliating you. Degrading you, hurting you.'

'If he rejects me I'll be like Jatta. My girdle's off and I still haven't given my gift.'

'Damn your gift, Eva! It's more like a curse.'

'He's trying to puzzle out how it works,' Eva whispered. 'He tells me so! He's trying to find a mechanical explanation. As if I'm his machine. I think he consulted *Lyle*—'

'Elmer couldn't be so gauche!' Maybe her brother could be as naive as that. As well as treating his bride as some living machine . . . or animal. Hurting her clumsily, oblivious to her feelings.

'Your Lyle knows about making love, doesn't he? Doesn't he?'

Nikki's heart skipped a beat. '*My* Lyle?'

'Aren't you likely to—?'

Nikki shuddered. 'I don't think so. I really don't think so any longer.'

'Lyle knows about love.'

'Probably. Yes. Why should I want him for that reason? Why should I desire a man of experience who has gaily dipped his wick where he pleases? Why should I welcome him, myself all fresh and unused?'

'At least he'd know *how*! If Lyle knows my gift's going begging he might—'

Alarm, alarm. 'That's a dangerous thing to be thinking, Eva.

366

I'm not asking you to save your gift for Elmer, understand. He doesn't deserve you.'

'He has to, or I'm such a fool. Nikki: Elmer says that a man ... penetrates deeper ... from behind. The curve of the ... tool ... matches the curve of my tunnel. There must be something high up in me which bursts the first time and releases the virility. The virus, whatever it is. Into the man's organ, to make him a longlife.'

A sash ran up a long slanting shaft to the skylight. Snaring the end of the cord, Nikki pulled. High above, the pane lifted. Not to admit more light; light wasn't wanted. Hopefully a breath of fresh air.

'I'm sure he asked Lyle for advice . . .'

'And Lyle recommended whipping you harder?'

'Not unless he was hoping to make me hate Elmer!' Eva began shredding her kerchief. 'It's dangerous, isn't it?' One strip of lace, then another. 'Elmer's obsessed with getting the ceremony right. He can't. This upsets him.'

'It upsets you too! That's rather more vital.'

'Elmer doesn't try *too* hard. He hasn't broken my flesh.'

'Because he *respects* you, is that it?' Nikki almost gagged on the words. 'How can I bear to speak to him?'

'Don't speak to him. Not about this. Be my true sister. I could have helped Jatta more, but I didn't understand at the time. What's going to happen now that my father's dead? Will there be no more daughters like me? After Minnow and Ester and Sal and Kaisa and Martha and Mary and the new one, Hanna? Maybe it'll all be over.'

'How can it be over when genial Osmo bespeaks a woman off into the wilderness to drown herself because she frustrated him? How can it be over while we play lord and ladies and maidens and cheer proclaimers as heroes? When will a woman ever proclaim, and what will her words be?'

'My mother—'

'Crazy queen hen with her clutch of chicks! Our world's possessed by power.' Nikki spat. 'I hate it now that it's done this to Elmer. To you; it's you who matters.' Eva's comforter paused, panic-stricken. 'I mustn't hate ... or I'll be consumed with hatred. I'll be poisoned. It's you who should be hating. Yet if you start to—'

'*I'll* go over the hill. Into another valley. I know it. Jatta had *courage*. I'll need it too. Help me have it!' Eva faltered. 'I'll be

367

very careful that Lyle doesn't . . . seize a chance. We'd be giving a fine new tale to the cuckoos, wouldn't we just? Adultery and vengeance. The ruin of this keep. I wouldn't want any of that, Nikki. It would tear me apart too; destroy me. Elmer will learn how to love. Let's put on brave faces.'

Brave faces in the stifling gloom under a high-up square of buttery brightness. For a while the two women nuzzled one another wordlessly brow to brow.

Then they left the cubicle to walk along the faded glade through shadow and brilliance towards Elmer's useless brass dwarf.

When they stepped from the lift, on the third floor, a yowl of misery and appeal greeted them. In the distance a black and white cat lurched into motion along the waxed floorboards of the panelled corridor, hauling its hindquarters.

'Nikki-Nikki,' the cat cried plaintively.

Nikki and Eva hurried towards the animal. Windows at each end of the corridor were a long way apart. The middle reaches were comparatively dim. Nikki thought that her pet had soiled his backside; that Tommi was trying to wipe his fur clean by dragging his bum along the floor.

Tommi's hind legs weren't doing anything at all. Only his front legs were striving.

'Nikki!'

The weight Tommi had put on before hibernation had stretched his skin. Losing surplus mass during the long sleep had made his coat loose, a size or so too large for the body within. This floppiness was as nothing compared with the sheer bonelessness of his back legs.

'His spine's broken . . .'

'Broken?' Nikki knelt, tucking in her frock so as not to smother Tommi.

'By a trap—'

'We're on the third floor.'

'By a dog's jaws—'

'There's no blood . . . Tommi, what happened? Are you hurting?'

The cat's pupils were dilated wide: mad black marbles, full with panic. Tommi stretched out his neck and licked Nikki's hand. The purrs were thunderous. She had never heard her pet throb so loudly. He was appeasing her, appeasing whatever unknown force had immobilized his hind legs.

'What happened, Tommi?'

'Maybe he ate some poison.'

'Down in Elmer's workshop . . . some chemical. Speak to me, Tommi! What did you eat?'

'Meee!' moaned the cat, obsessed with this calamity which had overtaken its precious and only self. 'Meee!' Tommi resumed purring in bewildered fright.

'We must make him vomit,' said Nikki. 'Salt down his throat on a spoon. Wait with him Eva. Don't move, Tommi. Be back in a moment. Be all right soon. Soon.'

Nikki fled along the corridor past the main south stairway to the private family dining room, and through to a little pantry adjacent. In less than a minute she was back with a bowl of salt and a spoon.

By then, attracted by the cat's cries, her father had arrived. He was purring to a halt in his wheelchair. His fingers rested over the control buttons – his wrist strapped to the chair-arm. Sunken dark eyes peered from his jaundiced parchment countenance.

'The cat's a cripple now, eh?' His voice was a rustle of dead leaves.

'He's poisoned. I'm going to make him sick, Dad! Eva, help me open his mouth.'

'He'll bite . . .' Nevertheless, Eva crouched and pulled the cat's jaws apart. 'Why should I care if he hurts me?'

Nikki managed to insert some salt, spilling much more. Tommi choked and coughed. His pink tongue lapped fretfully.

'Stop it, silly girls,' croaked Henzel. 'He caught my sickness from sitting on me when I can't shrug him off. Heating me up like an oven. Would you force salt down *my* throat? Send for Moller. Send for the priest for mana's sake. And for Mother Grünwald, you sillies!'

Nikki glared a solitary dagger at her father for his condescension. Was Eva's complaint about Elmer *silly*, too? If whipping his newly-wed wife was *curative*, maybe Elmer was behaving perfectly sensibly!

'He'd probably lap piss at this moment if you gave him a saucerful,' croaked her paralysed father. 'Send for Moller and Ma Grünwald.'

Voices were ascending the stairway. Excited voices. Elmer's

369

and Lyle's and others'. As the owners of the voices appeared, Nikki swung round to see burly bald bailiff Andersen and a white-coated baker from over in the north wing, dusty with flour – along with her brother and Lyle who were wearing stained overalls.

'Eva, my goose! Father, Nikki! Osmo was shot down. That was a month ago—' Elmer paused to recover his breath.

'A cuckoo came by the bakery.' On the bailiff's cranium a purple birthmark might have been the dropping of a bird which had gorged on mustaberry. The baker – Bergman – nodded brightly. He'd been honoured by a cuckoo visit.

Nikki stared coldly at her brother who was so gawkishly excited. Only Lyle registered her expression.

'Shot down by an arrow?' Her father's voice was a rattly husk. 'A crossbow quarrel, or what?'

'By a *quarrel* certainly, Dad! Not of the crossbow kind—'

'Tommi's been poisoned!' cried Nikki. Wasn't Elmer aware of the sprawled, panting cat? Did he suppose that she and Eva were playing with puss on the floor?

At least her father took heed. 'Andersen,' he rasped, 'send for Mother Grünwald and Moller urgently, will you? Tell them our cat's dying.'

'He can't be dying! Don't let Tommi hear that.'

All sympathy, Lyle hurried to kneel by Nikki and Eva. He reached out his hand towards the distressed cat, then thought better of this manoeuvre. 'How did it happen, Nikki?'

'In your workshop, maybe?'

'No, no, he wasn't down there. He hates the place now. How could he possibly have got all the way up here in that state?'

'By dragging himself? To find me!'

'What's wrong with Tommi?' Elmer asked at last.

Andersen was persuading the baker to be an errand boy. 'Lord Henzel wants them *now*. That's what urgent means—'

'Cuckoo told *me*. I'm the witness—'

'We know what it said. You told us.'

Bergman dusted off his hands indignantly. 'Not even a drink with his lordship while I'm telling him.'

Plunging a hand into his tunic pocket, Andersen produced a half-mark. He pressed the coin into a large white hand. 'Buy one, buy several. Just send the priest and the witch. Bring them with you! Come back yourself.'

In a flurry of haste the baker departed down the stairs, sandals slapping.

'Don't try to shift the animal yet,' Henzel rasped irritably. He was tired at having to assert himself. 'What quarrel are you talking about, son?'

Lokka emerged from a doorway further along. Her horsy face was startlingly white with cosmetics above a long creamy muslin gown buttoned up to her throat. On sighting Eva her placid mask enlivened with a smile – of thankfulness? *She couldn't suspect Elmer's cruel incompetence*, thought Nikki.

'Mother! There's a cuckoo tale concerning Osmo—'

Henzel shut his eyes until his wife had walked round into view directly in front of him.

'Why is our cat—?'

Lyle rose. 'We'll know soon enough, Lady Lokka.'

Lokka smiled down at her daughter-in-law who chose to remain crouched beside Nikki and the loudly purring, prostrate cat. Its front claws flexed in and out against Nikki's knees. Memories of comfort. Was Eva's pose a mime of someone abasing herself to avoid being hurt? A parody of submission?

'The quarrel between Osmo and that Juke Nurmi fellow flared up again – right up into the sky,' related Elmer. 'Nurmi hit Osmo's sky-boat with a missile while it was flying back from Sariolinna towards Maananfors. Osmo's boat went out of control away to the west, on fire. Poor Osmo must be dead.'

'What's the origin of this story?' his mother asked cautiously.

'Juke Nurmi himself, would you believe? He turned up at Pohjola Palace and bragged how he put paid to Osmo.' Elmer said to his kneeling wife, 'My duckling, your mother has taken a shine to the mutie, so it seems! In her distress. And with the everything machine causing problems, too.'

Eva mustered a serene dignity. 'A shine to Juke Nurmi? She did invite half a sky-boat load of muties to our wedding to liven things up, remember?'

Sore point.

With Elmer, a minor sore point. It had been very much sorer with Osmo, given his attitude to mutants. The arrival of the mocky-men in Sariolinna was the reason why Osmo had not stayed to witness Elmer finally blessed with the bride they had both competed for.

That was the nominal reason. Osmo and Elmer had contested for Eva in friendly rivalry. Which of them would be able to bring the alien machine to life? Mechanical aptitude versus mana. The latter had lost out, perhaps due to Elmer's instinctive expertise being mana-rooted anyway. The two friends hadn't actually quarrelled at the outcome. Yet Osmo had been galled. Honour obliged him to swallow his gall. Then Lucky invited mutants as wedding guests.

So very much had happened recently, reflected Nikki. *Including her gentle brother becoming a whipper of his newly won wife.* She mustn't let fury at his behaviour warp her – though she was truly infuriated.

A sore point, Elmer's conduct. A very sore point for Eva. Abominably so! Unacceptable. Yet an echo of much else, as Nikki had begun to realize since Osmo's 'splendid' performance at the gala. 'Impeccable,' Gunther had said of that. Some such word of extravagant praise. Nikki had been fool enough to let Elmer experiment with Tommi on Gunther's behalf – so that the lord of dreams could recapture the soul of a dead woman whom he loved so madly that he wore part of her *skull* in a box chained to his chest. Had Gunther's Anna loved him equally, growing old while he remained ever-youthful thanks to her gift?

'Don't you care about Tommi?' demanded Nikki.

'Of course I care,' said Elmer. 'I want to know what's wrong. I need to know. That cat's our pioneer hibernator—'

'And Osmo kidnapped Minnow Sariola too,' added Lyle.

'*Minnow*?' cried Eva. 'What do you mean?'

'Probably she's dead too . . .'

When Tommi had woken up from three months' sleep back at the end of January while all the world was as white as Lokka's face – after Tommi finally stumbled away from Elmer's electro-cradle, sluggish and feeble – what deep dreams had the pet reported to his hopeful interrogators?

Having wings.

Leaping into the air.

Flying through the sky after cuckoo birds.

Finding their nests on a cloud.

A great big soft warm nest full of cuckoos.

Where he went to sleep.

And dreamed that he leaped into the air. Flew through the sky to a soft, warm nest.

And slept. And dreamed, and flew.

This was enough to reassure Elmer; and he had set to work

on the full scale – the Gunther-size – hibernation monitor.

'What kind of missile was it, Son?' rasped Henzel. 'Something out of that Pandora's box you opened for Queen Lucky?'

'No, Dad. The machine didn't start producing till after I'd left. With my bride.' Elmer chewed on his knuckle as if a thorn had lodged in it. 'Osmo had already flown away. Nurmi only went to Sariolinna after he shot at Osmo's sky-boat. Seems he got the missile from the Isi – in exchange for a doll, of all things.'

Not long after Lucky's everything machine had assembled itself (a feat which Osmo had failed to achieve, unlike brother Elmer) and after Lucky had despatched the newlyweds and Lyle to Loxmithlinna in her own sky-boat with her blessing: that was when the machine began manufacturing bizarre weaponry, according to cuckoo tattle. Which was also when Bertel had been killed by that fellow Minkle Kennan who was hanging around the court obsessed with gaining a Sariola bride . . . Keeping tracks of events, reflected Nikki, *might save her from being plagued by fury.*

While her poor dear selfish cat lay throbbing on the floorboards, debate proceeded above its head, and hers.

'Now Lucky is sponsoring Osmo's assassin?' asked Lokka, crestfallen.

Eva darted a glance up at Lady Loxmith. 'Juke Nurmi protected my sister – he looked after her and Jack.'

Demon Jack Pakken had arrived at Lucky's palace back in March in a stolen Isi sky-boat. He was the pilot. Jatta's miracle child was already in his adolescence . . .

Eva squinted at her husband. 'Juke Nurmi never laid a hand on Jatta . . .' She raised her eyebrows in a fashion which might possibly have been construed as coquettish.

'He certainly betrayed his own sister at the gala,' Elmer said sternly. His candid, cadaverous face was righteous. 'Do you know why, my goose? Because he loved her *too much*.' His long slender bony fingers were clenching and unclenching.

'Save us from being loved too much!' exclaimed Nikki. She could have torn out the peacock ribbon from her hair, the coaly hair from her scalp. She mustn't. Mustn't yield to mania. Now she had an inkling of how mania could infest a person. At that party once upon a time mania had infested Elmer temporarily. Now he had become a grimmer case. She refused infestation.

She refused the blandishments and malice of manic emotion. Somehow she must sympathize. How could she ever sympathize with the vile furtive obscenity Elmer was inflicting upon Eva? Was she a dewy doe, and he a lumbering stag? She must be stronger than him. Resistant.

Her brother paid little heed to her enigmatic outburst. 'The missile was one that seeks heats. The heat of engines. Why did the Isi give him a missile?' This was what Elmer wanted to know.

'To put paid to Osmo, presumably.' Lyle adjusted the gold-rimmed glasses on his snubby nose, the better to focus upon this conundrum.

'Why should the Isi help Nurmi?'

'To stir up trouble.'

'Which Isi are we talking about?' croaked Lord Henzel. Elmer had to turn to Lyle for a reminder.

'According to Bergman the cuckoo said it was the Velvets.'

'Who live way beyond Saari.' Puzzlement knit Elmer's brow. 'Poor old Osmo couldn't have annoyed *them*.'

'Maybe he did. But how?'

'Poor Minnow,' muttered Eva.

Exasperation flared in Nikki, despite her resolution. 'Maybe the Isi heard from cuckoos how Osmo treated Juke Nurmi's sister at the gala! Maybe they thought it was unfair.'

Still her cat lay in abject distress, its nose pressed against her knee.

Lyle chuckled. His frizzy halo of hair seemed like a crazy golden crown. 'Do you think so, Nikki? The aliens aren't averse to misusing human women,' he reminded the group. He glanced down at Elmer's wife. His expression *seemed* innocent enough. 'Witness your own sister, Eva. Witness that peasant girl Jack Pakken brought to Pohjola Palace with him . . .' He slapped his brow theatrically, jolting his glasses. 'Hell, I'm a fool. Where did what's-her-name, Eyeno Nurmi, get that false eye of hers from? The eye that fooled Osmo? The eye she tore out and smashed!' He gazed at the distressed cat, reminiscing. 'When Gunther was here he was talking about spying on people's . . . dreams, wasn't it? By using some mana-mirror.'

Lokka frowned. 'I do remember that.'

'What are dreams but something you see inside of you? Eva, in Pohjola Palace you have some mirrors which let you see what your trained dogs are looking at a couple of keys away, don't you?'

Eva nodded cautiously.

'What if you fitted a tiny mana-mirror inside someone's eye socket disguised as an eyeball? You might be able to spy on what someone is perceiving keys and keys away. Hundreds of keys away. Without the person even suspecting – if they thought they had received the false eyeball as a gift pure and simple. You've put your finger on it unwittingly, little Nikki.'

Little Nikki? Was she now downgraded in Lyle's view compared with the *gifted* Eva? Unwitting little Nikki, who hardly realized the significance of what popped out of her lips . . .

Elmer's dark mellow eyes were troubled. 'A spy-lens in a totally plausible eye? It's an idea. I'm not sure *I'd* know how to begin to make such a device . . .'

'Maybe that's because it isn't only a machine,' snapped Nikki. 'It looks like something human. More human than your brass dwarf upstairs. It looks like a real human eye.' She mustn't be *strident*.

Her brother directed a mystified grin at her. 'I suppose the Isi might know how. When she threw her eye away, thanks to Osmo, they lost their observer. That must have enraged them.'

The *goof* did not know what was wrong. He had no idea.

'What might a mutant poet girl witness that was interesting?' mused Elmer. 'The gala? Cuckoos would be cackling about the gala. It beats me.'

Lyle smirked fleetingly at Eva and offered her a hand to help her rise. She shook her head. 'Minnow too,' she muttered.

Bergman, the baker, bustled from the stairway out of breath. The mana-priest followed close behind. Ruddy-featured, and with flame-red hair, Moller practically glowed with rude health.

'I'm here, Lord Henzel,' he announced in an exuberant, ringing tone.

'I sent a *boy* for Ma Grünwald,' Bergman told the bailiff.

'My cat collapsed,' said Nikki.

Unbuttoning his charcoal jacket with a triple flip of his fingers, Moller swooped down beside Nikki. 'Your cat collapsed, Miss Loxmith,' he confirmed.

Moller was given to stating the obvious. He would always establish the skin, or shell, of a situation before proceeding to less visible circumstances. 'Mana be with me,' he murmured. Shutting his eyes, he passed flexing hands slowly over Tommi a finger's breadth above the fur. The longer hairs poking from the panting cat's coat served as his guide. Moller was in contact with

375

Tommi yet at the same time hardly touching the cat at all.

'Maybe this Juke is an agent of the Velvet Isi,' Lyle was saying to Elmer. 'Just like his sister. Now he has insinuated himself into Lucky's court.'

Elmer sucked in his cheeks, considering this possibility.

'Just *who*,' added Lyle, 'was supposedly looking after Jatta and her kid when the Isi grabbed the boy?'

'Juke Nurmi was,' agreed Elmer. 'No, wait a moment.'

Lyle didn't wait. 'After Demon Jack escapes to Sariolinna, Juke turns up there too. If Jack Pakken genuinely *did* escape from the Isi.'

'Hang on, this doesn't mesh somewhere. Damned if I can put my finger on it.'

'Ah, isn't that because Nurmi supposedly got his missile from the Velvets? Whereas it was the Brazen Isi who took the boy?'

'Juke Nurmi couldn't be an agent for two Isi factions at the same time. They're rivals.' How angular Elmer seemed.

'Probably Juke didn't sell Jack Pakken to the Isi after all.'

'That's right.'

Nikki began paying more attention to Lyle's drift. He was suavely leading Elmer along in one direction then in another direction, sowing a little doubt here, a little confusion there, trapping him into minor contradictions – all in an apparently innocent fashion, had Eva not been part of his audience.

'Naturally,' continued Lyle, 'we *assume* the various Isi are rivals. Are they really?'

'Come again?'

'Maybe the Isi don't think in those terms. Maybe their activities complement one another's. What was special about the poet girl that they put a spy-eye in her? What was she likely to see? We'll never know now that Osmo put paid to her. So the Isi put paid to Osmo.'

'I'm getting befuddled . . .'

'That's the idea. The Isi strategy.'

And Lyle's? It all sounded such an innocuous conversation (although about weighty matters, or at least weighty implications) yet it was really a game of cat and mouse, with Elmer playing the part of the unwitting mouse, squeaking in response whenever a paw slapped him in a new direction. Elmer didn't know. Nor could Henzel or Lokka realize. Lyle was acting as Elmer's *adviser*, wasn't he? In anticipation of his future role at Lord Elmer's side.

'Suppose, on the other hand,' Lyle carried on amiably, 'that what's-her-name, Eyeno Nurmi, actually knew she was a spy . . .' Lyle seemed capable of continuing in this meandering vein for as long as he pleased, leading Elmer by the nose. A house of cards: did Eva appreciate such cleverness? Eva was paying more heed to the talk above her head than to Moller's hand-passes over Tommi, but she was shivering as she listened.

Could Lyle contrive to relieve Eva of her gift without Elmer ever being aware of this? Until Elmer began to age, and Lyle didn't?

'Brave faces, sister,' Nikki whispered. Eva nodded, determination in her eyes.

The mana-priest's hands had been hovering over Tommi's hindquarters, fingers twitching. Now he looked up.

'I can sense a massive blood clot blocking the vein that drains the hind limbs and pelvis. That's why the hind legs are paralysed. Iliac thrombosis, to be exact.'

'Paralysed,' croaked Henzel.

'Do you mean Tommi wasn't poisoned after all?'

'No, Miss Loxmith. This is most unusual in a cat. Could be due to prolonged inactivity . . . The animal's muscle tone is strangely flaccid.' Unlike the purrs, which continued remorselessly.

Prolonged inactivity.

'Is Tommi in pain?'

'More in panic. He's lost touch with half of himself.'

'What can we do?'

Moller's hands, which had diagnosed, now spread apart impotently. 'I wouldn't pin too much hope on Mother Grünwald. The clot could break up and lodge in the heart. That's what I'm sensing.'

'Elmer should build a cart on wheels for his hindquarters,' Nikki said bitterly. 'With a shit tray attached to it!'

'Nikki!' chirped Lokka.

Her brother swept back his mop of black hair. 'A cart's no use for a pernicketty cat. For a dog, perhaps . . .'

'Or even for a man,' said Henzel.

Bending right over, Nikki laid her cheek next to Tommi's head. 'Tommi, Tommi, we're so sorry. You'll have to be brave.'

'Meeee,' moaned the cat.

'Even for a *man*.' Elmer repeated himself uneasily. 'If this happens to a cat, it could happen to a man. It might happen to Gunther . . .'

'I'll carry your pet with me, Miss Loxmith, to a quiet place. A very quiet place.'

'Remember that he can speak! He understands you.'

'Not fully; not just now. I'll carry him very carefully. Mother Grünwald will help me ease him.'

'Where is she? Where is she, Andersen?'

'On her way, Miss Nikki,' promised the bailiff, though he sounded unsure of this.

'Soon,' said Elmer. 'Soooon.' Causing Nikki – to her annoyance – to begin crying. Soon comes death, not a bowl of fish.

'I'm coming with you, Mister Moller.' Nikki sobbed.

'And I'll come too,' said Eva.

Moller frowned. 'This cat . . . only has one future. It might distress you both.'

'Am I scared of being hurt?' Eva asked the mana-priest.

The bailiff clapped his hands as a sweaty kitchen-lad in shorts and string vest erupted into the corridor, calling out, 'Sir!'

'This'll be Ma Grünwald—'

However, this lad wasn't a forerunner of the wisewoman. Following behind came a well-built young man with blond hair lapping his shoulders. His brown corduroy shirt and breeches and boots were travel-stained. At the topmost step he stumbled as if he might have continued mounting more steps which weren't there at all. His boot crashed on to the floor as he recovered his balance. He looked muddled. Perhaps he was exhausted.

The newcomer's brow was broad. His was a frank, open face, though the corners of his mouth drooped. His blue-eyed gaze wandered over the group, not quite connecting with anyone as yet.

He hitched his shoulders to galvanize himself into action. To Elmer's consternation he announced, 'I'm Lord Beck's nephew, Cully.'

An early dinner time. Curtains wide open, evening sunlight slanting. The gleaming brass automaton fed Lord Henzel. Lokka was in her pink glitterbug gown. Eva wore violet silk to complement her tattoos. She and Nikki and the newcomer sat opposite Lyle and Elmer; however Nikki hardly touched her portion of fish pie . . .

Just before Mother Grünwald had slid a sharpened harnie quill into Tommi's neck and blown through it, the pet had stared at Nikki and mewed hopelessly.

Then he had whimpered a couple of words, which might or might not have been *love you*. A last appeal. Or a last desperate ploy, since Tommi had never previously said such a thing to her. Still, it almost broke Nikki's heart.

Love you. If indeed those had been the words.

Very soon Tommi's heart stopped too, and his eyes became glassy. Fish: not soon. Never ever again. Thanks to Elmer's wretched cat-cradle.

On the unexpected arrival of Gunther's nephew, Elmer had leapt to the conclusion that something was amiss with the full-size version of the hibernator monitor.

Tommi had emerged from the junior version in January. By mid-April, when the last of the ice and snow had almost all gone, Elmer had completed Gunther's commission to his own complete satisfaction. The contraption resembled a bizarre coffin without a lid, softly padded inside so that the dream lord wouldn't succumb to bed sores. Wires and dials. Isi powercells in triplicate. A four-month clock (to be on the safe side). An arousal device. Other gadgets which Nikki's brother and Lyle enthused about . . .

The two men had loaded the cradle on board the *Sea Sledge* for the wending journey by lake and river-chain to Castlebeck. Ten days later, Elmer and Lyle returned, mildly disgruntled. Gunther had put on more weight yet he was experiencing the qualms of a bashful bridegroom. To confront his dearest dream after so long! He wouldn't make use of Elmer's machine immediately. That would be too precipitate. Now that the machine was safely in his keep Gunther would contemplate the cradle for another couple of weeks or three. He would meditate a while longer on his forthcoming dream-quest.

Nikki was glad she hadn't gone along to Castlebeck for an early springtime outing (give or take some late flurries of snow). For Gunther ordered his dead wife's casket to be moved up from the crypt to his private chamber to rest on low trestles alongside the hibernation monitor. He did not yet re-open the tammywood coffin to lay bare his wife's bones, but he did request from Elmer a cable with clips at both ends to link the little skull-box which the dream lord wore on his chest, with some part of Anna Sariola's skeleton. Taken aback by this untechnical notion, Elmer had nonetheless complied.

When Lyle reported this zany aspect of Gunther's plan – relating it with a certain mischievous relish to compensate for a 'financial disappointment' – Nikki had felt very queasy. To sleep so deeply, clipped to a skeleton. To sleep, courtesy of gland-juice from serpents which shed their skins. Gunther's wife had shed not only her skin but all of her flesh. The symbolism seemed sinister.

Maybe Gunther had intended to fluster Elmer. It transpired that the dream lord hadn't quite amassed enough tithes to pay Elmer the two hundred golden ors which were still outstanding . . .

While Nikki's brother and Lyle were at the dream lord's keep, Cully certainly hadn't been in residence. Nor had Gunther said anything as to his nephew's whereabouts. Yet here the young man was now, at dinner in the aitch-house, acting oddly.

'No, nothing's wrong with Uncle Gunther,' Cully assured Eva once again.

Elmer smiled fondly at his wife's excessive concern. 'Cully has told us six times by now! Gunther began hibernating, when was it *exactly*?'

Cully's broad brow creased. 'Ah . . . June the . . . mm. In the first week.'

'Can't you remember exactly?' pressed Eva. 'Didn't your uncle originally want you to look after his keep while he slept? So I hear. Why has he changed his mind?'

'Yes, Uncle Gunther changed his mind,' agreed Cully.

'Maybe he was wise to,' Nikki whispered to Eva. 'I wouldn't want this fellow to look after my . . .'

My cat.

She had forgotten momentarily that Tommi had died a few hours earlier. She still expected Tommi to come begging round the dinner table, if he could insinuate his way into the dining room. *Fish pie tonight.* A maid in starched apron dallied in the pantry where Nikki had rushed for salt. Stinging grains to thrust stupidly and well-meaningly into her paralysed pet, tormenting him with thirst perhaps.

Lokka cleared her throat. 'Nikki, this young man's our guest.'

'I'm less than a guest, I'm afraid!' Cully's countenance was full of innocent apology. 'Uncle Gunther sent me here to work for you.' His hand jerked so that he nearly upset his beer glass. 'I shouldn't be imposing on you like this, at dinner. I really should be eating in the kitchen.'

380

'Eat in the kitchen? Work for us?' asked Elmer. Comprehension dawned on Elmer. 'Oh, because of the *money* Gunther still owes . . .'

Cully flushed. 'Yes, he owes money, doesn't he? My uncle owes money. He sent me here to work for you instead of looking after the keep; and he sent me with a bit of money too. It grieves me to tell you I had an accident on the way. Some men attacked me.'

'Attacked you?'

Elmer frowned imploringly at his wife.

Cully drooped. 'I was hit over the head, you see.' Eva peered at his tumble of blond hair but failed to see. 'I find I'm forgetting things . . .'

'Such as where you were for ages while your uncle was searching for you?' Eva glanced at Nikki for confirmation.

'Exactly!' said Cully. 'Precisely. I feel such a fool. I know I had to come here to work for you. And pay the money. But I lost it.'

'Do you believe any of this?' Eva murmured to Nikki, her lips hardly moving at all.

'You ought to be home at Castlebeck while your uncle's asleep,' said Elmer.

A panic gripped Cully. 'No, I mustn't do that. Mustn't. It's a matter of honour! Uncle Gunther's honour, my honour. I must work here. *Please.* I can turn my hand to most things from mucking out stables to, well, most things. Mucking out would be fine.' He eyed Lord Henzel, whose mirror was angled to reflect Cully. 'I'm not a true nephew, you know, sir. I oughtn't to be at your table. It's an impertinence.'

'You seem an amenable young man,' Lokka said to soothe him. 'We'll settle on some suitable work for you tomorrow. Don't you agree, Elmer?'

Her son nodded, but Eva was persistent.

'Can you describe these men who attacked you, Cully?'

'There were three of them, Mrs Loxmith . . .' As if this was a description. Conscious of the inadequacy of his account, Cully strove to relate an ambush somewhere in some woods. The details were woefully deficient. There'd been one assailant with long blond hair, who sounded like Cully himself. And a burly bald fellow, who bore a suspicious resemblance to Andersen the bailiff. Along with a red-haired man, who might have been the Loxmiths' mana-priest – the third man wore a mask, so Cully could only see his hair. The trio had quickly pulled a hood over their victim's head, before knocking him unconscious. Thus he hadn't seen too much. Lyle, rather than Elmer, signalled furtively to Eva to desist from further questions. She shifted awkwardly on her cushion.

'Are you enjoying your pie?' Eva asked their guest instead – she didn't really want to heed any of Lyle's suggestions.

The young man's face lit up. 'Oh *yes*. It's so tasty.'

Despite the bundles of herbs at the window a fat suckerfly had hummed its way into the room. Cully's gaze followed the insect as it veered this way and that. How fascinated he seemed by its random route.

Tommi had been so good at catching flies. Clapping them between his paws. Even snatching them from mid-air in his jaws. Gotcha.

'No,' vowed Cully, 'I mustn't go back to Castlebeck till Uncle Gunther's awake again. I must pay off his debt, mustn't I? I must do some honest work.' He brushed back his long hair and looked around the table, smiling gratefully and sadly at everyone.

'That young man's under a sway,' said Lokka afterwards, over coffee. Cully had pleaded fatigue and departed to his guest room. Next morning, as was his wish, he would relocate to a humbler lodging in the aitch-house.

'A sway,' mused Elmer, ill at ease.

'Don't you know about such things?' asked his bride softly.

'Seems harmless enough, if a bit ham-handed . . .'

Lyle glanced fleetingly at Elmer's own large bony hand; and Eva leaned forward as if to ease herself.

'He intrigues me rather.' Her tone suggested that Elmer's assistant, by contrast, did not intrigue her. 'This reluctance to go back to his uncle: I wonder what the true reason is?'

'I suppose we should try to find out for Gunther's sake,' Lyle said to Eva.

'Yes, I ought.'

'Don't interfere with a sway,' advised Lokka.

Now Eva had a little project to help distract her from the damned outrage Elmer was inflicting on her. And from the news about Minnow, coming on top of her father's murder. That distraction, thought Nikki, was probably good. Nikki's fingernails idly raked the tablecloth, cat-like. Why didn't Elmer have scratches on his cheeks, as he so richly deserved? Yet that would be undignified. Eva prized her dignity.

Tomorrow Nikki must really quiz her bosom confidante about

– yes, what Eva knew of Demon Jack, who had *saved* a woman from indignity . . .

Unlike Elmer. Or Osmo, who inflicted it egotistically. Unlike Lyle, for that matter.

The sisters-in-law would talk and talk together. What might they be able to plot which would alter circumstances?

26 · IN THE DOME OF FAVOURS

The first that Eva knew of Jack's arrival in Pohjola Palace was from an excited Minnow. Bundled in a coat of tawny tarandra fur, the junior sister raced into Eva's lamplit chamber – sending the door crashing back against the panelling – and spun around twice as if this was the only means by which Minnow could possibly slow down.

'Jatta's boy's come, Evie!' Minnow tore open the toggles of her coat. Melting flakes flecked the fur and her frizzed-out hair, though it hadn't snowed recently. Snow clung to her peaked leather boots. She stamped. 'Cuckoos, it's boiling in here.'

The pot-bellied stove was indeed radiating heat, though not stiflingly so far as Eva was concerned. She sat in white-satin chemise and underskirt at a dressing table littered with spangled combs, brushing her hair. Outside, the afternoon night was gathering in, the sky a purple velvet casing for the arc of silver sickle which hung a slim bright awning above frigid mountain peaks as if a slice of ice had floated loose weightlessly from the greater ice below.

'He's a young man now! Looks sixteen if he's a day.'

'Do you mind shutting my door? What are you talking about?'

Minnow threw her coat towards the bed, which was intricately carved with all manner of knots: splices and hitches, reefs and figure-eights and sheepshanks. These tangled decoratively along the foot and sides, attaining a mazelike profusion upon the huge headboard.

'Warming up for her wedding to whomever,' the elfin girl informed herself. She slammed the door. 'Younger sisters make do with fires of peat to toughen themselves. Jatta's boy flew a little Isi sky-boat here, Evie. Jack brought a woman with him

383

too – she's been a prisoner of the Jutties. Unmen used her to look after him – bears quite a resemblance to a Sariola, she does. Such a wind came with him. What a wind when he landed. Tossing a ton of snow into the air. I was right there in the sky-boat yard. All our Evie's busy about is dolling her tresses,' she added breathlessly. And added again, 'He *does* look sixteen if he's a day! He's grown up as fast as a mushroom. I mean, that's really important. Maybe he'll *die* of old age in another year or two.'

'Calm down . . .' By now Eva was piling up her hair hastily and thrusting combs into the mass to pin it. She shook her head to see what might tumble loose. Little did. 'Do I look decent?'

Minnow giggled. 'Evie, you're still in your underskirt.'

'I know that, sprite!'

'I can see the dent of your girdle.'

'Does Jatta know about her boy yet? Does Mother know?' Eva headed for a narrow wardrobe towering near the stove and chimney-pipe to pluck out a thick green woollen dress. No, not this one, but the burgundy one.

Minnow seized her coat again to sling round her shoulders. 'So why did I need to shut the door when she'll be out through it in two flicks of a lamb's tail? That's what I'm wondering, aren't I?'

Guards had steered Jack and Anni to the Dome of Favours. The stained glass of the cupola above was blanketed with snow, a patchwork of compressed wool dyed faintly blue and pink.

Godlike and gauche, a fresco of hairy heroes in homespun garments strode around the curving wall, illuminated by the hanging oil lamps. In the gaps between those swaggering figures, bodies a quarter their size were suspended at all elevations and angles. Seemingly children at first glance, those were likewise grown men, and a fair few were women. Between the pygmy figures floated many other persons, aslant and askew, who were still more diminutive. Amidst whom, tinier folk were in turn blown about willy-nilly as if on a breeze.

Thus a mass of humanity receded into imaginary distance. Or emerged from it. A jigsaw of people giant and medium and wee crowded the interior surface of the dome-chamber: an audience extended in time and space. Up on a scaffold, mumbling to himself, a bearded artist in smock and beret was painstakingly adding a further miniature inhabitant to the mob. He painted with a tiny brush upon the chest of one giant; for yes, there were bodies within bodies. On second or third glance this became evident. Creases in garments were actually little limbs. Tiny men and tiny women inhabited the blowing hair of heroes.

Petitioners would come to the Dome of Favours to appeal to Queen Lucky or Prince Bertel or, more sensibly, to the palace chamberlain. Suitors would present themselves here. Would they be ranked as heroes or midgets?

A dozen sofas formed a loose half-circle before a carved and padded throne. Their upholstery was a brown and cream tapestry of woven faces large and little. Faces within faces. Dozens, hundreds of faces gaping expectantly in different directions. All wanting something.

Very soon, as word spread, the dome grew almost crowded – quite as if figures were leaping out of the fresco, though actually people were entering by any of five different arched doorways. Minnow and Eva arrived first by a hair's-breadth, to gape at Jack and the young woman who clung to his arm.

Ester and Sal and Kaisa scampered in together with a trotting guard, followed by an indignant yet fascinated Mrs Simberg. Clerks and maids came, consumed with curiosity, risking a scolding for leaving their tasks. Mana-priest Serlachius, his face ruddier than ever from the rush. With him, that guest from Earth, Roger Wex with all the pockets in his cloak. Wiggy Wethead. Cooks and carpenters. A minstrel with his harp.

The Dome of Favours was a public hall, though the decor inhibited most residents of Pohjola Palace from idling in it very often to court or to hobnob. At times one felt that one might be pulled into the all-encircling fresco, to shrink and diminish. As for sitting upon so many woven faces, why, those might bite or prick up their ears!

More spectators arrived by the moment, including stout black-clad Nanny Vanni with baby Hanna in her arms, and a guard whose boredom had evaporated like steam from a hot hob. Here came lanky chamberlain Linqvist in formal frock-coat, white kid gloves, knee breeches, and broad crimson cummerbund, a powdered white wig upon his head.

Prince Bertel took loping elastic paces, golden epaulettes bouncing upon his shoulders. Lucky herself followed close behind, in a long gown of deepest purple and a velvet cloak trimmed with bluish verrin-fur. Her sapphire tiara was planted askew. Raven hair strayed every which way as if the Queen had been raking it with her fingers just before word came.

385

Through another doorway hurried spiky-haired Jatta. Jatta stared with a shock of recognition at the young woman with the large dusky eyes and chubby cheeks who was clasping her protector. She gazed at that escort himself incredulously.

Jack wore a glossy one-piece livery of coppery hue, a black glyph upon one shoulder. A Juttahat livery, such as she had seen upon her boy's abductors. He was Jatta's own height, and of wiry build. There was about him such a sense of dancing energy held in check. His skin was the colour of cinnamon, his eyes amber, his jet hair as cropped as Jatta's own.

He was Jack. Certainly he was Jack. Jack, transformed. Taken away from her, then restored after seemingly fourteen or fifteen missing years – which had been no more than six months. Jatta felt very much older than her own years, as though it were she who had aged prematurely. She stepped hesitantly towards him.

'Jack? Fastboy?'

How radiantly he smiled at her. 'Jatta Mummy, do you remember the robberbird I threw through the grove to make it fly again? Do you remember the lake where I learned to swim while Juke made you tell him stories?' His voice was a mellow tenor, the accent teasingly exotic.

'Oh yes . . .' Tears welled in her. 'I do, I do.' It was him.

His woman companion was trembling. Her blue woollen gown wasn't as thick as it might have been for a winter's journey. Relief and anxiety were written on her face in equal measure. In her free hand she clutched a crumpled filmy bundle. The serpent-skin suit, of course. That body-stocking with which the Brazen Isi had controlled her . . .

'This is Anni,' Jack explained.

'I remember you . . .' Anni's teeth chattered. 'You weren't able to—'

Weren't able to save her from slavery. Jatta was wearing a suede tunic over calfskin trousers, but two of the guards sported long grey cloaks over their padded white winter leathers. 'Give her your cloak,' Jatta told one of them. She helped drape Anni.

Jatta's mother had paused by the scaffolding to view the encounter. Above her, the artist had slipped his brush between his teeth and spliced his fingers together while he watched. The joints cracked explosively.

'Mikal,' the Queen called up to him whimsically, 'how soon will you be done?'

Mikal pulled off his beret and peered down. 'I'm cramped, your Majesty . . .'

'But how soon?'

'It's endless.' He twisted the beret in his fists like a dishcloth. 'Essentially it's endless. If I finish all these mini-figures I'll have to fit micro-figures inside 'em, won't I? The number increases all the time—'

'Why are you wearing a Juttie costume here?' Jatta asked her son. 'Couldn't you change?' Such a trite question – rather than '*What happened to you during the whole of the last six months and more than twice that many years of your life?*' A motherly question perhaps; a broody hen question.

'To point to where I've been, Jatta! So as not to seem to be an impostor.' Jack didn't call her Mummy now. Indeed, she wasn't a broody old hen at all. She was a scant few years older than he looked.

Lucky strolled to the throne and seated herself, with Bertel in attendance. He whispered something in her ear but she shook her head.

'Fastboy,' she called, 'can *you* help Mikal finish this fresco? By speeding him up?'

'I can help the wind and the light and the cold, Grandmother. The light that stuns a creature, the cold that chills them. That's how we escaped. I can hurry the birds and beasts, but it isn't good for them. I can make flowers bloom, but they'll die.'

Lucky began to question him. Could he or his lady companion understand the jargon of the Juttahats? Some, was the reply. Not enough. Hardly sufficient to follow fluent hisses and clicks. Those who supervised him and Anni had spoken in Kalevan.

Why had they let him escape? Because of the light that stuns. The cold that chills.

'Show us, Fastboy. Show my mana-priest, so he'll understand. You won't hurt him, will you?'

Jack shook his head. 'He won't move for a while after . . . And the light and cold will leak.'

Spectators withdrew up against the fresco of huge heroes and smaller persons and smaller still. Lucky summoned the nearby guards, who drew their lightpistols as a precaution.

Jack smirked. 'Light's fast. Far faster than me. I once tried to catch light moving but I couldn't. Because it's so fast, a person can seem frozen.' He walked away from Anni and Jatta to face the portly mana-priest, who eyed him calmly. The pupils of Jack's own eyes dilated. 'Try to run away from me, fat man.'

Hands upon his belly, Paavo Serlachius breathed slowly and deeply, scorning the jibe and Jack's glare. He had no intention of being mesmerized.

'Feet, be fleet,' the priest chanted. 'Toes, to go. Shanks' ponies skipping.' He launched himself away from Jack.

Began to.

Briefly all the light in the Dome of Favours seemed to gather around Jack. Conversely for a moment Serlachius became a pitch-black silhouette, an unmoving image captured by the flash. Spectators rubbed their eyes as snowflakes swirled within the dome – but the panes in the cupolas hadn't given way beneath their burden. Hoar-frost iced the priest's curly hair as if his head was a florid cake. In the hush, many muffled voices muttered. Linqvist, who had seated himself on one of the sofas, rose slowly, though his motion pantomimed haste. The sofas were talking quietly to themselves, but soon were inaudible.

Serlachius stood poised, half-turned to hurry away, going nowhere, doing nothing. Not a finger twitched.

What Jatta had felt for a few seconds was a state of perfect balance. She might have been at the centre of everywhere, and thus she experienced no need to move anywhere at all. Indeed, she had possessed no ability to move . . . How different from the itchy haste with which that popinjay van Maanen had formerly afflicted her!

Osmo, whom sister Eva had taken something of a shine to at the gala, regardless of his contempt for a fugitive burdened with a young child . . . Eva had also taken a shine to Osmo's bosom pal Elmer Loxmith. What might Elmer's quirk be, which Eva was blithely disregarding?

Jack had shone just now, like the sun. Jack had saved Anni from the Juttahats. This Anni had been their slave, with whom Jarl practised love-making . . .

Suspicion dawned in Jatta. Might Anni have been compelled to . . . initiate Jack similarly? After being a proxy mother to him? Hence the snake-skin garment she retained as a souvenir?

What a misgiving, so soon after her boy's wonderful – and daunting – return to his mother! Anni deserved befriending; Jatta owed that to her. Pohjola Palace must seem as alien to Anni as the Isi nest. Anni's teeth were chattering. Jatta took the young woman's hand and squeezed it comfortingly. In a sense,

Jatta was the author of Anni's misfortunes. Snatched from her farm, Anni had acted as the puppet substitute for Jatta, erotically and then maternally.

'That's really impressive, mm?' Minnow had sidled up. Jatta's younger sister gawped at Anni. 'Poor you, being a body-slave. How did it *feel*?'

Jack clapped his hands. Performance over; though not in the case of the mana-priest. Not yet. Serlachius still aped a statue. Jack yawned; he returned, erratically, towards the throne. 'I'm so tired,' he said. 'So hungry.'

'Bring tisane of mustaberry and sweet tarts,' Lucky ordered her chamberlain. Linqvist jerked a gloved finger at two nearby maids. The maids curtseyed and fled – of course that's really why they'd been here in the Dome of Favours. To await such an order.

If this miracle youth was tired, now was surely the time to ask him questions. Such as how he had navigated his way from the Brazen Isi nest to Sariolinna through the wintry sky. Could he see clearly in bad light? In darkness too? How had he known which way to head?

'My mother talked about Pohjola, Grandmother. What other Great Fjord is there up here in the north? Just a question of flying till I found it. Where else should I come to? I want to serve you. You're the Queen.' An eager young squire was Jack.

'And now you're reunited with your mother,' mused Lucky. 'Quite a while before I'm reunited with myself . . .' Bertel rested a hand gently on his wife's shoulder. She nodded fretfully. 'How could you be sure my Jatta was here?'

Jack rocked on the balls of his feet. 'Your sky-boat came to the valley where the sheep were on fire. You must have taken my mother home. My father said so to quieten me.'

'Your Juttie daddy . . . the zombie. Yes, how is he?' Lucky darted a droll glance at Jatta.

'Oh quite,' whispered Minnow. 'That's vital.'

'He has nearly forgotten who I am, Grandmother. They gave him a mind of his own. They let him have his head. He was a prodigy they'd made, a marvel among Juttahats—'

Jarl. A prodigy. Yes.

'Now they have to enter his mind to direct him for his own sake. He jerks and lurches so. He's disgusting.' Jack peeped at his mother shyly, pity and puzzlement on his young face, which was now weary. How could she have embraced such a person as Jarl? Yet if she had not done so, Jack wouldn't even have existed.

'So you're seeking your own identity,' said Lucky. Her tone was kindly. 'Aren't we all? At least some of us are.'

Jack was born of myself, and myself, thought Jatta. *Really, I'm his identity . . . The key to it. He had to come here to find the key to himself.*

'You wouldn't have fled to serve Grandmother otherwise.' The title obviously amused Lucky. Grandmother of hundreds, mostly dead. Great-grandma'am of thousands. 'You must resent me for abandoning you. Once in the womb, twice at Speakers' Valley. Well, *don't you resent me?*'

Jack shook his head so innocently. Anni was tensing up, no doubt anxious that sanctuary might be refused.

'Excuse me, Your Majesty,' interrupted Wex. Though Lucky scowled, the agent from Earth persevered.

'Your Majesty —'

{An appeal to her megalomania!}

'— the young man must be a mine of information about the Isi, even if he mayn't appreciate all that he knows right now.'

{Might half of his brain be Juttahat? Could he have been programmed?}

Wex twitched. 'We mustn't be too suspicious, not after his demonstration of will power, merely because he's a hybrid —'

{This is dubious biologically.}

'It isn't dubious, because the Isi hope to control human beings by means of,' and Wex gestured at the serpent skin garment clutched in Anni's hand, neglecting to name it. 'Or by any other means, Your Majesty.'

A mischievous smile puckered Lucky's lips and dimpled her cheeks. Already one maid had rushed back, bearing a silver tray of blueberry tarts in rye crust. Jack wolfed one tart, guzzled the next, and merely worked his way through the third while the maid stood simpering before him.

'With Jack's help we might be able to impel a certain Isi to spill its knowledge. Together we might —'

'Together,' echoed Lucky. 'Your motto, eh?'

{She's mocking us.}

'You and yourself together haven't made much progress so far, have you, Wex?'

Wex glanced around the chamber which seemed so crowded, not merely by spectators but by all those figures in the fresco, faces in the sofas. *{Everyone knows there's a mage in the dungeon.}* 'Yes, everyone knows there's a mage in the dungeon,' Wex agreed.

390

Lucky laughed. 'You're coming apart at the seam, my jester! So how shall *I* ever reunite myself?'

What did she mean? Reunite herself?

{*Don't mention the everything machine just now.*} 'Everything,' Wex mumbled plaintively.

Lucky heard him. 'Reunite everything, and everyone? Hold a party for all my dead daughters?'

It was true that Roger Wex was cracking. People weren't meant to have a voice in their heads unless they accepted it implicitly and totally. His starvation appeased for the moment, Jack had dropped half a tart back on to the tray. 'This dear voice in my head!' exclaimed Wex. 'Closer than a brother. Do you have one too?' he demanded of the dark-skinned youth. 'No, you don't. Of course he doesn't. But because I do, together we might crack the mage.'

'Was it like that for you?' Minnow asked Anni breathlessly. 'A dear voice in the head? A voice you couldn't disobey?'

Serlachius had begun to move at last. Ponderously he continued his manoeuvre to decamp from Jack, though Jack was no longer in his immediate vicinity. The younger Sariola girls giggled as the priest took one slow giant stride then another. Already Serlachius was recognizing a discrepancy between his intentions and achievement. Correcting his headlong plunge, he tottered and nearly fell. His right arm swung out as counterbalance. Hoar frost was melting from his hair. His ruddy face gleamed damply as he turned to seek Jack.

A cry of: 'Cuckoo in the palace—'

'Cuckoo coming—'

'Shut the doors at once!' bawled Lucky.

Spectators scurried to obey her.

All five doors swiftly banged shut to seal the Dome of Favours.

'Is there no privacy?' she demanded, eyeing the audience of daughters and maids and craftsmen, and nanny and governess and Wex. 'Snow-cuckoo, Bertel? It must have been roosting in some nook. I hope they throw it a chick.' Especially she eyed Wex.

{*Privacy is the friend of shameful thoughts, Wethead, of solitary fantasies and antisocial desires. Juttahats exhibit no mana-manias; nor do you. You must concentrate more clearly. You mustn't feel resentment. I am you.*}

'Shut up a moment! You're stopping me from concentrating.'

'Wex,' cooed Lucky, 'are you speaking to me?'

'No, your Majesty. Not at all. I was saying that together the young man and I might succeed—'

'—in rendering our mana-mage absolutely taciturn? Or completely contradictory? You needn't plead on behalf of my miracle grandson, Wex. Of course he must stay here with me.'

With me. With Lucky.

Not exactly with Jatta.

Yet of course Jatta would be seeing Jack constantly. Talking to him. Learning of his capsuled life till now. Absorbing his existence. Discovering how a child could mature in a mere six months; and what he had become. While, equally, Jack would chatter to her, to discover who he was at heart, and how. Jatta would tell him everything freely, gladly. Any barrier of privacy between them would be poison. He needn't be another Juke, squeezing her secrets out of her before bartering her to her mother in exchange for a getaway from the Isi. Jack had rescued Anni from the Isi. Perhaps Juke had rescued Jatta likewise? The Brazen Juttahats had brought Anni along with them to Speakers' Valley in her serpent skin. Would they have snatched Jatta too? Abducted a Sariola daughter? Maybe not. Lucky might have declared war on them in rage. Juke hadn't really saved Jatta at all. No more than he had protected his all too beloved sister.

Her fast boy had certainly saved Anni.

Now he was *eager* to serve his ever-youthful grandmother. Keen as mustard. How else could Jack be close to Jatta, source of his being, unless he ingratiated himself with Lucky? Did he sense himself growing older at a breakneck pace?

Don't torment yourself.

He'd been separated from Jatta for six months – and almost his entire youth. How distant did he feel from her?

'Would you like to share my room with me, Anni?' Jatta invited. 'Live with me, for company? Unless . . .' Jatta couldn't help glancing at the serpent skin suit hanging loose from Anni's fist.

'Wouldn't you be hoping to share a room with Jack?' piped up Minnow, all ears. 'I mean,' she gabbled to herself softly, 'Anni and Jack might very well be *intimate*, seeing as he took the trouble to rescue her so romantically and maybe our Jatta doesn't suspect such a thing . . .'

Of course Anni heard. Jatta too.

'Jack and I don't,' mumbled Anni, tongue-tied.

Minnow was all enthusiastic innocence.

'We haven't, honest.' Anni's tone betrayed the peasant she'd once been – once upon a time, before being groomed by Juttahats. 'We wouldn't. Jack wouldn't, even if I—'

'Oh,' Minnow told herself, 'so the Jutties must have tried to bring it about. I suppose they would want Jack to breed with a woman . . .'

'Be quiet,' snapped Jatta, though without too much conviction.

'Recently too, otherwise Jack wouldn't have been big enough . . .'

'Shut up, Minnow.'

'We escaped,' Anni told Jatta, 'and I brought the skin with me so that no other woman would ever have to wear it. I suppose they can produce more skins like this one. I didn't need a skin to make me rear your boy, Jatta, once I knew him. He was my only comfort. You aren't jealous of me, are you, Jatta?'

'Don't pay attention to Minnow.'

Anni flushed. 'Jealous that I raised your boy, I mean.'

Jealous? Jatta should thank Anni, just as Jack had thanked her by freeing her. She *was* thanking her; she was offering to share her chamber with this luckless marvellous woman who had survived body-slavery and the lustful rehearsals of Jarl masquerading as a man.

Revulsion at the thought of this slavery swept through Jatta – and disgust at her own captivation by that radiant cocksure phoney lover.

Disgust. Outrage.

Jatta gasped. She wasn't under Jarl's sway any longer. The sway had gone from her. It had dissolved, evaporated. She had beheld her alien lover as a zombie. Yet that spectacle hadn't truly altered the sway. Jarl had persisted within her. He had been like some indelible tattoo. Now Jack's presence dislodged that other presence within her. She was free – because Jack was here, her dusky amber-eyed son.

'I'm free,' she whispered in amazement.

'I'm really just a peasant girl,' said Anni. 'You're a princess.'

Free, because her fast boy was here in the flesh, grown almost to manhood. She was released, just as Anni had been released. Jack had displaced Jarl utterly.

To the refugee woman Jatta said, 'We're closer than sisters, Anni.'

393

'Oh *well* now,' said Minnow.

Eva was making her way towards Minnow and Jatta and Anni – in a more dignified and leisurely manner (though strands of her hair were coming undone from the combs). Her smile was suave.

'I'm so happy for you, Jatta. It's all working out so nicely after all.'

Silly vain Eva, silly pert Minnow. Both so sure of themselves.

By now Paavo Serlachius – not one to hold a grudge, or display rancour publicly – had recovered his composure sufficiently to applaud Jack with several resounding hand claps. 'Quite a master of the mysterium,' was his lofty comment. And Jack? He looked almost asleep on his feet.

Lucky called to her chamberlain: 'Mister Linqvist, arrange a room for my grandson. Somewhere near my quarters. We'll continue this interview later. As for Jack's companion—'

Jatta spoke up. 'Mother, I'm sharing my room with Anni.'

Lucky laughed. 'Very wise. Very caring. You can chatter and natter to her about your mutual interests. Let the cuckoo in now, Paavo. Sing it a story, tell it a tale. See if there's snow on its plumes. Make sure it has a chick to chew. Wex, you might take a look at that serpent-skin suit. Try it on for size. See if your better half can use it to control you thoroughly. Mikal, carry on painting.'

27 · INTERROGATION OF A SNAKE

If Bertel could bear to don such a pompous uniform of gold braid and epaulettes to please Queen Lucky, why, Roger Wex could stoop to wear a see-through body-stocking made of serpent skin if this stratagem might help to unlock the secrets of an alien mana-mage.

Even if the suit in question had been fashioned for a woman's body. {*It has been rendered supple and elastic. Distinctions of gender are individious.*} He was well aware of that.

Even if the suit had been used for sexual slavery. {*Regard this as an exorcism and redemption.*} Just so.

Wex felt naked and vulnerable beneath his cloak as, lantern

in hand and shivering, he descended a broad spiral stairway into the underbelly of the palace to rendezvous with Lucky and Jack and the mana-priest at the vault which served as dungeon. {*Body-shame is the partner of body-exploitation. Desire without respect should be psychologically impossible. What is often seen is not a secret.*} Wasn't that a fact?

{*Be warm; stop trembling.*} Actually, the serpent suit seemed to hold in his own body heat tolerably well for so flimsy a garment. Flimsy but tough. {*You are tough in spite of Paula Sariola's mockery. She is petulant at being thwarted. Her jibe about wearing the snakeskin may prove to have been an inspired suggestion.*} But of course. The captive mage was from the Brazen nest and it had brought the woman Anni to Speakers' Valley. It understood the snakeskin suit. {*It may try to control the wearer. I shall block its control. I may discover how an Isi mage goes about this. Needless to say, the whole human race could not forcibly be clad in cast-off serpent skins as an alternative to controlling our minds directly. Even if our own experiment has no significant results, at least Paula Sariola will have been taken at her word. Outfaced, upstaged by you, my Wethead.*} Would he look more impressive in the body-stocking if he dispensed with his wig as well as his cloak?

Wex had reached the bottom of the spiral. Along a dark corridor: an all too familiar pool of lamplight. A pair of guards stood attentively outside the mage's large cell. Table and chairs and stove were set outside for their creature comforts during the winter-long vigil. The other two guards would already be within, lightpistols covering the Juttahat chained to its stone ball, and its serpent master. {*Juttahats fail to use mana-power. Yet Jarl cast a sway over Jatta to seduce her. The Isi made him have his own mind. His own will. He was unique. Still, he was loyal to the Isi and his own kind.*} Wex walked along the corridor, gaberdine cloak clutched around him. The guards acknowledged him. Cards and coins lay on their table.

The liveried Juttahat had hoisted its master and stood like a bandsman with a stout brassy instrument coiled around chest and shoulders – except that the Juttahat was really the instrument. Serlachius was peeping warily into the clouded mana-lens in its silver hoop. The shaman from the tundra, whom Lucky had detained in Sariolinna for the past six months, chirped quietly from behind a mask of iridescent greens and blues. The mask was meant to mimic a robberbird. '*Crukk, crukk,*' he said. '*Crukk-crukk-crukk.*' His tin discs tinkled. Jack wore his Juttahat livery – which was almost identical to that worn by the serpent's mouthpiece except for a different black glyph upon his shoulder. Lucky had been scratching noughts and crosses in the sand with the tip of her scarlet boot.

Her tiara twinkled in the light from numerous massive candles. 'You're late,' she told Wex.

Bertel was warming his hands at a stove. The flue rose up the granite wall like some rampant black snake itself, to squeeze through an aperture of the same girth cut high up in the vault and surrounded with spikes. Split little minty logs formed a neat stack. Regurgitated lamb and piglet bones, a small heap. Burning wood scented the air with a fresh clean tang.

Of course Wex was late. He had argued with himself about wearing briefs or a sash or an informal scarf around his loins either underneath or on top of the body-stocking. The snakeskin fabric was split between the legs. Any priapism, and he'd be sure to protrude.

{We shall dampen your reflexes. Yours is a well-tuned body. We exercise you isometrically, and in tae-kwon do, tai-chi, and kung-fu.}

To be sure, but the mage might still somehow afflict him with priapism. This could be a gross breach of etiquette in front of a queen.

{In a sauna all is seen.}

Sariolas didn't seem to patronize palace saunas.

{You have not detected this, but virgin daughters wear unusual girdles. I have noted definite signs. Minor matters of posture and pleat. This odious archaic contrivance guards their chastity. We shall safeguard your decorum through inhibition.}

A discreet little apron might have been a good idea.

{Trimmed with lace? Borrowed from a chambermaid? Ridiculous and coy! Anni wore the skinsuit and nothing else. Jatta told Eva this. Eva told Minnow. We overheard Minnow relating this to herself, though you failed to notice. The human brain is largely unused. Yours is being used to a greater extent, my Wethead. Lucky expects you to perform just as Anni performed. If Lucky does not expect this we shall astonish Lucky.}

Hence, his late arrival at the interrogation. The dispute persisted.

The brazen serpent appeared tarnished today. Its once shimmery scales were dull shingles in the candlelight. There was a milky cast to its eyes. When Jack shuddered, the Isi shivered.

'Are you warm enough to talk, Honoured Mage?' Lucky asked solicitously. 'Is your den hot enough? Are you sick?'

The long, scaly head swayed from side to side as if the alien was experiencing difficulty in seeing her. Surely it wasn't going blind? Its forked tongue flicked out. Faint pastel bubbles of light drifted up from its sharp little horns.

'Being disturbed again.' The mouthpiece sounded irritated on its master's behalf. The Isi's blurred gaze drifted back towards Jack in his Juttahat attire. A tart odour wafted from it, briefly souring the fragrance of burning mintywood.

'Are you ill, Mage? You don't look very well.'

'I think it's getting ready to shed its skin,' Jack confided to his grandmother.

{*Highly likely! The outermost layer of skin is dead by now. New skin and scales have formed beneath with precisely the same pattern of ochre and rust. Its lymph system secretes a thin layer of fluid to separate the old skin from the new. During the day before the moult this fluid will be re-absorbed. Its eyes will clear. We believe this is how Isi biology operates, akin to that of terrestrial snakes. A serpent is a bio-form, just as a tree is a form of growth rather than a species. Right now the mage must be feeling vulnerable.*}

Wex related this to Lucky.

A puff of light fizzled feebly above the mage's head. '*Crukk-crukk,*' chirped the shaman.

The serpent peered at Jack as sharply as it could. 'Wearing our servants' clothing. Hoping to dizzy us?' asked its body-slave.

Jack spoke some hissing, clicking words of Juttahat.

'You being whom?'

'I'll tell you if you tell the Queen all she wants to know. I promise you'll find the answer worth your while!'

{*He is a child in many respects. Such eagerness.*}

'Why finding your answer so valuable?' The mouthpiece's gland-slits leaked a few dewy beads while the serpent strove to see Jack. 'If so, we must be knowing the answer already!'

Jack tensed himself in concentration. 'Tell the Queen everything she wants to know about the everything machine.'

'Everything about everything?' The Juttahat displayed its purple tongue. It coughed huskily and softly. The serpent's sides heaved in a seeming mimicry of laughter at the enormity of this demand. A scent of caramel prevailed briefly.

Jack stirred the air briskly with his left hand. 'Fog that hides, be gone. Light, reveal.'

The twenty fat candles flared up, flames dancing high. Serlachius held out the mana-mirror, which was no longer so opaque. All of the increased illumination seemed to focus dazzlingly upon the tarnished mage in its bearer's arms. The mouthpiece shut its eyes.

'I'll be Juttahat,' said Jack. 'I'll be the voice of the mage. I'll speak about the everything machine. I'll seize thoughts from the mage's mind.' His right hand plucked and clawed.

The mouthpiece jerked and the Isi hissed, displaying fangs.

'*Crukk!*' said the shaman, masked as the bird which would steal food from a plate then even the fork as well.

'Everything machine, great Mage!'

{*Jack doesn't know what she wants from the machine.*} Unless Lucky had confided in Jack, of course. {*Confide in someone who is essentially a child?*} Lucky might tell a child secrets she wouldn't tell to an adult. {*Jack wants to please his grandmother so that he can stay near to his mother, and learn all about his origin. Or else he is a mystery to himself.*} Jarl Pakken could have told him all about that origin. {*Jack's origin was his mother's womb, and the line of Lucky. He had to meet his grandmother. He may not have more than a few years to live. His urgency is extreme.*}

'The everything machine!'

Bertel's hope that the man with two minds might establish an intimate connection with the Juttahat, and thus with the Isi – a persuasive, forceful, mimetic rapport whereby to pick the mage's mind – had proved futile. On how many occasions had the shaman croaked and danced and drummed in the dungeon to avert hostile mana? How many times had the priest brandished the mirror circumspectly? How often had Wex and his better half tried to align themselves mentally with the shackled Juttahat?

On twenty occasions within the first month of Bertel's delivery of the agent from Earth to his wife! And all in vain. The mage remained equivocal and terse. Mainly it demanded the return of the stolen piece of equipment to Isi custody. Wex had learned precious little about the machine from those early interrogation sessions. Afflicted with a defensive dementia on the subject, Lucky was not about to confide more than Wex could make the mage reveal, which amounted to a few obscure conundrums.

By the end of that first month in Pohjola Palace, as the northerly winter loomed, it was evident that Wethead Wex wouldn't succeed in browbeating the mage. Whence dated Wex's decline to the status of a mascot. As such, he provoked either glee or exasperation. Yet at least had become established as a fixture around the court. Like a favourite Spitz hound yapping at its own reflection.

In January, at the time of the snow festival, Lucky had finally decided to let Wex inspect the machine. Doubtless the mage did know words which would command the device into action – but the mage was taciturn. Surely this Earthman posed no threat to Lucky's sovereignty or to her private plans. Maybe Wex himself (or his better half) might *stumble* upon a means of triggering the machine. Consequently, one frigid day two horse-drawn sleighs had set out from the palace by way of the Zig-Zag Gate . . .

A narrow covered roadway from within the palace complex veered left, then right, then sharply left again before emerging into a large square from which much wider streets radiated into Sariolinna town.

On either side of the exterior gate heroic ice sculptures stood sentinel, sustained by mana-spells as well as by the bitter cold. One was of a warrior with Bertel's wistful features, wielding a glittering sword. The other was Lucky, five metres high in ice armour, a fanciful crown of spun-ice upon her head suggestive of a three-tiered wedding cake. The sickle she brandished honoured her sky-origin and her harvest: of daughters, and of the wealth of a world. On the final afternoon of the snowfest two days hence, so long as there wasn't a blizzard, these ice figures would march ponderously down Sariola Boulevard to the nearby harbour while fireworks exploded overhead, drenching the snow with colour. Out across the frozen white-carpeted fjord they would tramp, following a line of poles flying a spectrum of pennants, while shamans danced and drummed on shore to urge the sculptures forward. Tipsy spectators would wager on how far those statues of ice could be shifted. To the yellow pole, to the green, to the blue? Perhaps, this year, to the violet pole? Wherever the images of Lucky and her consort halted, there they would remain until the fjord finally thawed, the actual day of their submergence offering another pretext for bets.

Smaller sculptures in ice or snow stood here and there along Katarina Avenue which cut through the town diagonally, and which the two sleighs took as their route. A bard with a harp, its strings of ice. A prancing goat with a man's features. A giant leaperfish balancing on its tail. Outside snowy-capped timber buildings, portable ornamental lampposts of wrought iron reared on tripod legs, their lanterns aglow with burning oil throughout this week. Horse-hauled sledges fitted with spring-loaded flukes for braking slid smoothly along over the slippery impacted snow. Skiers glided, packs on their backs. Children skidded as fast as they could along narrow runways. Top-heavy kick-sleighs scooted at chancy speed, propelled by foot, the steerers yoiking warnings. The noon sky to the south was a deep turquoise, draining into pink, the pearly rim of the sky-sickle almost resting on the mountain peaks. In other directions the heavens were sombre, funereal. Soon it would be afternoon night again.

Bells jingled. Horn calls tootled. In the front sleigh, with Lucky, rode Wex and Bertel and Linqvist, all bundled in furs. The escorting sleigh carried guards in white padded winter leathers, and General of the Guard Viktor Aleksonis, distinguished by a double-breasted greatcoat and a scarlet bicorne hat with plumed cockade {*resembling an old-time admiral's headgear. Or General Napoleon Bonaparte's*}. Who was he? {*He lost a war one winter in a snowy country.*}

Pedestrians applauded when Queen Lucky passed by. They thumped their gloves together. Their breath puffed out. Cheers were quite visible in the chilled air. Silence too would have been evident.

Ice daggers hung from gutters. Trees wore intricate combs of hoar frost. In lamplit Lucky Square serrated glassy spears rose several metres high from a fountain as if the onset of freezing, three months earlier, had been instant – a mana-sculptor had been at work.

A gaunt unkempt fellow had darted from behind the fountain, coat tails flapping. He shrieked at the light still lingering in the southern sky.

'I proclaim, I proclaim!'

Lucky waved to rein in. The pony veered into a low snow bank to brace itself and slow the sleigh. A hundred metres away the hysteric raved.

'I bespeak the sun. Can you see it rising from the ice? The ice steams! The snakes have frozen the sun.'

Of course he was no proclaimer. No proclaimer – even a Tycho Cammon – would have tried to command the sun. To attempt such a futile endeavour would have been to strain at a vast impossibility – and to risk rupturing oneself, tearing one's muscles apart; the muscles, also, of the mind.

The man's gaze lit upon the sleighs.

'Do you see the Queen?' he bellowed. 'Black Queen, Queen of

darkness! Where's the blonde Queen hiding, Queen of sunlight? We are all dead here! Our real selves live in the sun.'

Lucky had stood up, transfixed by his wild words.

'Our sunlight selves, and the sunlight Queen – she's the *real* Queen!'

His ravings had really affected Lucky. 'Give the lunatic light!' she cried.

In the accompanying sleigh four guards rose as one, aiming lightrifles and lightpistols.

'Don't!' For she had already changed her mind.

Light was faster than words, though. Light had lanced on its way. The hysteric's coat burned. He screamed, he fell.

'*Why did you do that?*' Lucky squealed at Marshal Aleksonis. A bunch of bloodflowers seemed to bloom in the snow against the fallen man. No, merely blood itself. {*And now, too late, she wants to talk to the dead man. Data: Paula Sariola was once blonde-haired. After she made contact with the Ukko entity her hair was black as coal for ever after.*}

'The Swan has him now,' Aleksonis called back. 'He can't insult our Queen any more.'

Lucky sank back alongside Bertel. 'Sweet mana, he might have *known* in his frantic mood.' {*Known what? We should remember this.*} 'He might have divined.'

Her prince was staring at the corpse. 'Looks so easy to die. One moment bawling at the sky and the next moment *iced . . .*'

'Don't become melancholy on me, Bertel! Swear to me you won't.'

'I won't,' he assured her. 'How can I?' Hauntedly he smiled. 'My love won't let me weep.'

And the sleighs had continued onward.

After crossing town and then some way beyond, they came to the fortress in the fjord. Stout low curtain walls ringed a small island a few hundred metres offshore, commanding the approach from the west to Sariolinna harbour. The drivers urged the ponies down a gentle slipway near an iced-up boatyard and on to the snow-clad frozen firth. Horns hallooed as the sleighs sped swiftly across.

Granite blocks loomed around a broad iron gate with a lock in the shape of an ear. General Aleksonis quit his sleigh to whisper into this metal lug, careful not to freeze his lips to it. Chains rattled. Grating, the gate opened slowly inward on little wheels set in curved rails recessed into the stone flags.

In the darkening courtyard six sentries stood woodenly to attention. Snow clung to them. Each held a projectile rifle with bayonet upright. Of course they stood woodenly. What else but wooden soldiers would be coated in snow? Fully life-size, the sentries wore large cylindrical peaked hats seeming more like ornamental hatboxes, rendered taller still by a fluffy white capping. {*Those hats are called shakos, my Wethead.*} Knee-high boots. Dark uniforms, which might have been blue, with trimmings which might have been orange, showed vaguely through the deposit from blizzards. The snow covering the courtyard appeared perfectly smooth and unblemished by footsteps until the advent of the ponies and sleighs, and their passengers who now dismounted. The last gloaming lingered, though stars were already prickling overhead. The sleighdrivers lit bright lanterns, passing these out to the well-padded white-clad guards.

'Attention!' barked the General.

Those wooden sentries were already ram-rod rigid.

{*A different sort of attention, my Roger.*}

The six soldiers began to pay attention. Their wooden stance relaxed. They stamped their boots; they slapped their coats and breeches. They shook their shakos, dislodging snow. The butts of their rifles thumped up and down. Those sentries weren't wooden now; they were living breathing men. Puffs of fog wreathed their dark faces.

'—Brr, it's cold.'

'—Brr, it's mid-winter.'

'—Bitter enough to freeze the balls off a Pootaran monkey.'

'—Off a wooden monkey, right?'

{*Data: a monkey was a triangular brass frame. It held a pyramid of spherical iron missiles for launching from a primitive large gun. In very cold weather brass shrank more than iron because of the different coefficients of expansion, and contraction, of the respective metals. Thus balls sometimes fell off. These soldiers are unlikely to know this. Their idioms are fossils.*} The sentries were fossils of a different kind: people who had been turned not into stone but into wood – wood which could become flexible as flesh again upon command. {*On the island of Pootara the black rationalists make wooden monkey-puzzles as well as puzzle-spheres and boxes. Monkey-puzzle is also the name of a prickly tree. Words melt and mix.*} Was Wex's wetwear disconcerted by this enchanted garrison?

'—Who goes there?'

'—It's Lady Luck.'

'—*Your Majesty!*'

402

'—General, *sir!*' Rifle butts slammed upon the snow. Lucky waved a hand in greeting.

'They're hard men, these,' she told Wex. 'Very hard men. No human raiders or Jutties would ever break into this fortress with impunity, would you say?'

Wex found it hard to say.

'Hard men. Woodmen.' She gestured at the donjon rising murkily from the courtyard, crowned at one corner with a stubby tower. 'Two score more are waiting inside. Oh, look now!' She pointed. On the low battlement of the thick curtain wall a pair of silhouettes patrolled. Her fort was coming to life. Light flooded on to the snow from several windows in the main building, towards which the party now headed, leaving the sentries to march to and fro.

'Woodmen,' Wex repeated. This was perfectly true, but what exactly did she mean?

'How?' he asked.

'You've heard of Tapper Kippan?'

{*The Forest Lord. A longlife. His keep lies approximately two hundred keys south-west of Landfall—*}

Wex nodded impatiently, and the Queen laughed.

'Both of you have heard! This was his gift to me when he wooed and wedded, hmm . . .'

'Edith,' prompted Bertel.

'Thirty years ago.'

'Thirty-five.'

'No, I'm sure it was thirty. Or maybe not. The Kippans know wood secrets, don't you see? It's different down there in the southerly forests. Here a young shaman will climb into a tree to seek the star in the sky which is his and his uniquely. There he eats a mushroom and *becomes* a tree for a year and a day—'

{*This confirms reports. A mutated fungus lives in symbiosis with a certain tree called the mootapu—*} 'If you transfuse the sap into a man's blood, he can be made wooden and insensible; then flexible subsequently.' Lucky beamed at Wex.

They were nearing the doorway to the donjon. Wex nodded uncertainly at General Aleksonis who had ordered the wooden soldiers to become animated.

'Don't you need a proclaimer on hand to do this?' {*Can commands be stored in advance?*} 'Can commands be stored?'

'My commander here at the fortress *is* a proclaimer. Or should I say *was*? Not a major proclaimer, understand. More of a captain

403

proclaimer. He and his men are a unit. They all spring into action if an intruder comes. The same sap flows in all their blood. He was able to bespeak them all to service, and thus himself too.'

'You mean he *volunteered* for this sort of life?' {*Do the Isi know about this method of controlling people?*}

'I assure you that they dream very pleasantly indeed while they're wooden. And they will live for a very long time.'

'Your wooden soldiers are totally obedient?'

'And fearless; and as hard to wound as a tree. Why shouldn't they be loyal to the youthful mother of Kaleva? Why not, Wex? They're very special people, my fifty wonderful woodmen.'

'I'm sure.' If only she was equally forthcoming about the everything machine. What she really wanted it for.

The Captain stood in the doorway of the donjon, which an oil lamp now illuminated. His dark blue uniform was faced with crimson and gold lace. A tufted, crimson pompom rose high from one side of his shako, on the front of which a silver plate was engraved with a stylized tree. He wore a side-arm and a sabre. His face, completely hairless, had a distinct grain to it and was of a light reddish-brown hue.

'Madam,' he said, 'all is well, as always.'

'Thank you, Captain Bekker.'

'The fortress stays secure. The Isi machine is safe. It's good that we have an important machine to safeguard. But I've been wondering: what does the machine do? I ask in case it starts to do anything of its own accord.'

'Why, Captain, it does everything. Everything the heart desires. And so far,' she added petulantly, 'nothing at all. Tell me, Captain Bekker, what would you yourself wish for?'

The officer considered this question gravely, more out of deference than because he was racking his brain.

He slapped his scabbard with a gloved hand. 'I'm a soldier, ma'am. I would wish for cleverer weapons. More advanced ones, more cunning ones.'

{*This would be inadvisable. The Isi seem to maintain a definite balance of stimulus and response in their dealings with the human race, my Roger. And who would these cunning weapons most likely be used against but the servants of the serpents?*}

'You and your men are my best weapons, Captain. My paragons.' Lucky was being gracious.

Still, the officer sighed. 'We're never used as warriors. A fighter sometimes hopes to become a hero . . .'

404

'I wouldn't wish to lose any of my fine set of soldiers!'

{*I'm sure the Queen understands about this balance of power. That it shouldn't be upset. Thus she holds these wooden soldiers in reserve, as it were.*}

Said Bekker, 'The dreams are my bounty, a sumptuous reward indeed.' His gloved hand rose to brush his dark hard face. 'Still, I would quite like to wear a large moustache. While I'm awake, and on duty. A moustache of strong bristles so as to look perfectly military . . .'

Lucky inclined her head as if she sympathized thoroughly with such an ambition. She hugged her furs around herself and shivered. Taking this hint, the officer turned and led the royal party into the banner-hung hall of the donjon.

'Is there a kitchen anywhere?' asked Wex.

'Naturally,' replied Linqvist. His powdered wig was like a snowy hat. 'But we aren't staying overnight. Unless, of course, the Queen decides that we are.'

If anything the interior of the building was more frigid than outside. Logs of mintywood lay stacked in a massive stone fireplace.

'Wait here,' General Aleksonis told the accompanying guards.

'Shall I light a fire with my pistol, sir?' asked one. Aleksonis shook his head.

A stone stairway mounted from the hall. Several short corridors led off at ground level. At the end of one, waited a soldier with a lantern.

The party entered a substantial vaulted chamber. Hanging from brackets, several oil lamps burned. Mere slits of windows cut deep furrows through one thick wall, framing thin rectangles of darkness. Three sentries stood to attention in their blue uniforms and tall shakos, holding bayoneted rifles upright: the honour guard for a globular brassy apparatus resting on a low plinth of black marble.

Wex stared at the Isi device.

A fat sphere twice as large as a very big pumpkin squatted upon a rotundly bifurcated base. On top, balanced a smaller sphere the size of a human head. Centrally upon the head was set a fist-size metal topknot. Scores of similar protuberances studded the flanks of the apparatus, inviting fiddling and twisting. To a certain extent the ensemble resembled a pot-bellied stove. In another regard an obese, legless torso with voluptuous buttocks, the arms reduced to small swollen stumps, the head equipped with jug-ears. All in a brassy alloy. With so many knobs and lumps and nubs of assorted sizes. Inviting twiddling.

{*My Roger, this is plainly modelled on the humanoid figure at the heart of the Mandelbrot set of infinite iterations. That set contains itself within itself again and again for ever. This cannot be the actual everything machine itself.*}

'Could this object be a hoax?' asked Wex. A prank, to make an ass of the Queen . . .

Lucky stamped her boot crossly to crush such a concept. 'Absolutely not! Of course if you have so little confidence . . . ! If that's your best suggestion! Why did I bother bringing you here?'

'I'm sorry. I was merely exploring the possibility.' {*It must contain the essence of an everything machine within itself; and everything manufacturable must be stored in abstract within that machine.*} Wex groaned. 'I don't know *how* you know it's genuine. Even if the Isi told you so – why would they tell you? Even if their mage confirms that's what this contraption is, how can you be sure? Your Highness,' he added diplomatically.

{*Presumably this Mandelbrot model contains a brew of nano-assemblers of molecular scale programmed to construct a general manufacturing unit of more substantial bulk. The construction unit would need to be bulkier, maybe very much more massive. I hypothesize that the assemblers would be liberated from this vessel and would then cannibalize non-organic matter from their surroundings. I specify non-organic matter, since otherwise the device would be lethally dangerous to whoever activated the unit and perhaps to many onlookers.*}

'Could this be a booby-trap?' Wex asked himself.

'Of course not,' retorted Lucky. 'The Brazen Isi intended it for their own use. Tell him exactly how we acquired it, General. Tell him how we're sure what it is.'

At last!

{*The material cannibalized could be anything at all if the nano-assemblers can demolish and rebuild individual atoms—*}

'Tell him, General Aleksonis. Before we all freeze.'

This, the General proceeded to do, with some swagger which might perhaps have introduced distortions of detail.

Three summers earlier a shuttleship had crashlanded in inhospitable terrain several hundred keys to the north-west of Sariolinna. Vilely inhospitable terrain. Nomads over a wide area witnessed its descent. Within a week word reached Pohjola Palace. The shuttle couldn't be of human ownership, otherwise cuckoos would already surely be tittle-tattling. Must belong to the Isi. Obviously had been way off course. Out of contact? Lost, so that the serpents had no idea where it was? An armed expedition set out by sky-boat commanded by the General in person. (And later word came of an Isi Ukko in the southern sky.)

The alien craft had come down in an area of undulating bog-land interrupted by thrusts of forest. Many trees had no firm soil to anchor their roots. They sprawled along the ground, twisted cripples raising branches in supplication. When any wind blew, clusters of razor-reeds whipped to and fro, quite capable of slicing a man's exposed flesh. Ideally no skin should be exposed. It was summertime – and bug-hot, related Aleksonis.

Gnats clouded the air. Gads and sweatsippers, stingflies and piss-in-your-eyes zizzed and whirred. The General's men wore hoods with veils of gauze. Gloves and boots and stout leathers. So hot in this gear. Your vision was constantly blurred by sweat and gauze and mists of gnats. You could easily blunder into one of the stagnant pools of putrid black water masked by mats of moss from which ferns sprouted. You could stray into a quaking morass. Heaps of sodden hay clogged your path like the matted gingery hair of giants which had been sucked under and suffocated. Mats of leathery leaves were slippery as grease. The air reeked of pollen. A scum of pollen and peat-dust lay on ponds in which poisonous bladders floated. Everything – plants and insects, earth and air and musty water – was festering with activity during the short torrid summertime, fruiting further rot.

Had they not already spied the shuttle from the air – sprawled on a great nest of crushed saplings – they would probably never have found it.

The sky-boat landed on an esker ridge only a few keys distant. When this region had been glaciated in the distant past some ancient stream had flowed under the ice and deposited gravel, a stretch of which remained blessedly bare. Only a few keys from the crash site. Even so, it took Aleksonis's men upwards of two hours to traverse the intervening bogs. (Could the journey really have been so vile?)

Juttahats wearing soiled Brazen livery had formed a loose picket around the shuttle, taking every advantage of crippled tree or camouflaged pool. They fought fiercely – suicidally, ber-serkly – with searing light and explosive bullets and finally with long knives to repel the intruders. (Surely those Jutties must have been tormented by gads and piss-in-your-eyes, and maybe by thirst and hunger?) They killed two of the General's men (only

407

two?) and injured a third before all were despatched by light and bullet and sticks of dynamite.

On board the shuttle, amidst wreckage, the Juttahat pilot survived with both legs broken and other injuries. Suckerflies seethed on gore like living bandages. Dead flies littered the deck. The pilot was in a bizarre state of mind like someone fungus-fugueing. A brassy machine – this very one – was secured to the hull by well-padded clamps. The injured Juttie clung to the base of the device, beseeching it as if it was the golden idol of some tubby faceless god, limbless though with many knobs. Or maybe the pilot now mistook the cargo for a Brazen Isi master coiled round upon itself in a rotund pile, but comatose. The Juttie clicked and hissed in its own jargon, then broke into Kalevan as if this deity must surely understand one language or the other.

'Being able to make any apparatus we are desiring . . . whether for finding whatever is lost, we being lost . . . whether for mounting and riding away in leaps and bounds . . . whether for tracking mana . . . whether for gaining control . . . whether for . . .' (Aleksonis imitated its voice, and Lucky's eyes gleamed.)

The Juttahat seemed oblivious to the arrival of the General and his men. From its superstitious pleas to the pot-bellied roly-poly, Aleksonis gathered that the device could produce *anything*. Or at least a very wide range of exotic objects.

When they began to unclamp its god from the wall, the pilot had struggled fiercely, seeming demented. (Or did it scuffle feebly?) It clutched at knobs. Its tongue jutted out. Froth flecked its lips. Gland-slits oozed. Aleksonis shot the alien through the head as a *coup de grâce*.

It took six hours to transport their prize safely through the pitfalls of the bogs.

Would the Isi have sacrificed a *shuttle* in order to play a prank upon Lucky? Would they have crashed their craft in such a remote place, where no one might have come across it if nomads hadn't happened to see it descending?

Those nubs and knobs invited twisting and twiddling.

Wex approached the inert machine and laid his palms upon it. Not the faintest throb; no vibration. He twisted one knob, then another. Then a third. {*A veritable multitude of controls – unless these are decorations. A multitude of decorations. Perhaps they should all be twisted simultaneously?*}

'Perhaps they all ought to be twisted simultaneously.'

'Twiddle-twaddle,' said Lucky. 'How could sixty people all crowd close enough at the same time? The meaning of so many knobs must be that they aren't meant to be used. They're just there to bewilder. To lead the uninitiated astray. Have you no better idea?'

'Maybe what matters is the order in which they're touched?'

{*Approximately one hundred and twenty knobs little and large, times one hundred and nineteen, times one hundred and eighteen, et cetera, all the way down to times two. The result is a very large number of combinations, requiring thousands of years to run through the series.*}

Lucky smirked. 'Maybe you and your better half would like to stay here with my wooden soldiers and try that out? I'm sure it would only take a while. A few centuries ago I studied some mathematics on board our mining ship.'

'Maybe that isn't the best way,' agreed Wex.

So they had returned to the palace.

Concentrated candlelight lanced through the mana-mirror to bathe the mage's head brightly. Molten wax had pooled in the sand beneath the sconces. Though lacking any wicks, those puddles flickered with light. The prison chamber was torrid. The serpent rocked from side to side, almost overbalancing its Juttahat bearer. It was hissing constantly. The air reeked of grease and soaked dog.

'Shed light on *everything*,' chanted Jack, over and over. Then he paused. 'Hurry up, snake. Shed light.'

'How do I start the machine?' demanded Lucky. She glanced derisively at Wex for a moment before repeating her question to the mage.

The mana-mirror in Paavo Serlachius' hand was aswirl with rainbows inside rainbows, spinning around. Of a sudden the spectral vortex stabilized. The mirror clearly displayed Jack's features. Jack, now.

A moment later: a younger face.

A younger one still.

An even earlier face: of a skinny infant.

A baby.

A *foetus*.

'Knowing the answer now.' The Juttahat's voice was slurred, though a hint of mocking triumph sounded.

And a younger foetus.

Lucky stamped her foot peevishly. Serlachius shook the mana-mirror and spat on it. '*Crukk-crukk-crukk,*' croaked the shaman.

'Being the same boy whom our best of servants was causing to sprout in your daughter's womb, Queen Paula.' The Juttahat staggered.

'Yes!' cried Jack.

A small, simpler foetus floated there in the mirror. If it became an embryo – if it became a blastula – if it returned to its very beginning, what effect might this have upon the youth himself?

{*High time to intervene, Wethead. Seize the serpent from its slave. Displace the slave, using tai-chi. It will collapse like a puppet whose strings are cut. Replace it with yourself and ourself. Hold the snake so that it cannot bite. It will be shocked and it will try to control us.*}

'Your Majesty —' Wex shed his cloak, displaying himself for all to see in the glassy honeycomb of the snakeskin body-stocking.

'Wex!' barked Bertel. 'Cover your loins in front of my wife. Cover them this instant.'

Lucky stared incredulously at the Earthman for several seconds before hilarity convulsed her. She shook, she puffed. Her laughter could hardly escape. Confused, Wex snatched the curly black wig from his head. Adhesive strips ripped, exposing two penny-sized steel discs implanted on the right side of his depilated cranium. He was clutching the wig in front of his groin, a bush of hair.

'What's the meaning?' gasped Lucky. 'What's the *meaning* of this—' A guffaw burst from her.

At least the foetus in the mirror had stopped shrinking and simplifying. The Isi mage reared, milky gaze fixed blurredly on Wex.

{*It senses the suit. Knows it. It knew Anni. You must drop the wig. And act.*}

The voice in his head had told Wex. He launched himself towards the rampant serpent and its porter. His hips slammed. The blades of his hands prised. His forearms levered. His whole body thrust and pivoted.

Jack was dancing a burlesque of Wex, imitating, helping him.

Stunned, the Juttahat slipped. Smoothly Wex relieved it of the serpent's weight. A kick at the Unman's feet, and it toppled upon the sand. The snake's slave made no attempt to rise. Wex had the mage secure in his grip.

Or did he? The skin suit was somewhat slippery . . .

Wex flexed his muscles, exerting measured force with his biceps, triceps, flexors, pectorals. Regardless, the serpent's body was sliding.

He braced himself, his whole body becoming a ballet of musculature. A harsh oily odour assaulted his nostrils. Bubbles of
pastel lights popped before his eyes. The tumbled Juttahat was
writhing sinuously in the sand, moaning.

{*Pretend to be Juttahat, heeding the voice of your master, submissive to its will.
Become Juttahat yourself. Let the Isi be your god within. Let snakeskin mould
your movements. Let a channel open into its mind. I will safeguard you.*}

The mage's skin was tearing.

Coming loose.

Hissing like angry cats, the mage surged. Its mass heaved out
of Wex's grasp. It welled forth – leaving him clutching a coiled
tunnel of discarded skin; squeezing the air from it, collapsing it.
The mage thumped down upon the sand, twisting to cushion
itself. Its pristine self. Newly revealed scales shone lustrously.
Glyph patterns of rusty ferric and ochre brown were bold and
crisp. At first glance. Only at first glance.

The great serpent had moulted violently. {*Prematurely.*} Scraps
of dead skin clung here and there. Already the mage was rolling
to try to dislodge these.

A patch of new scale was twisted, another torn off as if the
skin had been branded with an ugly hand-shaped emblem.

The Isi writhed. Its head reared to inspect itself, pupils glossy
black once more, dilated and glaring.

'Being disfigured,' the Juttahat wailed on its behalf, beating
its palms on the sand. 'Being mutilated!'

The serpent coiled around itself to hide a hand-mark on its
side. Wex's hand-print. What should he do with the vacated skin
which hung down masking his loins? Offer it to Lucky as a souvenir? *At least I extracted something from the Isi. Namely,
itself . . .*

'Crukk-crukk,' croaked the shaman; and the mana-priest eyed
Wex scathingly.

Lucky blinked at the Earthman, wobbling between mirth and
wrath. The former mood ascended. What was the point in entertaining a clown who'd come all the way from Earth if he did not
amuse?

'Fiasco, Wethead,' she said. 'Don't ever try to be a midwife.'
Her laughter peeled, echoing in the vault.

{*In case you try to squeeze the baby out of its mother.*} 'I'm perfectly
aware of that,' Wex said aloud. {*My Roger, we are much better placed
as an agent with this persona as a fool.*} 'Thanks for your advice.'

Jack – Juttahat impostor – darted to snatch the sloughed

411

snakeskin from Wex. He balled up the skin and slung it into the
alcove where the Isi was accustomed to roost. A gob of spittle
followed. Candles were guttering, almost burned to the base. The
mage writhed in a passion of self-disgust. Wex made haste to
recover his cloak, and then his wig.

28 · WHERE ONE STATUE STOOD BEFORE

Minnow had begun to sympathize with Roger Wex because she
habitually talked to herself. So did the Earthman.

By confiding in herself Minnow solved puzzles about people,
and reassured herself. Being quite little and still looking no older
than fourteen – well, maybe fifteen at a stretch – could be a pain.
Since Jatta's homecoming, Minnow noted that Eva had begun to
treat her rather more as an equal. Valued her opinion. Now that
Jatta's boy had also arrived in the palace, *well*!

Whistling, Minnow sauntered along arcaded Perfume Passage
which housed a herbal pharmacy and a laboratory for processing
civet from the anal glands of arctic billygoats and musk from
the penile sheaths of bull tarandras – a Sariola monopoly. The
air was cool but heady. She was intent on finding Jack Pakken,
who bobbed about the rambling palace unpredictably. Quite
likely he'd be with Jatta or Anni or both, but she did rather wish
to corner Jack on his own.

She came upon Wex instead.

The Earthman was sitting on the pedestal at the foot of a
lamplit statue of Minnow's mother. The effigy was twice as large
as life, regally robed, and composed of black and white stones
jigsawed together with the craftiness of a Pootaran puzzle. Not
so much a chequerboard as a chequerbody. Minnow just *knew*
that, given a few hours, it should be possible to prise the entire
effigy apart and reconstruct two smaller female figures in its
place. One black, one white; one twin nice, the other perverse.

In her pointy-toed boots Minnow tiptoed up behind Wex (that
green cloak, the curly black wig). She had lost her silly retired
guard Max who sometimes tried, demeaningly, to check on her
whereabouts just as if she was a really junior daughter, merely
because she rather resembled one. Was Minnow likely to be kid-

napped out of the heart of Pohjola Palace in the depths of winter? Hadn't she recently taken to wearing a sharp knife on the belt of her tunic? She would probably have asked herself these questions *sotto voce* had Wex not been muttering audibly.

'What do you *want* from the machine?' he was asking. 'What do you *want*, Lucky Sariola?'

Wex wasn't exactly talking to *himself*. It was surely the statue he was addressing, but perhaps his second self was interrupting him silently.

'No privacy, that's the problem,' Minnow couldn't help but comment.

Wex gave a start. 'Princess Minnow!'

'Do you mind?' She perched beside him on the pedestal, and clutched her blue breech-clad knees up to her chin. 'I don't want to tease, Mister Wex.' She gazed earnestly into his close-set brown eyes. His eyelids fluttered as if something within was taking refuge, or was trying to prevent him from gazing into her eyes in turn.

'Jail bait,' he mumbled. 'What does that mean?'

'You're having a frustrating time here, aren't you?' She teased at her frizzed-out mane, and pulled one hair loose.

He flushed; he sat on his hands.

'We ought to be friends, you and I. I mean to say, I have problems; I don't mind telling you. Being little as I am. Will a suitor truly want me as his bride, and love me, looking quite like a child?'

Wex pursed his lips. 'Some men on Kaleva might, for that very reason.'

'Or will he only pretend? Actually, I was looking for Jack. I'm really glad I came across you instead.' Jack had grown so swiftly and surely, unlike her. Jack was her opposite, and consequently fascinating. Despite his mana-power and spates of vigour he was disadvantaged. He'd had hardly any chance to reach her own state of maturity, had he? He was still a child. Thus he was akin – and opposite. Jack knew all about the Brazen serpents' underground palace! Or something at least. Quite like a hero. Like a hero too he had rescued a slave woman – even if Anni was a peasant; though what did that matter?

'You were talking to the statue, Mister Wex. I suppose that's a change from talking to oneself. A statue will neither agree nor answer back. Unless of course it's a person who's been proclaimed into a statue . . .' She cocked an eye up at Lucky's stone face, one plump cheek white, the other black. 'What do you want from your machine, Mother dear? That's what Mister Wex is asking you.'

A porter passed by, balancing a tray of fragrant hessian bags on his head. Puckishly Minnow slid her sharp little knife from its sheath as if she might sneak after him and slit a bag or two. Instead she twisted around and prised the point of the blade into a thin seam in her mother's stone robe where black met white. When Minnow removed her hand, the knife remained precariously implanted. Cautiously she twanged the hilt once. Twice, and the blade fell out. The knife clattered on the tiled floor.

'Are you planning to carve your initials on your mother's knee, Princess?'

'No, no, now listen. This should appeal to you – with the two of you being joined up together, so to speak . . .'

She explained her theory about this statue which had been standing here at the end of Perfume Passage since whenever: that it was actually two statues in one, or at least could be converted into a pair of smaller versions side by side. There was ample space for two effigies on the pedestal. *Obviously* you should deconstruct from the head downwards, otherwise the upper parts might topple on to your toes. The nose should be tweaked out first to gain access. Or one of the ears must be twisted and pulled. Most likely an ear, black or white.

'To reach an ear, you'll have to lift me up, Mister Wex. Will you? Will you tell me all about Earth while we work? I promise I'll tell you what my mother wants most in all the world – she told me when I was a *really* little girl by way of scaring me. Most people don't pay enough attention, do they? Gosh, I can tell you things just as if you're *me*.'

'Can't I simply tell you about Earth? Must we demolish a statue?'

'Oh, you see that's all part of it! Part of my mother's dream.'

An elderly sweeper wandered along the passage, pushing a broom. A laundress with a big white bundle hurried by in the opposite direction, nagging a little girl who stumbled at her heels, half-blinded by a second bundle. 'Keep up, keep up! Don't drop the wash or I'll fettle you—'

'People will think we're *meant* to be taking the statue apart. Why else would we be doing it, Mister Wex?'

Wex shuffled. 'It'll be in keeping with my other exploits.'

*

'Hold me tighter!'

Wex increased his grip on Minnow's hips. Already the effigy had been dismantled as far down as the bosom. Notched chunks of smooth stone lay in two piles, one black, one white. To twist and pull out the left ear had indeed been the first point of entry. For ten minutes Minnow had deftly been applying a kind of isometric finesse to the components of the statue, tugging, swivelling, pushing, lifting free. After each capture, Wex lowered her to deposit another small piece on its heap, then hoisted her up again. Really, she was an ingenious young lady, even if she might land him in hot water. It was quite true that they had a rapport. He could feel it. {*Beware.*}

And while he lifted and held and lowered her, which was easy for one of his physique who exercised scientifically on a daily basis, he had started telling her about the homeworld.

'What a huge number of *places* Earth seems to have,' was her opinion. 'No wonder people stay close to home.'

'Travel that's unnecessary wastes resources and pollutes.'

'And all those languages too. It must be terribly confusing. Though with all those places how can everywhere be so crowded? Ah, that's why you don't eat animals – there's no room left for them!'

'No, we must leave space for animals – our ancestors damaged so much of the web of life already.'

'Aha.' Another piece came free. Wex lowered. Minnow stacked. Wex lifted her.

'Do you dream about Earth or about here, Mister Wex?' she asked from up above him; and against him.

'Ah. Well. My partner stays active while I'm dormant. So it dominates. My dreams echo its activity. Usually it plays chess with itself, so that's what I dream. But that's fine. Ordinary dreams try to solve problems symbolically, don't they?'

'Poor you,' was her comment. She squirmed to readjust her position. 'You're strong, but you're a softer person than when you first came to court. I suppose failure mellows a man if it doesn't make him wretched. Not that you're a failure! Minnow should wash her mouth out. Ah.' Yet another piece.

Down, and up again.

Wex confided in her about his abortive use of the snakeskin body-stocking – abortive of the moulting serpent; and she giggled, then tutted. 'I must make friends with Anni, that's really important . . .'

'Please do!'

'And tell you what I discover? Ah, now here's a naughty twist. A Pootaran *definitely* made this statue—'

Presently they were able to work side by side, both standing on the pedestal, and the deconstruction speeded up. Down past the waist.

Did Wex's companion oppress him? Why no, it was a comfort not to be alone. Juttahats must feel this way, though to a much greater, more imperative degree. A comfort, yet sometimes confusing, especially of late. Couldn't be true that he was cracking up. Helping a mischievous girl take a statue apart wasn't eccentric in the circumstances; it was a symbolic act.

'Quite right,' agreed Minnow.

'Your mother's dream,' Wex reminded her.

How had it come to be *him* of all people on Earth who was chosen to be a wethead? Who was Roger before he became Roger-plus, with the joined-up mind?

'I was in the Pee-Pol,' Wex explained. 'The Peace Police, serving the people.' He almost trapped himself in a tongue-twister. 'People, Pee-Pol,' he repeated, as if imitating a cuckoo. 'Everyone should really police herself, himself.'

'As your other half polices you?'

'People and police should ideally be one and the same, do you see?'

She saw a white stone which needed joggling to remove.

'I was in intelligence, Minnow.'

'And now intelligence is in you. Symmetrical!' Black piece and white piece, clasping each other like hands.

Numerous residents of Pohjola Palace had passed by (some more than once) during the hour it took to dismantle Lucky's statue. Stare as they might (or might not), no one had thought to interfere. At last, two considerable heaps of pieces confronted a bare pedestal.

Time passed more taxingly now. While Minnow picked through the black pile, hoping to find a former section of shoulder or cheek which might form part of a new smaller foot, Wex thought he saw how to make a start on a shorter white statue. Alas, opportunist intuition didn't help at all. So he began arraying the white pieces side by side in neat rows to form a grid of stone chunks, all of which he would be able to scan in unison.

'Mister Wex?' prompted Minnow.

His hands continued shifting pieces.

'Roger!'

'Eighty-eight pieces times eighty-seven times eighty-six,' he told himself.

'My mother's dream is to find herself. She's convinced that her Ukko copied her, and that the copy is what came back to rejoin her parents because her hair was blonde and afterwards it was black as ink. She thinks she's still really in the Ukko, sane and cheerful. Or in some part of the Ukko that's separate from it now. Split off from it, just as she was split off from herself. She wants to find that part, and herself—'

Wex eyed her distractedly. 'I'm dreaming, Princess. Dreaming. I'm seeing a grid and eighty-eight white chesspieces made of stone, all of different shapes, though not vastly different. That's forty-four pieces a side. My wetwear's absorbed in the game. How can white play against white, unless we really concentrate? I'm dreaming. I heard you, yes. We heard you. I'm dreaming, and I'm awake.'

Minnow jumped up. 'Pay attention, Roger! It's really important.'

'The wooden soldiers pay attention in the fortress. I *am* paying attention. We are. How to put Lucky together again. How to start the machine so that she'll put herself together.' His hands turned over smooth notched chunks of stone. The shadows which the pieces cast seemed to irritate him. He tried to brush those away. 'I'm Roger Wex of the Pee-Pol, Princess. A person of the people.'

She shook her head sadly. She nibbled at skin alongside her thumbnail, biting a morsel loose.

'And what,' demanded a frock-coated figure in a white periwig, 'is the meaning of this? Where's the *statue*?'

Lucky's chamberlain stared disbelievingly at the empty pedestal, at the heap of black stones, at the neat array of white rubble which was almost blocking access to Perfume Passage. And at Wex on his knees, and at Minnow standing by. Had someone finally blown the whistle on their escapade, or was Linqvist's arrival on the scene pure chance? The chamberlain seemed to be struggling to associate the absent effigy with the parade of white and the pile of black stones.

'Well,' said Minnow. 'It's like this . . . We thought. There ought . . .'

'Yes, Miss?'

'To be two statues rather than one!' she concluded in a rush.

Like some lofty wading bird with a crimson stripe around his waist the chamberlain stalked about in agitation. With white kid glove he picked up a smooth black fragment and peered.

'The Queen . . .' he murmured. He might have been holding a highly irregular goblet, and proposing a toast.

'I think that's an inside bit,' Minnow said helpfully because she noticed notches protruding on all sides.

'Or-dure.' Linqvist pronounced the word slowly, almost in a tone of wonder.

'Or-dure . . .' It was the closest to obscenity which his sense of decorum would allow him to approach.

'What did you hope to find inside, Miss Minnow? A jewel? A map? A key to a secret door? *You'll put this all back together as it was,*' he told Wex. 'Even if it takes all the rest of today and all night.'

'Put the Queen together again as she was,' agreed the Earthman. Some spectators were gathering now, intrigued.

'Even if it takes all night, do you hear?'

'I'll help,' said the initiator of this mischief. 'Just in case it takes longer than all night—'

'*No*, Miss Minnow. Please indulge me, and go somewhere else entirely.'

'We'll be able to manage,' Wex assured the empty air midway between Minnow and the chamberlain. 'Myself and me on our own. Once we organize the blacks. Once we can see the whole pattern. A sculptor thought it all out originally, didn't he? Or she.'

'Please, Miss Minnow.'

Minnow felt busy, busy. Possessed by an itch to stir events. 'Bye, then,' she said to Roger Wex, and skipped away.

Jack's manner of settling down in the Brazen Isi nest had involved rushing pell-mell around its tunnels, windmilling his way wildly (though without collisions) into yellow-lit chambers, grottoes, workshops, crypts, halls and hibernacula, subterranean gardens, piglet pens where massive sows farrowed, a hangar housing a space-boat . . . Junior Juttahats in elastic gold lamé scampered with him, chirping and sibilating; and soon he was

to don the same gear, though he never exactly became chums
with any of the alien youngsters in the nest, nor could he ever
understand them properly. It was a while before he realized that
these juniors rushed with him from place to place – places perfectly familiar to them – not merely because he rushed, and so
caused them to rush, but because voices in their noddles told
them to imitate him so that he in turn might come to copy them.

'Did you miss me?' Jatta finally asked him.

'Of course I was missing you,' was his answer. A knowing
child again, his eyes were wide with curiosity and concern. 'You
weren't being there! Just Anni. I wasn't crying. I was running
too fast for sobs.'

Jack's perspective on his life with the Isi and Juttahats was
enfolded in upon itself, events six months previously adjoining
those just a few weeks since. He was such an amalgam of young
man and child, proud of his growth and powers yet anxious that
he was leaving himself behind – outdistancing himself so quickly
that he might race through manhood, might rush from the world
having hardly been in it except for one long sleep-strobed flash
which illuminated all of his experiences equally. His life curled
up around him as a child might curl up. Yet he was darting
briskly towards a precipitate future.

'Crying, running,' echoed Anni. 'Oh don't you go ing-ing this
and ing-ing that like a Juttie. It's past.'

'I'm remembering the nest —' And his memories were continu-
ous with the present, folded around it, circling.

'You haven't spoke to the Queen that way, have you? Nor
should you neither to your mother. I tried to keep Jack talking
straight just like a human,' she told Jatta. 'Even if that's how
the interpreter Jutties always talked to him while they were
studying the bairn. And even if I wasn't brought up too fancy
myself.'

Brought up. By her parents. Did she hope to go back home to
the farmstead from which Juttahats had abducted her?

'I don't mean that we're crowding each other, Anni!' Jatta
hastened to assure her. 'I don't mean that at all.'

Jatta's chamber, with two beds in it, still seemed moderately
spacious. Several large mirrors now hung on the walls upon the
woodland tapestries, opening windows into reflection rooms
easily accommodating beds and chests and dressers and more
upholstered twins of chairs (one occupied by Jatta, one by Anni,
while Jack knelt on a rug by the tubby stove). The mullioned

window framed wintry darkness and some glint from snow and stars – curtains were open wide, offering another space, albeit a chilly one. The lamplight was mellow.

'Home?' enquired Anni. 'The body-slave of a Juttahat returns *home* to a glad welcome? *Better she'd died, better she'd died.* I can hear it already. Oh but I'm sorry,' she said hastily to Jatta, 'I don't mean you. Just me.'

'I understand.'

'What's home, anyhow? Has Jack come back home when he was never here before?'

For the major part of the lad's life to date what constituted *home* had been the great underground nest of the serpents and their servants. The glow of apricot light, the fruity air, the twangs and chimes resounding seemingly at random – and a personal den of alien hydroponic plants and furniture either looted or bartered for. The mage who had initiated the project of seducing a Sariola daughter was absent, abducted by Lucky herself as if in perfect reciprocation, tit for tat. It was that selfsame mage which now tarried in the palace dungeon, aloof and evasive. Management of the miracle boy could hardly devolve even partly upon Jarl the impostor – the Juttahat with a mind of his own – on account of his moribund state. Another Isi mage took charge, using interpreter mouthpieces . . .

. . . as Jatta was now discovering from Anni and from her son who told her their tale day by day, like two cuckoos relating somewhat divergent visions of events.

In the Brazen nest there had originally been six mana-mages, sporting those sharp little horns; and then there were five – out of perhaps forty serpents, and a hundred times as many Juttahats.

'Like dogs with owners,' said Anni, 'the Jutties are given a *reason* for their lives by the Isi. A compelling goal. You might say as Jarl gave me the same treatment when I was in the snake-skin suit, so that I'd love my duty!' The body-stocking in question had been a sloughed skin of the mage (who was now downstairs), mana-magicked by that dignitary.

'It was 'im as caused Jarl to happen—'

In his buoyant pride at being such a prodigy – a kind of honorary Isi – Jatta's future lover had bragged to Anni about his special endowments. ('Oh, I was *privileged*, weren't I!') Seems the mage had presided at Jarl's conception, casting an enchantment, spraying smells, biting the Juttie female with a cocktail of juices

420

it had dreamed up. Juttie females, of whom there were about a hundred in the Brazen nest, weren't much different to look at from the males when they were in their livery. Out of their livery – well, Anni didn't know; nor Jack neither. Parenting didn't matter to Jutties particularly, though swelling and birth was an experience. Any Juttie was a parent to the kids in elastic gold lamé. Inner voices guided behaviour, and offspring grew so quickly. After Jarl had been born – already an oddity – additional surgery and mana-massage shaped him into the persuasive semblance of a human being. ('Small wonder he fell apart so easily after you Sariola-ed him! He was so artificial.') The mage, Jarl's mentor, educated the phoney human since Jarl didn't hear helpful voices. Groomed him. Finally, when he was full-grown, gave him a doll to play with – Anni.

The mage's motive: to steal a royal daughter's gift? To breed a kind of hybrid human who could manipulate mana but be amenable to control by Isi? To sabotage Queen Lucky?

Isi rarely had single motives. Nor did all Isi necessarily share the same clusters of motives or methods.

Jarl's mentor was known as Imbricate, which meant overlap, though the mage's scales were not especially arranged like shingles on a roof. More of an allusion to motives partially concealing other motives. Maybe Imbricate even had a motive for being locked in the vault downstairs in Lucky's palace. Maybe it was trying to attract voices into its own mind – human voices, which would tell it of Lucky and her schemes from close at hand.

The mage which supervised Jack in the absence of Imbricate was known to Anni and Jack as Brille-Estivan. *She who slept in summer* – with a nod of acknowledgment in the name to the polished scales which would cover her lidless eyes like little mirrors. When she shuttered those dark eyes the scales gleamed, reflecting in miniature what the eyes no longer perceived in an ordinary manner.

Brille-Estivan was a luminary, a phosphormeisterin who could illuminate darkness till the objects of scrutiny blazed. Who better to shed light on the mind of the fast boy? Whereas Imbricate had principally been a somaseer, a body-adept.

Yet Jack always possessed a will of his own; and Brille-Estivan's supervision of him was slacker than Imbricate's might have been. Maybe the two serpents were rivals. Or else Brille-Estivan's approach was different from Imbricate's.

'Being with Jack saved me from going completely loopy, I'd say,' declared Anni.

Kept underground, but not otherwise greatly confined, Jack had grown apace. He had socialized with Anni, who told him tales of naughty nakkis. He had mingled with Juttahat striplings who were also growing rapidly and with a much surer sense of inner purpose, verging on the obligatory. What was *his* purpose? He had flexed and ripened his elemental talents. The casting of light – to the delight of Brille-Estivan, who viewed him as midway between a protégé and a puppy-dog in training. The calling of wind or chill. The hurrying of creatures. The forced growth and blooming of certain creamy waxen flowers.

When Lucky had sent deflowered Jatta to fend for herself in the forests well south of the Great Fjord, a cuckoo had called the unfortunate princess to a well-stocked hut – in the same way as a cuckoo had led Jatta to find Jarl warbling beside that little lake near Lokka. Had servants of Imbricate provisioned that refuge hastily for her? Made sure that it was well enough stocked to last all winter long? If they knew where Jatta was, why not abduct her and carry her back to the Brazen Isi nest south-east of Landfall to gestate and bear her boy there?

'You might have miscarried from the shock,' suggested Anni. 'Smells in the nest might have mixed up your boy while he was being made . . .'

Imbricate, downstairs, would know perfectly well what its own plan had been. Or did it nurse several partial plans? Was its idea of a plan rather different from human notions of what constituted a plan – akin, perhaps, to Lucky's own foibles? Caprices such as abandoning a pregnant daughter in the forests as winter drew near.

'Mebbe your mother knew about the refuge,' said Anni. 'You were always one for gallivanting around in the wilds, weren't you, Jatta? So you've told me. Your mother thought you could cope. She didn't want a wild child born anywhere in her vicinity.'

Jack grinned. 'I'm wild because I was formed and born in the woods!'

'. . . and it's nature that you control.'

'Oh, my Fastboy, no one could have known that you'd have such mana in you,' exclaimed Jatta.

When Imbricate learned about Jack, from cuckoo tattle – learned of a male descendant of Lucky endowed with major mana – the mage set out in search of the fast boy. And caught him at Speakers' Valley. But the mage lost its own freedom. And Brille-Estivan, with different goals, became responsible for Jack.

'Until I was skipping the nest.'

'Don't -ing, Jack. You aren't a Juttie.' He still wore their shiny gear.

A tap on the chamber door. Two taps. Three. As if someone knew a code; though it was a code which nobody else shared.

Minnow opened the door. She limped into the room as if bothered by a twinge of cramp. Gazed at Jack, Anni, finally Jatta. 'I was wondering if you wanted anything. If there's anything I can *do* for you—'

'Have you been listening at the keyhole?' Jatta enquired. 'Your knees look creased.'

The younger daughter hastily brushed herself down. 'Oh, I wouldn't. Now would I?' she asked herself; and flexed her right leg to straighten the muscles.

'Maybe you're in training to be the local cuckoo?'

Minnow sighed exaggeratedly. 'Well, the world's so full of puzzles, isn't it just?'

'Bearing names such as Brille-Estivan, for instance? Or Imbricate?'

'Or Demon Jack.' Jatta's son grinned. A few snowflakes glittered in the air and vanished.

'I *think*,' confided Minnow by way of diversion, 'that Roger Wex has taken a fancy to me. I was wondering what you'd advise?' All innocence, she added, 'Of course I can ask Evie what she thinks . . .'

'I'm sure you will.'

'But well *you*, Jatta . . .'

'I already consorted with an alien?'

'All of us did that,' Anni said sadly. 'In our different ways.'

'*Exactly*. With that stuff in his head Wex is almost an alien, wouldn't you say?' Minnow loosened a button. 'Ooh, it's nice and warm in here.' She perched herself expectantly on Jatta's bedspread.

Lucky paced the portrait gallery from end to end and back again, with Bertel keeping step. Snow coated the skylights. A couple of oil lamps on slender tripod tables afforded sufficient illumination for Lucky to peer at images of herself, and herself, and herself again. Stout Granny was snoozing in her armchair, the goosefeather duster – her wand of office – clutched in a lardy old hand.

'Be damned to the mage,' snapped Lucky. 'Jack may have been *its* idea in the first place, that's true. If it thought Jatta might have been fertile, and her child special. A mana-kid! Fruit of Sariola loins. Fruit of the fruit of Lucky. Linked to me. Thus, a potential tool for finding the hiding place of my own true self, and commanding that place . . .' She paused in front of the mana-mirror aswirl with fog. 'Our mage may have divined this could happen. Be damned to it – Jack's here with us now.'

'He is, my dear.'

'It's the *machine* we need to perform. I need it to make me a detector. A location device. A mana-aerial. Something to find and control the place where I really am, Bertel.'

'The place where you really are,' he echoed faithfully. 'In the Ukko-child. If there is one.'

'Do you suppose that wretched Kennan fellow actually knew its whereabouts by sheer chance? If that's what he *was* hinting at! Ragnar Kennan, right?'

'Whose son I met at the gala. Not a family I'd trust too much, charmer though the young man might be.'

'Kennan isn't a name on my guest list. What a pity our Wethead didn't prove much help with the everything machine . . .' Lucky chuckled at the very thought of Wex and her tone grew merry. 'I'm thinking that we ought to hold a competition between science and mana.'

'How do you mean, my love?'

'In the persons of Osmo van Maanen and Elmer Loxmith, who else? Proclaimer laureate versus engineer. The prize: longlife. Eva likes them both well enough, doesn't she? Come spring, sap'll rise as ever. Van Maanen will be done mourning his mother.'

'Invite them *both* here, Paula? At the same time – is that wise?'

'I was thinking more of *summoning*. As soon as the snow has gone. I can't bear to wait much longer, Bertel. I just can't tolerate it. A useless mage, a useless Wex . . . *Who's there?*' she called out along the pinacothek.

Granny awoke – or ceased feigning sleep. Brandishing her duster, the old woman heaved herself up. 'Who's in Granny's picture gallery? Oh it's yourself, your Majesty. I fair thought you stepped out of one of the paintings—'

'*Who's there? Show yourself!*'

A shadowy figure detached itself from a door jamb. 'Mother, Mother!' A girl's voice.

'Ester?'

'It's me, Mother. Minnow.' The girl hurried closer. 'Please don't be hard on Mister Wex – he'll put your statue back together again just as it was, I promise, even if it takes all night. Wasn't entirely his fault, you see.'

'Statue? What statue? What has the wethead done now?'

'Black and white statue. Top of Perfume Passage.' Minnow managed to sound breathless as if she had sprinted all the way, though in fact she had arrived from the opposite direction. 'I'm to blame, Mother. I put him up to it, though really he put me up to it in the sense that he had to lift me or else I couldn't have reached – hasn't Mister Linqvist told you about it yet?' Minnow's eyes widened. 'Maybe he was scared to!'

'My natter, my chatter . . .'

'No, Mother, Jatta's with Jack and Anni.' Minnow clapped a hand to her lips.

'Run along now,' advised Bertel. 'Your mother and I were trying to talk.' Which prompted the elderly custodian to flick her duster in the girl's direction.

'What happened to my statue?'

Was Lucky on the brink of laughter or rage?

'We took it apart, Mother, him and me.' Of a sudden Minnow sounded far younger than her years. 'To see if we could make two separate statues with the pieces. It always seemed so *big* to me, the way it was. Unfairly big.' Such wistful appeal in her voice.

Lucky scrutinized her petite daughter. 'When you're wed,' she declared, 'you can live in a doll's house full of dolly furniture.'

'Oh I'm not that short,' Minnow reassured herself.

'Evie, Evie!'

Tricked out in her best burgundy gown, with five spangled combs in her hair, Eva was on her way to the palace ballroom, salvation of one's sanity during the long dark winter – even if Sariola daughters were only allowed to dance with one another or with the chamberlain or the tangomeister or a visiting suitor.

'Evie, it's decided. A contest over you!' Minnow posed triumphantly. 'Whoever can start the you-know-what wins you.'

'*Whoever?*'

'Out of Lord van Maanen and Elmer Loxmith.'

425

Eva relaxed. 'Oh, that's all right then . . . How do you know?'

Minnow waved a hand dismissively. Such an insignificant detail. 'Mother's bound to tell you soon. What are Osmo and Elmer *like*? Tell me again. I'll tell you how Jack and Anni fared in the Isi nest—'

29 · TANGO TIME

When Lord Osmo van Maanen landed his sky-boat in the walled airfield of Pohjola Palace during the first week of May, he was accompanied by Marko and Hannes and Victor Rintala, though not by Sam Peller.

Sam had practically insisted on remaining at Maananfors. With the first arrival of spring, Juttahats of the Brazen Isi had begun appearing in the hinterland south of the turquoise lake. A pair of alien scouts were sighted. A couple more. A farmer shot a Juttie; a Juttie knifed a forester. Nothing serious as yet; nothing menacing. Yet in Sam's suspicious soul such *symptoms* weren't to be neglected. Now that Johanna was dead, somebody had to pay proper attention.

During the course of the winter Osmo's thoughts had fastened ever tighter upon his mother's dying wish, as a gyrebird with a soarfowl in its claws. *Do not die, Son. Never die.* Those words, relayed by the cuckoo, haunted him. Osmo squeezed and devoured them, but could never digest them so that they would disappear. Johanna's last words echoed and re-echoed, multiplying many times over. Osmo twisted them into a braid – and that braid was the rope of his mother's hair. From the grave she who had lacked mana proclaimed at him imperatively now. Effectively, he was bespeaking himself – not in his own words but in hers. *Do not die. Never die.* She had died. If he disobeyed, he would die too. So her death would be wasted. Ultimately who had killed her but himself? Gyrebird-like, he circled around the points at issue. Longlife! To be gained surely by an act of mana – although misdirected mana had put paid to his own mother's life. To be won by claiming a Sariola daughter. Eva, of course. Elegant, luscious Eva.

Never die. Were the words which he clutched to himself prey

426

– or predator? Those words specified his destiny. The rope of his mother's hair had encircled her head thrice, except when she let it down to wash. Winterlong, her dying words bound him similarly, skull and brain. He began to panic that some other suitor might win Eva. Naturally he remained anxious as to the possibility – the *rare* odds – of becoming zombie. He despised himself for such funk.

Whom could he confide in? Who could give him final permission to carry out his mother's wish? He did feel obscurely that he needed some additional approval, some added impetus to change his life so radically – even though it might be high time to do so; although the time might be overdue! Who could advise? Not Alvar, puffing on his pipe, bound up in his chronicles. Not Sam. No, not Sam.

Trusty Elmer, then?

What, stake his claim for Eva by confiding in Elmer, who might be nursing similar notions of his own? Not that Elmer could exactly be viewed as a *rival* . . .

When Prince Bertel called by communicator to invite – practically to summon – Osmo to Sariolinna, Osmo rode out to Asikkala to speak to Victor Rintala. Why, it was Vivi's father who needed to approve. The gruff farmer had promised Osmo his right arm in support.

Consequently, Osmo flew northward to Lucky's domain with Vivi's father at his side. Victor Rintala was representing the countryside, as it were – the ordinary folk of the van Maanen territory. Moustached Marko of the town watch was the epitome of Maananfors itself. Hannes, a strapping – and sharp-witted – groom with a thatch of wild blond hair, was a man of the keep. Such an escort was a mark of Osmo's fair-minded liberality. On the return journey, with Eva Sariola – Eva van Maanen – beside him, Hannes could stretch out in the sky-boat's storage space where a certain stone man had once been stowed en route from Speakers' Valley.

On arriving at Pohjola Palace, where patches of compact snow still lingered in shady nooks, Osmo was delayed by Lucky's chamberlain for half an hour so that the Queen and her consort could receive him appropriately in the Dome of Favours.

Of favours, and of faces. Faces in a crowd of onlookers; faces frescoed upon the walls; faces peering from the upholstery of sofas.

When Linqvist led Osmo in, he was followed by Marko and

Hannes who carried between them a white marble bust of a girl thrusting upward in supplication, or perhaps fulfilment, from out of a roughly hewn base. A gift for the Queen from the sculpture park in Maananfors. Not an ostentatious gift exactly – after all, Osmo had been *invited* to woo – but simply a perfect and unique offering which had left a bare plinth in the park. A girl in exchange for a girl. Flesh in exchange for stone. And alluding to Osmo's victory over Tycho Cammon . . .

. . . whom the mutie Juke Nurmi had later revived, to murder Vivi Rintala. Her father wore a wistful expression as he brought up the rear behind the heavy burden, though perhaps he was veiling his wonder at being in the Queen's palace far in the north.

Lucky Sariola sat regally on a throne, gorgeous in gold-trimmed crimson gown and tiara, cheerfully hopeful. Expectant, though not currently *expecting*, so far as Osmo could discern. A nurse held a baby girl swaddled in a quilted wrap. Bertel simpered encouragingly.

Eva smiled at Osmo brightly. *Eva*. The doorway to his dream. Spangled combs clasped raven hair which would let down well below her shoulders. She was dressed in a cascade of white embroidery. Osmo bowed, bending his breeches knee, on to which a scarlet ribbon rosette had long since been sewn back.

A bearded artist squatted on an elevated platform, brush in hand as if about to record Osmo's arrival for posterity.

Others. Many others.

Osmo noticed a roly-poly dwarf made of polished brass, with black rubber wheels for feet and a winking 'tronic panel set in its chest. Tech from somewhere other than Kaleva, to be sure! Its eyes were red glass; its mouth was a grating. Twin antennae sprouted from its head. Half a dozen brass hands jutted from its barrel body, flexible fingers waggling slowly.

Now where had Osmo seen such a contraption before? Why of course: in the exercise gallery of the aitch-house at Loxmithlinna, when he'd been paying a visit to Elmer a couple of years ago . . .

Elmer's brass dwarf. A clammy chill assailed him.

This fabricated dwarf was tubbier than the one in the gallery. In many regards it was different. All those silly hands protruding from it. The red eyes, the 'tronic panel: tech from off-world. Elmer collected such items whenever he could lay hold of them.

The lanky engineer *wasn't* here in this frescoed dome. Unless he was crouching behind other spectators so as to keep out of sight. Why should Elmer be crouching? Why should he be here at all? As it happened, as it *happened*, Osmo hadn't notified his friend that he was due to fly north ... Where was the need to? Elmer had already serviced the van Maanen sky-boat quite recently and pronounced it to be in fine condition. Tell him as a courtesy, by communicator, merely because Elmer had maybe shown a certain gauche interest in Eva?

Marko and Hannes were setting the bust of the girl down, directed by a wave from Bertel, close to the preposterous brass humanoid.

'A thousand thanks for your gift, Lord Osmo,' said the Queen. Her smoky eyes, framed in that youthful face so full and fresh, were quite captivating. She raised the ruby ring which glinted on her right hand as if he should advance and kiss it, yet even while he hesitated the hand relapsed on to her knee. 'For your mana-gift, of course – which is owing to myself, ultimately, isn't that so?'

Alvar had never said anything whatever about the van Maanen family being descended from an early daughter of Lucky's ... Osmo must have looked blank, for the Queen continued with a playful smile, 'Without my Ukko, without the way to Kaleva, what would you have been? If you had been anything at all, Lord Osmo! All of you, except dear Bertel, are of my doing. Of my making. Are you not?'

'We all owe you our admiration,' Osmo said tactfully.

'Owing mana to me, you shall repay me with your service. And I shall repay you in turn with a willing daughter of mine, and with longlife, if you succeed. A hundred thanks too for that lovely piece of sculpture. A Wikström, isn't it?' Lucky focused upon a young Sariola girl in the crowd – who looked alarmed. 'You won't try to take this one apart, will you, my Minnow?'

The elfin girl shook her frizzy head and said several things swiftly to herself.

'That's my daughter Minnow, Lord Osmo. *Quite* mature and marriageable, despite her mischief! Be warned: don't let her lure you into any pranks at the ball this evening.'

Minnow flushed, and stared at the marble bust speechlessly. Anxiously, Osmo sought Eva again. She had moved coyly behind a portly mana-priest. Or perhaps deftly, to defer any public witticisms from her mother. It was *Eva* whom the Queen was offering Osmo as a bride. Wasn't it ... ? Surely not that other pixie of a daughter ... That would be a prank indeed. How could he

429

reassure himself on this score, in a way which wasn't crass?

'If I succeed,' he repeated. He was conscious of all the onlookers eyeing him. Unexpectedly, for once, he felt diminished rather than enhanced by an audience. The Queen's attitude appeared to be that he owed his entire existence and status to her – whereas Bertel's invitation had been so friendly and fulsome. What had the chamberlain called this reception room? The Dome of *Favours*. Was he merely a favour hunter?

'If you can bespeak an alien machine into action. My Brazen Isi everything machine!' Lucky stared defiantly around the room, at those – such as her chamberlain and her priest and her general – who must have known all about the matter, and at others who might not know at all. She was uttering a public challenge. Her consort laid a restraining hand lightly on her shoulder. She shook off his hand impatiently. *No*, she was rising. The Queen stepped forward. She stroked her hand over the head of the fat metal dwarf.

'My brassy alien machine,' she declared – confusing Osmo further. Was that contraption of metal hands and rubber wheels and winking lights really the Isi machine?

She chuckled at his perplexity. 'No, but it looks quite like it.' With her other hand she caressed the sculpted white hair of the marble maiden. 'Which shall it be? The marble, or the metal?' As if she was choosing between—

—*two gifts, from two suitors*.

Elmer must be here in the palace.

Without having told Osmo his intention. The heroes painted around the walls oppressed him now, rather than exhilarating him. All those figures pressed in upon Osmo as if to wrest a prize from him when it was within his grasp – when he had nerved himself at last to risk the zombie gamble.

'I take it, Your Majesty, that you also invited Elmer Loxmith to compete for your daughter *Eva's* hand.'

Eva's hand. Eva's. Not that Minnow girl's. How could Elmer compete? He wasn't a proclaimer, a manameister. He would be no more than a goad, a foil. This must be the Queen's mischievous intention. An alien machine was involved. Elmer was a dab hand at tinkering with machinery. No doubt mana was at the root of his talent. Yet really, what comparison was there between Osmo and the engineer? Poor dupe Elmer, lured here to tease Osmo. Elmer's heart beating pitter-pat. Doomed to disappointment.

Lucky was studying Osmo, eyebrow cocked quizzically.

'The question is, your Majesty, does Loxmith know that I'm invited too?'

Lucky smiled sweetly. 'He does by now. But this is *your* welcoming to our palace. I do thank you for this piece of sculpture. If this girl could speak, what would she say? She looks as though she wishes to say something. Can you make her talk?'

'She was never alive . . .'

'Surely Wikström used a model.'

Again Osmo was caught off balance. The Queen implied that if he was really able to command a machine to come to life, then he ought to be able to do as much for a bust with lips and nose and eyes. Bertel nodded at him encouragingly. Spectators were agog, though Victor Rintala had clenched his fist – Victor seemed aggrieved at his lord's reception hitherto. Eva was watching intently, excited. The tip of her tongue curled upon her upper lip, moving moistly from side to side.

There could be no thoughts within the marble, other than those with which admirers invested the bust, courtesy of the sculptor's skill.

Stooping, Lucky squeezed one of the dwarf's several hands. Its red eyes blinked. A song quavered forth in a husky voice – through its grille of a mouth.

> *Sky-sickle shines upon the sea*
> *Silver combs in your hair*
> *You're as far away from me*
> *Without a care, without a care . . .*

As Lucky relaxed her grip, the brass dwarf stopped singing. How had Elmer managed the trick? By cobbling together bits of tech . . . It was a greater feat to massage marble to say something; though what might Osmo make the girl's lips say? *I'm leaping free, to my destiny?* Pohjola Palace must be a privileged prison so far as Lucky's daughters were concerned. *I'll ride on his horse, to far Maananfors.* Not that Osmo had travelled the hundreds of keys on horseback – nor by water.

How had Elmer come here? In the *Sea Sledge* by way of lakes and rivers, then part way along the Great Fjord? He must have set off days earlier than Osmo, yet still arrived first. He must have been invited first.

Osmo breathed deeply.

'Stone,
'Be bone,
'And flesh upon bone.
'Marble lips
'Part
'And speak
'From the heart.'

Speak his own thoughts ventriloqually. His own aspirations. His breathings-out, from his soul.

The girl's marble lips were pouting. Parting. Her carved eyes still stared upward fixedly but her mouth had become supple.

Never die, Son. Live long. Leap free to destiny.

No, his mother's voice mustn't issue from those lips. His mother's ghost mustn't be drawn into that immortally young marble head.

Ride a fine horse into Maananfors. When he returned home he would certainly do that – with Eva mounted in front of him, to show her to all the townsfolk, their new châtelaine.

Whose voice, ideally, should speak from those lips but Eva's? Unfortunately he had not heard Eva's accents for many months. Lucky's own ripe husky tones were in his mind right now. *She* was the mother who should speak by proxy. She was the one who would give her lovely hen into his care.

A wind sprang up inside the Dome of Favours, self-born within that large circular room. White insects careered through the air. No, those were frantic flakes of snow. The blank-eyed marble girl opened her mouth wider.

And squealed.

Squealed without any meaning to the noise – other than distress – as a draught of breath rushed from her lips.

The noise she made was more devoid of meaning than a scream. Not even a stuck-pig sort of squeal. It was the voice of something that had never had a mind but now was compelled to express itself.

A Juttahat was in the room now. Grinning at Osmo tauntingly. Ach, it was a cinnamon-skinned human youth with short dark hair dressed in golden Juttahat livery. Why would a human being dress as a slave of the Isi? Out of decadent affectation? To suggest some *affinity* with aliens? Some spurious brotherhood?

Beside the youth: surely a sister of Eva's? With her black hair cropped spikily. A purple suede tunic sewn with strips of brightly coloured felt . . .

Suppose that her tunic was grubby and torn. Suppose that her face was dirty and fatigued. Who else could it be – but Jatta Sariola whom he had exiled to live with muties? As recognition dawned on Osmo, the young woman continued scanning him dispassionately as if he was a portrait of himself rather than a person.

Eva's elder sister. Back home in the palace once more – after consorting with *Juke Nurmi* the mutie proclaimer; that's what a cuckoo had tattled. Nurmi had tried to set a zombie on Osmo even after being trounced and humiliated thoroughly. Where was Nurmi now? Did Jatta know?

Disconcerting thoughts danced wildly in Osmo. He certainly hadn't expected to find Jatta at court, and present at his very welcoming – if indeed he was as warmly welcome as he had imagined would be the case, and as Bertel had led him to believe! The Queen had banished Jatta in a rage. Later she came to her errant daughter's rescue – after a fashion. To find that same daughter here now in seemingly good favour – *condoned*, and staring at him with such evident self-possession: this perplexed him. Had he walked into some kind of trap? Would there be recriminations?

He had acted justly in regard to Jatta, hadn't he? Prince Bertel had been reassuring about the matter at the gala. There must be ethnic purity or muties might become commonplace. Mockeries of men – on a world where alien mockeries served sly serpents.

The marble girl had simply squealed. Who *was* that young fellow-me-lad, the Juttie impersonator? A wet-behind-the-ears proclaimer?

'Jack!' called out the Queen. A flurry of blue snow twinkled up in the air, dyed by light from the stained glass of the cupola.

'Yes, Grandmother?'

'You're worrying our guest.'

Jack.

Demon Jack.

Fastboy Jack.

Jatta's son, whom Osmo had last seen as a far more junior urchin.

Already an adolescent. Grown so swiftly. So abnormally. A proclaimer of some kind, who could interfere with Osmo's best

433

efforts. Why, that bust of the girl had already frozen solid again without Osmo's own say-so. Frozen to marble. Reverted. If it had frozen to ice instead – as that flutter of snow hinted – Osmo's courtship gift might have slowly begun to melt before his eyes, making a fool of him. The fast lad respected Queen Lucky well enough not to attempt such a jape.

To *attempt* it, perhaps . . . which was not to say that Jatta's brat would have succeeded! Osmo had merely been caught off guard. Was her Jack – the Queen's grandson – here to test him? Of a sudden all seemed sinister . . . and intentional. Part of Lucky's legendary mad mischief.

Caprice was the sharp edge of her shrewdness. She was pushing Osmo, spurring him. Well then, he must welcome her roguery! And the presence of Elmer, and of Demon Jack too, as foils. Otherwise he would merely be proclaiming at some inanimate alien device without a clear sense of its makers and its origin. To contend against Elmer was a *boon*. To contend, in a sense – since Elmer's mana was purely mechanical. Not a matter of passion and power.

Osmo gazed again at Eva, desiring her. That teasing starflower tattooed on her cheek, another visible upon her neck: the beginnings of a private pathway to the soft unopened gates of life. How did she diverge from his memory of her, nurtured progressively throughout the winter? When he had been in Yulistalax, that damned ephemeral intoxication with the mutie poetess witch had led him astray from Eva, who alone was worthy of him; as he would be worthy of her.

'You shall dance with my daughters at the ball tonight,' announced the Queen gleefully. Quirky dimples puckered her fresh chubby cheeks. 'Welcome, Lord Osmo, proclaimer laureate! May you succeed abundantly.'

Had she said *daughters*? Dance with more than one daughter? If only Johanna could have been waiting in whatever suite chamberlain Linqvist would show him and his escort to, twiddling her Pootaran puzzles on his behalf, solving problems even in darkness by touch alone.

The palace ballroom was frescoed all along two walls and in between the tall windows of the third wall, which were curtained with ruched pink satin. The fourth wall, except for its wide double doors, was mirrored to expand an already abundant space.

In this case the many painted figures weren't heroes. In *trompe l'oeil* hundreds – probably thousands – of elegant partners danced, swirling yet stationary. The fictive women wore shoulderless cascading ballgowns, the men black tails or fanciful uniforms. The parquet floor was of hard-wearing northern sylvester wood. Stained alternately orange and a rich blue, its blocks were shaped like stylized shoeprints. A huge crowd of shoeprints dovetailed into one another, shuffling forward or backward incessantly. So it seemed from out of the corner of one's eye whenever a large enough gap opened up among the actual dancers and hopeful loiterers thronging the ballroom. The shoeprints extended in perspective far into the illusory dancefloor beyond the walls.

Acetyline illuminated the lustred prismatic chandeliers. A long buffet table offered buns and dumplings, cream pancakes, sliced pork and leaperfish, ox tongues in aspic, goose and roe and sausages, braised tarandra calf kidneys and sweetbreads, as well as cordials and juices – though no ales or spirits. The Queen had no wish for frenzy to erupt at her ball.

The music, naturally, was tango in a minor key, perfect for public courtship. There'd be none of the wild drumming and yoiking and prancing of a Lucky's Day fest tonight. Which was why Loxmith had craftily inserted a tango song into his preposterous tubby brass dwarf – which 'quite looked' like that alien machine still to be encountered. (*Had Elmer been told of that resemblance in advance? Or was he perhaps still oblivious?*) Twangy percussive melody, wistful and plaintive, conjured the slow manoeuvres of the dance during which strangers could become closer, through which intimacies could emerge quite decorously.

A clear rhythm dominated: *Chum! Chum! Chum!* Since the Queen herself was present, the chamberlain presided over etiquette. Lanky Linqvist – in freshly powdered wig and new apricot cummerbund – held two fans, a red and a blue. Any particular man and woman might only dance twice in succession. When the chamberlain opened his blue fan, a man might invite a woman. When he opened the red, that was the woman's privilege.

The tangomeister presided over hearts. He and his four bandsmen – on accordion, violin, guitar, and cymbals – wore matching black breeches and lace shirts. The meister additionally sported silver ribbon rosettes on his knees, and a polka-dot cravat. He was a portly, personable man of middle age with wavy greying hair. A drooping squint to one eye conveyed a sentimental soulfulness, which was amply matched by his mellow baritone voice.

435

It was as if that eye focused upon some other scene than the ballroom – not even upon the *trompe l'oeil* extension of the ballroom, really, but upon some ideal vista far away, some far shore of impossible happiness.

He would sing two songs, then step forward to make himself available as a partner for the ladies' rounds – singing while he danced – then return to sing alone, alongside the quartet.

> 'Why don't we part
> 'Before we start
> 'To fall in love with one another?
> 'Why not save ourselves the bother
> 'Of two broken hearts?'

Really, the meister was a proclaimer in a minor key, a projector of wistful tender emotions. His sentiments could possess one's soul, gentling and caressing until the singer seemed to have become one's very own mouthpiece, one's true voice – and the true, yearning voice of everyone present. How could one entertain wild passions of rage and lust and spite while this meister was singing?

A riff on the accordion, a ripple of cymbals, a final guitar twang. Applause.

Now was the time to address Elmer, who had led *Eva* from the dance floor, and was returning to the far end of the room to lurk with Lyle Melator. Thus far, Elmer and Osmo had only exchanged distant formal nods as if an embarrassing truce prevailed between the two friends – who were now rivals.

Elmer had spruced himself up for once. A smartly cut maroon jacket with white lapels and many brass buttons. A pea-green waistcoat. Breeches to match. How awkward he looked. Perhaps the gear had belonged to Lord Henzel, kept in some chest in the paralysed man's chamber.

As Osmo approached, Lyle Melator slipped away casually in the direction of the buffet, leaving Elmer to hold his own. Elmer gazed after his assistant in a mild panic, then stood his ground, apprehensive – yet emboldened; determined, in a gauche and forthright way. His gaunt face jutted as if tempting Osmo to hit him on the chin.

'Actually,' said Osmo graciously, 'I'm glad of the competition, even if it's a little lopsided. Don't you think so in your heart, Elmer?' He chuckled. 'Oh, I shan't bespeak you into doubting yourself. That would be quite unfair. The Queen wouldn't like it one bit. Relax, Elmer. You'll be as welcome as ever to visit Maananfors.'

Elmer leered. Perhaps he intended a more urbane riposte, but what he blurted out was, 'With Eva?' His tone sorted ill with the sweet pathos of the tangos.

'Odd, isn't it, that the brass toy you brought for the Queen bears a strong resemblance to a certain alien machine we're supposed to monkey with?'

Elmer's face betrayed that he had no knowledge of this similarity. He rallied, however – by supplying Osmo with a missing fact.

'She sent a sky-boat to collect me specially. So I suppose she thinks we're well matched – at least as far as machines go!'

He hadn't come in the *Sea Sledge*, after all.

'And I say you're a foil.'

'A fool?'

'Now would I ever say that? You'll enhance me, Elmer. You'll help me by being here.'

A small hand plucked at Osmo's sleeve as another tango began. It was that sprite of a girl, Minnow. The chamberlain was flourishing a red fan. Eva had been veering to and fro, her intentions apparently set on Osmo. She was waiting for Osmo to walk away from Elmer, her previous partner. Her younger sister had barged in.

'I'm allowed to dance with a suitor, Lord Osmo,' piped the girl. 'And you're certainly that.'

Her pert face amid that frizzed-out hair: Sariola features in dainty diminutive. Eva looked thunderously peeved as Osmo slanted his elbow reluctantly to accommodate Minnow's small hand in his and rested his other hand upon her shoulder. Her free hand wandered some way towards the small of Osmo's back. Otherwise their bodies didn't touch as they shuffled slowly leftward.

> 'An Ukko's in the sky tonight, dear heart;
> 'A cuckoo's keeping its eye on us two lovers—'

The meister sang sentimentally as he moved around the floor of wooden footsteps, idly guiding a frumpy ginger-haired woman whose eyes glistened moistly.

'I'll be wedding a fine fellow too one day,' Minnow was telling herself, and Osmo. 'Shouldn't be any taller than you. You're

437

about right. I like moustaches. If I was a boy I'd grow one, then I'd look older right away. Could you proclaim me a bit taller, by any chance? *Could you?*'

'Stretch you, girl? I wouldn't advise it! I can imagine that would *hurt* – for a long time afterwards.'

'Tycho Cammon hurt people horribly. How brave to face him. Or how silly! I'm not sure which.'

'Neither of those,' Osmo told her. 'It was something which had to happen. Things sometimes have to happen. If they don't, you can go crazy. Have you never felt a tide of compulsion pulling you along? It's a tide that I know how to channel, but still it can be stronger than even my will.'

> 'Now I'm as far away from you as any Ukko,
> 'And the cuckoo is our only voice,
> 'Mocking me that you still love me,
> 'Cheating you that I have made . . .
> '. . . another choice, another choice—'

Melancholy could also become an obsession. This had been the risk during the months after Johanna died. As time went by, shafts of lightning had cut through the gloom in Osmo: the lightning of Eva.

Osmo permitted himself a swagger. As a result Minnow tipped against him, momentarily unbalanced. The firmness of her hip thrust against his thigh. Springlike, she jerked away from his body.

The Queen was dancing slowly with her tangomeister. Looking away and over her shoulder, he sang of somewhere far off, some blissful meadow where his sweetheart waited, yearning for him to join her if only he could find the way to her; and Lucky's dusky eyes were moist with emotion.

Osmo, at last, was hand in hand with Eva.

'My father's forever gathering stories for these chronicles of his,' he was saying. 'Ah, it's a harmless obsession! He can tell you rousing tales of the old days till the cows come home. I suppose Elmer told you that *his* dad's a cripple, and Lady Loxmith has become morose on that account?'

'But,' said Eva sweetly, 'Lokka might snap out of her doldrums if Elmer acquires a bride.'

'Did you know that his keep was once afflicted by dread? Alvar, my dad, knows all about that sort of thing.'

438

The tangomeister warbled with such persuasive feeling. Bodies circled elegantly without bumping. Acetyline hissed faintly. The combs in Eva's hair twinkled. So did her eyes. What a scintillating hen she was. The starflower on her cheek was so perfect a complement. And the star on her wrist, as he held her hand. How many such tantalizing little tattoos did her gown hide? Perhaps one adorned a breast. Perhaps there were none at all except for those which were visible now! In which case she was nudity itself.

'Oh, Osmo, I'm in two minds – quite like poor Roger Wex!' Eva nodded sidelong at where the Earthman stood by the buffet. 'Do you know that he took one of my mother's statues to *pieces*? I hasten to add it was a Pootaran puzzle-statue; he didn't use hammer and chisel. I'm sure you'll have better luck with the Isi machine than he had, by all accounts. I'm quite banking on you, Osmo.'

'That's what I need to hear. As I see it, Elmer's here – quite innocently – primarily to stimulate me. I always appreciated his innocence, so why should I bear any grudge?'

Later, as Linqvist held up a red fan, a hand clasped Osmo's elbow firmly.

'May we dance, my lord?'

Jatta. Her expression was unreadable. Momentarily Osmo feared a knife thrust, and caught her hand in his. Her unnatural son was watching, poised on the balls of his feet. The tangomeister sang:

> 'Why did you send me so far away
> 'To a land beyond the seas?
> 'You loved another, but now every day
> 'I shall trouble your heart with unease—'

'Did you request this song especially?'

'How strange that *you* might become my brother-in-law,' Jatta replied quietly. 'Don't you think that a woman who can give longlife with her love might be something of a mutie herself? Something of a freak? Usually a man simply puts something into a woman, yet here's a case where a woman puts something into a man.' This was robust gross talk. She voiced it blithely enough as a mere matter of fact. Had he described Elmer as an innocent? Compared with this young woman, her sophisticated sister Eva was innocence indeed.

439

'I suppose I should . . .' He could not apologize. '. . . should redeem myself in your eyes.'

'You can't. Proclaiming is an exercise of power, and power eventually oppresses. You might have bested Tycho the tyrant – one *man* pitting himself against another corrupted *man* – but you felt free to oppress me, then that one-eyed poetess too.'

'Juke Nurmi's sister . . .'

'She was *his* victim too, so I hear. Eva told of her experiences at the gala with such exhilaration. Eyeno Nurmi was a shuttlecock caught between the two of you.'

> 'Why did you send me so far away
> 'To the land beyond the lakes—'

'A shuttle*hen*, perhaps? I wasn't "free" to oppress her. I was almost possessed – because of the link between her and . . . a certain death which hurt me.'

His gaze flicked towards Victor Rintala who was standing awkwardly on his own, abashed at being in the Queen's ballroom.

Jatta twitched in surprise. 'That man . . . is Vivi Rintala's *father?*'

'He's a farmer.'

'Here in support of your ambitions? How . . . charitable of him.' Her tone was mocking. 'His daughter was a shuttlecock too . . .'

'Or hen.'

'Joking is the last resort of selfish people who happen to be clever. Eyeno Nurmi was a *person.*'

Jatta was sanctimonious, it appeared. Her hair was deliberately abominable. A shorn, jagged mess.

'Nurmi, Nurmi. How the name dogs me, as if he's a terrier with his teeth in my shin. How did I offend him to begin with? Surely you must know. You were with him at a crucial time.'

'How? Oh, by being you. Having power by birth and by *freak fortune* too.'

'A fortune shared by him! Proclaiming is an exercise of wondrous mana—'

'—coming from our Ukko patron? Along with lust and mania! What a god to adore. I'm angry at what Juke caused to happen to your mistress, even if I owe Juke a debt.'

'To be repaid how?' Osmo must have winced, for she smiled faintly.

'Revenge makes the avenger a puppet. A shuttlecock. Usually a crowing *cock.*' Was she being obscene at him?

440

'Your mother's a woman of power,' he reminded Jatta.

The guitarist strummed his strings. The accordionist squeezed bittersweet melody from the mechanical heart in his hands as it pumped in and out in rapport with the hearts of the listeners.

'Your boy's a mana-meddler, and a wild one.'

'Oh I shan't set *him* on you – like a terrier.'

'Well,' Osmo said lamely as the song was winding towards its close, 'at least this tango has brought us together, in a manner of speaking.'

'You sent me so far away,' she echoed. 'And Eyeno too.' Pulling herself free from him prematurely before the final bars, she sauntered off.

'You never knew Eyeno Nurmi,' he called after her in protest. 'Why should you care?'

Aside from a parting shrug, Jatta paid no heed to this reasonable question.

Eyeno. Nurmi. The name was a double pain – almost as if the wench was still alive. Usually one danced twice in succession with the same partner. Osmo stood alone on the floor of footsteps, abandoned.

30 · THE ORIGIN OF EVERYTHING

Three well-sprung carriages – black-lacquered, with lines and curlicues of gilding – conveyed the royal party to the shore of the fjord, west of Sariolinna town. Woolly clouds scudded. Chilled breezes swept down from the white heights across the firth, combing the thawed water into foam-flecked waves, brushing phantom rivers upon its expanse. A reverberating boom – as if a salute had been fired from the fortress. Ice was slumping from one of those peaks. At first the avalanche appeared to dawdle, even though it would be tearing rocks loose. When the mass hit the fjord a good three keys away, water plumed up into the veil of snow still descending. Briefly a great tree with lacy foliage seemed to rear out of the firth before collapsing upon itself.

A scruffy bottle-green cuckoo had alighted on the final coach. When the party transferred to the ketch-rigged barge to be ferried the few hundred metres to the fortress island, the bird fluttered to perch upon the mizzen head. It stared down attentively. Chunks of melting ice, afloat, had permutated into strange amphibian creatures. The heavy barge wallowed, luffing, into the chilly gusts. Two of the sturdy dun draught-ponies neighed fretfully on shore. A hookbeaked greymew keened, hunting choppy waters for the fractured silver of a fish.

And here was the challenge in the lamp-lit vaulted chamber within the donjon: a big brassy pot set upon a bigger cauldron studded all over with knobs. The head and torso of an obese Copperman (though actually brazen) resting on a polished legless bum upon a black marble base.

'Oh now I see!' exclaimed Elmer, whose gift to the Queen hadn't been entirely dissimilar to a dwarf parody of the Isi device. He hadn't known – Osmo could read Elmer clearly enough.

The blue-clad sentries in their fanciful tall headgear withdrew stiffly to stand by window-slits. Their ruddy-faced officer murmured a report to General Aleksonis. Something very *odd* about those soldiers and their Captain . . . An image came into Osmo's mind of neatly carved wooden toys cradling tiny metal guns inside a toy fortress which he and the other visitors were roaming in miniature. *Boom, boom* – cannons fired mutedly from the battlements (another mass of ice must have cracked free from a peak).

Elmer's mana-priest, Moller – who, with Lyle Melator, comprised the Loxmith entourage – was arguing with the Queen's own priest, Serlachius, in support of the Loxmith bid to activate the brassy machine. The Earthman, Wex, kibitzed on this tolerably polite dispute, injecting nuggets of wisdom to the irritation of both priests. Shifting his weight from one leg to the other, Wethead Wex seemed to be favouring one side of his mind then the other side, rather than either of the disputants. Flame-haired Moller was florid of feature, and Serlachius's cheeks were similarly flushed. The commander of the fortress completed a rubicund trio – except that there was something peculiar about that officer's flesh, a polished timbery grain to it . . .

'The mysterium—' Serlachius was saying.

'A fundamental energy organizing space–time reality,' interrupted Wex, 'harnessed by the Ukko entities, and diffused throughout the north of this planet in the manner of a magnetic field—'

Marko and Hannes had accompanied Osmo to the fjord fortress, riding in the carriage along with himself and Aleksonis. Victor was absent. Pleading an overwhelming preoccupation, the farmer had asked to stay behind at the palace. Late last night, a jolly palace chef had bidden him to dance. From her he – whose body was tattooed with mushrooms – had learned of a certain stimulating, invigorating fungus which sprouted early in the northern spring on sodden dead vegetation newly thawed out. So he claimed. The next morning the cook would share a bowl of these with him – they soon lost their efficacy. So Rintala said. He must be more of a mushroom cultist than he had declared – or denied – in the sauna at Maananfors prior to Vivi's funeral. Or else he was simply an admirer of a certain buxom chef. Though annoyed at his desertion, Osmo was reluctant to frustrate Vivi's father.

Now that the moment had come, maybe Rintala simply hadn't wished to be present at Osmo's victory . . .

Serlachius clapped his hands sharply several times to silence the platitudes of Moller and the buzzings of Wex.

'Shall I pronounce a blessing over this enterprise, your Majesty?'

The Queen nodded gratefully. She seemed glad to delay the proceedings for just a little longer in case disappointment should devastate her. When Eva pouted impatiently, Osmo directed a reassuring smile in her direction. She did not quite acknowledge him. Dignity, and common sense, forbade her from openly favouring either suitor prematurely.

'Mana be with us, and with all practitioners of the mysterium which is the kernel of everything, the succulent nut, as we are its shell. Mana be with those who bespeak events into existence, and with those who massage the muscles of the world —'

Osmo's confidence soared. Yet guileless Elmer did not appear downcast. The engineer's long bony fingers were manipulating air in an antic fashion, twisting and turning imaginary knobs.

'May this machine perform for our Queen today!'

'Bertel, my love . . .'

The Prince produced a golden or from a fob pocket in the waistband of his uniform.

'You toss it, Bertel – we're in your hands.' Lucky was trembling, which offended her. She plucked the coin from her husband. 'No, I shall do so.'

Lucky was going to throw a coin to decide which suitor should make the first attempt upon the alien machine. Up until this

hour the question of order of precedence hadn't even occurred to
Osmo. He was minded to protest, especially while Elmer was
busily twiddling his fingers like some conjuror limbering up for
a demonstration of sleight of hand. What was the alternative –
that the two men should perform simultaneously? In that case
there'd be no certainty as to which of the suitors had succeeded.

A gold or bore the Queen's head looking leftward on one side,
and looking rightward on the reverse; hence various jokes about
two-faced ors. Lucky clenched her fist, shut her eyes, twirled
round twice quite girlishly, and directed her closed hand – at
Osmo.

Her voice wavered. 'Will it be left, or right?'

Wex was swaying like a metronome or a spastic semaphorist.
'Right,' called Osmo.

The Queen tossed the coin aloft. It tumbled, bounced, rolled
on its rim on a collision course with Osmo's brass-buckled shoe.
He jerked his foot aside. The coin executed a tight circle, teetered,
then was settling. Out of the vibrating blur emerged a little
silhouette which for a moment longer might be either, or.

Leftward. The Queen's golden face looked leftward.

And Elmer failed.

The lanky engineer had approached the Isi machine as a wrestler might. His hands shifted this way and that way, seeking a
grip on its hundred-some knobs. His long slender fingers roved
yet never more than grazed those tempting protuberances before
he would reposition himself, edging further around the burly
mechanism. Always more knobs remained out of sight and just
out of reach. How could he encompass them all at once? He
couldn't. He sucked in his cheeks deeply as if those might meet
within and cling together. Presently he had begun gently patting
groups of knobs, seemingly at random. Crook-kneed, he circled
ever so slowly around that great brazen pumpkin with the faceless head perched upon it.

Ten minutes had passed thus; and still he *did* nothing. It was
all preparation.

The Queen's patience had failed; and therefore so had he.

Osmo addressed the machine.

'Fat Brassman, your origin is alien. Juttahat fingers made you
for the handless serpents who cannot clutch a knob – except in

444

their mouths. Words and thoughts must stir you; as mine shall stir yours—'

An *everything machine*. What was the origin of *everything*? What great word could express and unlock entirety, totality, unbounded potential? The name Ukko perhaps?

This brassy apparatus was only a doll compared with an Ukko, even if nested within it there lurked a whole potential toyshop of gadgets. Should he proclaim at it imperatively the story of Copperman who marched out of the sea and swelled in size till he was as tall as a tree? So as to force the machine to grow? Osmo shut his eyes.

Dolls, toys . . .

As if in a dream he felt himself shrink. The whole fortress also diminished, round about him, donjon and gatehouse and battlemented walls. Lucky's sentries were toys. The Queen was too, and her Prince and her daughter and General and Chamberlain. They stood about him like little mobile models carved in wood and painted perfectly. The fortress was the setting for a complicated game employing wonderfully realistic pieces. He himself was player and piece. As was Elmer. The aim of the game was to make the brass homunculus move. Rotate, open up, expand, perform.

Osmo envisaged this vaulted chamber at the heart of the donjon where the players were set out. He imagined himself as an enormous child crouching outside its toy, squinting through a window-*slit*. A great blue eye like a segment of sky. The wall was on hinges. *Open up, wall!* The child reached in with chubby fingers to set the brass piece in motion by . . . pushing down on the sphere at its apex . . . to make it spin like a top.

'Spin, brass top!' he bespoke. 'Whirr, and whirl! Gyrate within! Rotate!'

The whole universe was spinning around him and around the machine. Clouds of stars gusted by in uncountable numbers, while he and the brass top balanced unmoving at the heart of creation. The knobbly globe of the everything machine reflected all of this starlight. Of a sudden the starlight was within the machine, counter-rotating. The machine had become transparent. It enclosed a whole cosmos of scintillating sparks, packed densely together.

Osmo snapped open his eyes – to be greeted by a bright blur. Everything was unfocused. His heart thumped; his blood raced. His whole body felt as though it was rotating inwardly. Every morsel of him was fluttering as if his flesh might fly apart, as if his organs might dismember themselves. More in a rage than panic, more in exasperation than despair, he knew that his bespeaking had rebounded upon himself from an unswayable target.

'Flesh, be still,' he roared. 'Heart, be calm. Eyes, be clear.'

His sheer pique saved him from a seizure to which terror might have condemned him. Gradually he recovered his equilibrium. By and by he could see clearly again.

The brass machine stood impassively as ever.

Thus it was Elmer's turn again; the engineer's second chance. When Elmer failed once more, what should Osmo do for an encore? He still felt nauseated and unsettled. Surely he had *almost* activated the machine.

The engineer hunkered by the brass device. His eyes appeared crossed. He too must be seeing a blur, of knobs. He hummed tunelessly, as if to conjure a corresponding hum from within the alien apparatus.

Of a sudden his right hand darted forward – to pull out a knob and twist it clockwise. Then another. And a third. At the same time with the heel of his left hand he slammed the first knob.

The machine throbbed.

It was active. An indigo glow formed an aura around the device – almost outside of the visible spectrum, a breed of shadow in which threads of energy spiked like crackling blue hairs. Elmer retreated circumspectly.

Eva led the applause.

'I *caused* this to happen,' Osmo insisted indignantly. 'Did you see all the stars, all the sparks of energy inside it swirling round? I almost burst myself – didn't everyone see how I strained? Afterwards it only took a little push. The push of a knob.'

Elmer laughed lightly, deliriously. 'The proper knobs, yes the proper ones. That's what I was intent on grasping. A symmetrical arrangement. Didn't really matter which knobs, where.'

'Once the machine was primed by me! I really must insist—'

'You didn't start the machine.' In Elmer's tone there was exultation. Eva hugged him. He dared to stoop and kiss her on the lips, to press her against him.

'Just so!' exclaimed the beaming Queen, while Prince Bertel grinned amenably. 'We award you the hand of our daughter Eva,

Elmer Loxmith. We grant you all of her, and longlife too.' The Earthman Wex added his voice: 'Congratulations, Loxmith, we're impressed—' The Queen eyed her jester. 'You, and yourself as well?' She clapped her hands delightedly.

'However, let me sound a note of—'

'*Madam*' – from the Captain, urgently.

The purring Isi machine was beginning to change shape. Its broad brass bum was spreading out.

Within an hour the donjon had effectively become a shell. An enlarged arched entrance gaped wide enough and high enough to accommodate a carriage and ponies. The lone tower still rose from one corner – though empty of floors or stairway – and the mass of the outer structure survived. Indeed the donjon appeared as sturdy as ever, except that it was hollow save for the large mechanism which now squatted amidst powdering debris.

What a crashing and crumbling there had been. Such clouds of dust, now largely dispersed. Shrieks of outrage from the Queen had punctuated her melancholy contemplation of the donjon's seeming demise and the apparent ruin of her hopes. Several times she had been on the verge of rescinding her award to Loxmith even though Wex had ventured to reassure her. {*Justifiably, in the event, my Roger.*}

'It's clearing enough space for itself and what it might be called on to produce,' Wex had told Lucky. 'Let's wait and see.'

Which the visitors had all done, from a safe distance at the far end of the courtyard. And the watchful cuckoo too, perched on a battlement.

'My *fortress*,' the Queen had protested. She had clenched her teeth grimly as, out of sight, more masonry crashed down inside the donjon sending dust billowing into view.

Captain Bekker and General Aleksonis had been all for Lucky leaving the island right away, and had directed hostile glances at Wex. Two of Bekker's sentries advanced stiffly to the very threshold of the largely invisible devastation – bracing themselves against possible debris – and called back very little by way of reports. Eva had wrung her hands, and Loxmith appeared lugubrious. Van Maanen was lost in bitter reverie. Prince Bertel began elevating himself on his toes, pumping himself up and down as if to see better. {*Thinking of dashing boldly into the building. Opportunity for accidental death.*}

Wex had positioned himself in front of Lucky's consort. 'It may

447

be,' he mused aloud, 'that everything machines are somewhat chancy contrivances—'

'Her Majesty ought to leave,' Bekker advised again; but Lucky shook her head crossly.

'How so, Wethead? Why wait till now to tell me?'

'At last we have an example of one in action. Of Isi design, admittedly. I can imagine machines like this in use on dead moons, manufacturing things . . . I don't suppose the Isi minded letting one loose on Kaleva.' {*Chancy? Nanotech machines must be exactly programmed. The device is merely reconfiguring its environment as a preliminary to operations.*} 'I agree. We won't be harmed. What I mean, your Majesty, is that it might create unexpected artefacts.'

Downcast: 'Oh I only required one product from it.'

'Yes?'

She had ignored him. The donjon continued to quake within. Bertel had abandoned his notion.

As they waited, a change came over the sky. Spring weather was notoriously capricious. Clouds piled against one another till the sky was rumpled pewter, tinctured with urine, threatening a return of snow. Beyond the low curtain wall, over the firth, the greymew – or another of its ilk – screamed its hunger at submerged fish. The sea-bird plummeted, then it rose back into view with silver wriggling in its claws. Had the bird been *bescreaming* its prey to surface? The cuckoo shifted its scaly head in the mew's direction, registering its departure towards the shore where it could tear up its meal.

Eventually the donjon had become calm, and dust had settled.

First, sentries filed into their gutted former headquarters, bayonets outstretched. Next, Captain Bekker entered to survey what onlookers could already glimpse. Way inside the new entrance, fluted brassy columns flanked an aperture as large as the entrance itself. These served as entry into a cave of glossy metal set in the heart of what had recently been the donjon.

Wex followed, while General Aleksonis delayed an impatient, anxious Lucky.

A grooved tower resembling a curious silo soared – open at the front to expose a spacious metal cavity. Its interior was peppered with little nozzles which seemed the inverse of the former knobs that had sprouted from the brassy Mandelbrot man. Wex sneezed. The air was hot and acrid and still full of tiny motes. These drifted slowly towards the aperture, to be sucked into the nozzles. A baffle could slide down to shut the {*assembly chamber, is what this is*}. Pipes descended into the floor where flagstones and metal had flowed together. To Wex the tower seemed rooted like a tooth. {*With a tap root. Feeder roots will be spreading out even now far underground to fill its storage vat with demolished matter sucked in for transmutation. Source of energy: fission? There's no evidence of intrusion into our brain or body by the nano-motes.*}

In a groove to the right of the assembly chamber a small bulge was swelling out. A brassy little globe emerged on a stiff stalk. A blank eyeball, cupped within lips. {*Control interface. Grasp it. Address it.*}

As Wex was reaching out, Captain Bekker jerked him aside. The sheer power of that man – muscles like solid timber, except that they flexed! His voice was a rasp.

'The Queen's privilege, I believe.'

From a distance, lodged temporarily between two sentries, Wex watched Lucky whisper to that little globe she had placed her fingers upon; and listen; and whisper again. Avidly she talked to Bertel.

'Captain Bekker,' she cried, 'guard this machine from anyone but me, do you hear? I'll return soon. Right now, I have a wedding to arrange.' {*The machine may need time to calibrate itself.*} 'Come along, husband. Come along, my jester.'

When Lucky swept out into the courtyard once more, wreathed in smiles, she advanced upon Elmer and held up her ruby ring to be kissed.

This done, he stared around, relieved and triumphant. 'Cuckoo, cuckoo,' he yelled boyishly to the eavesdropping bird on the battlement, 'tell the tale of how Elmer Loxmith activated Lucky's everything machine, and won Eva Sariola as his bride!' At whom, he winked. He strode over to Osmo, who looked so dismayed and disbelieving. 'Dear friend, will you proclaim at my wedding?'

Words dribbled from Osmo's lips. 'At *your*. . . wedding? *What . . . ?*'

The Queen smirked. 'Ah, benevolence fills me to the brim. How can I ever express such happiness?' She clapped her hands. 'I know! I shall invite the parents of that fellow who helped my girl. I'll send my sky-boat to collect them from their hovels. Won't that be magnanimous? The merest paupers welcomed to my palace. Well, Elmer?'

Of course her future son-in-law nodded agreeably – the foible seemed of no special instant significance.

For a moment or two.

Then understanding dawned.

'But . . .'

How would he possibly protest? Should he sully this fine moment by bickering with Eva's mother? What could he possibly say? And for whose sake?

Osmo heard himself growl – as if his body had understood Lucky's import even before his mind completely absorbed the meaning.

The fellow who helped my girl.

The girl being Jatta.

This must have been Jatta's idea – to punish him, to humble him, to tear him apart inwardly. *Mummy, Mummy, if Lord Osmo doesn't win wouldn't it be such fun, wouldn't it be really rich to. . .* whisper, whisper in the madwoman's ear.

The fellow who helped my girl. Juke Nurmi. Mutie Juke. Invite his freak mum and dad to the festivities – mana alone knew how bizarrely warped they were! That'll chase Osmo keys and keys away with a flea in his ear. That'll really sicken him. And teach him.

Vile bile churned in Osmo's belly. Clenching his teeth and forcing his face to stay rigid, he lumbered a few paces away from Elmer before his *rival* could say or do . . . nothing whatever, sweet nothing. Gawkish lunk, making appealing cows' eyes at Osmo. And at Eva.

Never die, Son. Never die. In cuckoo tones his mother's words mocked him.

A few snowflakes capered. Demon Jack wasn't here in the fortress, however. Just the dismal clouds above. Crazy Lucky wasn't even bothering to watch him with malicious relish. She was staring back gleefully at the shell of the donjon housing the wonderful gift which he himself had caused to come into being. Only to be cheated, insulted, swindled in favour of his once best friend – so that he was doubly despoiled. Gall flooded him.

Say nothing for the moment; do nothing – till you can slip out of Sariolinna with your balls intact.

That evening, Osmo kept to his guest suite, along with Marko and Hannes and Victor Rintala. Afar, he could hear drunken

450

singing. He wore his knife and his lightpistol – which Elmer and Lyle had overhauled for him after the events of the Lucky's Day feast some nine months previously . . .

Osmo paced to and fro past a linen-draped table bearing cold cuts and pickled fish and oat rolls and cheese and spirit, none of which he touched. Marko and Hannes were crestfallen and uncomprehending. Vivi's father seemed secretive – gruffly reticent in his indignation, as if the slap upon his lord's cheek also bruised his daughter's memory. Occasionally Victor nodded his bleached gingery head, but at what inner decision? They would leave the next morning if the weather had cleared. Maybe even if it hadn't. Fly back to Maananfors empty-handed, empty-hearted.

A thump on the door.

Hannes opened to . . . Bertel. The Prince thrust past, epaulettes bouncing. An open bottle of vodka was in one hand.

'I came to . . . *apologize.*' Lucky's consort pouted out the word affectedly as if the word meant something entirely different. He sounded distinctly tipsy, and not contrite so much as combative. Challenging Osmo to contradict him.

'Accept my apology.' Bertel was peremptory. 'A *prince's* apology, by the way!' When Osmo withdrew a few paces, Bertel pursued with a hectic swagger, challenging – life itself, possibly! He waved the half-empty bottle at his insulted guest.

'Accept a drink, damn it.' Those words weren't slurred at all. His inebriation was less than one might suppose. The Prince leered. 'I thought you might be a little vexed, mm?' Waving the bottle, he caught Victor Rintala a glancing blow; for the farmer had moved to Osmo's aid. 'Why you butting in, then? What's it to you? How dare you?' Bertel shoved the farmer in the chest. Advancing, he pushed him again. Victor drew back, only to attract a further buffeting. Bertel seemed intent on driving Victor halfway across the room, unless the farmer resisted.

Vivi's father merely smiled darkly. 'Wait, now. You.' And stepped backward again.

Even in his anguish Osmo spared a moment to wonder why Victor was showing such restraint. Out of respect for Prince Okkonen-Sariola, father of Kaleva? Victor didn't sound particularly deferential. Out of fear of the consequences if his temper flared? A scuffle; a knife thrust; a death . . . The terrible repercussions of those consequences if Lucky's husband met his death in a bedchamber brawl!

'*Wait, now.*'

Abandoning Victor in apparent disgust, Bertel surveyed Hannes and Marko. 'What are you two oafs staring at?'

'Are you trying to provoke us all, sir?' Osmo asked with a grim courtesy.

'Naturally you'd be riled. Your mignon egg's been snatched away. Can't unwrap it now, can you? I invited you here. Don't bother yourself too much. Longlife isn't all roses.'

'Isn't it now?' remarked Victor gruffly.

Never die, Son. Never die.

'Anyway, you failed. Eh, van Maanen? You failed. So: no hard feelings, mm?' The bottle jerked toward Osmo more like a weapon than a peace offering. 'You fluffed the contest.'

'I did *not* . . .'

'Pooh-pooh,' scoffed Bertel. 'I see you're wearing your pistol. Restores the manhood, eh?' Brightly the Prince eyed Osmo's retinue as though they might applaud his sally of wit. 'And I invited him here, so I fancy I ought to make some show of apologizing, don't you think so, chaps?' Bertel was definitely trying to madden Osmo.

Osmo breathed deeply. 'I proclaim that you'll *get out of this suite* toot-sweet and stay well away from me. This is spoken, Prince, this is spoken.'

He nodded at Hannes and Marko as managers of skittish stallions and miscreants, in case Bertel might prove immune to being bespoken.

Within instants the Prince was in retreat, practically fleeing. At the threshold Bertel glanced back, relief and regret mingling in that parting glimpse.

A wedding attended by muties. By a fat mutton-headed peasant woman with long trailing hairy arms, and a gimping hunchback with the head of a goat: Osmo dreamed confusedly of this. It was he himself who was being wed. A mana-priest with two heads presided. Both noddles were those of Wex, the Earthman – they kept knocking together, and apologizing. The best man was Juke Nurmi. He was armed to the scowling teeth with long knives, and also with a sword. Its serpentine blade was akin to a giant corkscrew which had been hammered flat and sharpened. Nurmi also toted a lightpistol.

'Short life, short life,' the mutie proclaimer promised.

The bride was Eyeno Nurmi. She began reciting about stars in jars, and wars and whores. She was ravishing, except that her

452

glass eye hung loosely upon her cheek on a short silver chain.

'Short life to you, brother-in-law.'

'See all the stars in a jar—'

Eyeno's mother bleated. Desire and disgust warred in Osmo. He really must restore that eye of Eyeno's to its socket otherwise her brother's prophecy would come true. 'Excuse me—' He lifted the glass eye to replace it – and looked right into it.

A myriad twinkling stars whirled within. Suddenly those stars streamed from the eye to circle Osmo's head like glitterbugs. He was blinded to the belligerent brother and the two-headed priest and the appalling uncouth parents. Now that her eye was back in its rightful place it reflected a meadow where waxen flowers bloomed. Gorgeous Sariola girls in gauzy gowns skipped around a gross yet ghostly figure. A naked man. The man was turning this way and that, hands outstretched in appeal. Ducking, one of the young women ran right through his girth. She entered his sagging belly and emerged from his beefy buttocks. That long blond hair, that chubby cherubic face . . . The man was Lord Beck. It was the dream lord. Like vast cupped wings, woodlands and lakes curved upward, following the contours of the false eyeball.

'Gunther!' cried Osmo. He mustn't spin round, else he would see his sworn enemy again. With that snaky-bladed sword poised at his back. If he didn't swing round Nurmi might run him through, just as the Sariola sisters ran through the vast man, one by one. A man so overweight, yet with no weight at all to impede their passage.

Pain pierced Osmo.

He woke with a terrible cramp. Rearing, he clutched at his calf muscles to knead them like dough. 'Relax,' he snarled at his ligaments. 'Unknot yourselves!'

Never die.

Soon he lay still, thinking of the dream. His own dream, to begin with . . . Then it had seemed that Gunther was dreaming too, in tandem, dreaming of a real scene somewhere into which the fat lord was struggling to project himself. Osmo was dreaming Beck's own dream, though from a different perspective – that of Eyeno Nurmi, through whose eye Osmo had entered that lovely, strangely upcurving terrain . . . of death? Surely the mutie poetess had drowned herself long since?

Why had his muscles cramped so vilely? Because he'd been thwarted. Hamstrung in his hopes.

In the morning he woke dully. Thin bands of sunshine sliced through chinks in heavy curtaining. The light lacerated Osmo's whole being as the events of the previous day flooded back. Nausea squirmed in his empty belly. He wished daylight away. The sun and the hour and the turning of the world weren't bespeakable. His pee-hard cock taunted him.

Padding through the adjoining chamber to visit the privy, he passed Marko and Hannes, both slumbering on couches. He couldn't see Victor. Was the farmer visiting the closet?

The outer door was unbolted, top and bottom. *Anyone could come into the suite.* As Osmo paused, the latch rose – raised softly by someone outside who wished to avoid a click and a clack. Slowly the stout door edged open.

'Victor—?'

Abandoning stealth, Vivi's father entered.

'Took some of our things to the sky-boat, I did, so we could get on our way the faster.'

'It isn't as if we're taking a trousseau with us, Victor—'

'Ought to be on our way, and swiftly. Soonest left is soonest forgotten. I'll wake the lads.' Indeed, Marko was already stirring. 'Rouse yourself there!' the farmer chided. 'What kind of watchman outsleeps his master? Rise and shine. We'll be on our way with the ducks. Quaack, quaack.'

Osmo seized Victor's right hand and hauled him to the window where he tore the curtain aside. The flood of light brought Marko and Hannes stumbling from their couches, rubbing their dazzled eyes. Swollen contusions marked one side of Victor's hand. Deep scratches. A smear of blood.

'I'm not seeing this . . .' Better not to know till later. 'Did you kill him?' Osmo whispered, to measure the urgency of their departure.

The farmer guffawed. 'Oh, I had this from a bitch – a Spitz in the sky-boat yard. Wuff, wuff.' He was fibbing. (*Wait now, you.*)

'Let's get out of here quickly,' ordered Osmo. He fled to relieve himself.

Osmo piloted the sky-boat west along the Great Fjord to avoid crossing high peaks. Then he swung south by way of a lesser firth. At the far end of this inlet the vessel climbed over densely forested hills cupping azure tarns. Osmo was following the obvious route, which would also be the swiftest route to Maananfors keep seven hours away at full velocity. Ample alcohol in the tank. He held the speed at a steady ninety keys so as not to strain the engine.

'Well?' Osmo demanded at last, over his shoulder. He hadn't wished to commence any further enquiry until they were well outside of the domain of Lucky. Sitting behind him, Victor had kept mum. Marko and Hannes respected their lord's silence. Besides, being aloft in a sky-boat was still a novel experience for them. The vessel itself produced noise enough to make an absence of chatter seem natural. The motor throbbed. The tail propellers whirred. Wind whistled into the intake pipes. The fuselage vibrated constantly.

'Well, Victor?'

'Look round, Lord Osmo.' The farmer sounded smug.

The sky-boat was flying level and true five hundred metres above a long lake flanked by low hills thickly tufted with trees.

Leaning back, Victor tugged open the hatch of the storage bay in which they had formerly stowed that marble bust. A figure wriggled within, roped hand and foot – barefoot – and muffled with torn linen. The bare legs jutting from a nightgown were those of a girl. Her hair was a frizzy bush. She blinked out at her kidnappers indignantly. Her mouth munched on her gag as she swallowed words.

Minnow Sariola.

'We shan't be returning empty-handed,' Vivi's father said proudly. 'Here's a lively hen for you. Bit me, she did, in fact. As you noticed. Quite a minx – might need a spot of bespeaking afore she settles down. Knocked an old fellow over the head as was snoozing outside her door, I did. Swan didn't come for him, so that's fine. No swan'll ever come for you now; not ever, Lord Osmo, once you lay this hen in a nest. Tuck-tuck, and doodle-do.'

Minnow Sariola. Instead of Eva. Minnow, hooked out of the palace.

A kid.

No, not a kid at all. Already set her heart on wedding a fine fellow. Preferably with a moustache. Osmo being about right; hadn't she said so herself? She might regard being abducted as romantic. Didn't look too appreciative right now . . .

Absurd!

Never die, Son.

How very galling to Prince Bertel and Queen Lucky.

Never die. 'You can't be very comfortable in there,' Osmo called in an effort at gallantry.

'*Unnngggh*—' The noises of the sky-boat almost drowned the girl's muted protest.

'I apologize!' Rather as Bertel had apologized to him the previous evening . . . Let crazy, cheating Lucky fly into a fury. Why, this was how heroes won their brides! 'Hannes, stuff the rest of our sacks in there with her for padding. And your coat.' Minnow couldn't exactly join them in the little cabin. Might be unpredictable. Stay in there, where Marko – being shorter – would have curled up on the return flight had events fallen out differently.

'Better shut the hatch again to hold her in – in case she rolls. I do beg pardon, little Princess! This is how champions win their loves, isn't it?'

'*Unnngggh*—'

'Don't worry, we'll open the hatch now and then. We'll land if you need . . . necessities.'

All attention had been on the cubby hole where Minnow lay curled in her nightgown, while Hannes bolstered her. 'Lord Osmo!' cried Marko. He tore at his lord's sleeve. 'Ware hill – we'll hit it!' The lake had ended.

However, the watchman was panicking unnecessarily. Osmo steered up and over easily.

They landed twice en route, descending each time on tilted rotors bumpily upon a different bleached pebbly lake-shore. Being a father – and since the alternative would be demeaning to Osmo – Victor attended to Minnow's necessities. He carried the kicking princess out behind bushes. On returning, the farmer would hold her to slake her thirst with lake water. He slipped her gag temporarily but kept her outcry well away from Osmo who paced the strand, stretching his legs. ('Now quit your cackle, my pecking young biddy – it isn't the chopper you're facing but a first-rate granite coop to queen it over.' *Splutter*: 'And how do you fancy you'll be received at the keep!') Afterwards Victor restored her tidily to the storage compartment amid those lumpy improvised cushions.

Osmo would navigate southwestward along the Valtimo to the bend where that wide river swept due west to avoid the Saddle-back Twins. He would fly a course between those two sprawling hills, just a couple of hours from home by air-boat even with a head-wind against them. Brindled Isi territory lay a score of keys off to the west; forests where few men ventured. Maybe he should try to raise Sam on the communicator to forewarn him and Alvar. *I'm bringing a bride. She just isn't the one we expected.* Very likely some Brindled Juttahat would be listening patiently day after day for infrequent transmissions. Brindleds were usually cordial. Neutral, at least. Plausibly so. Better not to alert them.

Anyone would have flown that way.

Something with a tail of flame leapt from the woody flank of the eastern Twin. A speeding firework. Heading towards the sky-boat.

How his face had leered from the fireworks over Lake Yulista.

The flametail was closing rapidly. Purposefully. Osmo banked the sky-boat and veered westward at full thrust. The vessel climbed diagonally across the western Twin.

An incandescent eruption threw the sky-boat. The left side of the canopy shattered, showering the occupants with shards. A fat little wheel flew away through the air. Blood ran from Marko's forehead. Yet the watchman leaned out, wiping his brow as he did so. He craned his neck. 'There's another one coming—'

The sky-boat responded. Propellers were still racing. Wind battered Marko, and Hannes behind him. Eyes watering, Osmo climbed. Dive, and they'd fly faster – but then he might hit the swell of the hill.

'Get back in, Marko!'

The second explosion tipped the sky-boat over to port. Sliding in his seat, Osmo clutched the control column, causing the vessel to pitch even more acutely. Uttering an incredulous cry, Marko tumbled out. He was gone. He'd be falling, falling.

In vain Hannes had hurled himself forward to try to seize Marko, if only by the feet. Unbalanced, Hannes clutched for Marko's former seat. The seat shifted. A flailing hand thumped the surviving half of the canopy. The resulting thunderclap could have been that of a wingbrace snapping. A sizeable section of the curved airshield sheered free, catching the groom in the neck. Blood spurted. Gurgling, hands clamped upon a severed artery, Hannes collapsed, half over the seat. The man was choking. Life-blood sprayed the littered floor. Another piece of canopy fell, catching Osmo a glancing blow on the shoulder before bursting into smaller pieces.

Osmo was fighting, nursing, cursing. The sky-boat veered to starboard. Hannes was dying. Marko would have hit the ground like a sack of grain which the blow would burst open. Maybe he'd impacted violently upon a tree and hung broken like a cruel parody of a shaman. Wind buffeted the exposed cabin. A propeller was screaming.

'Our tail's smoking—'

'Die, fire – be smothered!' bellowed Osmo. 'This is spoken! We shall not burn.' Did the fire heed him? No way to see its source. *Fire burn bones to ash.* How well he remembered howling those words at Tycho Cammon's soul-pyre, on the lake-shore at Maananfors. *Flames crack and crumble.* Ice and winter's chill: those were the thoughts to hold dear now. Fire melts frost, melts ice and quenches itself. He was shivering, perhaps with shock.

Never die.

Minnow . . . better that she remained where she was, securely padded. The engine was knocking – or was the princess banging her heels against the inside of the hatch behind Victor? Cool, cool, numb the tongues of flame. Shivers would be his salvation. How could he shiver so much unless he was freezing? The litter of fragmented canopy was icicles. Glassy icicles, not flames. The whole sky-boat was *cold*.

How many keys had they flown off course, on a gradual descent? Controls had locked up. Rods had probably failed, damaged by the explosions. Elmer would know. Triumphant Elmer, damn him! The sky-boat had frozen as if sheathed in invisible ice. It was a turbulent projectile boosting towards the west to collide eventually with the horizon. A thin streamer of smoke smudged the sky, but no fire flared. Fire was foxed. The boat was paralysed – try to rekindle its life and a frustrated inferno would engulf the vessel. Hannes had died long since.

Rotors wouldn't swing to slow the boat. Treetops rushed beneath. Foliage tore at the undercarriage as the sky-boat barely cleared yellovers and horzmas. Water stretched ahead.

As if remembering its previous descents and compelled to re-enact them – even though crippled now – the sky-boat plunged across the lough towards a stony shore.

Osmo roused from unconsciousness to an insistent thumping which corresponded with the beat of his headache. The crumpled sky-boat lay askew, half-beached. Hannes's corpse was jammed against him. A body lay ashore amid boulders. A bleached gingery head jutted at an oblique indignant angle. Victor.

Thump.

In wrestling the heavy groom aside, Osmo bloodied his hands. He wiped the palms vigorously on his breeches. Then he picked his way to the rear, and tore open the hatch assisted by a kick from within.

He eased Minnow out. Bare-legged and bound, her nightdress rucking up. No blood on her. No spasm of agony; no bones seemed broken. In her wide eyes: a chaos which she was trying her best to control. He ungagged her.

'She needs her hands free, doesn't she? Ooh, my wrists! Let me *see*, it's really important!' she gabbled. 'If I don't see I'll go *mad.*'

'Shhh, precious.' His head throbbed as he untethered her hands, then her feet.

Minnow sat up amidst the wreckage. She straightened her nightdress. She massaged her shanks – all the while staring hither and yon like a bird wary of attack from any quarter. She staggered to her feet. 'Ouch—' Stare, stare, everywhere. At Osmo with blood on him. At dead Hannes. At the ruin of the sky-boat, at Victor's corpse, at the lake, at the forest, at the sky. At Osmo, frantically. Her teeth chattered as if she was trying to tell herself a dozen things at once.

'What *happened?*' burst from her.

'Someone shot us down . . .' Osmo held his head. 'Be still, pain. Easy, brain.'

'This is a shambles; and where are we? Does anybody have any idea, who isn't dead? They're dead, all right, dead! Here's a pretty kettle of fish, with a Minnow dumped in it. And and and, *what*' – she stabbed a finger towards the chartreuse quiffs of a curver tree a hundredsome metres away – 'what is *that* meant to be when it's at home?'

Dangling under the bendy tree, only noticeable now that she pointed it out, hung a green band twice the size of a barrel hoop. A cloud cloaked the sun. As shadow swept across the forest's edge the hoop seemed to stay softly aglow with its own intrinsic light. By night it must shine out over the lough.

Lyle had taken over the task of applying white paint to Elmer's face in this final hour before the marriage. Stripped to the waist, the bridegroom had already coated his own neck and bony shoulders and chin and cadaverous cheeks. When it came to the flesh around his mouth and eyes the engineer's hand had quivered.

'Just as well Osmo isn't wedding her,' quipped Lyle. 'He'd have spent half the day preening himself, then what would he have done about that moustache of his? Bleached it? And ended up looking rather like Sam Peller.'

True enough, under his mop of black hair – held back from his brow by a net – Elmer appeared to have put on years, along with the cosmetic paint on which Lucky had insisted. His image in the dressing-table mirror was as blanched as a corpse, supposedly to highlight the longlife with which he was about to be gifted by wedding a Sariola daughter.

'Could you shut your right eye now?'

Elmer squinted as Lyle peered through the gold-rimmed spectacles astride his snubby nose and delicately applied a thinner brush to the upper lid. Then to the lower.

'Don't open yet. Let it dry.' A sly smile puckered Lyle's lips. 'When I wed, perhaps you'll paint me green.'

Elmer answered without overly moving his mouth: 'Whatever for?'

'Green for freshness and pristine innocence, what else?'

'But you aren't—'

'The girl may wish to believe it.'

Girl? What girl? *Nikki?*

'Or on the other hand, not. Remember that party in the aitchhouse when you got merry? With the shopkeeper's wife?'

'Um,' said Elmer noncommittally, 'why mention that?'

'Oh I don't know. Practice makes perfect – left eye now.'

Obediently Elmer shut his other eye and tolerated the gentle tickle of the brush hairs. Was some beldame, or Lucky herself – or Jatta – currently offering Eva the fruits of experience while adorning her? Similarly Elmer himself was due for an interview with his new mother-in-law shortly after the ceremony, when she would confide a very special word to him.

'A spot of practice hasn't helped Osmo, eh? Lucky will slaughter him sooner or later for his effrontery.'

'Meaning that we shouldn't attempt a reconciliation too soon?'

'Could be inadvisable.'

'Inadvisable on the Queen's account? Or mightn't Osmo be satisfied with Minnow – is that what you think?'

'We'll need to watch out.'

With the paint on his eyelids still drying, Elmer was unable to watch anything at all; blindly he listened to advice.

The fact that Osmo and party, decamping without a by-your-leave, had kidnapped Eva's younger sister from her bed had been common knowledge around the whole palace by mid-morning on that disconcerting day a week earlier. This would have been so in any event once a maid discovered Max, a retired guard, tied to the foot of the empty bed, head pounding and a gag between his gums. But also a couple of cuckoos had found their way into the palace. One was definitely a witness to the awakening of the everything machine. For days thereafter the two birds were to haunt the palace, squawking for their supper, snooping, and regaling any attentive ear.

To a considerable extent the Queen's fury was sidetracked by her preoccupation with the towering apparatus at the fortress. A necessary sequel to its activation was the business of arranging nuptials. She wouldn't dream of doing otherwise than reward Elmer promptly. Yet not quite *immediately*. Her mischievous whim of inviting mutants to the celebration was fortified unshakeably by the knowledge of how offensive Osmo had found this proposal. Consequently Bertel must fly off to . . . where was it, Outo? Down beyond Niemi. Her consort must fly there in person to press invitations upon Juke Nurmi's parents and upon any other of those warped villagers whom he could corral. He must bring back a troop of them toot-sweet. He must *insist*.

But wasn't General Aleksonis to chase after Lord Osmo with a gang of guards – or even with some of Lucky's wooden soldiers, tough and seasoned – to try to kill the proclaimer and free Minnow from his clutches?

'I'll massacre that scoundrel,' Lucky assured Roger Wex in the hearing of a cuckoo – so that her daughter's abductor would hear of her vow by and by. 'But in my own good time. A *bad* time it'll be for that robberbird van Maanen, make no mistake. I'll burn him to ashes right where he toasted Cammon's bones. I'll blot out his soul. His pleas won't matter a scavvy's fart.' She stared at the cuckoo, perched on a chandelier in her Filigree Parlour which resembled a giant bird's cage. The oval wall of the chamber was clad in a vine of convoluted golden wirework, except where an oval window stood open upon the rooftops of the palace like some watchful eye with an intricate web of glittering veins inside it.

'Let him hear, let him fear. Let him wait for his fate.'

'Ah,' said Wex, 'but it might take van Maanen days on end – nights on end, I suppose – to talk the girdle off Minnow.'

What do you know about her girdle?

'I assumed . . . We deduced . . .'

'Did you, my jester? A hot-shot proclaimer such as van Maanen should be able to loosen her soon enough.'

'There may still be time if we go after Minnow. I want to go after her, your Majesty.'

Lucky studied Wex incredulously. 'You? Why you?'

'I like Minnow. We like her. *I* like her.'

She giggled. She cocked her head. 'Are there three of you now? When did you conceive this quaint affection? When Minnow showed you how to make two statues out of one?'

Unwilling to have his feelings mocked, Wex prevaricated. 'Maybe Jack'll want to go too – in the little sky-boat he brought with him when he rescued Anni. The rescue boat.'

'You aren't making off with any sky-boat of mine!'

'Any? Do you mean you have more than two? Another at the fortress – hidden away. Is that it?'

The cuckoo listened avidly.

{*Of course airships – dirigibles – would be the ideal form of transport, my Roger. But in the early days there were a series of fatal accidents. The profile of a slow-moving airship attracted mana-storms and lightning bolts.*}

Wex adjusted his wig, though it wasn't askew.

'When I catch van Maanen,' vowed Lucky, 'I'll have a ring of proclaimers turn him to stone. He'll be a statue standing in a fire-pit. Or up to the chin in a pit of shit. Something foul.'

But not yet. Nor hastily. She could do without a troublesome interruption to her private project of finding herself – courtesy of something yet to be produced by the everything machine; that was evident. She didn't want a disruption with unpredictable spin-off – one which might divert a portion of her strength (even perhaps her wooden soldiers).

'I need more proclaimers around me.' She gazed directly at the cuckoo as if issuing a recruitment call. 'When I go to war I intend to flatten van Maanen quickly.'

'Meanwhile Minnow—'

'Chase after them, Wethead, if you like. Cross the fjord. Go overland, with my blessing. I'm tired of your presence.'

Wex patted his cloak of many pockets. {*If we call Conway to ask for a sky-boat from Landfall she'll be well advised to refuse. If an Earthkeep sky-boat is used for a mission perceivedly on behalf of Lucky, that will seem partisan and favouristic. Landfall ought to remain neutral. I must regrettably overrule any such proposal.*} Surely haste was of the essence in Minnow's case? {*Regrettably! There are higher considerations, my Roger.*} The wetwear must nurse some tenderness for Minnow too. Or was his invisible companion merely indulging Wex?

Quietly: 'Minnow talks to herself . . .'

'A fellow spirit! She already knows where her other self is – inside her own head.'

Wex persisted. 'You'll be sending a sky-boat south to collect your wedding guests—'

'Heading south-westward, not south-east. Be off with you, Wethead. Soppy for a girl: who'd have believed it? I'll roast van Maanen once he's stone. I'll crack his petrified nuts.' But not immediately. 'Coo-coo cuckoo: go and screech for a proclaimer who hates van Maanen's guts!'

Hark at the story; hear the tale. When the royal sky-boat (winter-white with vermilion eyes) returned to Pohjola Palace on an evening five days later, it disgorged Bertel, and half a dozen nervous mutants in raggy finery – and also the Dame of Niemi's son, Minkie Kennan, heir of the selfsame Ragnar Kennan who had once tried to swindle the Queen. The mutants and young Kennan were duly received in the Dome of Favours. Quite an audience goggled. Minkie carefully distanced himself from the freaks.

Arto Nurmi had come to Pohjola, gnomish and pointy-eared, with hearing to rival any cuckoo's. Father of van Maanen's *bête noir*, no less. The Queen was delighted to clasp both of the glove-maker's six-fingered hands. Her own hands were sheathed in white lace for the occasion. Arto subjected those lace gloves of hers to close scrutiny. He might have been meeting the gloves rather than the wearer.

'Second only to your son, Arto Nurmi, you're very welcome here.

'Um,' mumbled Arto, 'maybe my Juke made good in your eyes, your Highness. He made bad afterwards at the gala.'

'Oh no, goodfellow. Your Juke tried to humble van Maanen.'

'Where's Juke got off to these days?' Arto demanded dolefully, as if Queen Lucky might surely know.

'I hope he'll come here,' Lucky assured the glovemaker. 'I hope he'll hear the cuckoo call.'

'Maybe he's off a-visiting the velvet snakes, as he did when he went with our Eyeno for her false eye.' A tear leaked from Arto. 'I'm hoping my home won't fall down with me not there to hear it creaking. We know our place, you see.'

'Your place is here right now, good sir. Won't you introduce your fellow guests?'

Arto extracted his hands from her grasp and splayed five fingers and a thumb as if to assist in these introductions. He crooked his thumb. 'Well, there's Lammas—'

Lammas was covered in curly grey wool except upon his sweet face and his palms. Shorts hid his loins.

'—who's a bit of a singer, your Highness, in the tango style.'

Lucky clapped her hands delightedly. 'He'll croon in the ballroom after the wedding.' Lammas bowed awkwardly, then he scratched a tufty thigh.

'And there's Pieman.' Whose skin was a yellow pastry crust. 'He can whistle a tune.'

'And enjoy a fine pie at a feast, I'll be bound.' Pieman shuffled. Maybe he didn't care to eat anything suggestive of himself.

'Knotty.' Whose hessian tunic seemed to be an outgrowth from his ridgy stringy brown skin. Knotty held an old fiddle and bow. Arto consulted his hand, deliberately downplaying his own intelligence.

The final two guests were a wizened old woman and a chubby adolescent girl. The old woman bent almost double in a perpetual bow. Her head angled askew so as to peer at what was in front of her. The girl wore a saucy, petulant expression on her rosy face. Her blonde hair was in bushy pigtails. Her chest – under a billowy blouse – seemed to host several bosoms. The old woman clasped the girl firmly by the hand.

'Goody Hilda – she's our healer from Halvek – brought June with her, hoping as you might lay your saintly hands on the girl to banish her problem.'

'What problem's that, goodfellow?'

'June's from Halvek too, you see, your Highness. If anyone

464

touches her, as they well might try to, she promptly gives them a disease. Right away. They soon give others they touch the disease.'

'A love disease.' Lucky winced.

'All kinds of diseases! Raging thirst, and maddening itch, and the shivers and the shits, beg pardon. Goody Hilda can control June, but Goody mightn't be alive much longer. While Goody holds June's hand the girl's harmless to touch.'

'Harmless,' croaked the bent old humpback woman. She eyed Lucky acutely. 'If June ever conceives babes while she's like this, they'll be a right *plague*. I know it – there'll be four at once.' Breasts bobbing, June managed a curtsey. 'Mebbe her affliction's a protection again' this happening. June attracts men something chronic, you see—'

'Not me,' commented Minkie, aloof.

'—unless I'm holding her hand, I was about to say.'

The Queen darted a glance of interrogation at her husband. Bertel mimed amazement. First he'd known of the infectious aspect of June. Lammas scratched himself a few times and grinned sheepishly. Had those hands of his previously strayed towards June while the twisted old woman was looking the other way? No – he was emphasizing Goody Hilda's message. Heroes in the walls and faces in the sofas seemed to peer anticipatively through the ranks of onlookers. A cuckoo shared the scaffold with the mural painter.

'You expect me to lay my hands on her?' Lucky laughed appreciatively. 'Why, you've brought June here as your protection, haven't you? Your insurance for a safe journey home.'

'Oh no,' the wisewoman protested lopsidedly. 'Your saintly hands are the reason. Seeing as your royal family has, beg pardon, a smidgin of *zombie* love sickness in its organs, as is well known, along with the blessings of longlife, if you follow me.'

'I follow you, all right. The girl's your safe conduct. What impertinence. What ingenuity. I'm impressed.'

Elmer looked uneasily at Eva. His bride-to-be tossed her turban of coal-black hair dismissively.

'Enough, enough,' cried Lucky. 'Let me know more about June, Goody Hilda – if any of it's true – but not right now. You mutants are cordially welcome here in my palace. Let no one lay an unfriendly finger upon any of them. And you' – she eyed Ragnar Kennan's son more coolly – 'are welcome as well. I suppose.'

Minkie, dolled up in a waistcoat of green and scarlet stripes, lavender breeches and scarlet kneesocks, took a few steps forward.

'Your Majesty, it's such a privilege and intense *pleasure* for me' – he glanced fleetingly, avidly, at sumptuous Eva – 'to be received at your court merely because I offered the shelter of my humble keep to your noble consort. Oh, and a few litres of alcohol as well. To fuel the sky-boat, needless to say! I'm already overwhelmed' – another peek at Eva – 'at the beauty of Sariolinna. I rejoice that my father's transgressions' – he lowered his voice sadly – 'don't weigh against me. Since I'm now *intimately acquainted* with what my father was proposing—'

Lucky waved a hand to cut short his spiel. 'Just don't repeat history, sir.'

Minkie beamed as if she had bestowed an accolade.

'Why ever did you invite *him*?' she quizzed Bertel once they had retired to the portrait gallery and were alone – except for drowsing Granny, who cocked an ear.

'I met him at the gala, my love, you'll recall. Kennan invited me to Niemi Keep. Niemi's on the way to the mutant villages. We couldn't very well fly all day and all night—'

Minkie had been such a charming, thoroughly engaging host. Not that Bertel was fooled.

After several centuries of life Bertel Okkonen-Sariola wasn't one to succumb hastily to blandishments other than those of his wife, which indeed weren't blandishments as much as imperatives. Bertel had lived altogether too long. Far, far too long.

The handsome young fellow with the chestnut curls and nut-brown eyes was a rapscallion in paragon's guise. Reformed by his marriage to Kyli of Saari? Not exactly! News of the impending wedding of Bertel's daughter, on whom Minkie had set doting eyes quite briefly at the gala, filled young Kennan with a passionate restlessness. Tidings of the kidnapping of Eva's junior sister – next in line to wed – increased his agitation. Salt on a hen's tail! Bertel could sense these surgings in Minkie's soul. Unlike Kyli Kennan.

Kyli, late of Saari, was thrilled by a royal visit. She was also roundly pregnant and not quite the same Kiki-liki as Minkie had first ravished . . .

Itchy frustrations were afflicting her spouse. What had Kyli brought him, after all, but a dowry wherewith to renovate the keep

– and clogs of responsibility? Burdens (a major one now evident in her belly) could age a fellow! Could tie him down, weigh him down, sap his vitality.

Here in Minkie's home lounged Prince Bertel, hundreds of years old and still quite as spry as a cockerel (with a little pot belly). Potent, for a fact. Still coupling fertilely. Still treading his ever-fresh hen, and maybe some other lasses too, judiciously. (He'd need to be shrewd with volatile Lucky always in the offing.) Bertel could read Minkie easily.

Young Kennan began to drop hints about a secret he knew which could well merit the hand of a Sariola daughter, theoretically speaking.

Now as to this business of kidnap . . .

Deplorable in the case of a royal daughter. Went without saying. In Minkie's case a certain dear chick had bewitched him; bespoken his heart. A different case entirely. A Sariola daughter deserved a proper wedding. Ah, to admire the spectacle of a Sariola wedding – with younger sisters as bridesmaids, perhaps? What were the names of those younger daughters of Bertel? Ester, ah yes. How old was she?

Dame Inga had eyed her son reproachfully. Her censure seemed equivocal. Inga knew her son, just as she had known his daddy. She was aware when a bee was buzzing in his bonnet, drowning out sensible counsels.

Kyli, hostess to a prince, was blithely oblivious to the undercurrents.

An introduction to court for Minkie might fully rehabilitate Kyli in the eyes of her father. Reinstate her.

How unfortunate it was that, given Kyli's advanced condition, she herself oughtn't to travel, should an invitation be given. One must take care on such a journey. Extreme care, such as Minkie would take. Should an invitation be forthcoming. Any glimpse of hideous mutants might imprint upon the baby in her womb. Minkie would take great care, wouldn't he?

Bertel had allowed all of this to roll over him persuasively. He positively invited himself to be bluffed. He had lived for far too long. Minkie was a plausible rascal prone to wild and impetuous ways such as the shedding of blood (at least the coppery blood of Juttahats). His father, Ragnar, had been such a quarrelsome man. Bertel had lived too long.

His face duly painted white, Elmer entered the Dome of Favours somewhat gawkishly, squired by his honour guard of mana-priest Moller and Lyle Melator. Elmer's new white shirt, crusted with embroidery and with such a wide collar, allowed a glimpse of matching white neck and bony shoulders. The palace tailor had furnished snowy breeches, belted in silver. Soulflowers woven of white ribbon decorated his knees. Miniatures of these adorned the silver buckles of his ivory-leather shoes.

A tinselled shaman drummed out a heartbeat. Half a hundred huge candles illuminated the crowded dome, the walls of which were thronged with heroes large and small. (Mikal, the perpetual painter, cast a dubious eye at greasy gases trembling upward to escape through a vent in the faceted blue and pink eye of the cupola.) The crimson-gowned Queen sat enthroned. Prince Bertel stood alongside her, stroking his wispy goatee. The tattooist perched on a high stool next to an empty chair to which a tray of needles and pigments was hinged. Portly and dignified in his grey serge suit, Paavo Serlachius attended Eva. The bride was crisscrossed with silk sashes of orange and lemon hues and bound with belts of gold brocade around her bosom and belly and thighs. On her high-piled coiffure a chaplet of starflowers perched, the violet petals softening the inky darkness of her hair. She was juicy sweet fruit in rich wrappings. Ripe fruit a-flower.

Daughters Jatta and Ester and Sal and Kaisa and Martha in descending order, and even Mary (hand held tightly by Mrs Simberg) and baby Hanna (in old Nanny Vanni's arms) wore tunics large and little which were mazes of vivid felt strips, rectangular rainbows within rainbows. Most held posies of star-flowers; Jatta held her son's arm. Dusky Jack was in Juttahat livery still.

Minkie shuffled fretfully from foot to foot. He clasped and unclasped his hands. He thrust them deep into his pockets. Anything to immobilize his paws. He'd totally failed to gain the Queen's ear. Once burned, twice shy. She scorned his bait.

Was crazy Lucky even interested in a certain place of wishes-come-true beneath a certain lake? Her mind seemed to be aimed inflexibly elsewhere. By now he'd heard the cackle of a cuckoo, and enough palace gossip: an alien machine ensconced in her fortress had infatuated her.

Small chance he'd had of addressing the Queen, to be sure! Or Eva, either. For which he blamed Bertel. In Niemi, Bertel had acted so invitingly. Now he had clammed up. He turned the cold shoulder. Wouldn't even listen to Minkie's hints that Kyli might have begun to pall on him, that perhaps he'd be prepared to forsake her if a radiant opportunity presented. Ah, the need for delicacy in this matter! For wiliness. Leeway for his charm to operate. Of course he couldn't possibly confide the family secret till after he'd ploughed a virgin daughter. Really, our Minkie had been made an ass of.

Watching appetizing Eva waiting beside the mana-priest, Minkie felt hot with anguish. Frustration incubated an egg of rage, and rampage. Whatever could he *do*? A couple of guards were forever keeping an eye on him. There would be no repetition of the kidnapping of Minnow. *Her* younger sister, Ester, was only thirteen or fourteen, damn it. Hardly ripened. Must he ingratiate himself long term in hopeful anticipation? Patiently, sedulously sow seeds, which weren't exactly the seeds he felt eager to sow right now? He felt so agitated, foiled and fooled. Van Maanen had owned his own sky-boat in which to speed away. Minkie didn't.

What a bashful virgin Elmer Loxmith seemed in his white outfit and cosmetic paint as he approached his orange and lemon and golden bride. How he gaped at Eva.

Serlachius recited from a brassbound copy of the *Book of the Land of Heroes*:

> 'Bridegroom, dearest of my brothers,
> 'Wait a week, and yet another,
> 'For your loved one is not ready . . .'

Naturally Eva was ready. She was more than ready. Yet this was the way the ritual must proceed in the case of a royal wedding. Stuttering slightly, Elmer duly expressed his impatience and eagerness. Jatta advanced to fulfil a duty which would have fallen upon Minnow had Eva's junior sister not been abducted – the jocular tormenting of the bride so as to bewilder spiteful nakkis who sour milk and wedlock.

Jatta sounded more grim than droll as she warned her sister, 'Beware! You'll be exchanging your own dear mother for a harridan. You'll be swapping your comfy bed for a hard one. You'll be leaving your lenient daddy for a martinet. Your dad will very likely choke on smoke in the sauna while trying to cleanse his tears.'

'Woe, woe,' Eva replied.

'Be off with you, bought hen!' Bertel told Eva gruffly. 'This isn't a deal worth celebrating.'

'It is, it is,' insisted Eva. Momentarily she sounded anxious – as though her post-nuptial party might be cancelled on a whim. But Lucky took Eva's hand and placed it in Elmer's. Serlachius blessed the couple, and the assembly applauded.

Elmer sat in the vacant chair for the tattooist to commence his work. Short and bald and wiry, this artist sported a witty and eloquent tattoo of spectacles upon his brow – the spectacle bows running down behind his ears – as if he had pushed the glasses up the better to concentrate. Unbuttoning the groom's shirt, the tattooist exposed Elmer's right shoulder. He swabbed a patch of skin clean of paint with sterilizing spirit. The craftsman consulted Eva's outstretched wrist. The tattoo would be a star-flower just like hers. Elmer winced when the needle pricked his flesh, then composed himself stoically.

Pumpernickel and smoked tarandra tongues; mushrooms in sour cream; rye porridge served in sylvester bark; goose and dumplings and pots of roe . . . and a mocky-man combo playing the tango in that ballroom which fooled the eye that the *salon de danse* was even more spacious and thronged than in reality.

Arto conducted – or pretended to – waving six-fingered white kid gloves. Pieman knocked crusty knuckles on borrowed cymbals. Knotty nursed plaintive, though sprightly, melody from his fiddle. Now and then Knotty tensed a muscle and sawed the bow across the strings of his skin as well as the violin, producing an ethereal haunting chord. Lammas sang with such a heartfelt tremolo.

> 'My body's a beast's, not a man's,
> 'Yet my heart's as human as yours.
> 'Dear girl, my duckling, I beg of you
> 'Don't close, don't lock your doors . . .'

The tangomeister listened with increasing approval. So did the regular accordionist and guitarist and violinist spruce in their lace shirts and black breeches. What might have been absurd – pathetic – was instead so poignantly believable.

Lammas sang again and again, while dancers slow-stepped sideways.

*

'That woolly fellow definitely has a voice,' Moller said to Serlachius at one point. 'A voice indeed. A tongue.'

Paavo Serlachius was quite as affected as Moller. Both ruddy-faced men now saw eye to eye. Those eyes of theirs were moist with sentiment.

'A definite touch of the mysterium,' agreed Serlachius. 'A vista beyond the world. His words seem like ordinary words but aren't. They're like the echoes of words, resounding far away then returning. They've died and come back to life to haunt us. They've been lost but unexpectedly are home again.'

'Well put, brother. Very well put. I find myself thinking of old acquaintances. When you were studying at Tumio did you happen to run across a Jussi Haavio? Quite a dandy fellow. He consorted with Pootarans a fair bit.'

'Did he have a taste for sailors?'

'No, he was interested in their tenets. Their wooden puzzles are defences against the mysterium, he said. Like hexes hung on the doorposts of their minds. Miniature mazes in wood, to twist mana aside. Trap the mysterium, maybe. Jussi Haavio's the priest in Forssa now, by the way.'

'He must have been in Tumio after my time, Pappi Moller . . . There's supposedly an Isi maze somewhere in the forests a good way north-west of Maananfors, if I may mention a name that's anathema now.'

Moller nodded. 'Viper's Nest. The mutant mage's lair. That's a death-maze, isn't it?'

'Ah, but what precisely is a death-maze?'

'A maze where men get killed when they try to penetrate it.'

'I'd say it's a mana-maze which the Brindleds built to magnify their mutant mage's concentration.'

'Or to keep a banished Viper safe and sound. I suppose a Tapper Kippan might negotiate his way into it, being a woodlord—'

'Lord Kippan worries too much about his skin, I hear,' said Serlachius.

'In case it turns into bark, rather like our cymbal player there?'

'In case it gets seriously punctured by a hatchet man. You're aware that we have a mage in the dungeon? Name of Imbricate. Would you care to inspect it? With the Queen's consent . . .'

Minkie Kennan was all ears, though ostensibly enraptured by the mutant's song.

'The voice of sorrow is silence,

471

'And the name of absence is, ah my lost Rita.
'I'd chance almost any violence
'From her false lover just to seat her
                'By my side,
                'By my lonely side—'

'But *Mother*,' said crop-headed Jatta, 'Wex could *easily* have flown in the sky-boat to Loxmithlinna.'

'Along with newlyweds? On a mission of vengeance? Don't be absurd, my natter.'

'He could have flown part of the way and saved days and days of travel. Maybe saved Minnow from *rape*.'

'Wethead was so impatient to be on his way.'

'From rape, do you hear! What sort of mother—'

'Mother of a multitude, my dear. Please don't be hectic at your sister's wedding ball.'

'But—'

'Listen to me, my chatter, I was raped of my soul. Of my very soul. I'm an echo, an ever-living echo. How do you think I endure for so long?'

'You've no idea,' Bertel told his hundredth-some daughter. His gaze flicked away from her. 'Why don't you dance? Why not dance with Minkie Kennan?'

'With *him*?'

'While your indulgent daddy dances with your own dear mother.'

Elmer stepped sidelong across the footstep parquet with his bride. His hand slid and detected the girdle beneath her wrappings of brocade belts and bright sashes. She giggled momentarily, then looked haughty.

Now he knew what that firmness on her haunch was. He knew the word of loosening. That word was . . . he almost whispered it audibly, but no one must overhear.

The word was: *Whipper-snapper*.

A droll joke of Lucky's . . . Maybe all men less than a century old were whipper-snappers in her estimation. Different words would release other Sariola daughters' girdles. No doubt those other words were all equally facetious in their implications. This would serve neatly as a seal of secrecy. What proud husband would blab about how he was a *whipper-snapper*?

*

Wedding guests who hailed from upcountry towns were enchanted by the sweet singing of the sheepman. A true tango singer ought to come from a humble background. This sharpened his perception of the contrast between the real and the ideal. Lucky's tangomeister himself had been of peasant stock before he acquired a stouter figure and ribbon rosettes and a cravat. What was humbler than the condition of a mutant? On account of his voice – and his mood – these connoisseurs of tango could forgive Lammas his mutation. They could take him to their hearts – just as he in turn raptured theirs.

A deputation approached the Prince.

Would Lammas care to tour Lucky's domain for a few weeks, or more, along with the mutant threesome, the fiddler, percussionist, and gloved conductor?

'Why not!' exclaimed Bertel. 'Top-notch idea.' He beckoned to Minkie, and explained the circumstances.

'Would you like to travel around the north country for a few weeks with the mutie combo, Kennan? As their impresario?'

Minkie gaped at the Prince.

'You're from the same region as the muties, after all. Local pride, eh? Our sky-boat will hardly be flying you home till the mutants are ready to return, now will it?'

Minkie was appalled. He did *not* appreciate this proposal. Oh no, sir, no. And no again.

'In that case you'll be obliged to hang around court for a few more weeks, eh Kennan?'

Next, the Queen heard of the proposed tour. Why, this was ideal! What a double slap in the face for van Maanen. Meantime, Goody Hilda and June the Diseased could stay in the palace. June seemed such a presentable, outgoing lass. She *interested* Lucky.

'You used to love hiking around the countryside,' the Queen remarked to Jatta. 'Maybe *you'd* like to guide Lammas and his friends. Give them the benefit of your experience.'

'*No, Mother!*'

Speedily Jack was by Jatta's side, frowning at his youthful grandmother.

'Maybe not,' conceded Lucky.

'Perhaps,' Bertel suggested amiably to Minkie, 'you might become better acquainted with June? Exert your charms. Charm her and cure her.'

Minkie glared daggers at the Prince, and Bertel smiled blithely.

> 'There's a girl who's going away
> 'On the very next day, the very next day
> 'For ever, and a Sunday.
>
> 'There's a girl who's broken my heart,
> 'And tomorrow morn my hen will depart.
> 'In the arms of an upstart she'll play.
>
> 'Tomorrow night she'll bare her breasts.
> 'In a goose-feather bed she'll be caressed—'

32 · Bright Stones and Bones

The ballroom was empty but for Minkie. It was a week since Elmer and Eva Loxmith had departed from Lucky's domain. But not Minkie, though he wore his long tawny leather campaign coat as a shroud over his redundant finery.

Minkie danced slowly with an empty spirit bottle held out in his hand. That bottle had been his partner off and on (lurking in one of his sagging pockets) for the past day and a half. A sip here, a sip there. Now she was empty. Lighter to dance with. He blew across her neck and she warbled at him.

The pink satin drapes were partly open, exposing white net curtaining bright with trapped daylight – as split skirts might expose petticoats. Minkie studied the innumerable blue and orange shoeprint blocks marching in procession, then diminishing in *trompe l'oeil* so that there was no real way of numbering them even if he resorted to such an asinine means of whiling away his time. If he squinted, patterns emerged. All sorts of novel dance steps. Steps he might have taken; but hadn't. Call this routine the Prance. Already the Prance was sliding into some other permutation. On the walls – in that unreachable space of painterly illusion beyond the walls – thousands of elegant ballgowns and stylish black tails swirled motionlessly.

'Woo woo,' said his bottle.

'Woo who?' he asked her. He swung round to cast a bale-ful glance at the mirrored wall. He had left one of the double doors ajar on his entry. In the silvered glass alongside posed his image.

'Highly presentable fellow-me-lad, eh Miss Bottle?' Should he hurl her at the mirror to express his utter exasperation? 'Surely there's a last drop left in you?' He squeezed tight. 'If there isn't, I'll throw you for sure. If you'll give me a fiery kiss – just a tiny little one'll do – well, what would you say to a waltz?'

Did the mirror shimmer? Minkie blinked. He could swear there was movement in the far distance of the *trompe l'oeil*. Beyond the multitude of diminishing dancers something dark rushed towards the ballroom – a shadow shape.

Nothing whatever moved in the wall.

He felt such a premonition of impending arrival.

Minkie dropped Miss Bottle when a headless black steed halted halfway along the ballroom.

A gust buffeted him. A coaly mount with two riders, one hunch-ing behind the other . . . how could it halt when it hadn't moved to begin with? Only air had moved.

Death: it was death come to fetch him. Not in the guise of a swan but of a jet-black pony. Or giant dog. Death was looking in the wrong direction for the moment. Not a large creature, smaller than a pony. Terror made it seem bigger. Maybe it had shrunk down from shadow-size, condensing. Might it be a dwarf steer? He saw horns! His heart thumped. His fingers fumbled vainly for the sheath-knife in an inner pocket.

Two riders on a beast which had appeared from nowhere! As the beast wheeled round, Minkie saw what was actually before his eyes rather than what his panic conjured. Astride a black machine on a double saddle sat Jack Pakken garbed as a Juttie – his hands on those twisty horns – and Prince Bertel wild-haired behind him.

The steed was a machine. Mostly made of metal. Two slim tall wheels at the rear. A steerable leg at the front. Two stubby snouts jutted from the curved bars which Jack was clasping. Those looked remarkably like gun barrels.

As soon as Bertel caught sight of Minkie, he dismounted. He noted the empty bottle lying on the parquet floor. He raised an eyebrow.

'If it isn't young Kennan, entertaining himself! Jack, be a good grandson and fetch my Paula's tiara from the chest in our

475

chamber. If it isn't in the chest, try the big armoire. We'll take the tiara back with us. That'll prove where we got off to, won't it now? Right inside the palace. So much for security if anybody can jump through walls, and jump, jump, jump away again!'

Jack scrambled from the machine. This remained upright on its three wheeled legs. Jatta's fast boy scurried from the ballroom, leaving Bertel alone with Minkie.

Bertel began to brag in an affected drawl which was especially irritating. Languid and swanky.

Seemed that this everything machine was *capital* at producing weapons, whatever else one might wish from it. A dozen projectile guns to begin with as hors d'oeuvre!

Next, this Juttahat jump-bike.

Young Jack had seen a toy version of just such a vehicle while he was being raised in the Brazen Isi nest. Serpents hadn't deployed any such devices on Kaleva hitherto. Maybe the jumpbike was a recent invention of theirs. Experimental, don't you know? It must leap through mana-space to arrive where the rider hoped to be (rather like my wife's Ukko, do you follow?). Taking little leaps one after another. With a *certain* element of oblique unpredictability, it seemed. Like the jinking of a flycatcher through a cloud of gads and piss-in-your-eyes.

'Piss-in-your-eye,' repeated Bertel.

Jutties themselves mightn't be too spunky at steering such a jump-bike – or even at coaxing it to jump in the first place. Unless there was a mana-mage along for the ride. Or some serpent sitting on their shoulders. Jack had jumped the bike right along the courtyard in the fortress on his first attempt, then back again, while Lucky looked on. Here one second, there the next, here again an instant later.

'Of course *you've* never even been near our fortress, Kennan . . .'

The machine operated *thus* and *thus*. Simple as pie.

'Even you could steer it, drunken, I suppose . . .' Bertel nodded at Miss Bottle.

Just look at these twin guns mounted on the handlebars, fired by a squeeze *here*, and *thus*. You could imagine a squad of Jutties jumping into combat, appearing, firing, disappearing – though a snake coiled around each trooper might need to risk its skin at the same time. When were snakes ever found in the midst of a fight?

'Oh, once in Speakers' Valley when our Jack was snatched as a child, I admit. Imbricate wasn't personally involved in the violence—'

Minkie found Bertel's attitude unbearably patronizing – and Jack had been gone quite a while, for a fast boy. Jack must be turning the Queen's chamber over in his search for that elusive tiara.

The *In-between* on a jump-journey wasn't disconcerting at all. So Bertel had found. The In-between was akin to a flash of darkness – if Minkie could grasp such a concept – succeeded by the new location.

The Prince sauntered away from the vehicle to pick up the fallen bottle. Bertel caressed this casually and suggestively while Minkie in turn wandered towards the jump-bike.

'Oh yes, *do* sit down before you fall down, Kennan.'

The saddle may have been perfectly contoured for a Juttahat bum. To a human being it felt ridgy, although Minkie's coat served as padding. The right handlebar ended in two segments, blue and silver, ornamented with black glyphs. The left handlebar sported a single red segment. Those could all be twisted.

'Motion and headlight on the right, guns on the left. Jack worked that out soon enough. Where *is* the lad? I hopped on behind him for the second test-ride, you see. Try the light, Kennan. The silver bit.'

Minkie turned the appropriate segment. The resulting beam was invisible in the daylight of the ballroom, but a reflection glowed brightly in the mirror-wall. Minkie swung the handlebars so that the light fell on Bertel instead.

Blue segment. The machine throbbed softly and moved forward by a couple of wheel turns.

'You need spunk to jump the bike, Kennan.' Bertel stroked the bottle. 'Why did you ever come here?' he murmured to himself, audibly enough.

Cold chilled Minkie's groin.

He was in Speakers' Valley once again, loitering beside the Prince and Eva. Juke Nurmi's curse was withering him so that beauty and desire became meaningless, robbing him of his essence, gelding his spirit . . .

'. . . no harm in you sitting on it, eh? I admire your lavender breeches. Maybe they're on the tight side. What's there to squeeze? Drunken shrunkencock.'

Minkie howled.

Twisted *red*.

Bertel's white-uniformed chest erupted bloodflowers. He was staggering backwards from the staccato thunder. A mirror beyond him had exploded into icy daggers. The ballroom resounded with the drumming detonation of bullets and percussion of collapsing glass. The prince had tumbled. His lifeblood pooled on the floor of footsteps.

Terrible silence, punctuated by the tinkling fall of a few last fragments of mirror.

'Grandad!'

A figure in coppery livery jerked the door wide. Amber eyes surveyed the bloodied body, the bike. All the light in the room seemed to flood towards that appalled young cinnamon face.

Minkie had already twisted the blue part of the handlebar.

He was astride the jump-bike in the Dome of Favours. That painter in his smock and beret gawped down at Minkie. Upholstered faces stared from sofas as if intent on reporting his presence. What confusion could he cause to assist his escape?

The bike skidded on sand in a gloomy granite vault. A couple of huge candles fused to sconces by their wax offered scant illumination. Many other candles were unlit.

A figure – *Jack* – leaped on to the bike from behind Minkie. A figure encumbered by a great brassy tuba – which thumped against Minkie's shoulders.

Wasn't Jack at all. It was an honest-to-mana awful Juttie supporting its serpent master. A reek of sour fruit filled Minkie with nausea. Puffs of pastel light popped. He was in the damned dungeon under Pohjola Palace. With a Juttie clinging to him. An Isi looming over his head. He writhed. He shrieked. He tried to fight clear of the alien and its coiling burden. He almost quit the bike.

The Juttie was clutching him.

'Jumping!' it urged. 'Jumping out of this place!'

Of course, of course. Jumping. Not lying sprawled on the sand amongst bones in a dungeon waiting for Lucky to come for him like a frenzied verrin.

He twisted blue.

Flash of darkness.

Sunlight, a street descending harbourwards.

478

Sails of sloops and yawls. High mountains beyond wide water. A pony reared, whinnying, throwing its rider. A cart collided with an iron lamppost, knocking it askew. The bike rolled on at a leisurely pace down the brick-paved roadway. Voices shrieked – not at Minkie but at what he wore on his back: a Juttie and a rearing snake. A chain dangled from a shackle round the Juttie's ankle. A loose arm's length of links dragged over the brick paving. The alien must have been fettered to something which had remained behind in the dungeon. Its touch and its master's odours offended Minkie mortally.

A crossbow quarrel twanged into the pink sign of a leaperfish outside an inn. Fired too high – Minkie recalled that first illusion of shadowy mass when the jump-bike first appeared in the ballroom. People were scattering. Another quarrel zinged past.

Urgently the Juttie shouted in his ear: 'Jumping to the quayside! Long-jumping over the sea and beyond the mountains! *Maaginen* Imbricate is helping.'

He twisted blue.

The leap beyond the fjord and the peaks, from the wharf, was a longer darkness in which he felt he was choking, unable to catch a breath. He gulped in the sweet air and green dazzle of a wooded valley. Goats fled. A robberbird screeched.

'Long-jumping twice!'

Suffocating blackness – and a sloping meadow flanked by evergreens. Not a creature to be seen, not a farmhouse, not a scribble of smoke in sight. The Juttie would be well advised to hurl Minkie off the bike in this meadow or the next if it wasn't too hampered by its master's coils.

Minkie twisted red, firing the guns rowdily as a distraction. He stabbed his right elbow hindward into the startled body-slave's solar plexus, praying that the creature possessed a plexus in its abdomen. He butted his head back savagely, crunching his skull into a scaly coil. Did a rib or two snap under the impact?

Swinging to leftward on the rebound, he stiff-armed his gasping passenger. He swept the slave and the injured Isi from the saddle.

Twisted blue.

From the far end of the meadow he stared back at the much diminished figures tumbled in disarray.

Blue twist: and a lakeside, harnies hooting.

Blue twist: an overgrown forest dell, timber in every direction.

479

Minkie stared through the crowding fronds for the sun to set his course south-east.

To Niemi? Homeward?

He'd killed the Prince. He'd snuffed out Bertel Sariola. He'd murdered *Crazy Lucky's husband.* He had ended a marriage four centuries old from which sprang all those daughters who gave longlife to their spouses. If *he* couldn't gain one of them! He never would have while Prince Bertel was around . . . If our Minkie couldn't – despite the impediment presented by Kyli – then who ought to? Who ought to, for mana's sake?

Kyli, hmm. Yes, Kiki-liki. This was really becoming very unfortunate. Kyli, who was carrying his heir . . . a tush he cared about an heir! What advice would Snowy stutter out? Really, this was all so unfair. The Prince had fooled and insulted and provoked him hatefully.

Longlife, hmm. A short and nasty one for our Minkie if the Queen ever caught up with him. When she found him. If she found him.

Shrunkencock, indeed. No man could tolerate that. He'd been possessed, was the truth of it. Beguiled, compelled – to act out his daddy's destiny again. Fooling with the Sariolas, infuriating people, fleeing from reprisals. Worse, far worse than Ragnar's fault – he'd murdered Lucky's consort.

Bertel wanted to be killed. The Prince had invited being killed. Deliberately he had driven Minkie to distraction, then posed in front of a gun. Bertel was sick of Lucky and her ways. Her schemes, her whims, her passions. Minkie had done the Prince a service.

And himself, none at all, damn the man. There should be no question of guilt. The Prince had incited him from the moment that Minkie and those muties arrived at Pohjola Palace. Would anyone else understand this? Could anyone else have an inkling?

Kyli, hmm . . .

Minkie wrung his hands.

Bertel had lured him to Sariolinna, hadn't he just? That was plain as pie now. Belatedly.

Kiki-liki would forgive him. He could charm forgiveness from her. After all, he hadn't been responsible. In what guise would she hear the news? That her husband of recent vintage had made a play for a Sariola daughter, all too willing to forsake his Kiki-liki? He hadn't really done any such thing. Not openly. Not so as people other than Bertel would be aware.

480

Kyli might just hear that her Minkie had quarrelled bitterly with the Prince on account of delays in letting him return home from court. Minkie Kennan was supposed to defer to the time-table of a warbling mutie who looked like a sheep? That was cause enough for a hot-blooded fellow-me-lad – who had promised his mother that he would behave himself.

Ach, but he mustn't feel that he himself was to blame. Bertel was. Lammas was. Even *Ragnar* was – for establishing a pattern (which had surely boiled up in Minkie's blood) of irking people homicidally. For sewing a glove which his son now wore.

'It's Loom Lake for me,' Minkie announced to the trees. He scanned warily in all directions in case a cuckoo might be roosting somewhere in the foliage, green against green.

'Coo-coo,' he called. None was anywhere in the vicinity. It would be a dull cuckoo indeed that sat in the middle of nowhere on the merest offchance. If one had been present, he could have sent his love to Kyli and Inga – whenever, if ever, they might receive such a message. A caution too, that a Kennan had seriously offended the Queen.

Ragnar hadn't found life in the bolthole hidden away under that distant lake at all humdrum, so Minkie recalled. A place where dreams could come true. Paradise, of a sort. Could be splendid. Pity Snowy couldn't be with him. It would be idiotic to stop at Niemi.

Way beyond where the damned Muties lived, among a hundred nameless lakes, one in particular was shaped like a rhomb. Mana-mists drifted thereabouts. Steep cliffs balanced huge boulders on their brows.

Jump by jump by little jump, all the way across the land, preferably keeping out of sight: might take a couple of days, kipping in woods overnight. By the time he found the lake he'd be famished.

'Loom Lake, here I come.'

Twist blue.

First, Jack had dashed to Jatta to break the news to her, and for help. *What should he do?* En route to the ballroom Jatta had sent a guard to find Serlachius urgently, then Linqvist.

Scant time passed before the chamberlain was sending riders at a gallop out to the fortress. Well within the hour the Queen was back in her palace. The continuing absence of Bertel and Jack had troubled Lucky. She had already left the fortress. The ketch-rigged barge was nearing shore when the messengers arrived.

Now, in the ballroom, Lucky was as she had never been before . . .

'What Kennan stole may have been just what you needed from the everything machine—'

Lucky stared at Jatta as if her remaining grown-up daughter was merely some tormenting reflection of herself who had stepped out of an unshattered mirror. Two of the ruched curtains had been torn down to cover the corpse. Serlachius knelt beside that pink mound intoning a plea to the swan. 'Bird of death, Thief of breath—'

'Shut up, shut up,' Lucky bawled at the mana-priest. What was this offspring saying?

'If that bike can leap through mana-space to wherever you want, Mother—'

Reproachful but wary, Serlachius continued in a soft mumble.

'Bertel can't heal himself of a shattered heart, Serlachius! That bike was a *weapon*, my chatter.' Lucky's teeth chattered. 'Who can I talk to, now? Who knows me? Four hundred years, four centuries, and he deserted me, would you believe it? Who do I talk to?'

Softly: 'I'm—'

'You're saying anything that comes into your head just to distract me, as if *I'm* the fool. Next it'll be: oh, Minnow needs saving, by the way, otherwise there won't be many more daughters left. There can't be any more after Hanna, not now!'

Amidst the orange and blue woodblocks were several ghost footprints of blood. Jack still held the tiara, dangling limply.

'Shall I put that trinket on my head?' Lucky shrieked at Jatta's son. 'Shall I be the perfect Queen? Is that why you have it in your hand? The bike was a weapon,' she repeated to Jatta, 'just like the guns it gave me first of all. It's an Isi joke cooked up between the mage and Minkie Kennan.'

'Between them? That's impossible, Mother—'

'I'll be needing *more* weapons, for sure. Many more jump-bikes and guns and whatever else it can spew out. For when I ravage . . . what needs ravaging.'

A guard smirked foolishly. General Aleksonis froze him with a glare before the Queen could notice.

'It's well enough known that Kennan hated the snakes and their slaves—'

'Amongst whom you've been one: a snakeslave's strumpet.'

Jatta flushed.

Words jerked from Jack. 'Grandfather asked me to fetch your tiara so we could jump back to show you.'

'And now you don't know where to put it? Do you imagine anyone would steal from me? I'd wall them up alive for a hundred years. I'll wall Kennan up.'

'Don't call my mother a strump's pet,' Jack muttered miserably. 'I tried to freeze Kennan with light but I was a moment too late. He already jumped.'

'Fastboy was too late?'

'Yes!'

'How fast did you come here with Anni in that little Isi sky-boat, Jack?'

'On the wings of the wind, Grandmother,' Jatta's son answered proudly.

Lucky stabbed a finger at him. 'Why didn't you chase after Kennan right away on the wings of your famous wind?'

Jack's glance in his mother's direction was barely more than a flicker, but Lucky noticed. Her smoky eyes widened.

Jatta gestured at the hump under the pink curtains. 'Mother, I told him not to – in case Kennan killed my boy as well.'

'You told him not to . . .' Lucky sagged. 'If only you'd gone on tour with the mutants . . . Is that really *Bertel* under there?'

The mana-priest peered discreetly under the blood-stained drape.

'Fool!' she yelled. 'I mean, is it *really* Bertel? Didn't he want me to keep the jump-bike? Didn't he wish me to ride away on it to wherever my soul is prisoner?' Lucky sounded like some devastated child whose toy, and thus whose world, had been snatched away. She rounded on Jatta. 'The bike was only a weapon, nothing else. I wouldn't have known where to leap to. The bike's the weapon he chose . . .'

'Mother!'

'You're trying to distract me from grief, my interfering natter. From rending and tearing. Destroying!' Clawlike, Lucky's fingers raked the air so fiercely it seemed as if the air indeed tore like tissue paper.

'So I am,' admitted her daughter defiantly.

'All to save your boy from a tiny risk. And to save me from realizing . . .' The hush preceding her next words was awful. '. . . that Bertel betrayed me – that he chose his own death.'

'That's a wild thought, Mother. You can't be sure—'

'Can't I? Minkie Kennan will know for sure. He was alone with Bertel. Bertel sent Jack for my stupid tiara. Prove yourself, Demon Jack! Bring Kennan back here for me to question before I kill him. Go with him, General,' she bellowed at Victor Aleksonis. 'My hero who braved so many gadflies and Jutties to bring me the everything machine! Then I'll know whether it's really Bertel or not under there – won't I, Jatta?'

Eager to quit the Queen's presence, Aleksonis was already heading towards the doorway, gesturing impatiently at Jack. Jack was on the point of bounding after him when the Queen called, 'Wait! Give me the tiara first. How can you handle the murderer and the mana-mage and its slave with a coronet in your hand?'

'I'll freeze them with light, Grandmother,' promised Jack as he handed over the tiara.

'Make sure you send our big sky-boat out too, Aleksonis – with the eyes.'

From the threshold the General spoke in a loud whisper: 'And the sky-boat at the fortress?'

'My sentries must stay on full alert. Who can I rely on now?'

Her lanky chamberlain, in frock-coat, cummerbund, and wig, cleared his throat. 'Funeral arrangements,' Linqvist murmured to Paavo Serlachius, who was still down on his knees.

Lucky wandered towards the covered corpse. Her pace was sluggish. She might have been dragging her scarlet – her blood-red – boots through an invisible morass. Stooping, she laid the half-circle of bright sapphires upon the stained satin shroud. Linqvist glanced at her non-plussed. She pulled off her ruby ring too and cast it upon the corpse.

Serlachius was quicker on the uptake. Those items were for burial.

'Bright stones, stiff bones,' he chanted. 'Prince Bertel's soul remains whole, remembering itself.'

'And who,' Lucky enquired of her mana-priest again, 'is actually under here?' Her voice quivered. 'I did value his fidelity, Paavo. I can't be constant to myself, not while the real me's missing. But he could be faithful. He could.' Her tone pleaded for understanding.

'Minkie Kennan *murdered* him, Mother,' said Jatta. 'Daddy couldn't have planned any of this. The jump-bike. Kennan being in the ballroom – drunk.' She had noticed the empty bottle.

'Sending Jack off on a wild goose chase . . .' Lucky shook her head. 'He murdered himself, to escape me. How could he? *How?* Yet I know it, just as if I've always known it! Who do I confide in now? There's only myself to trust. But where am I? No, Bertel couldn't have cheated me after all this time. He couldn't . . . could he?'

It was late the following afternoon before Jack and the General returned, along with a passenger.

As the trio entered the Dome of Favours, Lucky imagined for a moment that Aleksonis and the fast boy had succeeded in bringing Minkie Kennan back with them . . .

Bertel's coffin of tough fireproof purple tammywood rested on golden brocade. From beneath the brocade peeked the iron runners of a sledge. Bertel's flamboyant golden epaulettes lay detached on top of the box, flanking a braided peaked cap. It was as if a peculiar bird with broad bill and stubby decorative wings had been positioned there to suggest a soul roosting sag-bellied upon the body-box. Next evening, the coffin would be lowered into a stone sarcophagus in a wee crypt below the palace. A daughter, dead in childhood two centuries earlier, rested down there, unremembered till now except by an ancient candle stub.

The populace of the palace and town had been filing through the dome to pay their respects, abbreviatedly. People could hardly absent themselves. Linqvist had seen to this. But nor did mourners wish to linger unduly in the presence of the Queen at such an unsettling time.

Enthroned, Lucky kept vigil clad in black crêpe. She seemed wrinkled and haggard, decrepit. A black veil almost hid her features. Through this veil she could watch the file of diffident spectators virtually unseen. Her mana-priest sat awkwardly on a sofa near the brocade-swathed catafalque clutching a pouch of indigo baize. Next to him, a sandy-haired young proclaimer. Jatta perched defiantly and mutely on another sofa. Her mother hadn't allowed her to wear black for Bertel. Every half minute, a shaman hung with metal trinkets and ribbons and scaly bird-plumes thumped his drum. A cuckoo had taken up residence on painter Mikal's vacated platform. The Wikström bust of the girl – van Maanen's gift – had been exiled to a storeroom. Elmer Loxmith's roly-poly dwarf brass mannequin remained. Rolled back against a hero-frescoed wall, its eyes glowed red.

Lucky fancied that the brown-skinned youth tricked out as a

Brazen Juttahat, and her General in his greatcoat and cockaded two-horned hat, had brought Kennan with them. She threw up her veil.

However, the newcomer was walking of his own free will. He wasn't being pushed at knifepoint. Greasy fawn hair swept back from his brow. His eyes were an icy blue. Clad in a soiled grey travelling cloak, he was taller than Kennan. Rather more athletically built.

Lucky knew heartache. And remembered who the newcomer was.

'Madame,' announced Aleksonis, 'we're grieved to report that the absconders eluded us.'

Not simply: *we failed to find them*. Her General was being verbose to make what he said seem more authoritative.

By now Lucky felt far less concerned to question a captive Minkie Kennan. He might say something about Bertel which she would loath to hear. That Bertel had actually *invited* Kennan to kill him. That Bertel had paid his assassin with the newly manufactured jump-bike, which would let the assassin skip away. Allow him to escape along with the mage Imbricate. This, at Bertel's suggestion too? Liberating an alien prisoner hinted how Bertel had been a prisoner too, and now was free . . .

A raid on Niemi – vendetta against the Kennans – might open a horrible wound when she was on the point of finding her lost self.

Bertel, Bertel, *why*? Did he fear that when she found herself she might no longer have needed him in the same way, or even at all? Bertel feared this prospect and couldn't bear it? Surely he hadn't intended to spoil her time of joy and fulfilment? To punish her for their life together! For their long, long life. That was unthinkable.

It was treachery, complete infidelity. An aching wound, dealt by her own dearest friend and lover, father of all her daughters (who hadn't really been a friend at all). She couldn't bear to know this.

'We ranged far and fast to the south-west, your Majesty. Far faster than I've ever flown, in fact. Demon Jack hurled us along on a wild wind. Even after nightfall we searched by sickle-light and starlight. We must have travelled a third of the way to Saari, and no exaggeration. Then Jack had to sleep.'

Jack was yawning right now, rocking to and fro on his heels.

'In the morning we raced west ahead of the sun in case Kennan had tried to elude us by taking a roundabout route. Maybe after crossing the Great Fjord Kennan had headed south-west. Towards Maananfors, rather than towards Saari and Niemi—'

'*Maananfors*.' Lucky growled the hateful name.

Jack was stumbling towards the sofa where his mother sat waiting for him.

'You didn't change your original aim, did you?' the Queen called out. 'You didn't think you might try to rescue a kidnapped daughter belatedly instead of catching a murderer?'

Unheeding, Jack sunk upon the sofa. He nodded asleep.

'No, absolutely not,' insisted Aleksonis. 'We thought Kennan might try to take refuge in your enemy's keep.'

Refuge with van Maanen. That was where *ravaging* should be directed – at Osmo van Maanen. Kennan must simply be killed – quickly, somehow or other – before he had time to tell lies. (Could he possibly *brag* about the killing of his host, the Prince, father of Kaleva?) Kennan must be extinguished. Van Maanen must be ravaged.

'There's good news, Your Majesty; and sad news too.'

Their passenger stepped forward, his expression a mongrel blend of diffidence and defiance.

The man spoke with gruff assurance. 'I was waiting between the Saddleback Twins for van Maanen to fly back to his keep. I fired Isi missiles at his sky-boat. The boat sped away westward out of control and burning. I shot van Maanen down. I . . . did not know that he had stolen a daughter of yours.'

Appalled, Jatta hid her mouth and nose. Her eyes stared so wide, unblinkingly, at Juke. He hadn't noticed her yet.

One of the onlookers must have clutched a hand of the brass automaton. Its voice throbbed into song:

> *You're as far away from me*
> *Without a care, without a care . . .*

Bertel! Far away from her. Without a care.

Minnow . . . killed by accident, along with van Maanen. Saved from violation by a violent death. Van Maanen dead too, and her vengeance aborted. But also fulfilled by this outsider – whom she had wished to invite to Eva's wedding. Here he was: Juke Nurmi. Sometime protector of Jatta. He had accomplished her

487

wish willy-nilly. Van Maanen's executioner. His assassin. A handsome relentless fellow, haunted by demons in the heart. He had stolen her revenge from her. He had also carried it out. And killed Minnow in the process, unknowingly.

Wouldn't there very likely have been a Sariola daughter on board that sky-boat returning to Maananfors? If van Maanen had succeeded in arousing the everything machine surely there would have been. Juke Nurmi would have fired his missiles regardless. Eva would have died instead of Minnow.

Missiles obtained from a faction of the serpents . . . by what guile?

Lucky twisted about on her throne in her satin weeds of grief. How alone she was, never mind her chamberlain and General and mana-priest and her remaining grown-up daughter and her daughter's boy, and everyone else. Alone, alone, without her full self. Without her husband.

She had sent out a call for proclaimers. One sat on the sofa beside her mana-priest. Here was Juke Nurmi.

As if Nurmi knew her thoughts, he said, 'You sent out a call, Queen Lucky. At a farm I heard a cuckoo. I began heading north.'

'To tell me that I no longer needed proclaimers to pit against Lord Osmo? To tell me this in person? To collect a reward?'

'When your little sky-boat passed over, I bespoke a minty to flare.'

The General nodded vigorously. 'The tree exploded like a maroon.'

Juke Nurmi had acted the coward in Speakers' Valley. He had betrayed his own sister – sacrificed her to van Maanen to save his skin. But he had risked going to the Isi for help in his revenge.

Nurmi stood before her steadfastly, even though he had been responsible for a daughter's death. Well, he had protected another daughter, hadn't he? Maybe he hadn't been heading north in the hope of reward – but to bring about his own doom. His sister was avenged. Guilt on her account gnawed his heart. Only a Queen could judge him. What an arrogant, proud presumption!

Ach, was this man also obsessed with committing suicide by proxy?

'You aren't the sort to hang yourself from a tree, are you!' Lucky barked at him. Nurmi stiffened. 'Or to leap into a lake!' As van Maanen had ordered the man's sister to do.

'Did you know,' she asked, 'that your father is touring my territory at present?'

'What? My . . . father?' Nurmi's face said all the rest. Fastboy and the General hadn't told him. He hadn't heard of the wedding invitation through cuckoo-cackle, though he had heard of van Maanen's summons to the Northland . . . The Isi must have *flown* him to a suitable place for an ambush.

'Which Isi did you go to, Nurmi?'

'The Velvets . . . They gave the false eye—'

'—to your sister? Why would they do that?'

'My father's here? Is that true?'

He dared to question her word?

'Arto Nurmi the glovemaker; the very same. I invited him to Princess Eva's wedding with Loxmith, because you protected Jatta. It's Eva you would have shot down if a certain other lord had wedded her instead.'

A groan escaped from Juke Nurmi. Jatta had at last uncovered her face. For the first time Juke really noticed her sitting on the sofa of staring faces – and realized who she was among so many others, and why Demon Jack had gone there to rest after his exertions. Jatta was eyeing the agent of her sister's assassination with pity and utter dismay.

Bertel. Bertel. Lucky had actually forgotten about her dead husband for several moments. She had forgotten the contents of the body-box. Forgotten why she was dressed in black satin . . .

The recurrence of the memory was anguish. To direct her fury at Nurmi would be to kill Bertel all over again, with herself playing the role of Kennan, accomplisher of suicide. It would be she herself who had killed her husband.

She *had not* driven Bertel to suicide. His long, long life had soured of its own accord. He hadn't shared her passion to find her full self. For him there was no other self to be found. Impending success in this quest had made Bertel fear that he would lose her, the anchor of his soul. Before this could happen he had disposed of himself. Poor weak man.

Lucky said lightly to Juke, 'You'll want to be here to greet your father on his return from their tango tour. Lammas was a great success at court. That werewool has a magical voice.'

Juke seemed awestruck at the notion of respect for his mutant father and kinsfolk.

Someone had jogged the damned brass dwarf again.

Sky-sickle shines upon the sea

A salty tear leached from Lucky. She dried her cheek with her veil.

'*You* must have a magical voice too, Juke Nurmi! Setting sheep ablaze, and suchlike. I have a machine which needs nursing if it's to deliver what I want. Though of course,' she added, 'new weapons are what we need too, if the Isi are giving missiles to assassins now.' She grinned lopsidedly. 'The Isi may covet what I want, for themselves.'

Bertel. Poor weak man. Betrayer, of himself. In the final accounting who else did people betray but themselves? Who else did a person discover but themself?

'Nurmi,' prompted Lucky, 'an old acquaintance is waiting to greet you.'

The assassin blundered towards Jatta. At his approach her sleeping son awoke instantly, alert. Juke halted, gazing at Fastboy's crop-headed mother.

'Jatta, I'm truly sorry about your little sister—'

'Could you possibly say,' Jatta asked him, 'that you're sorry about your *own* sister too?'

33 · THROUGH VIPER'S MAZE

Once again Osmo and Minnow arrived back at the lakeside near the green hoop hanging from the curver tree. A column of flies hummed above the wrecked sky-boat as if a faint ghost of Hannes bestrode his corpse. Mist lazed over the lake and insinuated through the woods.

Mana-mist: there was power hereabouts, and it was frustrating the castaways. Perhaps they could have left by the same route they arrived by, except that Osmo's vehicle would never fly again.

Amongst the trees they had spied aspects of other hoops hanging half-hidden in the distance, just as slashes of paint might blaze a trail. They had been unable to reach a single one other than the first. However, they had come across a human skeleton still in scraps of rotted clothing, and lacking a head. The skull itself had lain several metres further on, perched upright.

'*He* can't bespeak us a route,' Minnow told herself indignantly, back again at the lakeside. 'How about Kaleva's champion proclaimer?'

'I don't know the origin of these hoops, do I?'

'Does he still have a headache?'

Minnow was dressed baggily in Victor's black breeches and starched white shirt with sleeves rolled up. Victor had neglected to bring a bundle of Minnow's day clothes from her chamber when he kidnapped her. The farmer's stripped body lay crook-necked amid the boulders, his tattoos on display: a mound of morels and chanterelles and horns of plenty. Minnow's feet were wrapped abundantly in strips of cloth ripped from other garments in the packs which had cushioned her. Osmo had sliced off the breeches at the knees and had cut an extra hole in the belt so that it would pull tighter. Togs of a dead man. Minnow's attitude had been: 'He dragged me into this – so now he can dress me!'

Somewhat earlier . . .

Never die, Son. Johanna's dying command had echoed in tandem to the thumping of his head. Osmo had almost lost his life in the sky-boat. Marko and Hannes and Victor had all died shockingly. Being lost in a wilderness was hazardous. Here he was with a Sariola daughter who could give him longlife. Then his body would recover speedily from minor injuries, just as Gunther had healed of Cammon's blow by the morning after. Minnow could give him protection. His head had thudded, and corpses lay nearby. The notion of seizing his abducted bride with seductive bespeakings was absurd, absurd. The idea wasn't *wholly* absent from Osmo's mind – as Minnow, still in her nightgown, must have detected.

'Well,' she'd said after her ankles and hands were free, 'so now *it's* going to happen, I suppose. What every woman waits for with a flutter of the heart and loins.'

'No,' Osmo had said lamely, 'I have a headache.'

She had regarded him with incredulity. Then she giggled.

'Excuse me, but isn't that meant to be what *I* say by way of an excuse? The hero abducts the maiden in her nightie. He survives a disaster. Then . . . he has a headache? I agree this isn't a very suitable bridal bed. But why else did you kidnap me?'

'I didn't tell Victor to kidnap you.'

'You might as well have told him.'

Victor, Victor.

Embarrassments had multiplied for Osmo. She would have the shirt off Victor's back as a penalty. And the breeches off his legs. And she did.

When she was about to change she said to him, 'By the way, you'd better look the other way in case I offend your romanticism. I'm having my bloodflow at the moment.'

'You're having . . . ? You aren't.'

'Should I have arranged not to, to save us inconvenience? Somehow I don't seem to have brought any spare bungs with me.'

Blithely she proceeded to explain in some detail how dried spongemoss from the tundra absorbed twenty times its weight in *ooze*. Tied round with thread, enclosing a pull-string, and packed in a waxed tube for storage, this was ideal for *bunging* inside oneself . . .

'I'll make do with a rag, my lord.'

While she had changed, he had turned his back.

And now they were back once more by the water, their knapsacks almost empty of food. Evening was imminent. The nearby hoop glowed. Away in the forest hung hints of other luminous arcs.

Minnow needed a coat.

Hannes's gaberdine, retrieved from the storage compartment of the wreck, served her purpose once Osmo had cut off half a metre from its length. They built a fire of branches, which he lit with his lightpistol and a few hot words. Wading (after first stripping off vermilion socks and buckled leather shoes) Osmo bespoke a couple of trusters to slide into his hands, and toss ashore.

They filled their bellies with the charred fish spitted on sticks. Minnow wiped her licked fingers on the shortened black breeches which came down to her shanks. Osmo washed his hands scrupulously, though there was already dried blood from Hannes on his own breeches and on his once splendid waistcoat. A ribbon rosette was missing from one knee . . .

. . . the same rosette which he had once given brusquely to his mother as a favour.

(*Never die . . .*)

'Was that enough for you?' he enquired of his captive princess. 'Do little creatures like leppis need a snack during the night-time too?'

She puffed herself up scornfully in her ballooning garb.

'Huh!'

Then she chuckled. 'You're thinking of nakkis, aren't you, Osmo? Could be all sorts of naughty nakkis in these woods, creeping closer.'

It was true. She was right. Oh, maybe not in the superstitious peasant sense. But what had hung these hoops in these woods?

'Actually, I'm a bit scared too,' she admitted. 'You'd better protect me. Right?'

Light was failing. Huge vaporous serpents of mist were wallowing. The hoop glowed balefully. It could have been their route-plan. A perfect circle. Twice they had set off through the woods. Twice they had returned to the selfsame place on the shore where the sky-boat had crashed.

'Scared, eh?' Not of himself. Nor of the corpse in the boat. Nor the body among the boulders.

Rage at Minnow's mother took hold of him. If it hadn't been for Lucky's cheating, he wouldn't be here at all!

'I wouldn't be here either,' she muttered to herself.

'Did I say something, girl?'

'You looked at me as if *I'm* responsible.'

Lucky had invited *muties* to Elmer's wedding, knowing perfectly well how Osmo would feel about such an insult. The Queen was malice and madness incarnate. All because her precious daughters had a rare gift to give to the daring; to those who would take it.

Minnow said carefully, 'My sister Jatta was bespoken away through the woods by a certain fine fellow with a buzz in his bonnet. She had to sit beside lakes breakfasting on a truster then spilling her soul to somebody else with a buzz on the brain, who was apparently protecting her. Does this sound familiar? Oh dear, is your headache coming back?'

'I'm being trapped in a pattern . . . I can feel it. There's a mana-pressure. Events are mirroring, mocking.'

Nurmi was a mocky-man masquerading as a proper person who could proclaim . . .

Minnow's teeth chattered. 'Trapped by hoops, trapped by mana-mists full of nakkis. Isn't it nice? Let's concentrate on protection – just in case passions start surging out of control.'

'The poetess,' Osmo muttered, unwilling to pronounce Eyeno's name. In Yulistalax he had been possessed by passion. When he had banished that passion his own mother died in the backwash.

493

Who had shot the sky-boat down? Juttahats? Must be Juttahats. Of the Brindled persuasion? Maybe Sam had been justified in his paranoia.

'Good, now you're thinking—'

This region of forest was an Isi playground. A mana-playground. Those hoops hadn't been hung up by human shamans, for a fact. That skeleton they'd come across: some human adventurer had died violently, decapitated.

To learn; to find some weapon with which to pay Queen Lucky back!

Never die. Longlife. Zombie. Lucky's elfin daughter.

'Now he's stopped thinking. He's going round in circles.'

With an effort Osmo gathered his wits. 'We'll be warm. Fire stay bright. We'll be safe. Nothing shall roam near us. Nothing reach us. This is spoken, this is spoken.'

Minnow mumbled to herself persistently while she lay on the other side of the fire from Osmo. 'I'm sure this is a lumpy mattress, isn't it? What a jar of pickles. Here's her future husband not knowing a bit about bungs, nor wishing to neither. Has a bung of his own, but he's never been bunged. We'll not go into girdles. Tomorrow's troubles, hmm? No wise words from Mummy. Jatta's Jarl was a kettle with a different spout. Steamy, hey? Oh yes, roll over. Lumps and bumps and humps—'

'Will you shut up?' hissed Osmo across the fire.

'Maybe the word for a girdle's gurgle-gurgle. Haven't cleaned our teeth lately, have we?'

'Please shut up till the morning. This is *spoken*! Not a word more!'

Minnow uttered no more actual words but she hummed through closed lips till dreams claimed her. 'Mm, mm – MMM – mmmm, mm, m, MM!'

Lemon mists clung to water and woods, stealers of morning sun-gold. After washing separately, then breakfasting together on another pair of compliant fish, Minnow asked Osmo, 'Do you really need to know the origin of the hoops?'

'It would help! I'd know the right name for them, wouldn't I? They must be Isi gadgets. Supposedly there's a monstrous mutant mana-mage—'

'As bad as that?' she asked archly. 'Mutant *and* monstrous at once, and a mage?'

'—expelled by the Brindleds. Maybe it's a voluntary recluse.

494

These hoops could form part of its prison – or its refuge. They deflect intruders. Alternatively, they stop the mage from straying. Its name is Viper.'

'My mother – if you'll pardon a rude word – keeps a mana-snake in our palace without too much trouble. A deep dungeon and a few guards seem enough. Ah but this one is mum-mum-mum. Much more mighty, hmm? Mutant and marvellous. Mum, mum.'

'Will you stop mumming at me, Minnow?'

'Mumming, indeed. *He's* tied to his mother's hamstrings and can't snap free.'

'What do you mean by that? My mother's dead.'

'Minnow snapped free, didn't she? Now she'll have to make the best of it.'

'*Hamstrings* is the wrong word,' protested Osmo. 'Surely you mean apron strings.' He didn't want to contemplate the memory of Johanna.

Minnow's retort was scornful. 'What's the *right* word to say to a Minnow in these circumstances? We'd best go and visit this Viper unless we want to stay here all week. Who gives a hang about the origin of these hoops? Their destination's more important, where they lead to. They're a route. If,' and she marvelled at herself, 'we jump through them instead of trying to walk past them.'

Tugging at his moustache, Osmo considered her proposal.

By ducking his head slightly, he was able to step through the first suspended hoop. Leaping wasn't required. In those baggy black shorn-off trousers, and hugging the gaberdine coat around her waist, Minnow needed to take a higher step.

Fifty metres away in the misty woodland two green hoops were now fully visible, off to the left and off to the right. The route to each was a simple path which had totally eluded them previously.

'You were right, damn it!' He breathed deep. 'I don't trust the left-hand way . . . I'm sensing resistance. Obstacles.'

They had scarcely taken a dozen steps along the rightward route when: *Crukk, crukk.* An iridescent bird, its plumage a shimmer of blues and greens, had flown through the hoop in their wake to perch in a curver.

'Is that a cuckoo? A baby one?' Minnow cupped her hands

around her eyes. 'It's hard to see. It could tell us things . . . Coo-coo-coo,' she called.

'That's a robberbird, not a cuckoo,' Osmo told her. 'They steal things that attract them. But they often give themselves away in their excitement. They imagine no one can notice where they are.' He held up his knife blade loosely so that it would catch the light.

Crukk – like a twig snapping sharply. The bird eyed the metal acquisitively.

A moment later Minnow had snatched the knife. She was on her knees at Osmo's feet. She clutched one of his shoes. Before he knew what she was doing she had sliced a silver buckle free. She threw it further along the path.

'My shoe!'

'It's still a lot better than my own footwear.' Nonchalantly she handed the knife back. 'Minnow took to wearing a knife,' she muttered, 'but she didn't think of wearing it in bed.'

Crukk. The bird launched itself out of the tree. It flapped over their heads; sped towards the fallen ornament.

Greenness enveloped the bird. Momentarily it seemed as though the would-be thief had adopted perfect camouflage. Then its body was flopping about on the path. A wing seemed to be missing.

'East way isn't necessarily the safe one,' said Minnow. '*Don't try to get your buckle back.*'

They returned to their starting point and took the left-hand way.

He was treading on blunt blades, not of herbage but of iron. The iron was heating up, and becoming sharper. Despite his shoes his soles burned painfully. Minnow was hopping along, squeaking, '*Ouch.*' He had to concentrate intensely to see woodland. Otherwise he saw a jagged wilderness of scorching metal.

'Ground, be cool and supple,' he proclaimed. 'This is spoken.' Resentfully Minnow clung to his arm for support.

'Be earth, not iron. Lose your heat.'

The path became ordinary again.

After they had stepped through the next hoop, a choice of three tracks confronted them. Each led to a hoop.

'The middle one feels bad,' said Osmo.

'Good, let's take it!'

*

A beast blundered through the undergrowth: a verrin huger than any which had ever attacked a flock of sheep. The brindled brown carnivore reared upright. Long bald whip-tail jutted stiffly as a counterbalance. Nostrils in its long hairy snout flared wide. Its eyes were mad moist beads. Claws raked out from its forefeet as it lurched towards Osmo and Minnow. Hissing, it bared yellow teeth as long as her thumbs. A scatter of bones lay beside the track, torn apart.

Osmo snatched for his lightpistol, and fired. A thread of radiance lanced the air. Behind the oncoming beast, a branch flared. Hotlight must have passed right through the animal.

Minnow shrieked: 'It's too big! Make it smaller!'

Of course it was unnaturally big.

'Verrin, verrin, stop and shrink,' Osmo bellowed. Again he fired in vain. The enormous verrin was almost upon them, snarling, naked tail whipping.

'Halt and shrivel! *This is spoken.*'

And the verrin did pause. Wild-eyed, it hesitated. It tottered. Those teeth, those claws, the straining cordy muscles of its neck and jaw . . .

'Make it smaller!'

'Shorten, dwindle —'

The beast began shrivelling and shrinking. Swiftly it collapsed down in size and stature. Within half a minute a bewildered musti crouched in its stead, slim and snake-tailed. Appalled at its diminished horizons, the normally feisty predator fled.

Osmo heaved sighs.

'I think,' Minnow said to herself, 'in this situation a hero needs to feel a sort of sublime confidence rather than bravado and bluster. Isn't that right? Absolutely right. Then it won't be so tiring to proclaim.'

'What do you know about it?' snapped Osmo. Her protector, her captor.

'I've learned a bit about heroism from Jatta – at least since Jack came back. Eva wouldn't have been much use in this pickle. Jatta's a hero, really.'

More than himself? That ragged, exhausted figure who appeared in his hall: how easily he had dealt with her then! Sprinkled salt on her tail to send her fleeing.

'Wasn't it a little conceited of you,' she asked with saucy insouciance, 'to take Tycho Cammon home with you as a statue?

497

A trophy. What did you feel when you defeated him? Grandeur and conviction?'

'Well yes . . .'

'I think we need rather more sublimity and less shoving people around in fits of pique. Maybe we should leave that to my mother.'

Sublimity. Grandeur. Conviction.

(*Never die.*)

They had reached the next hoop. When they had stepped through, they saw four green hoops inviting them to advance in different directions.

The floor of the misty woodland and the path itself writhed with countless thin striped brown snakes the length of a fellow's arm. Leathery white eggs speckled with ochre littered wide tracks. The vegetation was crushed flat as if a heavy barrel had rolled through the undergrowth. Infant snakes were hatching all the time. They sliced their way out of shells that resembled a great crop of oval puffballs. Vacated shells – torn open by the egg-teeth – sagged, drying out. Snakes on the path hissed malevolently, displaying fangs dripping beads of venom. When Osmo bespoke the path clear, almost immediately it filled up again with squirming bodies.

'Even a monstrous mutant mage wouldn't lay this many eggs,' remarked Minnow. 'I think *this* time we ought to shut our eyes and walk.'

'*What?*'

'Shut our eyes. Pay no attention at all. Think about something else entirely.'

Missiles exploding in the sky. Revenge on Lucky. Safety from snakebite by seizing longlife – on a bed of snakes . . .

'Do you wear a tattoo, Osmo?'

'Speaker's lips on the biceps of my arm – to give my words muscle.'

'Well, think of those. Keep your thoughts close to you. I'll talk to myself. Shut your eyes!' She tugged him along. 'Well, Minnow, what do you think about lips on arms? That's the sort of thing muties might actually have. Mouths high on their arms—'

'Don't you try to imply that I'm any sort of mutie!'

'What's he saying? Hit a sore nerve there. When such muties eat they have to lean right over their food and stick their shoulder on the plate—'

'That's absurd.'

'Of course they can still chatter with the other mouth. Can Osmo make words come out of the lips on his arm, I'm wondering? Can his arms argue with each other? Hey, lefty, you're lazy! Pull your weight. Ever seen yourself in a mirror, righty?'

'You're being preposterous.'

'Just don't open your eyes!'

'And here we are,' she said presently. 'You can look. We're here.'

They were beside the next glowing hoop.

No snakes nor eggs were visible behind Osmo and Minnow; only trees in thick mist.

'You're really useful,' he admitted.

'Hmm. Let's wait and see about that.'

'I mean it, Minnow.'

'Does he really? Is being useful the same as being precious? Wait till an infatuation seizes our proclaimer!'

The path led to a cave in a rocky hillock. A tunnel led downward. Its smooth yellow walls shone with a soft luminosity. From the deep interior came a sigh, as of something vast breathing.

Osmo and Minnow linked hands as they began their descent. The tunnel was only wide enough for two people walking closely side by side. Neither wished to precede the other.

The subterranean chamber they came to was as oval and leathery-seeming as a serpent's egg. Its hue was blue. A dense yet supple skin of sky appeared to have adhered to the cavern, diffusing light throughout: a membrane with a faint shingle pattern punctured by the mouths of several small passages. Osmo and Minnow paused on the threshold, hugging the wall.

The principal occupant of the lair could no more have poked its vast head into those shafts than it could have hauled its bloated body out of the blue egg by way of the tunnel to the surface. Why, its head was the size of a whole Simmental bull. The serpent mage must have been smaller when it first entered this den – unless the chamber had been specially created around it.

Was the monster still growing? Would it eventually fill this space to bursting point? One day, with a convulsive seismic heave and eruption of mana-energy, would it hatch itself free of its confinement and burst upward? A sharp tooth jutted from its upper lip. Drifting down from its horns, balls of pastel light like spittle bubbles burst upon this projecting fang.

Curled massively round upon itself, its head protruded from between two lower coils. Its tail jutted from between two other coils as if the monster had tied itself into a vast slack knot. As breath sighed in and out, the whole body slowly swelled and deflated and swelled again. Belly scales were dishes, the scales on its head were rows of miniature tents. Sepia ciphers decorated other scales. A Minnow could have thrust her fist into its facial pits. Viper's armoured body was a streaky ochre which shimmered iridescently as if secreting a gossamer film of oil.

Several amber-skinned Juttahats in beige livery attended the mage. One was polishing it with a pad. Another held a creamy waxen flower rising long-stemmed from a goblet. A third was hauling a netful of bones away.

Juttahat bones.

Viper must eat its own attendants. Juttahats must travel here from the Brindled Isi nest, guided through the hoops, to serve the mage and also obediently become its food . . .

Those body-slaves paid no attention to the two snoopers until the serpent lifted the scales from its eyes. Those scales were so thick that they were almost opaque. Revealed were vertical black pupils in orange irises.

Osmo stepped forward into the lair, followed by Minnow.

'Great Mage,' he called out, 'I'm the Lord of Maananfors. We're friendly with the Brindled Isi. *Being* Osmo van Maanen,' he corrected himself. 'Being friendly with the Brindleds. Coming into your keep with Minnow Sariola.'

The flower-bearer acted as mouthpiece. 'First humanbeing visitors since Taiku-Setala was coming here. Was Taiku-Setala telling you the route?'

'I don't – I'm not knowing any such person. My sky-boat crashing after . . .' (being shot down by the friendly Brindleds?) '. . . after an accident, returning from the north.'

'With a bride, who will be giving you longlife?'

'No,' yelped Minnow.

Osmo answered, 'Yes.'

The serpent contemplated the intruders. 'Where better to be consummating your noble wedding, Lord Osmo, than in this bower of rebirth? Where my shed skins are coating the walls, being transformed to celestial blue by the wishes of a *maaginen*.'

Now it was Osmo's turn to protest.

'Oh no, we must tie our knot at Maananfors, not here, great Mage.'

The enormous serpent stirred its coils. 'You not being friendly with Brindleds? This exalted Viper not being important enough to tie you together?'

'*Say something, Osmo.*'

'Human beings being bashful,' was his excuse.

'Insulting to be rejecting such an offer,' said the mouthpiece. It lifted the flower from its chalice and wagged it reprovingly. 'This wedding could be signifying symbolic union between the people of Maananfors and the Brindleds. Why else are you coming here? For what purpose?'

'To find a way out of the forest,' Minnow replied.

Osmo growled: 'For a weapon against the Queen.'

'Isn't that what *I'm* meant to be?' Minnow exclaimed. 'Isn't that why you kidnapped me?'

'Not at all! You're admirable. You're a precious treasure.'

'Oh there's a compliment. You'll be sublime yet.'

'Sublime, this union presided over by a *maaginen*,' said the mouthpiece.

'Fancies himself just because he's so big . . .'

The mage opened a mottled pink cave of a mouth. Inside lolled a long forked tongue the girth and rosy hue of a skinned sea-eel grown to full size. Tips of great fangs peeped from plump violet sheaths on either side of the upper jaw. Apart from those twin points, and the projecting anomalous egg-tooth, the serpent's mouth was toothless.

In growing so gargantuan, Viper must have lost all the rearward-jutting teeth which assisted the passage of prey down its gullet . . . Those must have softened and snapped off – or else been shed. Viper needed docile Juttahats to crawl into its mouth and thrust themselves down its neck, sacrificing themselves so that it could feed.

Bubbles of pastel light puffed from the mage's horns. Odours of cinnamon and oily vanilla assaulted Osmo and Minnow. The serpent's scales were shining lambently, reflecting the azure membrane which cloaked the walls. Those scales reflected the couple over and over in miniature, caught between the skin which the serpent still wore on its body and those sloughed transformed skins on the wall.

The den was an egg in which Viper was gestating monstrously. Minnow and Osmo were within the egg.

The flower waved mesmerically. Pastel light popped. The air reeked of heady fragrances.

Their bridal chamber was hung with blue silk – tent within tent of blue silk. Silk draped behind the bed and drooped above it. Sleek silk everywhere. The sheet on which Minnow lay, naked but for her velvety girdle, was slippery sapphire silk. Osmo, unclothed, was alone with Minnow. She, with him. Rampant, he approached to gaze down at her dainty butter-hue limbs, the little bubberry-tipped cones of her breasts – and the girdle which almost entirely eclipsed a little bunch of black hair, forbiddingly.

'Precious duckling,' he whispered as he knelt on the sheet next to her. He fumbled, and was frustrated.

She wriggled, she squirmed. 'Cock can't come inside my cave,' she muttered obstreperously. 'Mother never told you the word.'

'A word to unfasten this. Of course . . . there's a word which the girdle knows.'

The eager bridegroom did his best to speak gently. 'It'll soon tell me its secret name; for this is spoken.' He breathed deeply. 'I bespeak it to put the name into my head; to divulge what was said. Unbind, unwind, before and behind. Password slip into my mind.'

Minnow slithered on the silk and he restrained her, hands upon her hips, focusing upon the girdle.

A suggestion of a mouth full of mist loomed insubstantially alongside the bed. A great vague mouth. A shadow of Osmo's own lips, magnified . . . ?

Lips murmuring:

Star over Tundra . . .

The prompting hesitated, then resumed.

Robber in the Icy Palace . . .

A pause.

Laughing . . .

> *Insanely . . .*

Another pause.

Never . . .

> *Glancing up!*

Star-Tundra-Robber-Icy-Palace-Laughing-Insanely-Never-Glancing.

Stuh. Ruh. Ip – a name pronounced itself in his mind.

Stripling.

'Stripling!' Osmo cried. The word was a snub to his manhood. It was a mischievous insult.

As Minnow's girdle fell away, she rolled aside. In a trice she was on her knees. Before Osmo could clutch her to him she had propelled her naked body in sheer affront through those wide hazy lips which had helped him to discover the key.

He was kneeling nude in a blue cave crowded by the massive pulsing coils of Viper. Mouth agape, the mage was gagging. Jammed within that great mouth was Minnow. She hunched foetally around the sleek rosy sea-eel of a tongue. She clutched it to her chest. She clamped it with her legs. Osmo's garments, and Minnow's, lay strewn about.

He'd been *swayed*. Swayed.

So had she been likewise.

Except that Minnow had eluded the sway before consummation could occur . . .

Had Viper hoped to study the way in which a Sariola daughter conferred longlife on he who first ploughed her?

Viper's Juttahats shuffled about aimlessly. They seemed to have no idea what to do. Living food was in the master's toothless mouth but the meal wasn't behaving at all like willing victuals. Minnow had evaded the well-retracted fangs, and perhaps those were fragile or soft. By no means was she sliding down the mage's throat. Viper was tongue-tied.

The mage's eyes gaped, pupils full and glossy black. Minnow's eyes were wide too – yet she seemed not to be seeing either the den or her recently ardent admirer.

Minnow saw dark-orange dunes under a violet sky. A crimson sun, squashed oval by glassy air, wobbled upon the very horizon. Two bone-white Ukkos peered down faintly upon the tides of sand. Or were those millstones which floated on high really Ukkos at all? They were so perfectly rounded. Lucky's Ukko had been shaped more like an egg. Perhaps those were *moons* – which hadn't disintegrated into vastly long thin sickles arcing across the heavens . . .

To be entering into the proclaimer's psyche during those moments of the orgasm, of the little death, in the way that an Isi would be entering the mind of its servant!

The illusion of the bridal chamber being a great sway to be

503

casting. Casting lassos of concentrated thought with which to be reknotting reality! Could any mage other than this Precious One be succeeding in conjuring such a dream in her cave of liberated vision?

As the Ukkos of the Luminated Path through Starspace could be conjuring a dreamworld within their Resplendence, weaving mirages and echoes, braiding exterior events with the inner rainbow of their Being – Nourishing the Rainbow – while the rainbow in turn was tinting the hues of events in the world . . .

This world, where a cub Ukko was surely raising its rainbow self unseen; where this Precious One was mimicking its gestation so as to be swaying it . . .

This Precious One, who had been dreaming the Great Narration of the Arrival of the Wild Juttahats – these humanbeings – upon this world in an Ukko wherein Isi voyagers and their servants were being bones and dead echoes. So swaying other Ukkos to be bringing Isi here too, though never yet towards the humanbeing homeworld . . .

To be entering into this humanbeing proclaimer's essence. To be failing, tongue-tied in one's bespeaking by the little female's wild surprise leap, herself entering into this Precious One's head and self in a gesture both enforcing and constraining of this Enlightened Precious One.

('Huh, and I'm precious to Osmo too.')

Be leaving this Precious One. Believing me. Be leaving me. Leaving.

('That's what we were trying to do, Viper!')

Tongue twisting, time twisting, time's sinews tensing and stretching. In my egg-cave, days flying by outside. Sun winking, nights blinking. Precious One's design being blocked so close to its climax. Queen may be finding unseen Ukko. Ukko arising, erupting free, while this Precious One is bursting from her egg-cave in rapport.

('Oh I see, so I'm wasting your time, am I? A whole heap of your time – while your mind spills all over me like saliva.')

Junior female's mode of time-thinking is distracting this Precious One. Time flying.

('My heart bleeds. And what else besides? I didn't ask to come here and put on a mating demonstration for you.')

In the Great Narration of How The Ancestral Isi Once Were Entering The Ukko, that Ukko was declaring, 'To be carrying you

504

*to another star – but first I am demanding eighteen stories.' And
the Eighteen Stories are following—*

('I'm demanding a few things too before I'll remove this bung
from your big mouth! The first, being safe conduct.')

Their knapsacks full of Juttahat victuals, Osmo and Minnow
hiked through open woodland well beyond mana-mists and glowing hoops.

'Minnow, it's a chimney flower!' Sizzleflies were circling above
the solitary azure tube like a puff of smoke. 'Those don't show
themselves till the second half of June.'

'Told you so! Time was flying by, according to Viper.'

'I suppose, snake-charmer, if you'd chosen you might have left
me behind in its den . . .'

'Huh! That wouldn't have been very considerate of Minnow,
now would it?'

'Of course afterwards you'd have been all alone in the wilderness.'

'Like my sister, do you mean?'

'I'm sorry. Feel free to tell me when I put my foot in my mouth.
As opposed to the whole of yourself in a mana-mage's mouth!'

'A monstrous mutant's, don't forget.'

Minnow had actually communed directly with an Isi, and not
through the mouthpiece of a Juttahat. Not that Osmo personally
had heard a word of the encounter. Perhaps 'communed' was the
wrong concept. Enforced communion, maybe! She had glimpsed
an alien world with moons in the sky. The prodigious serpent
had been seriously fazed by Minnow.

'I'm going to tell the first cuckoo we see all about this,' promised
Osmo. 'That'll teach your mother a lesson. I suppose Viper hoped,
um, to learn the secret of longlife by observing us making, um
. . . love?'

'Not at all,' Minnow said pertly. 'Viper's very old. It was her
who coaxed an Ukko to bring the snakes to Kaleva. What Viper
wanted was for you to lose control of your will in a delirium of
orgasm. She might have been able to make you into a puppet.'

'You saved me from that . . .'

'Just so. I'm thinking,' she continued blithely – as if his aborted
nuptial assault had been a peccadillo unworthy of her attention,
'that the Ukkos must find our relationships with the snakes
richly entertaining. Otherwise an Ukko would never have
heeded Viper's persuasions. The Isi knew an Ukko had gone

missing. Must have discovered another intelligent species . . .'

Osmo pursed his lips. 'Now the Queen's hoping to commandeer this infant Ukko which is fledging somewhere on Kaleva – and gain all sorts of power for herself.' Anger boiled in him. 'Well, she won't, damn it!'

'The Isi hope she'll lead them to it. Then they can step in. Use this new Ukko to help them tame us wild Jutties.'

'Which is precisely why your wretched mother has to be foiled.'

'Yes. No. Maybe.' Minnow was of three opinions.

They had come to a foaming, boulder-strewn river. Late-flowering musktrees along the bank were in the final dwindle of their feathery ginger blooms. Fluff carpeted the waterside herbage, still scenting the air in its decay. Osmo scuffed his shoes – one buckled, one lacking – through this frail pot-pourri and inhaled. Perhaps reminded of the mage's odours, he enquired, 'What sort of, well, personality did Viper seem to you? Or doesn't that make much sense in the case of an Isi?'

'Oh well, the Precious One was rather *fond* of herself. Just like some people I could mention.'

'Your mother,' Osmo muttered darkly.

'I wasn't exactly thinking of her . . . Like me as well, for that matter. I'm fond of me.'

'I believe I am too, Princess. Fond. You're almost a shamaness – and you've saved me from death, and possession.'

'We try our best, my lord.' In those absurd shortened baggy breeches Minnow curtseyed, grinning impishly.

Osmo scuffed more pot-pourri. 'I do wish to wed you – willingly, Minnow. Voluntarily. After we get home to Maananfors together.'

'Oh now, but who's willing and who's volunteering?'

'If you'll allow me to?'

'Huh! So she loses her girdle and now *he's* coy! Still, she quite admires his moustache. Never mind other parts she was obliged to take a peek at . . . His inhospitality to Jatta had to be some kind of major *prejudice*. Not that we ought to brush *that* entirely under the rug . . .'

Minnow communed with herself while the Lord of Maananfors studied his despoiled shoe to which clung fading gingery fluff.

{When I said 'break a leg' I was wishing us luck, not giving you an instruction, my Roger!}

Wex favoured a crutch of firm purple tammywood as he gimped through mizzle along the shore of a grey lough. After catching his brace so often in underbrush he was grateful for this gritty strand. Tiny islands pimpled the water, each the toehold for a little crowd of trees which thrust outward as fulsomely as missing Minnow's frizzy hair.

'I can assure you a delay of this sort was the last thing on my mind,' Wex groused.

Laid up for ten days under a jut of rock in a slumber induced by his other self! *{To conserve our food supplies while your shin-bone knitted back together . . .}* Prompted by subtle isometric jiggling of the fracture performed while he lay comatose, yes indeed.

One consolation: the accident had occurred close to where an ancient tammy had collapsed against a neighbour, snapping off a convenient branch – a wooden limb to supplement his own hurt limb. Wex's left leg, swaddled from knee to ankle in clingbandage from one of the pockets in his cloak, wouldn't be reliable for a fortnight more or maybe a month – even with his second mind constantly monitoring and ministering. The majority of his boot was missing now, sliced off and discarded. His lower leg ached dully with each limping step he took.

{We're trying our best.} 'Are we?' Subconsciously – metaconsciously – might Wex's other self have been . . . a mite *jealous* of his devotion to the lass who chattered to herself? *{Don't be preposterous. After the security of the human race, your well-being is a prime concern. Our well-being, my Roger, remember! Besides, we overstayed our welcome in Pohjola Palace. High time to leave Queen Lucky's vicinity, in my estimation.}* So chasing after Minnow was just a convenient pretext for departure? *{She had become psychologically important to you.}* And how important was she to his other self? *{She certainly seems to complement us sympathetically.}* Meaning that his other self could acquire a sweetheart too? *{Wetwear hardly requires such flustering comforts. Though love might help stabilize you. The security of the human race is pivotal. I wonder whether I did inadvertently give you an instruction, which you carried out unwittingly?}* That wasn't a very clever instruction when it involved ten days in a recuperat-

ive stupor, and a gammy leg. {*Discomfort provokes bickering. I shall encourage the output of endorphins. Just watch your step, my Roger. Don't be slapdash.*}

Wex began to whistle as he limped along the shoreline. He spied a cuckoo winging over the water. A low scarp loomed from the woodland beyond the lake, vague in the misty drizzle.

Within the next few minutes {*six minutes and ten seconds, Kalevan planetary time, to be precise*} he had spotted two more cuckoos heading in the direction of that rocky butte. He felt buoyant, almost merry.

The stone butte rising amid the forest was a crusty loaf riven with cracks and apertures. Around its base: glossy larkeries, mustardy yellovers, and a high proportion of harper trees. Moisture beading the strings between the trunks and branches of the harpers showered Wex as those he passed between began to thrum. {*Stop whistling, my Roger.*} Gauzy mist drifted from several of the clefts in the butte. {*Mana-miasma. Something's afoot.*} He was basically a foot. Trusty foot, dodgy foot, and a tammy crutch. The lowest aperture was up a few metres of scree. The brace served to anchor him as he mounted slowly and carefully. Talus grated and shifted under his boots. The strain of keeping his balance {*lean forward slightly; and now our left foot*} made him break out in a clammy sweat. Yet he felt buoyed up. The weather was perspiring coolly.

That aperture was high and narrow. From somewhere within issued a muted cacophony of cuckoo voices. Now that he could support his weight against a rocky wall, Wex eased his body along sidestep by sidestep.

In a grotto, crusty with phosphorescent green lichen and ridged with rocky ledges, scores of the big talkative birds roosted and fluttered hither and thither from perch to perch. {*. . . fifty-two, fifty-three, fifty-four.*} Against the grotto-green, the birds' plumage was a disconcerting camouflage. The air was pungent. Droppings coated the floor. Here was a veritable conclave of cuckoos. {*A cuckoo-klatsch, an avian gossip circle.*} Birds eyed the human intruder but did not screech at him. They were too busy calling out to one another: *sing the story, tell the tale.* Several were hissing and klicking in alien cadences.

'—knifed a Pootaran sailor to death right inside the mana-bishop's palace. Though what was a rational mariner doing in there in the first place, you may well ask! The Pootaran agent in Tumio requested a blood-fee from Papin Jumala, no less—'

'—her baby was *born* a zombie, so the story goes. Born dead and alive at once—'

'—instead the hervy disembowelled the woodcutter—'

'—so she said to her husband, "Never again!"—'

'—the rope snapped, and the lad drowned himself headfirst down the well. Could the nakki nymph have been his own reflection? After they hauled the corpse out, the shaman poured half a barrel of oil into the well and tossed in a blazing rag. Everyone heard such a shriek from below—'

'—and every day the mad girl said to the leper tree, "Don't shrink from me, Karl. I love you." One morning the tree had shed most of its branches except for one on each side. Her father found her clinging to what was left of the leper tree. Those two branches were bent down around Kristina's shoulders. He had to saw her free. That same day near Kip'an'keep Karl hurt both of his arms very messily while he was showing off to Helga. Despite a proclaimer and a wisewoman, gangrene set in. Three weeks later Karl's arms had to be amputated. They gave him jointed wooden ones carved from leper branches. Leper wood's sensitive. The proclaimer could bespeak the arms so that they would move almost like real ones to do pretty much what Karl wanted. Those new arms of his would never bend to embrace Helga. Nor would his wooden hands caress her no matter how hard he tried—'

'—so the goat said to the farmer's wife—'

What a medley of tittle-tattle was bouncing to and fro. If cuckoos were telepathic, as Wex and his other self were convinced, why were the birds not communing silently mind to mind? {*Information overload, my Roger? Maybe they are jettisoning stories. Perhaps they are sending the stories they've acquired back to an auditor elsewhere. That auditor may be shaping a model of humankind and serpentkind. Consequently of its own nature. Consider how an Ukko demands stories. Stories are the links on which it hangs its thoughts. Somewhere right now an Ukko is harvesting this world hungrily. An Ukko is the master of the cuckoos. It altered these native birds just as it mana-mutated the tundra tarandras. It made the cuckoos robberbirds of news, to nourish . . . ah, its progeny. With serpents here, there are increasingly intriguing events. Thanks to mana, there are compulsions and obsessions. The progeny feeds and is formed.*}

A cuckoo darting to a new perch shat on Wex's boot.

'—the Queen's wooden soldiers—'

'—a knife duel upon a cow-hide, with the brothers tied to one another—'

'—new weapons are piling up. *Next* the everything machine produced an armoured war-wagon which careered away out of the fortress of its own accord. This vehicle plunged into the waters of the fjord, and presently re-emerged on to the shore.'

{*Listen.*}

'The war-wagon blundered away from Sariolinna and was lost sight of in the woods. That night, its eye-lamps glaring, it attacked a farm, burning the barns and farmhouse to the ground. Next night, it attacked a hamlet. Demon Jack Pakken went after the rogue vehicle along with Juke Nurmi. Jack would tame it for the Queen by means of the light that paralyses, or else the cold that numbs, or failing those the storm that arrests and over-turns—'

The cuckoo flapped away through babel towards the far side of the grotto.

So Juke Nurmi, van Maanen's bane, was in Lucky's realm assisting the Queen? This news could be the ideal pretext for claiming hospitality at Maananfors when Wex eventually arrived there! This might make the rescue of Minnow much easier . . . assuming that Lord Osmo hadn't already heard the same report about Nurmi from cuckoo cackle. If this proved to be the case at least Wex would be offering the Lord of Maananfors an earnest of good faith by telling him. {*Weapons* are piling up at *Lucky's fortress in the fjord. Tech weapons.*}

Wex could inform the kidnapper about those weapons, as another earnest. {*Not only rubbing salt into van Maanen's ego wounds, but also poisoning him with paranoia? Penelope Conway won't much relish this sort of meddling – all for the sake of a sentimental infatuation, my Roger, a quixotic personal quest.*} Wex most certainly wasn't infatuated; at least not in the fashion of Kalevan suitors. This mission was more a matter of honour and conscience. Of noble consciousness. {*If we snatch Minnow away from van Maanen in such circumstances we'll be behaving exactly like an agent of the Queen, not of Earth.*} Wex would escort Minnow to Landfall instead for sanctuary. {*To Penelope Conway, who had her womb removed to avoid such entanglements? Weapons are piling up in the north.*}

'How about you, Wetwear?' Wex exclaimed. 'How about you? Will it be *break a leg* again? Break the other leg too? Or are we seriously trying to rescue Minnow?' {*Belatedly! Lamentable that we need such a giddy goal to sustain us. We're surrendering to the tides of mania,*} *my Roger.*} Just so long as his wetwear bore this risk in mind, there'd be no harm. 'Both of us, right? You and me.'

In the phosphorescent green grotto the gossip-birds of like hue continued cackling nineteen to the dozen.

'War—'

'There'll be war, for sure—'

After a while the ammoniacal odour of bird droppings proved quite dizzying.

Minkie Kennan felt giddy. Positively light-headed in anticipation of bliss. He swirled Anna boisterously around in his arms at the carnival in the village street. Anna wore a lacy gown hung with hundreds of pink and rose ribbons. He was in his green and scarlet striped waistcoat (and those lavender breeches). Minkie was striped quite like a pollenfly, and Anna was the flower. As she twirled, her slender petals of rose and pink spun apart then hugged her body again. The gown that they ornamented – and had veiled in repose – was almost as flimsy as chiffon. How Minkie would have loved to be a more distant spectator of this gambol of fly with flower, and behold his partner more fully.

He was *almost* sure what Anna should look like underneath the petals and lace – give or take a mole or dimple or pucker here or there. Very like her sisters Gerda or Maria whom he had already bedded joyfully several times, most recently both at once. That had been a first for our Minkie, though his charm proved equal to the occasion. Anna would be unlike willowy sister *Inga*, whose cheeks were less chubby and buttocks more boylike, not to mention her peppering of freckles . . . Oh it had been quite a tease to tell Gerda and Maria apart. Minkie's perplexity, which he had played up, had richly amused those guileless chicks who nursed not a whit of jealousy, so it appeared.

Anna's ribbons lifted and swirled as masked couples cavorted. Four fiddlers sawed their bows so vigorously it was a wonder that they didn't snap the strings. None of the melancholy modesty of the tango hereabouts. Sausages and beer for all, served by buxom wenches from booths garlanded with paper flowers. Minkie's idea of a street party. Mummers paraded about, costumed as cuckoos and serpents, goats and velvet-horned tarandras. Minkie's dream of a palace dominated one edge of this village of white-painted timber houses. Slim marble towers of snowy hue soared gracefully, tipped with pennants.

Something like a yellow sun looked down upon the merry scene from high in the sky-bowl. A strange bowl, indeed: vistas of forest and lakes climbed ever upward, replicating themselves ever more diminutively.

Within that luxurious little palace was Snowy, twenty times over. Blotchy-faced stuttering Snowy served as valet and steward and cook and courtier and flunkey and as numerous guards.

None of those persons were really Snowy. Nakkis, nakkis, all of them. Amenable nakki lackeys. Just as the maids within the palace – svelte or curvaceous – were all nakkis who ministered to Minkie's pleasure. Just as the majority of the residents of this village, participants in the carnival, were nakkis.

Maria and Gerda and Inga and Anna and Gretel were something else. Likewise Paula. Minkie had become jaded with his nakki maids. They presented no piquant challenge whatsoever to a fellow of his mettle. The six lasses definitely possessed more *actuality*. They were reflections, to be sure. Echoes of women who had once lived. (In the case of Gerda and Maria, decidedly cuddly echoes!)

Nor was it hard to guess of whom they were echoes. They themselves might well have forgotten their former identities. But to Minkie – lately fled from Pohjola Palace – it was plain as mustaberry pie that the girls were Sariola daughters. They had each given longlife to some husband presumably now long dead. Here was their own prize: preservation in a kind of paradise at the age they had been when first they wedded whoever those lucky fellows had been.

Fellows who had died long since, presumably. The girls' amnesia saved them from heartache.

Paula, the pigtailed blonde, was the odd one amongst them. She behaved as blithely as any of her sisters. Yet she was the spitting image, the absolute twin, of Queen Lucky herself – with the startling exception that Paula was blonde. Uniquely blonde.

According to the legend of Lucky, hadn't she herself once been blonde? Before she first entered her Ukko, far away beyond all the stars in the sky? Was Paula not really a sister of Gerda and Gretel and Inga and Anna and Maria at all? Might she be a reflection of Lucky herself – of the young Lucky who once upon a time had entered her Ukko, to be transformed? When Minkie finally brought Paula to bed in his marble palace full of nakkis, might she remember her real identity in shock and bewilderment?

Oh, but what would she remember? Not her life on Kaleva!

512

Qualms as to Paula's reaction – bearing in mind a certain Queen's caprices – dampened (though did not extinguish) Minkie's ardour in that direction. Once he had ploughed all the dark-haired sisters, though, wasn't it inevitable that blonde Paula must complete the series?

The Queen wasn't dead. So how could her echo be here?

He swung Anna, laughing, around.

'Enough, enough,' she appealed.

'Let's quench our thirst, my goose. Then maybe some other thirsts too?'

She giggled gratifyingly.

From along the street brassy music swelled to engulf the fiddlers' tune. The nakki minstrels ceased their sawing as a band came marching along. Scarlet-uniformed bandsmen with jaunty peaked caps played on trumpet and tuba and trombone, cornet and cymbals and forest-horn. A harlequin-clad acrobat followed, somersaulting. A juggler tossed no fewer than five variously coloured clubs high in the air. Minkie seized a glass of beer for Anna, and one for himself. He admired her peachy skin, her sultry eyes, her coaly curls. He winked, he toasted her. The bandsmen halted nearby. *Rump-tump-tootle, poop-poopety-poo.* The acrobat pranced on his hands. The juggler's clubs rose even higher. In other circumstances children would have flocked to feast their ears and eyes. No kids hereabouts, though.

Kyli had been about to give birth to a child of his own, a squealing brat . . .

He'd had no real choice in the matter of fleeing here, had he? Not with the Prince's blood on his paws, oh no – even if that business had all been Bertel's fault, for a fact. May as well indulge himself to the hilt amidst such opportunities as these. Anyone sensible would.

When he had finally paused astride his jump-bike on that clifftop beside the great boulders, launching the vehicle and himself down into Loom Lake had taken such courage and faith and will power. He could afford to feel proud of himself. Rewards were definitely in order.

In a flash of darkness, the bike had jumped into a meadow. A clump of creamy flowers had seemed to question him, quite as if those waxen blooms were the eyes and ears and mouths of paradise. He'd refrained from twisting red and firing off some jubilant thunder and lightning from the guns to announce his arrival. The flowers had all nodded their heads in a certain direction, which he had taken, only crushing a paltry number of blooms under the wheels of his bike. The charming village, and the splendid keep with its maids and its Snowies, hadn't proved to be far away . . .

Yet how far was far in this domain? How close was close? Up the curving wings of the dreamworld unfolded an eye-fooling vista of repetition and variety wherein must lurk yet other villages harbouring the living reflections of other Sariola sisters. And nakkis. Maybe stranger residents besides.

'Um, Anna, did you ever meet a man called Ragnar? A touchy, tetchy man who rubbed people up the wrong way?' Minkie stroked Anna's ribboned, lace-veiled shoulder, and a lock of her coaly hair. 'Unlike me! Though quite like me in a way, I suppose . . .'

She pouted. 'I don't remember. No, I don't.' Defensively: 'Why should I wish to remember somebody with a bad temper?'

'Of course you wouldn't, my goose. Of course not. Forget I asked. How about us ducking out of sight for a while and paying a little visit to my palace?'

'All those fellows there with weeping acne . . .'

'—won't harm your lovely complexion. They'll keep out of the way.'

'Inga saw them.'

'You *shan't*. I'll blindfold you with my kerchief and lead you by the hand into the loveliest chamber you can imagine. A chamber of joy where we can play the finest game, Anna.'

She inclined her head, charmed. 'That sounds—'

'—delicious,' Minkie assured her.

Like wind over water, a ripple of excitement stirred the crowd.

'She's come back to us,' exclaimed a voice.

Heads turned. 'Oh it's *her*,' cried someone else. On tiptoe, Anna craned to see. The brass band fell silent.

'Lift me up, Minkie, will you?'

'*Of course*.' His hands gripped her hips, slipping amidst ribbons. He hoisted, sliding her up his frame. She pressed her palms down on his shoulders to support some of her weight.

'Who's coming, anyway? Another sister from another village?'

Elevated, Anna was staring over bandsmen and chattering mummers.

'I remember her now – of course I do!'

'*Who?*'

A rift opened. Approaching along the street strode a slender

514

woman with silky yellow hair falling loose. She wore a grey cloak over a ruffled white blouse and breeches of brown leather buckled with brass. Over one shoulder, a satchel. She gazed in bemusement at the marble towers rising just beyond the white wooden houses. Gazed with one eye, with her right eye. The other eye-socket was an empty hole into which her eyelids drooped.

'It's Eyeno! She's come back from travelling—'

Eyeno Nurmi.

Here, in his bolt-hole and paradise? The very same dolly chick for whom he had felt such a hankering. Whom her brother had forbidden to our Minkie by a proclamation which made him droop and dwindle. Whom van Maanen had bespoken to flee from Speakers' Valley to the edge of the world to drown herself in the deepest lake. Here, in his refuge?

She must be a reflection, an echo, a ghost. Phantoms were substantial hereabouts! Or else she was a nakki trickster, a double.

Where have you been all my life? Precious and dear. Where's the wench of my dreams? How can I forget? You'll be mine some day, poetess. A living, loving poem as potent as a charm . . .

With a new glass eye she would look as lovely as before. And without those discouraging leather breeches. Off-putting was the word. Off they ought to be put. He let Anna slide down him to stand on her own two feet again.

When the newcomer noticed our Minkie she halted, startled. Her lone eye widened. She bit on her lip. Disquiet and outrage possessed her.

'*You!*' The word was spat out.

'Minkie, at your service,' he called out to her. His hopes weren't dashed. Surely she was a reflection or a nakki. Her brother's prohibition needn't apply in this dreamland. He felt a chill creep over him.

'You, rutting with my maidens! Hoisting them!' As she advanced, her empty socket seemed to shine, moist with tears of indignation. '*How can you be here? How dare you be here?*'

She was flesh and blood. Of a sudden the flesh meant nothing to him, and his own blood was listless. She was real, alive, a hag without an eye. A termagent. How could he possibly have felt lured by such as her?

Or by ink-haired Anna with cheeks like buns and close-set piggy eyes? That simply wasn't true; he knew it wasn't – Anna was succulent, a feast for a fellow.

A banquet of ashes.

Eyeno Nurmi had leapt into his own Loom Lake, into his family's treasured secret place, to poison paradise for him!

'Go away!' he called.

'*You* can't proclaim to me.'

'Brother's sweetheart,' he jeered, 'leave me alone.' He felt sickened with ugliness. With hers. With his own – so murderous and faithless. With those grotesque bestial mummers. With the menacing juggler and the scary acrobat. Everywhere, eyesores. The upcurving bowl of forest was coated in mildew and gangrene. The sun's eye, so jaundiced. This was far worse than at the gala on that morning when she had passed by. On that earlier occasion the appreciation of beauty – desire for beauty – had faded away. Now beauty itself became repulsive.

'Keep away!' He was shaking. If she touched him, he would vomit.

Astonishment showed on Eyeno's face as she realized the effect her presence was having on our Minkie. She stepped back a pace, then another, measuring his reactions.

Anna *wasn't* hideous. Wasn't, mustn't, couldn't be. Proving that she wasn't would be his salvation. Seizing his dancing partner by the hand – which took quite some courage and will power – Minkie retreated, hauling Anna with him.

'But Eyeno's here,' she protested. 'I don't want to—'

'You will, you will,' he babbled. Arm around Anna, he forced her along the street. He carved a path through the carnival crowd.

'The loveliest chamber you can imagine – a chamber of joy – you and me. That's where we were going. You just forgot, that's all. You're always forgetting. I'll help you remember. You and me, my goose.' Already it was becoming almost tolerable to be so close to her who had been the object of his desire – and who would be this again, for his salvation.

'I don't know—'

'You'll know soon enough, I swear.'

'*Minkie Kennan!*'

Somewhere behind, Eyeno was trying to halt him with a reproachful, hectoring outcry. She couldn't do that to him. He hustled Anna onward.

'I'll twist my ankle!'

'Don't drag your heels, my joy, my treasure. No wait, I'll carry you.' He could bear to clutch Anna now. She still seemed quite like so many joints of beef. Not rotten beef, though. Hoisting her, he stumbled on at a trot.

'Isn't this an adventure?' he panted in her ear. 'Isn't this glamorous? Wait – till you see – my chamber (puff) – all decked with silk—'

He must put Eyeno out of his mind. Maybe she would go away.

'Shut your eyes, Anna, no peeping.'

Two strawberry-faced Snowies, armed with crossbows, stood on guard at the drawbridge. Minkie couldn't pause to set his darling down and blindfold her. 'Close your eyes, my duck. *Please*. Wait till I ask you to open them – or else you'll spoil the surprise—'

Glistening white towers with window embrasures soared high above. Scarlet and orange pennants fluttered.

So much iridescent silk in his bower, as if the wings of all the world's glitterbugs had been plucked and mellowed for the purpose. Ruched silk draped the walls. Bed hangings and canopy and sheets were sleek and shimmery. Padded pink satin covered the floor as if it were a dell of blushmoss, virtually demanding bare feet. The whole room seemed intended to slide a couple of people softly together into one another's embrace.

With a last struggle of protesting muscles, Minkie avoided dumping his burden so heavily that she would bounce. After the finale of two flights of stairs his heart thumped alarmingly. Sweat prickled tormentingly. He simply had to tear off his waistcoat and shirt, whilst gasping endearments.

Anna lay in her wrappings of ribbons and lace, regarding him with renewed if quizzical interest. Once again she was enchanting in his eyes. Gorgeous. His need was clamoursome. He hopped closer, tearing off shoes, nearly losing his balance entirely. His cock throbbed for this hen. He would groan and cry out, submerging her in his desire. He subsided upon the bed.

'So many fine feathers . . .'

Ribbons and lace, and peachy downy skin.

Both of them were as naked as plucked poultry now. As he slid inside her, Anna's eyes widened. She cried out a single slurred word.

What did she cry? *Enter? Hunter?* She squirmed. She was gawping at something beyond him. At *someone*, surely! Let it

517

not be a Snowy. Let a red-faced Snowy not have crept into the chamber to squint. Minkie swung his upper half around – and withdrew from Anna precipitately.

A huge naked man stood bunched in frustrated fury, clutching and unclutching his fists. His face was a baby's. He seemed about to bawl. Long blond hair straggled. Thin stripes streaked skin which looked a size too large for his nevertheless redoubtable frame. A silver chain was slung between rings in his nipples. From the central link dangled a locket. Bare-assed, Minkie scrambled from the silky bed, and held very still. Where was the nearest knife? How close were the nearest Snowies if he called out to them?

'Gunther, my *Gunther* . . . !'

Anna spoke the name as if she needed to practise it after long disuse so as to rediscover the meaning. She sat up, slipping, then recovering herself. She covered her lap with a web of fingers.

Wonder replaced misery on the big man's face.

'Anna, do you really know me at last?'

Convulsively one of his paws gripped the locket, concealing it. 'The years, the endless years . . .'

'We were one heart,' whispered naked Anna, spellbound. 'We loved, how we loved . . . Until, until I was old . . .'

Tears of joy trickled from the nude man's grey eyes. His gaze swung to inspect Minkie, with a poignant anguish. He waved his arm in a gesture which both included Minkie yet then seemed to brush him aside. Silk glistened beyond this Gunther, haloed him. Despite his hefty presence, there was an odd impression of weightlessness about the man, as though he dreaded floating away from where he stood.

'I've found you in my dreams,' he told Anna. 'In the deepest dreams a man ever dreamt.' This sounded very romantic to Minkie. He must be sure to remember those lines. Though what specifically did the words mean?

The man's face was vaguely familiar. Not his bare body! No one would readily forget that chain strung between the nipples. Yet the cherubic features, and the long blond hair, oh yes.

Try to visualize him with some clothes on.

Where? Where?

Not too recently.

Somebody at Saari? Someone visiting the court of Lord Helenius? Some time before Minkie's precipitate marriage? Maybe, maybe not. *After* his wedding to Kyli? (So what's our

518

Minkie up to then, starkers, in this bedroom of silk and satin? That is irrelevant. And perfectly excusable.) The only event of much substance prior to deceased Prince Bertel's infernal invitation to Lucky's palace was the trip to the gala in Yulistalax . . .

That jaunt with Kyli, where he'd set eyes on Eva Sariola, alas. Where Eyeno had such an alarming effect upon him. Please don't think about *her* . . .

Was it at the gala that he had seen the big man whose reflection echo was here now?

Someone proclaiming? No . . .

Someone spouting verses? About finding love in dreams, like some tangomeister?

Though the initiative was perhaps reckless, Minkie asked cautiously, 'Were you at last year's gala by any chance, sir?'

This enquiry did distract Gunther's attention from Anna, prompting him to growl, 'Why the hell are you with my wife?'

Galvanized – though still rejoicing – Anna snatched for her lace and ribbons to part-way cover herself. She shook her head in denial, dissociating herself from any real connection with Minkie. Joy seemed her main sentiment: joy of rediscovery, bliss at being reunited with this Gunther, and with herself, though above all with him.

'Ach, it doesn't matter,' exclaimed Gunther. 'It's been so difficult to reach you, Anna. The few times when I did you didn't know me.' Did she wholly know him yet? How questioningly, now – if elatedly – Anna was scrutinizing this Gunther's nipple-chains and his fully exposed figure, gross and puckered as if he were at once a glutton and a starveling.

Minkie felt as if he was participating in some strange mystery . . . gallingly enough, as a mere auxiliary, an item of furniture. The intruder – Anna's *husband*, in some bizarre fashion! – seemed determined to suppress the pangs of jealousy which the spectacle of his woman sporting with a lover should have provoked in any normal fellow.

'What this person did just now,' Gunther declared with as much certainty as he could muster, 'awoke the real you. That . . . person made you remember me at last, Anna.'

'Yes,' she agreed, all smiles and tears of happiness and ribbons and bare skin. 'Oh yes.'

Quickly Minkie pulled on his lavender breeches. 'I did promise I'd give you something to remember,' he chipped in.

'Where is this place?' Anna's husband was asking her. 'Are these really the shores of death?'

On with his shirt and waistcoat, though he spared no time to button the latter before stamping his feet into his shoes. Now he was decent.

'Seems I've been quite the matchmaker, haven't I?'

Gunther glared scathingly at Minkie. 'Who are *you*? What are *you*? Do I care a hang? Get out of here. Vanish.' Yet it was the big fellow who seemed curiously insubstantial.

Bolder now that he was dressed, Minkie cocked his head. 'This is my palace, you know. Why don't *you*. . . disappear?'

Anna gasped. 'Oh no.' The big man was quivering.

'Don't be saying that,' he growled. His brow knit in concentration. 'I dreamed my way here with all my will.'

'Dream yourself away, then,' suggested Minkie.

Definitely the interloper was struggling.

'Gunther—'

'Anna—' Gunther's voice sounded distant and quavery.

The gilded bedroom door swung open. In hurried a Snowy wearing bright red leathers, cradling a rifle. Under his bleached mop his face was a roseate pool in which his features floated. To some extent the hue of his uniform lessened the visual impact of his acne.

'Bu-bu-bu-bu-BOSS,' he stuttered, 'there's a blu-blu-BLOODY bu-bu-BIG kru-kru-kru-CROWD of villagers outside armed with a-a-a-a-AXES and sick-ick-ick-kick-SICKLES an' knives an' all. They've tu-tu-tun-TURNED against you!'

Minkie was through the door in a trice. As he brushed past Snowy, Anna cried, 'Don't go away!'

It wasn't Minkie whom Anna was imploring.

'Don't leave me, Gunther!'

('Anna—')

A wail of loss pursued Minkie.

Minkie freewheeled the Juttahat jump-bike into the wide arched doorway. To either side of him Snowies were aiming crossbows across the drawbridge at a besieging mob of nakki bandsmen, fiddlers, minstrels, mummers, wenches, erstwhile caperers at the carnival. Many of them were armed. All were incensed. The abusive crowd stretched back for a hundred metres and more.

'Lord Kennan's for the pillory!'

'—head on a pole!'

In the distance, Minkie spied Eyeno Nurmi, conductress of this assault. That damned one-eyed bitch was gesticulating, whipping up frenzy. The ugliness of the scene chilled him. Mummers tricked out as goats and tarandras were grotesque freaks, *monsters*.

Those were no longer nakki-people wearing disguises. Those were beasts upright on two legs.

The unnatural mob stank of animosity. In another moment its vanguard would be swarming on to the drawbridge, careless of crossbow quarrels or bullets from the Snowies. A broken tile landed beside Minkie, skittering away across the white-paved marble of the hall.

See red.

Twist red. Bullets erupted from the guns of the jump-bike.

A bandsman hefting an axe instead of trombone or trumpet lurched backwards. A nakki-cuckoo collapsed. The acrobat toppled. Bodies tumbled as Minkie swung those handlebars, twisting red, twisting red. Within seconds, the horde of enemies was in disarray – colliding, tripping, fleeing for shelter.

'We'll be back!' shrieked the harlequin-clad juggler from amidst the rout.

Rosy-faced Snowy grinned. 'It's wu-wu-wu-WAR, bu-bu-bu-BOSS!'

'It's wu-wu-*war*,' chorused two more Snowies, their faces raw pink glossy orbs.

War, in this dreamworld? War in paradise? Against nakki enemies – with nakki Snowies fighting by his side? His Snowies wouldn't turn against him so long as he led them vigorously enough – he must cling to that faith. Dismay and exhilaration plucked at our Minkie's nerves, making lunatic music. Of Eyeno Nurmi, bringer of ugliness, there wasn't any longer so much as a glimpse.

35 · A CUCKOO IN THE HALL

Cully had been living at the aitch-house for three weeks by now. Lucky's Day had come around again. It was the four hundred and third anniversary of that daynight in the void when the girl who would become Queen had entered the innards of her Ukko. At mana-priest Moller's urging the annual celebration was going ahead as usual despite the death of Prince Bertel – the murder of Eva's father – two months earlier. How could this apex of the calendar be altered? Ought it to be made into a *wake* for the Queen's consort? Certainly not! For the well-being of Kaleva, Loxmithlinna must toast Paula Sariola. This was a mana-day. Elmer and his bride must celebrate.

Eva found Cully helping with preparations in the banqueting hall. Occupying most of the second floor of the crossbar of the aitch, the hall offered a view across the water-yard and through the portcullis bridge south-westward over several keys of lake. Water lay leaden under unseasonably grey sky. Fireproof purple tammywood panelled the majority of the hall and the high ceiling too. Each of the tall windows wore a delicate external cage of wrought-iron foliage. A lad was carrying in an armful of candles for use that evening. Another lad balanced atop a tall stepladder, replenishing a chandelier. Elmer and Lyle had spoken of wiring the hall electrically in time for next year's feast. This wasn't wholly their decision to make. The great hall wasn't properly part of the family wing. The wider community of artisans who lived in the rest of the aitch-house deserved their say. Even if Loxmiths were lords, the tradition of the aitch-house was one of shared decisions as regards keep and town and countryside.

A brewer was tapping a barrel to test the dark ale. A scullion set down a tower of plates on one of the long tammy tables. With a feather duster on the end of a rod a maid flicked at a brass-framed portrait of the Queen painted last century or the century before – Lucky was smiling winsomely.

As Eva approached Cully, a plate slipped from his hands. China shattered on a hard floorboard.

'Damned clumsy oaf, but you're a curse,' swore Bailiff Andersen. He shook his bald head exasperatedly as if tempted to butt the young man. Cully stood so helplessly apologetic, the corners of his mouth drooping.

'I'm trying my best not to be, sir . . . My hands twitched. They aren't always quite my own.'

'So whose hands are they? Pah! Your uncle was well rid of you, young Cully.'

'You're right. Well rid of me.' Cully's frank open face looked momentarily haunted. 'I must pay the debt by staying here, mustn't I?' He flinched from Eva; then contrived a smile of appeal. *Don't ask me things, please.*

She would ask him. She would.

Cully's contradictory stories fascinated and baffled her. It wasn't so much that Eva could torment Lord Beck's nephew by day to compensate for her own nightly humiliation. Bashfully yet staunchly Elmer still inflicted *that* upon her in the silk-draped iron-clad bedroom. If such had been Eva's motive, Nikki might have withdrawn her outraged sympathy, her much-valued friendship. Eva couldn't have abided this loss. She did rather pity Cully – at the same time as she persevered in quizzing him mischievously.

That young man was under a sway, Lady Lokka insisted. On the contrary it seemed to Eva that Cully was doing his maladroit best to resist a sway. His clumsiness was one of the consequences of this inner struggle which he was unable to articulate. Eva felt sure that her continued probing, her needling, would break through the shell one day and crack him open. A blow on the head could hardly account for his confused state. (Perpetrated by a trio of robbers who were surely an invention!) Nor could Lord Gunther Beck's protégé genuinely be such a dolt.

Oh, those *stories*. Those lies, concocted seemingly on the spur of the moment to satisfy her curiosity, and deflect it from discovering the nub of the matter! Those fantasies, with which Eva subsequently regaled an incredulous Nikki. But not Elmer. Nor Lyle. Cully was Eva's personal project. She would only share it with her sister-in-law, at least until a revelation of the truth about the strange young man.

There was a definite theme to Cully's anecdotes of his past life. That theme might explain his reluctance to return to Castlebeck. It was quite at odds with his professed devotion to his uncle's honour. By rights Cully ought to have detested Gunther Beck . . .

Supposedly Lord Beck had quarrelled with Cal, Cully's father, a while before Cully's father was killed by Jutties. This bickering had been about Marietta, Cully's mother. Beck was infatuated with Marietta. Beck might have contrived Cal's death . . .

After that tragedy the dream lord took Marietta into his keep for a year or so – and into his bed for at least part of that time. Beck might even be Cully's biological father. But wait. One of Cully's earliest memories was of his uncle throwing the boy into a deep pool – in a presumed attempt to kill him. Soon afterwards, Beck tethered the child to a tree near a verrin's den.

Did this occur in the vicinity of Castlebeck? Cully could only have been a few months old at the time! Still regarding himself as wedded to his long-dead wife, Beck was anguished at his adultery. Then, in a remorseful change of heart, he adopted the boy instead. If the dream lord ever died Cully would be Beck's heir.

Cully had an older sister and a younger sister – Helga and Olga, whom he loved dearly, especially Olga. If Cal had died before Cully was conceived, who in that case was Olga's father? Beck, again? The Marietta episode seemed to have happened around the time Cully was born, and a while after he was born, and also during his adolescence.

The light which Nikki could throw upon Cully's stumbling confessions suggested that these were a jumble of fabrications both chronologically and with respect (or disrespect) to the character of Lord Beck. Just a year ago, Nikki had met Gunther Beck here in this very aitch-house. The dream lord might be under the sway of an obsession about his dead wife Anna. He had definitely not struck Nikki as someone who would try to drown an infant or feed him to a verrin. (Without success in either event!) Nor had Beck seemed likely to conspire with Jutta-hats to bring about the death of a human neighbour of his.

'Never mind about the plate,' Eva told the vexed bailiff. 'I want a word with Cully.'

She led the awkward young man out of the hall by the westerly door. Tempting smells of feast in the making drifted from a nearby kitchen. Adjacent, was a small refectory. A single oil lamp softly illuminated circular tables and lath-and-baluster chairs of hardwearing sylvester wood. A ceiling fan rotated, stirring warm savoury air. A leather-aproned cobbler from the west wing was gossiping with a saddler over Pootaran coffee.

Slumped in his seat across from Eva, Cully seemed resigned yet also wary and defensive. Brown cord shirt and scuffed breeches – opposite green satin gown and spangled hair-combs. An onlooker might have suspected that an assignation was in progress between the bluffly handsome fellow with his long hair and sensual lips – and this voluptuous lady. A rendezvous insisted upon by the latter, whereas the swain was reluctant and shy.

Beck's nephew (or his true son?) spilled coffee in his saucer as he raised his cup.

'So,' said Eva, 'sister Olga was born at least a year after your father's death, is that right?'

Cully nodded, then frowned. His coffee was too hot to drink.

'Burns my lips,' he muttered; and set the cup down clumsily.

'On the other hand *after* your dad's death your uncle gave sanctuary to your mother and both her daughters and yourself too.'

'Yes. No,' said Cully. 'You're confusing me. I forget.' He touched his blond-thatched skull gingerly. 'It's because of the bang on the head. How often do I have to tell you, Lady Eva?' His moist gaze begged her to desist.

Elmer whipped her for a while each night. Though not so as to break her flesh and draw blood. (If he finally drew blood, would that invigorate him?) By day for a while she whipped Cully with her words – for his own good. Eva steepled her fingers. Her coffee was going to last for a long time.

'It's as if there are two of you, Cully, who each lived two separate lives.'

'Two of me? How can there be? There's only me.'

'And a wicked uncle as well as a kind uncle.'

Cully's lip quivered as he spoke. He stared past Eva at the doorway, anxious to escape. 'I owe a lot to Uncle Gunther.'

'For having your dad killed? For trying to drown you? And feed you to a verrin?'

Abruptly the young man's fist crashed on to the tabletop. Coffee slopped from both their cups. Such pent-up feelings.

'I know that happened but it didn't,' he snarled. 'And I'm Uncle's son but I'm bloody well not. I honour him and I'll pay his debt.' Eyebrows raised, the cobbler and the saddler were exchanging glances.

'Many more smashed plates and botched jobs,' Eva said lightly, 'and you could well be packed off back to Castlebeck. In two flicks of a lamb's tail.'

'*Mustn't go there. Shan't.*' Nails grooved his palms.

'Shan't-can't,' she mocked. 'Why ever not?'

'Because! Why can't you leave me be?'

Saddler and cobbler were nodding sadly. 'Why can't you leave me be?' Was Elmer's bride attempting infidelity so soon after her wedding? Unexpectedly Cully rose, almost upsetting the table. A cup crashed to the floor.

Eva wagged her finger. 'Clumsy clogs.'

'Why am I clumsy? Why do you think?' Cully's face was

tormented. 'Don't push me, Lady Eva. Please, I'm begging you. And I'll not go back to Castlebeck.' Tears in his eyes, he blundered from the little refectory.

Definitely his shell was on the verge of cracking.

Another few knocks and the truth would spill from him, healingly, whatever that truth might be. Cully would be master of himself, not a victim. Nikki would be proud of Eva. Some day soon, cuckoos would cackle how Eva Loxmith-Sariola had cured Lord Beck's nephew of a sway which was crippling him. Eva's cruelty – such minor cruelty! – was an act of compassion. When Cully at last cried out a confession, wrung from some place within which remained obscure even to himself – which he sensed by reason of the shadow it cast, if not the substance; when he finally sobbed out the truth, astonished to recognize it and acknowledge it at last, in that moment when a locked door opened and light spilled through, Eva might similarly perceive how to cure Elmer of his lamentable impediment, which certainly gave *her* cause to lament ... and to nurse fury at her mother's mischief. Lucky's sting in the tail!

When Eva cured Elmer, Nikki could stop detesting her brother. Nikki couldn't truly detest Elmer. Consequently, her heart was in turmoil, tempting her towards mania, though she was well aware of this peril.

No more could Eva allow herself to loathe the husband who treasured her – *overly*, unable to violate her however much he tried. As yet he hadn't tried excessively. He mustn't, mustn't. Or must Eva first bleed?

She must find her sister-in-law to tell her how close Cully was to the hour of truth.

Events on the fourth floor of the south wing swiftly engulfed Eva in other concerns. Failing to find Nikki anywhere on the second or third floors – and knowing that Elmer's sister would not be haunting the ground floor workshops – Eva had been heading up by way of the stairs to the long gallery where she and Nikki frequently walked and talked together ever since that confession in the hidey-hole.

The main double doors to the suite of offices stood wide. Unaccountable bustle, on a feast day such as this! Lyle's raised voice, and Elmer's; Nikki's too.

A bearded clerk hurried out but darted back in again as Lyle shouted, 'Just a moment, Magnus!' At the far end of the corridor the lift disgorged Lord Henzel sitting rigid in his wheelchair, propelled by a lad. Nikki herself appeared in the doorway. Spying Eva, she cried:

'Quickly – Minnow's *safe!*'

A communicator call had come from the keep at Maananfors. From Osmo, none other. As its content spilled from an excited Elmer, Eva's exhilaration leaked away, and Nikki squeezed her sister-in-law's hand.

This office housed symbol ledgers and charts and clockwork calculators; and the radio communicator too. When the apparatus had chimed unexpectedly only Magnus and an apprentice clerk had been on duty. Magnus had taken the call, to hear Osmo's zealous steward Sam Peller declare that his lord wished to speak to his old friend.

By now Elmer's paralysed father was in the office too, and Lady Lokka, and Moller, and chunky Captain Haxell of the Defence Volunteers . . .

'Osmo's *enraged* at the Queen,' Elmer was explaining. 'He's talking war – real war against the Northland. Wants to know where I'd stand. Where we'd stand. With him or against him. Seeing as I wedded Eva. For which, so it seems, I'm forgiven conditionally. Osmo's meaning to marry Minnow, and she'll be marrying him gladly, as he puts it—'

This announcement astonished Eva. Hadn't Osmo kidnapped her feisty little sister by force? How could Minnow possibly feel *glad*?

'Can I call my sister on your communicator?' she asked. 'I'm sure Minnow'll tell me what's really happening.'

'There's a thought,' Elmer said fondly. 'If he'll let the two of you talk. He sounded hectic.'

'I fancy,' said Lyle,' we shouldn't chat to Maananfors until we work out exactly where we stand.'

Rolf Haxell nodded. Clad in a patchwork of leather – bottle-green and umber – the Captain was short and beefy. His was a head large in proportion to his height: broad and high-browed under a bristly grizzled crewcut. Chin and jaws were prominent. Little ears seemed handles too small for such a jug. Silver portcullis ear-rings dangled from the lobes. The flesh of his face was as pasty as a cow's tripe. A man who avoided the glare of the sun; but with certain characteristics of a mastiff, too.

'Minnow's Eva's own *sister*,' protested Nikki. 'How better to find out? At least women might tell each the truth.'

Lyle adjusted his gold-rimmed glasses – casting scorn on this suggestion, though without discourtesy. A wheeze from the crippled lord. A rasp. Lokka, her painted face white as snow, held up a hand for silence.

'What does Osmo mean by "real" war?' croaked her husband.

'That's the question in a nut-shell,' agreed Elmer. 'During Osmo's absence it seems Sam Peller began laying his hands on a large stock of powerful weaponry supplied by the Brindled Isi . . .'

Lokka was sceptical. 'Why would they do that?'

'Osmo sounded perfectly convincing, I assure you! We know that the Queen's receiving Isi weapons from her everything machine—'

'Which my clever brother brought to life,' said Nikki. 'Bravo, Elmer.'

'That was a Brazen Isi machine. The Brindleds must be trying to maintain a balance of power.'

'Oh I doubt that,' said Lyle.

'In case Lucky should go on the rampage against Osmo?'

Lyle laughed bitterly. 'More likely to provoke a rampage. Feed it. Give it plenty of fuel. Lucky hates Osmo's guts, and he isn't dead after all. Osmo detests the Queen on account of the mutie caper. Juke Nurmi shot his sky-boat down, and now Osmo's bane is Lucky's new favourite.'

'Meanwhile we're on Lord Osmo's flank,' pointed out Haxell.

'How do we stand?' said Elmer.

The Captain of the Defence Volunteers scratched, cat-like, at an ear. A little silver portcullis ring flipped to and fro. 'Time to lower you-know-what, I'd say. Declare ourselves neutral.'

Nikki was nodding hopefully.

Elmer sucked in his cheeks. 'I don't think that'll be quite good enough for Osmo. Not if I'm to atone for wedding Eva – even if he has Minnow instead – nor for giving Lucky access to weapons to use against him. That's how Osmo sees it. And in a sense he's right . . .'

Lord Henzel rasped quietly, 'Osmo has always somewhat over-shadowed you, Son.'

Elmer looked wounded. His dark mellow eyes surveyed the company. He sought Eva; then swept back his mop of black hair.

'Not in one respect, Father! A pretty crucial respect. A perfectly *gorgeous* respect.'

'Respect, indeed,' murmured Nikki despite herself.

Eva frowned – *not in front of other people, please*. There was no need. Nikki walked to the window to stare down into the water-yard, watched inquisitively by Lyle.

'I still want to talk to Minnow,' Eva told her husband – who hadn't yet proved himself to be a proper husband at all; whose attempts were painful to her.

'Of course,' agreed Elmer, 'but that might *bond* us prematurely to Osmo's cause.'

'Doesn't that rather depend on what Minnow says? She must have undergone a strange conversion to appreciate abduction like a piglet in a sack. Or else she's been thoroughly bespoken—'

'He said she'll be marrying him *gladly*—'

'Alternatively—' Eva bit on her lip. *Alternatively, Minnow was seduced so smoothly and sweetly, so competently and skilfully . . .* Maybe Eva didn't wish to know this.

And maybe she did – but not publicly, broadcast across Kaleva, overheard by any eavesdropper . . .

Would Minnow, cock-a-hoop, be tolerable?

Implications were dawning belatedly on Elmer. 'He'll be a long-life now,' he muttered, 'or soon will be . . .'

His mother smiled at him fondly. *So are you now, Son, so are you.* Elmer looked away.

'Willing to risk his skin in a war, even so!'

'Our skins too,' said Lyle, 'on the face of it.'

'Maybe Osmo hasn't any real choice, if the Queen's arming herself . . .'

'Do *you* have a choice?' queried Elmer's assistant. 'Do we? Does Loxmithlinna?' He eyed Haxell, seeking an accomplice – if the Captain of the Volunteers were not already a henchman, long since cultivated.

'I think,' Eva said, 'maybe I *oughtn't* to talk to Minnow just yet. Not openly by communicator.'

Elmer appeared relieved. So he ought to be.

'Lord Osmo lost his sky-boat,' said Haxell. 'It'll be a slow war on his side, to the extent that one small sky-boat would have helped him. Unless, of course, the Brindleds have given him some of these new jump-bikes we've been hearing about . . . Meanwhile the Queen can fly her troops to Maananfors. Or to here, I suppose, if we're in league with van Maanen . . .'

Lyle peered at the Captain. 'Our aitch-house would be a fine strong fortress to occupy within easy striking distance of Maananfors, wouldn't you say?'

'The Queen might try to *seize* the aitch-house?' Haxell flipped at his ear as if a stingfly was pestering him. 'If we don't have the support of Lord Osmo's new weapons? Either he takes us over, or she does: is that the score? The Defence Volunteers aren't going to like this choice, you know, Mister Melator.' Another flick. 'Even in the time of the Dread we were safe in our aitch-house.'

'Because nobody came here,' Lyle pointed out. 'Nothing hostile came. I'm thinking now about Lucky's wooden soldiers.'

Elmer darted a puzzled glance at his assistant.

'Those sentries at the fortress, Elmer. Invulnerable warriors, so I heard. As soon shoot a tree and expect it to fall down. Our aitch-house may be fairly invulnerable, but is the town? These days there are far too many souls to cram into our keep – supposing Lucky feels frustrated and decides to ravage. Of course if the Queen's ensconced inside of here we're practically inviting Osmo to attack the aitch-house.'

'What are you suggesting?' Elmer asked helplessly. He'd been led by the nose in two contrary directions.

Lyle spread his hands nonchalantly. 'It's your choice. Or rather, Lord Henzel's. With the concurrence of the Volunteers.'

'Aye,' agreed Rolf Haxell. 'What's best for everyone? Is being neutral a protection or a provocation?'

Eva moved close to her husband – in title, at least. 'Can't you decide?' she implored him. *Couldn't he summon up the spunk?* Nikki was keeping her back defiantly turned.

''Course,' added Haxell, 'with you being the instinctive engineer that you are Lord Osmo would want you on his side – whatever other reservations he might be feeling. Swanky weapons can go wrong, 'specially if they're recent gifts from the snakes . . .'

'I wonder,' mused Elmer, 'whether celebrating Lucky's Day might be seen as provocation in the circumstances?' Surely this was a simpler problem. But no; it was merely an aspect of the bigger problem. 'Supposing we were to cancel . . .'

'At this late hour?' The mana-priest would have none of this. 'Celebrating Lucky's Day is essential – and *normal*.'

Nikki swung round. 'I wonder whether they'll be celebrating Lucky at Maananfors as usual tonight? Can they possibly applaud her and attack her at the same time? Maybe there'll be a thanksgiving instead for Osmo's survival. Van Maanen's Day, hmm?'

'When's the wedding to happen?' Eva asked with sudden understanding. 'When, Elmer?'

'Osmo didn't say.'

'You didn't ask ... I don't suppose *we'd* be invited. Though he's inviting his guards into your keep. Into *our* keep. Don't you see, the marriage'll be tonight! When else? Osmo can honour Minnow instead of my mother. A Sariola substitute. He'll honour her,' Eva breathed, 'with his hand and with his body. Tonight, Elmer, tonight.' She was provoking him. Rousing him. Speaking in a code which, of the others present, only Nikki understood. Unless sly Lyle also knew.

Tonight must be the night. Her husband couldn't fail her on this night of nights. She would whip *him* with words. *Osmo's in bed with my sister now. He may be drunk but he's proclaiming himself potent. He's entering her successfully – isn't he, Elmer, can't you see? – just as he'll enter our keep. There's such a lascivious ripple of mana on the breeze tonight. Respond to it! Rise to the occasion, now! Night of nights. Osmo triumphs. You aren't less than him, oh no. You're Princess Eva's husband, not a sprat's spouse. Am I too sumptuous for you? Be jealous, Elmer! Very jealous. I surely am. Possess me!*

Elmer stared at Eva, transfixed. Surely he understood.

Yes, whip him with words. Enrage him. Bring him to the boil, so that he would toss away that lame, limp, ordinary whip. So that he would use his shaft instead. Eva almost felt herself to be a proclaimer. Her practice with Cully was paying off.

'Tonight,' echoed Elmer. 'Yes, you're right, my goose.' Did he really understand?

The banqueting hall was crowded to capacity. Aitch-house dwellers and townsfolk packed the long benches shoulder to shoulder. Bodies congested the floor – backs to the walls. People even perched around the edge of the dais where the Loxmiths and their guests sat at high table. All windows were canted open, to the extent that the exterior cagework permitted. Doors stood wide. Above the mass of heads loomed an ample reservoir of air and space beneath the lofty ceiling. Still, the hall was fairly reminiscent of a busy sauna.

Would there be enough goose and meatballs and pigs' trotters, sufficient blood-soup and loaves and pasties, adequate sausage

531

and slabs of fish? Perhaps! Gorging wasn't uppermost in guests' minds, even though many did gobble and swig to comfort themselves. Talk – and speculation, and exaggeration – was all of the likelihood of a war. Two harpists strummed. They were hardly heard. A cuckoo had negotiated its way through the wrought-iron foliage and clung to the open top of the window closest to the dais. Whenever it cackled, an urgent hush propagated from one end of the hall to the other: '*Hwisht, what's it saying?*' In the wake, a renewed surge of voices. Ebb and surge, ebb and surge.

'—I tell you van Maanen's going to attack us—'

'—because Elmer married Eva—'

'—Lucky's going to attack us—'

'—because Elmer and Osmo are allies—'

'—she has wooden soldiers whom you can't ever kill—'

'—van Maanen has war-bikes as can jump a key at a time, even right into a keep—'

'—right through the walls, so I've heard—'

'—the Brindled Jutties'll fight for van Maanen—'

'—mutie proclaimers'll fight for the Queen—'

'—and the aitch-house'll fall—'

'—so why ain't the portcullis down?'

The Dread was returning.

Eva had insisted on Cully being at the high table, seated between herself and Nikki. Lyle, on Nikki's far side; then Moller and Rolf Haxell at the end. Lord Henzel sat next to Eva in his wheelchair, flanked by the brass feeding automaton and by its builder Elmer sitting next to his white-faced melancholy mother. Elmer was drinking quite heavily but did that matter as regards tonight? He'd go 'over the hill', out of the valley of his diffidence. Eva was drinking too, and she was urging Cully likewise. At first the young man had tried to abstain, just as he had tried to refuse the invitation to feast with the Loxmiths.

The hall was hectic as Lokka arose, tall and ghostlike, robed in glitterbugs, her long face a snowy mask. She waited, waited as the din died and the two harpists quit plucking chords. Her husband's face was creased parchment. His sunken dark eyes surveyed her audience.

Lokka spoke with a tremulous dignity. 'People of Lox-mithlinna,' she said. 'My people, our people: a crisis has come, as you know. It's time that my husband should abdicate as your lord, and myself as your lady, in favour of . . . *Lord* Elmer, *Lady*

Eva, who will lead our aitch-house through this exigency—'

('—what's one of those, then—?')

('*Hwisht!*')

'—with your support and solidarity, which we re-affirm at this feast in honour of the Queen of Kaleva—'

('—who's on the verge of *attacking* us—!')

('—let's hope as yon cuckoo reports how much we admire the crazy lady—')

('—self-defence! Rolf Haxell has his head screwed on—')

('—Melator too; he'd make a lord to reckon with—')

('—swanky upstart, wouldn't trust the fellow—')

('—why shouldn't a boatwright's boy be boss—?')

('—Lord Elmer can build brass soldiers for us—')

('—slow as pond-slugs; and only after five years of fooling around—')

('—our Elmer's a cut above a puffed-up bully any day. We're *community*, laddie. We have a say. And *you're* having too much of one—!')

Soon Lokka sat down. Elmer rose, grinning ingenuously, to be acclaimed. He stretched out his hand, behind the automaton and his motionless father, to raise Eva to her feet.

Moller also stood, red hair aflame, face aflush. Vigour itself might have been erupting from out of his grey serge priest's suit and his stiff white wing collar.

'It's Lucky's Day today,' he called out ebulliently, as if anybody might be unaware of this fact. 'Thanks be for Lucky's daughters, especially for Eva, Lady of Loxmithlinna and of our harmonious keep—' Moller was modifying his usual blessing.

'Wouldn't you like to live for ever, Cully?' whispered Eva urgently. 'Like your Uncle Gunther?' *Really push him. Torment him. His shell will break.*

Din ebbed and flowed. Not even Nikki could hear Eva clearly.

'Like your uncle, hmm, Cully?'

Cully's teeth were clenched. 'He won't live for ever.' The words tore from him. 'He'll die. If I go back there.'

'What did you say?'

Cully's knife stabbed into a black sausage of blood and onions and barley on his half-full plate. 'Die, dreamlord, die.'

'What's that?'

'I can't, I shan't!' exclaimed Cully. 'Won't do it, whatever it is that I have to do.' He was gouging the sausage to and fro.

533

'No wonder your work's so slapdash. No wonder you break plates. Wouldn't you like to live for ever, hmm?'

'*Me?* But who am I?' Cully seemed in agony, as if on fire within. He drained his mug of ale. Froth flowed from his lips.

'Snakes and white flowers,' he hissed. 'Telling me my story, singing me my tale – of *never-was*. Now-being-true, now-being-true. Dreamlord'll be dying. Making a harlot of your mother. Throwing you in a pool to drown. Tying you as a verrin's supper. Never happened. *Happening.*' His voice was slurred yet mechanical. He was rigid yet about to crumble. He warbled quietly, 'Killing-ing-ing-ing.' An echo, reverberating in his brain.

Eva fell into the same lilt. 'No, *living*. For ever. Becoming longlife.'

Nikki was showing signs of alarm. Regardless of the flutter of her sister-in-law's hand, the mouthing of caution, Eva carried on her pursuit of Cully's soul.

'Being longlife, Cully,' she invited. Life and death seemed to be the point at issue in his terrible perplexity.

Cully's long hair scythed from side to side as he shook his head like a beast. 'Through you?' he gasped. 'Then killing the lord? Killing this lord instead?' He sounded like an alien.

'No, no, of course not . . .'

'Stop examining me, stop peering! Flowers on your skin. Harlot, mother wasn't being a harlot.'

His voice rose to a howl. 'Stop *looking*!' His hand smashed down upon his neglected food, freeing the knife from the blood-sausage. In a trice he had raised the knife. Already he was on his feet, chair crashing backwards – as he drove the metal at Eva's prying, abruptly terrified eye.

How Eva screamed . . . until Mother Grünwald had made many passes with her hands.

Blood stained Eva's cheek as she lay shuddering upon the floor behind the high table. Her head was cushioned upon Moller's grey jacket. The dinner knife had sprung the eyeball from its orbit. It had torn muscles. Completely severed the optic nerve. Eva's left eye was a ball of detached useless jelly lying on the floor. No one could bear to touch it. With a kerchief the wise-woman dabbed blood oozing from the vacant socket.

Bedlam in the banqueting hall had died down – the turmoil from which Cully had fled through the nearest open door. Lyle and Henzel and other guests had given chase, though not instan-

534

taneously. Bodies had collided in the panicking throng. Elmer knelt by his wife, aghast. Nikki, too, crowding the mana-priest who crowded Ma Grünwald. Lokka still sat, her chair swung round, shaking with shock. Her paralysed husband stared fixedly into the mirror which the automaton angled in front of him.

The scaly green cuckoo high up on the window gawked too. Scrabbling sideways, it shifted its vantage point.

'Bloodshed,' it croaked. 'Ukko-ukkoo, there'll be carnage.'

'Here, do you mean, cuckoo?' cried an artisan. 'Bloodshed in the future?'

The bird ignored his question.

'Coo-coo,' the man shouted, 'sing the story, tell the tale.'

'Ukko-ukkoo,' was the bird's response. If it was a response at all.

'How can it tell a tale that hasn't happened yet?' bawled another voice.

Eva began to gasp out some words. That single eye staring up at Elmer was fully alive, darkly bright. It was as though two soft linked creatures had lived in twin holes in a shell clad with softness. One had been torn out yet somehow the twin survived.

'Brazen Isi swayed Cully to kill his uncle,' she told those who were comforting her. 'They gave him such bad memories. He resisted those. Part of him fought back, even though he was so confused. He came here to stop himself from going to Castlebeck. What a fool I was. Now we know, don't we . . . ?'

'Hush,' soothed Ma Grünwald, 'you'll be all right, Lady Eva.'

'She'll be *all right*?' echoed Nikki.

'Yes! She will! She isn't dying.'

'Now we know, at the cost of her eye . . . She was doing it for you, Elmer,' Nikki told her brother.

'For me?' Elmer cast about helplessly.

'You wouldn't understand why.'

'Why would the Isi want Cully to kill Gunther?' he asked.

'—to kill his uncle,' persisted Eva.

'Why would they want that to happen?'

Nikki shrugged contemptuously. 'To stop him from dreaming his way to . . . Anna? That isn't why Eva was provoking Cully. You really don't know, Elmer.'

'No,' gasped Eva. But by way of appeal to Nikki. *Don't tell him. That she had been practising provocation. That Nikki knew all about the whipping.*

'Now that I'm . . . disfigured—' Eva's hand rose towards her face. Ma Grünwald restrained Eva's wrist. The arm became limp. The wisewoman passed her other hand over Eva's forehead, whispering a charm of easement.

'I'll look just like Eyeno, won't I?' asked Eva as she lay there, peering up half-sighted. 'Eyeno Nurmi at the gala, after she tore out her false eye . . . What will Osmo think if he comes here with his guards? What will he think when he sees me? Your one-eyed wife . . .'

'Don't,' begged Elmer. 'My goose, my treasure.'

'Still waiting to lay the magic egg,' murmured Nikki.

Gingerly, between thumb and forefinger, Moller picked up the eyeball which had lain nearby all along – impossible to touch, till now. He lifted it almost too gingerly. The eye nearly slipped from his grip. Carefully he placed it upon the table, not too far from Henzel.

'If you whip her feathers enough . . .'

Elmer flushed deeply.

'Don't,' appealed Eva. 'You'll ruin it all, Nikki.'

'Yes of course. I'll be quiet . . .' What fierce reproach was in Nikki's fawnlike eyes.

Lokka caught hold of a word. 'Ruin,' she repeated numbly, gazing down at Eva's bloodstained face.

Henzel's whole frame shuddered as if a jolt of electricity passed through his crippled body, lancing his paralysis momentarily. Had he just spied the eye upon the banqueting table nearby?

'Dad!' exclaimed Elmer.

The arms of the brass automaton swung erratically, then stopped abruptly. Henzel's spasm had also passed.

A distant creaking and grating . . .

Across the water-yard, the portcullis was descending. Boats dressed in bunting for Lucky's Day slumbered in evening sunlight spilling low through the bridged gateway between the onion domes. Someone was letting the massive grating down on its rails.

Were Cully's pursuers doing so? In case the runaway should try to steal *Sea Sledge*? That wouldn't be the reason. The Dread had come again.

Soon great prison bars of shadow elongated across the water-yard towards the banqueting hall.

'*Bloodshed*,' cackled the messenger bird, '*and war.*'

536

Hopping around, the cuckoo picked its way through the tendrils of iron foliage.

Taking flight, the cuckoo dived down between merrily-pennanted masts. It swooped along the water-yard then sped up and away through that portcullis which was no barrier to its passage at all.

The End of the First Book of Mana

The BSFA takes you beyond your imagination

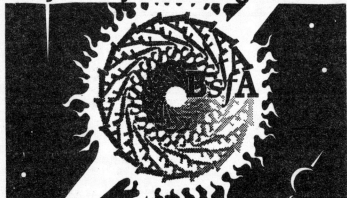

The British Science Fiction Association is your key to the many worlds of Science Fiction. You will discover everything you always wanted to know about SF in Britain — and more. Six times a year *Vector* brings you interviews, book reviews, and incisive articles in one of the leading critical magazines on SF. Six times a year *Matrix* brings you right up to date with all the news, plus film and magazine reviews. Six times a year *Paperback Inferno* gives you a searing overview of paperbacks in the UK. And three times a year *Focus* provides a unique forum for every SF writer in the country.

All this for just £12 a year. If you enjoy science fiction, join the BSFA. Write to Joanne Raine, Membership Secretary, 29 Thornville Road, Hartlepool, Cleveland TS26 8EW. In North America: Cy Chauvin, 14248 Wilfred St, Detroit. MI 48213, USA. Rates $25 sea/$40 air.

Recent titles available in VGSF

Prices correct at time of going to press (July 1994)

Master of Paxwax

PHILLIP MANN

It is the far distant future. Humanity has spread across the galaxy, systematically wiping out, imprisoning and enslaving every alien species, hostile or not. Now the galaxy is ruled by the Eleven Families, each supreme in its own, vast realm.

But beneath the surface of one dead and obscure planet lie the seeds of rebellion. For here, the survivors of the ravaged alien races have taken refuge, to plot their revenge on their barbaric conqueror – and the downfall of the human empire.

One man is chosen to be the instrument of their vengeance – but he doesn't know it. His name is Pawl Paxwax. He is the second son of the Fifth Family, and this is his story – a magnificent epic of far future intrigue, passion and tragedy.

'High class space opera with a welter of convincing aliens' – *White Dwarf*

£4.99   0 575 05572 3

The Fall of the Families

PHILLIP MANN

The second and concluding volume in Phillip Mann's epic of interplanetary revenge and tragedy.

Pawl Paxwax has established himself securely as Master of the Fifth Family, ready to take his place among the human rulers of the galaxy, and free to marry the woman he loves, Laurel Beltane. A time of peace and rebuilding should follow ... but it is destined to be short-lived, for the oppressed myriad alien species are now ready to initiate the final part of their plan to free themselves of the human yoke, and that means they must destroy Pawl's happiness to turn him into the instrument of their revenge.

Once again Phillip Mann's remarkable imagination brings to life an immense and colourful canvas of the far future.

£5.99   0 575 05787 4

Cloud Castles

MICHAEL SCOTT ROHAN

The Spiral: where past and present meet, where myth and legend infiltrate the mundane world, where Hy Brasil and Babylon are a short voyage away from Liverpool or Hamburg – via the cloud archipelagos.

You can't always find it – but it can always find you. And when it once again calls lonely business-man Steve Fisher he discovers that in the heart of hi-tech Europe a denizen from the dawn of time is reaching out to ensnare one of humanity's most sacred emblems. If it succeeds an apocalyptic struggle that has raged for millennia will be resolved – and a new, eternal dark age will begin.

Cloud Castles is fantasy on the grand scale, sweeping across Europe's past and present in a dramatic, panoramic story – a magnificent novel from the bestselling author of the *Winter of the World* trilogy.

£8.99   0 575 05563 4

Aztec Century

CHRISTOPHER EVANS

In her dreams, Princess Catherine could still see London burning, and the luminous golden warships of her enemies, the Aztecs, as they added yet another conquest to their mighty Empire . . .

Sweeping from occupied Britain to the horrors of the Russian front and the savage splendour of Mexico, *Aztec Century* is a magnificent novel of war, politics, intrigue and romance, set in a world that is both familiar – and terrifyingly alien.

'A sacrificial *feast* of a story – highly original sf from the first page onwards, an intriguing and compelling thriller to the end' – Robert Holdstock

'Christopher Evans is particularly brilliant at mixing a cocktail of the everyday and the wonderful to make a magical alternative history' – Garry Kilworth

'Intelligent, finely written, and towards the end, absolutely nail-biting' – Iain M. Banks

£4.99   0 575 05712 2

Blood and Honour
SIMON R. GREEN

A travelling player down on his luck accepts a job impersonating a prince. Unknowingly, he is plunged into a world where the Real and Unreal meet, where ghosts, apparitions and spies prove to be deadly; a world where all his theatrical skills are required, just to stay alive.

'A good book, a good read and fun ...' – *Vector*

£4.99   0 575 05545 6

Down Among the Dead Men
SIMON R. GREEN

There is a part of the Forest where it is always night, where the tall trees bow together to shut out the light. Men call it the Darkwood, and in living memory its denizens have threatened the Forest Land. Now the scars are slowly healing – until, in a clearing near the Darkwood's boundary, something buried deep beneath the earth begins to wake from its foul dreams ...

£4.99   0 575 05620 7